CROSSOVERS ²
EXPANDED
A Secret Chronology of the World

CROSSOVERS ²
EXPANDED

A Secret Chronology of the World

(1940–The Future)

Sean Lee Levin

Meteor House

Meteor House

ISBN 978-1-9454270-0-8

First Trade Edition

To Philip José Farmer, whose groundbreaking work
changed my life and those of many others

Acknowledgments

As Win Scott Eckert so correctly stated in the Acknowledgments of the original *Crossovers* volumes, "no work of this volume is created in a vacuum." Indeed, the present volumes owe much to the input of other people. Jay Lindsey provided much info on contemporary horror crossovers. Pete Rawlik filled in many of the gaps in my knowledge regarding some of the connections in his work. George Henry Smathers, Jr., aka "Henry Zeo Covert," provided me with much of the soap opera crossover info included in the appendix on television crossovers. Rick Lai's extensive knowledge of the pulps and other forms of popular fiction was invaluable. Chuck Loridans and Mark Brown's creative mythographic research regarding Dracula and Frankenstein forms the framework for many of the entries regarding those particular Children of the Night. Rather than list each specific piece of data I've received from people over the past few years, I will simply thank the following:

Matthew Baugh, James Bojaciuk, Andrew Brook, Dave Brzeski, Loki Carbis, Anthony R. Cardno, Salvatore Cucinotta, John L. French, Martin Gately, Greg Gick, Micah Harris, Andrew Henry, Matt Hickman, Matthew Ilseman, Rick Lai, Jay Lindsey, Brad Mengel, Bobby Nash, Adrian Nebbett, Jess Nevins, Kim Newman, Dennis E. Power, Pete Rawlik, Josh Reynolds, Charles R. Rutledge, Andrew Salmon, I. Ronald Schablotski, Art Sippo, B. L. Sisemore, John Allen Small, George Henry Smathers, Jr., aka "Henry Zeo Covert," Luke Van Horn, Alejandro Vasquez, and Chris Wike.

Thanks as well to my fellow members of the New Wold Newton Meteoritic Society, for their unwavering support and valuable feedback on my work. You're the best friends a guy could ask for. I owe Meteor House and its masterminds, Michael Croteau, Paul Spiteri, and Win Scott Eckert, for giving my first two books a home. In particular, Win has been my strongest supporter, and I am honored that he chose me to continue his amazing work with the original volumes. Win, you are a true friend, and it's a pleasure, as well as a privilege, to follow in your footsteps. Thanks are also due to Keith Howell for his stunning covers.

I cannot understate the impact the work of Philip José Farmer has had on my life. Phil, I miss you a great deal. I, Win, and many others owe you more than I can possibly say.

Last, but never least, I want to thank my parents, who believed in my abilities as a writer long before I did. Thank you for encouraging my creativity. It has all led up to these two massive books.

Sean Lee Levin

I first learned about holism from Douglas Adams. I was sixteen years old when the first *Dirk Gently* book was published and it fascinated me with this notion of the interconnectedness of all things. Strangely enough, what popped in my addled brain was that it was similar to this Wold Newton concept I knew a bit about. I can't tell you when I first read the words, Wold Newton, but I do know it was from Marvel Comics and I think it was on a letters page. It would have been the 1970s when I was still single digit age. My guess is that it was either *Conan* or *Kull* or *Tarzan* and likely a Roy Thomas or Don Glut story. At the time, I had never heard of Gnosticism, but I did understand that Wold Newton was secret knowledge, and thanks to my reading these Books of Knowledge of Good and Evil, I was a god . . . or at least a pagan in good standing.

This was not mere child's play. I recall my sophomore year of high school when a classmate, one Derek Buchanan who I lost all track of over the intervening decades, exchanged notes with me asking where he could find certain books, among them *The Hour of the Dragon* by Robert E. Howard. I wrote back the book was readily available from Ace Books as *Conan the Conqueror*. He replied he needed to read a particular version edited by Karl Edward Wagner, a name I knew from a Bantam Conan paperback I owned, *The Road of Kings*. Derek then passed me a note that read, "Have you ever heard of Wold Newton?" We discussed the meteor and the plausibility of these events in hushed tones. We ceased speaking when other students or the moderator came near. Other kids had drugs to buy and sell; we had contraband of a far more valuable nature. We had secret knowledge of the interconnectedness of all fiction.

Derek recommended I read *Tarzan Alive* and *Doc Savage: His Apocalyptic Life* by Philip José Farmer. I knew these titles well from a local used bookstore on the border of Cleveland and Parma called American Book & News. *Tarzan Alive* had been part of my last purchase there before it burned to the ground taking literally thousands of old paperbacks with it. I was heartbroken for years as there was so much I always intended to buy. Goaded by my classmate, I finally read Farmer's book and was enraged that he dismissed as fiction some of my cherished twenty-four volume matched set black Ballantine editions of Edgar Rice Burroughs' jungle tales with the stunning cover art by Neal Adams or Boris Vallejo. They meant as much to me as the dozen matched set white Ace editions of Robert E. Howard's *Conan* tales with the equally stunning cover art by Frank Frazetta. I spent much of my childhood wishing I could have been born in an earlier decade. Little did I appreciate then just how special my own era was for discovering fantastic fiction.

Back to this Farmer fellow who had the audacity to claim some *Tarzan* novels were fabrications while others were authoritative. What's more, he altered the internal chronology, changing dates and facts so that it worked for his own logic. I was filled with righteous indignation and . . . and envy. Yes, envy because what Farmer had done was brilliant in its audacity and invention. Now, I knew better than to accept as gospel what Farmer was stating, but he was so well read and had put so much thought into making this fiction live and breathe outside of the pages of these paperback reprints I loved that I knew his Wold Newton research was a sort of alchemy at work. Most importantly, the book contained references to other characters whose stories I read and it all started to tie together in a logical fashion, this inter-connectedness of all things I loved.

It will come as no surprise to say that as a child, I was different. I'm sure that's something everyone reading this also experienced. It was the most obvious impression of my childhood. I was different from my parents, my siblings, my classmates. I did not fit. I was like Tony and Tia from the *Witch Mountain* movies. I was stranded in a world where my dad was a machinist, my mother was a housewife, my sisters watched sitcoms, and we went to church on Sunday.

I knew there was something more to life. There was *King Kong* every Thanksgiving. There were Ray Harryhausen's *Jason and the Argonauts* and *Sinbad* trilogy and *Clash of the Titans* that, like *Conan* and *Kull*, taught me the real history of our world that was far more exciting than anything in the Bible. There was *Planet of the Apes*, one of my earliest memories from age three, that taught me over the years that science and evolution trumped the religious doctrine I was taught in parochial school. There was *Godzilla* and *Gamera* to teach me that other cultures had fiction and mythology so vastly different from our own that Western history books and philosophy could not be trusted to tell the whole story.

There were stories in my paperbacks and comic books that spoke of a pre-Cataclysmic world before the Great Flood. This seemed terribly relevant in the era when the search for Noah's Ark was not only fodder for episodes of Leonard Nimoy's *In Search of* series, but was even the basis for a theatrical docudrama. There were mythology books at our local library or ones "borrowed" from my sister's closet during summer vacation that revealed to me how Norse mythology mirrored much of the early chapters of Genesis. All of this suggested a world where secret knowledge was more true than what I would be told by authority figures at home, in school, or church.

One Sunday before Mass in the days when I served as an altar boy, I asked our pastor about Atlantis and spoke of what I knew from my secret books. Thinking I was reading Madame Blavatsky instead of Marvel Comics, he told me I should throw the books away. This convinced me to do the exact opposite of course, for it was clear others feared questions. Today, I have a full theosophical library on CD-ROM and still refer to my bookshelves as my Books of Knowledge of Good and Evil.

Fantastic fiction will let you live forever and be a god. It will open your eyes to the interconnectedness of all things and the Gnostic truths that must be whispered between those who know. The outside world will never understand and thank whatever deity you worship or fear because who wants to share these treasures with the ignorant masses? Phil Farmer led the way. Roy Thomas and Don Glut carried the torch high in their comic book scripts. Win Scott Eckert and Rick Lai and Sean Lee Levin and countless other Wold Newtonians have given us not only stories, but essays and studies and chronologies to devour. All are doing their bit to share this secret knowledge with fellow initiates.

Open the door to a new world where you will discover fiction you never dreamed of. Open your third eye to a world that exists within our own, but is invisible to those blind believing fools around us. Embrace the secrets. Absorb them. Discard some as you choose for none of it is gospel. Formulate your own theories and histories. And grow and grow and never stop glowing. That is what it is all about. That is why we are here. Now, explore and discover all that lies within these pages.

William Patrick Maynard
Parma, Ohio
April 2016

1940

Winter 1940; Summer 2011
A PLAGUE ON THE LAND

Moran's Pub, owned by Seamus Moran, is frequented by vigilantes. Seamus pours the owner of a fire opal another large Bushmill's, and thinks of his cousin Paddy and his bar uptown. Seamus thinks most of the vigilantes are killers, with two exceptions: "the green one was a man of peace, the pink one killed when she had to but mostly avoided it." Seamus, a leprechaun, asks the Nightmare to deal with trouble in his homeland, Eire, the spiritual plane of Ireland. In the 21st century, Detective Sergeant Bianca Jones of the Baltimore Police Department's homicide

division talks to Nemesis, the goddess of retribution, at Paddy's. Bianca thinks the Nightmare is "a character, like the Spider or the Pink Reaper," but Nemesis says he was real, and persuades Bianca to go back into the past to help the hero in Eire.

Short story by John L. French in Apocalypse 13, *Diane Raetz, ed., Padwolf Publishing, 2012. The shadowy vigilante with the fire opal probably needs no more introduction here. Paddy Moran and Nemesis are from Patrick Thomas' Murphy's Lore series. "The green one" is the Green Lama, while "the pink one" is the Pink Reaper, another character from the Murphy's Lore series. The Nightmare is a pulp-era vigilante created by French. The Nightmare became romantically involved with Nemesis in Thomas and French's book* From the Shadows. *Bianca Jones appears in her own series of stories by French. Bianca is wrong about the Nightmare and the Pink Reaper being fictional, and she is also wrong about the Spider's nonexistence.*

January
NAZIS IN PARADISE

Cliff Secord (aka the Rocketeer) accompanies a group dispatched by Howard Hughes to Tibet to steal a high-tech aircraft from Nazis seeking a lost valley. Another member of the group is Doctor Emme, who speaks several languages, including Tcho-Tcho.

Short story by Don Webb in The Rocketeer: Jet-Pack Adventures, *Jeff Conner, and Tom Waltz, eds., IDW Publishing, 2014. The Tcho-Tcho are a race of short hairless people that worship the Great Old Ones Lloigor and Zhar, and were created by August Derleth as part of H. P. Lovecraft's Cthulhu Mythos.*

Winter. John Perry and Chuck Marley begin fighting crime as the Black Fury and Kid Fury (*Fantastic Comics* #17, April 1941).

Winter
THE BLACK BAT AT BAY
Jim Anthony comes out of retirement when he is tasked by the N.Y.P.D. with capturing the Black Bat, who has been framed for murder. Anthony was recommended to Commissioner Warner by FBI agent Dan Fowler, with whom Anthony has worked before. Anthony also tells Warner, "A famous member of my fraternity once said that pertinence is purely a matter of perspective." The Bat attacks a group of criminals at the wrecked Comet Club, which was once owned by a man named Suydam, who died in 1921 in the same fire that destroyed the club. Gangster Gentleman Jack Schulz has a penthouse in the Shandor Building.

Short story by Josh Reynolds in Black Bat Mystery, Volume 2, *Airship 27 Productions, 2012. The Black Bat and Jim Anthony appeared in the*

pulp magazines Black Book Detective *and* Super Detective, *respectively. FBI agent Dan Fowler's stories appeared in* G-Men Detective. *Fowler and Anthony previously met in Erwin K. Roberts' story "Neighborhood in Peril" and Reynolds' tale "Proof of Supremacy." The fellow sleuth quoted by Anthony is either Sherlock Holmes or C. Auguste Dupin. Suydam is a relative of Robert Suydam from H. P. Lovecraft's "The Horror at Red Hook." The Shandor Building is from the movie* Ghostbusters. *Anthony must have permanently resumed his adventurous career after this, given his appearances in "The Carolingian Stone" and other stories.*

THE CAROLINGIAN STONE

Jim Anthony comes to the aid of Monsieur Chantecoq. The director of the Louvre is named de Felipone. Belphégor, aka Simone Desroches, has seemingly returned. Anthony has special dispensation from the Sûreté after "that business with the Vampires in Marseilles." Chantecoq compares Anthony's acrobatic feats to those of Francis Ardan. The false Belphégor is Jan Mayen, ally of the Nazi *Übermensch* Sun-Koh. Mayen compares Anthony to a modern day Bran-Mak-Morn. Anthony lunges at Mayen, driving him into a statue of Bal-Sagoth. The Louvre's Room of Barbarous Gods also includes statues of Rhan-Tegoth and Nodens.

Short story by Joshua Reynolds in Tales of the Shadowmen Volume 8: Agents Provocateurs, *Jean-Marc and Randy Lofficier, eds., Black Coat Press, 2011; reprinted in French in* Les Compagnons de l'Ombre *(Tome 12), Jean-Marc and Randy Lofficier, eds., Rivière Blanche, 2013. Jim Anthony appeared in pulp novels by Victor Rousseau Emmanuel, Robert Leslie Bellem, and W. T. Ballard. Chantecoq appears in a number of novels by Arthur Bernède, as well as the film serial* Belphégor. *De Felipone is a descendant of Andrea de Felipone, alias Sir Williams, from Ponson du Terrail's Rocambole novels. The Vampires are from Louis Feuillade's serial* Les Vampires. *Dr. Francis Ardan is from Guy d'Armen's novel* Doc Ardan: City of Gold and Lepers; *Jean-Marc and Randy Lofficier's adaptation and translation of the novel implied Ardan was actually an American pulp hero known as "Doc." Jan Mayen and Sun Koh appeared in separate German pulp series by Paul Müller, but had several crossovers. Bran Mak Morn is the king of the Picts in stories by Robert E. Howard. Bal-Sagoth is from Howard's story "The Gods of Bal-Sagoth." Rhan-Tegoth is from August Derleth's novella* The Lurker at the Threshold. *Nodens is a mythological figure who appears in both Arthur Machen's story "The Great God Pan" and H. P. Lovecraft's Cthulhu Mythos.*

DOMINO LADY VS. MUMMY

The Domino Lady, investigating a cult that has been killing various people in order to use their body parts to create a patchwork mummy, thinks it is a shame "that rascal Ravenwood" went back to New York. One of the cult's victims is Johnny Weissman, an Olympic swimmer turned actor who has starred in several Ki-Gor films.

A Return of the Monsters *one-shot by Nancy Holder, Bobby Nash, Rock Baker, and Jeff Austin, Moonstone Comics, 2011. The Domino Lady was created by an author using the nom de plume "Lars Anderson" and appeared in five issues of* Saucy Romantic Adventures *and one issue of*

Mystery Adventure Magazine. *Occult investigator Ravenwood was created by Frederick C. Davis and appeared in a series of stories in the pulp magazine* Secret Agent X. *The Domino Lady and Ravenwood first met prior to the 1939 events of Nash's story "Jazz," and would meet again in 1941 during the events of C. J. Henderson's novel* To Battle Beyond. *Ki-Gor is the jungle hero created by John Murray Reynolds, who went on to appear in stories by several authors using the pen name John Peter Drummond; since Ki-Gor is in the CU through other crossovers, the films starring Weissman must be inspired by stories of the real Ki-Gor. Weissman is obviously based on Johnny Weissmuller, who portrayed Lord Greystoke in a series of films, but the two cannot be conflated, as Weissmuller died in 1984.*

FEAR THE DARK

Richard Wentworth attends a charity benefit hosted by the Ravenwood Foundation, although Mr. Ravenwood himself is unable to attend. An amulet from a traveling museum currently on display at the fundraiser transforms a man into a monstrous creature, which Wentworth (as the Spider) must defeat.

Short story by Bobby Nash in The Spider: Extreme Prejudice, *Joe Gentile and Tommy Hancock, eds., Moonstone Books, 2013. Ravenwood, "the Stepson of Mystery," was created by Frederick C. Davis and had his own feature in the pulp magazine* Secret Agent X.

Spring
THE DEVIL'S NEST

The jungle hero Ki-Gor joins an expedition to the valley known as the Devil's Nest to find Brendan Barnes, the American heir to a great fortune. Barnes tells the group his family has been associated for years with the Jellyby Foundation in London, and therefore received regular reports on the Foundation's work in Borrioboola-Gha and other parts of Africa. One of Ki-Gor's traveling companions, Dr. John Moore of MI6's Department Q, refers to an expedition funded by a patron of the Royal Geographic Society to a nearby valley where a dinosaur allegedly exists: "Too close a follower of that old crackpot Challenger, I suppose . . . This is the Congo, not some cloud-shrouded neverland like Maple White Land."

Short story by Duane Spurlock in Jungle Tales Volume One, *Ron Fortier, ed., Airship 27 Productions, 2012. Ki-Gor's adventures were originally chronicled by several authors using the pen name "John Peter Drummond" in* Jungle Stories *from 1939 to 1954. In Charles Dickens'* Bleak House, *Mrs. Jellyby is a self-styled philanthropist who tries to ship downtrodden*

Britishers off to the African colony of Borrioboola-Gha so they and the natives can earn money through coffee growing. Moore is wrong about the dinosaur in the valley, and he is also wrong about Professor George Edward Challenger not having actually discovered Maple White Land, as his discovery of the plateau was recounted in Edward Malone's account (edited by Arthur Conan Doyle) entitled The Lost World.

Spring. U. S. Jones begins his war on crime. (*Wonderworld Comics* #28, August 1941.)

May
FAREWELL, MY ROCKETEER

Cliff Secord is forced to fly a group of Nazi agents to Colorado to find a treasure left there by visiting Aztecs a century ago. The leader of the group, Bauchmann, reminds Cliff of Jonas back in New York. Another member of the group, Ganos, once pursued some sort of large bird figurine. Cliff prevents the last remaining Nazi from murdering a tall, black-haired, blue-eyed man named Simon (who forged a treasure map to deceive the Nazis) and an equally tall, willowy blonde woman named Patricia.

Short story by Gregory Frost in The Rocketeer: Jet-Pack Adventures, *Jeff Conner and Tom Waltz, eds., IDW Publishing, 2014. Cliff encountered "Jonas" (actually the shadowy pulp vigilante) in Dave Stevens'* The Rocketeer: Death Stalks the Midway. *The large bird figurine is the Maltese Falcon, from Dashiell Hammett's mystery novel of the same name. The man and woman are Leslie Charteris' "laughing Robin Hood of crime" Simon Templar, alias the Saint, and his companion Patricia Holm.*

Summer. Jeff Crocket wages war against the Nazis as Captain Fight. (*Fight Comics* #16, December 1941.)

Summer

THE ROCKETEER: CARGO OF DOOM

The Rocketeer (aka Cliff Secord) battles a villain known as the Master. One of the Master's henchmen is Guptmann, who was subjected to brain surgery by the Master's greatest foe. The Master and the crew of his ship are carrying dinosaurs from "Skull—," a small, remote island near Sumatra. A few years ago, an expedition to the island captured a giant gorilla and brought it to New York, where it ran amok. The Master seeks revenge on the inventor of Cliff's rocket pack. The Master's employer refers to him at one point as "John Sunli—."

Four-issue miniseries by Mark Waid and Chris Samnee, IDW Publishing, August–November 2012. The Master is the bronze man's archenemy; he was portrayed as the inventor of Cliff's pack in Dave Stevens' original comic The Rocketeer. *His foe must have had a contingency plan that enabled him to survive his plunge into the ocean in the comic book miniseries* Doc Savage: The Monarch of Armageddon, *only to be killed at the end of this exploit. The giant gorilla is King Kong, and his and the dinosaurs' homeland is Skull Island. Given the references to it here, as well as its appearance in the film* Dead Alive *(aka* Braindead*), which is set in 1957, Skull Island must have returned to the surface at some point after it sank beneath the waves in November 1932, as seen in* Son of Kong.

DARK STREETS OF DOOM

The Masked Avenger, disguised as his ally and lookalike Curtis Van Leif, meets Commissioner Kirk Stanley at the Explorer's Club. The Masked Avenger uses a rocket pack designed by a famous scientist, Clark Savage. When the Masked Avenger is outnumbered by white slavers, at least two other vigilantes come to his aid.

Short story by Tom Johnson included as one-half of a Gryphon Publications Double Novel, revised and reprinted in Triple Detective #3, *Altus Press, 2009. "Kirk Stanley" is a pseudonym for Commissioner Stanley Kirkpatrick from the Spider pulp novels. The most famous rocket pack built by Doc is the Cirrus X-3, which was used by Cliff Secord for his adventures as the Rocketeer. A later model, the Cirrus X-9, appeared in Win Scott Eckert's story "The Eye of Oran," and the novella* The Scarlet Jaguar. *Doc must have donated a pack to the Masked Avenger. In the original version of this story, the heroes who help the Masked Avenger, though unnamed and not given any dialogue, were clearly the Spider and another shadowy pulp hero. However, in the revised version, the Black Bat and the Phantom Detective help the Masked Avenger out of his jam. Perhaps all four adventurers were actually independently investigating the disappearances of young street children, and decided to pool their efforts upon learning they were on the same trail, only to find the Masked Avenger was already on the scene. If so, this crossover confirms that all these pulp heroes coexist in the CU.*

THE DEATH'S HEAD CLOUD

Jim Anthony battles a madman who has created a fog that has a lethal effect on those it comes in contact with. Appearing or mentioned are: Inspector Craig; Malone; Joséphine Balsamo; Irma Vep; "that odd Persson woman"; Pickman; Dr. Death; Dr. Satan; "the Mephistophelean master of the Si-Fan"; Fantômas; the *Daily Sentinel*; Reid; Xonira; Reid Enterprises; Patricia Savage; the *Bugle*; the *Globe*; the *New York Inquirer*; the Sky Band; Police Commissioner Warner; the Kingscote School for Girls; St. Trinian's; the Minchin's Seminary; "a dance academy in Freiburg of dubious reputation"; the Black Bat; "that arachnid lunatic in the fright-wig";

Ellen Patrick; Margo Lane; "the Remmers that Wolfe sent around"; Maple-White Land; "a lama with an unfortunate predilection for the color green"; Ravenwood; and Captain Nemo.

Novel by Joshua Reynolds, Pro Se Press, 2013. Jim Anthony appeared in the pulp magazine Super Detective, *in stories written by Victor Rousseau Emanuel, Robert Leslie Bellem, and W. T. Ballard. Inspector Gordon Craig is from Robert Barbour Johnson's short story "Far Below." Malone is Detective Thomas F. Malone from H. P. Lovecraft's "The Horror at Red Hook." Joséphine Balsamo is Arsène Lupin's archenemy. Irma Vep is from Louis Feuillade's silent film serial* Les Vampires. *Persson is Una Persson, a recurring character in Michael Moorcock's Multiverse. Richard Upton Pickman is from Lovecraft's "Pickman's Model." Dr. Death's misdeeds were chronicled by Harold Ward in a titular pulp magazine. Dr. Satan's crimes were recounted by Paul Ernst in* Weird Tales. *The master of the Si-Fan is Dr. Fu Manchu. Fantômas is the vicious criminal mastermind created by Marcel Allain and Pierre Souvestre. Reid is Britt Reid, aka the Green Hornet. The* Daily Sentinel *and Reid Enterprises are both owned by Reid. Since Britt was based out of Detroit rather than New York, the reporter in this novel must be an employee of the* Sentinel*'s New York offices. Xonira is from Derrick Ferguson's novels*

Dillon and the Legend of the Golden Bell *and* Dillon and the Pirates of Xonira, *bringing Dillon into the CU. Patricia is the cousin of a certain golden-eyed pulp hero called "Doc." The* Daily Bugle *and the* Daily Globe *are seen in Spider-Man stories published by Marvel Comics. The* New York Inquirer *is from Orson Welles' classic film* Citizen Kane. *The Sky Band was an all-female group of criminals featured in a storyline in Lee Falk's comic strip* The Phantom. *The Black Bat appeared in stories by Norman A. Daniels in the magazine* Black Book Detective. *Commissioner Warner is also from the Black Bat stories. The Kingscote School for Girls is from Antonia Forest's novels about the Marlow family. St. Trinian's appeared in illustrated cartoons by Ronald Searle that were later adapted into a series of films. The Minchin's Seminary is from Frances Hodgson Burnett's book* A Little Princess. *The dance academy in Freiburg is from Dario Argento's horror film* Suspiria. *"That arachnid lunatic in the fright-wig" is the Spider. Ellen Patrick is better known as the Domino Lady, who appeared in stories by the pseudonymous "Lars Anderson" published in* Saucy Romantic Adventure. *Margo is one of the most loyal and trusted agents of the pulp hero who operates from the shadows. Remmers is the favorite beer of Rex Stout's rotund sleuth Nero Wolfe. Maple-White Land is from Arthur Conan Doyle's* The Lost World. *The "lama with an unfortunate predilection for the color green" is Jethro Dumont, aka the Green Lama, whose stories were written by Kendell Crossen for the pulp* Double Detective. *Ravenwood, "the Stepson of Mystery," is an occult detective appearing in stories by Frederick C. Davis in the pulp* Secret Agent X. *Captain Nemo is, of course, from Jules Verne's* 20,000 Leagues Under the Sea *and* The Mysterious Island.

September 13–17
THE INVISIBLE-BOX MURDERS

A New York newspaper called the *Daily Planet* appears.

A *Doc Savage* pulp novel by Lester Dent. *Dent wrote three stories for* All Detective Magazine *in 1934 featuring Foster Fade, "the Crime Spectacularist," who worked for a New York newspaper called the* Planet. *The New York* Daily Planet *may be a branch of the Metropolis* Daily Planet *Superman worked for as Clark Kent.*

September 25–27
RETURN TO HELL HOUSE

A group of scholars and psychic sensitives visits the notorious and haunted Belasco Mansion in Maine. A member of a previous expedition in 1931 was driven insane by the experience, and was shipped off to Castle Rock Asylum.

Novella by Nancy A. Collins in He Is Legend: An Anthology Celebrating Richard Matheson, *Christopher Conlon, ed., 2009, also printed as a standalone E-novella. This story is a prequel to Richard Matheson's novel* Hell House, *which is in the CU via references in Kim Newman's stories "Angels of Music II: The Mark of Kane" and "The Snow Sculptures of Xanadu." The town of Castle Rock, Maine recurs throughout Stephen King's interconnected fiction, providing further evidence* Hell House *takes place in the CU.*

Early Autumn
A CAT AMONG DOGS

Socialite Nina Hastings begins fighting the mob as the Black Cat. Rocky McFayne, publisher of the *Express*, tells his reporter Joe Roper to ask his friend at the *Daily Clarion*, Mr. Havens' paper, to use the *Clarion*'s resources to help them uncover the Cat's true identity. Joe agrees, saying Steve Huston owes him a favor.

Short story by Tom Johnson in Pulp Echoes, *Night to Dawn Magazines & Books, 2011. The Black Cat was a secondary character in the one-shot pulp* The Angel Detective, *which was published in July 1941. This story provides her origin, which went unrevealed in the original story. The* Daily Clarion *newspaper, its publisher Frank Havens, and reporter Steve Huston are from the Phantom Detective pulp novels by several authors using the pen names "G. Wayman Jones" and "Robert Wallace."*

Autumn
DEATH RIDES THE *VALKYRIE*

The Black Bat investigates a theft aboard a zeppelin. One of the suspects is reformed ex-con Rowland Clark. The Bat's assistant Silk Kirby scoffs at rumors of a "crime college" in upstate New York. However, after Clark seemingly commits suicide, the Bat reveals the crime college does exist, and Clark was rehabilitated there. Clark's murderer proves to be Kobold, a former member of the group of German adventurers known as the *Alle-Männer*.

Short story by Andrew Salmon in Black Bat Mystery Volume One, *Ron Fortier, ed., Cornerstone Book Publishers, 2010; released in a revised edition* as a standalone e-book by Timepiece Press in 2015. *The Crime College was founded and run by the man of bronze. Ostensibly a group of adventurers from the German pulps, the* Alle-Männer *(German for "All-Men") were actually created by Salmon, and also appear in his forthcoming novel* All-Men: The Shadow-Line.

ILSA'S CROSSING

Judex helps Marines Tom Grayson and Frank Corby smuggle Resistance member Ilsa Laszlo out of France. Judex is seeking the papers of a late scientist named Boroff, which are being used by the Nazis to create super-weapons. Grayson mentions War Wheels, while Corby refers to Haverlyte Rays.

Short story by Travis Hiltz in The Shadow of Judex, *Jean-Marc and Randy Lofficier, eds., Black Coat Press, 2013; reprinted in French in* L'Ombre de Judex, *Jean-Marc and Randy Lofficier, eds., Rivière Blanche, 2013. Judex is the title character of the classic French film serial. Tom Grayson and Frank Corby are from the serial* The Fighting Devil Dogs. *Ilsa Laszlo (née Lund) is from the movie* Casablanca. *Boroff is from the serial* S.O.S. Coast Guard. *The War Wheel is a weapon faced by DC Comics' heroic aviator Blackhawk; Captain America and Easy Company also dealt with a War Wheel in* Batman/Captain America. *Haverlyte is from the serial* Officer 444.

THE MASKED MARKSMAN'S COMMAND PERFORMANCE

Ed Race, the Masked Marksman, puts his skills to the test to prove to the FBI agents known as the Suicide Squad (Dan Murdock, Johnny Kerrigan, and Stephen Klaw) he is not a Nazi spy, and teams up with them to prevent the real enemy agents from blowing up the train on which they are traveling.

Short story by Emile C. Tepperman in The Spider *magazine, March 1942, crossing over Tepperman's Masked Marksman series, which appeared in* The Spider, *and the Suicide Squad tales, which appeared in* Ace G-Man Stories. *Ed Race is in the CU through an encounter with the Spider in Rich Harvey's story "One Death to a Customer." Similarly, the Suicide Squad is in through a reference in Stuart Shiffman's story "True Believers," which features or mentions many characters already in the CU, notably the Sâr Dubnotal.*

October
THE CASE OF THE GILDED FLY (OBSEQUIES AT OXFORD)

Gervase Fen has an epiphany about the murder he is investigating, and hopes Gideon Fell never becomes privy to his lunacy.

Novel by Edmund Crispin. The reference to John Dickson Carr's sleuth Dr. Gideon Fell reinforces Fen's inclusion in the CU.

November 1940–May 1941
OFFICERS AND GENTLEMEN

Guy Crouchback receives a letter telling him to report to the headquarters of Hazardous Offensive Operations in Marchmain House. Guy stays for a time at Mrs. Julia Stitch and her husband Algernon's villa while recovering from his experiences during and after the withdrawal from Crete. Major-General Whale refers to a story in the *Daily Beast*, saying Lord Copper has always held a grudge against the regular army. Mrs. Stuyvesant Oglander is mentioned as one of the women whose hair Trimmer cut in the 1930s.

The second novel in Evelyn Waugh's Sword of Honour trilogy. Marchmain House and Mrs. Stuyvesant Oglander are from Waugh's novel Brideshead Revisited. *Mrs. Julia Stitch and her husband Algernon Stitch are from* Scoop, *as is Lord Copper, publisher of the* Daily Beast *newspaper.*

December
AIRBOY/G-8

Davy "Airboy" Nelson teams up with his fellow pilot G-8 to battle the latest batch of giant bats cooked up by G-8's nemesis Herr Doktor Krueger.

Graphic novel by Chuck Dixon and Ken Hoover, Moonstone Comics, 2012. This crossover with G-8, a Wold Newton Family member, helps to bolster Airboy's presence in the CU. The giant bats are of the same breed as those seen in the G-8 pulp novel The Bat Staffel.

Late Autumn
HOLY DISORDERS

Oxford don and amateur detective Gervase Fen is disgusted when Scotland Yard becomes involved in the case he's investigating. There is talk of sending down Sir John Appleby to look into the matter.

This novel by Edmund Crispin takes place near the end of the Battle of Britain. Gervase Fen is already in the CU through a reference in James Anderson's novel The Affair of the Mutilated Mink; *the reference to Michael Innes' sleuth Sir John Appleby bolsters his inclusion.*

1941

Winter

BLACK BAT & DEATH ANGEL VS. DRACULA: ANGELS AND THE UNDEAD

The female vigilante Death Angel investigates the murders of several prostitutes at a monster-themed club. She comes face to face with the culprit: Count Dracula. The Black Bat comes to Death Angel's aid, but Dracula ultimately escapes, suggesting they will meet again.

Return of the Monsters *one-shot by Mike Bullock and Eric Johns, Moonstone Comics, 2011. Death Angel is an original character created by Bullock. The Dracula seen here is likely a "soul-clone." The exploits of the Black Bat, secretly D.A. Tony Quinn, were primarily written by Norman A. Daniels under the pen name G. Wayman Jones; he appeared in* Black Book Detective *from 1939–1953. The date is conjecture.*

ANDY HARDY'S BLONDE TROUBLE

Andy Hardy's father, Judge James K. "Jim" Hardy, is treated for tonsilitis by the Brooklyn-born Dr. Lee Wong How.

The fourteenth film in the Andy Hardy series. Dr. Lee Wong How is from the Dr. Gillespie film series, which is itself a spin-off of the Dr. Kildare films; Kildare and Gillespie originally appeared in stories by Max Brand. Since Dr. Kildare is in the CU, so are Dr. Gillespie and Andy Hardy.

MARRIAGE AND LOVE

Fibber McGee and his wife Molly attend a marriage encounter group. The other couples present are John and Blanche, Ronald and Benita, George and Gracie, and Dagwood and Blondie Bumstead.

Short story by Barbara Gratz in It's That Time Again 3: Even More New Stories of Old-Time Radio, *Jim Harmon, ed., BearManor Media, 2006. The McGees are from the radio series* Fibber McGee and Molly. *By extension, that show's spin-offs* The Great Gildersleeve *and* Beulah *also take place in the CU.* The Great Gildersleeve, *which began in 1941, had Throckmorton P. Gildersleeve moving into his deceased brother-in-law's estate. Since Gildersleeve is still Fibber's next-door neighbor in this story, it must take place before he moved. John and Blanche are the title characters of* another radio show, *The Bickersons. Ronald Colman and Benita Hume were a real acting couple that played fictionalized versions of themselves on the radio series* The Jack Benny Program. *George Burns and Gracie Allen were also real, but played fictionalized versions of themselves on the radio show* The Burns and Allen Show. *Dagwood and Blondie Bumstead are from the radio show* Blondie, *based on Chic Young's comic strip. Since Blondie and Dagwood are in the CU, so are the other couples.*

February
THE ROCKETEER/THE SPIRIT: PULP FRICTION!
The Spirit joins forces with the Rocketeer to battle the Octopus and his ally Benedict Trask, who are using an advanced television/matter transmitter stolen from a bronze-skinned inventor in an attempt to assassinate President Roosevelt.

Four-issue miniseries by Mark Waid, Paul Smith, Loston Wallace, Bob Wiacek, and J. Bone, IDW Publishing, 2013. The bronze-skinned inventor needs no further introduction.

April 22–May 3
THE KEEP
A group of Nazis stationed in a small castle in the Transylvanian Alps find themselves falling victim to the keep's owner, who appears to be a vampire. Among the books in the keep's library are the du Nord translation of *The Book of Eibon, De Vermis Mysteriis* by Ludwig Prinn, *Cultes des Goules* by Comte d'Erlette, *The Pnakotic Manuscripts, The Seven Cryptical Books of Hsan, Unaussprechlichen Kulten* by von Juntz, and the *Al Azif* by Abdul Alhazred.

The first novel in F. Paul Wilson's Adversary Cycle. The Cycle is part of Wilson's "Secret History of the World," which also includes his Repairman Jack novels and a number of other connected novels and short stories. The appearance of various tomes from the Cthulhu Mythos in The Keep *brings the Secret History into the CU, with the exception of the final novel in the Adversary Cycle,* Nightworld, *which involves apocalyptic events, and as such must take place in an AU. Rick Lai notes some of the connections between Wilson's works:* 'Implant *features a drug developed by GEM Plama, a fictional pharmaceutical firm which plays a larger role in the Repairman Jack novel* All the Rage. *At least three characters from* Implant *(a Presidential doctor, a Secret Service Agent, and an FBI agent) resurfaced in Wilson's* Deep as the Marrow. *The hacker/kidnapper villain of* Deep as the Marrow *was briefly mentioned in another Repairman Jack novel,* Legacies, *in which Jack also briefly visits the Gates house from Wilson's* Sibs. *There are more connections between Wilson's works than I have mentioned here.*

"Wilson's universe is connected to the Cthulhu Mythos (references in The Keep, The Tomb, and 'The Barrens') and the Greystone Bay 'shared world' horror anthologies. In the Greystone Bay series (edited by Charles L. Grant), there were Mythos references in stories by other authors. Joseph Payne Brennan's 'Jendrick's Swamp' in Doom City *features Ithaqua (the story was reprinted by Chaosium in* The Ithaqua Cycle*), and Thomas F. Monteleone's 'No Pain, No Gain' from* The Sea Harp Hotel *features Miskatonic University. Brennan also had his own occult detective, Lucius Leffing, investigating murders in Greystone Bay (see 'A Heritage Upheld' in* Greystone Bay*). Wilson's own Greystone Bay entry, 'Doc Johnson' from* Doom City*, became tied into his own universe through the story 'Feelings,' in Wilson's* The Barrens and Others. *'Feelings' features another Doc Johnson who was the brother of the title character from the Greystone Bay story. The Johnson from 'Feelings' lived in Monroe, a fictional community in Long Island, New York. Monroe figures in many of Wilson's works (*The Touch, Reborn, Legacies, All the Rage, *and others)."*

Spring

THE GONKY MOB COPYCAT CRIMES

Brian O'Brien (aka the Clock) forbids his young female sidekick Butch to accompany him on an investigation. Butch goads him by saying, "I should have teamed up with the Spirit—HE'D appreciate me!" O'Brien responds "The Spirit—bah!"

Story by George Brenner in Crack Comics *#25, Quality Comics, September 1942. The Clock, originally published by Centaur, was the first original masked hero to appear in comic books, and is more "pulpish" than many of those who followed him. The reference to the Spirit brings him into the CU. This story originally ran untitled; I have used the title given on the* Grand Comics Database *website.*

Spring 1941–June 1944

INGLOURIOUS BASTERDS

Sgt. Donny Donowitz is one of the Basterds. A pack of Red Apple Cigarettes can be seen at a table in the *La Louisiane* tavern.

2009 feature film directed by Quentin Tarantino. Sgt. Donowitz is the father of film producer Lee Donowitz from the film True Romance. *One* of the main characters of True Romance, *Alabama, is also mentioned in* Reservoir Dogs. *Red Apple Cigarettes also appear in* Pulp Fiction, Four Rooms, From Dusk Till Dawn, Romy and Michele's High School Reunion, Kill Bill: Vols. 1 and 2, *and* Planet Terror, *as well as several stories by Win Scott Eckert. Rick Lai notes, "The movie alters WWII history. In June 1944, Adolf Hitler, Joseph Goebbels, Hermann Göring, and Martin Bormann all die in a Parisian movie theater. Presumably real-life actor Emil Jannings perished there as well. References to 'Americans . . . on the beach' place these supposed deaths after D-Day (June 6, 1944). How does this square with history? All the answers can be found in the adventures of Doc Savage. In my Doc Savage chronology (The Revised Complete Chronology of Bronze, Altus Press, 2010), the events of* Violent Night *(aka The Hate Genius) transpired in June 1944. Hitler attempted to flee Germany only to be caught in Switzerland by Doc Savage. The novel asserted that Hitler had left a double in Germany to impersonate him. It was this double who was killed at the Paris cinema. The other Nazi leaders present were doubles as well. In my Doc Savage chronology, I argued that his foe Sown (The Screaming Man and* The Frightened Fish*) was behind Hitler's flight. All the doubles behaved like their originals in Paris because they were under the influence of Sown's mind control device. Sown arranged for Hitler's escape from Allied custody in Switzerland (the dictator arrived in Germany only to be nearly killed in the July bomb plot, Operation Valkyrie). As for Emil Jannings, he must have miraculously survived the attack on the Parisian movie house. He actually died in 1950."*

March
DEATH GHOST FROM THE FUTURE WAR
The Spider battles a test subject for the United States' Superior Soldier Program, who has gone insane from the combination of steroids with which he has been injected.

Short story by Rik Hoskin in The Spider: Extreme Prejudice, *Joe Gentile and Tommy Hancock, eds., Moonstone Books, 2013. The Superior Soldier Program is meant to be the same Super Soldier Program that created Captain America, who first appeared in* Captain America Comics #1 *in March 1941, the same date given by Hoskin for this story. Apparently, the tale takes place shortly before Steve Rogers was injected with the serum that gave him his enhanced strength and agility. However, in the CU, Rogers became Captain America in 1940. Probably the death of Dr. Reinstein, the creator of the serum, caused the U.S. government to seek other means to create a super soldier.*

May
EMERALD DEATH

Michael Hannigan arrives in Africa aboard a tramp steamer called the *African Queen*. Father Niles McKenzie learned a technique to conceal himself in darkness at a Tibetan monastery; the monk who taught him mentioned he also taught it to another American, a pilot named Allard who had spent time in the mountains following the Great War.

Novel by Bill Craig, Arctic Wolf Publishing, 2008. Michael "Hardluck" Hannigan first appeared as a much older man in Craig's novel The Mummy's Tomb, *part of a series set in the present day featuring Police Detective Jack Riley. The* African Queen *is from C. S. Forester's novel of the same name. Allard is the shadowy pulp hero. Although the year of this novel is given as 1939, the sequel,* The Sky Masters, *picks up immediately afterwards, and refers to the German invasion of France, which occurred in May–June 1940.*

THE SKY MASTERS

"Hardluck" Hannigan and his friend Gregor Shotsky (who first met each other aboard a steamer called the *African Queen*) throw in their lot with Abigail Grayson, who like her deceased father, Sir Edmond Grayson, the Earl of Graystoke, is a British Intelligence agent. The three rendezvous at a café in Casablanca called the Blue Parrot, which is owned by an obese man named Ferrari.

Novel by Bill Craig, 2009. The African Queen *is from C. S. Forester's novel of the same name. Abigail and her father are probably related to the Duke of Greystoke. The Blue Parrot and its owner Signor Ferrari are from the classic film* Casablanca.

May 1–4
THE GREEN HORNET MEETS THE AVENGER

The Avenger seeks to bring the Green Hornet to justice, but eventually discovers he is really a hero, and forges an alliance with him. Britt Reid's Uncle John appears. The Avenger tells Reid about two other crusaders for justice: one with intellect and strength far beyond those of mortal men, and another who preys on evil from the shadows, striking criminals from the darkest corners of their minds.

> Short story by Michael Uslan in the limited hardcover edition of The Green Hornet: Still at Large, *Joe Gentile, Win Scott Eckert, and Matthew Baugh, eds., Moonstone Books, 2012. Uncle John is John Reid, formerly the Lone Ranger. The other crimefighters mentioned by the Avenger are the bronze-skinned, golden-eyed pulp superman known as "Doc," and the pulp vigilante who operated from the shadows, respectively.*

Mid June
MURDER IN SOUND EFFECTS

Magician George Chance (aka the Green Ghost) is a guest on a radio show, along with *New York Comet* columnist Walt "Mr. Broadway" Whitley and others. When another guest is murdered, Chance's girlfriend Merry White goes to the *Daily Star* and sweet-talks Robb, the Morgue manager, into getting her a list of everyone who has been on the show for the last year. The Ghost, disguised as a consultant for Commissioner Standish, enlists the aid of Officer Burland in solving the case. Inspector Cramer prevents a criminal from shooting Standish.

> Short story by Erwin K. Roberts in George Chance: The Green Ghost Volume One, *Ron Fortier, ed., Airship 27 Productions, 2014. The Green Ghost appeared in pulp stories by G. T. Fleming-Roberts. "Walt Whitley" is a pseudonym for Walt Whitney, a Broadway columnist for an unnamed New York newspaper, who also fought crime as Bob Phantom, appearing in* Top-Notch Comics *in the 1940s. Officer Burland is Kip Burland, aka the Black Hood who appeared in* Top-Notch *and other comics in the same era. Both characters were published by MLJ, the company that would later be known as Archie Comics. Per the standard rules regarding references to superheroes' secret identities, this story only confirms Walt Whitney and Kip Burland have CU counterparts. It does not necessarily mean they ever donned costumed personas in the CU. The* New York Comet *is the paper for which Norman A. Daniels' pulp hero the Masked Detective works in his alter ego of reporter Rex Parker. The* Daily Star *is owned by Jim Anthony, a half-Comanche, half-Irish hero that appeared in the pulp* Super Detective. *Robb appears in Roberts' Jim Anthony story "The League of Dead Patriots" and the two-part novella "The Sons of Thor," and is mentioned in the story "Arsenic is Where You Find Her." Inspector Cramer is from Rex Stout's Nero Wolfe books.*

Summer. Teenager Chuck Chandler battles criminals and the Axis as Crimebuster. (*Boy Comics* #3, April 1942.)

July 2–4
HOMEFRONT

Lance Star investigates the murder of a Department of Justice agent during the annual charity air show hosted at his home base, Star Field in Long Island. Lance's operations manager Walt Anderson tells him Mr. Barnes has cancelled, as he had to take an unexpected trip to South America. The pilots who are able to attend the show include Calvin, Dalton, Santini, and Howard M. Murdock. Ferris Air, whose owner is named Carol, has a pilot demonstrating a new plane they're planning to introduce next year. Detective Barney Bishop works with Lance to find the murderer. Bishop's old acquaintance Ellen Patrick attends the show, and indicates it has been a few years since she was last able to attend Lance's benefit.

Short story by Bobby Nash in Lance Star: Sky Ranger Volume 2, *Ron Fortier, ed., Cornerstone Book Publishers, 2009. Air ace Lance Star is a character from the Canadian pulps. Mr. Barnes is an aviator who appeared in pulp stories by George L. Eaton. Calvin is meant to be the father of Theodore "T. C." Calvin from the television series* Magnum, P.I. *Dalton is the father of Jack Dalton from the television series* MacGyver. *Santini is Dominic Santini from the television series* Airwolf. *Howard M. Murdock is the father of H. M. "Howling Mad" Murdock from the TV show* The A-Team. *Ferris Air (also known as Ferris Aircraft) and its owner Carol Ferris are from the comic book exploits of the Green Lantern, though it is unconfirmed whether a CU version of the company's test pilot Hal Jordan ever donned an emerald ring that generated energy constructs and was powered by his own willpower. However, Jordan's predecessor as the Green Lantern, Alan Scott, has been established to have existed in the CU. Ellen Patrick is the alter ego of Lars Anderson's pulp heroine the Domino Lady. Detective Barney Bishop also appears in Nash's "Target: Domino Lady" and* The Domino Lady: Money Shot, *as well as Ron Fortier's "The Claws of the Cat." Both "Target: Domino Lady" and "The Claws of the Cat" appear in the anthology* The Domino Lady: Sex as a Weapon. *"Target: Domino Lady," set in 1936, mentions Ellen attending one of Lance's air shows.*

July
ATOLL OF TERROR

A mad vivisectionist working for the Nazis tells a captive Cliff Secord the British government forced him out of the country, just like Moreau before him.

Short story by Simon Kurt Unsworth in The Rocketeer: Jet-Pack Adventures, *Jeff Conner and Tom Waltz, eds., IDW Publishing 2014. Moreau, of course, is from H. G. Wells' classic science fiction novel* The Island of Doctor Moreau.

Summer
THE CRIMSON CLOWN—KILLER

The Crimson Clown goes undercover as a criminal at the Pink Rat in order to confront Boss Flannery. Later, in his true identity of Delton Prouse, he goes to a benefit for the Policemen's Widows Fund held by Nina Hastings. Prouse tells Inspector Blurney he is familiar with Rocky McFayne's newspaper, the *Express*, though it is not as large as Havens' *Daily Clarion*. Another guest at the benefit, Jasper Baldwin, was a member of the Gray Gang until Dan Fowler of the Feds brought the mob to justice. While hiding in the same office where Flannery and Baldwin are meeting, the Clown witnesses the Black Cat attempting to steal from them.

Short story by Tom Johnson in Pulp Echoes, Night to Dawn Magazines & Books, 2011. *The Crimson Clown was created by Johnston McCulley and appeared in* Detective Story Magazine *from 1926–1931. The Pink Rat dive bar is from the novels by Walter Gibson and others about a certain shadowy vigilante. The Black Cat (aka Nina Hastings) appeared in the one-shot pulp* The Angel Detective. *Like the Crimson Clown, the Black Cat was a Robin Hood-type adventurer, stealing criminals' ill-gotten gains and giving them to the needy. Frank Havens, publisher of the* Daily Clarion, *is from the Phantom Detective pulp novels. FBI agent Dan Fowler's exploits were chronicled in the pulp magazine* G-Men Detective. *Since the shadowy vigilante, the Black Cat, the Phantom Detective, and Dan Fowler are all in the CU, this crossover brings in the Crimson Clown. In the November 11– December 9, 1928 issues of* Detective Story Magazine, *McCulley had a serial entitled "Thubway Tham Meets the Crimson Clown." Thubway Tham was another series character of McCulley's who appeared in* Detective Story Magazine, *a lisping conman who preyed on those who rode the New York City subway system. McCulley also wrote "Thubway Tham and Mr. Clackworthy" in the February 18, 1922 issue of* Detective Story, *in which Tham met Christopher B. Booth's own grifter character, Mr. Amos Clackworthy,* who also appeared in that magazine. *Tham and Clackworthy crossed over again in Booth's "Mr. Clackworthy and Thubway Tham," published in the March 4, 1922 issue of* Detective Story.

PREY OF THE MASK REAPER

The Spider and the Black Bat reluctantly join forces to battle the Mask Reaper, who has been brutally murdering masked vigilantes and their loved ones across the country.

Short story by I. A. Watson in The Spider: Extreme Prejudice, *Joe Gentile and Tommy Hancock, eds., Moonstone Books, 2013.*

September 8
THE VAMPIRE OF NEW ORLEANS

The Continental Op is visited by a woman who claims to be Countess Marcian Gregoryi's sister. The Op visits the *Club de la Merci*, owned by Mafia Don Franco Vitelli. The club's singer is a woman named Ziska. Vitelli's chief competition is Irish gangster Liam O'Breane. The Countess is a member of a vampire order led by Count Saint-Germain, aka Szandor. The Op receives documents from fellow P.I. Teddy Verano referring to a string of scalpings and murders committed by a Countess Marcian Gregoryi in Paris in 1804. The Op also seeks advice on vampires from Professor Ruven van Helsing. Johann Georg Faust was turned into a vampire by Saint-Germain, and in turn transformed Countess Marguerite Karnstein.

Short story by Jared Welch in Tales of the Shadowmen Volume 10: Esprit de Corps, *Jean-Marc and Randy Lofficier, eds., Black Coat Press, 2013; reprinted in French in* L'Almanach des Vampires, *Jean-Marc and Randy Lofficier, eds., Rivière Blanche, 2014; and in* The Vampire Almanac (Volume 2), *Jean-Marc and Randy Lofficier, eds., Black Coat Press, 2015. The Continental Op is a private investigator created by Dashiell Hammett. Countess Marcian Gregoryi and Count Szandor are from Paul Féval's novel* The Vampire Countess. *Here, Szandor is conflated with the Count Saint-Germain, a historical figure who appears in a number of works of fiction, and was rumored to have been a vampire. Other accounts portray Saint-Germain as a mere immortal rather than a vampire. Probably there is more than one unaging individual using the name of the Count Saint-Germain. Don Franco Vitelli is a descendant of François Vitelli, a member of the* Frères de la Merci *from Féval's* Bel Demonio. *Liam O'Breane is a descendant of Fergus O'Breane from another Féval book,* The Mysteries of London. *Ziska is from Alexandre Dumas' play* The Vampire. *Teddy Verano is a P.I. created by French author Maurice Limat. Professor Ruven van Helsing is from*

Jean-Marc Lofficier's novel The Katrina Protocol; he is a member of the American branch of the family that also produced the vampire hunter Abraham Van Helsing, from Bram Stoker's Dracula. Countess Marguerite Karnstein is from Funeral Feast, one of Jeff Patrick's Dark Angel Chronicles series of e-books, and is presumably a relative of Carmilla Karnstein from J. Sheridan Le Fanu's Carmilla.

Late Summer
THE SEA WRAITHS

Secret Agent X battles a diabolical Nazi plot to attack the U.S. The *Clarion* and Jim Anthony's *New York Star* are mentioned as rivals to the *Herald* newspaper. Agent X, disguised as FBI Agent Wesley Greaves, requests aid from Commander Miles Messervie, Chief of Operations for the Special Intelligence Service, who playfully refers to his secretary as "Miss Tuppence" and "Miss Ha'penny," and has her send for Lieutenant Tanner, who can help get "Greaves" behind enemy lines. Tanner and "Greaves" are flown to France by Lance Star and his Sky Rangers.

Novel by Sean Ellis, Age of Adventure, 2009. Secret Agent X appeared in a titular pulp magazine. The Clarion newspaper is from the Phantom Detective pulp novels. Jim Anthony, the owner of the New York Star, appeared in the pulp magazine Super Detective. "Commander Miles Messervie" is better known as Vice Admiral Sir Miles Messervy (aka M) from Ian Fleming's James Bond novels. John Pearson's James Bond: The Authorized Biography of 007 states Messervy did not become head of the British Secret Service until January 1946, so the reference to Messervy as head of the SIS must be an exaggeration, though he may have been second in command of MI6 at this time. Messervy's secretary is Miss Moneypenny, also from the Bond novels. Bill Tanner is MI6's Chief of Staff in the Bond novels. Lance Star and his Sky Rangers are Canadian pulp characters who have been revived by modern authors, notably Bobby Nash. This book takes place in late summer, between the German invasion of France in May–June 1940 and the United States' entry into World War II in December 1941.

October
SKY PIRATES OF RANGOON

Cliff Secord, pretending to be asleep during a battle between the American Volunteer Group in Burma and a group of pirates in order to hide his secret identity, thinks "I bet this never happened to the Spirit."

Short story by Cody Goodfellow in The Rocketeer: Jet-Pack Adventures, *Jeff Conner and Tom Waltz, eds., IDW Publishing, 2014. Cliff actually met the Spirit in February.*

Autumn
DEPTHS OF HORROR

Thunder Jim Wade and a Japanese naval commander are abducted to the undersea city of Jahl-Ki, whose people worship Father Dagon and Mother Hydra. There, they are forced to battle various creatures in an arena, including the Gnophkeh, Dholes, and Byakhee. Wade remembers a military man named Knight telling him about a similar kingdom beneath the ocean off the coast of New England, which was bombed by the American military.

Short story by Frank Schildiner in The New Adventures of Thunder Jim Wade, *Tommy Hancock and Russ Anderson, eds., Pro Se Press, 2012. Thunder Jim Wade was the hero of five stories by Henry Kuttner, which appeared in the pulp* Thrilling Adventures *in 1941. Father Dagon, Mother Hydra, and the kingdom off the coast of New England (Y'ha-nthlei) are from H. P. Lovecraft's "The Shadow over Innsmouth." The Gnophkeh were created by Lin Carter as part of Lovecraft's Cthulhu Mythos. The Dholes were also created by Lovecraft, while the Byakhee are from Mythos stories by August Derleth. The military man named Knight is Richard Knight, who appeared in stories by Donald Keyhoe in the pulp* Flying Aces.

December
AS TIME GOES BY . . .

In Casablanca, Doctor Omega requests the aid of Rick Blaine, owner of *Rick's Café Américain*, who agreed to listen to the Doctor as a favor to Ferrari. Rick tells Omega Major Strasser will see to it he receives special treatment from neither the Vichy French nor the Nazis. He also says Captain Renault doesn't hand out letters-of-transit to just anybody. Rick is startled as he recognizes the song Sam, his piano player, is performing. In Germany, Omega's time-and-space ship, the *Cosmos* has fallen into the hands of Doktor Drexler and his son Frank. Several years ago, the Drexlers reigned havoc on New York City with Ironmen created by the elder Drexler, who was later falsely believed to be dead at the hands of the masked vigilante known as the Spider, who defeated them both. Afterwards, Frank started raving about vigilantes who dressed like spiders, bats, or cats, or who dressed in red, white, and blue or the Union Jack. Unbeknownst to father and son, the Doctor and his companion Fred are spying on them. The Doctor tells Fred not to touch a cube that has a powerful effect on Omega. Three months ago, the Doctor and Fred chose as the current power source for the *Cosmos* a meteor, which shared many properties with *vril* energy, that some believed originated from an exploding planet. This meteor had traces of solidified krypton gas and sometimes radiated a green glow. Omega calls Noel Essaillon, a Frenchman who has written about time travel, a fool. Back in the present day, the Doctor says as a backup plan, the Nazis will bury Doktor Drexler's newest batch of Ironmen to be awakened when the Fatherland has regrouped. Fred refers to them as "Sleepers."

Short story by Paul Hugli in Tales of the Shadowmen Volume 9: La Vie en Noir, *Jean-Marc and Randy Lofficier, eds., Black Coat Press, 2012; reprinted in French in* Les Compagnons de l'Ombre (Tome 15), *Jean-Marc and Randy Lofficier, eds., Rivière Blanche, 2014. Doctor Omega is from the novel of the same name by Arnould Galopin, as is his companion Fred and his ship, the* Cosmos. *Rick Blaine, his Café Américain, Ferrari, Major Strasser, Colonel Renault, and Sam are from the film* Casablanca. *Although the year of this story is given as 1942, this is incorrect. Rick Blaine's appearance here takes place concurrently with the beginning of* Casablanca, *which itself takes place in December 1941. Frank Drexler and his father battled the Spider in Norvell W. Page's pulp novel* Satan's Murder Machines. *The vigilante who dresses as a bat is the Batman. The vigilante who dresses as a cat is probably the Black Cat, aka Hollywood stuntwoman Linda Turner, whose adventures were published by Harvey Comics. The vigilante who dresses in red, white, and blue is Captain America. In the 1960s, Cap battled Drexler's second batch of Ironmen, known as "the Sleepers." The cube is the Cosmic Cube, which contains mysterious energies that allow its wielder to transform reality itself. In the Cube's first appearance, it was utilized by Captain America's foe the Red Skull. The Skull was also the one who originally proposed the creation of the Sleepers, though Doktor Drexler appears to have been the* one who actually produced them. *The vigilante dressed in the Union Jack is the aptly-named Union Jack, Cap's teammate in the superhero group known as the Invaders. Although most comic book superteams' exploits do not take place in the CU, it has been established a version of the Invaders existed in the CU, albeit for a much shorter period of time than their Marvel Universe counterparts.* The vril *energy is from Edward Bulwer-Lytton's novel* The Coming Race. *The meteor is a piece of kryptonite, a radioactive fragment of Superman's home planet Krypton, which is deadly to the Man of Steel. Noël Essaillon is from French author René Barjavel's science fiction novel* Le Voyageur Imprudent *(aka* Future Times Three*).*

THE MASKED DETECTIVE'S DEADLY TRAIL

The Masked Detective, impersonating a petty criminal, tells the doorman at an underworld dive in Hell's Kitchen Blinky McQuade sent him. Later, he tells Detective-Sergeant Gleason to contact Frank Havens, publisher of the *Clarion*.

Short story by Tom Johnson in Pulp Detectives, *Altus Press, 2010. The Masked Detective, alias Rex Parker, reporter for the* New York Daily Comet, *was created by Norman A. Daniels, and appeared in his own self-titled pulp magazine beginning in Fall 1940. Blinky McQuade is the criminal persona the Spider uses to infiltrate the underworld. Frank Havens and the* Clarion *are from the pulp exploits of the Phantom Detective. The date of this exploit is based on a description of a 1941 Buick as "new," along with the fact one of the murder victims in the story was rejected for military service, suggesting these events take place after Pearl Harbor.*

Christmas
BOY KILLER TO DIE TOMORROW

Mr. Mystic clears the name of a young boy sentenced to the electric chair with the help of the Spirit and Lady Luck.

Mr. Mystic Sunday strip by "S. R. Powell" (Bob Powell) in The Spirit Section, *December 28, 1941. This crossover brings together the Spirit, Mr. Mystic, and Lady Luck, all of whom were created by Will Eisner.*

Late Autumn
A PRESENT FOR HITLER

Reichsmarschall Hermann Göring sends Leo Saint-Clair (aka the Nyctalope) on a quest alongside Captain Maciste of the Italian *Bersaglieri* and Herr Doktor Merkwürdigliebe, a German scientist. Merkwürdigliebe mentions the works of Kepler and Dr. Omega.

Short story by Emmanuel Gorlier in The Nyctalope Steps In, *Jean-Marc and Randy Lofficier, eds., Black Coat Press, 2011; reprinted in French in* La Nuit du Nyctalope, *Jean-Marc and Randy Lofficier, eds., Rivière Blanche, 2012. The Nyctalope is the hero of a series of novels by Jean de La Hire. The immortal strongman Maciste first appeared in the 1914 Italian silent film* Cabiria, *went on to appear in several more films from 1915–1928, and was revived in the '60s for a new series of "sword-and-sandal" movies. Dr. Merkwürdigliebe will later be known by the English equivalent of his name, Dr. Strangelove, from Stanley Kubrick's film of the same name. Kubrick's movie ends with mankind being destroyed by nuclear warheads, and therefore must take place in an alternate reality to the Crossover Universe, thus making the Strangelove of the film a counterpart to the CU's Strangelove, who appears in Gorlier's story. Dr. Omega is the title character of a science fiction novel by Arnould Galopin.*

1942

Winter

SATAN'S MINIONS

Richard Curtis Van Loan (alias the Phantom Detective) points out Richard Wentworth and his fiancée Nita Van Sloan to his companions at a nightclub.

Short story by Tom Johnson in Classic Pulp Fiction Stories #1, *Tom and Ginger Johnson, eds., Fading Shadows Publications, June 1995; reprinted in* Pulp Detectives, *Altus Press, 2010. The cameo by Wentworth (the Spider's alter ego) and his beloved Nita reinforces the Phantom's place in the CU.*

THE CASE OF THE BLIND SOLDIER

The Green Ghost (George Chance) investigates the bizarre murder of an army Corporal. Agent Jeff Shannon of G-2 is also looking into the crime. Chance's aide Joe Harper seeks a lead at the Pink Rat. Commissioner Standish tells Chance Dan Fowler and his boys are moving in to clean up corruption at Fort Dix.

Story by Tom Johnson in Exciting Pulp Tales, *Altus Press, 2011. The Green Ghost (aka simply the Ghost) appeared in the pulp magazine* The Ghost, Super-Detective *(later retitled* The Ghost Detective *and then* The Green Ghost Detective*), and was created by G. T. Fleming-Roberts. Jeff Shannon is* better known as the Eagle, who appeared in stories by "Kerry McRoberts" (Norman A. Daniels) in Thrilling Spy Stories and Popular Detective. *The Pink Rat is an underworld dive bar from the pulp novels featuring the man Farmer identified as Allard Kent Rassendyll, who was the brother of G-8 and the half-brother of the Spider. FBI agent Dan Fowler was created by Major George Fielding Eliot, and appeared in the pulp G-Men Detective. The year is conjecture, though the story explicitly takes place during America's involvement in World War II. It must take place very early in the war, since Win Scott Eckert's "Chance of a Ghost" established that George Chance was recruited by the OSS shortly after war was declared and worked in that capacity for the duration. Chance returned to adventuring as the Green Ghost in summer 1945.*

February 7
TKO

The Rocketeer (aka Cliff Secord) battles a man with a propeller-bearing suit, although a swarm of bats rather than Cliff defeats the villain. Cliff gives his opponent's flying device to two of Doc's aides, one of whom is carrying a pig, and says now that he has returned their boss' prototype, the two of them are even. When the ape-like chemist asks Doc why he let Secord keep the rocket pack, he responds "Gentlemen, anyone can ignite an engine, but to soar like an eagle you need the heart of a lion . . . and that, my friends, takes a hero."

Story by Lowell Francis and Gene Ha in Rocketeer Adventures #2, IDW Publishing, *June 2011. Doc, his aides, and the pig are not referred to by name, but are easily identifiable. Dave Stevens' original comic* The Rocketeer *established Doc was the creator of Cliff's rocket pack. According to Rick Lai's* The Revised Complete Chronology of Bronze *(Altus Press, 2010), Doc served with the COI, the predecessor to the OSS, from December 1941 to March 1942, and his attorney aide was teaching a law class in February of that latter year. Doc and his aides must have made a brief trip to Los Angeles to work on the propeller device, which was stolen by Cliff's unidentified foe.*

Late February
BATTLE FOR L.A.

The Black Bat, the Phantom Detective, the Domino Lady, and G-8 join forces to battle Japanese forces that are planning an occult invasion of Los Angeles. Secret Agent X was previously severely wounded while investigating the planned attack in Chinatown.

A Return of the Originals *graphic novel by C. J. Henderson and Mark Sparacio, Moonstone Comics, 2010. This crossover confirms the Black Bat, the Phantom Detective, the Domino Lady, G-8, and Secret Agent X all coexist within the CU.*

RESOLUTION

The Spider and Ram Singh investigate the remains of corrupt Japanese millionaire Omaguri Sento's mansion. There, they encounter Sento's corpse, which has been possessed by an extra dimensional monster.

This short story by C. J. Henderson in the hardcover edition of The Return of the Originals: Battle for L.A., *Moonstone Comics, 2010, takes place concurrently with* Battle for L.A. *itself, which details the circumstances of Sento's death.*

Spring. Wrestler Bob White and his teenage manager Terry White begin fighting criminals and slashers as Nightmare and Sleepy. (*Clue Comics* #1, January 1943.)

Spring
THE EYES OF SATAN

The Phantom Detective attempts to end a gang war in New York. The Phantom's ally, Inspector Thomas Gregg, is doing his own part to end the conflict, aided by, among others, Timothy Scallot, Cardona, and Captain McGrath. The instigator of the war tells a group of fellow gangsters they should worry more about the Black Bat or the Masked Avenger than the Phantom.

Short story by "Robert Wallace" (Tom Johnson) in Double Danger Tales *#37, Tom and Ginger Johnson, eds., Fading Shadows Publications, March 2000; reprinted in* Triple Detective *#3, Altus Press, 2009. Timothy Scallot is from the Secret Agent X stories. Cardona is from the pulp novels featuring a certain slouch-hatted crimefighter, while Captain McGrath is from the Black Bat pulps. The Masked Avenger is Johnson's own original creation.*

THE INVISIBLE PIRATES

Marine biologist Doris Nixson shoots at the villain Tidakada to save Thunder Jim Wade's life. The weapon has no effect on Tidakada, who boasts he eats *vril* for breakfast.

Story by Nick Ahlheim in The New Adventures of Thunder Jim Wade, *Tommy Hancock and Russ Anderson, eds., Pro Se Press, 2012. The reference to the* vril *(from Edward Bulwer-Lytton's* The Coming Race*) strengthens the inclusion of Henry Kuttner's pulp hero Thunder Jim Wade in the CU.*

Summer

THE ROAD NOT TAKEN

The Nyctalope has been sent by the Vichy government to assassinate G-8, who is aiding the French Resistance. He attacks the pilot and his comrades Bull Martin and Nippy Westin, only to discover their mission is an honorable one. A group of allied officers meet to discuss dealing with the Nyctalope, and a British officer introduces a young naval officer named James Bond.

Short story by Matthew Dennion in Night of the Nyctalope, *Jean-Marc and Randy Lofficier, eds., Black Coat Press, 2012; reprinted in French in* La Nuit du Nyctalope, *Jean-Marc and Randy Lofficier, eds., Rivière Blanche, 2012. The Nyctalope's adventures were chronicled by Jean de La Hire; during World War II, he served the Vichy regime in France, collaborating with the Nazis. G-8's adventures during World War I alongside his comrades Bull Martin and Nippy Weston (spelled "Westin" in Dennion's story) were chronicled in pulp stories by Robert J. Hogan. James Bond needs no introduction.*

THE SPIDER'S WEB

Secret Agent X battles a German agent who is preying on New York City with giant Sind spiders from India. The existence of the spiders became known to the world in 1933, when their discovery was recounted in a book by Robert Wallace.

Short story by Tom Johnson published as "Horror's Monster" in Classic Pulp Fiction Stories #9, *Tom and Ginger Johnson, eds., Fading Shadows Publications, February 1996; reprinted as "Horror Monsters from Hell" in* Secret Agent X, Volume Two, *Ron Hanna, ed., Wild Cat Books, 2007, and as "The Spider's Web" in* Pulp Detectives, *Altus Press, 2010. A Sind spider appeared in the Phantom Detective pulp novel* The Jewels of Doom.

June

CODENAME: ECSTASY

The Rocketeer battles the Nazi group known as the Silver Legion, which is attempting to kidnap Hedy Lamarr in order to get their hands on her invention, the frequency hopper. When Hedy asks Cliff what they should do with a captured member of the Legion, he replies, "Leave that to me. I know a guy called Doc who's big on rehabilitation through applied brain surgery. If it works on criminals, it should work on Nazis, too."

Story by Nancy A. Collins in The Rocketeer: Jet-Pack Adventures, *Jeff Conner and Tom Waltz, eds., IDW Publishing, 2014. Dave Stevens' original comic* The Rocketeer *established Doc as the builder of the rocket pack used by Cliff Secord.*

July

THE HORROR OF HYPERBOREA

Thunder Jim Wade and his aides Dirk Marat and Red Argyle battle the Nazi mad scientist Baron Victor von Hammer and his son Franz, who have abducted Professor Isaac Levi in the hopes the scholar can lead them to the lost civilization of Hyperborea, planning to use its secrets to take over the world. Von Hammer is actually Baron Victor von Frankenstein, the illegitimate and long-lived son of the legendary Baron von Frankenstein and a barmaid he bedded while hunting his creation, while Franz is really one of the younger Baron's own creations. A Bedouin aiding Wade and company against Frankenstein's living corpses uses the language of ancient Stygia. The Bedouins invoke the name of Mitra. Levi's daughter Lise says her father witnessed the execution of a member of the Frankenstein family who created a creature that killed dozens of people in his and nearby villages, and a member of her mother's family lost an arm fighting against one of the Frankenstein monsters. This ruined his dreams of being a soldier, though he did become a police officer. Lise tells Wade about traps in Hyperborea, the first being the anger of Zath, the lord of spiders and the earth. Wade and company store their *Thunderbug* ship in a warehouse owned by a doctor colleague of Wade's who uses his vast fortune and amazing mind to save the world. Marat refers to the time Argyle destroyed an Oparian outpost by accident. Frankenstein, who has captured Wade and friends, tells Wade he once defeated Bulldog Drummond in London. Zath served Bel, the masked maker of chaos. A statue of Louhi, witch queen of Hyperborea, appears. The second trial of Hyperborea is the many mouths of Xotli, the Atlantean lord of blood. Wade, Frankenstein, and the others are attacked by the witch men of Hyperborea. Louhi tells Frankenstein she was ancient when his people were food for the Elder Worms and slaves to her people and their Acheron rivals, and only ancient Gagool and Ayesha have lived nearly as long as her. She subjects Wade and the rest to the Trial of Bori, and thinks of a barbarian who nearly killed her thousands of years ago.

Novella by Frank Schildiner, Pro Se Press, 2014. Thunder Jim Wade appeared in five stories by "Charles Stoddard" (a pseudonym for Henry Kuttner) in the pulp Thrilling Adventures *in 1941. The elder Baron Victor von Frankenstein and his creation are from Mary Shelley's* Frankenstein, *of* course. *The younger Victor was formerly known as Victor Saville, the protagonist of Robert Myers' novels* The Cross of Frankenstein *and* The Slave of Frankenstein. *Hyperborea is from Robert E. Howard's stories of Conan the Barbarian, as is Stygia. Mitra is a deity from the Conan tales. Bel is from the Conan story "The Queen of the Black Coast." Acheron appears in* The Hour of the Dragon *and other Conan tales. Bori is from Howard's essay "The Hyborian Age." The member of the Frankenstein family that was executed is from the Hammer film* The Curse of Frankenstein. *Creative mythographer Chuck Loridans has identified this member of the family as Victor Frankenstein III, the son of the former Victor Saville and the grandson of Shelley's Victor. The police officer who lost an arm to one of the Frankenstein monsters is Inspector Krogh from the Universal film* Son of Frankenstein. *Zath is from L. Sprague de Camp's novel* Conan and the Spider God. *Louhi is from de Camp and Lin Carter's Conan story "The Witch of the Mists." Xotli is from de Camp and Carter's novel* Conan of the Isles. *The witch men of Hyperborea are from de Camp and Carter's "Legions of the Dead." Wade's doctor colleague is the golden-eyed pulp hero known as "Doc." The New York warehouse owned by Doc is used for the storage of his many vehicles, and is disguised as the headquarters of a business called the Hidalgo Trading Company. The lost city of Opar in Africa is from Edgar Rice Burroughs' books about the jungle lord. Captain Hugh "Bulldog" Drummond is from a series of novels originated by H. C. "Sapper" McNeile, and continued after McNeile's death by Gerard Fairlie. The Elder Worms are a reference to Howard's Bran Mak Morn story "Worms of the Earth." Gagool is from H. Rider Haggard's first Allan Quatermain novel,* King Solomon's Mines, *while Ayesha is the title character of Haggard's novel* She *and its sequel and prequels.*

August
THE NAZI SPIDER STAFFEL
   John Masters, the allied pilot known as the Lone Eagle, rescues two French Resistance members from a prison camp with an unlucky number. The camp's Kommandant is a tall, thin colonel with a monocle, whose underlings include his secretary Helga, who flirts with an American army colonel, and an obese man named Sergeant Schultz. The Resistance members were contacted by an American secret agent about Germany's use of giant Indian Sind spiders. Masters encounters his old enemy R-47 and an elderly scientist called Herr Doktor K, who is experimenting with the spiders' venom, and believes Masters is actually his old nemesis, "G-" The Doktor's enemy has two aides, one of whom is a bull of a man, while the other is a tiny nippy kid.

Short story by Tom Johnson in Classic Pulp Fiction Stories *#16, Tom and Ginger Johnson, eds., Fading Shadows Publications, September 1996; reprinted in* Pulp Detectives, *Altus Press, 2010. The Lone Eagle appeared in his own self-titled pulp magazine beginning in September 1933; he was active during both World Wars. The prison camp (Stalag 13), its Kommandant (Colonel Wilhelm Klink), Helga, the American colonel (Robert E. Hogan), and Sergeant Schultz are from the television series* Hogan's Heroes. *The American secret agent is the pulp hero Secret Agent X; his battle with German agents utilizing Sind spiders was chronicled in Johnson's story "The Spider's Web." The spiders first appeared in*

the Phantom Detective *novel* The Jewels of Doom. *Herr Doktor K is G-8's nemesis Herr Doktor Krueger. Krueger must have survived the explosion of his cave headquarters in the graphic novel* Airboy/G-8. *In that story, Krueger was confined to an iron lung, whereas here he is merely wheelchair bound. Krueger must have made a partial recovery in the two years between the two stories. G-8's aides are Bull Martin and Nippy Weston. Since Secret Agent X, the Phantom Detective, and G-8 are in the CU, this crossover brings in the Lone Eagle and Colonel Hogan.*

September

THE LESSER OF TWO EVILS

A vampire turned centuries ago by Monsieur Goetzi of Selene defends his domain from Eckhart, a member of the Nazi Thule Society.

Short story by David McDonald in Tales of the Shadowmen Volume 10: Esprit de Corps, *Jean-Marc and Randy Lofficier, eds., Black Coat Press, 2013; reprinted in French in* L'Almanach des Vampires, *Jean-Marc and Randy Lofficier, eds., Rivière Blanche, 2014; and in* The Vampire Almanac (Volume 1), *Jean-Marc and Randy Lofficier, eds., Black Coat Press, 2015. Otto Goetzi and Selene are from Paul Féval's* Vampire City. *Eckhart is from "Everybody Hates Hitler," an episode of the television series* Supernatural.

1943

Winter. Colonel Moore Williams dons the flamboyant costume of the Flamingo to battle the Axis. (*Contact Comics* #1, July 1944.)

Early March

THE LEAGUE OF DEAD PATRIOTS

FBI agent Dan Fowler tries to apprehend gangster William "The Bill" Kennedy, but is forced off the road by the Domino Lady. When Dan complains about vigilantes interfering with the Bureau's affairs, his fellow agent Larry Kendal opines with many of America's able-bodied men at war, they can use all the help they can get. Fowler says that they're getting it, from Jim Anthony, the Ghost Squad, and Secret Agent X, all of whom operate with government sanction. However, he argues "clowns" such as the Shadow, Brother Bones and the Domino Lady are interfering loose cannons. After questioning Kennedy's henchman Joe McGoohan, Fowler heads to the Tule Lake internment camp. There, he meets Norman Takei and his young son George. Fowler eventually discovers the Domino Lady and McGoohan are allied against Kennedy. When Fowler asks McGoohan why he is involved in this case, "McGoohan" says the answer is right in front of him. Fowler sees an X etched in the mud, and says he should have known.

Story by Andrew Salmon in Dan Fowler: G-Man Volume One, *Ron Fortier, ed., Cornerstone Book Publishers, 2009. Dan Fowler was created by Major George Fielding Eliot and appeared in 112 issues of the pulp magazine* G-Men Detective. *The Domino Lady was created by an unidentified author using the nom de plume Lars Anderson and appeared in five issues of* Saucy Romantic Adventures *and one issue of* Mystery Adventure Magazine. *Jim Anthony appeared in the magazine* Super Detective; *his exploits were chronicled by Victor Rousseau Emanuel, Robert Leslie Bellem, and W. T. Ballard. The Ghost Squad were co-created by Salmon and Ron Fortier, and have starred in one novel to date, which featured a guest appearance by Fowler. Brother Bones is another hero created by Fortier. Secret Agent X starred in his own self-titled pulp magazine; he was created by Paul Chadwick and his exploits were continued by several others, all of whom used the pen name "Brant House." In this story, the master of disguise is using the alias Joe McGoohan. The hero of the shadows needs no further introduction. George Takei would grow up to portray helmsman Hikaru Sulu on the television series* Star Trek; *for an explanation of how the future events depicted in the* Star Trek *franchise and the franchise itself can coexist in the CU, see J. R. Rasmussen's story "Research."*

Spring

THE DEAD WORLD

A man named Innes refers to the Minunians, the Ant Men of Africa. Innes discovers the world at the Earth's core was created by an alien race called the Fashioners.

Short story by Innes, related to F. Paul Wilson via Gridley Wave, in The Worlds of Edgar Rice Burroughs, *Mike Resnick and Robert T. Garcia, Baen Books, 2013. The Ant Men are from Burroughs'* Tarzan and the Ant Men. *The description of the Fashioners makes it clear they are meant to be the Great Race of Yith from H. P. Lovecraft's "The Shadow Out of Time," thus connecting Burroughs' series set at the Earth's core to Lovecraft's Cthulhu Mythos.*

Summer

GUNS OF VENGEANCE

Tony Quinn (aka the Black Bat) and his girlfriend Carol Baldwin see a light coming from the *Clarion* Building. He resolves to ask the owner, Frank Havens, about it. Later, Commissioner Warner, Captain McGrath, and Inspector Thomas Gregg meet with Quinn, asking him to investigate the murder of a gangster. Soon afterwards, playboy Richard Curtis Van Loan and his girlfriend Muriel Havens (Frank's daughter) visit Quinn, stating they're looking for a worthy charity to which to donate some money. Quinn recommends they contribute to a fund for the widow of a murdered policeman. Later, Quinn, as the Black Bat, finds the Phantom Detective snooping around his office. The two ultimately part on amicable terms.

Short story by Tom Johnson in Pulp Detectives, *Altus Press, 2010. The encounters between the Black Bat and the Phantom Detective (aka Richard Curtis Van Loan), both in and out of costume, are near-identical to those shown in an earlier story by Johnson, "City of Phantoms" (*Triple Detective #4, *Altus Press, 2010). However, the accounts of the Black Bat's activities before and after their meetings in each tale are completely different. I have chosen to treat "Guns of Vengeance," the more recent account, as the "correct" one for CU purposes. It is worth noting "City of Phantoms" has a cameo by FBI Agents Dan Fowler and Larry Kendal from the pulp* G-Men Detective. *Although the two heroes say this is the first time they've met, this is clear fictionalization, as they crossed paths in 1939 during the events of Erwin K. Roberts' "The Sons of Thor," and again in 1941, as seen in the graphic novel* Return of the Originals: Battle for L.A. *"Guns of Vengeance" takes place during World War II, and the murdered policeman served two years in the army, suggesting the story takes place no earlier than 1943, two years after the United States entered the war.*

THE THIRD CRY TO LEGBA

John Thunstone quotes Jules de Grandin.

Story by Manly Wade Wellman in Weird Tales, *November 1943.*

NOIR

The mercenary known as the Black Sparrow joins forces with Miss Fury to search for a Templar treasure that is also being sought by criminals. The Shadow and Margo Lane appear.

Five-issue miniseries by Victor Gischler and Andrea Mutti, Dynamite Entertainment. The Black Sparrow is from Dynamite's Shadow series, which is for the most part compatible with the character's established history. Miss Fury was the title character of a comic strip by Tarpé Mills from 1941–1952.

July 7, 1943–October 1, 1944
DOGS OF WAR

The British agent Sparrow mentions the Nazis' Special Projects Division.

A five-issue Atomic Robo miniseries by Brian Clevinger and Scott Wegener, Red 5 Comics, August–December 2008. The Nazis' Special Projects Division is from the video game series Wolfenstein.

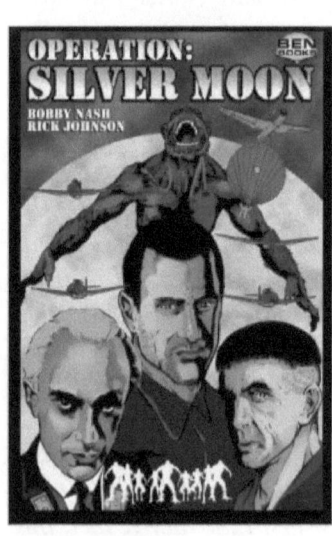

July 27–August 7
OPERATION: SILVER MOON

Tom Lupus, a werewolf agent of the U.S. War Department, teams with the vampire lord Vlas to prevent the Nazis from using an orb they have discovered to unleash the monstrous Army of the Black Death to spread havoc. General Heinrich Krieger says to Professor Hans Steir, the archaeologist who unearthed the orb, "This toy you've discovered may very well be the most powerful weapon known to man. Perhaps even more than that Jewish ark that was lost to us a few years ago. This artifact is the key to our total victory." An air strike on the Army is led by a pilot who refers to his men as Rangers.

Graphic novel by Bobby Nash and Rick Johnson, BEN Books, 2015. General Krieger is clearly referring to the events of the film Raiders of the Lost Ark, *bringing Tom Lupus into the CU. The pilots conducting the air strike are Lance Star and his Sky Rangers, Canadian pulp characters who have been revived in the modern day by Nash and others.*

August 1943–June 1951
UNCONDITIONAL SURRENDER
Virginia Crouchback remembers falling down the stairs at the Palazzo Corombona in Venice. The expatriate British poet Parsnip now writes for the American magazine *Survival.*

The third novel in Evelyn Waugh's Sword of Honour trilogy. Waugh's novel Brideshead Revisited *featured a party held at the palace of a Venetian named Vittoria Corombona. Parsnip previously appeared in Waugh's book* Put Out More Flags.

October 29–November 3
BLUE DEVIL ISLAND
On a Pacific island, a group of American pilots encounter a creature called Viran Ghurak, which sometimes appears as a black faceless man. One of the pilots is Max Collins, a native of "a small fishing village on the Maine coast."

Novel by Stephen Mark Rainey. The description of Viran Ghurak as a black faceless man suggests he is really Lovecraft's Nyarlathotep. Max Collins must be a member of the Collins family of Collinsport, Maine, as seen in the television series Dark Shadows. *Rainey has also written tie-in novels for that series.*

Autumn
HOOFS
John Thunstone tells Countess Monteseco he has to catch a plane to investigate a case with Judge Pursuivant.

Short story by Manly Wade Wellman in Weird Tales, *March 1944.*

THE SHADOW CALLING NICK CARTER
Nick Carter teams up with the Shadow and Margo Lane to battle a criminal mastermind called Vox.

Story written by Walter Gibson and illustrated by an unknown artist in The Shadow Comics *#12, Street and Smith, March 1944, reworked from "The Voice of Crime," an episode of the* Nick Carter, Master Detective *radio program cowritten by Gibson and Edward Bruskin, broadcast April 18, 1943.*

November 15–21
LIGHTS, CAMERA, MURDER!
Ed Race, the Masked Marksman, investigates the sabotage of a film being made by a friend of his. A grimy storefront set reminds Race of old Doc Turner's drugstore in Manhattan.

Short story by Rich Harvey in The Spider: Shadow of Evil, *Moonstone Books, 2012. Ed Race, the Masked Marksman, had his own series of stories by Emile C. Tepperman in* The Spider *pulp magazine. Doc Turner, a pharmacist and amateur detective, appeared in stories by Arthur Leo Zagat in the same magazine. Both Race and Turner encountered the Spider in 1934, as seen in Harvey's story "One Death to a Customer," bringing them both into the CU.*

1944

Winter
NUMBER SEVEN, QUEER STREET

Jerome Latimer, sidekick to psychic detective Miles Pennoyer, writes, "There are not many people who are fortunate enough to know these selfless and splendid people, the psychic doctors—and there are still fewer books that record the wonders they can do and are still doing. Algernon Blackwood's book *John Silence* was one of the first, and Dion Fortune's book *The Secret of Dr. Taverner* is another . . ."

Introduction to the collection Number Seven, Queer Street *by Jerome Latimer, edited by Margery Lawrence.*

ARSÈNE LUPIN VS. COLONEL LINNAUS

Colonel Peer Linnaus tells Oberleutnant Siegmund von Keller Sherlock Holmes was no match for Arsène Lupin.

Short story by Anthony Boucher in Ellery Queen's Mystery Magazine *Vol. 5, No. 19, 1944; reprinted in* The Many Faces of Arsène Lupin, *Jean-Marc and Randy Lofficier, eds., Black Coat Press, 2012.*

THE LETTERS OF COLD FIRE

John Thunstone's foe Rowley Thorne is unsuccessful in acquiring a copy of the *Necronomicon*, and instead acquires a book belonging to a student of the Deep School, an extradimensional school that provides students with instruction in sorcery.

Short story by Manly Wade Wellman in Weird Tales, *May 1944. The reference to the* Necronomicon *provides further proof John Thunstone's exploits take place in the CU.*

February
DOUBLE DIAMOND

San Francisco-based importer and amateur sleuth Gregory Hood's plane stops over in Chicago, where he winds up investigating the theft of a diamond formerly in the possession of one of the passengers. At one point, he calls lawyer John J. Malone for help.

Episode of the radio series The Casebook of Gregory Hood *written by Denis Green and Anthony Boucher, broadcast August 5, 1946. Craig Rice's lawyer John J. Malone is already in the CU, thus confirming Gregory Hood's inclusion.*

Mid March
THE SPIDER: SHADOW OF EVIL

Shakespeare, Montaigne, and John Raymond Legrasse are quoted on the subject of evil. Richard Wentworth tells Commissioner Kirkpatrick he'll be enjoying a fine meal at the Cobalt Club while Kirkpatrick is accepting a lifetime achievement award from the Ladies Auxiliary.

Novel by C. J. Henderson, Moonstone Books, 2012. William Shakespeare and Michel de Montaigne were real people, but John Raymond Legrasse, from H. P. Lovecraft's "The Call of Cthulhu," is not. Henderson has chronicled Legrasse's further exploits in a series of stories. The Cobalt Club is the club a certain vigilante visits when he impersonates a wealthy globetrotter. Wentworth celebrates his birthday, allegedly his fortieth, early in the book. However, Wentworth was born in 1891, which would make this birthday actually his fifty-third.

Spring
JOHN THUNSTONE'S INHERITANCE

Sabine Loel suggests that John Thunstone bring his friend Jules de Grandin along to investigate the supernatural phenomena at Bertram Dower House, but de Grandin and Dr. Trowbridge are busy with cases of their own.

Story by Manly Wade Wellman in Weird Tales, *July 1944.*

April
REQUIEM FOR A REGIME

The Nyctalope has been asked by Bob Morane to locate his friend, archaeologist Aristide Clairembart. The professor's Nazi captors wish him to verify whether what appears to be the Spear of Destiny is in fact the genuine article. The Nyctalope rescues Clairembart, but the two are soon confronted by Count Dracula, who seeks the Spear for his own nefarious purposes. A man named Harker, whose family has a long history of doing battle with Dracula, helps the Nyctalope fend off the vampire.

Short story by Chris Nigro in Night of the Nyctalope, *Jean-Marc and Randy Lofficier, eds., Black Coat Press, 2012; reprinted in* The Vampire Almanac (Volume 1), *Jean-Marc and Randy Lofficier, eds., Black Coat Press, 2015; and in French in* L'Almanach des Vampires, *Jean Marc and Randy Lofficier, eds., Rivière Blanche, 2014. The adventures of the Nyctalope (aka Leo Saint-Clair) were recounted in French pulp stories by Jean de La Hire. Adventurer Bob Morane and his friend Professor Clairembart are from novels by Henri Vernes (Charles-Henri Dewisme). Harker is Quincey Harker, son of Jonathan and Mina Harker, from Bram Stoker's* Dracula *and the Marvel Comics series* Tomb of Dracula. *The 1945 date given in the story is in error.*

July 1944–January 1945
TO DUST AND ASHES IN ITS HEAT CONSUMING
Five airplanes, including one piloted by Group Captain Victor Carroon, trail UFOs that have appeared above London. One saucer is followed by a plane flown by Flight Lieutenant Tug Carrington. In Mission Control, Captain Boothroyd and Air Commodore Lord George Beltham give orders to the pilots. Professor Bernard Quatermass dismisses Beltham's claim one of his fellow investigators is an enemy agent. Harry Dickson breaks up the argument. Dickson's protégé is a sergeant seconded from the Marine Police, Stanley Bulman, who mentions his nephew George.

Short story by Nigel Malcolm in Tales of the Shadowmen Volume 9: La Vie en Noir, *Jean-Marc and Randy Lofficier, eds., Black Coat Press, 2012; reprinted in French in* Les Compagnons de l'Ombre (Tome 13), *Jean-Marc and Randy Lofficier, eds., Rivière Blanche, 2014; and in* Harry Dickson vs. the Spider, *Jean-Marc and Randy Lofficier, eds., Black Coat Press, 2014. Professor Bernard Quatermass is the protagonist of several British television serials and films, including* The Quatermass Experiment, *which also features Victor Carroon. Tug Carrington is an ally of aviator James "Biggles" Bigglesworth in novels by W. E. Johns. Captain Boothroyd is the future Major Boothroyd, service armorer for the British Secret Service in the James Bond novels. Lord George Beltham is a later holder of the title once belonging to Lord Edward Beltham in Marcel Allain and Pierre Souvestre's Fantômas novels. Harry Dickson, "the American Sherlock Holmes," appears in pulp stories by Jean Ray and others. Stanley Bulman is the uncle of Detective Sergeant George Bulman, who appears in the TV series* The XYY Man, Strangers, *and* Bulman.

Summer. Copyboy Rusty Adams begins battling gangsters as Crash Kid. (*Cannonball Comics* #1, February 1945.)

Summer
DOMINO LADY'S THREESOME

Ellen Patrick, alias the Domino Lady, goes undercover at a burlesque house to investigate the disappearance of several showgirls. Violet Ray Brant, the Golden Amazon, is also working there undercover for the same reason. The two of them eventually team up with the ghostlike heroine known as the Veil to battle the alien from Mercury who has captured the girls.

One-shot by Nancy Holder, Howard Hopkins, and Silvestre Szilagyi, Moonstone Comics, 2012. The Domino Lady is firmly in the CU through encounters with Wold Newton Family members the Spider, the Avenger, and Sherlock Holmes, among others. The Golden Amazon appeared in stories by British-born author John Russell Fearn in The Toronto Star Weekly. *The Veil is an original character created by Howard Hopkins. This crossover brings the Golden Amazon and the Veil into the CU. The year is conjecture.*

LIGHTS! CAMERA! SABOTAGE!

Agent Palmer of the FBI assigns secret agent Jeff Shannon (aka the Eagle) to go undercover on the set of a film directed by a suspected saboteur.

Story by Bobby Nash in The New Adventures of the Eagle, *David White, ed., Pro Se Press, 2012. The Eagle's stories were chronicled by Norman A. Daniels under the pseudonym "Captain Kerry McRoberts" in the pulp magazines* Thrilling Spy Stories *and* Popular Detective. *Agent Palmer also appears in Nash's comic book* Lance Star: Sky Ranger–One-Shot! *(illustrated by James Burns) and the upcoming novel* Lance Star: Sky Ranger–Cold Snap. *His grandson is FBI Agent Harold Palmer, the protagonist of Nash's novel* Evil Ways, *as well as its forthcoming sequel* Evil Intent. *Both novels are part of a series of thrillers set in Sommersville, Georgia. Since Lance Star and the Eagle are both in the CU, so are the two Agent Palmers.*

THE DEAD MAN'S HAND

John Thunstone places a phone call from Pennsylvania Station, telling the person on the other end he's sorry he and Dr. Trowbridge can't come.

Short story by Manly Wade Wellman in Weird Tales, *November 1944. Thunstone is talking to Seabury Quinn's occult detective Dr. Jules de Grandin.*

October 8–Late November
THE BLACK BAT'S WAR (aka DRUGS OF DESTRUCTION)

Tony Quinn (aka the Black Bat) and his friend Senator Cliff Walker are both members of the Cobalt Club. Criminal Gunner McGlone helps the Bat and his chauffeur, ex-con Silk Kirby, out of trouble. Quinn tells his girlfriend Carol Baldwin another aide, Butch O'Leary, is out Christmas shopping for presents for his murdered sister's son.

Short story by Tom Johnson originally published as "Drugs of Destruction" in Double Danger Tales *#51, Tom and Ginger Johnson, eds., Fading Shadows Publications, March 2002, and reprinted as "The Black Bat's War" by "G. Wayman Jones" in* Triple Detective *#3, Altus Press, 2009. The Cobalt Club is frequented by a certain slouch-hatted, shadowy mystery man in one of his favorite disguises. Gunner McGlone is the identity the Phantom Detective uses to infiltrate the criminal underworld. Butch avenged his sister's murder in Johnson's Masked Avenger story "Crime's Last Stand."*

October 26. Events of "The Black Wave" by Brian Keene, in which a weapon created by Black Lodge for use during the second World War goes horribly awry.

Autumn
DOMINO LADY/SHERLOCK HOLMES: TANA LEAF MURDERS

The Domino Lady (aka Ellen Patrick) and Sherlock Holmes travel to Egypt to battle a cult that has allied with the Nazis. Ellen and the cult's victims are exposed to the tana leaf, which causes them to hallucinate.

Two-issue miniseries by Nancy Holder, Bobby Nash, Reno Maniquis, Nick Diaz, Matt Ross, and Kori Zick, Moonstone Comics, April–May 2013. Hitler is in power, and is implied to have been ten years ago, suggesting a placement in 1944 or 1945. Ellen twice refers to Holmes as being seventy-years-old. However, Holmes would actually be ninety-years-old in 1944. The royal jelly bee pollen elixir he created in 1921 must make him appear at least two decades younger than his actual age. Tana leaves are from the first series of Mummy films released by Universal Studios.

THORNE ON THE THRESHOLD
John Thunstone sends a letter to Jules de Grandin which states if anything fatal or disabling overtakes Thunstone within the next few days, de Grandin should act on the information contained in the letter.
Story by Manly Wade Wellman in Weird Tales, *January 1945.*

1945

Winter
CAPTAIN MIDNIGHT MEETS AIRBOY
Captain Midnight, captured by Japanese soldiers on a Vietnamese island, is rescued by Airboy, who reveals his fellow Airfighter Skywolf told him the leader of the Viet resistance is actually involved in illicit doings.
Short story by Chuck Dixon in The Captain Midnight Chronicles, *Christopher Mills, ed., Moonstone Books, 2010. This story confirms Captain Midnight, Airboy, the Airfighters, and Skywolf coexist within the CU. The Captain and Airboy seemingly meet for the first time during this story. This may invalidate Jim Harmon's theory, proposed in "The Life Story of King Kong," that Robert J. Hogan's pulp aviator G-8 assumed the alias of Captain Midnight after World War I, since the graphic novel* Airboy/G-8 *had the titular duo meeting for the first time in 1940. However, it is also possible this is fictionalization on Dixon's part.*

March
TWILIGHT (CREPUSCLE)
Gno Mitang decides the Japanese army must not use Godzilla against the Americans.
Short story by Emmanuel Gorlier, appearing as "Crepuscle" in Nyctalope: L'Univers Extravagant de Jean de La Hire, *Emmanuel Gorlier, ed., Rivière Blanche, 2011, and in English in* The Nyctalope Steps In, *Jean-Marc and Randy Lofficier, eds., Black Coat Press, 2011. Gno Mitang is a former ally of Jean de La Hire's hero, the Nyctalope. Godzilla (or Gojira) is from the classic 1954 Japanese monster film and its many sequels. Although the massive destruction to Japan seen in the Godzilla films is incompatible with CU continuity, this story does indicate Godzilla himself exists in the CU, though obviously the films cannot.*

Spring
CONFIDENCES DANS MA NUIT
Thomas Narcejac, recovering from his wounds in a WWII hospital, meets Arsène Lupin, Inspector Maigret, Dr. Watson, Father Brown, the Saint, and Pierre Véry.

Foreword to Confidences dans Ma Nuit, *a collection of short stories by Thomas Narcejac, Athénée, 1946, reprinted as* Usurpation d'Identité, Hachette, 1980. Pierre Véry is the creator of lawyer and amateur sleuth Prosper Lepicq.

THE FLAMING CURSE

The masked and winged hero Hawkman, looking into the background of a supposedly cursed man, receives some help from a retired detective who deduces his true identity.

Story by Gardner F. Fox and Joe Kubert in Flash Comics #69, National Periodical Publications, February–March 1946. The detective, though un-named, is clearly meant to be Sherlock Holmes. This crossover brings a version of Carter Hall, the Golden Age Hawkman, into the CU.

legends of new pulp fiction...

June

CHANCE OF A GHOST

George Chance's (aka the Green Ghost) friend Ned Standish, of the Kingsport Standishes, a *summa cum laude* graduate of Miskatonic University, has been accused of murder. Although Chance calls Standish "Commissioner," he is actually an Assistant Police Commissioner for one of New York City's boroughs, as are Weston, Kirkpatrick, Woods, Foster, Quistrom, Gordon, Warner, Hombert, and others. Chance refers to other vigilantes active at the time he began his career, such as the Black Bat, Captain Midnight, the Phantom Detective, the Domino Lady, and Ki-Gor. Chance's wartime missions began with liberating Professor Horatio Smith, who was something of a modern-day Scarlet Pimpernel, from a supposedly unescapable German prison camp. Subsequent missions for the OSS included a strange encounter with a hideously wriggling whitish worm at an abandoned chateau in Northern France and one with a revolting frog-mouthed, tentacle-lipped creature that accosted him in the sewers of Paris. Standish went over the file on flapper girl Toby Basinger's case with D.A. Skinner. A lookalike for Standish murdered Basinger, who killed an ex-girlfriend of Chance's, nightclub singer Angel de la Ruse. Chance's aide Joe Harper smokes Red Apple Cigarettes.

Short story by George Chance, edited by Win Scott Eckert in Legends of New Pulp Fiction, *Ron Fortier, ed., Airship 27 Productions, 2015; reprinted in* The Green Ghost Declassified, *forthcoming, Moonstone Books. The Green Ghost (aka the Ghost) appeared in the pulp magazine* The Ghost, Super-Detective *(later retitled* The Ghost Detective, *and then* The Green Ghost Detective*). Kingsport, Massachusetts and Miskatonic University are from H. P. Lovecraft's Cthulhu Mythos tales. Commissioner Weston appears in the tales of a vigilante who can cloud men's minds. Commissioner Stanley Kirkpatrick is from the Spider stories. Commissioner Woods is from the Green Lama's pulp exploits. Commissioner Charlie Foster is from the Secret Agent X tales. Commissioner Arthur J. Quistrom is from Leslie Charteris' novel* The Saint in New York. *Commissioner Gordon operated as a whispering vigilante in pulp novels by Laurence Donovan. Commissioner Jerome Warner is from the Black Bat stories. Commissioner Hombert and D.A. Skinner are from Rex Stout's Nero Wolfe novels. Captain Midnight is from the radio series of the same name. The Phantom Detective appeared in pulp stories by Robert Wallace. The Domino Lady is a pulp heroine created by Lars Anderson. Ki-Gor is a jungle hero who appeared in pulp tales by John Peter Drummond. Professor Horatio Smith is from the movie* Pimpernel Smith. *The Scarlet Pimpernel is from Baroness Orczy's novels, of course. The seemingly unescapable prison camp is Loki from Farmer's authorized Doc Savage novel* Escape from Loki, *which is also the source of the whitish worm, which Doc encountered in Baron de Musard's chateau during World War I. The frog-mouthed, tentacle-lipped creature is Dewer, who encountered occult detective Jules de Grandin in Seabury Quinn's story "The Bride of Dewer." Toby Basinger and Angel de la Ruse are from Howard Hopkins' Green Ghost story "Ghost of a Chance," although Basinger's name is Eckert's invention. Red Apple Cigarettes appear in a number of films, including* Pulp Fiction, Four Rooms, *and* Romy and Michele's High School Reunion, *as well as a number of other works by Eckert.*

Summer
THE SECRET OF THE AERO PLANE
Major Henderson and Captain Cody meet Captain Hercules Hurricane at a bar in Walkabout Creek, Australia. Henderson tells Cody during World War I, a splinter enemy group claimed to be empowered by Thor and the Norse gods. He also says Hitler allegedly lost major expeditions trying to find the Holy Grail and the Ark of the Covenant, and dispatches Cody to meet the enigmatic pilot Captain Aero.

Short story by Erwin K. Roberts at the Planetary Stories *website. Captain Cody and Major Henderson will later be known as Commando Cody and Mr. Henderson from the film serial* Radar Men from the Moon *and the television series* Commando Cody: Sky Marshal of the Universe. *The super-humanly strong Captain Hercules Hurricane appeared in the British comic* Valiant *during the 1960s and 1970s, though his stories were set during World War II. Walkabout Creek, Australia is from the film* Crocodile Dundee. *The German splinter group is the titular organization from Roberts' two-part novella "The Sons of Thor." The Nazi expeditions to find the Holy Grail and the Ark of the Covenant were seen in the movies* Indiana Jones and the Last Crusade *and* Raiders of the Lost Ark, *respectively. Captain Aero's exploits were published by the American comic book company Holyoke during the 1940s.*

WHEN THE SEA BLAZED AT TINIAN

Major (formerly Captain) Cody knows a Comanche shaman named Mephito.

Short story by Erwin K. Roberts at the Planetary Stories *website. Major Cody is the future Commando Cody of the serial* Radar Men from the Moon *and the TV series* Commando Cody: Sky Marshal of the Universe. *Mephito is pulp adventurer Jim Anthony's grandfather.*

HAPPY DEATH MEN

The Avenger, visiting the Midas Club under the guise of Juan Dyer, overhears a group of men talking about a series of gruesome murders. According to Burke at the *Classic*, the victims were all chosen at random. One man says he

would expect this if "that nutcase with the fangs and the fright wig" were still around, but he hasn't been seen in a couple months. "Dyer" and his companion, Ellen Patrick, join the conversation. The men who were already discussing the killings are Drew, an attorney; Dithers, the construction magnate; and Mann, a financial advisor. Dithers says the killers have horrible death's head grins, like the victims of poisoning murders in Gotham a few years ago. They are joined by Dr. Karl Walden and his companion, Lilya Zarov. Drew has instructed his daughter to stay indoors until the killings have stopped. When Zarov leaves, "Dyer" attempts to find her; upon returning, he finds Ellen and Walden have disappeared, and none of the others at the table remember them being there in the first place. Stepping into a back alley, the Avenger is attacked by one of the grinning murderers. In a flashback, Benson and Nellie Gray battle one of the so-called "Happy Death Men." As the monster attempts to crush him to death, Benson uses a technique taught to him by the yoga master Dekka Lan Shan and refined with instruction from another New York crime fighter to slow his heart rate in order to briefly deceive the creature into thinking he is dead. The creature is killed by Ellen Patrick, now in her other identity as the Domino Lady. Benson says the dead creature's skin tissue matches a strange polymorphic material similar to the residue at the scene of Justice, Inc.'s battle with a woman known as "The Countess," who seemingly died at the end of that affair. Benson states rich men have been disappearing, members of various clubs: the Explorers Club, the Cobalt, the Sphinx, the local branch of the Baltimore Gun Club, and the Discoverers League. Back in the present, Benson regains consciousness, finding himself, the Domino Lady, Nellie, Smitty, and Mac in the living room of a penthouse apartment. Benson realizes Lilya Zarov and the Countess are one and the same person, though her appearance has changed. Benson tells Walden unlike the Nazis, the United States has successfully created a supersoldier. Smitty asks if Walden is part of the Unholy Nine gang; Walden replies that group stole his organization's good name, or at least half of it. Mac refers to rumors of immortality elixirs such as Royal Jelly and the "Elixir of Life." Benson suspects Dr. Walden is far older than he looks, and Mac wonders if he once had a supply of a longevity elixir that ran out. Smitty remarks the Countess was reportedly disfigured around the time of the Russian Revolution, and it seems like she spent a long time looking like "a female Phantom of the Opera" despite her current difference in appearance. Benson suggests Walden is the "Baron" who assisted the Countess in her misdeeds last year, and she has changeable flesh like him. At the conclusion of the affair, Benson sends the last of the Death Men to a secure rehabilitation clinic in upstate New York that is run by a bronze-skinned doctor friend of his. Benson suggests to his comrades Walden may have escaped from them using technology similar to that used by a foe of this doctor, which in turn was based upon a "disintegrator" invented by Theodore Nemor. Nellie asks if perhaps Walden believes, as did a man called Rode Boeman whom they encountered a few years ago, there is more to Benson's condition than mere muscular paralysis.

Short story by Win Scott Eckert in The Avenger: The Justice, Inc. Files, *Joe Gentile and Howard Hopkins, eds., Moonstone Books, 2011. The Midas Club is from the Doc Savage novel* The Man Who Shook the Earth. *Burke, a reporter for* The New York Classic, *is an agent of the shadowy crimefighter, as is Mann. This crimefighter is the same one who helped Benson in refining his heart-stopping technique. The "nutcase with the fangs* and the fright wig" is the Spider. Attorney Carson Drew is the father of young amateur sleuth Nancy Drew. J. C. Dithers is Dagwood Bumstead's boss in Chic Young's comic strip Blondie. The Domino Lady, created by Lars Anderson, is one of the most famous pulp heroines. The poisoning murders in Gotham are a reference to Batman's archenemy the Joker. Dr. Karl Walden is meant to be Baron von Hessel from Philip José Farmer's Doc Savage novel Escape from Loki. Many questions about the Baron/Walden are answered in Eckert's story "The Wild Huntsman" (The Worlds of Philip José Farmer 3: Portrait of a Trickster, Michael Croteau, ed., Meteor House, 2012). The Countess Lilya Zarov is meant to be Lili Bugov, the Countess Idivzhopu, the Baron's mistress in Escape from Loki. In Farmer's novel, it is mentioned the Countess' family held manhunts; Lili's use of the name Zarov in this story is meant to imply she is related to General Zaroff from Richard Connell's short story "The Most Dangerous Game." The Countess' previous encounter with the Avenger's team was chronicled in Eckert's story "Death and the Countess" (The Avenger Chronicles, Joe Gentile and Howard Hopkins, eds., Moonstone Books, 2008). Dekka Lan Shan, also from Escape from Loki, is the grandfather of the Dekka Lan Shan who appears in "The Sapphire Death," a Peter the Brazen story by "Loring Brent" (George F. Worts). The Explorers Club and the Sphinx Club were both real clubs. The Cobalt Club is frequented by a certain aviator-turned-pulp hero. The Baltimore Gun Club appears in Jules Verne's novels From the Earth to the Moon, Around the Moon, and The Purchase of the North Pole. The Discoverers League is from the novel Hunt at World's End by Gabriel Kaufman. The supersoldier created by the United States government is, of course, Captain America. The Unholy Nine appear in Max McCoy's story "Feast of Fire," found in the limited hardcover edition of The Avenger Chronicles. The organization to which Walden belongs may be the Nine Unknown from Talbot Mundy's Jimgrim novels, and also may be the CU equivalent of the organization seen in Farmer's Empire of the Nine series, which takes place in an alternate universe. The Royal Jelly serum was created by Sherlock Holmes, and has provided him and his family and friends with extended lifespans; its existence was revealed by William S. Baring-Gould in his biography Sherlock Holmes of Baker Street. The Elixir of Life was created by Dr. Fu Manchu. The Phantom of the Opera is from Gaston Leroux's novel of the same name. The clinic in upstate New York is owned and run by the pulp hero nicknamed "Doc." Doc's encounter with a villain using similar teleportation technology to Dr. Walden's was chronicled in the pulp novel The Vanisher, while Theodore Nemor's disintegrator appears in Edward Malone and Arthur Conan Doyle's Professor Challenger story "The Disintegration Machine." Eckert first proposed the device from The Vanisher was *based on Nemor's creation in his story "The Vanishing Devil" (*Tales of the Shadowmen Volume 1: The Modern Babylon, *Jean-Marc and Randy Lofficier, eds., Black Coat Press, 2005). Rode Boeman is meant to be Red Orc from Philip José Farmer's* The World of Tiers *novels; Benson encountered him during the events of Christopher Paul Carey's story "Devil's Dark Harvest" (also found in* The Avenger: The Justice, Inc. Files*).*

ACCORDING TO PLAN OF A ONE-EYED TRICKSTER

The Avenger is visited by American government agent Tony McKay and a British agent named Jim. Jim tells Benson almost thirty years ago, Sherlock Holmes, whose brother was then head of the British Secret Service, fought a man called Baron Ulf Von Waldman, who appears to be the same person as Dr. Walden, whom Benson encountered last month. Walden's ally in his battle with Benson was the Countess Lilya Zarov. Walden has demanded Benson and his own ally in their previous conflict, the Domino Lady, come to him. Walden is renting Stonecraft Castle. One of Walden's past aliases is Larsen. Walden states Benson is a great scientist, perhaps second only to

another who lives in New York. Zarov once had her back broken by an enemy who was escaping from a prison camp Walden ran during the Great War. Prior to that, this enemy had slept with her, resulting in a pregnancy. Lilya used her shape-changing abilities, inherited from an extraterrestrial mother, to heal her injuries. Another member of her mother's race was defeated by "a doltish 'gentleman thief'" in the 1890s. Lilya's son went on to battle his hated father, who did not realize the truth about his parentage, as the son had changed his features so he would appear older. At the conclusion of the battle, Walden alludes to a future encounter with Benson's daughter.

Short story by Win Scott Eckert in The Avenger: Roaring Heart of the Crucible, *Nancy Holder and Joe Gentile, eds., Moonstone Books, 2013. This story completes the trilogy begun by Eckert with his stories "Death and the Countess" (*The Avenger Chronicles, *Joe Gentile and Howard Hopkins, eds., Moonstone Books, 2008) and "Happy Death Men" (*The Avenger: The Justice, Inc. Files, *Joe Gentile and Howard Hopkins, eds., Moonstone Books, 2011). Tony McKay is from Sax Rohmer's novel* Emperor Fu Manchu. *"Jim" is James Bond. Sherlock Holmes' encounter with "Baron Ulf* von Waldman" was chronicled by Dr. Watson in his tale "The Adventure of the Fallen Stone" (Sherlock Holmes: The Crossovers Casebook, *Howard Hopkins, ed., Moonstone Books, 2012), edited by Eckert. Holmes' brother, Mycroft, was portrayed as the head of the British Secret Service and one of the first to hold the title of "M" (a reference to the James Bond novels) in John T. Lescroart's novels* Son of Holmes *and* Rasputin's Revenge, *as well as Alan Moore and Kevin O'Neill's comic book series* The League of Extraordinary Gentlemen. *Dr. Karl Walden, alias Baron Ulf Von Waldman, is meant to be Baron von Hessel from Philip José Farmer's authorized Doc Savage novel* Escape from Loki. *In his essay "The Green Eyes Have It–Or Are They Blue?"* (Myths for the Modern Age: Philip José Farmer's Wold Newton Universe, *Win Scott Eckert, ed., MonkeyBrain Books, 2005), Christopher Paul Carey argued the Baron and Wolf Larsen (from Jack London's* The Sea-Wolf*) were aliases of the immortal XauXaz from Farmer's trilogy of novels about the ancient society known as the Nine, a theory elaborated upon and modified by Eckert in his story "The Wild Huntsman"* (The Worlds of Philip José Farmer 3: Portraits of a Trickster, *Michael Croteau, ed., Meteor House, 2012), among others. Countess Lilya Zarov is meant to be Lili Bugov, Countess Idivzhopu, from* Escape from Loki; *the use of the surname Zarov is meant to imply she is related to General Zaroff from Richard Connell's story "The Most Dangerous Game." In his essay "Who's Going to Take Over the World When I'm Gone?"* (Myths for the Modern Age)*, Eckert argued Doc's greatest nemesis was the result of Lili and Doc's sexual encounter in* Escape from Loki; *the shape-changing abilities shared by mother and child would explain how Lili was able to recover from her crippling and disfiguring injuries suffered at the climax of that novel, as well as why Lester Dent claimed in* The Fortress of Solitude *that Doc's foe "was not a young man," despite the fact he would have been only eighteen-years-old at that time. Doc is the New York resident who is possibly a greater scientist than Benson. The Domino Lady, created by Lars Anderson, is one of the most well-known pulp heroines. Stonecraft Castle was formerly owned by James D. Stonecraft, an oil magnate obsessed with immortality, who appears in Farmer's authorized Tarzan novel* The Dark Heart of Time. *The "doltish 'gentleman thief'" is A. J. Raffles; his encounter with a member of Lili's mother's race was recounted by his amanuensis Harry "Bunny" Manders in "The Problem of the Sore Bridge—Among Others," edited by Farmer. The Avenger and the Domino Lady's future daughter, Helen Benson, was first mentioned in Farmer and Eckert's novel* The Evil in Pemberley House. *The title of this story is a play on that of the Doc Savage pulp novel* According to Plan of a One-Eyed Mystic. *Eckert notes, "The shape-shifting abilities displayed by Lilya in this tale, in addition to having a direct Farmerian* *origin, are a very subtle nod to Christopher Paul Carey's position that Lili Bugov is actually John Sunlight after a sex change operation, as described in ['The Green Eyes Have It']. After all, a shape-shifter could easily change gender as well as appearance. While I still favor the mother-son theory, the story is my way of acknowledging multiple viewpoints, and the ground-breaking work Chris did in this area."*

DERRINGER SOCIETY

Gregory Hood investigates the murders of two fellow members of the Derringer Society, a club devoted to the classic science fiction character Dr. Derringer.

Episode of the radio series The Casebook of Gregory Hood *written by Denis Green and Anthony Boucher, broadcast July 8, 1946. The Dr. Derringer stories were first mentioned in Boucher's novel* Rocket to the Morgue. *Boucher modeled Derringer on Professor Challenger.*

BOTHON

R'lyeh is mentioned in this tale of Atlantis and reincarnation.

Short story by Henry S. Whitehead in Amazing Stories, *August 1946; reprinted in* West India Lights, *Arkham House, 1946. The reference to R'lyeh from Lovecraft's Cthulhu Mythos brings this story into the CU. Bothon is from Whitehead's Gerald Canevin story "Scar-Tissue," providing further evidence this story takes place in the CU.*

November
WHO MADE ME SUCH A WOMAN?

Kanoto Yoshimuta, who has lost her family in the atomic bombing of Hiroshima, accepts a ride from a man with gold-capped teeth and a Prussian hairstyle. The man tells Kanoto he knows how she has been trying to bribe fishing boats to take her to an obscure little island to collect specimens of its fungi, and he has already warned General MacArthur not to be eating mush-rooms anytime soon. Sakima, Haruchi, Doctor Natas, and Serizawa are also mentioned.

Short story by G. L. Gick in Harry Dickson and the Werewolf of Rutherford Grange, *Black Coat Press, 2011; reprinted in* The Monsters of Madame Atomos *by André Caroff, adapted and translated by Brian*

Stableford, Black Coat Press, 2012, and in French in Les Compagnons de l'Ombre (Tome 9), *Jean-Marc and Randy Lofficier, eds., Rivière Blanche, 2012. Kanoto Yoshimuta is better known as André Caroff's villain Madame Atomos. This story ends with her choosing her nom de guerre. The man with gold-capped teeth and a Prussian hairstyle is John P. Marquand's Japanese spy Mister Moto. The obscure island is from the movie* Matango *(aka* Attack of the Mushroom People*); those who ingest the mushrooms on the island are transformed into humanoid mushrooms themselves. Mura Sakima is a Japanese agent from the film serial* The Masked Marvel, *while Oyama Haruchi is a spy from the serial* G-Men vs. the Black Dragon. *Doctor Natas is from Guy d'Armen's novel* Doc Ardan: City of Gold and Lepers. *Jean-Marc and Randy Lofficier's adaptation and translation of d'Armen's book implies Natas is actually Sax Rohmer's Doctor Fu Manchu. Dr. Daisuke Serizawa is from the Japanese monster movie* Gojira, *which was released in the United States as* Godzilla. *Although the mass destruction seen in the Gojira/Godzilla films is incompatible with Crossover Universe continuity, Serizawa does have a CU counterpart, as seen in Michel Stéphan's story "The Red Silk Scarf."*

Early December
THE RIVET GANG

A duo named Ham and Monk confront Cliff Secord, telling him their employer, the inventor of Cliff's rocket pack, wants him to recover it from the Rivet Gang.

Story by Lisa Morton in The Rocketeer: Jet-Pack Adventures, *Jeff Conner and Tom Waltz, eds., IDW Publishing, 2014. Dave Stevens' comic* The Rocketeer *portrayed the pulp hero widely called "Doc" as the inventor of the rocket pack, although Doc was not referred to by name, nor were two of his aides who appeared alongside him in the comic, the dapper lawyer and the apelike chemist.*

1946

Spring
SWAN SONG (aka DEAD AND DUMB)

A journalist asks Gervase Fen for an interview for her series on famous detectives, adding she's hoping to also speak with H. M., Mrs. Bradley, and Albert Campion, among others.

Novel by Edmund Crispin. The references to Carter Dickson's (pseudonym for John Dickson Carr) Sir Henry "H. M." Merrivale, Gladys Mitchell's Mrs. Beatrice Adela Lestrange Bradley, and Margery Allingham's Albert Campion provide further evidence Gervase Fen is in the CU.

SHONOKIN TOWN

John Thunstone wishes the late Love-craft, who "knew so much about the legend of Other-People, from before human times, and how their behaviors and speech had trickled a little into the ken of the civilization known to the wakeaday world," and de Grandin could see and hear the Shonokins.

Story by Manly Wade Wellman in Weird Tales, *July 1946. The H. P. Lovecraft reference implies John Thunstone exists in the same universe as Lovecraft's Cthulhu Mythos. Jules de Grandin is an occult investigator created by Seabury Quinn.*

GOLDEN AMAZON VERSUS QUASIMODO, THE HUNCHBACK OF NOTRE DAME

The Golden Amazon, visiting Notre Dame Cathedral, tussles with a cult that has brainwashed Quasimodo into doing its bidding.

Short story by Sean Taylor in Of Monsters and Men, *Tommy Hancock and Joe Gentile, eds., Moonstone Books, 2014. The Golden Amazon appeared in a series of stories by John Russell Fearn in* The Toronto Star Weekly. *Apparently Victor Hugo was lying when he referred to Quasimodo's death in his novel* The Hunchback of Notre Dame, *and Quasimodo actually acquired extended longevity somehow.*

THE PHANTOM'S GHOST

Visiting France, the Green Ghost (George Chance) battles a successor to Erik, the Phantom of the Opera, who has apparently stolen the original Erik's remains.

Short story by Eric Fein in Of Monsters and Men, *Tommy Hancock and Joe Gentile, eds., Moonstone Books, 2014; reprinted in* The Green Ghost Declassified, *forthcoming, Moonstone Books. The Green Ghost appeared in the pulp magazine* The Ghost, Super-Detective *(later retitled* The Ghost Detective *and then* The Green Ghost Detective*). The remains in this story cannot be those of the real Erik from Gaston Leroux's novel, as he survived at least until the year 2002, when he appeared in Simon R. Green's* Nightside *novel* Hex and the City.

Summer

SCOTT-KING'S MODERN EUROPE

Scott-King once shared a luncheon at the British Embassy in Stockholm with Sir Samson Courteney.

Story by Evelyn Waugh published in an abridged version in Cornhill, *Summer 1947; reprinted as "A Sojourn in Neutralia" in* Hearst's International *combined with* Metropolitan, *November 1947, and in the unabridged version under its original title in* The Complete Stories of Evelyn Waugh, *Little, Brown and Company, 1998. Sir Samson Courteney is from Waugh's novel* Black Mischief.

ZOMBIES UNDER BROADWAY

The Green Ghost (George Chance) battles a zombie while his girlfriend Meriem White is being strangled by another zombie named Korga. In a flashback, Joe Harper, one of Chance's aides, suggests to Commissioner Standish he ask ex-mobster Vito Molinaro, who now runs a nightclub called the Zombie Hut, about disappearances in and around the Broadway theatre district. Harper, who smokes Red Apple Cigarettes, heard about some strange goings-on at the club a few months ago. At the Zombie Hut, Jeanette LaChance sings a love song. Molinaro recommends that Chance and Meriem speak with his press agents, Gerry Mills and Mick Steeger, about the strange events of a few months back. Mills and Steeger were ordered by Molinaro to go to the Caribbean island of San Sebastian to get him a real zombie for the Zombie Hut's opening. While there, they encountered a madman named Dr. Paul Renard, who was creating zombies himself. Professor Harris of the Manhattan Museum of Fine Arts was the one who suggested to Mills and Steeger that they find their zombie in San Sebastian. The still-living Renard's henchman is a man named Joaquin.

Short story by Win Scott Eckert and Eric Fein in The Green Ghost Declassified, *forthcoming, Moonstone Books. This story is an unofficial sequel to the 1945 movie* Zombies on Broadway, *which is the source of the Zombie Hut. San Sebastian appeared in both that film and the earlier* I Walked with a Zombie. *Many of the characters in this story are thinly-disguised versions of characters from* Zombies on Broadway: *Korga (Kalaga); Vito Molinaro (Ace Miller); Jeanette LaChance (Jean La Danse); Gerry Mills and Miles Steeger (Jerry Miles and Mike Strager); Dr. Paul Renard (Dr. Paul Renault); and Joaquin (Joseph). Miles and Strager were also the main characters in five other films:* The Adventures of a Rookie *(1943),* Rookies in Burma *(1943),* Girl Rush *(1944),* Radio Stars on Parade *(1945), and* Genius at Work *(1946). All of these films take place in the then-present day, with the exception of Girl Rush, which takes place during the Gold Rush of 1849. Perhaps Miles and Strager are in fact immortals, and somehow connected to two other long-lived bumblers who have had a number of misadventures over the years (see Dennis Power's article "Immortal Befuddled" on* The Wold Newton Universe: A Secret History *website). Red Apple Cigarettes are from the connected films of Quentin Tarantino and Robert Rodriguez, and also show up in a number of other books and stories by Eckert. Professor Algernon Harris and the Manhattan Museum of Fine Arts are from Frank Belknap Long's Cthulhu Mythos novel* The Horror from the Hills. *Eckert's story implicitly conflates Harris with the Professor Hopkins that recommends Miles and Strager journey to San Sebastian in* Zombies on Broadway.

Summer. First exploit of young adventurer Rick Brant and his pal Don "Scotty" Scott, *The Rocket's Shadow,* by "John Blaine" (Harold L. Goodwin and Peter J Harkins).

Autumn. Judy of the Jungle has her first recorded exploit. (*Exciting Comics* #55, May 1947.)

1947

Spring
BLEAK PROSPECTS
Private investigator Rip Kirby is in Paris looking for a stolen child adopted by a desperate mother. He tells Desmond, his butler-sidekick, he is "merely . . . borrowing from the greatest detective of them all! Did you ever hear of Mr. Sherlock Holmes and his Baker Street Irregulars?"

Rip Kirby *comic strip by Alex Raymond, April 23, 1948. Kirby's explanation treats Holmes and the Irregulars as real people, and thus brings him into the CU.*

ARSENIC IS WHERE YOU FIND HER
Shorty Morgan, aka the retired vigilante known as the Black Dwarf, is reunited with one of his past assistants, Arsenic Gaynes. Morgan tells his servant Dippy to take a picture of Arsenic to Robb at the *Clarion.* Another of the Dwarf's former assistants, Art "the Human Fly" Bellows, now works for Colonel Lane's Mammoth Circus, whose barker is Carney Callahan. Bellows lands his plane near a high school, and tells the coaches his appearance is a

publicity stunt for Blossom's Circus. Morgan calls FBI agent Dan Fowler to tell him the man who has been seen with Arsenic may be a spy. Bellows remarks Fowler is rumored to have worked with the Phantom, the Black Bat, and even Jim Anthony.

Short story by Erwin K. Roberts at the Planetary Stories *website. The Black Dwarf's adventures were published by the comic book company Harry "A" Chesler and appeared in* Spotlight Comics *and* Red Seal. *The* Clarion *newspaper is from the pulp stories of the Phantom Detective, who is the Phantom referred to by the Human Fly. Robb maintains the* Clarion's *"morgue"; he also appeared in Roberts' two-part novella "The Sons of Thor." Carney (or Carnie) Callahan, a barker for Colonel Lane's Mammoth Circus, appeared in the strip "The Barker" in* National Comics *and the series* The Barker, *both published by Quality Comics. Blossom's Circus is from Hugh Lofting's Dr. Dolittle's Circus. Dan Fowler's adventures appeared in the pulp* G-Men Detective. *The Black Bat was featured in* Black Book Detective. *Jim Anthony appeared in the magazine* Super Detective.

Summer
JUSTICE SERVED COLD

Private eyes Black Jack Justice and Trixie Dixon are hired by a wealthy woman to retrieve letters to an old flame from a blackmailer at the Metrolite Hotel.

Story by Gregg Taylor, Sami Kivelä, and Mark Hester at the Addictive Comics *website. The Metrolite Hotel is the home of one of the agents who works for a shadow mystery man. This crossover brings Black Jack Justice, the title character of a radio podcast series written, directed, and produced by Taylor for the* Decoder Ring Theatre *website, into the CU. The year of this story is conjecture, though the series takes place in the 1940s, and the story explicitly takes place after World War II.*

DECIMATOR SMITH AND THE FANGS OF THE FIRE SERPENT

Boxer Achilles "Decimator" Smith turns vigilante after the death of his sister. He meets inventor Abe Kaufman, who tells him, "When I was back east, I did some work for a few vigilantes you might say. I belonged to a kind of a loose association of scientists who helped out the best way we could." Abe's brother Rocco adds, "You heard of that bloodthirsty joker with the weird laugh and the slouch hat in New York? Abe designed a few gadgets for him through his operatives."

Short story by Gary Phillips in Black Pulp, *Tommy Hancock, Gary Phillips, and Morgan Minor, eds., Pro Se Press, 2013. "That bloodthirsty joker with the weird laugh and the slouch hat in New York" is the shadowy hero who likely needs no further introduction.*

December 24
FROSTBITE

In New York City, Dorian Gray encounters a woman in blue, who poisons him, though it does not kill the immortal. Before leaving, the woman identifies herself as Mina Harker.

A short audio drama written by Mark B. Oliver and directed by Scott Handcock, Big Finish Productions, 2014. Mina Harker is from Bram Stoker's Dracula, *of course. Mina's reason for attacking Dorian is as yet unrevealed, as is why she is using her maiden name, despite having divorced Jonathan Harker nearly fifty years ago, as referenced in* The League of Extraordinary Gentlemen.

1948

Spring
THE APPRENTICE

Simon Templar, alias the Saint, meets 12-year-old His Serene Highness Prince Malko Linge, who wishes to be his apprentice. Templar worries Chief Inspector Teal would arrest him for child endangerment. Prince Shamyl of Cherkessia is outbid on a painting that once belonged to Malko's family, but the ex-Nazi who bought the painting finds it has been stolen, and in its place is a card with two stick-figures drawn on it: one with a crown and one with a halo.

Short story by Brad Mengel in Tales of the Shadowmen Volume 7: Femmes Fatales, *Jean-Marc and Randy Lofficier, eds., Black Coat Press, 2010; reprinted in French in* Les Compagnons de l'Ombre (Tome 7), *Jean-Marc and Randy Lofficier, eds., Rivière Blanche, 2011. The Saint and Chief Inspector Teal are from the novels by Leslie Charteris. Prince Shamyl of Cherkessia is the alias Templar used in the story "The Prince of Cherkessia" in the collection* The Saint Intervenes. *Malko Linge is better known as* Son Altesse Sérénissime *(His Serene Highness, or S.A.S.) from novels by Gérard de Villiers and his ghostwriters.*

Summer
GODFALL

The Phantom, upon finding a hidden trap door, remarks "Mandrake would be proud."

The Phantom: Ghost Who Walks #8–12 by Mike Bullock and Silvestre Szilagyi, Moonstone Comics, March–September 2010. The Phantom makes the comment about Mandrake in #12. Despite the modern trappings of this story, it features the 20th Phantom, who has married Diana Palmer by this time, and thus must take place not very long after 1945. The exact year is conjecture.

DROP DEAD

Inspector Schmidt, Chief of Homicide for the New York Police Department, investigates an unscrupulous landlady's death alongside his amanuensis George Bagby and Richard Holmes, the preteen grandson of Sherlock Holmes.

Novel by George Bagby. This crossover brings the Inspector Schmidt mysteries into the CU.

October

THE SNARLING MAN

The Avenger and Justice, Inc. battle Lord Derek Gwynplaine, whose face is twisted into a permanent rictus, a recurring condition in his family. Gwynplaine states one of his forebears joined a circus in the early 1700s.

Short story by Christopher Sequeira and C. J. Henderson in The Avenger: Roaring Heart of the Crucible, *Nancy Holder and Joe Gentile, eds., Moonstone Books, 2013. Lord Derek Gwynplaine is a relative of Gwynplaine from Victor Hugo's* The Man Who Laughs. *Rick Lai notes, "The original Gwynplaine was supposedly disfigured by a British doctor using an early form of plastic surgery in 1690. Hugo's Gwynplaine was given a permanent smile. The modern Gwynplaine claimed that his family suffered from a disease called rictus brought about by eating contaminated grain on their estate. Rather than using plastic surgery, Hugo's maniacal doctor must have poisoned the earlier Gwynplaine with strychnine or some other toxin that causes rictus. Later, the poison must have been used to infect the grain on the Gwynplaine family's property. Victor Hugo's original Gwynplaine died childless, but he was survived by his half-brother. Presumably the later Gwynplaine was descended from his namesake's sibling."*

1949

Winter
DAD
A young boy rescues a woman named Glinda from cruel experiments and sexual abuse at the hands of the boy's own father. Glinda and the boy travel to a land that has a yellow brick road.

Short story by Jean-Marc Lofficier in Tales of the Shadowmen Volume 9: La Vie en Noir, *Jean-Marc and Randy-Lofficier, eds., Black Coat Press, 2012. The boy is from Richard Matheson's 1950 short story "Born of Man and Woman." Glinda the Good Witch is from the Oz books by L. Frank Baum. It has been established there are several alternate versions of Oz accessible to and from the CU, including that depicted in Philip José Farmer's* A Barnstormer in Oz. *It is uncertain whether this Glinda is from one of these versions, or a previously unseen one. The year of this story is conjecture.*

Summer
SHOWDOWN AT STEAM TOWN
A man named Leo hitches a ride with two young men named Dean and Sal. Sal says Dean has problems with his family on his father's side, and therefore he is tense when meeting people from Britain. They are nearly crushed by a massive creature. They are led to a place called Steam Town by an elderly Native American named Little Beaver. They meet a young woman named Fran Reade, whose grandfather built Steam Town. Little Beaver refers to atomic bomb testing sites such as Los Alamos, White Sands, and Gamma Base. The creature that attacked Leo, Dean, and Sal turns out to be an ant that has grown to gigantic size due to exposure to radiation. Fran helps drive off the ant (as well as another of its kind) with a steam-powered automaton built by her great-grandfather.

Short story by Travis Hiltz in Night of the Nyctalope, *Jean-Marc and Randy Lofficier, eds., Black Coat Press, 2012; reprinted in French in* Les Compagnons de l'Ombre (Tome 12), *Jean-Marc and Randy Lofficier, eds., Rivière Blanche, 2013. Leo is Jean de La Hire's hero Leo Saint-Clair, aka the Nyctalope. Dean and Sal are Dean Moriarty and Sal Paradise from Jack Kerouac's classic Beat novel* On the Road. *Win Scott Eckert's essay "Who's Going to Take Over the World When I'm Gone? (A Look at the Genealogies of Wold Newton Family Super-Villains and Their Nemeses)" (*Myths for the Modern Age: Philip José Farmer's Wold Newton Universe, *Win*

Scott Eckert, MonkeyBrain Books, 2005) argued Dean was the great-nephew of Professor Moriarty. As a boy, Little Beaver was the sidekick of the title character of Stephen Slesinger and Fred Harman's Western comic strip Red Ryder. *Fran Reade is the great-granddaughter of dime novel inventor Frank Reade, and the granddaughter of his son Frank Jr., both of whom built steam-men. Gamma Base is from the exploits of Marvel Comics' the Hulk, although the CU version of the Hulk is much less powerful than his Marvel Universe counterpart, and his rampages are much less destructive. The giant ants are from the movie* Them! *The authorities must have covered up the ants' rampages in New Mexico and California in 1953.*

October
MADISON SQUARE GARDEN
Boxer Marcel Cerdan's sparring partner Steve Costigan once fought "Tiger" Valois. Cerdan and Costigan meet with lawyer Tom Hagen, who represents Vito Corleone. Hagen asks Cerdan to throw an upcoming match, but Cerdan refuses. Hagen meets with Don Vito, whose son Michael has been forced into exile in Italy by the vendetta of other mob families. The Nyctalope attends Cerdan's fight. The hero's old foe Gofrey Cultnom has been tasked by Corleone to use his mystic powers to affect Cerdan's performance. After Leo defeats Cultnom, Corleone assigns Roman Orgonetz to engineer Cerdan's death in a plane crash.

Short story by Emmanuel Gorlier in Night of the Nyctalope, *Jean-Marc and Randy Lofficier, eds., Black Coat Press, 2012; reprinted in French in* La Nuit du Nyctalope, *Jean-Marc and Randy Lofficier, eds., Rivière Blanche, 2012. Marcel Cerdan was a real boxer. Sailor Steve Costigan's two-fisted exploits were chronicled by Robert E. Howard; he fought "Tiger" Valois in "The Bulldog Breed." Don Vito Corleone, his son Michael, and his* consigliere/lawyer/adopted son *Tom Hagen are from Mario Puzo's novel* The Godfather, *as well as the film trilogy directed by Francis Ford Coppola. Michael Corleone also appears in Puzo's* The Sicilian, *bringing in that novel as well. The Nyctalope is the hero of French pulp novels by Jean de La Hire; he battled Cultnom in de La Hire's story "Night of the Nyctalope." Roman Orgonetz is a professional assassin and agent of the spy cartel SMOG in Henri Vernes' novels about adventurer Bob Morane.*

Autumn
THE MYSTERY OF THE MENACING MANUSCRIPT
Novelist Dan Holiday becomes involved in a mock murder mystery weekend at a publisher's mansion, but one of the other guests is truly killed. Another guest is actress Margaret Grace, who decades earlier was married to

popular motion picture director Harvey Fitzroy, who made headlines when he was arrested and convicted for murdering his girlfriend.

Short story by Bobby Nash included in the audiobook Box Thirteen: Adventure Wanted! *Radio Archives, 2014. Margaret Grace was first mentioned in Nash's story "Target: Domino Lady," which depicted her husband's downfall. Margaret was also mentioned in Nash's Ravenwood tale "Jazz."*

December 1949–January 1950
MIDNIGHT IN MOSCOW

The Shadow has dinner with four other men at a brownstone on West 35th Street owned by an obese man. One of the men is bronze-haired and is apparently scientifically inclined, while another sarcastically comments on the fat man's attitude. A framed picture of a monument hangs on the homeowner's wall. As they leave, the Shadow chats with the fourth man, John, whom he addresses as "My Lord." John's wife Jane spends Christmas in Baltimore, but they return to Africa for New Year's. One of the Shadow's female agents kills a drug dealer who is trying to sell to a redheaded youth wearing a varsity jacket with the word "Riverdale" inscribed on its back.

Six-issue miniseries by Howard Chaykin, Dynamite Entertainment, 2014. The brownstone on West 35th is owned by the rotund detective Nero Wolfe, while John is the jungle lord. The other two men present at the dinner are the bronze-skinned pulp superman known as "Doc" and Bulldog

Drummond. *The Shadow, Nero Wolfe, the jungle lord, Doc, and Bulldog Drummond were all identified as Wold Newton Family members by Philip José Farmer. The framed picture is in fact a photograph of the real monument to the Wold Newton meteor. The redhead in the Riverdale jacket is Archie Andrews, whose high school misadventures have been the subject of comics published by a company named after him for over seventy years. Presumably, the Archie of the CU aged normally, and was not an eternal teenager like his Archie Comics Universe counterpart.*

1950

Spring
THE DEVIL YOU KNOW
The Nyctalope battles aliens who have assumed the identities of the married men in the town of Harrisville, CA.

Short story by Roman Leary in Night of the Nyctalope, *Jean-Marc and Randy Lofficier, eds., Black Coat Press, 2012; reprinted in French in* Les Compagnons de l'Ombre (Tome 12), *Jean-Marc and Randy Lofficier, eds., Rivière Blanche, 2013. The aliens will later make another attempt to infiltrate Earthly society, as seen in the 1958 film* I Married a Monster from Outer Space.

TARZAN VE MANDRAKE MÜCADELESI (THE STRUGGLE BETWEEN TARZAN AND MANDRAKE)
Mandrake and Lothar visit Dakar in Africa. Lothar tells his master about Katopi, a plant which grants invincibility to those who ingest it. The plant is guarded by Lord Greystoke in "the jungle of the lions." Traveling to the jungle, Mandrake conjures animals to attack Lord Greystoke, but the ape lord defeats them. Impressed by Lord Greystoke's courage and strength, Mandrake decides not to take the plant, and he and Greystoke part as friends.

Short story by Selami Münir Yurdatap in a 16-page comic booklet of the same name.

Summer
THE WOLFF THAT ONE HEARS
Archaeologist François Bordes explores the caves at Lascaux, and finds a stone with a tablet inside, which has strange writing inscribed upon it. Trying to decipher the inscriptions, he searches a book by his colleague Aristide Clairembard. An hour later, he discovers similarities between the writing and samples recorded by Professor Lidenbrock in Iceland in the 19th Century. According to Clairembard, only one person was able to decipher the text

unearthed by Lidenbrock: Robert Wolff, a professor at Traybell University in Busiris, Illinois. Traveling to Busiris to meet with Wolff, Bordes and his American colleague encounter Dr. Oscar le Rouge.

Short story by Jean-Marc and Randy Lofficier in The Worlds of Philip José Farmer 2: Of Dust and Soul, *Michael Croteau, ed., Meteor House, 2011. François Bordes was a real archaeologist, geologist, and scientist, who also wrote science fiction novels under the pen name Francis Carsac. This story reveals where Bordes got the idea for his novel* Ceux de Null Part *(Those from Nowhere). Professor Wolff (aka Jadawin) and Dr. le Rouge (aka Red Orc) are from Farmer's* The World of Tiers *series. Traybell University appears in Farmer's novel* Traitor to the Living; *alternate universe versions of the University appear in Farmer's stories "The God Business" and "Seventy Years of Decpop." Busiris, Illinois is a recurring stand-in for Peoria in Farmer's works. Professor Aristide Clairembard (or Clairembart) is one of the allies of adventurer Bob Morane in novels by Henri Vernes. Professor Otto Lidenbrock's Icelandic expedition was chronicled by his nephew Axel Lidenbrock and edited by Jules Verne into a book entitled* Journey to the Center of the Earth. *This story is set in the early 1950s, and Bordes is described as "barely thirty." Since Bordes was born in 1919, 1950 is the most likely year for it to take place.*

THE DUFFY'S TAVERN MATTER

Insurance investigator Johnny Dollar looks into the case of a car that crashed through a window of Duffy's Tavern.

Short story by Steve Thompsen in It's That Time Again 3: Even More New Stories of Old-Time Radio, *Jim Harmon, ed., BearManor Media, 2006. Johnny Dollar, from the 1949–1962 radio series* Yours Truly Johnny Dollar, *is in the CU through C. J. Henderson and Joe Gentile's novel* Partners in Crime. *Therefore, this crossover brings in Duffy's Tavern, from the 1941–1951 radio show of the same name.*

Late November
COLD BLOOD

Sergeant William Beef's biographer, Townsend, tells him he needs a unique quality to make him famous as a detective: "You must resemble an alligator every few pages, like Mrs. Bradley, or talk like a peer in an Edwardian farce, like Lord Peter Wimsey. Or use bits of exclamatory French, like Poirot." Theo Gray asks Beef to look into the death of his friend, Cosmo Ducrow. Townsend thinks, "How different, I could not help reflecting, was the conversation of Holmes and Watson while they sat waiting for their clients not half a mile away." Noting there are better known detectives than he, with better reputations, Beef asks Gray why he did not consult Poirot, to which Gray responds he was engaged on another case. When Beef asks the same about Albert Campion, Gray replies Campion was not interested. Beef says he wonders where Gray will be if he refuses the case, to which Gray responds "On the phone to Inspector French . . ."

Novel by Lionel Townsend, edited by Leo Bruce. Gladys Mitchell's Mrs. Bradley, Dorothy L. Sayer's Lord Peter Wimsey, Agatha Christie's Hercule Poirot, Arthur Conan Doyle's Sherlock Holmes and Dr. Watson, Margery Allingham's Albert Campion, and Freeman Wills Crofts' Inspector French are all in the CU; therefore, this crossover brings in Sergeant Beef. Beef's cottage, where he first meets with Gray, is in Lilac Crescent, and was chosen for its proximity to Baker Street. Holmes and Watson were no longer living at 221B Baker Street in 1951, so Townsend must have meant their conversations in years past.

Winter
CITY WITHOUT GUNS

Batman and Robin travel to London to study Scotland Yard's methods. The Yard has a collection of portraits of famous crime fighters. However, the Dynamic Duo's own picture has been ripped from its frame. After apprehending a fugitive American criminal with the aid of British Batman fanatic Chester Gleek, the duo discover the portrait was originally donated by Gleek, who indignantly reclaimed it after seeing that it was placed alongside paintings of such "inferior" detectives as Sherlock Holmes.

Story by Bill Finger, Dick Sprang, and Charles Paris in Detective Comics #196, *National Periodical Publications (later known as DC Comics), June 1953.*

THE ANOMALY OF THE EMPTY MAN

Lamb is consulted by his friend Inspector Abrahams regarding the mysterious disappearance of James Stambaugh, who left only his clothes behind. Lamb visits Dr. Horace Verner, who is between seventy and a hundred, and tells him about the mystery. Verner tells Lamb the record he is about to play for him is of the greatest dramatic soprano of the century, and compares her favorably to some others, including Lena Geyer. Verner says in this recording lies the solution to Stambaugh's disappearance, and begins telling him a tale of an incident in the autumn of 1901. Verner was a great fan of the soprano, Carina, whose lovers seemed to all commit suicide. Verner's cousin, also a great admirer of Carina, investigated

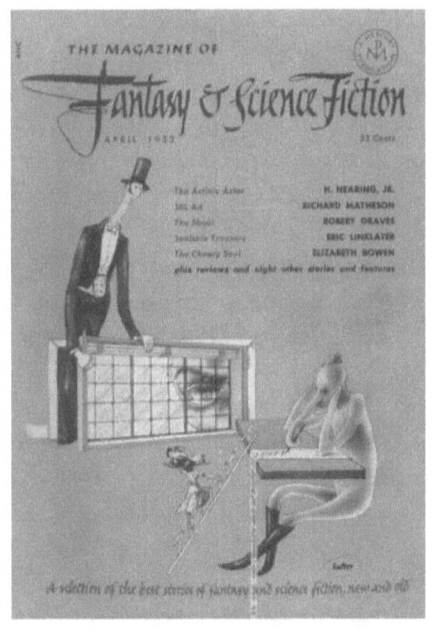

her unexplained death. After her passing, men began disappearing in a manner similar to Stambaugh's vanishing, including the Bishop of Cloisterham. Both Verner (who worked as an occult detective) and his cousin were hired by the family of one of the victims to investigate. Verner's cousin called him "a man of singular accomplishments," and Verner remarks his cousin, as his (Verner's) great-uncle Etienne used to remark of General Masséna, was famous for the accuracy of his information. Verner's cousin mentions his Boswell.

Short story by Martin Lamb, edited by Anthony Boucher in The Magazine of Fantasy and Science Fiction, *April 1952, and reprinted in* The Misadventures of Sherlock Holmes, *Sebastian Wolfe, ed., 1989. Martin Lamb also appears in Boucher's novel* The Case of the Seven of Calvary, *as well as the short story "The Way I Heard It." In "The Adventure of the Norwood Builder," Dr. Watson says "a young doctor, named Verner," a distant relative of Sherlock Holmes, bought his former Kensington practice. Carina is from the Holmes story "The Adventure of the Retired Colourman." Of Lena Geyer is a 1936 novel by Marcia Davenport. The cathedral town of Cloisterham is the setting of Charles Dickens' unfinished novel* The Mystery of Edwin Drood. *Verner's great-uncle is Doyle's Brigadier Etienne Gerard, who made the remark about Masséna in "How the Brigadier Slew the Fox" (aka "The Crime of the Brigadier.")*

Early January
THE TRUE COST OF DOING BUSINESS

Crime boss Buonaparte Ignace Gallia and his henchman Tee Hee Johnson meet with Colonel Bozzo-Corona of BlackSpear Holdings in Paris. Tee Hee nearly had his arm bitten off by an alligator named Albert. Gallia was recently assaulted by a group Tee Hee believes were the Union Corse, an event which seemingly resulted in the death of Baron Samedi. Gallia corrects him, saying their would-be killers were not Draco's men but members of Matarese's group. The Colonel notes Gallia's aliases include Mr. Big and Doctor Kananga, the soon-to-be-master of the island of San Monique. Leading Gallia and his men into the Pilaster Bank, the Colonel offers Gallia the Treasure of the Black Coats.

Short story by Frank Schildiner in Tales of the Shadowmen Volume 9: La Vie en Noir, *Jean-Marc and Randy Lofficier, eds., Black Coat Press, 2012; reprinted in French in* Les Compagnons de l'Ombre (Tome 12), *Jean-Marc and Randy Lofficier, eds., Rivière Blanche, 2013. Buonaparte Ignace Gallia, aka "Mr. Big" and his henchman Tee Hee Johnson are from Ian Fleming's second James Bond novel,* Live and Let Die. *In the 1973 film adaptation of the novel, Mr. Big's true identity is instead given as Dr. Kananga, dictator of the Caribbean island of San Monique, and he has another prominent henchman, the enigmatic Baron Samedi. The film also portrays Tee Hee as having previously had an arm bitten off by an alligator named Albert, although he has both arms in the novel. Given that* Live and Let Die *takes place in January–February 1952, this story must take place directly before Mr. Big and Tee Hee's fatal encounter with James Bond. Marc-Ange Draco leads the Union Corse in the Bond novel* On Her Majesty's Secret Service. *Colonel Bozzo-Corona is the leader of the criminal organization known as the Black Coats in novels by Paul Féval. BlackSpear Holdings is the name by which the Black Coats are known in the 2000s, as depicted by Jean-Marc Lofficier in his novel* The Katrina Protocol *and his Martin Mystère graphic novel, cowritten with Alfredo Castelli,* The Treasure of the Veste Nere; *this story establishes the BlackSpear name was already in use in the 1950s. The Matarese crime family is featured in novels by Robert Ludlum. The Pilaster Bank is from Ken Follett's novel* A Dangerous Fortune.

February–March 6
TO THE DEVIL A DAUGHTER

Lieutenant-Colonel William "Conky Bill" Verney (also known as C. B.) tricks the Satanist Canon Copely-Syle into believing they have met before. The Canon concludes they must have met at a house at Lord's used as a headquarters by a man named Mocata, who had a conflict with a White Magician of greater power than himself while searching for the Talisman of Set, and was later found dead outside a house called Cardinal's Folly in Worcestershire. C. B. tells the Canon, ". . . to people like ourselves, it is common knowledge that it was their magicians producing large numbers of homunculi which led the White Powers to destroy the whole continent of Atlantis by fire and flood."

Novel by Dennis Wheatley. Mocata died in battle with the Duke de Richleau, as recounted in Wheatley's The Devil Rides Out. *Cardinal's Folly is the Duke's home. Since the Duke de Richleau's exploits take place in the CU, so do the events of this novel. The version of Atlantis' destruction described by C. B. is depicted in another Wheatley novel,* They Found Atlantis. *After the events of this novel, C. B. married Molly Fountain, and the couple appeared as main characters in Wheatley's* The Satanist.

Summer. When several of his fellow comedians are robbed, Jack Benny hires vacationing private eye Richard Diamond to protect his fortune. ("Vacation in Hollywood" by Michael Leannah in *It's That Time Again 3: Even More New Stories of Old-Time Radio*, Jim Harmon, ed., BearManor Media, 2006).

December
UNDEADSVILLE
The current Slayer is Zoe Kuryakin, an 18-year-old first generation Russian Jew, who says she has no family she's aware of, except for her cousin Illya, who is a few years older than her and attending college in the Ukraine.

Short story by Michael Reaves in Buffy the Vampire Slayer: Tales of the Slayer, Volume 4, *Gallery Books, 2004. Zoe's cousin is Illya Kuryakin from the television series* The Man from U.N.C.L.E. *If Zoe is eighteen in 1952, she would've been born around 1934. Since Illya was born in 1933, he would be only one year older than Zoe, not "a few years older." In 1952, Illya was in the Russian Navy doing intelligence work, so perhaps his alleged college attendance was a cover story of some sort.*

INFESTATION 2: 30 DAYS OF NIGHT

A group of vampires battle the Old Ones in the Arctic. Miskatonic University is mentioned.

One-shot by Duane Swierczynski and Stuart Sayger, IDW Publishing, 2012. The vampires are from the comic book 30 Days of Night. *This story is part of a multiversal crossover that features the Old Ones waking up and attacking different worlds, so therefore it doesn't bring in any of the other continuities featured, though the DangerGirl cameo in the final issue probably takes place in the CU.*

1953

January 26–July 21
NICK & JAKE

Nick Carraway and Jake Barnes become friends, and encounter a number of famous people of their era. Appearing or mentioned are: Alden Pyle (aka Alden Pyle Carraway); Larry Darrell (aka York Harding); Irving Sheinbloom; Thomas Fowler; Robert Cohn; Mary Richards; Helen Fowler; Lady Brett Ashley; and Lamont Cranston.

An epistolary novel by Jonathan Richards and Tad Richards, Arcade Publishing, 2012. Nick Carraway is from F. Scott Fitzgerald's novel The Great Gatsby. *Jake Barnes, Robert Cohn, and Lady Brett Ashley are from Ernest Hemingway's book* The Sun Also Rises. *Alden Pyle, Thomas Fowler, his wife Helen, and York Harding are from Graham Greene's novel* The Quiet American. *This novel identifies Pyle as Carraway's son. Alden adopts his middle name, his mother's maiden name, as his own surname during the course of the book. Further, York Harding is treated as the nom de plume of Larry Darrell, from W. Somerset Maugham's novel* The Razor's Edge. *Irving Sheinbloom (originally Steinbloom) is from Christopher Guest's film* A Mighty Wind. *Mary Richards is from the television series* The Mary Tyler Moore Show. *The Lamont Cranston appearing here is not the real globetrotting millionaire, but rather the laughing, shadowy vigilante, who frequently assumes Cranston's identity when the latter is out of the country.*

Winter
ENTER THE DEVIL

The Harbor City police commissioner asks Officer Frank Devlin to become a vigilante. Devlin replies, "Well, now, do you want me dressing up as a bat or a spider or something? Or should I just blend in with the shadows?" The Commissioner replies, "Criminals are a superstitious and cowardly lot, but I'd rather them be afraid of a crazy cop with a license to kill."

Short story by John L. French in Classic Pulp Fiction Stories *#19, Tom and Ginger Johnson, eds., Fading Shadows Publications, December 1996; reprinted in* The Devil of Harbor City, *Wild Cat Books, 2004. Devlin is referring to Batman, the Spider, and the pulp hero of the shadows. Later stories establish Devlin (aka the Devil) exists in the same universe as both the shadowy hero and French's hero the Nightmare, and therefore his exploits take place in the CU.*

Spring
THE DEVIL YOU KNOW

Cursed musician Johnny Nickle meets Campbell Silver, who mentions his name is derived from his mother's side of the family, and who is interested in the super-natural. Reference is made to the films of Kit Langford, and Johnny plays "Lament for a Trumpet."

Story by Brad Mengel in Charles Boeckman Presents Johnny Nickle Vol. 1, *Pro Se Press, 2013. Nickle appeared in "Run Cat Run" by "Charles Beckman Jr." (Charles Boeckman) in* Dime Mystery, *December 1949. The death of Kit Langford was told in Beckman's "How to Kill a Corpse" (*Dime Detective, *June 1953).*
*"Lament for a Trumpet" was written by Big Lip, whose murder was solved in Beckman's "The Last Trumpet" (*New Detective Magazine, *April 1953). All three stories are collected in* Suspense, Suspicion & Shockers, *von Boeck-mann Fiction Factory Publications, 2012. Campbell Silver's mother is a member of the Campbell family from the television series* Supernatural.

Summer
NESTOR BURMA GOES WEST

In the Arizona desert, French private investigator Nestor Burma flips between radio channels. One describes a so-called devil girl claiming to be from Mars terrorizing the guests at an inn in Scotland, while another refers to Ellinson's daughter, Doctor Harold Medford, and Agent Robert Graham. Burma is seeking the former adventurer Jim Anthony. Burma thinks Doctor Cornelius and similar masterminds were more anarchic than he was during Anthony's heyday. Burma's client is Pam Rive, who met Burma at the Fiat Lux Agency, sparking jealousy in Hélène. Rive wishes Burma to find her

daughter, who is seeking her biological father, Anthony. Burma and his car are nearly trampled by an elephant-sized tarantula. Burma contacted Ardan, who owed him for a case involving Adélaïde Lupin in 1946, about Anthony. Anthony had several run-ins with a Nazi *ubermensch* named Sun Koh in the 1940s. Pam and Anthony's daughter, Vera Pima, appears and reveals she is a member of *Les Vampires*. Anthony reveals Pam and Vera are the daughter and granddaughter, respectively, of Irma Vep, with Pam also answering to that name. Anthony worries about how his wife, Dolores Colquitt-Anthony, is going to react to the news of his having an illegitimate daughter. Anthony compares the invisible jets the Vampires are using to Mayen's atomic vessels. Thinking about what it must have been like for Vera to have grown up as the daughter of the Great Vampire, Burma compares it to his own paternity, thinking Arsène Lupin is no patch on Irma Vep. Anthony says the tunnels beneath his home once housed an entire civilization stretching across the Southwest; his friend Harley Warren and a man called Raven-wood had an encounter with the inhabitants of K'n-Yan, one of their cities. Vera has eidetic memory, and knows everything there is to know about *Les Vampires*. Anthony remarks Interpol or SNIF would find that information very useful. He also quips invisible jets went out of fashion with consulting detectives and rubies filched from Asian idols. Pam says her own father's name was synonymous with terror in his time, and Anthony is as brutal as any Cimmerian or Pict from the *Nemedian Chronicles*. After Pam's death, Anthony asks Burma to help Vera establish a new identity. Vera chooses Vera Gemini as her new alias.

Short story by Josh Reynolds in Tales of the Shadowmen Volume 9: La Vie en Noir, *Jean-Marc and Randy Lofficier, eds., Black Coat Press, 2012; reprinted in French in* Les Compagnons de l'Ombre (Tome 12), *Jean-Marc and Randy Lofficier, eds., Rivière Blanche, 2013. Nestor Burma is the head of the Fiat Lux detective agency in novels by Léo Malet; his secretary is Hélène Châtelain. The radio broadcasts are references to the 1954 science fiction films* Devil Girl from Mars *and* Them! *respectively. Although the year of 1954 is given for this story, I have adjusted it to 1953 in order to allow enough time for the events of these two movies to occur and be*

fictionalized in film versions. Jim Anthony appeared in the pulp Super
Detective; *Dolores Colquitt, daughter of Senator Colquitt, was his girlfriend, and this story reveals that they eventually wed. Doctor Cornelius
Kramm is the ruthless scientist and criminal mastermind featured in Gustave
Le Rouge's* Le Mystérieux Docteur Cornélius. *The tarantula is from the
1955 giant monster film* Tarantula. *Dr. Francis "Doc" Ardan is from Guy
d'Armen's* Doc Ardan: City of Gold and Lepers. *In Jean-Marc and Randy
Lofficier's adaptation and translation of the novel, it is implied Ardan is
actually the bronze-skinned pulp superman widely known as "Doc"; in* Doc
Savage: His Apocalyptic Life, *Philip José Farmer revealed that this man's
true surname was Wildman. Adélaïde Johnston Lupin is the daughter of
Arsène Lupin and American journalist Patricia Johnston, who appears in* Les
Milliards d'Arsène Lupin. *Adélaïde appears alongside Ardan in Win Scott
Eckert's stories "The Eye of Oran" (*Tales of the Shadowmen Volume 2:
Gentlemen of the Night, *Jean-Marc and Randy Lofficier, eds., Black Coat
Press, 2005) and "Les Lèvres Rouges" (*Tales of the Shadowmen Volume 3:
Danse Macabre, *Jean-Marc and Randy Lofficier, eds., Black Coat Press,
2006). The 1946 reference is to "Les Lèvres Rouges," which also features
Nestor Burma and adopts Jean-Marc Lofficier's theory that Burma is himself
an illegitimate son of Arsène Lupin, thus making him Adélaïde's half-
brother. Doc Wildman and Adélaïde's daughter Patricia Wildman is the
protagonist of the novel* The Evil in Pemberley House, *cowritten by Eckert
and Philip José Farmer. Sun Koh and his ally Jan Mayen are the protagonists
of two German pulp series (or* heftroman*) by Paul Müller that crossed over
with each other.* Les Vampires *are from Louis Feuillade's film serial of the
same name, as are the alleged first Irma Vep and the Great Vampire, the title
held by the group's leader. In the CU, another woman used the name Irma
Vep before the one who appeared in* Les Vampires, *as seen in Reynolds'*
Phileas Fogg and the War of Shadows *and Kim Newman's* Professor Moriarty: The Hound of the D'Urbervilles. *Therefore, Pam Rive is actually the
third Irma Vep. Harley Warren is from H. P. Lovecraft's stories about
Randolph Carter, a scholar exploring the Dreamlands. K'n-yan is from
Lovecraft's revision of Zealia Bishop's story "The Mound." Occult detective
Ravenwood, the "stepson of mystery," had his own series of stories penned
by Frederick C. Davis as a back-up feature in the pulp magazine* Secret
Agent X. *SNIF, or the Service National d'Information Fonctionnelle, is
from the Langelot young adult spy novels by "Lieutenant X" (Vladimir
Volkoff). Before* Les Vampires' *use of such a vehicle, the superheroine
Wonder Woman piloted an invisible jet. The consulting detective reference
is to Sherlock Holmes, while the reference to rubies filched from Asian idols
is meant to evoke Wilkie Collins'* The Moonstone. *Irma Vep II's father is*

meant to be Fantômas, the so-called "Lord of Terror." Fantômas first met her mother in Travis Hiltz's tale "A Dance of Night and Death" (Tales of the Shadowmen Volume 3). They must have had a later sexual encounter that resulted in the birth of Irma Vep II, aka "Pam Rive." The Cimmerians are the people of Robert E. Howard's Hyborian Age hero Conan. Howard cited a book called The Nemedian Chronicles as his source of information about the Hyborian Age. The Picts are the people of another Robert E. Howard hero, Bran Mak Morn. Vera's choice of alias is a reference to the band Blue Öyster Cult's song "The Revenge of Vera Gemini."

DEAL WITH THE DEVIL

Sergeant Benjamin Campbell dismisses the idea of Frank "the Devil" Devlin hiding in darkness: "That was what that guy in New York would do. Devlin's not one to play with shadows." The Police Commissioner introduces Devlin to Michael Shaw, a New Yorker who owns a private investigation agency, whose services he has enlisted to clean up the courts in Harbor City. Shaw refers to underworld hangouts in New York such as the Pink Rat and the Black Ship.

Story by John L. French in Double Danger Tales #13, *Tom and Ginger Johnson, eds.,* Fading Shadows Publications, *February 1998; reprinted in* The Devil of Harbor City, *Wild Cat Books, 2004. The Pink Rat and the Black Ship are underworld dives from the exploits of a certain shadowy vigilante, "That guy in New York," who commands a network of loyal agents. Michael Shaw operated in the 1930s as the vigilante called the Nightmare, as seen in a series of stories by French.*

THE DEVIL'S WAKE

Frank "the Devil" Devlin is apparently killed by men working for New York City gangster Wolf Hopkins. Hopkins planned his attempt on Devlin's life with a Harbor City crook at the Red Thorn in New York, which has the same reputation as the legendary Pink Rat and Black Ship, bars where the police dare not go. The Police Commissioner, Sergeant Benjamin Campbell, and private investigator Michael Shaw attempt to avenge Devlin's death, but he turns out to be very much alive.

Story by John L. French in Double Danger Tales *#14, Tom and Ginger Johnson, eds., Fading Shadows Publications, March 1998; reprinted in* The Devil of Harbor City, *Wild Cat Books, 2004. In the 1930s, Wolf Hopkins was the archenemy of Michael Shaw, who was active as the vigilante the Nightmare, as seen in another series of stories by French. The Pink Rat and the Black Ship are underworld dive bars from the pulp novels by Walter Ginson and others about a shadowy vigilante with a large network of agents.*

DEVIL'S END

Frank Devlin finally ends the menace of Wolf Hopkins. Afterwards, he and his bride-to-be Angela Martinelli accept a job with Michael Shaw's private investigation firm.

Story by John L. French in Double Danger Tales *#22, Tom and Ginger Johnson, eds., Fading Shadows Publications, November 1998; reprinted in* The Devil of Harbor City, *Wild Cat Books, 2004. This tale picks up immediately after "The Devil's Wake."*

1954

Winter

THE MYSTERIOUS ISLAND OF DR. ANTEKIRTT

The Nyctalope, Robert Morane, Bernard Prince, a Boy with a cowlick who is a noted journalist, the Boy's Dog, and his drunken friend, the Captain, do battle with Monsieur Ming, Dr. Julius No, and Emilio Largo on the island fortress Antekirtta. Prince was recommended for the expedition by the American Bonisseur de la Bath, as Morane's friend Ballantine was sidelined by a twisted ankle. Antekirtta was created by Count Mathias Sandorf, alias Dr. Antekirtt. Hugo Drax once led an expedition to Antekirtta. The Boy is friends with a brilliant but absent-minded Professor. Largo was recommended to Ming by Blofeld. Ming's Shin Tan aided No in escaping the vengeance of the Si-Fan and others. The Boy says the Professor's experiments with electricity nearly burned down the Diva's villa. Ming reflects on an affair in China involving Dr. Natas and the Blue Scorpion. The Nyctalope and crew encounter Sandorf's aging comrade Point Pescade.

Short story by David L. Vineyard in Tales of the Shadowmen Volume 7: Femmes Fatales, *Jean-Marc and Randy Lofficier, eds., Black Coat Press, 2010; reprinted in French in* Les Compagnons de l'Ombre (Tome 8*), Jean-Marc and Randy Lofficier, eds., Rivière Blanche, 2011; and in* The Nyctalope Steps In, *Jean-Marc and Randy Lofficier, eds., Black Coat Press, 2011. The Nyctalope is the hero of a series of novels by Jean de La Hire. Robert "Bob" Morane and his friend Bill Ballantine are featured in a series of books by*

Henri Vernes (Charles-Henri Dewisme); Monsieur Ming, aka "The Yellow Shadow," is his arch nemesis, the leader of the Shin Tan. Bernard Prince is the protagonist of the eponymous Belgian comic by "Greg" (Michel Regnier) and Hermann Huppen. The Boy is Tintin; the Captain is Captain Archibald Haddock; the Boy's Dog is Milou (Snowy in the English translations); the Professor is Professeur Tryphon Tournesol (Professor Cuthbert Calculus in the translations); and the Diva is Bianca Castafiore; all of these are from the comics by "Hergé" (Georges Remi). Other comics by Herge connected to Tintin via crossover cameos and references include Quick and Flupke; The Amiable Mr. Mops; and Jo, Zette and Jocko. References from Ian Fleming's James Bond novels: Dr. Julius No is from Dr. No; Emilio Largo is from Thunderball; Hugo Drax is from Moonraker; and Blofeld appears in Thunderball, On Her Majesty's Secret Service, and You Only Live Twice. Antekirtta, Count Mathias Sandorf, and Point Pescade are from Jules Verne's novel Mathias Sandorf. Bonisseur de la Bath is Hubert Bonisseur de la Bath, aka CIA agent OSS 117, who appeared in 88 novels by Jean Bruce. The Si-Fan is the criminal organization led by Dr. Fu Manchu in Sax Rohmer's novels. Dr. Natas is from Guy d'Armen's novel Doc Ardan: City of Gold and Lepers; in Jean-Marc and Randy Lofficier's adaptation and translation of the book, it was strongly implied Natas was actually Fu Manchu. The Blue Scorpion is an enemy of Peter the Brazen in stories by "Loring Brent" (George F. Worts).

Spring
THE TINY DESTROYER
Ikano Kato shows Jean Kariven a figurine called a Dogu. Kariven mentions *le Frelon Vert* saving his resistance cell from a German baron with nasty dueling scars. Kato suggests perhaps someday his and Mr. Reid's sons will take up their mission. Reid's cousin, a former FBI agent named Martin, was killed in California. The Dogu previously belonged to a Dr. Melcher. The Dogu is a parasite created by the evil alien Denebians. A member of the Polarians, the Denebians' rivals, confronts Kariven and Kato.

Short story by Frank Schildiner in Tales of the Shadowmen Volume 7: Femmes Fatales, *Jean-Marc and Randy Lofficier, eds., Black Coat Press, 2010; reprinted in French in* Les Compagnons de l'Ombre (Tome 9), *Jean-Marc and Randy Lofficier, eds., Rivière Blanche, 2012. Jean Kariven and the warring Polarian and Denebian races are from novels by Jimmy Guieu. Mr. Reid is Britt Reid, aka the Green Hornet; 'le Frelon Vert" is the French translation of his alias. Ikano Kato is the Hornet's chauffeur and ally in the war on crime. NOW Comics' continuation of the Hornet's exploits in the 1980s and 1990s revealed the Green Hornet seen in the 1960s television* series was the original Hornet's nephew, Britt Reid II, while the Kato in that series was Hayashi Kato, son of the elder Reid's partner. The German baron with nasty dueling scars is Baron Wolfgang von Strucker, archenemy of Nick Fury and leader of Hydra, as seen in various Marvel Comics. Reid's cousin Martin is Dick Martin from the film Black Dragons. Martin was played by Clayton Moore, who later played the Lone Ranger on television. The Green Hornet radio series established Britt Reid was the Lone Ranger's great-nephew. Dr. Melcher is also from Black Dragons.

A MOMENT OF PERFECT HAPPINESS

Leo Saint-Clair, formerly known as the Nyctalope, encounters Dr. Adrien de Villiers-Pagan in Saigon. Photographer Mike Kovac occasionally shares drinks with English reporter Thomas Fowler, who is acquainted with an American man named Pyle. Pyle is in love with a Vietnamese girl named Phuong.

Short story by Roman Leary in The Nyctalope Steps In, *Jean-Marc and Randy Lofficier, eds., Black Coat Press, 2011; reprinted in French in* Les Compagnons de l'Ombre (Tome 8), *Jean-Marc and Randy Lofficier, eds., Rivière Blanche, 2011. The Nyctalope is the hero of a series of French pulp novels by Jean de La Hire. Dr. Adrien de Villiers-Pagan created the adventurer's artificial heart. Mike Kovac was played by Charles Bronson in the 1958–1960 television series* Man with a Camera. *Thomas Fowler, Alden Pyle, and Phuong are from Graham Greene's novel* The Quiet American. *This story takes place during the events of that novel, and shows a major scene in it from Leo and Kovac's respective points of view. Although the year is given as 1951, this must be incorrect, as Jonathan Richards and Tad Richards' novel* Nick & Jake *takes place before* The Quiet American, *and is set in 1953, being firmly tied to historical events from that year.*

Summer

THE DEATH BIRD

Jean Kariven meets with Albert Campion. Campion's valet, Magersfontein Lugg, mentions Sexton Blake. Campion shows Kariven documents originally belonging to Mr. Tobin, a Nazi spy. The weapon described in the documents is stored in a house built and owned by the Mocata family, the last member of which reportedly died in an occult ceremony some 20 years ago. Kariven, Campion, and Lugg find themselves in the middle of a conflict between a Polarian and a Denebian.

Short story by Frank Schildiner in Tales of the Shadowmen Volume 8: Agents Provocateurs, *Jean-Marc and Randy Lofficier, eds., Black Coat Press, 2012; reprinted in French in* Les Compagnons de l'Ombre (Tome 12), *Jean-Marc and Randy Lofficier, eds., Rivière Blanche, 2013. Jean Kariven and the rival alien Polarian and Denebian races are from novels by Jimmy Guieu. Sleuth Albert Campion and his valet Lugg appear in novels by Margery Allingham. Sexton Blake is one of the most enduring British penny dreadful detectives. Tobin is from Alfred Hitchcock's film* Saboteur. *The last of the Mocatas is from Dennis Wheatley's novel* The Devil Rides Out, *part of his series about the occult detective the Duke de Richleau.*

Late August
DON CAMILLO AND THE SECRET WEAPON
Mayor Peppone and Smilzo bring a Soviet spy to the priest Don Camillo's church for sanctuary. A British agent receives instructions from Mr. Hawthorne to bring in the Russian. Hawthorne's secretary is Anita Hutchens. The Soviet has stolen a microfilm containing research on a biological weapon called "the Satan Bug." Hawthorne assigns Eva Kant as the English agent's translator. The Russian spy, Avakoum Zahov, tells Don Camillo he is a fashion designer whose employer is in Clerville, and mentions that Princess Ann recently visited Italy.

Short story by Matthew Baugh in Tales of the Shadowmen Volume 8: Agents Provocateurs, *Jean-Marc and Randy Lofficier, eds., Black Coat Press, 2011; reprinted in French in* Les Compagnons de L'Ombre (Tome 10), *Jean-Marc and Randy Lofficier, eds., Rivière Blanche, 2012. Don Camillo is the protagonist of a series of comedic novels by Giovannino Guareschi; Mayor Peppone and Smilzo are also from the Don Camillo books. The British agent is James Bond. Mr. Hawthorne is from the novel* Our Man in Havana *by Graham Greene. Anita Hutchens (or Hutchins) is from the film* Three Coins in the Fountain. *The Satan Bug is the titular germ warfare agent from Alistair MacLean's novel. Eva Kant is the lover of the master criminal Diabolik in comic books by Angela and Luciana Giussani; Clerville is the town out of which the two operate. Avakoum Zahov first appeared in Andrei Gulyashki's novel* The Zahov Mission. *Gulyashki wished to have Zahov fight James Bond in a sequel. However, Gildrose Publications threatened to sue Gulyashki if he went through with his plans; thus, the book, when published, had Zakhov fighting a spy identified only as 07. Princess Ann is from the film* Roman Holiday.

Summer

THE YOTH PROTOCOLS

An FBI agent named Sarlowe thinks of centers of eldritch activity, such as the Warren site in the Big Cypress, the Martense molehills, and "certain secret cellars where a certain artist had painted certain pictures and almost certainly been eaten." He also thinks of Inspector Craig and his Special Detail in the subway tunnels beneath New York, as well as worms in the earth. Sarlowe's partner Indrid Cold is described as having a wax-like face. It is stated there are worse things in Heaven and Earth than dreamt of in Alhazred's philosophy. The local "old ones" include the Shonokins and

the *K'n-Yani*. Sarlowe reminds Cold of the Yoth protocols. A circular stone covering the stairs leading to the mound where the *K'n-Yani* live was placed there after the Zamacona Cylinder was unearthed. "The batrachian hillbillies in Massachusetts" and N'Kai are mentioned. Cold is the only person who ever used the Voormithadreth Corridor and hadn't rotted from the inside out. Cold identified Valusian spectrum radiation within the mound. The Russian necromancer Grigori Petrov refers to the Zann Concerto and the maw of Leng. Cold asks Petrov if he was planning to let Tsathoggua's children loose to do his dirty work. Sarlowe quotes, "Evil the mind that is held by no head."

Short story by Josh Reynolds in World War Cthulhu: A Collection of Lovecraftian War Stories, *Brian M. Sammons and Glynn Owen Barrass, eds., Dark Regions Press, 2014. Sarlowe is a relative of occult detective Baxter Sarlowe from Reynolds' novel* Wake the Dead. *The Warren site in the Big Cypress is from H. P. Lovecraft's story "The Statement of Randolph Carter." The Martense molehills are from Lovecraft's "The Lurking Fear." The secret cellars where an artist painted pictures and was eaten are from Lovecraft's story "Pickman's Model." Inspector Craig and his Special Detail are from Robert Barbour Johnson's story "Far Below." The worms in the earth are from Robert E. Howard's Bran Mak Morn story "Worms of the Earth." Indrid Cold is an allegedly real person connected to the supposed Mothman sightings in 1966. His wax-like face implies Cold is a member of* the wax-masked race of creatures seen in Lovecraft's "The Festival," which is the source of the quote, "Evil the mind that is held by no head." Abdul Alhazred, the mad Arab, is the author of the Necronomicon in Lovecraft's Cthulhu Mythos. The Shonokins are from Manly Wade Wellman's John Thunstone stories. The K'n-Yani, Yoth, the Zamacona Cylinder, and N'Kai are from Lovecraft's revision of Zealia Bishop's story "The Mound." "The batrachian hillbillies in Massachusetts" are a reference to Lovecraft's "The Shadow over Innsmouth." The Voormithadreth Corridor is connected to Mount Voormithadreth from Cthulhu Mythos stories by Clark Ashton Smith. Tsathoggua is also from Smith's Mythos tales. Valusian spectrum radiation is a reference to the kingdom of Valusia in Robert E. Howard's Kull stories. The Zann Concerto is from Lovecraft's "The Music of Erich Zann." The plateau of Leng appears in a number of Lovecraft's stories. The year is conjecture, though the story implicitly takes place in the 1950s, during the Cold War.

1956

Winter
JEALOUS LOVER

The debut of private investigator Al Diamond. Police Captain Jules Leopold appears briefly.

Short story by Edward D. Hoch in Crime and Punishment, March 1957. *Al Diamond (later renamed Darlan) would go on to appear in several more stories by Hoch, while Captain Leopold would appear in his own series of stories. Since Leopold is in the CU through a later crossover with Hoch's character Nick Velvet, so is Diamond/Darlan. In real life, an editor changed Diamond's last name after a few stories to avoid confusion with the title character of the radio and television series* Richard Diamond, Private Detective. *Since Richard Diamond is also in the CU, perhaps Al Diamond was a relative of Richard's who changed his last name to Darlan to avoid being compared to his kinsman.*

Spring
SHIFTING SANDS

Colonel Chinstrap appears.

Episode of the British radio comedy series The Goon Show *broadcast January 24, 1957. Colonel Chinstrap is from another radio series,* It's That Man Again. The Goon Show *was brought into the CU by a reference to Neddie Seagoon in David McDaniel's novel* The Rainbow Affair. *One of the regulars on* It's That Man Again, *Mrs. Mopp, appeared as a young woman in*

The League of Extraordinary Gentlemen, Volume II, *further cementing that show's inclusion. Colonel Chinstrap reappeared in a 1959 episode of* The Goon Show *entitled "Who is Pink Oboe?"*

Summer
HOUSE OF THE LIVING DEAD
Hellboy, adventuring as a masked *luchador* in Mexico, is tricked by a mad scientist into fighting the Frankenstein Monster, who said scientist found in a traveling carnival. A vampire also appears.

Graphic novel by Mike Mignola and Richard Corben, Dark Horse Books, 2011. The vampire, though not

named, is clearly meant to be the Christopher Lee version of Dracula. The Frankenstein Monster seen here also appears in his own miniseries, Frankenstein Underground.*

1957

Winter
THE ROBOTS OF METROPOLIS
Doctor Omega battles the mad scientist Rotwang in the city of Metropolis. Omega's companions Tizairou, Denis Borel, and Fred appear, as does a female robot created by Rotwang, who also possesses robots called Volkites and an earthquake ray created by the Atlantean Unga Khan. Omega tries to convince Rotwang to abandon his feud with the Fredersons. Omega views Rotwang's additions to the ray's control devices, including replacing the radium core with Lunarium and using oscillation overthruster circuitry as part of the targeting mechanism.

Short story by Travis Hiltz in Tales of the Shadowmen Volume 7: Femmes Fatales, *Jean-Marc and Randy Lofficier, eds., Black Coat Press, 2010; reprinted in French in* Les Compagnons de l'Ombre (Tome 9), *Jean-Marc and Randy Lofficier, eds., Rivière Blanche, 2012. Doctor Omega, Tiziraou, Denis Borel, and Fred are from Arnould Galopin's novel* Doctor Omega, *which has been translated and adapted by the Lofficiers. Rotwang, the City of Metropolis, Rotwang's female robot, and the Fredersons are from*

Thea von Harbou's novel Metropolis *and Fritz Lang's classic film adaptation. Although Hiltz indicates this story takes place in the future, Jean-Marc Lofficier's story "J. C. in Alphaville" reveals that Metropolis is actually in a pocket dimension in the Outlands (from Jean-Luc Godard's film* Alphaville*) created by Rotwang in 1954. The exact year in which this story takes place is conjecture. The Volkites, the earthquake ray, and Unga Khan are from the serial* Undersea Kingdom. *Lunarium is from George Tucker's novel* A Voyage to the Moon. *The oscillation overthruster is from the film* The Adventures of Buckaroo Banzai Across the Eighth Dimension.

Spring
SHAKE, RATTLE AND ROCK!

Officer Paisley appears, as do E. Joyce Togar, Evelyn Randell, and Kate Rambeau Sr.

1994 television movie directed by Allan Arkush, named after but otherwise unrelated to the 1956 film of the same name. Officer Paisley is played by Dick Miller, who played a character named Walter Paisley in A Bucket of Blood, *among others. Given the Officer's apparent age, he is most likely Walter's father or uncle. Kate Rambeau Sr. is played by Dey Young, who also played a character named Kate Rambeau in Arkush's film* Rock 'n' Roll High School. *Presumably Kate Sr. is the mother of the Kate Rambeau who attended Vince Lombardi High School in the late 1970s. E. Joyce Togar is played by Mary Woronov, who appeared in* Rock 'n' Roll High School *as Principal Evelyn Togar, while Evelyn Randell is played by P. J. Soles, who played Riff Randell in the same film. Perhaps E. Joyce and Evelyn are the mothers of Ms. Togar and Riff respectively.* Rock 'n' Roll High School *also spawned a sequel,* Rock 'n' Roll High School Forever. *Presumably some aspects of the former film at least (such as a mouse exploding after being subjected to the Ramones' music, as well as the presence of that mouse's human-sized, dress-wearing mother) were exaggerated for comic effect.*

Autumn
FACES OF FEAR

Christiane Génessier, who has been disfigured in an auto accident, is attacked in her dreams by a blade-fingered, fedora-wearing being who feeds on fear. This demonic figure mentions an "S-Mart flunky" who used the *Necronomicon* to send him back in time. Christiane is saved by Judex. Her surgeon father dismisses Dr. Crane, whose use of a fear serum on Christiane allowed the being to strike, and threatens to have him deported. Dr. Génessier notes the slasher's assault has further disfigured her, and decides he will need to take more drastic steps to restore his daughter's former beauty. Dr. Orloff assists Génessier.

Short story by Matthew Dennion in Tales of the Shadowmen Volume 7: Femmes Fatales, *Jean-Marc and Randy Lofficier, eds., Black Coat Press, 2010; reprinted in French in* Les Compagnons de l'Ombre (Tome 9), *Jean-Marc and Randy Lofficier, eds., Rivière Blanche, 2012, and* L'Ombre de Judex, *Jean-Marc and Randy Lofficier, eds., Rivière Blanche, 2013; and in* The Shadow of Judex, *Jean-Marc and Randy Lofficier, eds., Black Coat Press, 2013. Christiane Génessier and her father are from Jean Redon's 1959 novel* Les yeux sans visage *and a 1960 film adaptation by Georges Franju. I have adjusted the date of this story from 1959 to 1957 to give more time for the events of the novel to occur and be written up by Redon. The blade-fingered individual is Freddy Krueger from the* A Nightmare on Elm Street *film series. The "S-Mart flunky" (Ash Williams) and the* Necronomicon (*properly the* Necronomicon Ex Mortis; *not to be confused with the* Necronomicon *featured in the Cthulhu Mythos) are from the* Evil Dead *film series. Ash used the* Necronomicon *on Freddy in the comic book miniseries* Freddy vs. Jason vs. Ash. *Judex is the title character of the 1916 film serial directed by Louis Feuillade, which was remade by Franju as a full-length film in 1963. Dr. Jonathan Crane is better known as Batman's enemy the Scarecrow, who debuted in 1941. Génessier must not have researched Crane's background very thoroughly. Dr. Orloff is from Jesús Franco's film* The Awful Dr. Orloff *and its sequels. The Awful Dr. Orloff was set in 1912, and featured Orloff murdering women and surgically removing their facial skin in order to restore the beauty of his disfigured daughter, as Génessier did in* Les yeux sans visage. *Orloff must have suggested to Génessier shortly after the events of this story he adopt Orloff's own methods.*

1958

February 2
THE THREE SISTERS
In the far-distant past, the Dying Earth magician known as Rialto the Marvelous buries an Ioun Stone on the Moon to be discovered in the millennia to come. Another stone is discovered one hundred thousand years later on Earth by the necromancers of the dark kingdom of Acheron. In Egypt in the 14th Century B.C., a young woman named Hecate discovers the same stone after consulting Stygian scrolls. In France in 1642, Henri-Jean de

Sainte-Claire routs a group of alien Invaders using the stone. Sainte-Claire discovered he had acquired the power to see in the dark after a duel with Cyrano de Bergerac. In 1657, Sainte-Claire creates a harness based on Cyrano's notes in order to travel to the moon. In present-day Morocco, the Nyctalope (aka Leo Saint-Clair, Henri-Jean de Sainte-Claire's descendant with identical powers) enters a former secret military base hidden inside a cavern. Among the cave's contents are a partially disassembled Martian tripod, a crate of radium-powered weapons from Helium, and the rocket ship *OLB-1*, designed by Professor d'Olbans, which the Nyctalope used to explore the vagabond planet Rhea. The hero was once married to the Professor's niece Veronique. Leo mounts a recreation of Engineer Korrides' Lightning Projector on the rocket. He set up the base with friends from the CID in 1939, and began his adventurous career after his father was murdered by Sadi Khan. Less than six months ago, Leo surrendered himself to the French authorities. He was brought before two men: Geo Paquet of the *Direction de la Surveillance du Territoire* and Roger Noël of the *Service National d'Information Fonctionnelle*. Leo had asked Commissaire Ferret to let him meet with someone from the Intelligence services regarding a matter of national security. When Sadi Khan murdered Leo's father, he stole the stone that had been in the family for centuries. Leo thought the metal powder Cyrano used in his trip to the Moon may be a variant of the Z-4 element invented by Professor d'Olbans, which Leo used on his travel to Rhea. Before he surrendered, Leo discovered from a contact in the OSS, his distant cousin Hubert Bonisseur de la Bath, the stone was now in the possession of Stalin, who planned to send Soviet cosmonauts to the Moon.

   Short story by Emmanuel Gorlier in The Nyctalope Steps In, *Jean-Marc and Randy Lofficier, eds., Black Coat Press, 2011; reprinted in French in* Les Compagnons de l'Ombre (Tome 8), *Jean-Marc and Randy Lofficier, eds., Rivière Blanche, 2011. This story spans several centuries, but the date used for this entry is based on the Nyctalope's perspective. Rialto (or rather Rhialto) the Marvelous and the Ioun Stones are from the Dying Earth books by Jack Vance, which likely take place in an alternate future. Acheron and Stygia are from Robert E. Howard's Conan novel* The Hour of the Dragon. *The Invaders are from the television series of the same name. Cyrano de Bergerac is an historical figure who also appeared in a play by Edmond Rostand. Cyrano's trip to the moon was described in his novel* Comical History of the States and Empires of the Moon. *The Nyctalope, the OLB-1, Professor d'Olbans, his niece Veronique, the planet Rhea, Engineer Korrides, the CID, Sadi Khan, and Z-4 appear in a series of novels by Jean de La Hire. The Martian tripod is a reference to H. G. Wells'* The War of the Worlds.

Helium is a city on Mars (aka Barsoom) in Edgar Rice Burroughs' novels. Geo "The Gorilla" Paquet and the Direction de la Surveillance du Territoire appear in spy novels by Antoine-Louis Dominique. The Service National d'Information Fonctionelle (SNIF) is from the Langelot young adult spy novels by Vladimir Volkoff. "Roger Noël" is the alias of Capitaine Montferrand, the head of SNIF's Protection division. Commissaire Ferret is from Henri Vernes' Bob Morane novels. Hubert Bonisseur de la Bath (aka OSS 117) appears in espionage novels by Jean Bruce.

Autumn. Walter Paisley, a waiter at a beatnik café and would-be sculptor, achieves his dream via murder. (*A Bucket of Blood*, 1959 feature film directed by Roger Corman.) Despite appearances, Walter must have actually hanged a hollow sculpture of himself and escaped before the police could apprehend him.

1959

Summer

THE HOT ROCK

John Dortmunder attempts to break fellow professional thief (and occasional actor) Alan Greenwood out of prison. Greenwood plans to change his name to Alan Grofield after the escape.

The first Dortmunder novel by Donald E. Westlake. A professional thief named Alan Grofield appears in Westlake's Parker novels, written under the pen name "Richard Stark," and is also the protagonist of four other novels written under the Stark pseudonym. Can the two Alan Grofields be the same person? Another Dortmunder novel, Nobody's Perfect, *claims Greenwood became a successful television actor under his original name. This seems exceedingly unlikely, since Greenwood would be wanted by the police for his prison escape. Since both the Parker and Dortmunder series have links to the CU, it is more likely the reference in* Nobody's Perfect *is a distortion, and the two Grofields are indeed one and the same.*

93

July
THE ALGERIAN DILEMMA

Investigating terrorist attacks in Algeria, the Nyctalope seeks information from some old friends affiliated with French Military Intelligence, with whom he has worked on and off since the 1930s, most recently during the Antekirtta affair. He later faces the terrorist, the son and heir of his old foe the Djinn, who has been using Aladdin's Lamp to spread chaos. The villain flees, and the Nyctalope thinks he will neutralize the Lamp by using the method of the Seal of Solomon taught to him by his friend Jules de Grandin.

Short story by Emmanuel Gorlier in Night of the Nyctalope, *Jean-Marc and Randy Lofficier, eds., Black Coat Press, 2012; reprinted in French in* La Nuit du Nyctalope, *Jean-Marc and Randy Lofficier, eds., Rivière Blanche, 2012. The Nyctalope's adventures were recounted by Jean de La Hire. Antekirtta is from Jules Verne's novel* Mathias Sandorf; *the Nyctalope's trip to the island was chronicled by David L. Vineyard in "The Mysterious Island of Dr. Antekirtt" (*Tales of the Shadowmen Volume 7: Femmes Fatales, *Jean-Marc and Randy Lofficier, eds., Black Coat Press, 2010). Dr. Jules de Grandin's battles with occult forces were chronicled by Seabury Quinn.*

1960

Spring
WITH THE COMPLIMENTS OF NESTOR BURMA!

Private eye Nestor Burma discusses a case with his secretary Hélène involving the Maître d' of *Picratt's*. Burma is hired by former film director Leni Riefenstahl. Burma is abducted by a group of men, but is rescued by a British astrophysicist, who tells him his captors are the Atomos Organization. The professor was working for the organization while leaking info about them to the OSS. Eventually he convinced his superiors to let him leave the Atomos Organization, exchanging information with them about the group known as SMOG in return for his dismissal. The Atomos Organization's leader is Madame Atomos. Burma and the professor are met by Bob Morane and Hubert Bonisseur de la Bath, aka OSS 117. Unfortunately, the professor has been poisoned by Madame Atomos, leaving him a simple-minded mute. Though his title was Professor Bean, the OSS agents usually called him Mister Bean.

Short story by Nestor Burma, edited by Michel Stéphan in Tales of the Shadowmen Volume 8: Agents Provocateurs, *Jean-Marc and Randy Lofficier, eds., Black Coat Press, 2011; reprinted in French in* Les Compagnons de l'Ombre (Tome 8), *Jean-Marc and Randy Lofficier, eds., Rivière Blanche, 2011, and* La Saga de Mme. Atomos (Tome 7) *by Michel Stéphan, Rivière Blanche, 2013. Nestor Burma and his secretary Hélène Châtelain were created by French crime novelist Léo Malet.* Picratt's *is from Georges Simenon's novel* Maigret and the Strangled Stripper. *Leni Riefenstahl was a real person, most famous (or infamous) for directing the Nazi propaganda film* Triumph of the Will. *Madame Atomos and her organization appear in novels by André Caroff. Bob Morane and SMOG are from a series of novels by Henri Vernes. OSS 117 is the protagonist of a novel series by Jean Bruce and his successors.* Mr. Bean *is the title character of a British television comedy series.*

Autumn
THE THREE DOCTORS

Dr. Fu Manchu has been captured by Princess Alouh T'ho, maddened by her many defeats at the hands of Leo Saint-Clair. Alouh T'ho wishes to spill his blood upon the Heart of Ahriman, draining the souls of every human on Earth and giving the Princess' Blood Worshippers eternal life. Doctors Mystere and Omega come to Fu's rescue. Omega says the spilling of Fu's blood onto the Heart will create a charged vacuum emboitment, but the Princess carries out her plan anyways. After Omega presses a button on a stick, Mystere finds himself the captive of Dorje, driven mad by his defeats at the hands of James Schuyler Grim. Omega and Fu Manchu appear, and fail to save him. Omega resets time once again, only to find himself the captive of Ming Tsai Tsou, aka the Yellow Shadow, maddened by his defeats at the hands of Bob Morane. The spilling of Omega's blood onto the Heart of Ahriman will drain Omega's *wathan.* Fu and Mystere come to Omega's rescue. Ming recognizes Fu Manchu as his old associate, Dr. Natas. This time, Omega manages to accomplish his goal.

Short story by Jean-Marc and Randy Lofficier in Doctor Omega and the Shadowmen, *Jean-Marc and Randy Lofficier, eds., Black Coat Press, 2011; reprinted in French in* Les Compagnons de l'Ombre (Tome 9), *Jean-Marc and Randy Lofficier, eds., Rivière Blanche, 2012. Doctor Omega is from the novel by Arnould Galopin; the Lofficiers' adaptation and translation implied Omega was actually the CU counterpart of the Doctor of* Doctor Who *fame. The charged vacuum emboitment is from the* Doctor Who *serials "Full Circle" and "Logopolis." Alouh T'ho is a foe of Leo Saint-Clair (aka the Nyctalope) in novels by Jean de La Hire. The Heart of Ahriman is from*

Robert E. Howard's Conan novel The Hour of the Dragon. *The insidious Dr. Fu Manchu was created by Sax Rohmer. Doctor Mystere appears in several novels by Paul d'Ivoi. James Schuyler "Jimgrim" Grim and his enemy Dorje are from novels by Talbot Mundy. Dorje died in the book* Jimgrim, *but perhaps a side-effect of the emboitment brought him briefly back to life. Bob Morane and his enemy Ming Tsai Tsou (aka Monsieur Ming) are from novels by Henri Vernes.* Wathan *is from Philip José Farmer's Riverworld novels. The year is conjecture based on the fact Ming and Morane have had several encounters by the time this story takes place.*

1961

Winter. Professional thief Parker's first recorded exploit, *The Hunter* by Richard Stark (pseudonym for Donald E. Westlake).

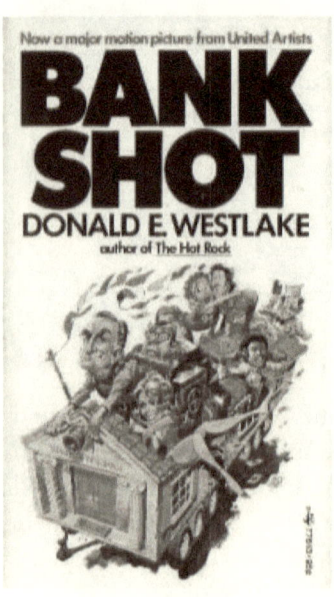

Spring
BANK SHOT
John Dortmunder literally steals a bank guarded by the Continental Detective Agency.

Novel by Donald E. Westlake. The Continental Detective Agency is from Dashiell Hammett's Continental Op stories. Since the Op is in the CU, so is Dortmunder. The guards would pop up several more times in the Dortmunder series; not all of those appearances will be listed here.

October
THE TSAR BOMB
Captain America's shield and a picture of Hellboy hang on the walls of Atomic Robo's offices.

Story by Brian Clevinger and Scott Wegener in Atomic Robo/Neozoic Free Comic Book Day 2008, *Red 5 Comics, May 2008, reinforcing Atomic Robo's inclusion in the CU.*

October 30–November 1
BIG LITTLE MAN
Miguelito Loveless lives out his old age in a V.A. hospital in Fort Bayard, NM. He reminisces about his old nemesis James West, and reflects on others besides himself who created giant toys, including the Toyman,

John Sunlight, and Sumuru. The bane of his present existence is Nurse Ratched, who previously worked at a sanitarium where a troubled patient committed suicide and another patient attacked her. Loveless' past nemeses include West, Lecoq, Paladin, Bulldog Drummond, and Bat Masterson. Fantômas was one of those who dared not speak his name. Loveless was granted an age-retarding serum by his colleague Count Manzeppi, and was friends with Walter Jameson, Voltaire, and Antoinette. Loveless served during World War II on the Allies' side as Michael Donovan; his friend Karl Glocken informed him of German atrocities, and he served for a time in British Intelligence alongside Commandant Bob Morane and Sir Dennis Nayland Smith. Loveless' late son attempted to follow in his footsteps after Miguelito faked his death. Loveless was pen-pals with Dr. Cyclops.

Short story by David McDonnell in Tales of the Shadowmen Volume 7: Femmes Fatales, *Jean-Marc and Randy Lofficier, eds., Black Coat Press, 2010; reprinted in French in* Les Compagnons de l'Ombre (Tome 8), *Jean-Marc and Randy Lofficier, eds., Rivière Blanche, 2011. Dr. Miguelito Loveless, James West, Count Manzeppi, Voltaire, and Antoinette are from the classic television series* The Wild Wild West. *Miguelito's son is Miguelito Loveless, Jr., from the television movie* The Wild Wild West Revisited; *although that film claims Loveless died several years before, McDonnell reveals here Loveless staged his death. The Toyman is one of Superman's most enduring foes. Sunlight is the arch nemesis of the bronze-skinned pulp superman, while Sumuru is the female criminal mastermind created by Sax Rohmer; the circumstances under which those two miscreants created giant toys are unrevealed. Nurse Ratched is from Ken Kesey's novel* One Flew Over the Cuckoo's Nest. *Lecoq is Emile Gaboriau's sleuth. Paladin is from the television series* Have Gun–Will Travel. *Bulldog Drummond is from the series of novels by H. C. "Sapper" McNeile and Gerard Fairlie. Bat Masterson is an historical figure who was played on television by Gene Barry. The diabolical Fantômas was created by Marcel Allain and Pierre Souvestre. Walter Jameson is the immortal from "Long Live Walter Jameson," an episode of* The *Twilight Zone. Karl Glocken is from Katherine Anne Porter's novel* Ship of Fools; *in Stanley Kramer's film adaptation, Glocken was played by Michael Dunn, who also played Loveless on* The Wild Wild West. *Bob Morane is the hero of a series of novels written by Charles-Henri Dewisme under the pseudonym Henri Vernes. Sir Dennis Nayland Smith is the implacable foe of Dr. Fu Manchu. Dr. Cyclops is a mad scientist engaged in miniaturizing humans and the title character of the 1940 film.*

1962

Spring

BASIL SEAL RIDES AGAIN (aka THE RAKE'S REGRESS)

The final tale of Basil Seal and Peter Pastmaster.

Short story by Evelyn Waugh in The Complete Stories of Evelyn Waugh, *Little, Brown and Company, 1998. Basil Seal was the protagonist of Waugh's novels* Black Mischief *and* Put Out More Flags. *Peter Pastmaster, who first appeared in* Decline and Fall, *is the son of Waugh's recurring character Lady Metroland.*

July

OPERATION STARFISH

James Bellmore is a Marine attached to the Joint Advisory Committee on Korea (JACK) as the assistant to the organization's number two man, Colonel Doctor Wingate Peaslee, also known as the Terrible Old Man. The name of the agency is a front for their battles against eldritch horrors. Bellmore and Peaslee travel aboard the USS *Miskatonic* to Johnston Island. Bellmore had a fight with a midshipman who decided to sample a bottle from his case of Remmers Imperial Stout. Bellmore's friends in London, Steed and Drake, suggested he develop a hobby. Having taken up cooking, Bellmore sends some of the foodstuffs to his friends, though mostly to Brenner, a Swiss chef he briefly studied under in New York. Bellmore meets Adam Royston of British Experimental Research Group, Unit 3. The *Miskatonic* uses a Tillinghast Resonator to lure the monsters on the island to be killed, including the Hounds of Tindalos.

Short story by Peter Rawlik in Kaiju Rising: Age of Monsters, *Tim Marquitz and Nickolas Sharps, eds., Ragnarok Publications, 2014. Wingate Peaslee is from H. P. Lovecraft's "The Shadow Out of Time." His nickname of "the Terrible Old Man" is a nod to Lovecraft's story of the same name. The USS* Miskatonic *is named after the Miskatonic Valley, the setting of many of Lovecraft's Cthulhu Mythos tales. Remmers is Rex Stout's detective Nero Wolfe's favorite beer. Wolfe's Swiss chef is Fritz Brenner. Steed is British spy John Steed from the television series* The Avengers *and* The New

Avengers, *while Drake is John Drake from the television series* Danger Man *(aka* Secret Agent*). Adam Royston is from the movie* X the Unknown. *The Tillinghast Resonator is from Lovecraft's story "From Beyond." The Hounds of Tindalos are from Frank Belknap Long's titular tale.*

Summer
ROUSE HIM NOT
John Thunstone states his friend Judge Keith Hilary Pursuivant owns a sword cane with a silver blade just like the one he possesses.
Short story by Manly Wade Wellman in Kadath #5, 1982.

REPOSSESSION
Hellboy battles a demon hunter who is seeking notes left behind by Abdul Alhazred, author of the *Necronomicon.*
Short story by Barbara Hambly in Hellboy: Oddest Jobs, *Christopher Golden, ed., Dark Horse Books, 2008. The connection to the Cthulhu Mythos strengthens Hellboy's inclusion in the Crossover Universe. Hellboy has had crossovers with a number of other characters; only those that easily fit into CU continuity will be included here.*

October 18–24
COLD WAR, YELLOW FEVER
Mitchell Peel is an operative of the Joint Advisory Committee on Korea (JACK), receiving orders from Colonel Doctor Wingate Peaslee, aka the Terrible Old Man. Peaslee tells Peel and other JACK agents Esteban Zamarano was sent to Banes, Cuba as part of Operation Mongoose to enlist his family's aid. The Zamaranos bought six volumes from the sale of the Church of the Starry Wisdom Library, including what appears to be a Spanish-language edition of *The King in Yellow.* After contact was lost with Zamarano, another agent traveled to Banes, and disappeared himself, though not before sending the message, "Where is the Yellow Sign?" The Soviets are willing to neutralize the threat, but Peaslee says Washington does not want to see another Gizhinsk, particularly so close to the U.S. borders. Peel and company work with Major Romero of the Cuban Security Forces and Agent Tanya Romanova of Soviet Army Intelligence to deal with the situation. Romanova refers to documented cases of childrens' minds being stimulated to see the universe in ways adults cannot, such as the Paradine children and "that village in Winshire." After the mission, a traumatized and disfigured Peaslee is retired to a minimum security facility near Arkham, Massachusetts.
Short story by Pete Rawlik in World War Cthulhu: A Collection of

Lovecraftian War Stories, *Brian M. Sammons and Glynn Owen Barrass, eds., Dark Regions Press, 2014. Mitchell Peel is related to David Conyers' series character Major Harrison Peel, an NSA consultant who appears in stories set in the milieu of H. P. Lovecraft's Cthulhu Mythos. Wingate Peaslee is from Lovecraft's story "The Shadow Out of Time"; his nickname of "the Terrible Old Man" is an homage to Lovecraft's story of the same name. The Church of the Starry Wisdom is from Lovecraft's "The Haunter of the Dark." Arkham, Massachusetts is the setting of a number of Mythos tales. The King in Yellow is from Robert W. Chambers' short story collection of the same name, and was incorporated into the Cthulhu Mythos by Lovecraft in his story "The Whisperer in Darkness." The Yellow Sign is also from Chambers' book. Gizhinsk and "that village in Winshire" are from John Wyndham's novel* The Midwich Cuckoos. *Agent Tanya (or Tatiana) Roma-nova is from Ian Fleming's James Bond novel* From Russia, with Love. *The Paradine children are from the short story "Mimsy Were the Borogroves" by "Lewis Padgett" (Henry Kuttner and C. L. Moore).*

1963

Winter. John Keith's first recorded mission for the American Policy Executive (A.P.E), *Overkill* by Norman A. Daniels.

H.P. LOVECRAFT, H.R. WAKEFIELD, JESSE STUART, JOHN METCALFE, CLARK ASHTON SMITH, FRITZ LEIBER, ROBERT E. HOWARD, CARL JACOBI, WILLIAM HOPE HODGSON, J. RAMSEY CAMPBELL, FRANK BELKNAP LONG, J. VERNON SHEA, JOSEPH PAYNE BRENNAN, JOHN POCSIK and others.

OVER THE EDGE

NEW STORIES OF THE MACABRE

Edited by AUGUST DERLETH

Spring
CASTING THE STONE

An occultist's library includes *The Book of Eibon, Cultes des Goules,* Judge Pursuivant's *Vampiricon,* and John Thunstone's *Myth Patterns of the Shonokins.*

Story by John Pocsik in Over the Edge, *August Derleth, ed., Arkham House, 1964. The* Book of Eibon *and* Cultes des Goules *are tomes associated with the Cthulhu Mythos, and were created by Clark Ashton Smith and Robert Bloch respectively. Judge Keith Hilary Pursuivant is the protagonist of a series of stories by Manly Wade Wellman; The* Vam-piricon *is mentioned in the Pursuivant stories. John Thunstone is another Wellman hero, who sometimes battled the man-like creatures known as the Shonokins; however, the book* Myth Patterns of the Shonokins *is Pocsik's invention.*

May 11–August 25
THE DAY OF THE JACKAL
A British official notes the head of the SIS is known to play cards with his top agents at Blades.

Novel by Frederick Forsyth. Blades is M's club, where he often plays cards with James Bond. Blades is a fictional club based on Ian Fleming's club, Boodles. The SIS is the correct name of the British external security agency, although it is often incorrectly called MI6, as for instance in the James Bond films.

1964

Spring
THE VOICE OF THE MOUNTAIN
A sorcerer's assistant named Alka used to be a librarian at Miskatonic University in Arkham, Massachusetts.

A Silver John novel by Manly Wade Wellman, Baen Books, 1984. Miskatonic University is a staple of H. P. Lovecraft's Cthulhu Mythos.

THE SCHOOL OF DARKNESS
John Thunstone and a number of allies (including Judge Pursuivant) battle Rowley Thorne at a symposium on American folklore.

Novel by Manly Wade Wellman, Doubleday, 1985.

Summer
THE SINCEREST FORM OF FLATTERY
The master criminal Diabolik is imprisoned in a private clinic by Doctor Garrick, who attempts to convince him he is Horace Ralph Valmont, an employee at the Depository Bank of Zurich. Diabolik's lover Eva Kant and nemesis Ginko are mentioned. Garrick eventually reveals himself as Fantômas. He mentions several of his imitators: Fantômases in Mexico and Argentina, Kriminal, Killing, and Satanik.

Short story by Jean-Marc Lofficier in Tales of the Shadowmen Volume 7: Femmes Fatales, *Jean-Marc and Randy Lofficier, eds., Black Coat Press, 2010; reprinted in French in* Les Compagnons de l'Ombre (Tome 7), *Jean-Marc and Randy Lofficier, eds., Rivière Blanche, 2011. Diabolik, Eva Kant, and Inspector Ginko are from the long-running Italian comic book series created by Angela and Luciana Giussani. The name Horace Ralph Valmont evokes both Horace Velmont, one of Arsène Lupin's aliases, and Ralph Valmont, the villain of Mario Bava's 1968 film* Danger: Diabolik. *The Depository Bank of Zurich is from Dan Brown's novel* The Da Vinci Code. *Fantômas is "the Lord of Terror" created by Marcel Allain and Pierre*

Souvestre. *The Mexican Fantômas is from a series of comic books published by Editorial Novaro in the 1960s. The Argentinean Fantômas is from Julio Cortázar's novel* Fantomas contra los vampiros multinacionales. *Kriminal and Satanik are the respective protagonists of two Italian comic book series by Max Bunker and Magnus. Killing was the subject of an Italian photo comic ("*fumetti*") in the '60s. All three of the aforementioned characters were influenced by Fantômas, as was Diabolik. It is worth noting one of Satanik's foes, the vampire Baron Wurdalak, also appeared in Bunker and Magnus' spy parody comic* Alan Ford.

Autumn
ALPHAVILLE, UNE ÉTRANGE AVENTURE DE LEMMY CAUTION

Lemmy Caution searches for his fellow secret agent from the Outlands, Henry Dickson. Both Dick Tracy and "*Guy l'Éclair*" have disappeared in Alphaville before Dickson.

*1965 feature film directed by Jean-Luc Godard. Lemmy Caution is an American detective appearing in mystery novels by Peter Cheyney. Here, he is played by Eddie Constantine, who also portrayed the character in several non-science fiction films. Henry Dickson's name is a nod to pulp character Harry Dickson, who appeared in German, Dutch, Belgian, and French pulp magazines. Jean-Marc Lofficier's "J. C. in Alphaville" (*Tales of the Shadowmen Volume 6: Grand Guignol, *Jean-Marc and Randy Lofficier, eds., Black Coat Press, 2010), which serves as a prequel to* Alphaville, *reveals Henry is Harry's son, and both Henry and Lemmy were sent to Alphaville by Mr. Klamm and Herr Erlanger from Franz Kafka's* The Castle. *"Guy l'Éclair" is the name by which Flash Gordon is known in France. Klamm and Erlanger must have also sent Gordon and Dick Tracy to Alphaville, although they presumably resurfaced soon after these events.*

Late Autumn
BAD MEDICINE

When Lenore Case suggests to Britt Reid Dr. Fang may be the one who is framing Reid's alter-ego, the Green Hornet, for spreading an apparent plague, Britt responds Fang is dead.

Short story by Vito Delsante and Win Scott Eckert in The Green Hornet Casefiles, *Joe Gentile and Win Scott Eckert, eds., Moonstone Books, 2011. Dr. Fang's apparent death occurred in Eckert's story "Fang and Sting" (*The Green Hornet Chronicles, *Joe Gentile and Win Scott Eckert, eds., Moonstone Books, 2010). She is the daughter of the original Dr. Fang, who appeared in his own radio series in the 1930s, and the granddaughter of Dr. Shan Ming Fu, better known as Dr. Fu Manchu.*

1965

Spring

THE SNOW SCULPTURES OF XANADU

Charles Foster Kane Jr. invites Orson Welles to his father's decaying estate, Xanadu. In 1949, there were reports an American black marketeer found dead in the Vienna sewers was Kane Sr.'s illegitimate son. Welles meets Dr. John Montague, whose published account of his investigation into the notoriously haunted Hill House in Connecticut Welles has read. In para-psychology texts, Xanadu has replaced Borley Rectory, the Loren Home, the Freiburg Tanz Akademie, the Overlook Hotel, and the Belasco Mansion as the world's most haunted house.

Short story by Kim Newman in Interzone #51, David Pringle and Lee Montgomerie, eds., September 1991; reprinted in Best New Horror 3, *Stephen Jones and Ramsey Campbell, eds., Carroll & Graf, 1992, and* Famous Monsters, *Pocket Books, 1995. Charles Foster Kane Sr. and Jr. are from Welles' film* Citizen Kane. *The American black marketeer is Harry Lime from Carol Reed's 1949 film* The Third Man. *Both Kane Sr. and Lime were played by Welles himself. Dr. John Montague and Hill House are from Shirley Jackson's novel* The Haunting of Hill House. *Borley Rectory is a real Victorian mansion that was dubbed the most haunted house in the world, although this was later exposed as a hoax. However, the CU version of the Rectory probably really is haunted. The Loren Home is from William Castle's film* House on Haunted Hill. *The Freiburg Tanz Akademie is from Dario Argento's film* Suspiria. *The Overlook Hotel is from Stephen King's book* The Shining. *The Belasco Mansion is from Richard Matheson's novel* Hell House.

ENDEAVOUR

Detective Constable Endeavour Morse is seconded from the Carshall Newtown police force to Oxford to investigate the murder of a 15-year-old girl. In the end, Morse decides to transfer to Oxford full-time. Morse's new landlady tells him the other two lodgers are named Goldberg and McCann.

Pilot movie for the television series Endeavour *broadcast July 1, 2012.* Endeavour *is a prequel to the television series* Inspector Morse, *which was based on a series of novels by Colin Dexter. Carshall New Town (or Newtown as it is spelled here) is the setting of Angus Wilson's novel* Late Call. *Goldberg and McCann are from Harold Pinter's play* The Birthday Party. *Several episodes of* Endeavour *contain references to people, places, and things from other works of fiction, including some that have already been confirmed as existing in the CU.* Inspector Morse *also received a spin-off,* Lewis.

FUGUE

Constable Morse attempts to apprehend a serial killer whose methods are based on the deaths of characters in various operas. Chief Superintendent Bright calls in Dr. Daniel Cronyn, an expert on serial murders, as a consultant on the case. Cronyn refers to killings in the States in the last ten years: the Starkweather case, the bodies in the swamp at Fairvale, and DeSalvo in Boston.

Episode of Endeavour *broadcast July 14, 2013. Charles Starkweather and Albert DeSalvo were real serial killers. The bodies in the swamp at Fairvale are a reference to Alfred Hitchcock's film* Psycho, *based on Robert Bloch's novel of the same name. Since* Psycho *takes place in the CU via a reference in Christopher Farnsworth's novel* Red, White and Blood, *so does* Endeavour.

Summer
ROCKET

Constable Morse looks into the death of a worker at a munitions factory owned by the Broom family, which occurred during a visit by Princess Margaret. The factory's union shop steward is Reg Tracepurcel. The youngest Broom, Johnny, boasts to Morse his car is the new Bellini.

Episode of Endeavour *broadcast July 21, 2013. The Bellini is a fictional brand of car driven by Raymond Delauney in the 1960 film* School for Scoundrels. *Some elements of this episode's plot reference the British film* I'm All Right Jack, *which featured a character named Bertram Tracepurcel. Perhaps Bertram and Reg are related.* I'm All Right Jack *starred Terry-Thomas, who also played Raymond Delauney in* School for Scoundrels. *The plot is also heavily influenced by the movie* The Lion in Winter, *but none of the references to that film count as crossovers.*

STANLEY AND HIS MONSTER

Young Stanley Dover secretly has a pet monster. Stanley finds a copy of *The Heterodyne Boys Big Book of Fun* in his attic, and shows it to his parents. Stanley's mother Sheila informs him about the Boys: "according to contemporary sources, they were real people, like Doc Savage, or the

Shadow." Occultist Ambrose Bierce (who may or may not be the writer of the same name) is hunted by Nightgaunts, and mentions Moxon. The demons Remiel and Duma appear, as does the Phantom Stranger, and John Constantine is mentioned.

Four-issue miniseries by Phil Foglio and Chuck Fiala, DC Comics, February– May 1993. The reference to the shadowy pulp vigilante and the bronze man as real people brings this series into the CU. Stanley and the Monster first appeared in comics in 1966, and therefore I have placed this series in 1965. The Hetero- dyne Boys also appear in Foglio's comic Girl Genius, *which is set in a Steampunk world ruled by mad scientists. Since the* Heterodyne Boys seen here are very different than those seen in Girl Genius, *it can be assumed they are those Boys' CU counterparts. The* Stanley and His Monster *versions of the Heterodyne Boys also appeared in a Munden's Bar backup story in the comic* Grimjack. *Matthew Ilseman writes, "The setting of* Grimjack, *the interdimensional city of Cynosure, is a nexus of different realities. You can travel from one universe to another by crossing the street. Since Wildwood Cemetery from* The Spirit *is part of Cynosure, then that would be where it intersects with the CU. There are many cameos from CU characters in the series. The pulp hero of the shadows, in particular, shows up a lot in the issues drawn by Tom Mandrake. There are references to Michael Moorcock's multiverse. Grimjack also appears in Roger Zelazny's Amber series. Cynosure was also the setting of crossovers between other comic characters published by First, including Nexus and Dreadstar." The Nightgaunts are from H. P. Lovecraft's Cthulhu Mythos tales. Moxon is from the historical Ambrose Bierce's story "Moxon's Master." Remiel and Duma are from Neil Gaiman's comic book* The Sandman. *That series has too many strong ties to DC Comics continuity to be included in the CU wholesale, so Remiel and Duma must have CU counterparts. It is shown in* The Sandman *that the Endless exist across the multiverse. The Phantom Stranger first appeared in a comic book that ran from 1952–1953, and was revived in 1969. John Constantine first appeared in the comics in 1984; either his CU counterpart was born and active much earlier, or this Constantine is a relative of the 1980s occult adventurer.*

Autumn
HOME

Endeavour Morse investigates the hit-and-run killing of an Oxford don. One of the suspects in the case is retired gangster Vic Kasper, who is now persona non grata with Sid and Gerald Fletcher. Later, one of Vic's employees tells the ex-criminal's son Vince (who is secretly in a partnership with the Fletchers on a construction deal) Thorpey is on the phone.

Episode of Endeavour *broadcast July 28, 2013. Gangsters Sid and Gerald Fletcher are Jack Carter's bosses in the 1971 film* Get Carter. *One of the gangsters in* Get Carter, *named Thorpe (also referred to as "Thorpey"), is an old acquaintance of Jack's. Thorpe must have worked for the Fletcher brothers for a time before switching his loyalties to rival crime boss Cyril Kinnear.*

1966

Winter
32 CADILLACS/DROWNED HOPES

Members of the Dan Kearny and Associates agency repossess a Cadillac stolen by John Dortmunder and his gang of thieves.

Joe Gores' DKA novel 32 Cadillacs *and Donald E. Westlake's novel* Drowned Hopes *both chronicle this encounter from different POVs. This crossover reaffirms the DKA agency and Dortmunder's coexistence in the CU.*

DANGER-A-GO-GO

Private investigator Honey West teams up with secret agents Miles Drake (alias Captain Action) and Derek Flint to battle Drake's old foe Dr. Anton Nova, who is being paid by the Red Chinese to use 8-track tapes to brainwash American soldiers for espionage purposes.

Honey West, Captain Action, and Flint *one-shot by Gary Phillips, Ben Hansen, and Kevin Caron, Moonstone Comics, 2012. Honey West and Derek Flint already have independent links to the CU; this crossover brings in Captain Action. Allegedly, Honey's father and Flint thwarted an assassination attempt on then-candidate John F. Kennedy seven years before. Since Hank West died in 1955, this cannot be accurate.*

Spring
FEED YOUR HEAD

John Steed visits Silver Sands, a seaside resort for retired spies, to investigate the death of a fellow agent, and discovers the Russians have infiltrated it. On her way to rescue Steed, Mrs. Peel drives past a sign that reads "St. Mary Mead–25 Miles; Walmington-on-Sea–50 Miles; Silver Sands–10 Miles."

Steed and Mrs. Peel: We're Needed #1–3 by Ian Edginton and Marco Cosentino, Boom! Studios, July–September 2014. Silver Sands appears to have been intended as a more benevolent (not to mention voluntary) retirement community for British spies than the Village (from the TV series The Prisoner*), and therefore it can be assumed the agents there are less high-risk to have at liberty than Number 6 and his neighbors. St. Mary Mead is the home of Agatha Christie's spinster detective Miss Marple, while Walmington-on-Sea is the setting of the British sitcom* Dad's Army*, bringing that show into the CU.*

THE WALLS OF NIGHT

Dr. Richard Kimble, a fugitive hunting the one-armed man who framed him for his own wife's death, passes Del Floria's Tailor Shop in Seattle.

Episode of the television series The Fugitive *broadcast April 4, 1967. As with its counterpart in New York, the Seattle Del Floria's Tailor Shop must disguise the entrance to the local headquarters of U.N.C.L.E. This connection brings* The Fugitive *into the CU.*

Late Spring
TROVE

Constable Morse investigates an apparent suicide, a missing girl, and the theft of valuable Anglo-Saxon treasures from Beaufort College, with the first two cases turning out to be intimately connected. Miss Great Britain, Diana Day, launches Burridge's Spring into Summer Fashion Collection. Morse passes a billboard advertising Grimsby Pilchards, and interviews Diana's manager Val Todd, whose wife tells him Mr. White from Play-Tone called. In Soho, Morse visits the third floor office of the apparent suicide, a private investigator, which is in a building that also hosts the Pacific All-Risk Insurance Co.; the Ex-Officers' Employment Bureau, Est. 1917; and R. Duck, Theatrical Agent, 4th Floor. Later, Morse questions Todd about his connection to the missing girl, who has turned up dead. Todd's wife interrupts again, to tell him Lane from SCDP is on the phone.

Episode of Endeavour *broadcast June 29, 2014. Burridge's Department Store is from the film* Trouble in Store. *Grimsby Pilchards appeared in "The*

Bowmans," an episode of the British sitcom Hancock, *bringing comedian Tony Hancock's fictional persona Anthony Aloysius Hancock into the CU. Mr. White is the talent agent for Play-Tone Records played by Tom Hanks in the 1996 film* That Thing You Do! *which is set in 1964. The Pacific All-Risk Insurance Co. is from Billy Wilder's film noir* Double Indemnity. *Evidently Pacific All-Risk has offices in both America and Britain. The Ex-Officers' Employment Bureau, Est. 1917, is one of the alleged businesses in the building in Fitzrovia that is actually the headquarters of the intelligence agency WOOC(P) in Len Deighton's Harry Palmer novels. Apparently WOOC(P) also kept an individual office in Soho. In the 1987 film* Withnail and I, *set in 1969, Withnail's Uncle Monty, an actor, says his first agent was "Raymond Duck . . . four flights up at Charing Cross . . ." At some point after the end of his representation of Uncle Monty, Duck must have taken up a new office in Soho. Obviously, he preferred his offices to be on the fourth floor. Lane is Lane Pryce, co-owner of the advertising agency Sterling Cooper Draper Pryce (SCDP), as seen on the television series* Mad Men, *which is set in the years 1960–1969. In "The Moms," an episode of the sitcom* 30 Rock, *Liz Lemon's mother reveals she once worked at Sterling Cooper, SCDP's forerunner, thus bringing that show into the CU as well.*

Summer
DEATH IN THE DESERT
Honey West is hired to investigate sabotage at the *Casa del Gato* club in Las Vegas, and winds up working with Thomas Hewitt Edward Cat, co-owner of the club, who is investigating the "accidents" at his business partner Pepe's request.

Honey West & T.H.E. Cat #1–2 *by Trina Robbins and Silvestre Szilagyi, Moonstone Comics, 2013. Private eye Honey West appears in a series of novels by G. G. Fickling, as well as a 1965–1966 television series. Thomas Hewitt Edward Cat, his business partner Pepe Cordoza, and the* Casa del Gato *club are from the 1966–1967 TV series* T.H.E. Cat. *Cat, a former acrobat and cat burglar turned freelance bodyguard, normally operates out of San Francisco, where he runs another* Casa del Gato.

Mid July
NOCTURNE
Constable Morse investigates a murder at a museum, and visits a girls' school in Slepe that was having a field trip to the museum when the man was killed. A signpost giving directions to Slepe, Midwich, and Crampton Hodnet is seen. One of the students is named Bunty Glossop, and the groundskeeper's son is Billy Karswell. Morse also questions an elderly couple

that visited the museum on that day, Nahum and Tabby Gardiner of Kingsport, Massachusetts. Morse walks past a billboard for Grimsby Pilchards, which has graffiti on it of the name "Titch Thomas." Morse and his superior, Detective Inspector Fred Thursday, visit the College of Arms in London, where the victim was formerly employed. They are told Sir Hilary is on holiday. The murder soon turns out to be connected to an unsolved homicide from a century ago, which was investigated by Detective Constable Cuff.

Episode of Endeavour *broadcast July 6, 2014. Midwich is from John Wyndham's novel* The Midwich Cuckoos. *Crampton Hodnet is from Barbara Pym's novel of the same name. Bunty Glossop is probably a member of the Glossop family seen in P. G. Wodehouse's Jeeves novels, while Billy Karswell and his father Wilf are likely relatives of Karswell from M. R. James' story "Casting the Runes." Despite the slight difference in the spelling of their surnames, Nahum Gardiner may be a relative of Nahum Gardner from H. P. Lovecraft's "The Colour Out of Space." Kingsport, Massachusetts is a recurring locale in Lovecraft's Cthulhu Mythos. Grimsby Pilchards are from "The Bowmans," an episode of the British sitcom* Hancock. *Titch Thomas is from Philip Larkin's poem "Sunny Prestatyn." In Ian Fleming's novel* On Her Majesty's Secret Service, *Sir Hilary Bray is a genealogist at the College of Arms whom James Bond briefly impersonates. Detective Constable Cuff may be related to Sergeant Cuff from Wilkie Collins'* The Moonstone.

Autumn

BAD MAN'S BLUNDER

The Green Hornet and Kato battle embittered heir Jess Logan and his Korean friend Shin-Cho Hahn, who have adopted similar masked personas and equipment to the heroes in order to sabotage a memorial to Jess' late father. Shin-Cho tells Jess about "Max, you know, my brother-in-law? The one who served in Korea? He was always trying to get a discharge by wearing—." Britt Reid tells Lenore Case about his and Kato's recent battle alongside caped comrades against a colonel.

Short story by John Allen Small in The Green Hornet: Still at Large, *Joe Gentile, Win Scott Eckert, and Matthew Baugh, eds., Moonstone Books, 2012. Shin-Cho Hahn's brother-in-law is Max Klinger from the television series* M*A*S*H. *Klinger frequently wore women's clothes*

in hopes of receiving a Section 8 discharge from the military. Shin-Cho's sister is Soon-Lee Hahn, whom Max married in the series finale of M*A*S*H. The Klingers went on to appear in the spin-off series AfterMASH. The caped heroes with whom the Hornet and Kato worked are Batman and Robin, as seen in "A Piece of the Action" and "Batman's Satisfaction," a two-part episode of the 1960s Batman television series. During that adventure, the heroic quartet battled the villainous Colonel Gumm and his henchmen. Per CU continuity, the Dynamic Duo the Hornet and Kato worked alongside were the second Batman and Robin team, consisting of Dick Grayson and Bruce Wayne Jr., respectively.

THE WORLD WILL END IN FIRE
In a flashback to 1958, Hayashi Kato arrives in Africa aboard the *Bantu Wind*, a ship captained by a tall and imposing African.

Short story by Richard Dean Starr in The Green Hornet: Still at Large, *Joe Gentile, Win Scott Eckert, and Howard Hopkins, eds., Moonstone Books, 2012. The* Bantu Wind *and its captain, Simon Katanga, are from the film* Raiders of the Lost Ark.

November
SWAY
Constable Morse traces a pair of stockings used as a murder weapon to Burridge's Department Store.

Episode of Endeavour *broadcast July 13, 2014. Burridge's Department Store is from the movie* Trouble in Store.

December
NEVERLAND
Constable Morse visits the law offices of "Vholes, Jaggers, Lightwood, Solicitors" in the course of a case.

Episode of Endeavour *broadcast July 20, 2014. The members of the law firm must all be descendants of lawyers from the works of Charles Dickens: Mr. Vholes (*Bleak House*); Mr. Jaggers (*Great Expectations*); and Mortimer Lightwood (*Our Mutual Friend*).*

1967

Winter
A THING OF BEAUTY
Sanford Biggs accepts a contract to kill the Green Hornet and Kato, and steals the Black Beauty for his museum, housed aboard his cargo carrier, the *Bigg Dipper*. The items in Biggs' museum include a glowing

green meteorite; the remains of a crashed experimental airplane that had been shot down over Switzerland in 1939; the mask, hat, and pistols of a famous lawman in the old west; and a bat-shaped metal throwing weapon. The Hornet recognizes the lawman's equipment. In the aftermath of the Hornet's battle with Biggs, everything in the museum is tagged, labeled, and accounted for, except for one empty case. The Hornet (aka Britt Reid) tells his ally, D.A. Frank Scanlon, the case contained an heirloom stolen from his family many years ago, which belonged to his grandfather.

Short story by Bobby Nash in The Green Hornet Casefiles, *Joe Gentile and Win Scott Eckert, eds., Moonstone Books, 2011. The glowing green meteorite is a piece of kryptonite, one of the few substances that can kill Superman. The experimental airplane belonged to the Canadian pulp hero Lance Star; its destruction at the hands of Star's foe Baron Otto Von Blood is depicted in Nash's upcoming novel* Lance Star: Sky Ranger–Cold Snap. *The lawman of the old west is John Reid, aka the Lone Ranger. The* Green Hornet *radio series revealed Britt Reid was the Lone Ranger's great-nephew. NOW Comics' Green Hornet comic established in turn the Green Hornet from the 1960s television series was Britt Reid II, the original Hornet's nephew. Therefore, Britt Reid II is actually John Reid's great-grandnephew, not his grandson. Perhaps John passed on his mask, hat and pistols to his nephew Dan Reid Jr., Britt Reid II's grandfather and the original Green Hornet's father, and they were stolen from him. The bat-shaped metal throwing weapon is one of Batman's batarangs.*

BATMAN '66 MEETS THE GREEN HORNET

Batman and Robin once again work reluctantly with the Green Hornet and Kato to defeat General (formerly Colonel) Gumm, who is now partnered with the Joker.

Six-issue miniseries by Kevin Smith, Ralph Garman, Ty Templeton, and Jon Bogdanove, co-published by DC Comics and Dynamite Entertainment, August 2014–January 2015. This story serves as a sequel to Batman, Robin, the Hornet, and Kato's first battle against Gumm in the Batman *TV series two-part episode "A Piece of the Action" and "Batman's Satisfaction."*

Spring
DON'T ASK

John Dortmunder once again crosses paths with guards working for the Continental Detective Agency. The country of Klopstokia is mentioned, as is the Frankenstein family.

Novel by Donald E. Westlake. The Continental Detective Agency is from Dashiell Hammett's stories about the Continental Op. The Frankenstein family needs no explanation at this point. Klopstokia is from the film Million Dollar Legs.

BATMAN '66 MEETS THE MAN FROM U.N.C.L.E.

Batman, Robin, and Batgirl join forces with Napoleon Solo and Illya Kuryakin when THRUSH has several of the Caped Crusader's foes broken out of Arkham in exchange for their joining the organization. Mr. Freeze and the Siren steal a ray gun called a "moleculator" from a facility in London. One of the scientists at the facility is named Dr. Quatermass.

Six-issue miniseries by Jeff Parker and David Hahn, 2016. Dr. Bernard Quatermass is from the British science fiction television serial The Quatermass Experiment *and its sequels.*

NOW THAT WOULD BE TELLING

The Green Hornet meets with former doctor Samuel Langhorne Chan, who says his niece married a man from Boston named Winchester some years ago.

Short story by Bradley H. Sinor in The Green Hornet Casefiles, *Joe Gentile and Win Scott Eckert, eds., Moonstone Books, 2011. Winchester must be either Boston native Charles Emerson Winchester III from the television series* M*A*S*H, *or else a relative of his.*

Summer. Broadway producer Max Bialystock and accountant Leo Bloom produce ex-Nazi Franz Liebkind's musical *Springtime for Hitler*, hoping they will make more money with this seemingly sure fire flop than a hit, as recounted in Mel Brooks' 1968 feature film *The Producers*. Leo Bloom is likely a relative and namesake of Leopold Bloom from James Joyce's *Ulysses*, and thus a member of the Wold Newton Family.

June
HONEY WEST & T.H.E. CAT: A GIRL AND HER CAT

P.I. Honey West is visited by Dr. Isabella Fang, who smokes Red Apple Cigarettes. Dr. Fang hires Honey to recover an alleged rubella vaccine she developed, as well as a pocket watch, which have both been stolen by Dr. Karl Stipier. Accepting the case, Honey asks another Los Angeles-based detective named Scott to handle her other cases in the meantime, and travels to San Francisco. Honey's old flame Johnny Doom, now a CIA agent, comes to her aid alongside two men she dubs Gray Suit and Blondie. Honey and Johnny book a room at the St. Francis hotel, although Gray Suit recommended the Hotel Carlton. Johnny reveals to Honey the "vaccine" is actually a biological weapon of a class the government has codenamed "Satan Bugs," and Gray Suit and Blondie are members of a worldwide organization that is in regular conflict with a criminal organization and "secret nation" that has tried to form an alliance with an Eastern secret society known as the Si-Fan. Johnny calls another government agent, Derek, for information about Stipier and Fang. Derek says there are fearful whispers about Fang at The Dragon of the Black Pool in Chinatown. Honey tells Johnny she thinks she recognized Derek's voice from a couple recent cases. Honey and Johnny are abducted by Dr. Fang's grandfather, Dr. Shan Ming Fu, the leader of the Si-Fan. One of Shan Ming Fu's minions is a sumo wrestler. At the elder doctor's recommendation, Honey enlists the help of Thomas Hewitt Edward Cat, former circus aerialist and cat burglar turned owner of the *Casa del Gato* nightclub and bodyguard, to retrieve the biological agent. Honey came to Cat's aid in Las Vegas a year ago. Besides Cat, Honey also meets his friend Pepe Cordoza and Captain McAllister of the SFPD. Stipier bought the mansion Silverstone West, which was built in the 1940s by an eccentric multi-millionaire named Tipton, from an employee of the latter's named Michael Anthony. A man with a bowler hat and an odd rifle attacks Honey and Cat as they flee Stipier's mansion with the Satan Bug and the watch. Honey's great-grandfather, James, was a major during the Civil War, and later was involved in government work. Cat did some bodyguard work for a scientist named Dr. Quest last year; Quest's wife was killed and his son was in danger. An agent for Intelligence One now guards the Quests. Honey was instructed in judo by a man named Macreedy, while Cat was taught how to tie knots by a young escape artist named Tony Blake. Honey arranges for a friend named Ben, who works at County General Hospital, to make a capsule that can pass for the real Satan Bug in order to deceive Shan Ming Fu. Blondie remarks Mr. Baldwin, the head of his organization's primary enemy's San Francisco offices, will be disappointed by Shan Ming Fu's continued refusal to form an alliance with them.

Novel by Honey West, edited by Win Scott Eckert and Matthew Baugh, Moonstone Books, 2014. Honey West is a private investigator featured in novels by "G. G. Fickling" (Gloria and Forest Fickling). In the novel Bombshell, *set in 1964, Honey and bounty hunter Johnny Doom are offered employment in the CIA. Honey evidently turned down the offer, as she had several adventures as a P.I. between* Bombshell *and* A Girl and Her Cat, *which were depicted in Fickling's novels, the 1965–1966 Honey West TV series, and several stories and comics published by Moonstone. In the novel* Honey on Her Tail, *which takes place three years after this book, Honey finally becomes a CIA agent. Dr. Isabella Fang is the daughter of the villainous Dr. Fang, who had his own radio series in the 1930s. Isabella encountered the Green Hornet and Kato in 1964 during the events of Eckert's story "Fang and Sting" (*The Green Hornet Chronicles, *Joe Gentile and Win Scott Eckert, eds., Moonstone Books, 2010). In 1974, Isabella and her grandfather would once again encounter the Hornet in Eckert's "Progress" (*The Green Hornet: Still at Large, *Joe Gentile, Win Scott Eckert, and Matthew Baugh, eds., Moonstone Books, 2012). Dr. Shan Ming Fu is better known by the nom de guerre Dr. Fu Manchu; Dennis E. Power revealed the Devil Doctor's birth name in his article "The Devil Doctor: The Early History of Fu Manchu" (found on the website* The Wold Newton Universe: A Secret History*). The Si-Fan is the secret society run by Fu Manchu in the novels by Sax Rohmer. Red Apple Cigarettes have appeared in a number of films, including* Pulp Fiction, From Dusk Till Dawn, *and* Romy and Michele's High School Reunion, *as well as several other stories by Eckert. The watch is a working (albeit inferior) replica of one of the distorters used by the warring Capellean and Eridanean races in Philip José Farmer's* The Other Log of Phileas Fogg. *Dr. Karl Stipier is meant to be Baron von Hessel from Farmer's Doc Savage novel* Escape from Loki; *von Hessel also appears under a variety of aliases in other stories by Eckert. The other detective in Los Angeles is Richard S. Prather's Shell Scott. Gray Suit and Blondie are Napoleon Solo and Illya Kuryakin from the television series* The Man from U.N.C.L.E. *U.N.C.L.E.'s greatest foe is the criminal organization THRUSH, which*

attempted to form an alliance with the Si-Fan in David McDaniel's novel The Rainbow Affair. The man in the bowler hat is an unnamed THRUSH agent seen in The Rainbow Affair. Ward Baldwin is in charge of THRUSH's San Francisco offices in McDaniel's novels. The Hotel Carlton is the home of Paladin in the television Western Have Gun–Will Travel. The term "Satan Bug" is derived from Alistair MacLean's novel The Satan Bug. Derek is spy Derek Flint from the movies Our Man Flint and In Like Flint. Honey encountered Flint during the events of the Moonstone comic Honey West, Captain Action, and Flint: Danger-a-Go-Go. The Dragon of the Black Pool restaurant in San Francisco's Chinatown is from the movie Big Trouble in Little China. The sumo wrestler, Tak, will later battle Fu Manchu's rebellious son Shang-Chi, as seen in the comic book Special Marvel Edition. Thomas Hewitt Edward Cat, Pepe Cordoza, and Captain McAllister are from the 1966–1967 television series T.H.E. Cat. Honey's 1966 encounter with Cat was recounted in the two-issue Moonstone comic Honey West and T.H.E. Cat: Death in the Desert. John Beresford Tipton and Michael Anthony are from the television series The Millionaire. Tipton's estate in that series was called Silverstone; Silverstone West is Eckert and Baugh's invention. Honey's great-grandfather is Secret Service agent James West from the classic television series The Wild Wild West. Dr. Benton Quest, his son Jonny, and Intelligence One are from the animated TV series Jonny Quest. Cat's replacement as the Quests' bodyguard is Roger "Race" Bannon. Honey's judo teacher is John J. Macreedy from the film Bad Day at Black Rock. Tony Blake is the title character of the television series The Magician. Ben Casey, a doctor at County General Hospital, is from the television series that bears his name. The Ben Casey episode "For This Relief, Much Thanks" began a two-part story that ended with "Solo for B-Flat Clarinet," the first episode of Breaking Point, bringing in that medical drama as well.

Summer
HIGH HEELS AND HEDONISM
Honey West goes undercover as a waitress at a Chicago nightclub in order to investigate the disappearance of an employee's daughter. Honey and reporter Carl Kolchak, who moonlights at the club, discover the girl has been abducted by the club's owner to use as a virgin sacrifice.

Honey West and Kolchak one-shot by Janet L. Hetherton and Ronn Sutton, Moonstone Comics, 2013. Kolchak is portrayed as a copyboy in this story, which seems unlikely given he would be forty-five at the time of these events. Kolchak began working for the Las Vegas Daily News in 1963 after repeatedly being fired from several newspapers in other cities, including Chicago. He must have briefly left the Daily News in 1967 to work for another Chicago paper before being fired again and returning to Vegas.

TRUE BELIEVERS

Appearing or mentioned are: Mr. Conway; the Sâr Dubnotal; Simon Ark; Shangri-La; Father Perrault; Annunciata Gianetti, aka Madame Arcati; Visualization of the Cosmic All; Rudolph Arcati; the Diogenes Club; Collinwood Manor; a Hellmouth; Prince Abduel Omar, aka Semi-Dual; modern white magicians in New York's Greenwich Village; John J. Malone; Joe the Angel; Kenneth J. Malone; Maggie Cassidy; Captain Danny von Flanagan; Dolly Dove; UBS news anchorman Howard Beale; Anthony Nelson; Maurice Minnifield; Jane Arden; detective agencies in Chicago, like Continental or Nathan Heller's A-1; the Sâr's meeting with Judex at Notre-Dame in the course of the gargoyle adventure; Lacey Raintree, aka Lakota Rainflower; "Spats" Colombo; Little Bonaparte; Little Caesar; Scarface; Robbo; the Big Boy; detective Tracy; Jeff Lebowski; Moris Klaw; Klaw's grandson Stephen, a member of the FBI's "Suicide Squad"; Dr. Spektor; the Arcane Order of the Black Sun; Aloysius Trelawney, aka Rowley Thorne; the Temple of the Dark Truth; Hugo Chantrelle; Northside 777; Ivo Shandor; Nephren-Ka; *The Ruthvenian*; the *Cultes des Goules*, attributed to the Comte d'Erlette; Sidney Redlitch and his books *Magic in Mexico* and *The Witches of New York*; Honeysuckle Cottage; Bludleigh Court; an Arisian; an electric pentacle; John Thunstone; Lieutenant Samms; Special Unit 2; and a Dirac communicator.

Short story by Stuart Shiffman in Tales of the Shadowmen Volume 10: Esprit de Corps, *Jean-Marc and Randy Lofficier, eds., Black Coat Press, 2013; reprinted in French in* Les Compagnons de l'Ombre (Tome 15), *Jean-Marc and Randy Lofficier, eds., Rivière Blanche, 2014; and in* Sâr Dubnotal 2: The Astral Trail, *Jean-Marc and Randy Lofficier, eds., Black Coat Press, 2015. Robert Conway, Shangri-La, and Father Perrault are from James Hilton's book* Lost Horizon. *The Sâr Dubnotal is an occult detective appearing in French pulp stories by an unknown author. Annunciata Gianetti and Rudolph are two of his assistants; here, Gianetti is conflated with the spiritual medium Madame Arcati from Noel Coward's play* Blithe Spirit. *Simon Ark appears in stories by Edward D. Hoch. The Visualization of the Cosmic All and the Arisians are from the Lensmen books by E. E. Smith. Lieutenant Samms is an ancestor of Virgil Samms from that series. The Diogenes Club is from Arthur Conan Doyle's Sherlock Holmes stories. Collinwood Manor is from the television series* Dark Shadows. *The Hellmouth is a reference to the show* Buffy the Vampire Slayer. *Semi-Dual was featured in tales by J. U. Giesy. The modern white magician in Greenwich Village is Marvel Comics' hero Doctor Strange. John J. Malone is a lawyer featured in books by Craig Rice. Joe the Angel, Maggie Cassidy, Captain Danny von Flanagan, and Dolly*

Dove are also from the John J. Malone books. Kenneth J. Malone is the protagonist of Randall Garrett and Laurence Janifer's novels Brain Twister, The Impossibles, *and* Supermind. *UBS and Howard Beale are from Sidney Lumet's film* Network. *Anthony Nelson is from the TV series* I Dream of Jeannie. *Maurice Minnifield is from the show* Northern Exposure. *Jane Arden is the title character of a comic strip created by Monte Barrett and Frank Ellis. The Continental Detective Agency is from Dashiell Hammett's Continental Op stories. Nathan "Nate" Heller's A-1 Detective Agency is from a series of books by Max Allan Collins. Judex is*

*from Louis Feuillade's film serial of the same name; the Sâr encountered Judex in Matthew Baugh's story "The Gargoyles of Notre-Dame" (*The Shadow of Judex, *Jean-Marc and Randy Lofficier, eds., Black Coat Press, 2013). Lakota Rainflower and Dr. Adam Spektor are from Donald F. Glut's comic book* The Occult Files of Doctor Spektor. *The Ruthvenian appears in many of Glut's interconnected comics, books, and films. "Spats" Colombo and Little Bonaparte are from the movie* Some Like It Hot. *Little Caesar is from the gangster movie of the same name. Scarface is the title character of a 1932 film by Howard Hawks. Robbo is from the movie* Robin and the 7 Hoods. *The Big Boy and Tracy are from Chester Gould's classic comic strip* Dick Tracy. *Jeff "The Dude" Lebowski is from the movie* The Big Lebowski. *Moris Klaw is from Sax Rohmer's story collection* The Dreaming Detective. *The Suicide Squad, whose members included Stephen Klaw, appeared in stories by Emile C. Tepperman in the pulp magazine* Ace G-Man Stories. *The Arcane Order of the Black Sun is from R. L. LaFevers' Theodosia Throckmorton books. The leader of the Order in LaFevers' books is Aloysius Trawley, whom Shiffman here identifies with Rowley Thorne, the archenemy of Manly Wade Wellman's occult detective John Thunstone. Jasper Thorne, an ancestor of Rowley's, appears in Matthew Baugh's story "Mysterious Dan's Legacy." Presumably, Trawley/Trelawney took the name Thorne in honor of his forebear. The Temple of the Dark Truth is from Anthony Boucher's Fergus O'Breen story "The Compleat Werewolf," while Hugo Chantrelle is from Boucher's book* Rocket to the Morgue. *Northside*

777 is a reference to the film Call Northside 777. *Ivo Shandor is from the movie* Ghostbusters. *Nephren-Ka is from H. P. Lovecraft's "The Haunter of the Dark." The* Cultes des Goules *is from Robert Bloch's story "The Suicide in the Study"; its author, the Comte d'Erlette, was named after Bloch's fellow Lovecraft disciple August Derleth. Sidney Redlitch and his books are from John Van Druten's play* Bell, Book and Candle. *Honeysuckle Cottage is from P. G. Wodehouse's Mr. Mulliner story of the same name, while Bludleigh Court appears in another Mr. Mulliner tale, "The Unpleasantness at Bludleigh Court." The electric pentacle is a reference to William Hope Hodgson's* Carnacki the Ghost-Finder. *Special Unit 2 is from the television series of the same name. The Dirac communicator is from James Blish's story "Beep," later expanded into the novel* The Quincunx of Time. *The* Quincunx of Time *and many of Blish's other works are set in a common future, one of many potential ones for the CU.*

Late July
THE GRAY LINE BETWEEN

Dr. Martin Luther King tells Britt Reid by choosing the path of nonviolence, like Jesus, Moses, Mohammed, Gandhi, Buddha, and his own great uncle, Britt will be one instrument in the effectuation of change in America.

Short story by F. J. DeSanto, Michael Uslan, and Joe Gentile in The Green Hornet Casefiles, *Joe Gentile and Win Scott Eckert, eds., Moonstone Books, 2011. Britt Reid's great-uncle is John Reid, the Lone Ranger. This story takes place during the Detroit race riots, which began on July 23, 1967.*

Edited by Joe Gentile and
Win Scott Eckert

Autumn
UP IN SMOKE

The Green Hornet shares his father and great-great-uncle's belief in bringing down evil wherever he finds it.

Short story by Deborah Chester in The Green Hornet Casefiles, *Joe Gentile and Win Scott Eckert, eds., Moonstone Books, 2011. The Hornet's great-great-uncle is the Lone Ranger.*

December 25, 1967–February 24, 1989
THE AUTOBIOGRAPHY OF FBI SPECIAL AGENT DALE COOPER:
MY LIFE, MY TAPES

Thirteen-year-old Dale Cooper receives a tape recorder on Christmas Day, 1967, and continues to record the details of his life throughout the years. On March 30, 1968 at 7 P.M., Dale writes, "Have just finished reading about Sherlock Holmes in *The Hound of the Baskervilles.* I believe Mr. Holmes is the smartest detective who has ever lived, and would very much like to live a life like he did. It is the Friends School belief that the best thing one can do in life is to do good rather than do well. I believe that in Mr. Holmes I see a way to accomplish this." On February 10, 1969 at 3 P.M., Dale, having discovered a corpse, says "I am trying to think the way Holmes would think but I mostly want to throw up." On August 17, 1975 at 9 P.M., Dale, having just learned that his girlfriend deliberately started a forest fire, recalls, "I believe it was Holmes who said that truth is often arrived at by two roads pointing in very different directions." On November 20, 1988 at 11 P.M., Cooper, now a Special Agent with the FBI providing records for his secretary, Diane, comments on his boredom with the mundane cases the Bureau has been assigning him: "Holmes used cocaine, an alternative I find unacceptable. What I need, what any detective needs, is a good case. Something to test oneself to the absolute limit. To walk to the edge of the fire and risk it all. The razor's edge. Are there any great cases anymore, Diane? Is there a Lindbergh kidnapping, a Brinks robbery, a John Dillinger, a Professor Moriarty?" On February 24 of the following year, he is sent to the small town of Twin Peaks, WA to investigate the murder of a teenage girl found wrapped in plastic.

Series of recordings by Dale Cooper, transcribed by Scott Frost, Pocket Books, 1991. Coop's reference to Holmes as "the smartest detective who has ever lived" establishes he and Holmes coexist, as does his reference to Moriarty alongside two real crimes and a real criminal, thus reinforcing the place of Agent Cooper and the television series Twin Peaks *in the CU.*

1968

Spring
INCIDENT AT HOI BINH

Mack Bolan clears his fellow soldier Niles Barrabas of charges of massacring innocent civilians in Vietnam.

Short story included in The Executioner #63: *The New War Book, 1984. Niles Barrabas is from Jack Hild's* Soldiers of Barrabas *series, which takes place in the 1980s. This crossover brings Barrabas into the CU.*

Summer
STING OF THE YELLOWJACKET

The Green Hornet once again battles his former fiancée Laura Cavendish, aka the Yellowjacket.

Short story by Howard Hopkins in The Green Hornet Casefiles, *Joe Gentile and Win Scott Eckert, eds., Moonstone Books, 2011. Laura Cavendish is a descendant of the Lone Ranger's foe Butch Cavendish; she first appeared in Hopkins' story "Flight of the Yellowjacket" (*The Green Hornet Chronicles, *Joe Gentile and Win Scott Eckert, eds., Moonstone Books, 2010). The original Green Hornet radio series established Britt Reid was the Lone Ranger's great-nephew.*

September
HEARTS OF THE RISING SUN

Captain Action battles Dr. Evil alongside the aged (but still skilled) Black Bat in Japan.

Novel by Jim Beard, Airship 27 Productions, 2014. This crossover further confirms Captain Action's inclusion in the CU. The Captain's archenemy Dr. Evil is unrelated to Austin Powers' foe of the same name.

Late Autumn
THE BLACK WIDOW

Britt Reid suggests to his reporter Mike Axford the Green Hornet (actually Reid's alter ego) may have saved Axford and a businessman from the clutches of the Black Widow because he was simply being a good citizen, protecting the rights of the people of Detroit. Axford retorts they're talking about the Green Hornet, not Batman.

Short story by John Everson in The Green Hornet Casefiles, *Joe Gentile and Win Scott Eckert, eds., Moonstone Books, 2011. The Green Hornet and Kato of the 1960s (the nephew and son respectively of the adventurers of those names active in the 1930s-1950s) teamed up with the second Batman and Robin team (Dick Grayson and Bruce Wayne Jr.) in the Batman television series two-parter "A Piece of the Action" and "Batman's Satisfaction."*

December
REFLECTIONS IN GREEN

Captain Action and the Green Hornet and Kato are manipulated into battling each other by the insidious Dr. Eville while attempting to rescue a Chinese scientist whom Eville has abducted.

Short story by Matthew Baugh in Captain Action Winter Special, *Moonstone Comics, 2011. Dr. Eville (also spelled Evil) is not to be confused with Dr. Evil, archenemy of British agent Austin Powers.*

QUEEN OF HORROR

A Democracy Pictures employee named Penworthy is instructed by his boss, Nat Katzman, to find a new angle for their horror movies. Magazine editor "Gorry Hackerman" suggests to Penworthy he find a female monster movie star. Penworthy chooses the beautiful Mildred Strudd, whom Katzman renames Adriana. Adriana is spectacularly successful, though she expresses distaste for having to play a werewolf. Katzman tells Adriana he loves her, but she turns into a very real werewolf and attacks him.

Story by Don Glut and Dick Piscopo in Vampirella #2, *Warren Publishing, November 1969; reprinted in* Vampirella Archives, Volume One, *Dynamite Entertainment, 2011. Democracy Pictures is a recurring movie studio in Glut's interconnected fiction. "Gorry Hackerman" is a thinly-veiled version of the legendary Forrest J. "Forry" Ackerman, whose Crossover Universe counterpart also appears in Philip José Farmer's* Blown *and David McDaniel's* The Vampire Affair. *The month is conjecture based on a mention of the movie* Barbarella, *which was first released on October 10, 1968.*

1969

February 14
AULD ACQUAINTANCE

The Green Hornet and Kato come to the aid of the Hornet's agent Tim Nektosha, whose loved ones have been targeted by the Yellowjacket, aka the Hornet's former fiancée Laura Cavendish. Kato reveals to Tim the Hornet's ancestor was a masked gunfighter who was assisted by a Potawatomi, whose own closest living relative in the present day is Tim himself. Laura's great-grandfather was a foe of the gunfighter and Potawatomi. Laura's goons kidnap Tim's potential girlfriend, Hanomah Return of the Tsichah tribe.

Short story by Matthew Baugh in The Green Hornet Casefiles, *Joe Gentile and Win Scott Eckert, eds., Moonstone Books, 2011. The masked* gunfighter who is the Green Hornet's ancestor is the Lone Ranger, as established in the Green Hornet radio series. The Ranger's Potawatomi companion is Tonto, while Laura's great-grandfather is their foe Butch Cavendish. The Hornet's previous battles with the Yellowjacket were chronicled by Howard Hopkins in his stories "Flight of the Yellowjacket" (The Green Hornet Chronicles, Joe Gentile and Win Scott Eckert, eds., Moonstone Books, 2010) and "Sting of the Yellowjacket" (The Green Hornet Casefiles). Hanomah Return is a relative of Tsichah policeman David Return from Manly Wade Wellman's stories "A Star for a Warrior" and "A Knife Between Brothers." Both she and Tim first appeared in Baugh's story "The Inside Man" (The Green Hornet Chronicles). The Tsichah are a fictional Native American tribe also mentioned in Wellman's John Thunstone story "The Golden Goblins."

May
REVENGE OF THE YELLOWJACKET
The Green Hornet has his final battle with the Yellowjacket, aka his former fiancée Laura Cavendish, daughter of John Cavendish.

Short story by Howard Hopkins in The Green Hornet: Still at Large, *Joe Gentile, Win Scott Eckert, and Matthew Baugh, eds., Moonstone Books, 2012. Laura and John Cavendish are descended from the Lone Ranger's foe Butch Cavendish. The Green Hornet radio series established the Hornet was the Lone Ranger's great-nephew, while NOW Comics' take on the character established the Green Hornet from the 1960s TV series was Britt Reid II, the nephew of the original Hornet. Therefore, Britt Reid II is the great-grandnephew of the Lone Ranger.*

Summer
THE GAUNTLET
There are rumors gangster Caesar Castillo came into power after his boss Miles Prince, the self-styled Prince of Hollywood, was arrested by Hollywood detectives in the late '30s.

Short story by Bobby Nash in The Green Hornet: Still at Large, *Joe Gentile, Win Scott Eckert, and Matthew Baugh, eds., Moonstone Books, 2012. Miles Prince's downfall was recounted by Nash in the story "Target: Domino Lady." This crossover confirms the Domino Lady and the Green Hornet coexist within the CU.*

THE ROADS NOT TAKEN
A cop turned soldier in Vietnam named Remo is greeted by a sentry

named Michael Long, also a cop in civilian life. Remo's platoon mates have nicknamed him the Destroyer, just as others in the group have been dubbed the Exterminator, Hannibal, and Sergeant Mercy. Remo considers becoming a soldier of fortune when his tour of duty ends, "like that Rainey fellow people [keep] talking about." Remo can see himself like James Bond, traveling the world to protect America. A visiting soldier tells a group of listeners about how he cleared a fellow soldier of the allegation of a massacre at Hoi Binh. This soldier, named Bolan, also tells them a story he heard from a guy named Spenser in Korea.

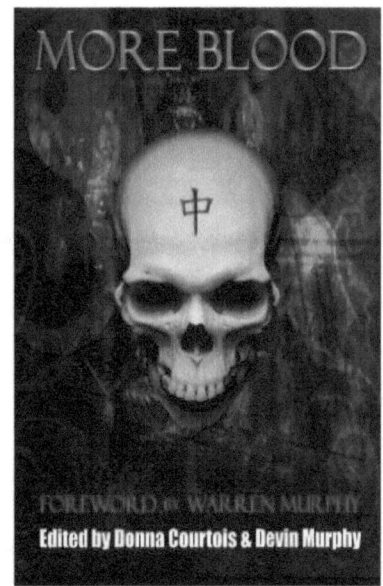

Short story by Brad Mengel in More Blood: A Sinanju Anthology, *Donna Courtois and Devin Murphy, eds., Destroyer Books, 2014. Remo Williams is the hero of the Destroyer novels, created by Warren Murphy and Richard Sapir. Michael Long (later known as Michael Knight) is from the TV series* Knight Rider. *The Exterminator is John Eastland from the movies* The Exterminator *and* Exterminator 2. *Hannibal is John "Hannibal" Smith from the TV show* The A-Team. *Sergeant Mercy was the wartime nickname of Mack Bolan, aka the Executioner, the vigilante created by Don Pendleton. Bolan cleared the name of Niles Barrabas in "Incident at Hoi Binh," included in* Executioner #63: *The New War Book. Barrabas is the protagonist of another series,* The Soldiers of Barrabas *by Jack Hild. Jim Rainey is the hero of Peter McCurtin's* Soldier of Fortune *series. James Bond needs no explanation. Spenser is Robert B. Parker's future private investigator.*

1970

January–June
THE DOGS OF WAR
   Kurt Semmler once served in the OAS, a French terrorist group, under Colonel Marc Rodin.
   Novel by Frederick Forsyth. Colonel Rodin is from Forsyth's novel The Day of the Jackal, *which takes place in the CU via a reference to M's club, Blades, from Ian Fleming's James Bond novels.*

Spring
SAINT AND SINNERS

A mysterious woman hires private eye Teddy Verano (accompanied by the succubus Mephista, who possesses the body of actress Edwige Hossegor) to rescue her nephew Simon, whom Satanist Steven Marcato and his wife wish to use to resurrect a master of dark magic named Morcata, Steven's uncle, who died many years ago in battle with the Duc de Richleau. Verano's father helped the Duc and his friends deal with the remainder of Morcata's cult. Verano says the Phantom is back and controls the Paris Opera House again.

Short story by Frank Schildiner in Tales of the Shadowmen Volume 11: Force Majeure, *Jean-Marc and Randy Lofficier, eds., Black Coat Press, 2014. Teddy Verano, Mephista, and Edwige Hossegor are from French horror novels by Maurice Limat. The original Teddy Verano series by Limat, which began in 1936, portrayed Teddy as a somewhat mundane private eye, though some of the threats he faced were exotic. In 1963, Limat revived Verano as a full-fledged occult detective who frequently battled Mephista. This story reveals the Teddy Verano of the '60s onward is the son of the original Teddy Verano of the 1930s-1950s. Simon Sinestrari is from the movie* Simon, King of the Witches. *Steven Marcato and his wife Minnie are from Ira Levin's novel* Rosemary's Baby. *Morcata (originally spelled Mocata) died in battle with the Duc de Richleau in Dennis Wheatley's novel* The Devil Rides Out. *The Phantom is from Gaston Leroux's novel* The Phantom of the Opera.

QUEST FOR MYSTERY!

Scooby-Doo, Shaggy, Fred, Velma, and Daphne team up with Jonny Quest, Hadji, and Race Bannon to rescue Dr. Quest from the clutches of Dr. Zin.

Scooby-Doo Team-Up #10 by Sholly Fisch and Dario Brizuela, DC Comics, July 2015.

Summer
THE RADICAL/THE PEOPLE VS. SAYDO

Radical activist Jim Saydo is arrested by patrolmen Pete Malloy and Jim Reed for a series of bombings, and subsequently prosecuted by Deputy District Attorney Paul Ryan.

Two-part story beginning on the television series Adam-12 *on October 6, 1971, and ending on* The D.A. *on October 8. Since Officers Malloy and Reed from* Adam-12 *are in the CU, so is Paul Ryan, who was the protagonist of two TV movies and the television series* The D.A.

August 4, 1970–September 9, 1986
OUTLAWS

A meeting about bank robberies being committed by a group of young radicals is held in the offices of Ward Keane, District Attorney of Plymouth County. The criminals are later put on trial for murder, with Special Assistant Attorney General Terry Gleason acting as prosecutor. The landlord of the Broad Street Grille is quoted in the *Boston Commoner.*

Novel by George V. Higgins, Henry Holt and Company, 1987. Keane and Gleason were first mentioned in Higgins' novel Impostors, *which takes place in the CU, thus bringing in this novel as well. The* Boston Commoner *newspaper appears in a number of Higgins' books, including the aforementioned* Impostors; *the Jerry Kennedy series;* Wonderful Years, Wonderful Years; Victories, *a sequel to the novel* Trust; *and* Bomber's Law.

October
THE MAN INSIDE

Tim Nektosha, a member of the Potawatomi tribe and agent of the Green Hornet, is arrested while serving as the Hornet's driver in Kato's absence. Tim's fiancée, Hanomah Return of the Tsichah, seeks help from the Hornet's alter ego, Britt Reid.

Short story by Matthew Baugh in The Green Hornet: Still at Large, *Joe Gentile, Win Scott Eckert, and Matthew Baugh, eds., Moonstone Books, 2012. Tim Nektosha has appeared in two previous stories by Baugh, "The Man Inside" (*The Green Hornet Chronicles, *Joe Gentile and Win Scott Eckert, eds., Moonstone Books, 2010) and "Auld Acquaintance" (*The Green Hornet Casefiles, *Joe Gentile and Win Scott Eckert, eds., Moonstone Books, 2011); he is a relative of the Lone Ranger's Potawatomi companion Tonto. The Green Hornet radio series established Britt Reid was the great-nephew of the Lone Ranger (aka John Reid), while NOW Comics' take on the character revealed the 1960s Hornet was the original hero's nephew, Britt Reid II, making the younger Britt John Reid's great-grandnephew. Hanomah Return is related to Tsichah policeman David Return from Manly Wade Wellman's tales "A Star for a Warrior" and "A Knife Between Brothers." The Tsichah are a fictional Native American tribe whose hereditary chieftain, Long Spear, appears in Wellman's John Thunstone story "The Golden Goblins."*

1971

Summer
DEAD SKIP/PLUNDER SQUAD

P.I. Dan Kearny, investigating the attempted murder of one of his agents, visits the house where professional thief Parker is planning a heist.

Joe Gores' DKA novel Dead Skip *and "Richard Stark's" (pseudonym for Donald E. Westlake) Parker novel* Plunder Squad *each describe Kearny and Parker's meeting from the respective authors' own characters' points of view.*

DON'T POINT THAT THING AT ME

Art dealer Charlie Mortdecai visits specialized automobile body maker Mr. Spinoza, who is willing to consider restoring or recreating various brands of car, including Hirondelles.

Novel by Kyril Bonfiglioli, 1972. Leslie Charteris' hero Simon Templar, the Saint, drove a fictional brand of car called the Hirondelle (also spelled Hirondel). This reference confirms Charlie Mortdecai in the CU.

1972

Winter
ZENITH'S END

Zenith the Albino has maintained his youth throughout the decades due to an elixir given to him by "Manchu."

Short story by Zenith, edited by Stuart Douglas in Zenith Lives!: Tales of M. Zenith, the Albino, *Stuart Douglas, ed., Obverse Books, 2012. Zenith was given the elixir vitae by Dr. Fu Manchu.*

March
KOLCHAK THE NIGHT STALKER: THE LOST WORLD

Carl Kolchak has heard about two professors from Duke University who seem to run into the bizarre almost as much as he does. Falling asleep, Kolchak enters the dreamplane.

Novel by C. J. Henderson. The two professors from Duke University are Drs. Hugh Blakely and William Boles, who appear in a series of stories by Henderson and Bruce

Gehweiler that are collected in Where Angels Fear. *The dreamplane is from Henderson's novels featuring Teddy London, a private eye who regularly encounters the supernatural. This novel takes place two years after Kolchak's first encounter with a vampire in* The Night Stalker, *i.e., 1972. Once again, contemporary references such as the Internet and Secretary of State Hillary Clinton are ignored in order to maintain Kolchak's adventures in their original time frame.*

Spring

ASSIGNMENT: THE AHAB APPARITION

A group of young ghost hunters and their talking dog Goober come to the aid of the Partridge kids, who are vacationing in Peaceful Cove, where a mansion is haunted by the ghosts of Captain Ahab and Moby Dick.

First episode of the animated series Goober and the Ghost Chasers, *broadcast September 8, 1973. The Ghost Chasers are a group of youths who investigate supernatural occurrences a la Scooby-Doo and Mystery, Inc. However, most of the ghosts Goober and company face are real, and they work for a magazine on the supernatural, rather than being private investigators. Perhaps Goober is a relative of Scooby's, explaining their common talent for speech, though Scooby doesn't share Goober's ability to turn invisible when scared. Perhaps someone fed Goober a variant on John Hawley Griffin's serum. Moby Dick and Captain Ahab are already firmly in the CU; therefore, this crossover brings in Goober and the gang. The Partridge kids are from* The Partridge Family, *thus bringing that show and its spin-off* Getting Together *into the CU. The Partridges appeared in eight of the sixteen episodes of* Goober and the Ghost Chasers.

BRUSH UP YOUR SHAKESPEARE

Goober and pals come to the Partridge kids' aid when their concert is canceled due to Macbeth's ghost attacking the Globe Theatre.

Second episode of Goober and the Ghost Chasers, *broadcast September 15, 1973. This crossover brings* William Shakespeare's play Macbeth *into the CU.*

FROM HERE TO INFINITY!

Joshua Kale, leader of the Cult of Zhered-Na and potential ally of the Man-Thing, uses magic to show the members of the Cult the history of their namesake, an ancient Atlantean sorceress. Zhered-Na worshipped the god Valka, and was given a vision of the future by her deity.

Adventures into Fear #15 by Steve Gerber, Val Meyerik, and Frank McLaughlin, Marvel Comics, August 1973. Valka is from Robert E. Howard's Kull stories. The Man-Thing is already in the CU through his encounter with Shang-Chi; this crossover reinforces his inclusion.

Summer
THE SINGING GHOST
Frankenstein's Monster III tricks the Partridge kids into coming to his mansion so he may steal Danny Partridge's voice. Goober and the Ghost Chasers prevent this from happening.

Fourth episode of Goober and the Ghost Chasers, *broadcast September 29, 1973. It is as yet unknown which of the many monsters created by members of the Frankenstein family is "Frankenstein's Monster III."*

IS SHERLOCK HOLME?
Goober and pals travel to England to investigate a series of thefts at a haunted mansion, aided by Detective Sergeant Roger Sherlock, a relative of Sherlock Holmes.

Thirteenth episode of Goober and the Ghost Chasers, *broadcast December 1, 1973. Since Sherlock Holmes is not known to have any ancestors with the surname Sherlock, it is possible Roger's full name is Roger Sherlock Holmes, and he shortened it for professional reasons.*

APACHE BLOOD: A GOOD DAY TO DIE
Dalton Hollick is compared to Mark Hardin, the Penetrator.

Story by Brad Mengel (writing as Edward T. Johnson) in Blood & Tacos: The Beginning, *Creative Guy, 2013. See the 1981 entry for* Quaking Terror *for the Penetrator's connection to the Crossover Universe.*

1973

Winter
BUTCHER'S MOON
The American Alliance of Machinists and Skilled Trades is mentioned.

A Parker novel by "Richard Stark" (Donald E. Westlake). The American Alliance of Machinists and Skilled Trades is from Westlake's novel Killy. *Since the Parker books take place in the CU, so does* Killy.

SUMMIT CHASE
Remo Williams asks a gangster, "How's Mack Bolan doing?" A female British agent's handler is James, a field agent grounded due to catching an S.T.D., who is said to have a series of books based on him.

The Destroyer *#8 by Warren Murphy and Richard Sapir. Mack Bolan, aka the Executioner, is Don Pendleton's vigilante character. James is, of course, James Bond, whose womanizing has finally caught up with him. Brad Mengel notes Bond's grounding with an S.T.D. is also reflected in the framing sequence of John Pearson's* James Bond: The Authorized Biography of 007.

Spring
SHIP OF FIENDS!

Spider-Man attempts to intercept a cruise ship whose passengers include a doctor who has developed a new vaccine which could cure his Aunt May's illness. Unfortunately, Dracula seeks to destroy the vaccine for reasons of his own, and he and Spidey briefly cross paths. The Human Torch has a cameo.

Giant-Size Spider-Man #1 by Len Wein, Ross Andru, and Don Heck, Marvel Comics, July 1974. This version of Dracula is the same one seen in Marvel's Tomb of Dracula *series, which is largely compatible with Crossover Universe continuity. Since a version of Spider-Man is already in the CU through other crossovers, it is likely this story occurred in the CU as well. The Human Torch and his teammates in the Fantastic Four have also already been included in the CU.*

THE YEAR OF THE DRAGON

"Kung fu monk-master" and CIA agent Victor Mace investigates the theft of a Ming Dynasty statue worth about five million dollars. A Chinese rep asks for the assistance of the Death Merchant or the Murder Master, but the CIA tells him they're both busy.

Kung Fu #4 by "Lee Chang" (Joseph Rosenberger), Manor Books, 1974. Rosenberger's hero Richard Camellion, aka the Death Merchant, is already in the CU. Therefore, this crossover brings in both Victor Mace and the Murder Master, who appeared in a three-volume series of novels by Rosenberger for Manor around the same time as the Mace books.

April–June
SOMETHING NASTY IN THE WOODSHED

Charlie Mortdecai visits his old tutor, John Dryden, at Scone College, and encounters Bronwen Fellworthy for the first time. A Miss H. Glossop appears.

Novel by Kyril Bonfiglioli, 1976. Scone College is from Evelyn Waugh's Decline and Fall. *Miss Glossop may be a relative of Honoria Glossop from P. G. Wodehouse's Jeeves stories.*

June
THE LAUREL AND HARDY MURDERS
Would-be detective Hilary Quayle and her private eye boyfriend Gene look into the murder of a comedian at a banquet held by the Sons of the Desert, a nationwide Laurel and Hardy fan club of which Gene is a member. One of the club members suggests calling in Nero Wolfe.

1977 novel by Marvin Kaye. The reference to Wolfe, a Wold Newton family member, brings Hilary and Gene, who appeared in a total of five novels by Kaye, into the CU. The dates given in the book fit the year 1973.

Summer 1973–April 1974
JOYLAND
The GS&WM Railroad and the tabloid *Inside View* are mentioned.

Novel by Stephen King. The GS&WM and Inside View *appear often in King's interconnected fiction.*

1974

Winter
COLLINWOOD POSSESSED
During his previous conflict with Barnabas Collins, Viking wizard Morath battled the embodiment of his good side, resulting in his being thrown into a bizarre limbo, where he encounters a caterpillar-like creature playing chess with a man with white hair. The caterpillar recommends he use the Eye of Agamotto, a doorway to the dimensions which is floating overhead, to escape. Morath says somewhere on Earth is the Orb of Agamotto, the key to those dimensions. Traveling through the eye, he emerges at the Greenwich Village dwelling of a practitioner of mystic arts, where a woman cries out, "Stephen!"

Dark Shadows #34 by John Warner and Joe Certa, Gold Key, November 1975. "Stephen" is Doctor Stephen Strange, the Sorcerer Supreme. Strange's Sanctum Sanctorum is in Greenwich Village. The Eye and Orb of Agamotto are both from the Doctor Strange comics. The caterpillar is Agamotto himself, who took the form of a caterpillar in the opening storyline of Strange's second ongoing series. Though drawn differently than in Marvel Comics' accounts, the white-haired man is meant to be the villainous Silver Dagger from the same storyline, while the woman is Strange's paramour Clea. It is worth noting a flashback in that story featured the future Silver Dagger reading the Vatican library's collection of books about the black arts, including the Necronomicon. The connection to Dark Shadows reinforces Doctor Strange's inclusion in the CU.

Spring
THE GREAT MORTDECAI MUSTACHE MYSTERY
Charlie Mortdecai returns to Scone College to investigate the murder of Bronwen Fellworthy.

Novel by Kyril Bonfiglioli and Craig Brown, 1999. Scone College is from Evelyn Waugh's Decline and Fall.

THUNDERHEAD
Cyclone Daisy uncovers the wreck of the *Pegasus*, a slave ship that crashed off the coast of Western Australia after a plague broke out. Jim Hawk, a pilot in the Outback who works with both the Flying Doctor Service and the Northern Territory Police, combats a new outbreak of the plague and an attempt to steal the ship's captain's gold. The ship is found by two young children, who say, "We'll dig up the pirate's treasure," and "And the bones of Captain Blood."

Air Hawk and the Flying Doctors comic strip storyline by John Dixon, September 1975. The reference to Rafael Sabatini's Captain Blood brings Jim Hawk into the CU. Brad Mengel writes, "Trying to date the story is a little tricky. There was a Cyclone Daisy in 1972, but it hit the East Coast of Australia. The story can't be moved to the East Coast, as the slave ship was sailing from Africa with a cargo of slaves. I'd place the story in 1974 and suggest that writer and artist John Dixon gave the wrong name to the cyclone."

Summer
THE SCARLET JAGUAR
Patricia Wildman, the current Duchess of Greystoke, and her allies Charles Peter Parker and Helen Benson do battle with the deadly Scarlet Jaguar. Pat uses a side kick her karate teacher in Detroit taught her to break down a door. A statue in Pemberley House that was brought back by Sir William Clayton from Greece in the 1820s has been turned to blood-red glass. Pemberley House once belonged to the Dukes of Greystoke, and before that to Pat's distant relative Fitzwilliam Darcy, the owner of the manor in the 1790s and early 1800s. Parker was formerly a member of the investigative firm Knight Errant Limited and a Scotland Yard inspector. Emma

An Original Pat Wildman Adventure

THE SCARLET JAGUAR

WIN SCOTT ECKERT

Ponsonby hires Pat and Parker's firm, Empire State Investigations (ESI), to investigate the disappearance of her father, who is the British ambassador to Xibum, the Central American nation formerly known as British Hidalgo. Emma's aunt was once the secretary to a British Secret Service agent, who recommended ESI to Emma. The home of Alex de Winter, the High Commissioner of Xibum, is called *Casa Delgado*, which is very close to the name of a nightclub in San Francisco de Winter and his wife Marianne once visited. Violet Holmes visits Pat and Parker. Violet was the best friend of Pat's mother Adélaïde; her father Mycroft once held the highest position in the Secret Service, and her son Clive is also in the family business. Violet bought the neighboring estate of Fogg Shaw not long after Patricia moved into Pemberley. Violet mentions both M and Parker's uncle. She also says hijacked nuclear missiles and assassins from the KGB's Ninth Section, formerly SMERSH, are more the Secret Service's speed than the Scarlet Jaguar. Parker asks whether the Diogenes Club could deal with the threat, but Jeperson and company are otherwise occupied. Pat was trained to swing through trees by Penelope Smith, née Penelope Gray, who in turn learned the skill from her own father. Pat's father learned a method to disable a person by pinching certain nerves from a Frenchman named Senak. Helen's father was a colleague of Doc Wildman's in the 1930s and '40s, while her mother fought crime as the Domino Lady. Pat, Parker, and Emma are attacked by some of the remnants of a "secret nation" that evolved out of the ashes of Professor Moriarty's criminal organization. This organization uses a bird as its symbol. Pat's father helped set up a counter organization to this group in the 1940s, working with the United Nations, which supposedly put the criminal organization permanently out of business. Pat places a phone call to private investigator Kent Lane. Her amphibious jet has the name Pennor Lumber Company on it. Xibum is a merger of British Hidalgo with a neighboring country taken over by an Englishman named G. Emory Partridge in 1956, and liberated by the United Network Command (the same organization Pat's father helped found) in 1957. Partridge resurfaced in England in 1964. Kent Lane arranged for a government agency he once worked with called the CACO (Coordinating Authority for Cathedric Organizations) to provide Pat and her allies with fake passports to Xibum. Marianne de Winter smokes Red Apple cigarettes, as did Pat's mother. Pat refers to a number of villainous women, including Madame Elisabeth, who battled her grandparents; the self-styled Countess Cagliostro, who had a running conflict with her maternal grandfather; Irma Peterson; and the progeny of the Devil Doctor, which include a backstabbing daughter and a granddaughter called Isabella Fang who has wreaked havoc in Detroit, San Francisco, and other places. Pat and Helen battle two of the Scarlet Jaguar's henchmen, one of whom remarks the ladies are built like *Playpen* centerfolds. Pat, Helen, and Parker travel to the hidden Vale of the Blue People, which houses a Mayan population, to find the abducted Emma. Pat studied with some of the preeminent archaeologists of her time, including Littlejohn, Jones, and her own father. The Mayans' leader, King Bahlam, has an aunt who has gone into seclusion because of her great sadness. Pat uses a *baritsu* move on one of the Blue People. A bizarre occurrence in the 1930s left Helen's father with frozen, moldable features, which he was able to use to change his appearance; Parker remarks Hamilton Cleek, "the man of forty faces," was said to have had the same ability. Pat uses the Cirrus X-9 rocket pack invented by her father to escape from the Jaguar's headquarters. The Scarlet Jaguar was led to a village containing one of the "secret nation's" former bases by a Dr. von Hessel.

Novella by Win Scott Eckert, Meteor House, 2013. The Scarlet Jaguar is a sequel to Philip José Farmer and Eckert's novel The Evil in Pemberley House. *Pat Wildman is the daughter of Dr. James Clarke Wildman, Jr., aka Doc Wildman, whose adventures formed the basis for Lester Dent and other authors' tales of the man of bronze. Pemberley itself is from Jane Austen's* Pride and Prejudice, *as is Fitzwilliam Darcy. Charles Peter Parker is the nephew of Dorothy L. Sayers' sleuth Lord Peter Wimsey, and the son of Lord Peter's sister Lady Mary and Inspector Charles Parker; Eckert has conflated him with Peter Parker from the British adventure television series* Knight Errant Limited. *Helen Benson is the daughter of Paul Ernst's avenging pulp hero (whose surname was Benson) and Lars Anderson's Domino Lady (aka Ellen Patrick), one of the most famous pulp heroines. Eckert alluded to a possible romance between Benson and Ellen in a trilogy of Avenger stories published by Moonstone Books. Pat's karate teacher is Hayashi Kato from the 1960s Green Hornet television series. Sir William Clayton, the younger son of the 3rd Duke of Greystoke (who was present at the Wold Newton meteor strike), is from Farmer's biographies* Tarzan Alive *and* Doc Savage: His Apocalyptic Life. Tarzan Alive *established the Dukes of Greystoke lived at Pemberley House. British Hidalgo is from Avram Davidson's book* Lime-killer!*; here, it is conflated with the country of Hidalgo from the series of pulp* novels about a bronze-skinned crimefighter. *Emma's aunt is Loelia Ponsonby, James Bond's original secretary (later replaced by Mary Goodnight) in Ian Fleming's novels. M is Bond's superior. Bond battled the terrorist organization SPECTRE, which had hijacked a pair of nuclear missiles, in the novel* Thunderball. *SMERSH was a real Soviet agency that appeared in several of the early Bond novels. Alex de Winter is a descendant of William de Winter, who is in turn a descendant of Milady and Lord de Winter from Alexandre Dumas'* The Three Musketeers. *Jean-Marc Lofficier first revealed William's existence in his creative mythographic essay "Will There Be Light Tomorrow?"* (Shadowmen: Heroes and Villains of French Pulp Fiction, *Black Coat Press, 2003); he was present at a conclave in Wold Newton to decide the outcome of the French Revolution, during which the fateful meteor strike occurred. These events were depicted and elaborated upon in Eckert's story "The Wild Huntsman"* (The Worlds of Philip José Farmer 3: Portraits of a Trickster, *Michael Croteau, ed., Meteor House, 2012). The nightclub in San Francisco is Casa del Gato, which was owned by the title character of the 1966–1967 television series* T.H.E. Cat. *In the Marvel Comics series* Master of Kung Fu, *the character of Clive Reston is strongly implied to be the son of James Bond and the great-nephew of Sherlock Holmes. Eckert and Matthew Baugh co-created Clive's mother, "Shrinking" Violet Holmes, the daughter of Sherlock's brother Mycroft, who cheated on her husband Charles Reston with Bond. Violet also appears in Eckert's story "The Eye of Oran"* (Tales of the Shadowmen Volume 2: Gentlemen of the Night, *Jean-Marc and Randy Lofficier, eds., Black Coat Press, 2005). Adélaïde Johnston Lupin Wildman is the daughter of Maurice Leblanc's gentleman thief Arsène Lupin and American journalist Patricia Johnston, whom he met in* Les Milliards d' Arsène Lupin. *Adélaïde also appeared in "The Eye of Oran," as well as another story by Eckert, "Les Lèvres Rouges"* (Tales of the Shadowmen Volume 3: Danse Macabre, *Jean-Marc and Randy Lofficier, eds., Black Coat Press, 2006). Doc Wildman appeared in those stories under the alias of Francis "Doc" Ardan (Jean-Marc and Randy Lofficier's translation and adaptation of Guy d'Armen's* Doc Ardan: City of Gold and Lepers *strongly implied "Ardan" was really a young Doc). Fogg Shaw, which once belonged to Phileas Fogg from Jules Verne's* Around the World in Eighty Days, *was mentioned by Farmer in both* Tarzan Alive *and* The Other Log of Phileas Fogg. *The Diogenes Club is from the Sherlock Holmes stories. Kim Newman has done several stories about Richard Jeperson, a Club member active in the 1960s-1970s, which adopt the premise, first proposed in the film* The Private Life of Sherlock Holmes, *the Club is a front for the British Secret Service. Penelope Smith was once known as Miss Gray, a member of a justice-focused crimefighting organization in the 1940s. She married her teammate, Smith. Penelope's father is the jungle lord, as theorized by Chuck Loridans in "The Daughters* of Greystoke" (Myths for the Modern Age: Philip José Farmer's Wold Newton Universe, *Win Scott Eckert,* ed., MonkeyBrain Books, 2005). *Senak is a Vulcan (from* Star Trek*) stranded on Earth; Eckert first mentioned him and his teaching of the nerve pinch to Doc Ardan (aka Doc Wildman) in "The Vanishing Devil"* (Tales of the Shadowmen Volume One: The Modern Babylon, *Jean-Marc and Randy Lofficier, eds., Black Coat Press, 2005). The "secret nation" is THRUSH from* The Man from U.N.C.L.E. *television series. David McDaniel's tie-in novel* The Dagger Affair *revealed THRUSH grew out of the criminal empire headed by Professor Moriarty, Sherlock Holmes' greatest foe. Eckert revealed Pat's father helped found*

U.N.C.L.E. (the United Network Command for Law and Enforcement) in his story "Doc Wildman: Out of Time" (Farmerphile: The Magazine of Philip José Farmer #6, *Christopher Paul Carey and Paul Spiteri, eds., October 2006). G. Emory Partridge is from* The Man from U.N.C.L.E. *episodes "The Gazebo in the Maze Affair" and "The Yukon Affair." U.N.C.L.E. seemingly destroyed THRUSH once and for all in David McDaniel's unpublished novel* The Final Affair; *however, U.N.C.L.E. battled a revived THRUSH in 1983, as seen in the reunion TV movie* The Return of the Man from U.N.C.L.E.: The Fifteen Years Later. The Scarlet Jaguar *reveals that some of THRUSH's former soldiers were hired as mercenaries by the Scarlet Jaguar after the events of* The Final Affair. *Kent Lane first appeared in Farmer's story "Skinburn"; he is the son of Allard Kent Rassendyll (whose shadowy tales were told by Walter Gibson and others in a series of pulp novels) and one of his female agents. CACO is also from "Skinburn." In the Doc Savage novel* Waves of Death, *Doc's cousin Patricia has a plane disguised with the name of the Norpen Lumber Company. Red Apple cigarettes have appeared in several films, including* Pulp Fiction, From Dusk Till Dawn, *and* Four Rooms, *as well as several stories by Eckert. Madame Elisabeth is the fictional vampiric version of the historical Elisabeth Bathory seen in the film* Daughters of Darkness. *Doc Ardan (aka Wildman) and Adélaïde fought Elisabeth in "Les Lèvres Rouges." Joséphine Balsamo, the Countess Cagliostro, is one of Arsène*

Lupin's greatest foes. Irma Peterson is from H. C. "Sapper" McNeile and Gerard Fairlie's Bulldog Drummond novels. The Devil Doctor is Sax Rohmer's Fu Manchu; his daughter is Fah Lo Suee. Isabella Fang is Fu Manchu's granddaughter and the daughter of the title character of the radio series Doctor Fang; her activities in Detroit were chronicled in Eckert's stories "Fang and Sting" (The Green Hornet Chronicles, Joe Gentile and Win Scott Eckert, eds., Moonstone Books, 2011) and "Progress" (The Green Hornet: Still at Large, Joe Gentile, Win Scott Eckert, and Matthew Baugh, eds., Moonstone Books, 2012). Isabella's exploits in San Francisco are recounted in Eckert and Matthew Baugh's novel Honey West and T.H.E. Cat: A Girl and Her Cat. Playpen *is an adult magazine that has appeared in* The X-Files, Lost, Special Ops Force, *and several other television series and films. The Vale of the Blue People is meant to be the Mayan valley from the novels featuring a certain bronze-skinned doctor. Littlejohn is one of Doc's five aides. Jones is, of course, Dr. Henry Jones, Jr., better known as Indiana Jones. King Bahlam's aunt is from the pulp stories of the aforementioned bronze doctor. Baritsu, a Japanese system of wrestling, is from the Sherlock Holmes story* "The Adventure of the Empty House." *Hamilton Cleek appeared in novels by Thomas Hanshew. The Cirrus X-9 is a later model than the Cirrus X-3 rocket pack seen in the Rocketeer stories by Dave Stevens and his successors. The original story that introduced the Rocketeer revealed Doc built the X-3. The X-9 previously appeared in* "The Eye of Oran." *Dr. von Hessel is meant to be Baron von Hessel from Farmer's authorized Doc Savage novel* Escape from Loki; *Eckert has revealed a number of other misdeeds committed by the slippery Baron under a variety of aliases in several of his stories, most notably* "The Wild Huntsman."

MR. MOODY'S AMAZING HATS

The wealthy Mr. Moody has a collection of "hats worn by the most famous men in history," each of which apparently compels him to imitate those men when he wears them. The hat of "Raffles—the notorious European jewel thief" causes Moody to steal his neighbor's necklace at a garden party.

Story by Jack Sparling in Beyond the Grave *#2, Charlton Comics, October 1975. This story treats E. W. Hornung's gentleman thief A. J. Raffles as a historical figure, placing it in the CU.*

August 2–10
STATESIDE DEBUT

In 1991, the vigilante known as the Voice, convalescing at a clinic, tells his nurse the story of how he became a crimefighter. Returning home from Vietnam, his plane made a stopover in Hawaii, where he visited Chang Apana, a former member of the Honolulu Police Department and the alleged model for the character of Charlie Chan. He mentions the first master, who had a maxim about eliminating the impossible. Some say the first master is still alive and living in Tibet, or else he acts as the oldest beekeeper in the United Kingdom; he also wrote monographs. Investigating a cabal he heard rumors of in Saigon, the future Voice is confronted by his own father. One of the men injured by the soon-to-be hero, Mr. Jones, is treated by his honorary uncle, Dr. Fairchild. The cabal was actually a gathering of Independent Operators, part of a network set up by the Voice's uncles Dan and Richard, both former civilian federal agents. After a falling-out with J. Edgar Hoover and the McCarthyites, the two joined an all-branches military group called JANIG in the mid 1950s. The sting operation was designed to capture people wishing to destroy the network; however, many of those people turned out to be individuals on the side of justice investigating rumors of the network's existence. These included Steve McGarrett, a naval officer named Magnum, members of Robert Ironside's team, Dan Briggs, Jim Phelps, King Farriday, Napoleon Solo, John Keith, Amos Burke, Alexander Scott and Kelly Robinson, and JANIG's own Steve Ames.

Short story by Erwin K. Roberts in the magazine Double Danger Tales, *Fading Shadows Publications; reprinted and revised on the* Planetary Stories *website. This crossover brings Roberts' pulp-style hero the Voice into the CU. In real life, Chang Apana was indeed the real-life basis for Charlie Chan; however, Chan was a very real individual in the CU. Nevertheless, Max Allan Collins' Nate Heller novel* Damned in Paradise *establishes Apana had a CU counterpart. The first master is Sherlock Holmes. The Voice's father is Secret Agent X, a pulp hero created by "Brant House" (Paul Chadwick). Mr. Jones was a plastic surgeon turned disguise artist who appeared in Dennis Lynds' story (written under the house name Robert Hart Davis) "The Man of a Million Faces,"* Mike Shayne Mystery Magazine, *June 1968. Dr. Jeffrey Fairchild, alias Dr. Skull and the Skull Killer, battled the villain known variously as the Octopus and the Scorpion in two one-shot pulp magazines. Dan is Dan Fowler, G-Man, who was created by Major George Fielding Eliot and appeared in the pulp* G-Men Detective. *Richard is*

Chinese-American Secret Service agent Richard Wong, created by Lee Fredericks, who appeared in G-Men and G-Men Detective. JANIG (Joint Army Navy Intelligence Group) and Steve Ames are from the Rick Brant juvenile adventure novels by "John Blaine" (Harold L. Goodwin and Peter J. Harkins). One novel, The Flying Stingaree, had a cameo by Ken Holt, a young amateur detective appearing in books by "Bruce Campbell" (Sam and Beryl Epstein), while Rick loaned some of his gadgets to Ken in "Campbell's" novel The Mystery of the Plumed Serpent. Steve McGarrett is from the television series Hawaii Five-O. Magnum is Thomas Magnum from the TV series Magnum, P.I. Robert Ironside is from the television series Ironside. Dan Briggs and Jim Phelps are from the classic television series Mission: Impossible. King Farriday (or rather Faraday) is a spy character appearing in the short-lived comic book series Danger Trail, published by DC Comics in the early '50s. Napoleon Solo is, of course, from The Man from U.N.C.L.E. John Keith is from Norman A. Daniels' The Man from A.P.E. espionage novels. Amos Burke is from the television series Burke's Law and Amos Burke, Secret Agent, as well as the 1990s revival of Burke's Law. Alexander Scott and Kelly Robinson are from the TV series I Spy.

November
PROGRESS

Britt Reid witnesses Dr. Isabella Fang being shot by an unknown party. Isabella's grandfather is Dr. Shan Ming Fu, leader of the Si-Fan. She is treated by Dr. Hanomah Spottedhorse, whose husband Thomas, formerly Tim Nektosha, is now a tribal policeman on the Tsichah Reservation in Wyoming. Lenore Case speaks derisively of Britt's former love Laura Cavendish.

Short story by Win Scott Eckert in The Green Hornet: Still at Large, Joe Gentile, Win Scott Eckert, and Matthew Baugh, eds., Moonstone Books, 2012. Dr. Isabella Fang is the daughter of the title character of the radio series Dr. Fang. Dr. Shan Ming Fu is better known as the insidious Dr. Fu Manchu. Hanomah Spottedhorse (formerly Return) is a relative of Tsichah policeman David Return from Manly Wade Wellman's stories "A Star for a Warrior" and "A Knife Between Brothers." The fictitious Tsichah tribe also appeared in Wellman's John Thunstone story "The Golden Goblins." Tim Nektosha is a relative of the Lone Ranger's Potawatomi companion Tonto; the Green Hornet radio series established the Hornet was the Lone Ranger's great-nephew, while the NOW Comics series from the 1980s and 1990s identified the 1960s Green Hornet as the nephew of the original Hornet, thus making him the Lone Ranger's great-grandnephew. Tim and Hanomah previously appeared in Matthew Baugh's stories "The Inside Man" (The Green Hornet Chronicles, Joe Gentile and Win Scott Eckert, eds., Moonstone Books, 2010), "Auld Acquaintance" (The Green Hornet Casefiles, Joe Gentile and Win Scott Eckert, eds., Moonstone Books, 2011), and "The Man Inside" (The Green Hornet: Still at Large). The late Laura Cavendish, aka the Yellowjacket, was the great-granddaughter of the Lone Ranger and Tonto's foe Butch Cavendish; she appeared in Howard Hopkins' stories "Flight of the Yellowjacket" (The Green Hornet Chronicles), "Sting of the Yellowjacket" (The Green Hornet Casefiles) and "Revenge of the Yellow-jacket" (The Green Hornet: Still at Large), as well as "Auld Acquaintance."

1975

Winter

MAN BAT AND ROBBIN'

Scooby and the gang go to Gotham City to investigate monster sightings, and wind up working with Batman and Robin to pursue the source of the sightings, the Dynamic Duo's old foe Man-Bat.

Scooby-Doo Team-Up #1 by Sholly Fisch and Dario Brizuela, DC Comics, January 2014. This story takes place a few years after The New Scooby-Doo Movies, and Fred refers to Mystery Inc. and Batman and Robin previously encountering the Joker and the Penguin. Per CU continuity, this crossover features the second Batman and Robin team, Dick Grayson and Bruce Wayne, Jr.

WHO'S SCARED?

When the Scarecrow douses Mystery, Inc. and the Mystery Analysts of Gotham City with his fear gas, it's up to Scooby-Doo and Ace the Bathound, who as non-humans are unaffected by the drug, to save the day. The Mystery Analysts present for the meeting include Batman and Robin, Roy Raymond, Mysto, Doctor Thirteen, Kaye Daye, Slam Bradley, and Jason Bard. Paintings of Detective Chimp and Sam Simeon are also seen.

Scooby-Doo Team-Up #2 by Sholly Fisch and Dario Brizuela, DC Comics, March 2014. Roy Raymond, TV detective, appeared in Detective Comics from 1949–1961. Mysto, Magician Detective appeared in his own back-up feature in the same series in 1954. Doctor Terrence Thirteen, the Ghost-Breaker, appeared in Star-Spangled Comics from 1951–1952. Kaye Daye is one of the original Mystery Analysts of Gotham City that appeared in Batman in the 1960s and 1970s. Slam Bradley appeared in Detective

Comics *from 1937–1949. Slam's older brother Biff Bradley was involved in an affair on Dinosaur Island alongside several other adventurers in 1927, as seen in* Guns of the Dragon, *while Slam himself had an adventure with the third Batman and Robin team, the Elongated Man, and an elderly Sherlock Holmes in 1986, as seen in "The Doomsday Book." Jason Bard first appeared in a Batgirl story in* Detective Comics *in 1969 before spinning off into his own back-up feature, which ran until 1973. Detective Chimp (Bobo, a chimpanzee skilled at solving crimes) had a back-up feature in* The Adventures of Rex the Wonder Dog *from 1952–1959. Sam Simeon, a talking ape who works as a P.I. with the curvaceous and brilliant Angel O'Day, was featured in the comic* Angel and the Ape. *These characters are all CU counterparts of their equivalents in the DC Comics Universe.*

March 18–May 14
KOLCHAK: THE NIGHT STALKER AND DR. MOREAU

Mike Kelly   Mark Grammel

Carl Kolchak encounters the Lochley family, scientists who have discovered Doctor Moreau's island, where his beast-men have managed to reproduce and create a colony over the last century, and brought them back to the U.S. An enigmatic man named Dr. Clarke appears, and engineers the deaths of several beast-men. Kolchak, reading H. G. Wells' *The Time Machine*, notes Clarke used a brand of British-made dynamite not manufactured in over ninety years, and thinks he traveled a long way to wipe out the future of the "Mor-Lochs."

One-shot by Mike Kelly, Eric Stanway, and Mark Grammel, Moonstone Comics, 2013. Dr. Clarke is implicitly Wells' Time Traveler. The Traveler's use of the name Clarke is a reference to Philip José Farmer's biography Doc Savage: His Apocalyptic Life, *in which the Traveler's real name was given as Bruce Clarke Wildman. This story implies the beast-men are the ancestors of the Morlocks from* The Time Machine. *As with other Kolchak stories by Moonstone, mentions of the cloning of Dolly the sheep and other contemporary references are being ignored in order to maintain Kolchak's adventures in their original time period.*

Spring
HOLLYWOOD BOULEVARD

Talent agent Walter Paisley appears in this film about sleazy movie studio Miracle Pictures.

1976 feature film directed by Allan Arkush and Joe Dante. Paisley is played by Dick Miller, who earlier played a busboy turned murderous sculptor of that name in Roger Corman's 1959 film A Bucket of Blood. *Walter apparently committed suicide at the end of* A Bucket of Blood, *but given this and other film appearances by Miller as Walter Paisley, it seems obvious he must have staged his own death. One of those films is Dante's* The Howling, *where he was the owner of an occult bookstore. Since* The Howling *takes place in the CU, so too do Walter Paisley's other appearances. Given that he has a different occupation every time he appears, Walter's fugitive status likely requires him to change jobs frequently.*

INVASION OF THE CLONES

The half-Chinese Kung Fu expert Victor Mace was murdered by the same group that has captured Richard Camellion.

The Death Merchant *#16 by Joseph Rosenberger. Mace was the protagonist of the five* Kung Fu *novels written by Rosenberger under the pseudonym "Lee Chang," published in 1973–1974. The fourth* Kung Fu *novel mentioned both Camellion and another series character of Rosenberger's, the Murder Master.*

TROUBLE IN PARADISE

Velma and Daphne are invited to Paradise Island by Wonder Woman on Batman's recommendation, partly to learn the ways of the Amazons, and partly to help them stop the spate of mythological creatures that have been attacking recently. This is somewhat complicated by Fred, Scooby, and Shaggy being unable to set foot on the mainland due to the Olympian gods' edict.

Scooby-Doo Team-Up *#5 by Sholly Fisch and Dario Brizuela, DC Comics, September 2014.*

Summer
WHERE SOARS THE SILVER SURFER!

A Satanic cult brainwashes the Silver Surfer into attacking Dracula.

Tomb of Dracula *#50 by Marv Wolfman, Gene Colan, and Tom Palmer, Marvel Comics, November 1976. The version of Dracula seen in the* Tomb of Dracula *series has valid independent links to the CU, as does the Silver Surfer; therefore, this crossover likely takes place there as well.*

TRUTH, JUSTICE, AND SCOOBY SNACKS

When Caesar's ghost appears in the *Daily Planet*'s offices, Superman calls in Mystery, Inc. to help him find out the truth behind the haunting. It turns out to be the work of the Prankster, who transforms Superman into a monstrous form with Red Kryptonite. With the help of Superman's dog Krypto, as well as Scooby and Shaggy inadvertently drinking the serums that once gave Lois Lane and Jimmy Olsen superpowers, the gang saves the day.

Scooby-Doo Team-Up #9 by Sholly Fisch and Dario Brizuela, DC Comics, May 2015. Velma alludes in passing to the events of an earlier story, "A (Super) Friend in Need"; however, given that the Super Friends, as a superhero team, do not fit into the CU, this should be disregarded. Lois seems unaware that Clark Kent is Superman, even though CU continuity holds that she and Clark have been married for over two decades by this point. Lois must be merely keeping up appearances in front of her coworkers and Scooby and the gang in order to keep Clark's dual identity a secret.

GOTHAM GHOULS

Mystery, Inc. is summoned to Gotham City by Poison Ivy and Harley Quinn to help them end an apparent curse that has been on them since they stole an opal. The "ghost" responsible turns out to be Catwoman. Ultimately, the gang works with Batgirl to apprehend all three larcenous ladies.

Scooby-Doo Team-Up #12 by Sholly Fisch and Dario Brizuela, DC

Comics, November 2015. This Catwoman must be a successor to Selina Kyle-Wayne and a predecessor to the feline fatale who will later encounter Vampirella.

Autumn
NIGHTMARE IN ALGERIA

"Poor Shafik Jamal had neither the reflexes nor the experience of Richard Camellion. With the exception of Mack Bolan, another deadly crime fighter known as *The Executioner*, very few men had."

The Death Merchant #18 by Joseph Rosenberger. The reference to Mack Bolan reinforces the Death Merchant's place in the CU.

Winter

THE LOVECRAFTIAN DAMNATION

Marvin Richards, host of the television program *Challenge of the Unknown*, once again summons reporter Carl Kolchak, informing him Dr. Randel Penes is still alive and still in possession of the *Necronomicon*. Among the names that cursed tome has been known by are the *Kitah al-Azif*, the *Cultus Maleficarum*, the *Liber Logaeth*, and the *Necronomicon Ex Mortis*. Assisting them in dealing with this threat are Dr. Kirsten Helms and Madame Sarna La Rainelle. Paddy Moran from Bullfinches told Kolchak about La Rainelle, who worked with John Legrasse more than once, helped Anton Zarnak escape from the Tindolosi, and knew Marc Thorner, Ravenwood, and Jules de Grandin. Dr. Penes has merged with the creature he previously summoned, the Nyogtha.

A Kolchak: The Night Stalker one-shot by C. J. Henderson and Robert Hack, Moonstone Comics, 2010. This story serves as a sequel to Henderson's Kolchak story "What Every Coin Has," which featured Dr. Penes' previous use of the Necronomicon. In addition to the aforementioned tale, Richards also appeared in Henderson's stories "All That Glitters" and "A Forty Share in Innsmouth" and the graphic novel Kolchak: The Night Stalker–The Lovecraftian Horror. The Cultus Maleficarum is from Fred L. Pelton's "The Sussex Manuscript." The Liber Logaeth is a real book of alleged Enochian magic that was read by Queen Elizabeth I's astrologer John Dee, among others. The Necronomicon Ex Mortis is from Sam Raimi's Evil Dead films. Most creative mythographers treat Raimi's Necronomicon as a separate book from Lovecraft's tome, and therefore this reference may be in error. Leprechaun Paddy Moran and his bar Bullfinches (or rather Bulfinche's) are from Patrick Thomas' Murphy's Lore series of books. John Legrasse is from Lovecraft's classic story "The Call of Cthulhu," while Anton Zarnak is an occult investigator in several stories by Lin Carter and other authors. La Rainelle (or La Raniella) aided both men in Henderson's stories "To Cast Out Fear" and "Locked Room," and also appeared alongside Legrasse in Henderson's novel To Battle Beyond. The Tindolosi (or Tindlosi) are from Frank Belknap Long's tale "The Hounds of Tindalos." Mark Thorner is a policeman ally of Zarnak's. Ravenwood, "the stepson of mystery," appeared in stories by Frederick C. Davis in Secret Agent X. Occult investigator Dr. Jules de Grandin's exploits were chronicled by Seabury Quinn. The Nyogtha is from Henry Kuttner's Cthulhu Mythos story "The Salem Horror." Two television sets in a video editing room are showing the TV series Mystery Science Theater 3000, which debuted in 1988. This detail must be ignored in order to maintain Kolchak's adventures in their original time period.

A TRAVESTY

Film critic Carey Thorpe both commits and solves murders. The head of the Visaria Mission at the U.N. is murdered.

Story by Donald E. Westlake in the collection Enough. *Visaria is from Universal's Frankenstein movies, bringing this story into the CU.*

Spring
THE HOUSE ON WILLIS AVENUE

Jim Rockford teams up with young P.I. Richie Brockelman to find out whether the death of a fellow shamus was an accident or murder.

Episode of The Rockford Files *broadcast February 24, 1978. Jim Rockford is already in the CU through connections to Philip Marlowe and Carl Kolchak. Richie Brockelman first appeared in the 1976 TV movie* Richie Brockelman: The Missing 24 Hours. *After this episode, Richie began appearing in his own series, entitled* Richie Brockelman, Private Eye. *After that series ended, Richie met Jim again in a two-part episode of* The Rockford Files *called "Never Send a Boy King to Do a Man's Job."*

THE NINTH CONFIGURATION

Among the U.S. Army soldiers being treated by Colonel Vincent "Killer" Kane at an insane asylum based in a castle is astronaut Billy Cutshaw, who has a fear of dying in space.

Novel by William Peter Blatty. Cutshaw is meant to be the same unnamed astronaut who is told by a possessed Regan MacNeil he will die in space in Blatty's novel The Exorcist. *Since* The Exorcist *takes place in the CU, so does this novel.*

GRAND OPENING . . . UNDER FIRE

The Voice, present at a bank in disguise when a terrorist group holds the customers and staff hostage, thinks his Dad always said there would be days like this.

Short story by Erwin K. Roberts in Double Danger Tales *#57, Tom and Ginger Johnson, eds., Fading Shadows Publications, December 2002; reprinted in* Casebook of the Voice, *Modern Knights Press, 2014. The Voice's father is Brant House's pulp hero Secret Agent X.*

Summer

THE MAD FANTOMA MARK III

Fantoma Mark III, the grandson of the original Fantoma, kidnaps Fujiko Mine, and demands a ruby Lupin III recently stole from India's royal family as ransom. Fantoma intends to use the ruby as part of a laser satellite which will melt the Antarctic ice and flood all of Earth's cities, allowing him to take over the world.

Episode of Lupin the 3rd *broadcast October 9, 1978. The original Fantoma is a slightly renamed version of Marcel Allain and Pierre Souvestre's "Lord of Terror," Fantômas. According to this episode, Fantoma Mark III's satellite floods much of South America, and everyone in Rio de Janeiro is killed. This must be considered an exaggeration for the purposes of including this episode in CU continuity.*

1978

June

CHASTEL

Lee Cobbett and Judge Pursuivant team up to slay a vampire in Deslow, Connecticut.

Short story by Manly Wade Wellman in The Year's Best Horror Stories, *Series VII, Gerald W. Page, ed., 1979. Judge Pursuivant's eighty-seventh birthday is on the first day of this story; Wellman's "The Black Drama" established Pursuivant was born in 1891, hence the 1978 date.*

1979

Winter

BRACELETS, DEMONS AND DEATH

Vampirella's friend Cryssie Collins and special effects expert Harold Swillman find themselves in possession of the Hellbands created by Jedediah Pan, each of which can summon three demons. Swillman uses his Hellband to murder the guests at a gala party, and unintentionally causes Cryssie to be possessed by a demon herself.

Vampirella #92–93 *by Rich Margopoulos and Rudy Nebres, Warren Publishing, December 1980–January 1981. Jedediah Pan and the Hellbands are from "The Demons," a strip by Bill DuBay and Jose Ortiz that appeared in five installments in the Warren magazine* Eerie *in 1976.*

Spring. Private eye Amos Walker's first recorded case (*Motor City Blue* by Loren D. Estleman).

Spring. Events of *The Lime Pit* by Jonathan Valin, the first appearance of private investigator Harry Stoner.

Summer. Henry Po, investigator for the New York Racing Commission, begins his career (*The Disappearance of Penny* by Robert J. Randisi).

August
KENNEDY FOR THE DEFENSE
Boston-based defense attorney Jerry Kennedy tells his wife he cannot put private investigator Edward J. "Bad Eye" Mulvey on a case he is handling, and notes, "Cooper uses a guy named Spenser and says he's pretty good, but Spenser's one of those fresh bastards that thinks he's the sword of justice and goes running off to London every chance he gets, like he was trying out for his own television series."
Novel by Jerry Kennedy, edited by George V. Higgins, Alfred A. Knopf, Inc., 1980. The reference to Robert B. Parker's Boston-dwelling P.I. Spenser brings Jerry Kennedy into the CU.

December 24
CHRISTMAS, 24 HOURS
The professional assassin Golgo 13 is mistaken for a rapist by a hotel detective named Doll, who attempts to apprehend him.
1980 episode of Takao Saito's manga series Golgo 13. Golgo is in the CU through a later crossover with the series Kochikame, which also crossed over with Lupin III in the same special. This crossover brings in the title character of another series by Saito, Doll: The Hotel Detective.

1980

Spring
PLUTONIUM NIGHTMARE
The vigilante known as the Voice writes, "In the long run the police, as Nero Wolfe once told my Dad, have their legions of experts." He also gives many thanks to Uncle Simon and Willie, his British knife throwing mentors.
Novel by Erwin K. Roberts, Modern Knights Press, 2013. Nero Wolfe is Rex Stout's detective. The Voice's father is meant to be the pulp hero Secret Agent X. The Voice's knife throwing mentors are Leslie Charteris' hero Simon Templar (aka the Saint) and Willie Garvin, partner of Modesty Blaise in Peter O'Donnell's comic strip and novels. There are allusions in the Voice stories to other fictional heroes being the Voice's "honorary uncles," and therefore there is no actual genealogical relationship between he and the Saint that we know of.

November 21
STONE TEARS

Nelson LeHorn makes his yearly pilgrimage to the Susquehanna River petroglyphs, which include images of goat-men, lizard-men, and a giant snake LeHorn believes to be Old Scratch.

Short story by Brian Keene in his collections Unhappy Endings *and* Blood on the Page. *Nelson LeHorn is a background character in Keene's novel* Dark Hollow; *this story takes place a few years before the tragedy that befalls him and his family in that novel. The goat-men are a reference to the satyr from* Dark Hollow. *The lizard-men are probably the CU version of the Dark Ones who appear in the alternate world of Keene and J. F. Gonzalez' Clickers series. Old Scratch later appears in Keene's short story "Scratch." The date is derived from a character's reference to the fact they're revealing who shot J. R. on tonight's* Dallas. *That episode aired November 21, 1980.*

1981

Spring
WHEN MONSTERS MEET

Dr. Bruce Banner and Betty Ross are in Paris to meet with the Academy of Science. Betty is carrying a key that opens an underground gold vault. The namesake and great-great-great-great-great-grandson of Quasimodo kidnaps Betty, hoping both to plunder the vault and to have one of the assembled scientists mutate him into a "normal" human form. Bruce has been given a formula by one of his colleagues that could cure him of his double life as the Hulk, but winds up losing it, and it falls into the hands of Quasimodo. However, the formula seemingly lacks efficacy, and Banner turns into the Hulk and does battle with the hunchback. However, Quasimodo is finally cured of his deformities, and he and the Hulk make peace.

Episode of The Incredible Hulk *animated series broadcast October 9, 1982, adapted as "The Hulk Meets the Hunchback of Notre Dame!" by Bill Mantlo and Steve Mitchell in* The Incredible Hulk versus Quasimodo, *Marvel Comics, March 1983. The connection to Quasimodo from Victor Hugo's* The Hunchback of Notre-Dame *reinforces the Hulk's inclusion in the CU. The original Quasimodo must have fathered a child sometime after the events of Hugo's novel.*

May

THE CANA DIVERSION

Retired private investigator Brock "The Rock" Callahan investigates the death of another private eye, Joe Puma. Brock's friend Lenny Devlin tells him, "Buddy, compared with you, Sherlock Holmes was a bush-league rookie."

Novel by William Campbell Gault. Brock "The Rock" Callahan is in the CU through a cameo in Bill Pronzini and Marcia Muller's novel Doubles. *This crossover brings in Joe Puma, who starred in seven novels and as many stories by Gault between 1953 and 1961. Lenny refers to Holmes as if he were a real person.*

Summer

QUAKING TERROR

Mark Hardin battles Vlad Dosadan Magarac, Count Dracula. Magarac claims to be a descendant of the original Count Dracula, who was cruelly defamed by Bram Stoker.

The Penetrator *#45 by "Lionel Derrick" (Mark Kelly Roberts), Pinnacle, 1982.*

GEORGE V. HIGGINS

THE PATRIOT GAME

THE PATRIOT GAME

Department of Justice agent Pete Riordan investigates the sale of guns to the IRA. The seller is suspected to be Mikey-Mike Magro, who is being released from prison. Riordan suspects Magro is also seeking revenge against his former colleague Digger Doherty, brother of Bishop Paul Doherty.

Novel by George V. Higgins, Alfred A. Knopf, 1982. Pete Riordan first appeared in Higgins' novel Kennedy for the Defense, *which takes place in the CU via a reference to Robert B. Parker's P.I. Spenser. Mikey-Mike Magro, Digger Doherty, and Digger's brother Paul first appeared in Higgins' novel* The Digger's Game.

Summer. First case of private dick Ben Perkins, as told by Rob Kantner in "'C' is for Cookie."

October 1981–Winter 1982
NIGHT TRAIN

Lieutenant Michael Corvino of the NYPD, TV journalist Lya Marsden, and Professor Lane Carter investigate dark, otherworldly forces lurking in New York City's subway tunnels. Carter tells Corvino and Marsden about megapolisomancy, a mystical theory created by an early twentieth century occultist named Thibaut de Castries, who wrote a titular book about the subject. De Castries postulated as cities grow older and more defined, they take on a metaphysical life of their own, attracting paranormal beings. Besides de Castries' book, Carter searches a number of other volumes for hints as to what lurks beneath Manhattan, including *The Necronomicon* by Abdul Alhazred. Carter borrows an object called the "key of Cthulhu" from a friend at Miskatonic University in order to defend himself and his comrades against the underground creatures.

Novel by Thomas F. Monteleone, Pocket Books, 1984. Thibaut de Castries and his book Megapolisomancy: A New Science of Cities *are from Fritz Leiber's novel* Our Lady of Darkness. *Abdul Alhazred's* Necronomicon *and Miskatonic University are staples of H. P. Lovecraft's Cthulhu Mythos. Carter claims Miskatonic University is in Providence, Rhode Island, but Lovecraft located the college in Arkham, Massachusetts. Carter must have had a brief memory lapse.*

1982

Winter
A LIKELY STORY

The Italian restaurant *Tre Mafiosi* appears.

Novel by Donald E. Westlake. The Tre Mafiosi *restaurant also appears in Westlake's Dortmunder novel* What's So Funny? *as well as another non-series novel by Westlake,* Money for Nothing. *Since the Dortmunder books take place in the CU, so do* A Likely Story *and* Money for Nothing.

TILL DEATH DO US PART

The A-Team gets food from Hamburger Heaven, and Murdock also gets a Captain Bellybuster hat.

Episode of The A-Team *broadcast April 19, 1983. Hamburger Heaven and its mascot, Captain Bellybuster, first appeared in "Captain Bellybuster and the Speed Factory," an episode of the television series* The Greatest American Hero. *Since the A-Team are in the CU, so is that show's protagonist, Ralph Hinkley (aka Ralph Hanley).*

January–Late December
BLACK SWAN GREEN

Jason Taylor's classmates include Neal Brose and Clive Pike, while Mr. Nixon is his headmaster. Madame Eva van Outryve de Crommelynck tutors Jason in poetry. The Vicar of Saint Gabriel's' wife is Gwendolin Bendincks.

Novel by David Mitchell. Neal Brose appears as an adult in Mitchell's novel Ghostwritten. *Clive Pike and Mr. Nixon are from the short story "Acknowledgments," which features the now-grown Pike trying to get a book published by Timothy Cavendish, another character from* Ghostwritten. *Mitchell's story "Muggins Here" is a sequel to "Acknowledgments." Madame Eva van Outryve de Crommelynck and Gwendolin Bendincks are from* Cloud Atlas.

Spring
WAR MACHINE

Iron Man tricks the attacking ninjas known as the Masters of Silence into entering his simulation room, which he proceeds to plunge into darkness. One of the Masters counsels his teammates, "Remember the words of Master Zatoichi—'A warrior's eyes are the least of his senses.'"

Iron Man #282 by Len Kaminski, Kevin Hopgood, and Bob Wiacek, Marvel Comics, July 1992. The ninja's comments treat Zatoichi, the blind masseur and swordsman portrayed by Shintarō Katsu in a long-running series of Japanese films, as a real person. Both Iron Man and Zatoichi are in the CU; therefore, this story likely occurs there as well. I have moved this story from its 1990s setting to accommodate a more realistic timeline for Tony Stark's adventures.

Spring. Vietnam veteran, ex-cop, mystery writer, and amateur sleuth Mallory's first case (*The Baby Blue Rip-Off* by Max Allan Collins).

Summer
APPLEBY AND HONEYBATH

Retired Commissioner of Police Sir John Appleby and his friend, artist Charles Honeybath, investigate the appearance (and subsequent disappearance) of a body at the home of Terrence Grinton, a relative of Appleby's wife who has commissioned Honeybath to paint his portrait. Grinton says the shifting of county boundaries has pretty well done away with Barsetshire.

This 1983 novel by Michael Innes is a crossover between two of his series characters. Honeybath previously appeared in three novels: The Mysterious Commission, Honeybath's Haven, *and* Lord Mullion's Secret. *Since Appleby is in the CU, so is Honeybath. The county of Barsetshire was featured in the six* Chronicles of Barsetshire *novels by Anthony Trollope.*

IT'S A GOOD LIFE

Helen Foley first encounters Anthony Fremont, a young boy with powers that make him virtually omnipotent, at a bar owned by Walter Paisley.

Segment of the 1983 anthology film Twilight Zone: The Movie *directed by Joe Dante, based on the original* The Twilight Zone *episode of the same name, which in turn was based on the short story by Jerome Bixby. Walter Paisley is played by Dick Miller, who originated the character in the film* A Bucket of Blood *and went on to portray him in several more films, including two other Dante films,* Hollywood Boulevard *(co-directed with Allan Arkush) and* The Howling.

June
ASHES 2 ASHES

Ash Williams and the Wise Man track the *Necronomicon Ex Mortis* to an ancient temple that contains what appears to be Indiana Jones' skeleton.

Four-issue Army of Darkness *miniseries by Andy Hartnell and Nick Bradshaw, Dynamite Entertainment, 2004. This miniseries takes place concurrent with the first* Evil Dead *film. The skeleton's resemblance to Indy is odd, considering his appearances as an old man in the framing sequences of* The Young Indiana Jones Chronicles, *which are set in the 1990s, as well as his encounter with Lara Croft sometime before 2000, after apparently having been rejuvenated back to the prime of life.*

1983

Winter
DIAMONDS ARE A THIEF'S BEST FRIEND

B. A. Baracus runs into an old friend, Mario Ronda, who reveals he is an FBI agent, partnered with Bill Maxwell.

The A-Team *#1 by Jim Salicrup, Marie Severin, and Chic Stone, Marvel Comics, March 1984. FBI Agent Bill Maxwell is from the television series* The Greatest American Hero, *which was already connected to* The A-Team *by the appearance of the fast food restaurant Hamburger Heaven and its mascot, Captain Bellybuster, on both series. This reference furthers cements the two shows as taking place in the same universe.*

Spring. Events of "Rawhead Rex" by Clive Barker.

Spring
CRAZY DAZE

A parapsychologist interviewing Karen Barclay in the aftermath of her encounter with the killer doll Chucky mentions the town of Springwood, OH and its dream-killer.

Child's Play: The Series *#2–3 by Andy Mangels, Raine Szramski, and Mike Witherby, Innovation, July–September 1991. Springwood, Ohio is the hometown of dream-murderer Freddy Krueger, further proving the* Child's Play *movies (and comics) occur in the same world as the* Nightmare on Elm Street *movies. The Freddy reference is in #2.*

Summer. Boston P.I. John Francis Cuddy's first recorded case, *Blunt Darts* by Jeremiah Healy.

Summer
DYNAMITE PARK

Ben Perkins receives a hot tip from fellow Detroit private eye Amos Walker.

Story by Rob Kantner in Mike Shayne Mystery Magazine, *December 1984. Loren D. Estleman's P.I. Amos Walker is already in the CU; therefore, this crossover brings in Ben Perkins.*

BUTCHERS OF EDEN

Niles Barrabas recalls a meeting with John Macklin Bolan in Vietnam.

Soldiers of Barrabas *#3 by Jack Hild, 1984. John Macklin Bolan is meant to be Mack Bolan of the* Executioner *series, whose actual full name is Mack Samuel Bolan. In the* Executioner *novels published by Gold Eagle, Bolan uses the alias John Macklin Phoenix. This meeting seems to be separate from the one seen in the story "Incident at Hoi Binh."*

Late Autumn
FULL CONTACT

P.I. Miles Jacoby investigates a murder and a missing person case, which appear to be unrelated, but ultimately prove to be intimately connected. Jacoby asks Detroit-based detective Amos Walker to collect info about the missing girl's karate teacher. He later turns that case over to Henry Po for a time. Jacoby's investigation of the murder leads him to the Mysterious Bookshop, which has a sign in the window announcing an author named Mallory will be there later in the week to autograph books. Later, Jacoby calls a detective in Cincinnati named Harry Stoner and asks him to dig up info on a suspect.

Novel by Robert J. Randisi, 1984. P.I. Amos Walker is the protagonist of a series of novels and short stories by Loren D. Estleman. Henry Po, an investigator for the New York Racing Commission, is the protagonist of Randisi's novel The Disappearance of Penny, *as well as a number of short stories. Mallory is a mystery writer and amateur sleuth appearing in five novels by Max Allan Collins. Harry Stoner appears in a series of novels by Jonathan Valin. Since Jacoby is in the Crossover Universe, this crossover brings in Walker, Po, Mallory, and Stoner. Although the events of the previous novel,* The Steinway Collection, *set in 1976, supposedly occurred months ago, Amos Walker, Henry Po, and Harry Stoner debuted in 1980, and Mallory in 1983. Therefore, I have placed* Full Contact's *events in 1983, one year before its publication date.*

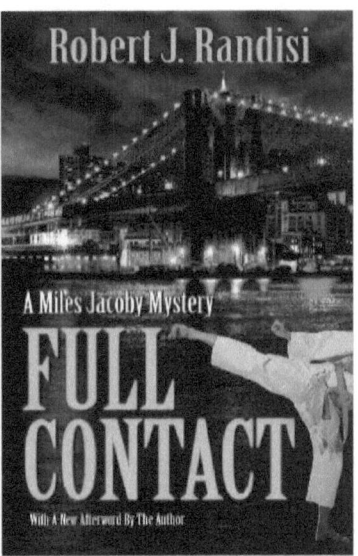

1984

Late February–Early March
FINAL JUSTICE

A Texas sheriff is gunned down by Sicilian gangster Joseph Palermo and his brother Tony. Deputy Thomas Jefferson Geronimo III fatally shoots Tony and arrests Joseph. Chief Wilson, Geronimo's superior officer, assigns now-Sheriff Geronimo to extradite the surviving Palermo to Italy. However, Palermo's fellow *Mafiosi* have the plane diverted to Malta and help him escape custody. Geronimo repeatedly attempts to capture Palermo, despite frequent reprimands for his methods from both Wilson and the Malta Police Department's Superintendent Mifsud, who eventually places Geronimo under house arrest in his hotel room. As part of a ploy to escape, Geronimo asks the officer standing outside his door if there was really a Falcon. The officer responds there was, right before Geronimo fakes chest pains and overpowers and ties him up.

1985 feature film directed by Greydon Clark. Wold Newton Family member Sam Spade's account of his investigation involving the Maltese Falcon was edited by Dashiell Hammett; since the officer says the statue actually existed, this film takes place in the CU. The date is based on the fact Malta is in the midst of Carnival when Geronimo arrives. Carnival is celebrated in Malta the week before Ash Wednesday, which fell on March 7 in 1984.

April
KILL FEE

N.Y.P.D. Lieutenant James Murtaugh attempts to apprehend a contract killer named Pluto, who picks his targets first and seeks money from people who stand to profit by their deaths only after the hit.

Novel by Barbara Paul. Lieutenant Murtaugh went on to appear in Paul's Marian Larch novels, which have already been established as taking place in the CU.

Spring
EXPLORERS

A newspaper bears the headlines "Kingston Falls 'Riot' Still Unexplained" and "Homewood School Teacher Reported Missing." Among the items in a junkyard is a sled inscribed with the word "Rosebud."

1985 feature film directed by Joe Dante. Kingston Falls is the setting of Dante's film Gremlins, *while the Homewood schoolteacher is Helen Foley from "It's a Good Life," Dante's segment of* Twilight Zone: The Movie. *In Orson Welles' classic film* Citizen Kane, *Rosebud was the name on Charles Foster Kane's sled as a child. Since Kane's sled was tossed into an incinerator at the end of* Citizen Kane, *Rosebud must be a brand name, and the sled in the junkyard another of the company's products. Since* Gremlins, *"It's a Good Life," and* Citizen Kane *take place in the Crossover Universe, so does* Explorers.

Spring. Private eye Nick Delvecchio's first recorded case, "The Snaphaunce" by Robert J. Randisi.

Summer
GHOUL

Young Timmy Graco and his friends find themselves battling a carnivorous ghoul in rural Pennsylvania. The boys are also troubled by the Sawyers' dog Catcher. The LeHorn family is among the mourners at Timmy's grandfather's funeral. The Ghoul knows of the Thirteen, including Behemoth and the Great Wurms, as well as the Siqqusim. It is also familiar with the "ancient race of subterranean swine-things." The *Daemonolateria* is mentioned.

Novel by Brian Keene. In Keene's novel Terminal, *Tommy O'Brien also mentions having been attacked by Catcher during his youth. The LeHorn family is from Keene's novel* Dark Hollow; *this appearance takes place less than a year before the tragic events that befell them in the flashback portions of that novel. The Thirteen are the main villains of Keene's mythos, thirteen ancient creatures who survived the destruction of the previous reality by God and now seek the destruction of the current reality, traveling from universe to universe bringing death and destruction; Behemoth and the Great Wurms* can be seen in Keene's Earthworm Gods *novels, and the Siqqusim are the main villains of his* The Rising *series. The subterranean swine-things are from* William Hope Hodgson's *novel* The House on the Borderland. *The* Dae-monolateria *is a fictional book of magic that appears in a number of Keene's works, including "Caught in a Mosh,"* Dark Hollow, *and* Ghost Walk.

June 30, 1984–April 7, 2025
THE BONE CLOCKS

Appearing or mentioned are: Dr. Marinus; Alan Wall; Hugo Lamb; Dominic Fitzsimmons; Felix Finch; Jonny Penhaligon; Kilmagoon Special Reserve; Elijah D'Arnoq; *Spyglass* magazine; Dwight Silverwind; and *The Voorman Problem.*

This novel by David Mitchell has connections to his other books, and therefore to the CU. Dr. Marinus, who is capable of reincarnation, is from The Thousand Autumns of Jacob de Zoet. *This incarnation of Marinus debuted in Mitchell's libretto for Michael Van der Aa's opera* Sunken Garden. *Johnny Penhaligon is a descendant of the Captain Penhaligon that appears in* The Thousand Autumns of Jacob de Zoet. *Alan Wall, Hugo Lamb, and Dominic Fitzsimmons are from* Black Swan Green. *Felix Finch and* Spyglass *magazine are from* Cloud Atlas. *The Afterword included in the paperback edition of this novel reveals Elijah D'Arnoq is the son of Mr. d'Arnoq, a minor character in* Cloud Atlas. *Kilmagoon Special Reserve is a fictional whiskey that recurs in Mitchell's works. Dwight Silverwind is from* Ghostwritten. *The book* The Voorman Problem *is the basis for the movie of the same name in* number9dream. *The section of the book entitled "Sheep's Head: 2043" takes place on an Earth ravaged by climate change, and therefore must represent an alternate future, which also appears to be the setting of Mitchell's story "The Siphoners." This section also has an appearance by Mo Muntervary from* Ghostwritten.

Summer. Actor and sometimes P.I. Jack Dwyer's first recorded case, *Rough Cut* by Ed Gorman.

October 26, 1984; November 5–12, 1955; October 27, 1984. Events of the feature film *Back to the Future.*

1985

Winter
THE HOLE IN THE WALL GANG

The Ghostbusters go to Arkham, Massachusetts to investigate hauntings at the home of a cheese magnate. Ray Stantz points out Miskatonic University to his teammates.

The Real Ghostbusters episode broadcast October 21, 1987. The Ghostbusters first visited Arkham and Miskatonic (both from H. P. Lovecraft's Cthulhu Mythos) in the episode "Collect Call of Cthulhu."

Spring
TWO MITES MAKE IT WRONG

Batman, Robin, and Mystery, Inc.'s attempt to apprehend the Spook and False Face is disrupted when the Fifth Dimensional imps Bat-Mite and Scooby-Mite, Batman and Scooby-Doo's self-proclaimed biggest fans, appear. Scooby-Mite uses his magical powers to make Mystery, Inc. more "contemporary," including providing them with "high-tech ghost-chasing gear!" After the Dynamic Duo and Scooby and the Gang convince the two pests to leave, another imp named Larry appears, proclaiming himself Robin's biggest fan.

Scooby-Doo Team-Up #3 by Sholly Fisch and Dario Brizuela, DC Comics, May 2014. Mystery Inc.'s high-tech "ghost-chaser" uniforms are clearly based on the Ghostbusters' uniforms, placing this story in the '80s. Per CU, continuity, this story features the third Batman and Robin team. Scooby-Mite also turns the gang into ponies briefly. Rather than treating this as a crossover connection to My Little Pony, it is preferable to interpret this as Scooby-Mite being familiar with the original toy line, which ran from 1981–1993. Larry is the CU counterpart of the character of the same name from the cartoon Teen Titans.

Late June–July
IMPOSTORS

Mark Baldwin, the CEO of a communications empire that includes the *Boston Commoner* newspaper, is friends with lawyer Roger Kidd.

Novel by George V. Higgins, Henry Holt and Co., 1986. The fictional Boston Commoner *appears in a number of Higgins' books, including his series about lawyer Jerry Kennedy, who is already in the CU. Roger Kidd is a supporting character in the Kennedy books.*

July
TOO OLD A CAT

Devlin "Trace" Tracy and his girlfriend Michiko "Chico" Mangini join the New York private investigation agency run by Trace's dad, ex-cop Patrick "Sarge" Tracy. Sarge's office is above Bogie's Restaurant & Bar. A Mafioso who hires Sarge to look into his wife's involvement with a cult says, "I heard there were some private eyes hung out downstairs in the restaurant." Sarge replies, "One's a broken-down pug and the other one's a one-armed communist." Detectives William "Tough" Jackson and Ed Razoni investigate the murder of the cult's guru.

Novel by Warren Murphy, 1986. The "broken-down pug" is Robert J. Randisi's private eye Miles Jacoby, while the "one-armed communist" is Michael Collins' P.I. Dan Fortune. Both detectives hung out at Bogie's (a real restaurant popular among mystery writers) in their respective series, and ran into each other there in Randisi's novel The Steinway Collection. *Razoni and Jackson were featured in another series of novels by Murphy that were published from 1973–1974.*

Summer
THE HEROIN CONNECTION

A character says, "This is not Africa and you're not with Mad Mike Quinlan and his Thunderbolts." The following comparison is made by Jon Skul: "There was only one other man as talented, and possibly more adept at quick-killing, that shadowy and legendary figure known as the Death Merchant."

First novel in the C.O.B.R.A. series by Joseph R. Rosenberger. The reference to Rosenberger's other series character Richard Joseph Camellion, aka the Death Merchant, brings C.O.B.R.A., a covert government agency operating outside the law proper, into the CU. Mad Mike Quinlan and his Thunderbolts are also from the Death Merchant novels.

CHOPPING MALL

Janitor Walter Paisley appears, as do gourmets Paul and Mary Bland.

1986 feature film directed by Jim Wynorski. Walter Paisley is played by Dick Miller, who first played the role in the film A Bucket of Blood *and went on to reprise it in a number of other films. Walter's apparent death here should not be taken at face value, just as his apparent death in* A Bucket of Blood *should not. Paul and Mary Bland are played by Paul Bartel and Mary Woronov, who originated the roles in Bartel's 1982 film* Eating Raoul.

Summer. P.I. Ryder Malone's first recorded case, *Jersey Tomatoes* by "J. W. Rider" (Shane Stevens).

September
GETTING UP WITH FLEAS
Devlin "Trace" Tracy is hired by his former employer at an insurance company to protect a freewheeling actor on the set of his latest film. Trace's office is above Bogie's Restaurant, which is frequented by mystery writers and other P.I.s; Trace says, "Now, Bogie's is getting out-of-town trade too. Only about a week before, there was this private detective from Boston who stopped in. He had a quiche cookbook under one arm and he ordered some kind of Yugoslavian beer and got drunk after two sips and then wanted to talk to the bartender about the meaning of courage." Detectives Ed Razoni and "Tough" Jackson investigate the hit-and-run murder of a man mistaken for the actor due to the star giving him his jacket.

Novel by Warren Murphy, 1987. The Boston private detective is Robert B. Parker's Spenser, though Trace is probably exaggerating his behavior somewhat. Murphy wrote a series of novels about Detectives Razoni and Jackson in 1973–1974. Trace first met the duo in Too Old a Cat. *Since* Too Old a Cat *and* Getting Up with Fleas *both state Trace is forty-years-old, they must take place in the same year.*

Autumn
A FRIGHT AT THE OPERA
The Ghostbusters attempt to rout Valkyrie ghosts haunting the Metropolitan Opera, encountering the Phantom of the Opera in the process.

Episode of The Real Ghostbusters *broadcast October 26, 1987. Erik, aka the Phantom of the Opera, is from Gaston Leroux's novel, which took place in 1881. Erik's longevity is doubtless due to his father being the Frankenstein Monster, as revealed in Jean-Marc and Randy Lofficier's story "His Father's Eyes."*

NIGHT OF THE CREEPS

Walt Paisley is the armorer for the police department of a small California town. A public restroom stall's wall has graffiti on it that reads, "Go Monster Squad!"

1986 film directed by Fred Dekker. Walt (or Walter) Paisley is played by Dick Miller, who originated the role in Roger Corman's film A Bucket of Blood, *and reprised it in a number of other films. The* Monster Squad *was Dekker's next film.*

1986

Early Summer
NO EXIT FROM BROOKLYN

Brooklyn private eye Nick Delvecchio attempts to recover a round objet d'art hocked by a mobster's stepdaughter which holds an unknown object of great value. Delvecchio asks Manhattan eye Miles Jacoby to follow his brother-in-law. Another P.I. both of them know, Henry Po, once recommended Jacoby enlist Delvecchio's help on a case that took him to Brooklyn. Delvecchio requires the help of a P.I. in Boston, so Jacoby gives him John Francis Cuddy's number.

The first Nick Delvecchio novel by Robert J. Randisi, 1987. Miles Jacoby and Henry Po are two other series P.I. characters created by Randisi, while John Francis Cuddy appears in novels by Jeremiah Healy. Delvecchio and Po both frequently appear or are mentioned in the Miles Jacoby books.

Summer. Los Angeles actor and private eye Saxon's first case, *An Infinite Number of Monkeys* by Les Roberts.

1987

April
A FISTFUL OF JUDEXES

Reporter Mattie Storin interviews Michel Kerjean, leader of the Judex Society, a security business dedicated to battling crime and corruption on the Channel Island of Jersey. The Society is named after a masked crime-fighter in Paris, before the War. Detective Sergeant Jim Bergerac of the *Bureau de Etrangers* intervenes when a group of Judexes at Diamante Lil's café become rowdy. An older detective named Teddy Verano helps him deal with the Judexes. On returning to the Bureau, Jim is greeted by his secretary, Peggy, who tells him Chief Inspector Barney Crozier wants to see him. Jim asks his former father-in-law Charlie Hungerford what the Law and Order committee plans to do about the Judex Society. The real Judex tells Jim Kerjean created the Society to discredit the vigilante, who he blames for the death of his grandfather, a criminal named Morales. Kerjean is backed by BlackSpear Holdings. Jim mentions his relationship with Susan.

Short story by Nigel Malcolm in Tales of the Shadowmen Volume 11: Force Majeure, *Jean-Marc and Randy Lofficier, eds., Black Coat Press, 2014. Mattie Storin is from Michael Dobbs' novel* House of Cards, *which features the appointment of a fictional Prime Minister of Great Britain, Francis Urquhart. Therefore, the Mattie Storin in Malcolm's story must be the CU counterpart of the character seen in Dobbs' book, which takes place in an AU. Michel Kerjean is the grandson of Robert Morales (née Kerjean) and his lover Diana Monti, who died in battle with the title character of Louis Feuillade's 1916 film serial* Judex. *Detective Sergeant Jim Bergerac, Diamante Lil, Peggy Masters, Chief Inspector Barney Crozier, Charlie Hungerford, and Susan Young are from the British police drama* Bergerac. *Teddy Verano is a private eye featured in books by Maurice Limat. BlackSpear Holdings is the name by which Paul Féval's criminal society the Black Coats is known in the 20th and 21st century, as seen in fiction by Jean-Marc Lofficier.*

Summer
HEARTLANDERS
Deadly Force investigates the Heartlanders militia group and finds their secret hideout. It is mentioned, "not even Goldfinger had the financial wherewithal to carve this hideaway out of solid rock." Later, three of the team are captured, and wait on the fourth member Calvin, to rescue them. One of the team says, "He's not James Bond, he's not even Julian Bond."

Deadly Force #3 by Mark Dixon, Jove Books, 1988. Given that the members of Deadly Force have all worked in the intelligence community, it makes sense they would have heard about Goldfinger's attempt on Fort Knox and James Bond's role in that. The fact James Bond is compared to Julian Bond, a real person, would confirm this. This crossover brings Deadly Force into the CU.

July
THE VANISHING VIRGIN
Nick Delvecchio is hired by the director of a play to investigate the disappearance of one of his actresses. Actor Jack Dwyer, who also sometimes works as a P.I., prevents the actress' murderer from killing Delvecchio as well.

Short story by Robert J. Randisi in An Eye for Justice: The Third Private Eye Writers of America Anthology, *Robert J. Randisi, ed., The Mysterious Press, 1988; reprinted in* Delvecchio's Brooklyn, *Five Star, 2001. Nick Delvecchio is already in the CU. This story brings in Ed Gorman's actor and P.I. Jack Dwyer.*

August
FULL CLEVELAND
Cleveland private investigator Milan Jacovich asks a fellow P.I. in Los Angeles named Saxon to look into the personal histories of some of the people involved in the case he's working on.

The second Milan Jacovich novel by Les Roberts. Saxon, the protagonist of another series of P.I. novels by Roberts, is in the CU through Robert J. Randisi's Miles Jacoby novel Stand-Up, *and this crossover brings in Jacovich.*

Autumn. Events of "Cabal" by Clive Barker, later adapted as the feature film *Nightbreed.*

Autumn
HELLRAISER/NIGHTBREED: JIHAD

In the upheaval following the destruction of the secret city of Midian, the Cenobites, the demons of order, launch a war against their enemies, the chaotic Nightbreed. The *Necronomicon* appears, and the Mad Arab, Cthulhu, and Shub-Niggurath are mentioned.

Two-issue miniseries by D. G. Chichester and Paul Johnson, Epic Comics, 1991, connecting the Hellraiser *series to the* Nightbreed. *The* Necronomicon, *the Mad Arab, Cthulhu, and Shub-Niggurath are, of course, all staples of the Cthulhu Mythos.*

THE DEAD OF BROOKLYN
Nick Delvecchio attempts to clear his priest brother of a murder charge, while simultaneously seeking the cause of an abusive husband's anger. Delvecchio asks his fellow P.I. Miles Jacoby to follow the husband. Later, he puts Sal Carlucci on the same job. Delvecchio hires Jacoby's friend Heck Delgado to defend his brother. Delvecchio considers turning the wife-beater case over to Jacoby, Carlucci, or Henry Po.

Novel by Robert J. Randisi, 1991. Miles Jacoby and Henry Po each appear in their own series of detective tales by Randisi. Lawyer Heck Delgado is a supporting character in the Jacoby books. Sal Carlucci is from Ed Gorman's novel The Night Remembers. *The plot of this novel was partially adapted from the short stories "Double Edge" (*Deadly Doings, *Bill Pronzini* *and Martin H. Greenberg, eds., Ivy Books, 1989) and "Turnabout" (*Deadly Allies: Private Eye Writers of America and Sisters in Crime Collaborative Anthology, *Robert J. Randisi and Marilyn Wallace, eds., Doubleday, 1992).*

December 24. Events of the movie *Die Hard.* The sequels include *Die Hard 2, Die Hard with a Vengeance, Live Free or Die Hard,* and *A Good Day to Die Hard.*

1988

Winter
THE BIRTHING OF THAT WHICH WAS
Tourists traveling up the Amazon River book a trip on a riverboat called the *Rita.*
Nightbreed #11 *by D. G. Chichester and Mark A. Nelson, Epic Comics, September 1991. The* Rita *is from the* Creature from the Black Lagoon *films.*

THE NEW YORK TIMES BESTSELLER!
SPENSER SCORES AGAIN!
ROBERT B. PARKER
"The best Spenser mystery novel in many a year!
—*New York Times*
PLAYMATES

February–Late March, September
PLAYMATES
Spenser visits Taft University, located in Walford, Massachusetts, to investigate a basketball star shaving points. Spenser's girlfriend Dr. Susan Silverman teaches at Taft.

Novel by Robert B. Parker. Taft University first appeared in Parker's non-series novel Love and Glory, *and would be mentioned in several Spenser novels following this one. The university is mentioned in other books by Parker: the Sunny Randall novels* Blue Screen *and* Spare Change; *the Jesse Stone novels* High Profile *and* Stranger in Paradise; *and the non-series novel* The Boxer and the Spy.

Early March–May 1
THE GRYPHON KING
Among the items donated to the University of Georgia's Rare Book Library by Professor Charles Bowman-Smith are Judge Keith Hilary Pursuivant's *Vampyricon* and *The Unknown That Terrifies.*
The reference to tomes written by Manly Wade Wellman's occult detective Judge Keith Hilary Pursuivant brings this novel by Tom Deitz into the CU. Some of the characters from this book go on to appear in the later volumes of Deitz' David Sullivan series, bringing those books in as well.

Spring
VIDEO NASTIES
Ghostbusters Egon Spengler and Peter Venkman discuss the inclusion of a flux capacitor in the Ecto-3, which may be of use "if Godzilla came to call."

The Real Ghostbusters #6 by James Van Hise, John Tobias, and Brian Thomas, NOW Comics, February 1989. Flux capacitors are originally from Back to the Future, thus bringing that film and its sequels into the CU, though clearly all the timeline tampering in the CU has averted that series' version of the year 2015. Although the massive destruction seen in the Godzilla films does not fit in with Crossover Universe continuity, Emmanuel Gorlier's story "Twilight" and Nick Pollotta's novel Doomsday Exam establish Godzilla does have a Crossover Universe counterpart, though he appears to have spent most of his existence in captivity.

TOAD ISLAND
The Ghostbusters investigate disappearances at the Toad Island theme park, and discover that Nogad has been abducting the customers in order to mate them with his ancestral people, the Deep Ones.

The Real Ghostbusters #8 by James Van Hise, John Tobias, and Rich Rankin, NOW Comics, April 1989. This story provides another link between the Ghostbusters and the works of H. P. Lovecraft; specifically, "The Shadow over Innsmouth." "Nogad" is Dagon spelled backwards.

Summer
RETURN OF THE KING
The Nightbreed battle the monstrous Rawhead Rex.

Nightbreed #13–16 by Clive Barker, D. G. Chichester, Mark Texeira, Dan Lawlis, and Ricardo Villagran, Epic Comics, January–June 1992. Rawhead Rex is from the eponymous story by Clive Barker.

December 24
DIE HARD 2
General Ramon Esperanza is the dictator of the Central American country of Val Verde.

1990 feature film. Val Verde first appeared in the movie Commando. It has also appeared on the television series Supercarrier and Adventure, Inc., as well as the comic book Sheena. Steven E. de Souza wrote all of the works in question. It also appears in the movie Jurassic Attack. The novelization of the film Predator places its events in Val Verde, although the movie Predators places them in Guatemala. Since the Die Hard movies and de Souza's version of Sheena are in the CU, so are Val Verde's other appearances.

Winter

CHILDREN OF THE BEAST

Jack Russell (who becomes a werewolf by night) utilizes a copy of Lemarchand's Mourning Scrolls to summon the spirit of his late father, hoping to learn a way to cure himself of lycanthropy.

Story by Len Kaminski, Jim Fry, and Brad Joyce in Marvel Comics Presents *#54–59, Marvel Comics, July–September 1990. Jack Russell, who originally starred in the Marvel Comics series* Werewolf by Night, *is already in the CU. Lemarchand is a reference to toy maker Philip Lemarchand, the creator of the Lament Configuration in the* Hellraiser *movie series, which has also been connected to the CU.*

THE CROWN JEWEL CAPER

The Black Cat steals an alleged treasure map leading to the Crown Jewels of France for antiquarian Hervé Marat, who calls the Kingpin to tell him the Cat is about to fall into a police trap. However, the female thief manages to escape the gendarmes. Inspector Gorlier is nevertheless glad they have recovered the fake map they planted, since it can be used as evidence, and they have outwitted the Cat. One of the gendarmes serving under Gorlier, Henri Poirot, is pleased to have an entertaining story to tell his great-uncle.

Story by Dwight Zimmerman, Mike Harris, and Joe Rubinstein in Marvel Comics Presents *#57, August 1990. Henri's great-uncle is, of course, Hercule Poirot. Julian Symons has placed Hercule's birth in 1864, which would make him 125-years-old at the time of this story; however, Rick Lai's essay "Partners in Crime: Fu Manchu and Carl Peterson"* (Rick Lai's Secret Histories: Criminal Masterminds, *Altus Press, 2009) provides a possible explanation for the Belgian sleuth's longevity. Both the Black Cat and the Kingpin have independent links bringing them into the CU.*

Spring
DOCTOR OMEGA AND THE PRODUCERS

Doctor Omega and his companion Cassandra Troy arrive in California in the 1980s. Suddenly, what appears to be an Electroman appears. However, he is actually an actor, who takes them to meet the film's producer, Max Bialystock. One of Bialystock's previous films was *Springtime for Hitler*. They run into Captain Langelot of the Service National d'Information Fonctionelle (SNIF). When Langelot tells Doctor Omega what they're facing is worse than the previous threats they faced together, Omega asks if it is vampires, Electromen, or Mr. T. Langelot reveals he has been selected as a consultant for a film based on his and the Doctor's encounter with the Electromen. A lawyer for the Bureau International de Documentation Industrielle, or BIDI, objects to the film's portrayal of the organization and its onetime leader, Madame Schasch.

Short story by Jean-Marc and Randy Lofficier in Doctor Omega and the Shadowmen*, Jean-Marc and Randy Lofficier, eds., Black Coat Press, 2011; reprinted in French in* Les Compagnons de l'Ombre (Tome 9)*, Jean-Marc and Randy Lofficier, eds., Rivière Blanche, 2012. Doctor Omega is from the novel of the same name by Arnould Galopin. Cassandra Troy is the title character of a comic story by the Lofficiers that appeared in* Mustang #310*. The Electromen are from* La Conspiration des Milliardaires *(The Billionaires' Conspiracy) by Gustave Le Rouge. Max Bialystock is from Mel Brooks' 1968 film* The Producers*. Max must have switched from producing musicals to films after serving his prison sentence, including a film version of his most successful show, Franz Liebkind's* Springtime for Hitler*. Langelot, SNIF, Mr. T, BIDI, and Madame Schasch are from the young adult spy novels by "Lieutenant X" (Vladimir Volkoff).*

GHOST IN THE MACHINE

When a New York skyscraper becomes intangible, Remo Williams and Chiun are sent to investigate. A self-proclaimed witch tries to use spells from the *Necronomicon*, and mentions several Lovecraftian deities.

The Destroyer *#90 by Will Murray.*

Summer
RADIATION WIPEOUT

Matt Hawke, the Avenger, makes reference to meeting Mark Hardin, the Penetrator.

The Avenger *#5 by Chet Cunningham, Chet Book Publishers, 2012. The fifth book in Cunningham's Avenger series was published in 2012, and updated the character so Hawke served in Afghanistan rather than Vietnam. However, it can be assumed the novel's events actually take place in the 1980s, as did its predecessors.*

SEPARATE CASES

Investigating the death of his fellow P.I. Andy McWilliams at Andy's wife Caroline's request, Miles Jacoby reads his files, and finds that Andy referred several cases to other detectives, including Jacoby's friend Henry Po, who usually investigates cases involving thoroughbred horse racing, and a man named Malone, who took a case in New Jersey. After Andy's death, Caroline took over his agency, and referred another case to a man Jacoby knows in Brooklyn, Nick Delvecchio. Jacoby discusses what to do with a murdered friend's saloon with another friend, Sal Carlucci, an ex-cop P.I. who runs a saloon in Greenpoint, Brooklyn. Jacoby also refers to a Boston P.I. who tends to push and prod until the guilty party comes after him rather than try to find some definitive evidence.

Novel by Robert J. Randisi, 1990. Henry Po and Nick Delvecchio are each the subject of other detective series by Randisi. The New Jersey P.I. named Malone is Ryder Malone, who appears in the novels Jersey Tomatoes *and* Hot Tickets, *both written by Shane Stevens under the pen name J. W. Rider. Sal Carlucci first appeared in Ed Gorman's novel* The Night Remembers. *The main character of* The Night Remembers, *apartment house manager and sometimes P.I. Jack Walsh, first appeared in Gorman's short story "Friends." Carlucci is also one of the protagonists of* The Black Moon, *a round robin novel whose authors include Gorman and Randisi, in which Sal at one point calls Jacoby seeking a recommendation for a detective in Lake Superior, Michigan. The Boston P.I. is Robert B. Parker's Spenser. This novel supposedly takes place a year after the Jacoby novel* Full Contact, *which has been dated to 1983. However,* Jersey Tomatoes *came out in 1986, and therefore I have instead placed* Separate Cases *in 1989.*

September 16–23
CRIME OF THE ARTS

The Voice teams up with a woman named Dana to take down the militia to which the man who disfigured her belonged. The hero uses his father's gas gun, and quotes the First Master Detective, "Watson, you see, but you do not observe." The Voice uses a meditative technique one of his honorary uncles taught him rather than go to sleep. The Voice compares a female scientist working with Dana's victimizer to the original Victor Frankenstein. The woman's father worked at a secret facility that reprogrammed people located near a town in upstate New York. The Voice calls his friend Curt Van Loan of Havens International Media. The Voice uses his Uncle Kent's mental trick to fall asleep nearly instantly, and teaches Dana his Uncle Jethro's technique for reducing pain without drugs. The Voice remembers seeing a picture of the militia's leader in the *New York Clarion*. The Voice thinks Matt Helm would have taken a practice shot at a tree, but he can't alert whoever is approaching. Dana compares the militia's headquarters to Fu Manchu's lair, but the Voice replies "If old Fu owned this place, we'd probably be dead by now."

Story by Erwin K. Roberts in Casebook of the Voice, *Modern Knights Press, 2014. The Voice's father is the pulp hero Secret Agent X, who was created by Paul Chadwick under the pen name "Brant House." The First Master Detective is Sherlock Holmes. The Voice's honorary uncle who taught him the meditative technique is Michael Traile, "the Man who Could Not Sleep," the archenemy of Donald E. Keyhoe's pulp villain Dr. Yen Sin. The reference to "the original Victor Frankenstein" is consistent with numerous books, comics, and movies in which relatives and descendants of Mary Shelley's Victor Frankenstein engage in experiments of their own. The secret facility near upstate New York is Doc's Crime College. Curt Van Loan is the son of Richard Curtis Van Loan, aka the Phantom Detective, who appeared in a titular pulp magazine by several authors using the pseudonym "Robert Wallace." Van Loan's girlfriend in the original pulp stories, Muriel Havens, is Curt's mother; her father, Frank Havens, was the publisher of the* New York Clarion *newspaper. Uncle Kent is the vigilante who stuck to the shadows, while Uncle Jethro is Kendell Crossen's pulp hero* The Green Lama, *whose real name was Jethro Dumont. The references to Matt Helm and Fu Manchu could be interpreted as allusions to fictional characters, but given the Voice's familiarity with a number of other heroes and villains, I am treating them as valid crossovers.*

October
HARD LOOK

Miles Jacoby travels to Tampa, Florida to search for a wealthy man's wife. Jacoby refers a case to Nick Delvecchio in Brooklyn while he's gone. A Boston P.I. who used to be a professional fighter like Jacoby is mentioned. Fred Carver puts Jacoby in touch with Lt. Alfonso DeSoto.

Novel by Robert J. Randisi, 1993. Nick Delvecchio is the subject of another series of detective novels and stories by Randisi. The professional fighter turned Boston P.I. is Robert B. Parker's Spenser. Florida-based private eye Fred Carver appears in a series of novels by John Lutz. Lt. DeSoto is Carver's best friend. This novel takes place a few months after the previous book in the series, Separate Cases. *Although the chronological*

references in the Jacoby books are often at odds with the publication dates of the debuts of the P.I.s referenced by Randisi, fortunately Delvecchio, Spenser, and Carver all debuted prior to 1989, and therefore Hard Look *does not need to be placed later chronologically than Jacoby indicated.*

Autumn
LORD OF THE LAND

Dr. Sam Cooper of the University of Nebraska travels to Tennessee to investigate legends of a "soul-sucker," and winds up face-to-face with the monster himself. Houdini's account of his imprisonment in the Pyramids is mentioned.

Short story by Gene Wolfe in Lovecraft's Legacy, *Robert E. Weinberg and Martin H. Greenberg, eds., Tor, 1990. Houdini's imprisonment in the Pyramids is a reference to H. P. Lovecraft's story "Imprisoned with the Pharaohs," thus bringing Wolfe's stories about Dr. Sam Cooper into the CU.*

1990

Winter
ROMAN HOLIDAY

Doc Brown and Marty McFly travel to Rome in 36 A.D. to return architectural plans Doc has borrowed. While there, they are helped out of a jam by a slave named Judah Ben-Hur.

Episode of the animated Back to the Future *television series broadcast October 5, 1991. The* Back to the Future *film series is in the CU through several crossovers. This episode brings in the events of Lew Wallace's novel* Ben-Hur: A Tale of the Christ.

Spring
BIGFOOT

After Tarzan saves his friend Prof. Philander from a group of belligerent men, Jane warns the professor someday he will go too far and Tarzan will not be around to protect him. The professor jokes in that case he will have to use his pugilistic skills as well as his mastery of *baritsu*.

Sunday Tarzan strip by Don Kraar and Gray Morrow, February 10, 1991. In "The Adventure of the Empty House," Sherlock Holmes told Dr. Watson he disabled Professor Moriarty at Reichenbach Falls by using 'baritsu, the Japanese system of wrestling." Professor Philander is from the Tarzan novels. Here, he is portrayed as an ornithologist. However, in Burroughs' novels he was the secretary to Professor Porter and an ex-history professor. Additionally, Farmer places the death of Burroughs' Philander in March of 1927. Most likely, the Philander seen in this story is a descendant of Burroughs' character.

RICOCHET

Newscaster Gail Wallens does a report on discredited Assistant District Attorney Nick Styles.

1991 feature film. Gail Wallens first appeared in the movie Die Hard, *which is already in the CU. Mary Ellen Trainor played Gail in both films, which were also cowritten by Steven E. de Souza and co-produced by Joel Silver.*

THE LAST SON OF THOR

The Voice encounters the remnants of the German nationalist group known as the Sons of Thor. The hero remembers his Uncle Dick, the father of his best friend Curt Van Loan, telling them about the Sons, and recommending the young boy ask his big Uncle Jim and Uncle Tony about them. Information about the Sons that came from the Ashton-Kirk estate was recently stolen from the locked archives of a local university.

This short story by Erwin K. Roberts, found in the book Plutonium Nightmare: A Novel of the Voice, *Modern Knights Press, 2013, is a sequel to Roberts' two-part novella "The Sons of Thor," which took place in 1939. The Voice is meant to be the son of Secret Agent X, the pulp hero created by "Brant House" (Paul Chadwick). His Uncle Dick is Richard Curtis Van Loan, aka the Phantom Detective, who appeared in his own pulp magazine. The Voice's Big Uncle Jim is Jim Anthony, who appeared in the pulp Super Detective. Uncle Tony is Tony Quinn, alias the Black Bat, who appeared in the magazine* Black Book Detective. *Ashton-Kirk was a detective created by John McIntyre for* The Popular Magazine; *the stories were collected in four books.*

Summer
THE THEFT OF LEOPOLD'S BADGE

Thief for hire Nick Velvet crosses paths with Captain Jules Leopold, head of the Violent Crimes Squad of the police force of an unidentified city in Connecticut.

Short story by Edward D. Hoch in Ellery Queen's Mystery Magazine, March 1991. This crossover brings together Hoch's series characters Velvet and Leopold. Since Nick Velvet is in the CU via a connection to Sherlock Holmes, so is Captain Leopold.

LAST CALL

A poem by William Ashbless is quoted, and the Yoyodyne Company is mentioned.

Novel by Tim Powers, the first chapter of the Fault Lines trilogy, followed by Expiration Date and Earthquake Weather. The poet William Ashbless was co-created by Powers and James P. Blaylock, and recurs throughout both authors' fiction. References to airplanes and blue jeans in the poem quoted in Last Call suggest this Ashbless is the 20th century California Cahuenga poet seen in Blaylock's The Digging Leviathan, but it is unknown whether he is the long-lived 18th–19th century Ashbless or a descendant. Yoyodyne is from Thomas Pynchon's novels V. and The Crying of Lot 49, as well as the film The Adventures of Buckaroo Banzai Across the Eighth Dimension.

OUT OF THE BLACKNESS

Baltimore police detective Bianca Jones investigates a series of bizarre rapes. A similar case happened recently in Arkham, Massachusetts. Crime Lab tech Joe Russo asked a Detective Armitage about the Arkham case. Bianca receives a fax from Arkham suggesting she check with London and call China Alley for possible leads. She goes to meet an informant at his bookshop, which contains copies of *Les Cultes des Ghoules*, *Las Reglas de Ruina*, *The Undead* by John Seward, M.D.; Holmes' *The Whole Art of Detection* and *Practical Handbook of Bee Culture*, and *The Dynamics of an Asteroid*. The bookseller, Morgan, tells Bianca the killings are related to a cult worshipping Shub-Niggurath, and mentions Tsathoggua.

Short story by John L. French in Here There Be Monsters, *Dark Quest, 2010. Arkham and Shub-Niggurath are from the Cthulhu Mythos stories of H. P. Lovecraft. Detective Armitage is doubtless a relative of Professor Henry Armitage from Lovecraft's "The Dunwich Horror." London is C. J. Henderson's private investigator Teddy London. The investigator in China Alley is Anton Zarnak, who was created by Lin Carter, and has appeared in stories by several other authors as well. Since Zarnak left our dimension during the 1998 events of Henderson's "The Door," "Out of the Darkness" must take place before that story.* Les Cultes des Ghoules *is from Robert Bloch's contributions to the Cthulhu Mythos.* Las Reglas de Ruina *is from Joseph S. Pulver Sr.'s Cthulhu Mythos novel* Nightmare's Disciple. *John Seward is from Bram Stoker's* Dracula; *another copy of his book* The Undead *appears in French's Anton Zarnak story "The Best Solution." Sherlock Holmes'* The Whole Art of Detection *was alluded to in Doyle's "The Adventure of the Abbey Grange," while his* Practical Handbook of Bee Culture *appeared in "His Last Bow." The Dynamics of an Asteroid *was penned by Holmes' greatest foe, Professor James Moriarty, as mentioned in* The Valley of Fear. *Tsathoggua appears in Cthulhu Mythos stories by Clark Ashton Smith. French and Patrick Thomas' book* Rites of Passage *establishes Bianca's first encounter with the supernatural happened shortly before Thomas' character Agent Karver joined the Department of Mystic Affairs. Thomas and C. J. Henderson's story "Family Ties" features Karver as an agent of the Department, as well as Zachery Goward, who died in Henderson's 1994 novel* All Things Under the Moon. *Therefore, Karver joined the DMA sometime before 1994, and "Out of the Blackness" occurred around the same time.*

A WORLD INSIDE

Bianca Jones, now working part time at Morgan's bookstore, is tasked by him to travel to Pennsylvania and retrieve the *Ravings of El-Hazred*, a collection compiled by Abd el-Hazred of incantations and rituals even more horrible than those contained in the *Necronomicon*. A group of occult enthusiasts utilizing the library of the *Ravings'* previous owner for a sacrifice discuss whether or not to use the *Book of Eibon* or Juntz' text before settling on the *Ravings*.

Short story by John L. French in Here There Be Monsters, *Dark Quest, 2010. Abd el-Hazred (or Abdul Alhazred) is the author of the* Necronomicon *in H. P. Lovecraft's Cthulhu Mythos stories. The* Book of Eibon *is a Mythos tome created by Clark Ashton Smith, while Friedrich von Junzt is the author of* Unaussprechlichen Kulten *in Mythos stories by Robert E. Howard. This story takes place a week after "Out of the Blackness."*

WITCH HILL

Sara Latimer inherits her great-aunt and namesake's house on Witch Hill Road in Arkham, Massachusetts, and discovers she is the reincarnation of her relative, and the Azathoth-worshipping Church of the Antique Rite to which the elder Sara belonged has plans for her. The younger Sara's friend Dr. Colin MacLaran appears, and Innsmouth, Miskatonic University, Cthulhu, the Whateleys, the Marshes, Robert Blake, and the Elder Gods are mentioned.

This novel by Marion Zimmer Bradley takes place in the CU via strong ties to the Cthulhu Mythos. Rick Lai writes, "Marion Zimmer Bradley created two occult detectives, Colin MacLaran and Truth Jourdemayne, whose adventures are interconnected. MacLaran is the investigator in Dark Satanic, The Inheritor, *and* Witch Hill. *Then MacLaren disappears from center stage and is only mentioned in the next three novels featuring Truth Jourdemayne,* Ghostlight, Witchlight, *and* Gravelight. *The last novel in the series,* Heartlight, *has MacLaran as the primary character and features appearances by Truth and characters from the previous six novels.* Heartlight *also retells the events of* Dark Satanic, The Inheritor, *and* Witch Hill *from a different perspective.* Heartlight *also reveals that MacLaran is the reincarnation of a character from Bradley's* The Fall of Atlantis *(which was originally published as two novels,* Web of Light *and* Web of Darkness*). The chronology of the series doesn't become clear unless you read* Heartlight. Witch Hill *had a reference that suggested its events transpire in 1971, but* Heartlight *puts the events of that novel in 1990.*

"In Witch Hill, *Lovecraft is mentioned as a real person co-existent with his creations, but MacLaran claims that Lovecraft invented the* Necronomicon. *Furthermore, MacLaran suggested the account of Robert Blake's death in 'The Haunter of the Dark' was distorted. In Lovecraft's tale, Blake died in his lodgings in Providence, Rhode Island, after visiting a church there. MacLaran asserted that Blake died in a church in Arkham. These inconsistencies between Lovecraft and Bradley can be reconciled by claiming that MacLaran (or Bradley) was spreading disinformation to mislead evil cultists. In* Gravelight, *it is revealed that the Church of the Antique Rite based its rituals on Comte d'Erlette's* Les Cultes des Goules *(The Cults of the Ghouls). This book was created by Robert Bloch in his Mythos stories,*

but he always called it Cultes des Goules. *Bloch never gave a history of the book, but Bradley supplied a background for the fictional tome (e.g. an English translation was published in London in 1816). The Mythos references from* Witch Hill *and* Gravelight *are reiterated in* Heartlight." *It is also worth noting that several characters in Bradley's Avalon series are implied to be the reincarnations of characters from* The Fall of Atlantis.

June
TANGLED JUNE
Dave Garrett, a disbarred lawyer turned private investigator in Philadelphia, contacts a fellow P.I. named Saxon to do some background work on a case.

Novel by Neil Albert. Les Roberts' actor and private eye Saxon is in the CU through Robert Randisi's Miles Jacoby novel Stand-Up. *This crossover brings in Dave Garrett. The first Garrett novel,* The January Corpse, *came out in 1991. The novels that followed were* February Trouble *(1992),* Burning March *(1994),* Cruel April *(1995),* Appointment in May *(1996), and* Tangled June *(1997). All of the novels take place in the month mentioned in their respective titles, and also in the same year.*

October 31
SATANIC, VERSUS
Occult detective Diana Tregarde teams up with Robert Harrison, a Bureau 13 agent.

Short story by Mercedes Lackey in Werehunter, Baen Books, 1999. *Bureau 13 is already in the Crossover Universe, and this tale brings in Lackey's character Diana Tregarde, who is also mentioned in* Black Magic Woman, *the first book in Justin Gustainis' Morris and Chastain Supernatural Investigations series.*

1991

Early Winter
NOT JUST A JOB
A man Freddy Krueger has chosen as his new human protégé gets a book from the Springwood library that features a chapter on Krueger, as well as "the infamous John Wayne Gacy, Ted Bundy, and Henry Lee Lucas, as well as less well-known deviants such as Michael Myers, Jason Voorhees, and the Sawyer family of Texas."

Short story by Nancy A. Collins in Nightmares on Elm Street: Freddy Krueger's Seven Sweetest Dreams, *Martin H. Greenberg, ed., St. Martin's*

Press, 1991. Gacy, Bundy, and Lucas are all historical serial killers. Michael Myers is from the Halloween *series of movies, Voorhees is from the* Friday the 13th *films, and the Sawyer family is from the* Texas Chainsaw Massacre *series of films, furthering the connection between these series.*

Spring. Reno-based female private eye Freddie O'Neal's first case, *Lay it on the Line* by "Catharine Dain" (Judith Garwood).

Spring
CAVEAT EMPTOR

The mercenary Terror, whose body is composed of parts from various corpses he has incorporated into himself, visits an occult expert named Rekrab whose collection includes a lacquered puzzle box.

Terror, Inc. #1 by D. G. Chichester and Jorge Zaffino, Marvel Comics, July 2002. The puzzle box is a Lament Configuration from the Hellraiser *film series, based on Clive Barker's story "The Hellbound Heart." "Rekrab" is Barker spelled backwards. Terror was originally known as Shreck, a character in Marvel's Shadowline imprint, which took place in an alternate reality to the mainstream Marvel Universe. He later immigrated to the reality where most of Marvel's heroes operate, encountering Wolverine and other heroes. Doubtless the Terror of the CU has a substantially different history.*

Summer
TERRIBLE ANTICIPATION

Lai Wan battles Bugg-Shoggog in the Dreamlands. Professor Zackery Goward, Kaman-Thah, and Nasht appear, and Theodore London, Dr. Henry Armitage, Kuranes, Celephaïs, de Marigny, Randolph Carter, Nyarlathotep, the Great Ones, Rice and Morgan are mentioned.

Short story by C. J. Henderson in Lai Wan: The Dreamwalker, *Moonstone Books, 2013. Psychometrist Lai Wan first appeared in Henderson's series of novels about P.I. Teddy London before being featured in stories of her own. Professor Goward is also from the Teddy London novels; since Goward died in the 1994 novel* All Things Under the Moon, *this story must take* place before it. Bugg-Shoggog, Dr. Henry Armitage, Professor Warren Rice, and Professor Francis Morgan are from H. P. Lovecraft's "The Dunwich Horror." The Dreamlands, Kaman-Thah, Nasht, Kuranes, Celephaïs, Étienne-Laurent de Marigny, and Randolph Carter are from Lovecraft's series of stories dubbed the Dream Cycle. Nyarlathotep and the Great Old Ones are from Lovecraft's Cthulhu Mythos.

RITES OF PASSAGE

Bianca Jones' captain in the Baltimore Police Department sends her to the Department of Mystic Affairs' academy to receive further training in battling supernatural menaces. While there, she begins a rivalry with a fellow cadet named Karver, who is secretly a former demonically possessed serial killer called the Carver Bianca brought to justice early in her career.

Novel by John L. French and Patrick Thomas, Padwolf Publishing, 2013. This story is a crossover between French's monster-fighting cop Bianca Jones and Agent Karver of the DMA, who first appeared in Thomas' Murphy's Lore series before spinning off into tales of his own. Since Bianca Jones is in the CU, so are Agent Karver and the other characters in the Murphy's Lore books and their various spin-offs. Contemporary references in the book must be ignored; Karver is active as an agent of the DMA in Thomas and C. J. Henderson's story "Family Ties," which must take place before 1994 due to the appearance of Professor Zachery Goward, who died in Henderson's novel All Things Under the Moon, *published in that year.*

1992

Winter
STUDS

Detective Constables Bob Louis and Dave Briggs are sent to the island of Jersey to work with Jim Bergerac on a case.

Episode of the television series The Detectives *broadcast February 24, 1993. Jim Bergerac, from the television series* Bergerac, *is in the CU through Nigel Malcolm's story "A Fistful of Judexes." Therefore, this crossover brings in the comedic misadventures of Louis and Briggs.*

STRANGERS IN PARADISE

Superintendent Cottam sends Detective Constables Louis and Briggs to the Paradise Club to investigate possible gang warfare. There, they encounter Danny Kane and Polish Joe.

Episode of The Detectives *broadcast March 3, 1993. This crossover brings in the television series* The Paradise Club.

FAMILY TIES (aka THE TIES THAT BIND)

Agent Karver and his partner Mandi Cobb of the Department of Mystic Affairs are transported to Newark by Terrorbelle, whose last motorcycle was wrecked by Murphy, the bartender at Bulfinche's Pub. Karver and Mandi recruit Lai Wan to aid in the search for Mandi's kidnapped nephew. Professor Zachery Goward drives the trio to the kidnapper's home, and later to the abandoned store where Mandi's nephew is being held.

Short story by Patrick Thomas and C. J. Henderson, appearing as "Family Ties" in Lai Wan: Tales of the Dreamwalker, *Marietta Publishing, 2007; reprinted as "The Ties That Bind" in* Dead to Rites: The DMA Casefiles of Agent Karver, *Padwolf Publishing, 2010. The Department of Mystic Affairs and Terrorbelle originally appeared in Thomas' Murphy's Lore books, and have appeared in spin-off books of their own. Lai Wan is a character from Henderson's Teddy London books, and has spun off into her own series of stories. Professor Zachery Goward died in the London novel* All Things Under the Moon, *which was published in 1994. Therefore, this story must take place before that book.*

Autumn
ALL THINGS UNDER THE MOON

Teddy London's battle with a millennia-old werewolf leads him to the Tibetan monastery of A'alshirie.

Novel by "Robert Morgan" (C. J. Henderson), Berkley, 1994. Several of Henderson's stories featuring Lin Carter's occult detective Anton Zarnak refer to Zarnak having studied under the masters of A'alshirie. This novel, the fourth in the Teddy London series, takes place a year after the first book, The Things That Are Not There, *which was released in 1992.*

1993

Winter
MEXICO IS FOREVER

Washington, D.C.-based P.I. Leo Haggerty asks another firm, Dan Kearny and Associates, to do some legwork in an inheritance case.

Novel by Leo Haggerty, edited by Benjamin M. Schutz, 1994. Dan Kearny and Associates (or DKA for short) is featured in a series of detective novels by Joe Gores. Since DKA is in the CU, so is Leo Haggerty.

THE LAND OF THE REFLECTED ONES

An occultist named Emerson gets more than he bargained for after purchasing an occult tome known as the *Aegrisomnia.* Other books in his collection include the *Necronomicon, Unaussprechlichen Kulten, De Vermis Mysteriis, Cultes des Goules,* Gantley's *Hydrophinnae,* Carson's *The Black God of Madness,* the *Book of Eibon,* the *Pnakotic Manuscripts,* the *Cthaat Aquadingen,* and the full *Revelations of Glaaki.*

Short story by Nancy A. Collins found in the collection Eternal Lovecraft, *Jim Turner, ed., Golden Gryphon Press, 1998. The* Aegrisomnia *is from Collins' stories of the monster hunting vampire Sonja Blue. The presence of the various Cthulhu Mythos tomes in this story establishes a link between the Sonja Blue stories and the Mythos, and so the CU.*

March
STRANGE BEDFELLOWS

L.A.P.D. Homicide Detective Charlotte Justice sees her superior, Lieutenant Stobaugh, speaking to Harry Bosch, and thinks he couldn't be trying to get Bosch transferred back to Robbery-Homicide. She wonders if Stobaugh intends to replace her with Bosch.

2006 novel by Charlotte Justice, edited by Paula L. Woods. The cameo by Michael Connelly's cop Harry Bosch brings Charlotte Justice into the CU. Bosch was reinstated to Robbery-Homicide in the 2005 novel The Closers.

Spring
WHO KILLED NICK HAZARD?

When a private investigator with a lot of enemies among his peers is murdered at a convention, Chief Amos Burke and his son Peter strive to solve the case. One of the other P.I.s at the convention is Chief Burke's old acquaintance, Honey West.

Episode of the 1994–1995 revival of Burke's Law *broadcast January 21, 1994. Anne Francis reprised the role of G. G. Fickling's sleuth Honey West, which she had previously played in "Who Killed the Jackpot?" an episode of the original* Burke's Law, *followed by the* Honey West *television series. Honey's surname is given as "Best" in this episode, but this is only a pseudonym (and a rather thin one at that) used for legal reasons. She must have returned to the P.I. business at some point after serving as a C.I.A. agent in the novels* Honey on Her Tail *and* Stiff as a Broad.

PUMPKINHEAD II: BLOOD WINGS

A witch possesses a copy of the *Necronomicon Ex Mortis.*

1994 feature film. The appearance of the Necronomicon Ex Mortis *from the* Evil Dead *series brings the Pumpkinhead film series into the CU.*

April
STAND-UP

Miles Jacoby investigates two cases simultaneously: the disappearance of a stand-up comic's floppy disk containing all his material, and the exact nature of a friend's involvement in a murder. Jacoby phones an actor and P.I. in Los Angeles named Saxon for information on comedians. He also asks Nick Delvecchio to look into a lawyer in Brooklyn connected to his friend's case. Jacoby has been to the race track before, once with Henry Po and once with Delvecchio. Seeking a P.I. in Vegas who knows someone who works security at the casino where the comedian last appeared, Jacoby can only find a woman in Reno named Freddie O'Neal, who knows somebody who knows somebody that works there.

The sixth and final Miles Jacoby novel by Robert J. Randisi, 1994. Saxon is a P.I. appearing in novels by Les Roberts. Nick Delvecchio is a Brooklyn P.I. whose cases have been chronicled by Randisi in three novels and nine short stories. Henry Po, an investigator for the New York Racing Commission, appears in Randisi's novel The Disappearance of Penny, *as well as a series of short stories. Freddie O'Neal appears in a series of novels by "Catharine Dain," a pseudonym for Judith Garwood. Supposedly, this novel takes place only a few months after the Jacoby novel before it,* Hard Look, *which I have placed in October 1989. However, Saxon refers to a recent case of his involving comedians, a reference to Roberts' 1994 novel* The Lemon Chicken Jones. *Additionally, the first Freddie O'Neal novel was published in 1992. Therefore, I have placed* Stand-Up *in April 1993, a year before it was published, rather than April 1990.*

Summer
A VOICE FOR JUSTICE

A gangster called Mister M suspects a hacker who is obtaining information on his men's crimes before they happen is a "Burbank" (communications man) for a vigilante such as the Voice.

Screenplay by Erwin K. Roberts in Casebook of the Voice, *Modern Knights Press, 2014. The term "Burbank" is derived from the name of one of the agents of the shadowy pulp hero whose tales were told by Walter Gibson and others; the agent specialized in communications.*

1994

Winter
TO BE MORE THAN HUMAN
Vampirella intervenes when her lover Adam Van Helsing, having taken the transformative drug Hyde-25, attempts to kill Samuel Bishop, aka the Jackass, whose great-great-grandfather's genes were altered by exposure to the drug a century ago.

Vengeance of Vampirella #9-10 by Tom Sniegoski, Buzz, Kevin Sharpe, Rod Ramos, David Perrin, and Caesar, Harris Comics, December 1994– January 1995. The drug Hyde-25 is originally from "Night of the Jackass," a strip by Bruce Bezaire and Jose Ortiz that appeared in the Warren magazine Eerie. *Samuel Bishop, the great-great-grandson of Claude Bishop from "Night of the Jackass," first appeared in "Return of the Jackass" by Tom Sniegoski, Jim Webb, and Steve Mitchell, Hyde-25 #0, Harris Comics, April 1995. The name "Hyde-25" is derived from Dr. Henry Jekyll's alter ego Edward Hyde.*

THE BLACK WIDOWS
Fourteen-year-old Jimmy Malone becomes the vigilante known as the Black Ghost to battle the vicious gang plaguing his community. After being wounded in battle, the Ghost is treated by an elderly husband and wife, Nash and Rose, who own a used bookstore. The two were once spies for the U.S. government. Nash later comes to the Ghost's aid in a gray facemask.

Short story by Tom Johnson in The Spider's Web, Night to Dawn, *2010. "The Black Widows" functions as an origin story for Johnson's hero the Black Ghost, who is brought into the CU by a mention in Gene Girardier's story "Incident on a Quiet Street." "Nash" is really Ford Duane, aka the Red Finger, an American counter-spy who appeared in twelve stories by Arthur Leo Zagat in the pulp magazine* Operator #5 *between 1934 and 1938. In the Red Finger stories, Duane's fellow agent and potential love interest is Patricia Ann Towndell, aka Flower. Apparently the two eventually married and took the aliases Nash and Rose.*

Spring
CASPER
Dr. Raymond Stantz unsuccessfully attempts to make Casper and his uncles leave the mansion they are haunting. Father Guido Sarducci also appears.

1995 *feature film. Dr. Stantz is from the movie* Ghostbusters *and its sequel, as well as the cartoon* The Real Ghostbusters. *Since the Ghostbusters are in the CU, this crossover brings in a version of Casper. Father Guido Sarducci is a character created by comedian Don Novello, who has portrayed him in several TV series (including* Blossom, Married . . . with Children, *and* Unhappily Ever After*) and specials.*

June 23
NOT GRATUM ANUS RODENTUM

Walter Skinner investigates a were-rat. At one point, Skinner and a group of homeless kids discuss the Herod slayings.

Short story by Brian Keene in The X-Files: Trust No One, *Jonathan Maberry, ed., IDW Publishing, 2015. The Herod slayings were depicted in Keene's story "Slouching in Bethlehem," which connects to other works by Keene.*

1995

Winter
THE HOUSE OF WAX (aka WAX SCULPTURE CASTLE MURDER CASE)

Teenage amateur sleuth Kindaichi Hajime, grandson of detective Kindaichi Kosuke, works alongside another teen detective, Edward Columbo, the nephew of a noted Los Angeles homicide detective.

Storyline in the manga Kindaichi Case Files *by Yōzaburō Kanari and Fumiya Satō. Kindaichi Kosuke appeared in a series of novels by Seishi Yokozimo. Edward Columbo is meant to be the nephew of Lt. Columbo from the television series* Columbo; *since the Lieutenant is in the CU, so are the Kindaichis.*

GRIEF

The evil Emir, foe of the Gargoyles, a race of ancient winged beings who turn to stone in the daytime, uses the Scroll of Thoth and sacred tana leaves to summon Anubis.

Episode of the animated television series Gargoyles *broadcast December 28, 1995. Tana leaves are from Universal's original cycle of Mummy films. The Scroll of Thoth is from the exploits of Simon of Gitta. In the third season of* Gargoyles, *the existence of the creatures is revealed to the world. Therefore, only the first two seasons can take place in the CU.*

Spring
VAMPIRELLA VS. THE EUDAEMON

Vampirella goes undercover at a sex club in Amsterdam, where the Eudaemon and his buddy Ed are tracking the same evil Vampi sensed. Vampi and the Eudaemon do battle, until the latter's foe Mördare begins a destructive rampage.

Vampirella Strikes #5 by David Quinn and Rudy D. Nebres, Harris Comics, June 1996. The Eudaemon is Bobby Formazzo, the son of a benevolent demon, who can transform into a massive magenta-skinned creature to fight the ruthless demon Mördare. This crossover brings him into the CU.

THE TIME OF FEASTING

The ancient language of vampires such as Victor Renquist includes the word "ftaghn."

The first novel in Mick Farren's Renquist Quartet series. "Ftaghn" is a variant on the R'lyehian word "fhtagn," from H. P. Lovecraft's Cthulhu Mythos. According to Farren, modern vampires evolved from the Original Beings, creatures created as warrior servants by a race of aliens that visited Earth thousands of years ago, who became known in legend as the Nephilim. The Original Beings were nine feet tall, had leathery skin and some vulnerability to sunlight, and were able to turn humans into similar creatures. The Nephilim also created a race of mediators between themselves and the humans called the Urshu (Watchers), who needed to hibernate for centuries. The Original Beings revolted against the Nephilim, and were nearly destroyed by their makers. After this, the Nephilim abandoned the Urshu and fled Earth. The Original Beings both mated with and infected humans, thus leading to the birth of the nosferatu. *According to Farren, vampires cannot survive direct exposure to sunlight, and, with few exceptions, the race no longer possesses the abilities to change shape, generate mist, or control animals. There is ample evidence there is more than one kind of vampire in the Crossover Universe, so there is no reason why Renquist and other vampires of his type cannot coexist with some of the more traditional vampires in the CU.*

RAZOR/MORBID ANGEL: SOUL SEARCH

Brandon Watts, an angel without a soul, helps Razor cope with her recent resurrection.

Miniseries by Everette Hartsoe, Georges Jeanty, Andrew J. Pepoy, and Albert Holaso, London Night Entertainment, September–December 1996. This series serves as a sequel to the miniseries Razor: Torture.

THE END OF BROOKLYN

Nick Delvecchio investigates the death of a former classmate, while also investigating an attempt on the lives of his father, who does not survive, and his godfather, who is a former Mafia don. Delvecchio asks his fellow private eyes Henry Po and Miles Jacoby to guard his godfather.

Novel by Robert J. Randisi. Po and Jacoby are two other series characters of Randisi's. The prologue and epilogue of this novel take place in 2010, fifteen years later. Delvecchio's investigation of his former classmate's death was adapted from the short story "Laying Down to Die" (Deadly Allies II: Private Eye Writers of America and Sisters in Crime Collaborative Antholo-gy, *Robert J. Randisi and Susan Dunlap, eds., Doubleday, 1994).*

INNOCENT MONSTERS

Detective Bianca Jones recruits psychometrist Lai Wan to investigate several brutal slayings around the United States. When Lai Wan replies aloud to Bianca's thoughts, Bianca remarks, "I bet Watson hated it when Holmes did that to him."

Short story by John L. French and C. J. Henderson in Lai Wan: Tales of the Dreamwalker, *William Jones, ed., Marietta Publishing, 2007; reprinted in* Here There Be Monsters, Dark Quest, *2010. Both French's Bianca Jones and Henderson's Lai Wan are already in the CU. Other Bianca Jones stories have treated Sherlock Holmes as a real person who exists in the same universe as Bianca.*

THE VRIL AGENDA

A young man named Dillon meets Jim Anthony at the New York branch of the Baltimore Gun Club, hoping Jim will teach him to fight evil. They soon find themselves in battle with Sun Koh, an Atlantean superman who seeks to acquire an Aerash Evocation Drive, which is powered by *Vril* energy, the primary power source used by a race of technologically advanced subterranean beings called the Vril-Ya. Appearing or mentioned are: Impey Barbicane; a potential teacher of Dillon's Jim says he has heard no longer lives in New York, but rather in Central America, where he has built a remarkable research complex, and allegedly married a Mayan princess, having two daughters he's training to continue his work; another one that lives on a small island off the coast of Maine, and refuses to have contact with any of his fellow adventurers, who never remarried or had children, but whose asso-ciates' own children still carry on his work, now operating his corporation on a global scale; a third potential teacher who is still active, but who Jim recommends Dillon stay away from; a fourth teacher, who Jim describes as an insane fanatic who may or may not be still alive; George Valentine; Ashanti "Shani" Garuda; Dan Fowler, director of the FBI, who Jim first met in 1938 while investigating what appeared to be a series of bank robberies; Otis "Alcatraz" Brown; Van Loan; the Machine; ComTeg; the Humanidyne Institute; F.L.A.G; *The Laws of Human History* by Karstev; *The Principles of Private Detection* by Clovis Anderson; Jimmy Holm; Vera Gemini; the first Irma Vep; Nestor Burma; Sturmvogel; Rolf Karsten; a league protecting the British Empire; Miskatonic University; Alaska Jim Hoover; Ludwig Minx; and Jan Mayen.

Novel by Derrick Ferguson and Josh Reynolds, Airship 27 Productions, 2014. Part II of the novel, "The Coming Race," takes place in 1937, and the crossovers in that section are listed in an entry under that year. Dillon is an original character created by Ferguson. This story serves as a prequel to his later adventures. The Machine is also from the Dillon stories. Jim Anthony appeared in stories by Victor Rousseau Emmanuel, Robert Leslie Bellem, and W. T. Ballard in the pulp magazine Super Detective. *The Baltimore Gun Club and Impey Barbicane are from Jules Verne's novels* From the Earth to the Moon *and* Around the Moon. *Sun Koh is from the German pulp series (heftroman)* Sun Koh, die Erbe von Atlantis, *written by Paul Müller under the pen name "Lok Myler." Ashanti "Shani" Garuda is from Dr. Art Sippo's short story collection* Sun Koh: Heir of Atlantis Vol. 1, *which portrayed several German pulp heroes as members of the Thule Society serving Sun Koh, including Sturmvogel from* Sturmvögel, mit Buchse und Toboggan durch die Arktis, Abenteuer zwischen Urwald und Prairie *by "F. L. Barwin" (Lisa Barthel Winkler and Fritz Barthel), Rolf Karsten from* Rolf Karsten, der Schrecken der Berliner Unterwelt, *Alaska Jim Hoover from* Alaska Jim, ein Held der Kanadischen Polizei *by "Big Ben" (Willi Richard Sachse) and "F. L. Barwin," Minx from* Minx der Geisterbeschwörer *and* Minx der Geistersucher, *and Jan Mayen from* Jan Mayen, der Herr der Atomkraft *by Müller. Alaska Jim met Sturmvögel in #199 of his own series, and also appeared in #49 of* Sun Koh, die Erbe von Atlantis, *while Sun Koh and Jan Mayen had*

several crossovers. The events of Sun Koh: Heir of Atlantis *are incompatible with those of Win Scott Eckert's "Captain Midnight at Ultima Thule," so Sun Koh's aides seen in* The Vril Agenda *must be counterparts of those in Dr. Sippo's collection, which takes place in an AU. Vril and the Vril-Ya are from Edward Bulwer-Lytton's novel* The Coming Race. *Eckert also connected Sun Koh to the* Vril *in "Captain Midnight at Ultimate Thule." Dillon's other potential teachers are the bronze man, the avenging man with shock white skin and hair, the shadowy pulp hero, and the Spider. The fates revealed here for Doc and the avenging vigilante conflict with the details of their later lives given in Philip José Farmer and Win Scott Eckert's novel* The Evil in Pemberley House. *However, Anthony's comments indicate his info on those two heroes' current whereabouts is only second-hand at best, and therefore it is very likely the stories he has heard about the two are false. Private eye George Valentine was the protagonist of the 1946–1955 radio series* Let George Do It. *FBI agent Dan Fowler appeared in the pulp magazine* G-Men Detective. *According to Erwin K. Roberts' story "Stateside Debut," set in 1974, Dan left the Bureau in the mid-'50s after a falling-out with J. Edgar Hoover and the McCarthyites, joining the group JANIG from the Rick Brant novels by John Blaine. Dan must have been reinstated to the FBI at some point between 1974 and 1995. Jim and Dan's 1938 meeting is the subject of Reynolds' story "Proof of Supremacy." Otis "Alcatraz" Brown, aka the Magician, first appeared in Ferguson's story "The Knobloch Collection Assignment," included in the anthology* Tales from the Hanging Monkey, Volume One. *Richard Curtis Van Loan is better known as the pulp hero the Phantom Detective. ComTeg is from the movie* The Killer Elite. *The Humanidyne Institute is from the television series* Misfits of Science. *F.L.A.G. (Foundation for Law and Government) is from the television series* Knight Rider. *Karstev's* The Laws of Human History *is from Eric L. Harry's 1999 novel* Protect and Defend, *which involves such events as the President of the United States being assassinated and China invading Siberia. The Karstev mentioned in* The Vril Agenda *must be the CU counterpart of the one seen in* Protect and Defend, *which takes place in an AU. Clovis Anderson's* The Principles of Private Detection *is from* The No. 1 Ladies' Detective Agency *series by Alexander McCall Smith. Jimmy Holm is the archenemy of Harold Ward's pulp villain Doctor Death. Vera Gemini is from Reynolds' story "Nestor Burma Goes West." Her alias is a reference to Blue Öyster Cult's song "The Revenge of Vera Gemini." Les Vampires and the first Irma Vep are from Louis Feuillade's film serial of the same name. Nestor Burma is a private eye appearing in novels by Léo Malet. The league protecting the British Empire is Alan Moore and Kevin O'Neill's League of Extraordinary Gentlemen. Miskatonic University is a staple of H. P. Lovecraft's Cthulhu Mythos. The year of the novel's main events is conjecture.*

Spring–Summer
THE CHAOS PROJECT

Maxim Gunn, an agent of the British Intelligence group known as the Organization, battles the evil Wanda Liszt, who is planning to conquer the world with the aid of Queen Sheba's Necklace. Wanda's father, Otto Liszt, had been cast in the mold of the great criminals, like Carl Peterson and Professor Moriarty.

Novel by Nicholas Boving, 1996, revised as part of the omnibus edition Maxim Gunn: The First Three, *Pro Se Press, 2014. Queen Sheba's necklace is from John Buchan's novel* Prester John. *Buchan's Richard Hannay novels contain references to John Laputa and Captain Arcoll, both of whom appear in* Prester John. *Carl Peterson is Bulldog Drummond's archenemy. Professor Moriarty needs no further introduction. Philip José Farmer identified Peterson as Professor Moriarty's grandson. All of these links bring Maxim Gunn into the CU.*

Summer
CONSPIRACY

Batman battles an Illuminati-like group. After defeating them, Batman leaves the evidence on Fox Mulder's desk, where it is found by him and Dana Scully.

Batman: Legends of the Dark Knight #86–88 *by Doug Moench, J. H. Williams III, and Mick Gray, DC Comics, September–November 1996. Agents Mulder and Scully (from* The X-Files*) are not referred to by name, but their likenesses are unmistakable. Per CU continuity, this story features the third Batman, Bruce Wayne Jr., whose father originally held the mantle.*

A DOZEN BLACK ROSES

The heroic vampire Sonja Blue encounters the vampire sect known as the Camarilla.

Novel by Nancy A. Collins, White Wolf Publishing, 1995. The Sonja Blue series is already in the CU via a mention of the Aegrisomnia, *an occult tome from that series, in Collins' Cthulhu Mythos story "The Land of the Reflected Ones." The Camarilla are from White Wolf's role-playing game* Vampire: The Masquerade. *The game presents a very different take on the nature of vampires than most accounts set in the CU, as well as a version of Dracula that is difficult to reconcile with most stories involving that infamous* nosferatu. *Therefore, this story must feature the CU version of the Camarilla, and does not import the continuity of* Vampire: The Masquerade *wholesale.*

Winter
REFRIED DEAD

Wynonna Earp, a monster hunting government agent who claims to be descended from Wyatt Earp, battles a mummy animated by tanna leaves.

Wynonna Earp #4–5 by Beau Smith, Pat Lee, Mark John Irwin, and Luke Rizzo, Image Comics, March–April 1997. Tanna leaves are from Universal Studio's original cycle of Mummy films, bringing Wynonna Earp into the CU.

Spring
DARKLOST

Victor Renquist and his Los Angeles-based vampire Colony fight human cultists who intend to free Cthulhu. A coven member named Julia thinks New Orleans vampires "had gone so far as to form a secret society called *Les Enfants du Sangre*, and had for a while been totally exploited by a *ronin* outcast *nosferatu* who had used the name Eccarius, until the creature had been nailed out in the sun by Cassidy, the notorious loner and wandering iconoclast, one of the few hobo diamonds left among the undead." Renquist "had lived through the era of the professional witchfinders and vampire hunters of the eighteenth and nineteenth centuries; the depredations of Kronos, Van Helsing, and the unspeakable Feldstein, all of whom had made a professional practice of entering the daytime refuges of his kind to impale with their wooden stakes . . ."

The second novel in Mick Farren's Renquist Quartet *series. Cthulhu is the most well-known of the Great Old Ones of H. P. Lovecraft's Mythos. Dr. Abraham Van Helsing is from Bram Stoker's novel* Dracula. *Kronos is from the Hammer film* Captain Kronos–Vampire Hunter. *Feldstein is an original character. Cassidy is from the comic book series* Preacher; *his confrontation with Eccarius and* Les *Enfants du Sangre was told in the one-shot* Preacher Special: Cassidy–Blood & Whiskey. *The* Preacher *series takes place in a universe where the American president (implicitly Bill Clinton) had a nuclear weapon dropped on the Navajo and Hopi reservations. Since no such event happened in the CU, the* Preacher Special: Saint of Killers *miniseries and* Blood & Whiskey *are being treated as the only* Preacher *stories to have definitely occurred in the CU. This novel is set one year after the events of* The Time of Feasting, *and was published in 2000.* The Time of Feasting *came out in 1996, and its events likely took place in 1995; therefore, references to the Columbine school shootings and other post-1996 events in* Darklost *must have been inserted by Farren in order to give the book a more "contemporary" feel.*

VAMPIRELLA VS. FLUFFY THE VAMPIRE KILLER

Vampirella goes undercover as a teacher at a high school to investigate a series of teen murders, and winds up working with a vampire-slaying student named Fluffy.

One-shot by Mark Rahner and Cezar Razek, Dynamite Entertainment, 2012. "Fluffy" is a thinly-veiled parody of Buffy Summers of the television series Buffy the Vampire Slayer, *and therefore it can be assumed in creative mythographic terms, she is indeed Buffy. However, the death of "Fluffy's" friend "Sallow" (Willow) must be considered a distortion. The date is based on the fact the principal of the school, who is portrayed as Vampirella's ally Criswell, states the previous principal was eaten. Two Sunnydale High principals were devoured: Robert Flutie (in the* Buffy *episode "The Pack"), and R. Snyder (in the two-parter "Graduation Day.") Since the events of "Graduation Day" resulted in the school being destroyed, I have concluded Criswell's presence is mere fictionalization and the principal is actually Snyder. Furthermore, the presence of "Fluffy's" vampire boyfriend "Cherub" (Angel) indicates this story takes place before the temporary removal of Angel's soul and his equally temporary death in Season 2. The high school being shut down at the end of Vampi and "Fluffy's" adventure is another distortion, as are references to the iPhone "There's an app for that" ad slogan, Ryan Seacrest, and Bristol Palin.*

July

EXPLOSIVE JUSTICE

Former police officer Bowen Chadwick (secretly the superpowered vigilante known as the Blaster) watches a news story on National News Net, a part of Havens International Media, delivered by Curtis Van Loan. In a flashback to the circumstances under which Chadwick gained his powers, Sergeant Sampson Jones tells Special Agent Simmons, "I do not care if the ghost of J. Edgar Hoover comes up to me with a request signed by the ghosts of Eliot Ness, Wyatt Earp, and Sherlock Holmes; I will not relinquish control of this environmental travesty." Van Loan later introduces Chadwick to another vigilante, the Voice, who needs his help against a right wing militia.

The Voice says, "If it weren't for the women and children in the compound, I'd be sorely tempted to use my honorary Uncle Dick's scorched earth methods. Go Mack Bolan on 'em." After the militia is defeated, a helicopter picks up the Voice and Chadwick; the crew of the aircraft refers to the pilot as String.

Short story by Erwin K. Roberts in Casebook of the Voice, *Modern Knights Press, 2014. Havens International Media is an outgrowth of the* Daily Clarion *newspaper owned by Frank Havens, an ally of the Phantom Detective (aka Richard Curtis Van Loan). The Detective's girlfriend in the pulp stories was Muriel Havens, Frank's daughter; Curtis "Curt" Van Loan is their son. Sergeant Jones is almost certainly mistaken about Sherlock Holmes being deceased, and was probably fooled by Holmes faking his death in 1957. The Voice's honorary Uncle Dick is Richard "Dick" Wentworth, better known as the Spider. Mack Bolan, the Executioner, is the protagonist of a series of novels by Don Pendleton and others. It has been suggested Bolan is Wentworth's son. The helicopter pilot is Stringfellow "String" Hawke from the television series* Airwolf.

Summer
21 DOORS
Detective Bianca Jones wonders if Shub-Niggurath could be behind the murder she is investigating. Her ally and part-time boss Morgan has Prinn's *De Vermis Mysteriis* alongside Holmes' *Practical Handbook of Bee Culture*, though Bianca makes sure *The Ravings of Abd el-Hazred* is still locked securely in a safe.

Short story by John L. French in Dark Furies: Weird Tales of Beauties & Beasts, *Vincent Sneed, ed., Die Monster Die! Books, 2005; reprinted in* Don't Turn the Lights On, *Diana Bocco, ed., Stonegarden.net Publishing, 2007, and* Here There Be Monsters, *Dark Quest, 2010. Shub-Niggurath is from Lovecraft's Cthulhu Mythos, while Ludwig Prinn's tome* De Vermis Mysteriis *is from Robert Bloch's own contributions to the cycle. The Ravings of Abd el-Hazred were penned by the "Mad Arab" Abdul Alhazred, who is the author of the* Necronomicon *in Lovecraft's mythos. Bianca previously encountered Shub-Niggurath and* The Ravings *in French's "A World Inside." Sherlock Holmes'* Practical Handbook of Bee Culture, with some Observations upon the Segregation of the Queen *was mentioned in Doyle's "His Last Bow."*

VIVA LAS BUFFY!
Wesley Wyndam-Price reads a book on demonology that has a picture of Idpa.

Buffy the Vampire Slayer *#51–54 by Scott Lobdell, Fabian Nicieza, Cliff Richards, and Will Conrad, Dark Horse Comics, November 2002–*

February 2002. The demon Idpa is from Scott Allie, Paul Lee, and Brian Horton's comic The Devil's Footprints, *also published by Dark Horse, bringing that miniseries into the CU.*

THE DEMON PLAN

MI5 sends Harry Pearce to recruit Maxim Gunn, now retired from the Organization, for a mission.

Novel by Nicholas Boving, 1997, revised as part of the omnibus edition Maxim Gunn: The First Three, *Pro Se Press, 2014. Harry Pearce is from the TV series* Spooks *(aka MI-5 in the United States). Since* Spooks *has already been included in the CU, this crossover further confirms Maxim Gunn's inclusion.*

JACKIE BROWN

During a trial run of a drug deal, Jackie Brown gets food from the Teriyaki Donut restaurant, while the woman who picks up the bag from her gets her meal from the Acuna Boys Tex-Mex Food restaurant.

1997 feature film directed by Quentin Tarantino. Teriyaki Donut is from Pulp Fiction. *The Acuna Boys Tex-Mex Food restaurant also appears in* Grindhouse. *In* Kill Bill: Vol. 2, *Bill's surrogate father, Esteban Vihaio, a pimp in Acuna, Mexico, leads a gang called the Acuna Boys, made up of the illegitimate sons of his prostitutes. Acuna Boys Tex-Mex Food is probably a legitimate front for Esteban and the Boys' illegal activities. This film is based on Elmore Leonard's novel* Rum Punch, *which has connections to other novels by Leonard. However, the protagonist of* Rum Punch *is a white woman named Jackie Burke, as opposed to the African-American Jackie Brown. Therefore, Elmore Leonard's connected fiction must take place in an alternate reality to the CU.*

Autumn
VAMPIRELLA VS. DRACULA

The Order of the Dragon attempts to replace their champion Dracula with Vampirella in a constantly repeating cycle of variations on the events recounted in Bram Stoker's novel.

Miniseries by Joe Harris and Ivan Rodriguez, Dynamite Entertainment, 2012. This story serves as an immediate sequel to Alan Moore, Gary Frank, and Cam Smith's story "The New European," found in the one-shot Vampirella/ Dracula: The Centennial, *Harris Comics, October 1997, and reprinted in the first issue of* Vampirella vs. Dracula. *The Dracula seen here is not Dracula-Prime, but rather a "soul-clone," who has had many run-ins with Vampirella.*

1997

Spring
TROUBLE TIMES THREE

The reformed jewel thief and masked government agent known as the Scarecrow teams up with the mercenary known as the Fox to take down a member of the villainous Corona organization.

Short story by Alanna Morgan and Debra Delorme in Double Danger Tales *#18–19, Tom and Ginger Johnson, eds., Fading Shadows Publications, July–August 1998. Delorme's hero the Scarecrow is in through a crossover listed below. This story brings in Morgan's character, the Fox, who went on to appear solo in the story "The Chinese Connection."*

HUNTER'S MOON

The Scarecrow joins forces with the Black Ghost.

Short story by Debra Delorme and Tom Johnson in Double Danger Tales *#20, Tom and Ginger Johnson, eds., Fading Shadows Publications, September 1998; reprinted in* Tales of Masks and Mayhem, *K. G. McAbee, ed., Mystic Toad Press, 2005. Johnson's modern pulp-style vigilante the Black Ghost is in the CU through a reference in Gene Girardier's story "Incident on a Quiet Street," which takes place in 2001. This crossover brings in Delorme's Scarecrow.*

OUT OF SIGHT

ATF agent Ray Nicolette appears.

1998 feature film directed by Steven Soderbergh, based on Elmore Leonard's novel. Ray Nicolette appeared in both that novel and another Leonard novel, Rum Punch, *although Leonard spelled his last name Nicolet.* Rum Punch *was adapted by Quentin Tarantino into the film* Jackie Brown, *although the protagonist was changed from the white Jackie Burke to the African-American Jackie Brown. Michael Keaton played Nicolette in both* Jackie Brown *and this film, and therefore it can be assumed the two movies take place in the same universe, with Leonard's original novels taking place in a separate reality.*

190

Summer
VARIATIONS ON A THEME

Sonja Blue encounters the revenant known as the Crow, a gay black man who has been sent to take out the white supremacists who murdered him and his lover.

Short story by Nancy A. Collins in The Crow: Shattered Lives and Broken Dreams, *J. O'Barr and Ed Kramer, eds., Del Rey, 1998; reprinted in* Dead Roses for a Blue Lady, *Crossroads Press, 2002. This Crow is not Eric Draven, who recently encountered Razor, but was resurrected by the same mystic crow. This crossover further confirms Sonja Blue's presence in the CU.*

September 15
THE MIND OF THE DEAD

Psychometrist Lai Wan comes to the aid of Carl Kolchak when they turn out to be investigating the same series of crimes.

Short story by C. J. Henderson in Sex, Lies and Private Eyes, *Joe Gentile and Richard Dean Starr, eds., Moonstone Books, 2009; reprinted in* Lai Wan: The Dreamwalker, *Moonstone Books, 2013. Kolchak also encountered Lai Wan in Spring 1997 during the events of Henderson and Joe Gentile's novel* Partners in Crime. *September 15 is a Saturday, placing this story in 1997 as well, after* Partners in Crime. *"The Mind of the Dead" does not address whether Kolchak and Lai Wan have met before.*

Autumn
UNNATURAL SELECTION

Some of Hellboy's past cases are mentioned, including something to do with pods in 1978, that shark thing in 1975, and an episode in New York with giant insects that mimic human beings.

Novel by Tim Lebbon, Pocket Books, 2006. The pod incident is a reference to the 1978 remake of the 1956 film Invasion of the Body Snatchers, *which was itself based on Jack Finney's novel* The Body Snatchers. *Miles Bennell and Becky Driscoll were renamed Matthew Bennell and Elizabeth Driscoll, while Jack Bellicec retained both halves of his name. The plot details and character names are otherwise completely different from the original film, and therefore it can be assumed the Bennell, Driscoll, and Jack Bellicec names were given to some of those involved in the second invasion of the pod aliens in order to create the illusion it was a retelling of, rather than a sequel to, the events of the original novel, which have already been included in the CU. "That shark thing" in 1975 is a reference to the movie* Jaws, *while the giant insects in New York that mimic human beings are a reference to the* Mimic *film series. Christopher Farnsworth's novel* The President's Vampire *revealed the title character, Nathaniel Cade, helped resolve the original Body Snatcher crisis, while* Red, White and Blood *implied Cade was also involved in the events of the first* Mimic *film. Perhaps Cade and Hellboy worked together on that adventure.*

1998

Summer
AVENGELYNE/PANDORA

Avengelyne and Pandora battle Avengelyne's friend Maria, who has been transformed into a human/demon hybrid. After Maria reverts to normal, she tells the two a story of an angel who fought a cult whose power came from the blood of Lucifer. The blood was given to a group of church elders for safekeeping, and discovered by Maria in the modern day, causing her transformation. Maria changes again, forcing Pandora to kill her. The ladies battle and defeat a human vessel of Lucifer.

Avengelyne/Pandora #0-1, by William Christensen, Mark Seifert, and Rick Lyon, Avatar Press, December 1999–January 2000. Avengelyne is already in the CU. Therefore, this crossover brings in Pandora, who has also met Razor.

THE CRACKED EARTH

Jack Liffey, a private eye specializing in cases involving missing children, visits his fellow investigator Ivan Monk's donut shop, hoping to obtain info on a Rastafarian man who beat him up.

Novel by John Shannon. Liffey is in the CU through an encounter with Wold Newton Family member Philip Marlowe in 2000. This crossover brings in Gary Phillips' P.I. Ivan Monk. In Shannon's Streets on Fire, *a client hires Liffey on Monk's recommendation.*

Summer–December 1. Events of the novel *Ghostwritten* by David Mitchell. The worldwide wars described in the section of the book entitled "Night Train" should be considered fictional. Also, the sentient computer program known as the Zookeeper must have abandoned its plans to destroy humanity, or else was thwarted before those plans could be carried out.

192

November

GHOUL GOBLIN

Chicago wizard-for-hire Harry Dresden battles an amphibious monster in Lake Michigan. Afterwards he thinks, ". . . My mind's already racing to figure out how I go about tracking the thing based upon limited knowledge. To say nothing of the possibility of there being any Missus and Junior Black Lagoons out there."

The Dresden Files *miniseries by Mark Powers, Jim Butcher, and Joseph Cooper, Dynamite Entertainment, 2013. Harry's comments suggest the monster he fought is related somehow to the Gill-Man from the film* Creature from the Black Lagoon *and its sequels. Several later crossovers establish the events of Butcher's* The Dresden Files *novel series take place in the CU, adding to the validity of this reference. This miniseries takes place between the novels* Fool Moon *and* Grave Peril.

Autumn

ANGEL SPOTLIGHT: DOYLE

Doyle is confused for someone named Mark Healy, which he says happens all the time.

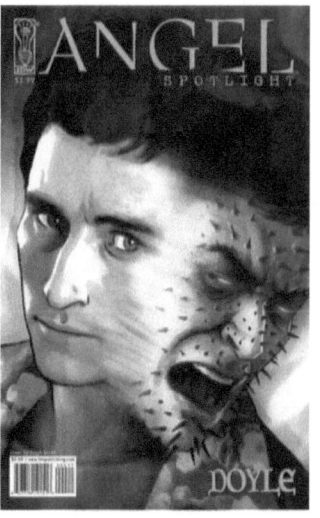

One-shot by Jeff Marriotte, David Messina, and Elena Casagrande, IDW Publishing, July 2006. Mark Healy is from the television series Roseanne. *Healy was played by Glenn Quinn, who also played Doyle on* Angel. *This crossover brings* Roseanne *into the CU, and by extension* The Jackie Thomas Show. *The final episode of* Roseanne *implied the entire series was actually a story written by Roseanne Conner that told a greatly distorted account of her life. Obviously, this should be disregarded for the purposes of incorporating* Roseanne *into the CU.*

1999

Winter

THE SUN FORTRESS

Maxim Gunn rescues the kidnapped Princess Alicia Flavia of Ruritania. Gunn, who is revealed to be a descendant of Rudolf Rassendyll, is also acquainted with a half-Chinese Shaolin priest in California.

Novel by Nicholas Boving, 2012, revised as part of the omnibus edition Maxim Gunn: Four, Five, Six, *Pro Se Press, 2014. Rudolf Rassendyll (from*

Anthony Hope's The Prisoner of Zenda *and* Rupert of Hentzau*) died un-married. Rudolf must have fathered a child out of wedlock sometime before meeting and falling in love with Ruritania's Princess Flavia during the events of* The Prisoner of Zenda. *This child would be Maxim Gunn's ancestor. The half-Chinese Shaolin priest is Kwai Chang Caine II from the television series* Kung Fu: The Legend Continues, *himself the grandson of the original Kwai Chang Caine from the Western series* Kung Fu.

February
CHOSEN PREY

A hacker named Kidd helps police detective and war game designer Lucas Davenport on an art-related matter.

Novel by John Sandford. In Stephen King and Peter Straub's novel Black House, *which takes place in the CU, Jack Sawyer is described as "a Lucas Davenport type," referring to the protagonist of Sandford's* Prey *series. This reference suggests Lucas Davenport is a real person who exists in the same universe as Jack. Kidd and a cat burglar named LuEllen are the protagonists of another series of novels by Sandford, and this crossover brings them into the CU. Kidd also has a cameo in a later* Prey *novel,* Silken Prey. *Another series character of Sandford's is Virgil Flowers of the Minnesota Bureau of Criminal Apprehension, who reports directly to Lucas Davenport. Davenport and Flowers frequently appear in each other's series.*

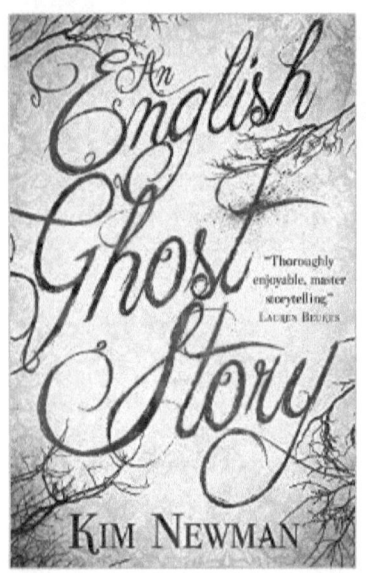

Spring–Autumn
AN ENGLISH GHOST STORY

The dysfunctional Naremore family moves into the Hollow, a haunted house once owned by Louise Magellan Teazle, the author of the Weezie books (inspired by her childhood in the Hollow) and the Drearcliff Grange series. The family reads a chapter about the Hollow in Catriona Kaye's *Ghost Stories of the West Country*. The chapter states the Hollow's "ghost trees" are described in a series of journal entries penned in 1879 by Timothy Bannerman, parson of the nearby village of Alder. In 1923, Kaye spent a night at the Hollow in the company of the trance medium Irene Dobson and the psychic investigator Edwin Winthrop.

Novel by Kim Newman, Titan Books, 2014. Drearcliff Grange is from Newman's novel The Secrets of Drearcliff Grange School. *Catriona Kaye and Edwin Winthrop are lovers who occasionally do contract work for the Diogenes Club (originally from the Sherlock Holmes stories), as seen in other tales by Newman. The Reverend Timothy Bannerman, the village of Alder, and Irene Dobson are from Newman's novel* Jago. *Irene also appears in Newman's story "Is There Anybody There?" At one point, it is stated it is "nearly the twenty-first century," suggesting a placement in 1999.*

April
SPEAKING IN TONGUES
Cop Konnie Konstantinitis suggests to Tate Collier and his ex-wife Bett they call her friend, FBI document examiner Parker Kincaid, to determine whether a note supposedly written by their missing daughter is a fake or not.

Novel by Jeffery Deaver. Parker Kincaid is from Deaver's novel The Devil's Teardrop.

Summer
DEMOLITION ANGEL
Carol Starkey investigates a bombing. John Chen appears, and Samantha Dolan is mentioned. Serial bomber Mr. Red eats at Big Kahuna Burger.

Novel by Robert Crais. Big Kahuna Burger has appeared in several films, most notably Pulp Fiction; *this reference brings the events of this novel into the CU. Carol Starkey would go on to appear in other books by Crais. John Chen and Samantha Dolan are from Crais' Elvis Cole novel* L.A. Requiem.

THE LEOPARD LEGION
At the request of his old friend, the Emir of Ladi, Maxim Gunn travels to Africa to deal with the Leopard Men, a mercenary army led by a megalo-maniac named Magunta. The Emir's security chief is the Scottish Alex Arcoll, whose great-grandfather investigated illicit diamond buying at the turn of the century. The elder Arcoll had a run-in with a man named Laputa, who wished to rule Africa. Prester John and an emerald necklace were also involved in this affair. Gunn learned how to appear seemingly from out of nowhere from a certain Shaolin monk of his acquaintance.

Novel by Nicholas Boving, 2012, revised as part of the omnibus edition Maxim Gunn: Four, Five, Six, *Pro Se Press, 2014. Alex Arcoll's great-grandfather, Captain Arcoll, and John Laputa are from John Buchan's novel* Prester John. *The Shaolin monk is Kwai Chang Caine II from the television series* Kung Fu: The Legend Continues.

Early October
GRAVE PERIL

Harry Dresden asks to be invited into a house that is a crime scene in order to fully work his magic. One of the cops suggests, "Like Dracula?" Harry replies the last he heard Dracula was in Europe.

Novel by Jim Butcher, 2001. Bram Stoker's version of Dracula is referred to as if he were real, confirming Harry Dresden's existence in the CU.

October 29–November
A QUESTION OF MEANING

A group of cultists travel to the Night Land, a future incarnation of the Dreamlands ruled by the Elder God Nodens.

Short story by Pierre V. Comtois in Sargasso: The Journal of William Hope Hodgson Studies *#1, Sam Gafford, ed., Ulthar Press, 2013. This tale connects William Hope Hodgson's novel* The Night Land *(which represents one of many possible futures for the CU) to the Cthulhu Mythos.*

Early December
THE X-FILES/30 DAYS OF NIGHT

FBI agents Mulder and Scully are sent to Wainwright, Alaska to investigate a grisly murder that proves to be the work of vampires. After the agents leave Wainwright, the surviving undead choose their next destination: Barrow.

Six-issue miniseries by Steve Niles, Adam Jones, and Tom Mandrake, WildStorm Comics, September 2010–February 2011. This crossover serves as a prequel to Niles' vampire comic 30 Days of Night, *which is set in Barrow, Alaska. This story likely takes place during* The X-Files' *seventh season, given that Mulder was not active as an agent for most of the two seasons that followed it.*

December
VOICE OF PAIN

FBI Agent-in-Charge Jeffrey Reynolds tells Police Lt. Ralph Adams he has been reading classified official reports about vigilantes such as the Voice. The most recent report was dated in the late sixties, and concerned a disguise artist referred to as Mr. Jones who worked for the Bureau. The Voice refers to

George Sanchez as "my Burbank." Reynolds considers asking his Great-Uncle Lynn about the vigilantes of the old days. Former police chief Cobbins refers to vigilantes (or "Independent Operators") who were involved in World War II, including an Australian who served with his country's military while wearing a mask and using the code name "the Phantom Commando."

Story by Erwin K. Roberts in Double Danger Tales #52, *Tom and Ginger Johnson, eds., Fading Shadows Publications, May 2002; reprinted in* Casebook of the Voice, *Modern Knights Press, 2014. Mr. Jones appeared in Dennis Lynds' story "The Man of a Million Faces," published in the June 1968 issue of* Mike Shayne Mystery Magazine *under the house name of Robert Hart Davis. Burbank is an agent of a shadow-cloaked pulp hero, specializing in communications. Reynolds' great-uncle Lynn is FBI agent Lynn Vickers, who appeared in stories by Bryan James Kelley in* Public Enemy *(later retitled* Federal Agent*). The Phantom Commando is an Australian comic character created by John Dixon who appeared in his own series from 1959–1970.*

December 31
THE DEVIL'S TEARDROP
Ex-FBI document examiner Parker Kincaid consults criminologist Lincoln Rhyme on a murder case.

This non-series novel by Jeffery Deaver features a cameo by Deaver's series character Lincoln Rhyme. Since Rhyme is in through a 2013 crossover, this novel takes place in the CU as well. Parker Kincaid went on to appear in two of the Rhyme novels, The Twelfth Card *and* The Burning Wire.

March 1999; March 2009

VOICE TO A NEW GENERATION
In 1999, a young girl named Emily visits the Poplar Park convention center with her friends, and winds up assisting the mystery man known as the Voice. The Voice expresses hope Emily will one day become an Independent Operator. Ten years later, Emily, now known as the Pulptress, battles a plot by Iranian fanatics to sabotage a space shuttle, and is herself aided by the Voice, who recognizes her. The Pulptress' friend Dillon is also mentioned.

Short story by Erwin K. Roberts in The Pulptress, *David White, ed., Pro Se Press, 2012. The Pulptress is the daughter of two of the greatest (unidentified) pulp heroes of all time. Orphaned as an infant, she was tutored by many of her parents' comrades to be the world's greatest hero. Roberts' hero the Voice and Derrick Ferguson's adventurer Dillon have already been established as existing in the CU; therefore, this crossover brings in the Pulptress. In Roberts' fiction, the "Independent Operators" are a network of vigilantes.*

Winter
THE ORANGE CURTAIN
Jack Liffey meets the elderly Philip Marlowe.

Novel by John Shannon. Liffey's encounter with Philip Marlowe, a Wold Newton Family member, brings him into the CU. Although Marlowe's age is given as 93, he was born in June 1900; therefore, he would actually be a few months shy of 100 at the time of this book's events.

Spring
AREA 52

Area 52 is a secret government storage facility in Antarctica where super-weapons, occult items, and other weird stuff are stored. Items held within Area 52 include wreckage from Roswell, the Ark of the Covenant, the Super-Soldier formula, Mjolnir, Wonder Woman's Lasso of Truth, the Time Machine, and an alien power ring that shoots green energy.

Four-issue miniseries by Brian Haberlin and Clayton Henry, Image Comics, 2001. The Ark of the Covenant is from the Book of Exodus, *but the version seen here is clearly the one seen in the first Indiana Jones film,* Raiders of the Lost Ark, *as it has an identical lethal effect when opened. Apparently, the Ark was moved to Area 52 from Area 51, where it was seen during the 1957 events of* Indiana Jones and the Kingdom of the Crystal Skull. *The Super-Soldier formula turned the frail Steve Rogers into Captain America. Mjolnir is the hammer wielded by the heroic god Thor; it must have passed into Area 52's hands millennia after Conan gave it to Crom, following the events of "What If Thor of Asgard Had Met Conan the Barbarian?" Wonder Woman's lasso is self-explanatory. The Time Machine is from H. G. Wells' novel of the same name. The alien power ring is the one wielded by the superhero Green Lantern.*

April 24–June
CONS, SCAMS & GRIFTS
Dan Kearny and Associates investigate a complex case involving gypsies. A pair of San Francisco cops referred to as Rosencrantz and Guildenstern consult L.A. Homicide detective Harry Bosch.

2001 novel by Joe Gores. DKA is already in the CU through a crossover with Dashiell Hammett's sleuth the Continental Op; therefore, this crossover brings in Michael Connelly's Detective Harry Bosch. Lawyer Mickey Haller, who appears in his own series of novels by Connelly, is Bosch's half-brother, and the two appear together in The Brass Verdict, The Reversal, *and* The Gods of Guilt. *All of Connelly's non-series novels are also connected to the Bosch series. Ex-FBI profiler Terry McCaleb appears in both* Blood Work *and the Bosch novel* A Darkness More Than Night. *Thief Cassidy Black, the main character of* Void Moon, *also appears in the Bosch novel* The Narrows. *Reporter Jack McEvoy appears in* The Poet *and* The Scarecrow, *as well as* A Darkness More Than Night *and* The Brass Verdict. *FBI Special Agent Rachel Walling appears in* The Poet *and* The Scarecrow, *and also in* The Narrows, Echo Park, The Overlook, The Reversal, *and* The Black Box. Chasing the Dime *features entrepreneur Henry Pierce, whose sister Isabelle was one of the victims of serial killer Norman Church from the Bosch novel* The Concrete Blonde.

June
SUMMER KNIGHT
Queen Mab inherits the debt Harry Dresden previously owed to the Winter Fae. Harry twice views Queen Titania with his Wizard's Sight.

Novel by Jim Butcher, 2002. Queen Mab and Queen Titania are from William Shakespeare's plays Romeo and Juliet *and* A Midsummer Night's Dream, *respectively, and went on to become recurring characters in the Dresden Files series.*

Summer
SHANGRI-LA
Lara Croft travels to the Immortal City of Shangri-La, and has to fight her way back out again.

Tomb Raider: The Series #11–12 by Dan Jurgens and Billy Tan, Image Comics, March–April 2001. Shangri-La is from James Hilton's Lost Horizon. *Both the one-shot comic* Tomoe/Witchblade: Fire Sermon *(set in 1995) and the* Army of Darkness *comic storyline* "League of Light Assemble!" *(set in 2008) portray Shangri-La as having been abandoned by its former inhabitants, but apparently a select few stayed behind.*

DRINKING MIDNIGHT WINE
Toby Dexter, a mild-mannered bookshop assistant in Bradford-on-Avon, follows a beautiful and mysterious woman named Gayle from Veritie, the real world, to Mysterie, the magical world. There, he learns he is a focal point, destined to play a major role in defeating Nicholas Hob, the Serpent's

Son and his ally, a fallen angel called simply Angel, who wish to raze both Veritie and Mysterie in order to allow Hob's father, the Serpent in the Sun, to remake them in his own image. Toby's shop sells the new English translation of the infamous *Necronomicon*, as well as the Bruin Bear and the Sea Goat books. Jimmy Thunder, God for Hire, once had a case involving Count Dracula's mandolin.

Novel by Simon R. Green. The Necronomicon *is from the Cthulhu Mythos stories of H. P. Lovecraft and others. Bruin Bear and the Sea Goat are from Green's novel* Shadows Fall. *Shadows Fall is one of many "towns you won't find on any map," largely populated by fictional characters and fictional representations of real people who have achieved reality through the world's belief in them. The town has at least six different Robin Hoods, who are seen arguing over which one of them is the closest to the real thing, and a few Merlins. Also, the real Jim Morrison, who faked his death, lives there. The book ends with the destruction of the town and the manifestation of Heaven on Earth, with everyone who ever died being resurrected, making it difficult to reconcile with CU continuity. However, later references make it clear the events of Green's Nightside and Secret Histories books are taking place before* Shadows Fall, *and given the number of alternate timelines and futures glimpsed in both series, it becomes simple enough to pinpoint the events of the novel* Shadows Fall *as one more possible future may or may not come to pass, while the town and its inhabitants continue to coexist with the rest of the CU. Count Dracula is from Bram Stoker's novel, of course. Several individuals mentioned in this novel go on to appear in the Nightside series.*

Autumn

THE DEATH OF BUFFY

Spike drops in on Rupert Giles to borrow a shear of Cytorrak, which he needs to finish off an acid demon he's knocked out behind the Sunnydale Municipal Building.

Buffy the Vampire Slayer #43–45 by Tom Fassbender, Jim Pascoe, Cliff Richards, Joe Pimentel, and Will Conrad, Dark Horse Comics, March–May 2002. Despite the different spellings, this is clearly a reference to Cyttorak, a god from the Marvel Comics Universe, best known for creating the Crimson

Gem of Cyttorak, the power source for the X-Men's foe the Juggernaut. Although the X-Men's adventures do not fit into CU continuity, the Crimson Gem was mentioned in Kim Newman's story "The Adventure of the Six Maledictions," and therefore we have independent verification Cyttorak has a CU counterpart. This storyline takes place between Seasons 5 and 6 of Buffy the Vampire Slayer.

Autumn 2000–Winter 2001
MORE THAN MORTAL

Nosferatu Victor Renquist visits England at the request of a female troika of his fellow undead, and becomes a witness to the Urshu known as Taliesin the Merlin's emergence from his centuries-long hibernation. Merlin's cocoon was unearthed in a mound excavated by students from Wessex University. The Duke de Richleau led a task force of specialists against occult forces utilized by the Nazis during World War II. Renquist thinks of the few English *nosferatu*, such as Sir Francis Varney, Barnabas Collins, and Lord Ruthven. A member of the female vampire troika, Marieko Matsunaga, used her powers of persuasion to seduce one of the Wessex students at a pub in Casterbridge in order to investigate the findings at the mound. Marieko is aware of Renquist's encounter with Cthulhu, one of the monstrous Old Ones. Renquist thinks the Scottish vampire lord Fenrior may preside over the largest community of their kind since a group of *nosferatu* and humans caused the dissolution of the Theatre Raoul Privache in Paris.

The third novel in the Renquist Quartet *series by Mick Farren. Wessex is a fictional region of England appearing in several novels by Thomas Hardy, including* The Mayor of Casterbridge. *The Duke de Richleau is featured in a series of novels by Dennis Wheatley. According to Farren, the Duke died in 1997 at the age of 93, whereas Wheatley's* Dangerous Inheritance *had the Duke dying in the 1950s, when he was in his eighties. Renquist must have been mistaken as to the Duke's age and time of death. Sir Francis Varney is from James Malcolm Rymer's* Varney the Vampire. *Farren claims Varney was impaled by a vampire hunter called Dr. Feisal in Persia, whereas Rymer's novel had Varney committing suicide by throwing himself into a volcano. However, Frank Schildiner's story "Fear from Above," set in the 1930s, reveals Varney survived plunging into Mt. Vesuvius, while Simon R. Green's novella "The Big Game," set in the 21st century, elaborates on the circumstances of how he survived. Travis Hiltz's story "The Mark of the Red Leech" depicts Varney's destruction in World War I, while Donald F. Glut and Jesse Santos' comic book story "Dracula's Vampire Legion" features Dracula resurrecting Varney and other infamous vampires in the 1970s. Varney must have been destroyed and resurrected several times. Barnabas Collins from the television series* Dark Shadows *is American, but the tie-in* novels by "Marilyn Ross" (pseudonym for Dan Ross) have Barnabas visiting England after first becoming a vampire, and only later returning to his native Collinsport, Maine. Lord Ruthven is from John Polidori's "The Vampyre." Farren claims Ruthven was captured by the Greek Orthodox Church and exposed to sunlight, killing him. However, Polidori's story had Ruthven walking around in the daytime. Perhaps the Church conducted a ritual that removed Ruthven's immunity to sunlight. If so, Ruthven's destruction was not permanent either, given his resurrection in "Dracula's Vampire Legion," as well as his appearance in the movie Countess Dracula's Orgy of Blood. Cthulhu and the Great Old Ones are from the stories of H. P. Lovecraft; Renquist and his coven encountered Cthulhu in the second novel in the series, Darklost. Raoul Privache is the vampire from John Metcalfe's short novel The Feasting Dead. Although there is no theatre in Metcalfe's novel, a Theatre Raoul Privache in Paris appears in Kim Newman's The Bloody Red Baron. The Theatre mentioned in More Than Mortal must be the CU version of the Theatre in the Anno Dracula Universe. Taliesin the Merlin's portrayal does not fit with other versions of Merlin in the CU, and therefore he is likely one of many individuals to use that name. Although Van Helsing is referred to as a real person in Darklost, Renquist believes in More Than Mortal that Count Dracula is merely the fictional creation of Bram Stoker. Rick Lai writes, "My theory is that the memories of Renquist and his Coven have been tampered with. Their telepathic ability has left them vulnerable to manipulation by a more powerful vampire. Who was this vampire? In Farren's novels, Renquist can be telepathically contacted by his former Master, Dietrich, who has retired to parts unknown. However, Dietrich can still contact Renquist telepathically. In The Time of Feasting, Renquist was nearly destroyed because he came into conflict with a rebellious member of his coven, Kurt Carfax, who had Dracula-like dreams of leading a vampire army. Dietrich must have recognized that Renquist would come into conflict with any vampires who saw themselves as world conquerors. Probably Renquist learned of Dracula's existence in the 19th century and wanted the coven, then led by Dietrich, to attack the megalomaniac. The wise Dietrich saw that the human vampire hunters would take care of Dracula, and could only persuade Renquist to back off by brainwashing him into believing that Dracula didn't exist. This was also done to the rest of the members of the Coven. A result of this brainwashing had the side effect of causing the Coven to believe that no vampires existed with Dracula's abilities (the ability to walk in sunlight, changing into bats and wolves, etc.) Dietrich was smart enough to leave the Coven aware of Van Helsing's existence since the occultist posed a formidable threat."

December. Events of "Red Wood" by Brian Keene.

Spring
DAY OF THE HUNTER

Searching for the cause of a sickness that is plaguing an African village, Tarzan enters a cave and discovers the journal of Professor Günther Klaustach, who in 1936 recorded how the "dark hunter" BlackJack sought to kill him. Just then, a cave-in occurs, and Tarzan somehow finds himself in 1936, where he teams up with BlackJack to prevent Klaustach from releasing a virulent toxin.

Sunday Tarzan strip by Alex Simmons and Eric Battle, January 6–May 19, 2002. BlackJack is Arron Day, an African-American mercenary active in the 1930s and '40s. He has appeared in comics, prose stories, and an audio play by Simmons; this crossover brings him into the CU.

KILLER BARBYS VS. DRACULA

The punk rock group the Killer Barbies battle Count Dracula. Dr. Seward appears, as does the Count's caretaker, Irina von Karstein.

2001 feature film directed by Jesús Franco. The Killer Barbies are a real punk group whose fictional counterparts previously appeared in Franco's film Killer Barbys *(both films used a different spelling for the band's name in the title, since Mattel would not let them use the name "Barbie.") The Dracula seen in this film is likely a "soulclone." Dr. Seward is doubtless a relative of the doctor from Stoker's* Dracula. *Irina von Karstein is played by Lina Romay, who played a vampire called Countess Irina Karlstein in Franco's film* Female Vampire. *Either the two Irinas are the same person using different versions of her surname, or else the two are related. It is also possible they are related to the similarly-named Karnstein family, whose members include another vampire, the title character of J. Sheridan Le Fanu's "Carmilla." It is worth noting there is a blind metaphysician named Dr. Orloff in* Female Vampire; *this character is most likely a relative of the title character of Franco's* The Awful Dr. Orloff *and its sequels.*

THE LOST LEVEL

An occultist named Aaron Pace discovers how to navigate the Labyrinth between worlds, and begins exploring other dimensions before ending up stranded in the Lost Level, a reality that can be journeyed to, but never returned from, and where things are constantly arriving from parallel realities. Pace mentions it was the Simon *Necronomicon* that introduced him to occultism as a child, but he didn't realize it was a fake, and it was many years before he laid eyes on the real *Necronomicon*. Nyarlathotep is mentioned in Pace's spell for opening doorways into the Labyrinth. In one of the alternate universes he visits, Tony Genova is President. When he meets a group of serpent men, the Annunaki, in the Lost Level, Pace compares them to tales of the Dark Ones, a race of lizard men he'd heard about in his studies. Mushroom men living in a swamp are referenced. Pace is familiar with the Void. He also knows about Globe Package Services and the Globe Corporation, and a robot employed by a future version of the company appears. Pace meets a cowboy, Deke, from another dimension, where a zombie plague wiped out civilization in the Old West. Deke mentions he was born in his world's version of Brinkley Springs, WV. Pace has knowledge of the Thirteen, and names Ob, Ab and Api in particular. Pace and his allies battle a giant Clicker. Pace is familiar with Black Lodge.

Novel by Brian Keene. The Labyrinth is a core part of Keene's connected fiction. The Lost Level is mentioned in Keene's novel Ghost Walk. *The* Necronomicon *and* Nyarlathotep *are from H. P. Lovecraft's Cthulhu Mythos. Tony Genova is from the* Clickers *novels by Keene and J. F. Gonzalez, where he is a mobster (as is his CU counterpart, who has appeared in other stories by Keene), and is also president in the world of* Clickers vs. Zombies. *The Dark Ones are also from the* Clickers *novels, though the species also exists in the CU, as Levi Stoltzfus mentions them in "Last of the Albatwitches." The mushroom men in the swamp may or may not be those infected with the fungus from Keene's* Earthworm Gods *novels. The Void is where Ob and the Siqqusim were confined until they were released in the alternate dimension of Keene's* The Rising. *Globe Package Services and the Globe Corporation exist across Keene's multiverse. Deke's homeworld is the world of Keene's short story "Lost Canyon of the Damned." The zombie virus, Hamelin's Revenge, is the same one that destroyed civilization in the 2000s in the world of Keene's* Dead Sea *and* Entombed. *The CU version of Brinkley Springs, WV was seen in Keene's novel* A Gathering of Crows. *The Thirteen are the main villains of the Labyrinth cycle. The Clickers are the crab-lobster-scorpion beasts that are the primary villains of the* Clickers *novels. Black Lodge is a government agency that recurs throughout Keene's fiction.*

Summer
LEVIATHAN

Mack Bolan vs. the Cthulhu cult on an oil rig in the Bermuda Triangle. Miskatonic University is featured.

The Executioner #276. *This is not the first time Mack Bolan has encountered Cthulhu worshippers: see the COMCON trilogy of Executioner novels, consisting of* Trigger Point (#262), Iron Fist (#264), *and* Ultimate Price (#266).

INCIDENT ON A QUIET STREET

Rockne "Roc" Callahan tracks down the owner of a dog he found, who remarks, "That name sounds familiar. Are you a football player or something?" He replies, "No, no, that's another guy." Later, while capturing a criminal, his opponent asks him who he is: "'The Grey Monk?' Jack questioned. 'The Black Ghost? Shadowhawke? Tell me, I gotta know!'"

Story by Gene Girardier in Double Danger Tales *#51, Tom and Ginger Johnson, eds., Fading Shadows Publications, 2002. The dog's owner has evidently confused Roc with William Campbell Gault's football player turned P.I. Brock "The Rock" Callahan. The Roc Callahan stories were originally set in the 1930s, but were later shifted to the present day with no major changes in the characters. I am treating Roc as a contemporary character for continuity purposes. The Grey Monk is a modern-day pulp-style hero created by John L. French. The Black Ghost, whose adventures are also set in the present day, was created by Tom Johnson. Shadowhawke (not to be confused with the similarly-named costumed vigilante Shadowhawk, who once encountered Vampirella) appeared in K. G. McAbee and Tom Johnson's story "First Flight," set in 1921. The reference to Shadowhawke in "Incident on a Quiet Street" would seem to suggest either the hero is somehow still active in the 21st Century, or a successor has taken up his mantle. Since Brock Callahan is in the CU, so are Roc Callahan, the Grey Monk, the Black Ghost, and Shadowhawke.*

THE NONESUCH HORROR

Sonja Blue is in New Mexico when a local sheriff, who happens to be a skinwalker, or werewolf, confiscates her signature weapon, a switchblade that can kill supernatural beings. When the sheriff shows it to a Native American medicine woman, she reveals: "'That is not just a knife, skinwalker! It is a thing of power, like the wolfcane,' referring to the totem-staff of the vargr, used for millennia by the alphas to denote their supremacy over the pack."

Short story by Nancy A. Collins in Dead Roses for a Blue Lady, *Crossroads Press, 2002. The wolfcane is meant to be the walking stick from* Universal Studios' *The Wolf Man, confirming Sonja Blade in the CU.*

KILLER INSTINCTS

William Lynch is trained in his quest for vengeance by a mysterious man known as Richard.

Novel by Jack Badelaire, Post Modern Books, 2012. From the hints dropped in the novel, Richard must be Richard Joseph Camellion, the Death Merchant. William's grandfather, Thomas Lynch, is the protagonist of the World War II-set *series* Commando *(*Operation Arrowhead, Operation Bedlam, Operation Cannibal, *and* Operation Dervish*) and the side series* Commando Resistance *(*The Train to Calais*).*

SOMETHING FROM THE NIGHTSIDE

John Taylor, a private detective in London with an innate talent for finding things, is hired to find a teenage runaway who has fled to the Nightside, a pocket dimension in London where it is always 3 A.M. John is originally from the Nightside, and has not been back in years. The railway station in the Nightside has graffiti with the name Cthulhu misspelled, as well as a list of destinations which includes Shadows Fall, Haceldama, and the Street of the Gods. John mentions Deathwalkers as among those who visit the Nightside. John sees a woman dressed as a punk reading a bible with blank pages, and realizes from her white on white unblinking eyes she is a graduate of the Deep School. John visits the bar Strangefellows. Bartender Alex Morrissey has a large glamour calendar behind the bar, showing Elvira, Mistress of the Dark in a series of photographic poses that would probably upset her greatly if she ever found out about them. John also visits the Hawk's Wind Bar & Grill, where it is still the 1960s and they have a jukebox the size of a TARDIS. Inside, John sees the Sonic Assassin showing off his new vibragun to the Notting Hill Sorcerer, the timelost Victorian Adventurer, the Amber Prince, all five Tracy brothers, and the whole Cornelius clan.

*Novel by Simon R. Green. Cthulhu is one of the Great Old Ones of H.
P. Lovecraft's Mythos. Shadows Fall is from Green's novel of the same name.
Haceldama is from Green's Deathstalker series of novels, which takes place in
another of the many possible futures for the Crossover Universe. The Street of
the Gods is from Green's Hawk and Fisher novellas* Winner Takes All *and*
The God Killer. *The Low Kingdoms, the setting of both the Hawk and Fisher
series and Green's Forest Kingdom series, must be in another dimension or a
pocket universe. Deathwalkers are from Green's novel* Drinking Midnight
Wine. *The Deep School appears in Manly Wade Wellman's John Thunstone
stories. Elvira, Mistress of the Dark is from the television series* Elvira's Movie
Macabre. *The TARDIS is of course the time and space vehicle belonging
to the Doctor, from the long running BBC series* Doctor Who. *The Sonic
Assassin is Michael Moorcock's English Assassin Jerry Cornelius, who used the
vibragun in* A Cure for Cancer. *Jerry Cornelius is one of many incarnations
of the Eternal Champion across Moorcock's Multiverse, and has been firmly
established as existing in the CU. The Notting Hill Sorcerer is Moorcock himself. The timelost Victorian Adventurer is Julien Advent, a recurring character
in the Nightside books. Advent is actually adventurer Adam Adamant (from
the television series* Adam Adamant Lives!*) using an alias, further connecting
the Nightside to the CU, although it is also obviously connected to multiple
alternate universes. The Amber Prince is Prince Corwin from the Amber series
by Roger Zelazny, which also crosses multiple universes. The Tracy brothers
are from the TV series* Thunderbirds, *created by Gerry Anderson, which probably takes place in an alternate future to the CU.*

THE MAN WITH THE GOLDEN TORC

Eddie Drood, aka Shaman Bond, is a member of the Drood (née Druid)
clan that protects the world from supernatural threats. He is suddenly inex-
plicably declared a rogue by his family, who set out to kill him. He strives
to learn the reason why. Appearing or mentioned are: a Time Agent whose
latest regeneration has gone terribly wrong, turning him inside out; the
Necronomicon; a Kandarian possessing amulet; the Old Ones; a Hyde using
a distillation of Jekyll's old formula; Rossum's Unionized Robots; a 1930s
powder blue Hirondel convertible sports car; Alice Little; Penelope
Creighton; Area 52; *taduki*; Martian red weed; the Arcadia Project; Vril
Power, Inc.; the Lurkers on the Threshold; Arne Saknussemm; Cave Carson;
a stuffed moomintroll; a statue of a black bird; a small black lacquered puzzle
box; the Holy Hand Grenade of St. Antioch; scrimshaw carved from the
bones of a great white whale; Baron von Frankenstein; and the Manx Cat.

*Novel by Simon R. Green. The Drood family name is a reference to
Charles Dickens' unfinished novel* The Mystery of Edwin Drood, *which has
been established to take place in the CU. Time Agents are from the television*

series Doctor Who *and* Torchwood. *The* Necronomicon, *the Old Ones, and the Lurkers on the Threshold refer to the Cthulhu Mythos of H. P. Lovecraft and others. The Kandarian possessing amulet is connected to the Kandarian demons from the* Evil Dead *movies. The reference to Hyde and Jekyll's formula is of course from Robert Louis Stevenson's* The Strange Case of Dr. Jekyll and Mr. Hyde. *Rossum's Unionized Robots is a reference to the play* R.U.R. *by Karel Capek, where the initials stood for Rossum's Universal Robots. In the play, a robot from the future explains how Rossum's robots became unionized. This likely takes place in an alternate future or an AU. The Hirondel sports car is the same kind of car Simon Templar drove in Leslie Charteris' Saint novels. Alice Little is meant to be Alice Liddell from Lewis Carroll's* Alice's Adventures in Wonderland *and* Through the Looking Glass. *Penelope Creighton must be an ancestor of Lady Penelope Creighton-Ward from the TV series* Thunderbirds, *which likely takes place in an alternate future. Area 52 is not an uncommon name in conspiracy fiction, but given that both are located in the Antarctic, it is likely the Area 52 burgled by Eddie is the one from the Image Comics series* Area 52. Taduki *is from H. Rider Haggard's* Allan and the Ice Gods. *Martian red weed is from H. G. Wells'* The War of the Worlds. *The Arcadia Project is from Green's Nightside novel* Hell to Pay. *Vril Power is from Edward Bulwer-Lytton's* The Coming Race. *Arne Saknussemm is from Jules Verne's* Journey to the Center of the Earth. *Cave Carson is a DC Comics character who explores under the Earth and has sci-fi tinged pulp adventures. The stuffed Moomintroll is from Tove Jansson's Moomin books. The statue of the black bird is the Maltese Falcon from the novel by Dashiell Hammett. The black lacquered puzzle box is from Clive Barker's "The Hellbound Heart," which is the basis for the* Hellraiser *movies. The Holy Hand Grenade of St. Antioch is from the film* Monty Python and the Holy Grail, *which is presumably an exaggeration of the true details of the quest for the Grail. The scrimshaw from the bones of a great white whale is a reference to Herman Melville's* Moby Dick. *Baron von Frankenstein is from Mary Shelley's* Frankenstein *and its continuations. The Manx Cat must be an AU version of the one seen in the First Comics series* Grimjack.

THE LIVING GODDESS

The deeply religious vigilante known as the Grey Monk battles Thuggee seeking a chest that has passed through many hands before coming to his own city. The history of the chest is shown through a series of flashbacks. One is set in Victorian London, and involves a Great Detective who is friends with a doctor (whose new bride has family in America), knows Baritsu, and is pursuing a Professor. Another takes place in New York City in 1939, and shows a vigilante who also has a guise as man about town

Michael Shaw gunning down Thuggee and Nazis seeking the chest at a museum.

Short story by John L. French in Souls on Fire: The Chronicles of the Grey Monk, *Wild Cat Books, 2008. The Great Detective is clearly Sherlock Holmes, though the 1892 date for the flashback must be incorrect, as that would place it during Holmes' Great Hiatus. 1886 is more likely, since William S. Baring-Gould's biography* Sherlock Holmes of Baker Street *states Dr. Watson married an American woman in that year. The vigilante in New York City in 1939 is Michael Shaw, aka the Nightmare, who has appeared in other stories by French.*

Summer 2001–Autumn 2002
DAEMONS ARE FOREVER

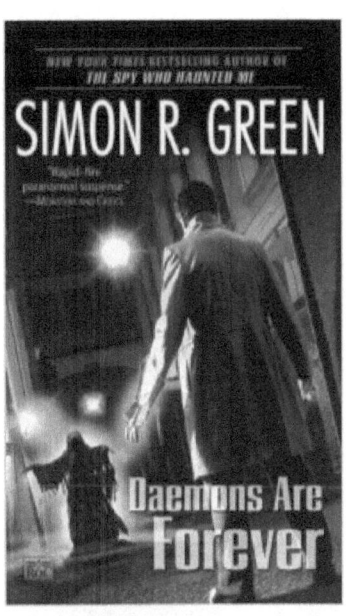

Eddie Drood, now leading the Drood Family, must find a way to drive out the Loathly Ones, demons that were brought to Earth during World War II to help fight the Nazis, before they summon the Hungry Gods to destroy the world. Appearing or mentioned are: a Hirondel sports car; Bruin Bear and the Sea Goat; Merlin's Glass; Vril Power, Inc.; Harry Fabulous; a ghost named Ash; a minor Norse godling; the Many-Angled Ones; the Celestials; *Renfield's*; a couple of Baron Frankenstein's more successful creations; Melmoth the Wanderer; Dracula; a French demon hunter named Mallorie; the Kandarians; Dr. Syn's Fly by Night Delivery Service; "this American gentleman and his giant rabbit"; Giles Deathstalker; a giant mechanical spider confiscated from an American mad genius in the Wild West; the Kessel run; and an Old One.

Novel by Simon R. Green. The Hirondel is a fictional brand of car driven by Leslie Charteris' hero Simon Templar, aka the Saint. Bruin Bear and the Sea Goat are from Green's novel Shadows Fall, *as is the ghost Leonard Ash. Merlin's Glass and Harry Fabulous are from Green's Nightside books. Vril Power, Inc. is a reference to the Vril Power from Edward Bulwer-Lytton's* The Coming Race. *The minor Norse godling is Jimmy Thunder from Green's novel* Drinking Midnight Wine. *"Many-angled ones" is a term originally used by Grant Morrison to describe the Lloigor of the Cthulhu Mythos in the superhero comic book* Zenith, *which must take place in an AU, but it has been adopted by other Mythos authors over the years. The*

Celestials are an alien race with untold cosmic power appearing in various series published by Marvel Comics. Renfield's, *of course, is named after Dracula's zoophagous minion. Baron Frankenstein's creations are a reference to Mary Shelley's* Frankenstein *and its many literary and cinematic continuations. Melmoth the Wanderer is from Charles Robert Maturin's novel of the same name. Mallorie may be a reference to the title character of the French horror film* Bloody Mallory. *The Kandarians are from the* Evil Dead *film series. Dr. Syn's Fly by Night Delivery Service is a reference to the Dr. Syn novels by Russell Thorndike. "This American gentleman and his giant rabbit" are Elwood P. Dowd and Harvey from the movie* Harvey. *Giles Deathstalker is from Green's* Deathstalker *novels, which take place in the far future. The giant mechanical spider is from the film version of* The Wild Wild West. *The Kessel run is from the movie* Star Wars: Episode IV–A New Hope. *The Old Ones are from H. P. Lovecraft's Cthulhu Mythos.*

August 24–Late October
NUMBER9DREAM

Eiji Miyake's quest to find his biological father in Tokyo brings him into contact with the Yazuka. In the process, he meets a Mongolian hitman named Suhbataar.

Novel by David Mitchell. Suhbataar previously appeared in Mitchell's book Ghostwritten.

October
THE CABINET OF CURIOSITIES

F.B.I. Special Agent Aloysius Pendergast investigates a series of killings that ultimately prove to be the work of his great-grand-uncle Antoine Leng Pendergast, aka Enoch Leng. Among the items in Leng's cabinet of curiosities is a giant rat from Sumatra. Archaeologist Nora Kelly also appears.

Novel by Douglas Preston and Lincoln Child. The giant rat from Sumatra is an implicit connection to the Sherlock Holmes stories. Calpurnia Pendergast, a relative of Aloysius, appears in Matthew Ilseman's Arsène Lupin story "A Theft of China," confirming Agent Pendergast's inclusion in the CU. Nora Kelly first appeared in

Preston and Child's novel Thunderhead, *which also featured reporter Bill Smithback, a supporting character from the Pendergast books. With this novel, Nora becomes a supporting character in the series as well. Most of Preston and Child's other collaborations are also connected to the Pendergast series by recurring characters, including* Mount Dragon, The Ice Limit, *and the Gideon Crew series, which so far consists of* Gideon's Sword, Gideon's Corpse, *and* The Lost Island. *The Pendergast novel* White Fire *involves an unpublished Holmes story, and Holmes himself is treated as fictional. Of course, Holmes was every bit as real as Pendergast. Perhaps the lost story was a completely fictional account penned by Dr. Watson, which Holmes did not allow Watson or Doyle to publish, given his well-known disdain for what he saw as Watson's sensationalization of his real cases.*

HARD AS NAILS

Former P.I. Joe Kurtz tells his ex-girlfriend Detective Rigby King about his background: "My mother was a whore. I didn't see much of her even before the orphanage. Once when she was drunk, she told me that she thought my old man was a thief, some guy with just one name and that not even his own. Not a second-story guy, but a real hardcase who would set up serious jobs with a bunch of other pros and then blow town forever. She said he and she were together for just a week in the late sixties . . . She said that he never wanted sex except right *after* a successful job."

Novel by Dan Simmons, Minotaur Books, 2003. Kurtz's father is Parker, a professional thief appearing in novels by "Richard Stark" (pen name for Donald E. Westlake). Since Parker is in the CU, so is Joe Kurtz. This novel, the third in the Kurtz series, takes place a year after the first novel, Hardcase, *which was published in 2001.*

Autumn

DARKEST HEART

Sonja Blue visits a New Orleans voodoo priestess, whose library includes a copy of Legendre's *Le Livre d'Absinthe.*

Novel by Nancy A. Collins, White Wolf Publishing, 2002. Legendre must be voodoo houngan Murder Legendre from the horror film White Zombie.

AGENTS OF LIGHT AND DARKNESS

John Taylor is hired to find the Unholy Grail from which Judas Iscariot drank at the Last Supper. Appearing or mentioned are: the Street of the Gods; description theory bombs; one of Baron Frankenstein's more successful creations; Leo Morn; the *Testimony of Grendel Rex*; Shadows Fall; winter wine; copies of the Maltese Falcon; the Warriors of the Cross; a crate marked *Antarctic Expedition 1936: Do not open until the Elder Ones return*; and Grendel's Bane.

Novel by Simon R. Green. The Street of the Gods is from Green's Hawk and Fisher novellas Winner Takes All *and* The God Killer. *Description theory bombs are a reference to description theory from Warren Ellis' comic book* Planetary, *which takes place in an AU. "One of Baron Frankenstein's more successful creations" is one of the many Frankenstein Monsters. Leo Morn and winter wine are from Green's* Drinking Midnight Wine. *Grendel Rex is a member of the Drood family turned into a self-proclaimed god in Green's Secret* Histories *novels. Shadows Fall is from Green's novel of the same name, which is also the source of the Warriors of the Cross. The Maltese Falcon is the legendary bird statuette from the eponymous novel by Dashiell Hammett. The Antarctic Expedition and the Elder Ones are from H. P. Lovecraft's* At the Mountains of Madness, *although that story actually takes place in 1929–1930 rather than 1936. Grendel's Bane is Beowulf's sword from the epic poem, bringing Beowulf into the CU.*

APPETITE FOR MURDER

Sam Warren, the Nightside's Detective, teams up with the transvestite superheroine Ms. Fate to apprehend a killer who has been eating parts of his victims' bodies in order to gain their respective powers and abilities. The Lone Ranger; Mr. Stab; and Arnold Drood, the Bloody Man are mentioned.

Short story by Simon R. Green in Unusual Suspects: Stories of Mystery & Fantasy, *Dana Stabenow, ed., Ace Books, 2008; reprinted in* Tales from the Nightside, *Ace Books, 2015. The Lone Ranger is self-explanatory. Mr. Stab and Arnold Drood, the Bloody Man, are from Green's Secret* Histories *series. Arnold is said to have been killed by his family last year. The first Secret Histories novel,* The Man with the Golden Torc, *refers to Arnold's death, but does not state when it occurred. Sam Warren describes John Taylor as a newcomer to the Nightside. Taylor moved to the Nightside in the novel* Something from the Nightside. *The Nightside and Secret Histories books contain crossover references to each other that affect the chronological placement of both series.*

Winter
THE LAST DETECTIVE
Elvis Cole runs into Harry Bosch. It is mentioned Bosch lives in the same area as Cole. Carol Starkey appears.

Novel by Robert Crais. Harry Bosch is not identified by name, but is described in such a way as to leave little doubt it is him. Elvis would also make a cameo in the Harry Bosch novel Lost Light. *Bosch is also mentioned in the novel* Cons, Scams & Grifts *by Joe Gores, one of the Dan Kearny and Associates novels. Carol Starkey is from Crais' novel* Demolition Angel. *With this novel, she becomes a recurring character in the series.*

UNDERLAND
Vampire Victor Renquist travels to "the Hollow Earth," actually a series of underground caverns that can be reached from various points on Earth. Renquist spent time in England during World War II monitoring an occult warfare unit working out of Ravenkeep Priory under the command of the Duke de Richleau. Marcus De Reske's attempts to raise Cthulhu are mentioned. Pelucidar is another of the Hollow Earth's names. A member of a serpentlike race called the Dhrakuh tells Renquist, "the English eccentric, Professor Challenger, had made it into one of the subsidiary caves, but never discovered a major underground city, unlike the Norwegian, Nielsen, and two years later, the Prussian, Erich von Stalhein, who had come with a well-equipped expedition funded by the Krupp family."

The fourth novel in Mick Farren's Renquist Quartet *series. The Duke de Richleau is from novels by Dennis Wheatley. Cthulhu is, of course, one of the Great Old Ones in the fiction of H. P. Lovecraft. Marcus De Reske was prevented by Renquist and his* nosferatu *coven from releasing Cthulhu in the second novel in the series,* Darklost. *The name "Pelucidar" is a variant on that of Pellucidar from the novels of Edgar Rice Burroughs. The land seen in* Underland *is clearly not Burroughs' world, but both this novel and Steven Utley and Howard Waldrop's story "Black as the Pit, from Pole to Pole" indicate there are many inner worlds. Professor Challenger appears in* The Lost World *and other works by Arthur Conan Doyle. Nielsen is not a pre-existing character, but Erich von Stalhein is the archenemy of W. E. Johns' heroic aviator Biggles.*

SPIKE: ASYLUM
Spike is hired by the half-demon Ruby Monahan's family to track her down. He discovers she is imprisoned inside the Mosaic Wellness Center, which has been designed to "cure" demonic beings. The Center was built by Ivo Shandor, who later went mad and decided humanity didn't deserve to live.

Five-issue miniseries by Bryan Lynch and Franco Urru, IDW Publishing, September 2006–January 2007. Ivo Shandor is the occultist who designed Dana Barrett's apartment building in Ghostbusters; *his descent into madness is referenced in that film.*

Spring
DILLON AND THE VOICE OF ODIN

Dillon battles the evil Odin, who is using a sonic device to menace the world. Dillon, whose catamaran is called the *Copperfin*, drinks a can of Tenku Beer. Double-O agents are mentioned in a flashback, and British Secret Service agent Gregory Tipp has an office on the tenth floor of the Transworld Consortium building, which is an elaborate front for the Service itself. At the headquarters of Odin's ally Dr. Numby, Dillon admires swords handcrafted by Domingo Montoya, one of the greatest sword-crafters who ever lived. The president of the United States meets with Doctor Michael Cadwallander, Director of Special Projects for the Henderson Institute of Alternative Technologies, and Milo Dane, head of the Omega Elite, the U.S. government's ultimate "dirty tricks" department. Dillon's friend Eli Creed drinks Old Dusseldorf beer.

Novel by Derrick Ferguson, iUniverse, 2003, republished in a revised edition by PulpWork Press in 2013 with a new first chapter. Dillon is already in the CU. Dillon's catamaran is named after the U.S.S. Copperfin *submarine seen in the film* Destination Tokyo. Tenku Beer *is from the film* Kill Bill: Vol. 1. *Double-O agents and Transworld Consortium are from Ian Fleming's James Bond novels. Domingo Montoya is the father of Inigo Montoya, one of the main characters of William Goldman's novel* The Princess Bride. *The Henderson Institute of Alternative Technologies is run by Dr. Sylvester Henderson, whose brother Mongrel has appeared in stories by Ferguson for Airship 27 Productions'* Mystery Men (& Women) *anthology series. Omega Elite has been mentioned in several of Ferguson's stories. Old Dusseldorf beer is from the television series* Magnum, P.I.

THE HADES PROJECT

A group of scientists accidentally open a doorway to Hell and release a demon that plans to free more of his kind. There is a reference to "a guy in England named Rusk, I think, used to strangle women using silk ties. They called him the Necktie Killer."

This novel by Justin Gustainis takes place in the Crossover Universe via a reference to one of the characters, Shari Sexpert, in Gustainis' Morris and Chastain Supernatural Investigations novel Evil Ways. *Robert Rusk, the Necktie Killer, is from Alfred Hitchcock's film* Frenzy.

May–June
ONE LAST HIT

Joe Portugal, an ex-rock star turned actor who keeps finding himself involved in mysteries, briefly meets private eye Jack Liffey.

Novel by Nathan Walpow, Uglytown Productions, 2003. John Shannon's P.I. Jack Liffey is in the CU through a meeting with Philip Marlowe, a Wold Newton Family member. This crossover brings in Joe Portugal.

Summer
CHARLIE'S ANGELS: FULL THROTTLE

Angel Natalie Cook accompanies her boyfriend to his reunion at Rydell High School.

2003 feature film. Rydell High School is from the film Grease *and its sequel. Since the* Charlie's Angels *television series and subsequent films take place in the CU, so do the* Grease *movies.*

KOSHIEN BOMBER CASE

Conan Edogawa and friends attend the high school basketball finals at Koshien Stadium, and wind up thwarting a suicide bombing. The game is between Kohnan High School's team (which includes Shigeo Nagashima) and the team for Ougane High School (whose members include Kazuhisa Inao).

Story by Gosho Aoyama in Detective Conan *Volume 43, 2003. Kohnan High School, Shigeo Nagashima, Ougane High School, and Kazuhisa Inao are from Aoyama's one-volume manga* 3rd Base Fourth. *Shinichi (or Jimmy in English) Kudo was a 17-year-old who used his deductive abilities to aid the police until members of the criminal Black Organization vengefully injected him with an experimental poison that transformed his body into that of a child. Shinichi, or Conan Edogawa as he was now known, enrolled in elementary school and formed a Junior Detective League with three of his classmates. As a cover for his detective work, Shinichi moved in with his best friend Ran Mori and her father Kogoro (named Rachel and Richard Moore in English). Since Conan Edogawa is in through a later crossover with Lupin III,* 3rd Base

Fourth *must take place in the CU as well. One of Conan's regular foes is Kaito Kuroba, aka Phantom Thief Kid, aka Kaitō Kid, the main character of another Aoyama* manga, Magic Kaito, *thus bringing in that series as well.* Magic Kaito *also crossed over with* Yaiba! *which is another series by Aoyama.*

MONSTER HUNTER INTERNATIONAL

After accountant Owen Pitt kills his boss upon learning he is a murderous werewolf, he is recruited by Monster Hunter International (M.H.I.), a company that kills monsters to cash in on secret government bounties. Owen is told *Creature from the Black Lagoon* was based on a true story, and that both H. P. Lovecraft and J. R. R. Tolkien based their works on stories they heard from monster hunters. M.H.I. battles the Old Ones. Upon hearing the main villain referred to as "C. O.," Owen thinks, "After having seen him, and feeling a taste of his power, calling the evil creature something so innocuous seemed a little silly. The residents of Tokyo didn't call Godzilla 'Big G.'" Earl Harbinger compares the agents of M.H.I. to famous monster hunters of the past, including Odysseus, St. George, Beowulf, and "Van Helsing with firepower." Julie Shackleford mentions "the Vanni Fucci incident in Dothan a while back."

Novel by Larry Correia, Baen Books, 2009. The references to Lovecraft, the Creature from the Black Lagoon and Abraham Van Helsing link Monster Hunter International *and its sequels into the CU. There is a CU version of Godzilla, as seen in Emmanuel Gorlier's story "Twilight" and Nick Pollotta's novel* Doomsday Exam, *but he appears to have spent his existence in the 20th and 21st centuries in captivity. Vanni Fucci is an actual historical person Dante placed in Hell in his* Inferno, *but the Dothan reference is specifically to Dan Simmons' short story "Vanni Fucci is Alive and Well and Living in Hell," a sequel to* Inferno *in which Vanni Fucci is briefly released from Hell and turns up on the set of a corrupt Alabama televangelist's program. This link also brings in Larry Niven and Jerry Pournelle's novels* Inferno *and* Escape from Hell, *which feature a sci-fi writer named Allen Carpentier who dies and ends up in the Hell described by Dante, as well as the television series* Reaper, *which made several references to Dante's various circles as real places in that show's version of Hell, and Gene Wolfe's story "Bed and Breakfast," set in a bed and breakfast near Hell, in which the narrator mentions Dante actually traveled to Hell.*

NIGHTINGALE'S LAMENT

John Taylor is hired to investigate a singer known as the Nightingale, whose singing inspires suicide. Appearing or mentioned are: a new edition of *The King in Yellow;* the password "Swordfish" to get into a nightclub; lots of monkeys doing manual labor (some of whom still have their wings); combat magicians; Nicholas Hob; miller medallions; Julien Advent, the timelost Victorian Adventurer; phasers and photon torpedoes; and the Murder Masque.

Novel by Simon R. Green. The King in Yellow is a play from Robert W. Chambers' book of the same name, which was incorporated into the Cthulhu Mythos by H. P. Lovecraft. "Swordfish" was the password to a speakeasy in the Marx Bros. film Horse Feathers. *The winged monkeys are from L. Frank Baum's* The Wizard of Oz. *Combat magicians are a reference to Warren Ellis' comic book* Gravel. *Nicholas Hob is from Green's book* Drinking Midnight Wine. *Miller Medallions are from the comic book* Grimjack. *Julien Advent is meant to be Adam Adamant from the BBC TV series* Adam Adamant Lives! *The Murder Masque is said to be the villain responsible for Julien Advent becoming timelost, which means he is intended to be the Face, the main villain from* Adam Adamant Lives! *Phasers and photon torpedoes are from* Star Trek.

THE DIFFERENCE A DAY MAKES

John Taylor and Dead Boy help an ordinary woman figure out why and how she came to be in the Nightside, and also try to reunite her with her husband. Appearing or mentioned are: the Maltese Falcon; Something from a Black Lagoon; one of Frankenstein's female creations; knockoff Hyde formula; a lipstick-red Plymouth Fury with a dead man grinning at the wheel; a great black beauty of a car, driven by an Oriental in black leathers, and a man in the back in a green face mask and a snap-brimmed hat; and worms from the earth.

Novella by Simon R. Green in Mean Streets, *Rock Books, 2009; reprinted in* Tales from the Nightside, *Ace Books, 2015. The Maltese Falcon is from Dashiell Hammett's private eye novel of the same name. Something from a Black Lagoon is a reference to the Universal horror film* Creature from the Black Lagoon. *Hyde formula is from Robert Louis Stevenson's novel* The Strange Case of Dr. Jekyll and Mr. Hyde. *The lipstick-red Plymouth Fury is the titular car from Stephen King's novel* Christine. *The man in the green mask and the Oriental in black leathers are the Green Hornet and Kato, with this particular pair probably being Paul Reid and Kono Kato, who began working together in 1993. Worms from the earth are a reference to Robert E. Howard's Bran Mak Morn story "Worms of the Earth."*

217

GHOST OF A CHANCE

J. C. Chance, Melody Chambers, and Happy Jack Palmer are field agents of the Carnacki Institute, a group devoted to investigating ghostly activity. Their latest case, a haunting in London's Oxford Circus Tube Station, bring them into contact with the ghost of a young woman named Kim Sterling, with whom J. C. falls in love; Natasha Chang and Erik Grossman, two members of the Institute's rival, the Crowley Project; and the Great Beast known as Fenris Tenebrae. J. C. boasts, "Remember . . . when the Ghostbusters have a headache; when the Scooby gang are having a panic attack; when Mulder and Scully don't want to know and the psychic commandos of the SAS are sitting in a corner crying their eyes out . . . Who do you send for? The specially trained field agents of the Carnacki Institute!" Melody refers to other Great Beasts, such as the Hogge or the Serpent. The head of the Institute, Catherine Latimer, refers to J. C.'s recent acquisition of a folio copy of the damned and utterly poisonous play *The King in Yellow*. Happy says they are not trained, equipped, or armed enough to deal with Great Beasts or Outer Monstrosities, or any of the Abominations. Natasha reminds Erik of the Case of the Horse Invisible, last year. J. C. doesn't know anyone who's actually encountered Frankenstein tech in the field before. He also has a Hand of Glory made from a monkey's paw.

Novel by Simon R. Green. The Carnacki Institute's name is a reference to occult detective Thomas Carnacki from William Hope Hodgson's book Carnacki the Ghost-Finder. *Since the Institute was founded in 1587, during the reign of Queen Elizabeth I, the Institute must have been named for an ancestor of Thomas', or else was later renamed after him. The Hogge is a reference to the titular being from the Carnacki story "The Hog." The Outer Monstrosities are mentioned in both "The Whistling Room" and "The Hog." The Case of the Horse Invisible must be connected to the Carnacki story "The Horse of the Invisible." The Ghostbusters are from the film of the same name and its sequel. The Scooby gang could be a reference to the talking dog Scooby-Doo and his monster-chasing comrades in Mystery, Inc. On the other hand, the Scooby Gang is the nickname Buffy Summers and her allies use for themselves on the TV series* Buffy the Vampire Slayer, *so it could be a reference to them. Either way, both Scooby-Doo and Buffy are firmly in the CU already. Mulder and Scully are from the TV series* The X-Files. *The psychic commandos of the SAS may be a reference to Warren Ellis' comic* Gravel. *The Serpent may be the Serpent in the Sun from Green's novel* Drinking Midnight Wine. *The play* The King in Yellow *is from Robert W. Chambers' short story collection of the same name. Frankenstein tech is named after the scientist from Mary Shelley's novel* Frankenstein. *The Hand of Glory made from a monkey's paw is a nod to W. W. Jacobs' short story "The Monkey's Paw."*

DILLON AND THE JUDAS CHALICE

Dillon, being chased by police through the city of Denbrook, tells his ally Wyatt Hyatt he took some training from a French race car driver named Vaillant. A potential client, Diogenes Morales, tells Dillon his former best friend, Cornelius Spoto, is plotting to overthrow the Caribbean island republic of San Monique. Dillon's comrade Reynard Hansen claims to have been trained by the Thieves Guild of Seville. Morales' daughter Fiesta attended the Higgins School of Higher Learning for Girls. Spoto worked with Dillon's enemy Cecil Henshaw in Parmistan.

Short story by Derrick Ferguson in Four Bullets for Dillon, PulpWork Press, 2011. *Dillon is already firmly in the CU. The city of Denbrook, created by Mike McGee, was the setting of nine serialized novels by various authors on the online fiction site* Frontier Publishing. *The French race car driver is the title character of Jean Graton's comic book series* Michel Vaillant. *San Monique is from the film version of Ian Fleming's James Bond novel* Live and Let Die; *since most of the Bond movies take place in an alternate universe to the CU, the San Monique mentioned in this story and Frank Schildiner's "The True Cost of Doing Business" must be the CU version of the island. The Thieves Guild of Seville is a reference to Miguel de Cervantes' short story "Rinconete and Cortadillo." The Higgins School of Higher Learning for Girls is named after Professor Henry Higgins from George Bernard Shaw's play* Pygmalion, *adapted as the stage musical* My Fair Lady. *Parmistan is a fictional country from the movie* Gymkata.

October
LOST LIGHT

Harry Bosch sees Elvis Cole driving his yellow 1966 Corvette and salutes the P.I.

Novel by Harry Bosch, edited by Michael Connelly. Robert Crais' detective Elvis Cole is not referred to by name, but his description is unmistakable. Prior to this book, Harry Bosch had an unnamed cameo in the Elvis Cole novel The Last Detective.

Autumn

HEX AND THE CITY

John Taylor is hired to investigate the origins of the Nightside. Appearing or mentioned are: six foot tall teddy bears of very little brain; three different Maltese Falcons; one of Baron Frankenstein's scalpels; the Mirror of Dorian Gray; old Carnacki the Ghost Finder; Kandarian demons; Alice's Restaurant; Wonka's Wonderous Warren: Chocolate with Everything; Rick's Café Imaginaire, run by Rick, whose slogan is "Everyone comes to Rick's"; a snark that turned into a boojum; Leo Morn; jabberwocky giblets that come with borogroves, which are always a bit mimsy; Cheshire Cat ice cream; the Street of the Gods; the Prospero and Michael Scott Memorial Library; Club Dead, exclusively for the many creations of Baron Frankenstein and his descendants; Julien Advent, the legendary Victorian Adventurer; Shadows Fall; Rats' Alley; Positronic Brains; Queen Mab; Titania; the Traveling Doctor; a singing rose; the Eaters of the Dead; an aristocratic French nobleman who wears a mask covering all but one eye, the left, who fled to the Nightside in the early 20th century to escape a Parisian mob, and who misses the opera; Luna and Gaea; Nicholas Hob; a moonchild; taduki; tanna leaves; and Orlando.

Novel by Simon R. Green. The six foot tall teddy bears of very little brain refer to the Winnie the Pooh stories of A. A. Milne. The Maltese Falcon comes from the classic detective novel by Dashiell Hammett. Baron Frankenstein's scalpel refers to either Mary Shelley's Frankenstein or one of the many films inspired by that novel. The Mirror of Dorian Gray refers to Oscar Wilde's The Picture of Dorian Gray, although there was no mirror in that book. Old Carnacki the Ghost Finder is from William Hope Hodgson's collection Carnacki the Ghost-Finder. Kandarian demons are from the Evil Dead film franchise. Alice's Restaurant is from the song by Arlo Guthrie and the film it inspired, directed by Arthur Penn. Wonka's Wondrous Warren: Chocolate with Everything refers to Roald Dahl's Charlie and the Chocolate Factory, bringing that book into the CU. Rick, the owner of Rick's Café Imaginaire, is clearly Rick Blaine from Casablanca, who must have relocated to the Nightside at some point. The snark that was a boojum refers to Lewis Carroll's "The Hunting of the Snark." Leo Morn is from Green's novel Drinking Midnight Wine. The jabberwocky giblets with mimsy borogroves refer to Lewis Carroll's "Jabberwocky," while Cheshire Cat ice cream is a reference to Alice in Wonderland.

The Street of the Gods is from Green's Hawk and Fisher novellas Winner Takes All *and* The God Killer. *The Michael Scott and Prospero Memorial Library refers to Prospero from William Shakespeare's* The Tempest. *Baron Frankenstein's* I Did It My Way *may be an AU version of Baron Frankenstein's* How I Did It, *from Mel Brooks' film* Young Frankenstein. *Baron Frankenstein and his descendants are a reference to Mary Shelley's novel and all the books and films inspired by that novel. Julien Advent, the legendary Victorian Adventurer, is supposed to be Adam Adamant from the BBC TV series* Adam Adamant Lives! *Shadows Fall is from Green's novel of the same name. Rats' Alley is from T. S. Eliot's poem "The Waste Land." Positronic brains are from the works of Isaac Asimov. Queen Mab is from William Shakespeare's* Romeo and Juliet, *while Titania is from Shakespeare's* A Midsummer Night's Dream. *The Traveling Doctor is intended to be the Doctor from the BBC series* Doctor Who; *although most of the Doctor's exploits take place in an AU, he does have a CU counterpart who frequently uses the name Doctor Omega. The Singing Rose is from Andrew Lang's poem of the same name. The Eaters of the Dead are Neanderthals from the novel of the same name by Michael Crichton, which is his retelling of the story of Beowulf. The aristocratic French ferryman is intended to be Erik from Gaston Leroux's* The Phantom of the Opera. *Luna and Gaea are the versions of those goddesses seen in Green's novel* Drinking Midnight Wine, *which is also the source of Nicholas Hob. The moonchild is a reference to Aleister Crowley's novel of the same name. One of the main characters in* The Moonchild, *Simon Iff, also appeared in a series of detective stories by Crowley. Taduki is from H. Rider Haggard's Allan Quatermain series, while tanna leaves are from the first series of Universal Mummy movies. Orlando is from the Virginia Woolf book of the same name.*

PATHS NOT TAKEN

John Taylor goes back in time to discover the origins of the Nightside. Appearing or mentioned are: Old Father Time; Time Tower Square; Shadows Fall; a Time Tunnel operated by the Authorities in the 1960s; Julien Advent; the Street of the Gods; one of Baron Frankstein's creatures; one of Frankenstein's descendants; a cat that can disappear at will; anti-life; Morlocks and Eloi; a pack of child-sized bipedal rats with disturbingly human hands; the Serpent; the Serpent's Son; Cthulhu; two giants throwing rocks at each other; and Rats' Alley.

Novel by Simon R. Green. Old Father Time, Time Tower Square, and Shadows Fall are from Green's novel Shadows Fall, *which probably takes place in an alternate future. The Time Tunnel reference suggests the Authorities were behind Project Tic Toc, the time travel experiment seen in Irwin Allen's television series* The Time Tunnel. *Julien Advent is intended to be Adam Adamant from the BBC TV series* Adam Adamant Lives! *The Street* of the Gods *is from Green's Hawk and Fisher novellas* Winner Takes All *and* The God Killer. *Baron Frankenstein's creation and descendants refer to Mary Shelley's* Frankenstein *and the many novel and film continuations of that story. The cat that can disappear at will is the Cheshire Cat from Lewis Carroll's* Alice in Wonderland. *Anti-life is from the DC Comics series* The New Gods. *The rats with disturbingly human hands are probably related to Brown Jenkin from H. P. Lovecraft's "The Dreams in the Witch House." Morlocks and Eloi are from H. G. Wells'* The Time Machine. *The Serpent and the Serpent's Son are from Green's novel* Drinking Midnight Wine. *Cthulhu is from Lovecraft's "The Call of Cthulhu" and many other stories by various authors. The two giants throwing rocks at each other are described in much the same way J. R. R. Tolkien described giants in the Misty Mountains in* The Hobbit. *Rats' Alley is from T. S. Eliot's poem "The Waste Land."*

SHARPER THAN A SERPENT'S TOOTH

John Taylor returns from the past to stop his mother from destroying the Nightside. Appearing or mentioned are: Rollerball t-shirts; a cyborg with golden eyes from an alternate future; a sonic screwdriver; a Water Baby; the Yellow Sign; Sneaky Pete; the Holy Hand Grenade of St. Antioch; the Door-mouse; the Bazaar of the Bizarre; Shadows Fall; Carcosa; Old Father Time; the Street of the Gods; a Kandarian punch dagger; Julien Advent, the Victorian Adventurer; Alf's Button Emporium; faeries hiding from the hordes of the Adversary; the Traveling Doctor; Colonial Marines; the Eaters of the Dead; Worms of the Earth; Time Tower Square; Elder Spawn; Dead-Eye Dick, who was featured in a series of dime novels; Rats' Alley; Haceldama; the Traveling Doctor; a blazer belonging to a retired secret agent, which has a button with the number six on it; and the Prospero and Michael Scott Memorial Library.

Novel by Simon R. Green. Rollerball is from William Harrison's story "Roller Ball Murder," which depicts a corporation-driven future that is one of several possible futures for the CU. The cyborg with golden eyes from an alternate future is one of the Hadenmen from Green's Deathstalker books. The sonic screwdriver is from the TV series Doctor Who, *while the Traveling Doctor is the CU counterpart of the Doctor himself. The Water Baby is from Charles Kingsley's novel* The Water Babies. *The Yellow Sign is from*

Robert W. Chambers' The King in Yellow, *and was incorporated into the* Cthulhu Mythos *by H. P. Lovecraft in the short story "The Whisperer in Darkness." Sneaky Pete is Pete Hutter from the television Western* The Adventures of Brisco County, Jr. *The Holy Hand Grenade of St. Antioch is from the movie* Monty Python and the Holy Grail, *although the events seen in that movie must have been exaggerated for comedic effect. The Doormouse is a member of a group of shapeshifting mouse hippies from Green's novel* Drinking Midnight Wine. *The Bazaar of the Bizarre is from Fritz Leiber's Fafhrd and the Grey Mouser short story of the same name. Shadows Fall, Old Father Time, and Time Tower Square are from Green's novel* Shadows Fall. *The Street of the Gods is from Green's Hawk and Fisher novellas* Winner Takes All *and* The God Killer. *Carcosa is from Ambrose Bierce's short story "An Inhabitant of Carcosa," which H. P. Lovecraft incorporated into the Cthulhu Mythos. The Kandarian punch dagger is connected to the Kandarian demons from the* Evil Dead *film series. Julien Advent is intended to be Adam Adamant from the TV series* Adam Adamant Lives! *In fact, at one point in the novel he is referred to as Adamant. Alf's Button Emporium is a reference to W. A. Darlington's fantasy novel* Alf's Button, *thus bringing that novel into the CU. The faeries hiding from the hordes of the Adversary are from Bill Willingham and Lan Medina's comic book series* Fables, *which is set in an AU. Colonial Marines are from the science fiction film* Aliens, *setting up the* Alien *franchise as another possible future of the CU. The Eaters of the Dead are from Michael Crichton's titular novel. Worms of the Earth are from Robert E. Howard's short novel of the same name, and like the Elder Spawn are connected to the Cthulhu Mythos. Dead-Eye Dick is a reference to an episode of the television Western* The Virginian *entitled "Dead-Eye Dick." Although the episode does not mention the Dead-Eye Dick dime novels are based on the adventures of a real person, it doesn't say they aren't either. Rats' Alley is from T. S. Eliot's poem "The Waste Land." The Traveling Doctor is the time-and-space-traveling Doctor of* Doctor Who *fame. The blazer with the No. 6 button is from the cult TV series* The Prisoner. *Haceldama is from Green's Death-stalker books. Prospero is from William Shakespeare's* The Tempest.

THE SPY WHO HAUNTED ME

Edwin Drood is chosen to compete against several other agents to solve a series of mysteries; the winner will gain all the secrets of Alexander King, the legendary Independent Agent. Appearing or mentioned are: Vril Power, Inc.; the Salvation Army Sisterhood; the Tracey Brothers; MI13; Leo Morn; Harry Fabulous; smoked black centipede meat; full-strength Hyde; Martian red weed; Universal Exports; Oz; SAS combat sorcerers; Shadows Fall; Oberon and Titania; the Djinn Jeannie; the London Knights; the Walking Man; the Traveling Doctor; the Old Wolf of Kabul; John Taylor; Walker; the Authorities; a small statuette of a black bird; two Pickman paintings; an unknown Shlacken; several copies of the Painting that Devoured Paris; a stuffed Morlock; a mummified monkey's paw; a small black lacquered puzzle box; the talking beavers of Narnia; Frankenstein monsters; the Lone Ranger and Tonto; Peaseblossom; the Collector; Puck; Mustardseed; Cobweb; Moth; Martians on huge metal tripods with metal claws, heat rays, and poisonous black smoke; Crouch End Towen; Black Air; use of a sword-umbrella as an old tradition in the British spy game; Strangefellows; Cathy Barnett; Lilith; and Queen Mab.

Novel by Simon R. Green. Vril Power, Inc. is a reference to the Vril power from Edward Bulwer-Lytton's The Coming Race. *The Salvation Army Sisterhood, Harry Fabulous, the London Knights, the Walking Man, John Taylor, Walker, the Authorities, the Collector, Strangefellows, Cathy Barnett, and Lilith are from Green's Nightside novels. This novel takes place between the Nightside novels* Sharper Than a Serpent's Tooth *and* Hell to Pay. *The Tracey (or Tracy) brothers are from Gerry Anderson's television series* Thunderbirds, *which probably takes place in an alternate future. MI13 and Black Air must be the CU equivalents of the British government agencies of those names seen in the Marvel Comics Universe. Leo Morn is from Green's novel* Drinking Midnight Wine. *Smoked black centipede meat is from William S. Burroughs' novel* Naked Lunch. *Hyde is a reference to the transformative formula seen in Robert Louis Stevenson's* The Strange Case of Dr. Jekyll and Mr. Hyde. *Martian red weed and the Martians on huge metal tripods are from H. G. Wells'* The War of the Worlds. *Universal Exports is a front for the British Secret Service in Ian Fleming's James Bond novels. The protagonist of Warren Ellis' comic book* Gravel *is an SAS Sergeant Major and combat magician. Shadows Fall is from Green's novel of the same name. Oberon, Titania, Peaseblossom, Puck, Mustardseed, Cobweb, and Moth are from William Shakespeare's* A Midsummer Night's Dream. *The Djinn Jeannie is from the television series* I Dream of Jeannie. *The Traveling Doctor is the CU version of the Doctor, of* Doctor Who *fame. The Old Wolf of Kabul is Bill Sampson, a British comic book character who debuted in the 1920s as the Wolf of Kabul. The small statuette of a black bird is the titular statuette from Dashiell Hammett's* The Maltese Falcon. *The Pickman paintings are a reference to H. P. Lovecraft's story "Pickman's Model." "Shlacken" is a reference to J. Sheridan Le Fanu's story "Schalken the Painter." The Painting that Devoured Paris is a CU version of the Painting that Ate Paris from Grant Morrison's run on the comic book series* Doom Patrol. *The mummified monkey's paw is from W. W. Jacobs' "The Monkey's Paw."*

The small black lacquered puzzle box is a Lament Configuration from the Hellraiser film series. The talking beavers of Narnia are from C. S. Lewis' The Chronicles of Narnia. The Frankenstein monsters are from Mary Shelley's Frankenstein *and its many sequels and adaptations.* The Lone Ranger and Tonto are self-explanatory. Crouch End is a real London neighborhood, but Crouch End Towen is the fictional Lovecraftian dark side of it from Stephen King's short story "Crouch End." In the television series The Avengers, *British spy John Steed used a sword-umbrella.* Queen Mab is from Shakespeare's Romeo and Juliet.

HOW DO YOU FEEL?

Dead Boy learns the true circumstances of his death, and takes revenge on those responsible. Appearing or mentioned are: Hyde extract; a lipstick red Plymouth Fury, with a dead man grinning at the wheel; the *Necronomicon*; the *King in Yellow*; and a combat magician.

Short story by Simon R. Green in Hex Appeal, *P. N. Elrod, ed., St. Martin's Griffin, 2012; reprinted in* Tales from the Nightside, *Ace Books, 2015. Hyde extract is a reference to Robert Louis Stevenson's* The Strange Case of Dr. Jekyll and Mr. Hyde. *The lipstick red Plymouth Fury is the titular car from Stephen King's novel* Christine. *The* Necronomicon *is a staple of H. P. Lovecraft's Cthulhu Mythos. The* King in Yellow *is from the eponymous book by Robert W. Chambers. Combat magicians are from Warren Ellis' comic book* Gravel. *Walker, the Authorities' Agent in the Nightside, appears in this story, placing it before* The Good, the Bad, and the Uncanny.

Late Autumn
BLOOD RITES

Harry Dresden says the White Council published the *Necronomicon*, knowing if too many people try to use a rite, it depletes the energy required to conduct it. Harry's mentor Ebenazar Blackstaff tells him half-demon mercenary Jared Kincaid once served Vlad Drakul, father of Dracula, and Dracula went to the Black Court as a form of teenage rebellion.

Novel by Jim Butcher, 2004. The references to the Necronomicon *and Dracula further cement Harry Dresden's presence in the CU.*

HELL TO PAY

John Taylor is hired to find the kidnapped daughter of immortal billionaire Jeremiah Griffin. Appearing or mentioned are: the Street of the Gods; the *Necronomicon* in the original Arabic; a Soylent Green special on the menu; Shoggoth's Old and Very Peculiar; Count Dracula; the Big Green Lizard; Morlocks; Martian red weed; Philip Marlowe; *The Canterbury Tales*; Kid Cthulhu; Old Father Time; the Maltese Falcon; Bruin Bear and the Sea Goat; Shadows Fall; ex-SAS combat magicians; a DeLorean still spitting discharging tachyons; Elvira, Mistress of the Dark; a Morlock; Jimmy Thunder; the Lady Orlando; Cobweb and Moth; and Queen Mab.

Novel by Simon R. Green. The Street of the Gods is from Green's Hawk and Fisher novellas Winner Takes All *and* The God Killer. *The* Necronomicon *and shoggoths are from the Cthulhu Mythos stories of H. P. Lovecraft and many others. Shoggoth's Old and Very Peculiar is a reference to Neil Gaiman's story "Shoggoth's Old Peculiar." Soylent Green is from Harry Harrison's novel* Make Room! Make Room! *setting up the dystopia of that novel as another possible future of the CU. Count Dracula is from Bram Stoker's novel* Dracula, *but the humorous portrayal in this book suggests the Dracula seen here may be a "soul-clone." The Big Green Lizard is a CU version of Godzilla from the 1954 film and its sequels. Presumably, this version of Godzilla has not gone on the massively destructive rampages seen in the films. Morlocks are from H. G. Wells'* The Time Machine. *Martian red weed is from H. G. Wells'* The War of the Worlds. *The reference to Philip Marlowe can be interpreted as to either a fictional character or a real person. Geoffrey Chaucer's* The Canterbury Tales *is mentioned by John Taylor as referring to Jeremiah Griffin within its pages. Kid Cthulhu is named for the Great Old One introduced in Lovecraft's "The Call of Cthulhu." Old Father Time, Shadows Fall, and Bruin Bear and the Sea Goat are from Green's novel* Shadows Fall. *The Maltese Falcon is from Dashiell Hammett's novel. The protagonist of Warren Ellis' comic book* Gravel *is a combat magician and former SAS Sergeant Major. The DeLorean spitting discharging tachyons is from the* Back to the Future *film trilogy. Elvira, Mistress of the Dark is from the TV series* Elvira's Movie Macabre. *The Morlock is from H. G. Wells'* The Time Machine. *Jimmy Thunder is from Green's novel* Drinking Midnight Wine. *The Lady Orlando is from Viriginia Woolf's novel* Orlando. *Cobweb and Moth are from William Shakespeare's* A Midsummer Night's Dream, *while Queen Mab is from Shakespeare's* Romeo and Juliet.

SOME OF THESE CONS GO WAY BACK

In the Nightside, conman Harry Fabulous is tricked by a fallen angel into murdering a woman. Taduki, tanna leaves, Martian red weed, black centipede meat, and the Jekyll and Hyde formula are mentioned.

Short story by Simon R. Green in Cemetery Dance *#60, Richard Chizmar and Robert Morrish, eds., Cemetery Dance Publications, May 2009; reprinted in* Tales from the Nightside, *Ace Books, 2015. Taduki is from H. Rider Haggard's Allan Quatermain novels and stories. Tanna leaves are from Universal Studios' original series of Mummy films. Martian red weed is from H. G. Wells'* The War of the Worlds. *Black centipede meat is from William S. Burroughs' novel* Naked Lunch. *The Jekyll and Hyde formula is from Robert Louis Stevenson's* The Strange Case of Dr. Jekyll and Mr. Hyde.

December 24
LUCY, AT CHRISTMASTIME

At Strangefellow's, Leo Morn meets with the spirit of an old acquaintance. The Mistress of the Dark and Darkacre are mentioned.

Short story by Simon R. Green in Wolfsbane and Mistletoe, *Charlaine Harris and Toni L. P. Kelner, eds., Ace Books, 2008; reprinted in* Tales from the Nightside, *Ace Books, 2015. Leo Morn is from Green's novel* Drinking Midnight Wine. *The Mistress of the Dark is Elvira from the TV series* Elvira's Movie Macabre. *Darkacre is from Green's novel* Shadows Fall.

2003

Winter
THE UNNATURAL INQUIRER

John Taylor is hired by the Nightside's most infamous tabloid, the *Unnatural Inquirer*, to search for a man who claims to possess a DVD showing evidence of the existence of the Afterlife. Appearing or mentioned are: the *Necronomicon*; the Street of the Gods; Martian red weed; Hyde; Jacqueline Hyde; big black monoliths on the Moon; the Old Ones; R'lyeh; Old Father Time; Lassie; Elvira; Rats' Alley; Julien Advent; a jukebox the size of a TARDIS; a collection of secret agents exchanging passwords and cheerful tall tales, while playing ostentatiously casual one-upmanship with their latest gadgets—pens and shoes that are communication devices, watches that hold strangling wires and lasers, and umbrellas that are also sword-sticks; an agent actually blinking on and off as he demonstrates his invisibility bracelet; the Traveling Doctor; the Strange Doctor; the Druid Doctor; Cthulhu; Shadows Fall; Haceldama; Deathwalkers; the Maltese Falcon; the King in Yellow; the Serpent in the Sun; a half-burned giant Wicker Man with a dead policeman inside it; a caricature of the Sonic Assassin, in his sixties greatcoat, gnawing on a human thigh-bone while making a rude gesture at the viewer; Queen Mab; a disembodied hand; a small featureless furry thing; tanna leaves; combat sorcerers; and a cricket bat enchanted by Merlin.

Novel by Simon R. Green. The Necronomicon, *the* Old Ones, R'lyeh, *and* Cthulhu *are from H. P. Lovecraft's Cthulhu Mythos. The* Street of the Gods *is from Green's Hawk and Fisher novellas* Winner Takes All *and* The God Killer. *Martian red weed is from H. G. Wells'* The War of the Worlds. *Hyde is a reference to the serum seen in Robert Louis Stevenson's* The Strange Case of Dr. Jekyll and Mr. Hyde, *which some Nightsiders use as a drug. Jacqueline Hyde is a descendant of Dr. Jekyll's. Her ancestor's serum turns her into a male Hyde. The two personas are in love with each other, but only come in contact when the transformation occurs. Big black mono-liths on the moon are from Arthur C. Clarke's novel* 2001: A Space Odyssey. *Shadows Fall and Old Father Time are from Green's book* Shadows Fall. *Lassie is from Eric Knight's novel* Lassie Come-Home. *Elvira is from the television series* Elvira's Movie Macabre. *Rats' Alley is from T. S. Eliot's "The Waste Land." Julien Advent is meant to be Adam Adamant from the British television series* Adam Adamant Lives! *The TARDIS is the time traveling vehicle used by the Doctor on the long-running British science fiction TV show* Doctor Who. *The Traveling Doctor is the Doctor himself. The pen communicator is from the television series* The Man from U.N.C.L.E., *while the shoe communicator is from the spy parody series* Get Smart. *The watches that hold strangling wires and lasers are from the James Bond movies; although the Bond of the CU is the version seen in the novels, there is no reason why he could not possess analogues of the watches owned by his cinematic counterpart. The umbrella that is also a sword-stick was wielded by British agent John Steed on the classic television series* The Avengers. *The agent with the invisibility bracelet is Sam Casey from the short-lived televi-sion series* Gemini Man. *The Strange Doctor is Marvel Comics' Sorcerer Supreme, Doctor Stephen Strange. The Druid Doctor is Doctor Anthony Ludgate Druid, another sorcerer appearing in comics published by Marvel. Haceldama is from Green's Deathstalker novels. Deathwalkers and the Serpent in the Sun are from Green's novel* Drinking Midnight Wine. *The Maltese Falcon is from Dashiell Hammett's novel of the same name. The King in Yellow is from Robert W. Chambers' titular collection of short stories. The dead policeman inside the half-burned Wicker Man is Sgt. Neil Howie from the 1973 film* The Wicker Man. *The Sonic Assassin is Michael*

Moorcock's spy Jerry Cornelius, one of the many incarnations of Moorcock's Eternal Champion across the Multiverse. The description of the Sonic Assassin gnawing on a human thigh-bone and making a rude gesture at the viewer is a reference to the artwork for Moorcock's Jerry Cornelius story "The Firmament Theorem" by Mal Dean on the cover of the 191st issue of the British New Wave science fiction magazine New Worlds. Queen Mab is from William Shakespeare's play Romeo and Juliet. The disembodied hand is Thing from the television series The Addams Family. The small furry thing is a Tribble from the Star Trek episode "The Trouble with Tribbles." Tanna leaves are from Universal Studios' original Mummy movie series. Combat sorcerers are a reference to Warren Ellis' comic book series Gravel, which features a former SAS Sergeant Major and combat sorcerer. The cricket bat enchanted by Merlin recalls Matt Wagner's comic book Mage, in which Merlin gives Kevin Matchstick, a reincarnation of King Arthur, Excalibur, which is now in the shape of a baseball bat. Whether this means Mage takes place in the same universe as the Nightside books is unclear.

THE BIG GAME

John Taylor battles Sir Francis Varney, the King of the Vampires, who is trying to turn the Nightside into a homeland for the undead. Appearing or mentioned are: Tsothagua Tequila; Jack Drood; the Street of the Gods; Kor; Julien Advent; Something from a Black Lagoon; the withered and mummified arm of the original Grendel monster, presented to the Adventurers Club by Beowulf himself, back in the sixth century; an ex-Ghost Finder; some kind of Boojum; the Suicide Club; Dracula; and Rassillonn's Restorative.

Novella by Simon R. Green in Tales from the Nightside, Ace Books, 2015. Sir Francis Varney is from James Malcolm Rymer's penny dreadful serial Varney the Vampire. Tsothagua Tequila is a reference to Tsathoggua, a Great Old One created by Clark Ashton Smith as part of H. P. Lovecraft's Cthulhu Mythos. Jack Drood is from Green's Secret Histories novels; his appearance here places this story before the short story "Question of Solace." The Street of the Gods is from Green's Hawk & Fisher novellas Winner Takes All and The God Killer. Kor is from H. Rider Haggard's novel She. Julien Advent is an alias for the titular hero of the 1960s British television series Adam Adamant Lives! Something from a Black

Lagoon is a reference to the Universal horror film Creature from the Black Lagoon. *The original Grendel monster and Beowulf are from the Old English epic poem* Beowulf. *The ex-Ghost Finder must have been a former member of the Carnacki Institute from Green's* Ghost Finders *series. The Boojum is from Lewis Carroll's poem "The Hunting of the Snark." The Suicide Club is from Robert Louis Stevenson's story of the same name. Dracula needs no introduction. Rassillonn's Restorative is a reference to the Time Lord Rassilon from the long-running British science fiction television series* Doctor Who.

FROM HELL WITH LOVE

The Droods go to war with Doctor Delirium and the Immortals over the Apocalypse Door. Appearing or mentioned are: U.N.C.L.E.; THRUSH; James Bond; S.P.E.C.T.R.E.; a Martian tripod; a Crystal Egg; the Danse Academy in the German Black Forest; Dracula; the Nightside; Shadows Fall; a Time War; the Carnacki Institute; Bradford-on-Avon; Carys Galloway, the Waking Beauty; the Howling Thing; Doctor Faustus; Indiana Jones; the Djinn Jeannie; the recently dead Griffin in the Nightside; the Lord of Thorns; Old Father Time; Jimmy Thunder, God for Hire; the Speaking Gun; Nicholas Hob, the Serpent's Son; the Collector; a Kandarian amulet; Castle Frankenstein; the Bride of Frankenstein; Area 52; and a bizarre alien city inside an Arctic mountain.

Novel by Simon R. Green. U.N.C.L.E. and THRUSH are from the television series The Man from U.N.C.L.E. *James Bond and S.P.E.C.T.R.E. are from Ian Fleming's novels. The Martian tripod is from H. G. Wells' novel* The War of the Worlds, *while the Crystal Egg is from Wells' short story of the same name. The Danse Academy in the German Black Forest is a reference to the horror film* Suspiria, *the first in a trilogy that also includes* Inferno *and* Mother of Tears. *Dracula is from Bram Stoker's novel. The Nightside is the setting of another series of novels by Green. Griffin, the Lord of Thorns, the Speaking Gun, and the Collector are also from the Nightside books. Shadows Fall is from Green's novel of the same name, which is also the source of Old Father Time. This Time War may be the CU version of the one seen in the television series* Doctor Who. *The Carnacki Institute is from Green's* Ghost Finders *novels. Bradford-on-Avon is a real town (the home of Green himself), but the version of it that appears here, is from Green's novel* Drinking Midnight Wine. *Carys Galloway, the Waking Beauty; the Howling Thing; Jimmy Thunder, God for Hire; and Nicholas Hob, the Serpent's Son, are also from* Drinking Midnight Wine. *Doctor Faustus is from Christopher Marlowe's play of the same name. Indiana Jones is from the film* Raiders of the Lost Ark *and its sequels. The Djinn Jeannie is from the television series* I Dream of Jeannie. *The Kandarian amulet is a nod to the Kandarian demons from the* Evil Dead *movies. Castle Frankenstein is* from *Mary Shelley's* Frankenstein. *The Bride of Frankenstein is from the Universal horror film of the same name. The Area 52 seen here is likely the one seen in the Image Comics series of the same name. The bizarre alien city inside an Arctic mountain is likely a reference to H. P. Lovecraft's* At the Mountains of Madness.

RAZOR EDDIE'S BIG NIGHT OUT

Razor Eddie, the Punk God of the Straight Razor, prevents a modernized version of Dagon from being installed in the latter deity's church in the Street of the Gods. Appearing or mentioned are: Rats' Alley; Jacqueline Hyde; and a small, winged monkey.

Short story by Simon R. Green in Cemetery Dance #55, *Richard Chizmar and Robert Morrish, eds., Cemetery Dance Publications, June 2006; reprinted in* Tales from the Nightside, *Ace Books, 2015. The Street of the Gods is from Green's Hawk and Fisher novellas* Winner Takes All *and* The God Killer. *Rats' Alley is from T. S. Eliot's poem "The Waste Land." Jacqueline Hyde is a female descendant of Dr. Jekyll who turns into a male Hyde; the two halves are in love with each other, but can never be together due to the nature of their condition. The small, winged monkey is from L. Frank Baum's* The Wonderful Wizard of Oz.

HUNGRY HEART

John Taylor is hired by a witch to recover her heart, which has been stolen by her ex-boyfriend. Appearing or mentioned are: one of Dracula's coffins, complete with original grave dirt and a certificate of authenticity; the mummified head of Alfredo Garcia, smelling strongly of Mexican spices; the mirror of Dorian Gray; and a phial of heart's blood from Varney the Vampyre.

Short story by Simon R. Green in Down These Strange Streets, *George R. R. Martin and Gardner Dozois, eds., Ace Books, 2011; reprinted in* Tales from the Nightside, *Ace Books, 2015. Dracula's coffin is from Bram Stoker's novel, of course. The mummified head of Alfred Garcia is from the film* Bring Me the Head of Alfredo Garcia. *The mirror of Dorian Gray is a reference to Oscar Wilde's novel* The Picture of Dorian Gray. *Varney the Vampyre is the title character of James Malcolm Rymer's penny dreadful serial.*

Mid Winter

JUST ANOTHER JUDGMENT DAY

John Taylor is hired by the Authorities that govern the Nightside to defeat God's enforcer, the Walking Man, who seeks to eliminate them and cleanse the Nightside of the wicked. Appearing or mentioned are: Shoggoth's Old and Very Peculiar; Delerium Treebeard; Dorian Gray's painting; Baron Viktor von Frankenstein; Sarah Kingdom; Julien Advent; Janissary Jane; Admiral Syn; Salvation Kane; Owen Deathstalker; the Black Lagoon; Grendel; Beowulf; the Street of the Gods; combat sorceresses; Kid Cthulhu; Old Father Time; the Unspeakable Abomination, which has tentacles and a three-lobed burning eye; the Darkvoid Device; the Howling Thing; Jacqueline Hyde; Elder Gods; and the Drood Family.

Novel by Simon R. Green. Shoggoth's Old and Very Peculiar is a reference to Neil Gaiman's short story "Shoggoth's Old Peculiar," while the shoggoth itself is from H. P. Lovecraft's Cthulhu Mythos. Kid Cthulhu is named for the Great Old One Cthulhu. The Unspeakable Abomination is meant to be the Outer God known as Nyarlathotep in Lovecraft's Mythos, one of whose personas has a three-lobed burning eye. The Elder Gods were created for the Mythos by August Derleth, and are enemies of the Great Old Ones. Delerium Treebeard is named after the Ent Treebeard from J. R. R. Tolkien's fantasy saga The Lord of the Rings. *Dorian Gray's painting is from Oscar Wilde's novel* The Picture of Dorian Gray. *Baron Viktor von Frankenstein is an alternate universe counterpart of Victor Frankenstein from Mary Shelley's novel* Frankenstein. *Sarah (originally Sara) Kingdom is from the* Doctor Who *serial "The Daleks' Master Plan." Julien Advent is meant to be Adam Adamant from the BBC TV series* Adam Adamant Lives! *The Howling Thing is from Green's novel* Drinking Midnight Wine. *Janissary Jane is from* The Man with the Golden Torc *and* Daemons are Forever, *the first two novels in Green's Secret Histories series. The Drood Family is featured in the* Secret Histories *books. Admiral Syn is a reference to Russell Thorndike's* Doctor Syn. *Salvation Kane is clearly a pseudonym for Robert E. Howard's puritan Solomon Kane. Owen Deathstalker is the protagonist of Green's Deathstalker novels, establishing the future seen in that series as one of many possible futures for the CU. The Darkvoid Device is also from the Deathstalker books. The Black Lagoon is from the Universal horror movie* Creature from the Black Lagoon *and its sequels. Grendel and Beowulf are both from the Anglo-Saxon epic poem* Beowulf. *The Street of the Gods is from Green's Hawk and Fisher novellas* Winner Takes All *and* The God Killer. *Combat sorceresses are a reference to Warren Ellis' comic book* Gravel, *whose main character is an ex-SAS Sergeant Major and combat magician. Old Father Time is from Green's novel* Shadows Fall. *Jacqueline Hyde is a female descendant of Dr. Jekyll (from Robert Louis Stevenson's* The Strange Case of Dr. Jekyll and Mr. Hyde*) who transforms into a hulking male Hyde.*

THE GOOD, THE BAD, AND THE UNCANNY

John Taylor escorts an elf across the Nightside, helps deceased P.I. Larry Oblivion look for his brother Tommy, and refuses to take Walker's place as agent of the Authorities that rule the Nightside. Appearing or mentioned are: Hydes; a cyborg from some future timeline with eyes glowing golden, mainlining a fierce and nasty future drug called Blood; taduki; Martian red weed; Queen Mab; Oberon and Titania; the Street of the Gods; Puck; the Sonic Assassin; the Time Tower; the Deep School; Salvation Kane; Old Mother Shipton; Indiana Jones; Mr. Stab; Miss Eliza Fritton, who used to run a private girl's school; the Carnacki Insitute; the Droods; the Vril Power Gang; the Nazi Skull; Jacqueline Hyde; the worms of the Earth; a stuffed water baby; giant albino penguins; an old-fashioned grandfather clock, with a cobwebbed human skeleton propped up inside it; a lizard serum; Julien Advent; Rats' Alley; Dr. Delirium; Wu Fang; and a Hand of Glory made from a monkey's paw.

Novel by Simon R. Green. The Hydes are individuals who use the formula that turned Dr. Henry Jekyll into Edward Hyde as a narcotic. Jacqueline Hyde is a descendant of Jekyll's who takes her ancestor's serum, which turns her into a male Hyde. The cyborg from a future timeline with eyes glowing golden is one of the Hadenmen from Green's Deathstalker series, which takes place in one of many possible futures for the CU. The Blood drug is also from the Deathstalker books. The drug Taduki is from H. Rider Haggard's novels and stories about hunter Allan Quatermain. Martian red weed is from H. G. Wells' novel The War of the Worlds. *Queen Mab is from William Shakespeare's play* Romeo and Juliet, *while Oberon, Titania, and Puck are from Shakespeare's* A Midsummer Night's Dream. *The Street of the Gods is from Green's Hawk and Fisher novellas* Winner Takes All *and* The God Killer. *The Sonic Assassin is Michael Moorcock's secret agent Jerry Cornelius, an incarnation of the Eternal Champion. The Time Tower is from Green's novel* Shadows Fall. *Salvation Kane is probably meant to be Robert E. Howard's heroic puritan Solomon Kane. The Deep School is an extradimensional school for sorcerers seen in Manly Wade Wellman's John Thunstone stories. Old Mother Shipton, Mr. Stab, and the Droods are from Green's* Secret Histories *series. Dr. Delirium goes on to become one of the main villains of the fourth* Secret Histories *novel,* From Hell with Love. *The Indiana Jones reference can* be interpreted as a reference to either a real person or a fictional character, but since both Indy and John Taylor are firmly established as being in the CU, we can accept this as a legitimate crossover. *Miss Eliza Fritton must be the same Miss Fritton who was the headmistress of St. Trinian's, a private school for girls, in illustrated cartoons by Ronald Searle. The Carnacki Institute is featured in Green's* Ghost Finders *series. The Vril Power Gang is a reference to the Vril power from Edward Bulwer-Lytton's* The Coming Race. *The Nazi Skull is a reference to Captain America's Nazi archenemy, the Red Skull. The worms of the Earth are from Robert E. Howard's Bran Mak Morn story of the same name. The stuffed water baby is a reference to Charles Kingsley's children's book* The Water Babies. *The giant albino penguins are from Lovecraft's novella* At the Mountains of Madness. *The old-fashioned grandfather clock with a cobwebbed human skeleton propped up inside it is from the movie* The Rocky Horror Picture Show, *bringing that film and its sequel,* Shock Treatment, *into the CU. The lizard serum is probably the one used by the Lizard, a foe of the Marvel Comics superhero Spider-Man. Julien Advent, a recurring character in the Nightside books, is meant to be adventurer Adam Adamant from the British television series* Adam Adamant Lives! *Rats' Alley is from T. S. Eliot's "The Waste Land." Wu Fang is a pulp villain created by Robert J. Hogan. The Hand of Glory made from a monkey's paw is a reference to W. W. Jacobs' story "The Monkey's Paw."*

A HARD DAY'S KNIGHT

John Taylor returns to London Proper for the first time in years to find out from the London Knights, the descendants of the Knights of the Round Table, why Excalibur has been delivered to him. He learns he is to grant the sword to the resurrected King Arthur, who will lead the Knights in thwarting an elven invasion of the Nightside. Appearing or mentioned are: Puck; the Church of the Riddle of Steel; the Street of the Gods; Julien Advent; R'Lyeh; the Old Ones; Mr. Stab; something from a Black Lagoon; the Yellow Sign; the Voorish Sign; Shadows Fall; Haceldama; Haven; a bunch of thugs in bowler hats, heavy eye makeup, and padded codpieces; Gaea (aka Gayle); Oberon and Titania; Queen Mab; Jersualem Stark; a quartet of fuzzy post-nuclear mutants with televisions implanted in their stomachs; the Doormouse; a branch of the Bazaar of the Bizarre franchise; Frankenstein blood; Carcosa; Scythia-Pannonia-Transbalkania; the legendary Apocalypse Door; a TARDIS; the Droods; *Butch Cassidy and the Cthulhu Kid*; Carys Galloway, the Waking Beauty; a couple of beat cops from some medieval city, waiting patiently for someone; all four Horsemen of the Apocalypse, playing bridge; and the Deep School.

Novel by Simon R. Green. Puck, Oberon, and Titania are from William Shakespeare's A Midsummer Night's Dream. *The Church of the Riddle of Steel is a reference to the Riddle of Steel from the film version of* Conan the

Barbarian. *The Street of the Gods and Haven are from Green's Hawk and Fisher novellas. The beat cops from a medieval city are Hawk and Fisher themselves. Julien Advent is meant to be adventurer Adam Adamant from the 1960s British television series* Adam Adamant Lives! *The Old Ones are from H. P. Lovecraft's Cthulhu Mythos. Mr. Stab, Jerusalem Stark, the Apocalypse Door, and the Droods are from Green's* Secret Histories *series. "Something from a Black Lagoon" is a reference to the Universal horror movie* Creature from the Black Lagoon *and its sequels. The Yellow Sign is from Robert W. Chambers' short story collection* The King in Yellow. *The Voorish Sign is from H. P. Lovecraft's "The Dunwich Horror." Shadows*

New York Times Bestselling Author

SIMON R. GREEN

"A macabre and thoroughly entertaining world."
—Jim Butcher, author of the Dresden Files

A HARD DAY'S KNIGHT

A NOVEL OF THE NIGHTSIDE

Fall is from Green's novel of the same name. Haceldama is from Green's Deathstalker novels. The thugs in bowler hats, heavy eye makeup, and padded codpieces are Alex and his droogs from Anthony Burgess' novel A Clockwork Orange, *which likely takes place in an alternate future. Gaea (aka Gayle) and Carys Galloway, the Waking Beauty are from Green's novel* Drinking Midnight Wine. *The Doormouse is a member of a group of mice who turned themselves into hippies via magic who first appeared in* Drinking Midnight Wine. *Queen Mab is from Shakespeare's* Romeo and Juliet. *The fuzzy postnuclear mutants with televisions implanted in their stomachs are the title characters of the BBC children's television series* Teletubbies. *The Bazaar of the Bizarre franchise likely includes the Bazaar of the Bizarre from Fritz Leiber's Fafhrd and the Gray Mouser tales. Frankenstein blood is a reference to Mary Shelley's novel* Frankenstein *and its many continuations. Carcosa is from Ambrose Bierce's short story "An Inhabitant of Carcosa," as well as* The King in Yellow, *and was incorporated into the Cthulhu Mythos by H. P. Lovecraft. Scythia-Pannonia-Transbalkania is from Avram Davidson's short story collections* The Adventures of Doctor Eszterhazy *and* The Enquiries of Doctor Eszterhazy. *The TARDIS is the time-and-space-traveling device used by the Doctor of* Doctor Who *fame. The title* Butch Cassidy and the Cthulhu Kid *melds the name of the movie* Butch Cassidy and the Sundance Kid *with that of Lovecraft's Cthulhu. In Terry Pratchett's Discworld novel* The Light Fantastic, *the Four Horsemen of the Apocalypse play bridge with the tourist Twoflower. The Deep School is a school of sorcery in Manly Wade Wellman's John Thunstone stories.*

FOR HEAVEN'S EYES ONLY

The Droods go up against a massive satanic conspiracy to bring about Hell on Earth. Appearing or mentioned are: Walker; the Nightside; MI13; Castle Frankenstein; Indiana Jones; the abandoned Danse Academie in Germany's Black Forest that had been a feeding ground for one of the Old Mothers; Area 52; the Iron Mann of the Plains; the London Knights; the Carnacki Institute; the Lord of Thorns; the Walking Man; Augusta Moon; description theory; the Oblivion brothers; Mr. Usher; monkey's paws; Bradford-on-Avon; John Taylor; Razor Eddie; a ghost named Ash from Shadows Fall; Jimmy Thunder, God for Hire; Night Gaunts; Sons of the Old Serpent; Jeremy Diego; and SAS combat sorcerers.

Novel by Simon R. Green. Walker, the London Knights, the Lord of Thorns, the Walking Man, Augusta Moon, the Oblivion brothers, Mr. Usher, John Taylor, and Razor Eddie are from Green's Nightside novels. Walker's appearance here takes place after the Nightside book The Good, the Bad, and the Uncanny. *MI13 is the CU version of the branch of British Intelligence seen in the Marvel Comics Universe. Castle Frankenstein is from Mary Shelley's* Frankenstein. *Indiana Jones is from the film* Raiders of the Lost Ark *and its sequels. The Danse Academie in the Black Forest is from the film* Suspiria. *Area 52 is likely a reference to the Image Comics series of the same name. The Iron Mann of the Plains is a shout out to Edward S. Ellis' "The Steam Man of the Prairies." The Carnacki Insitute and Jeremy Diego are from Green's* Ghost Finders *series. Diego's appearance here places this novel before his death in the* Ghost Finders *book* Ghost of a Smile. *Description theory is from Warren Ellis' comic book* Planetary, *which takes place in an AU. These monkey's paws are apparently made from the DNA of the one in W. W. Jacobs' "The Monkey's Paw," though they don't have the power of the original. Bradford-on-Avon is a real place, but the version referenced here is from Green's novel* Drinking Midnight Wine. *Jimmy Thunder, God for Hire, is also from* Drinking Midnight Wine. *The Sons of the Old Serpent are probably a reference to the Serpent in the Sun from the same novel. The ghost named Ash is Leonard Ash from Green's novel* Shadows Fall. *Night Gaunts are from Lovecraft's Cthulhu Mythos. SAS combat sorcerers are from the aforementioned Warren Ellis' comic book* Gravel.

THE BRIDE WORE BLACK LEATHER

John Taylor is getting ready both to marry Suzie Shooter and to become the Nightside's new Walker, and wants one last case as a private investigator, but his plans are interrupted by the arrival of the Sun King, a man who wants to let the sunlight in and put an end to the Nightside's endless dark. Appearing or mentioned are: the Maltese Falcon; Katherine Karnstein; the Jekyll & Hyde Reunion Dinner (for all those touched and affected by the Good Doctor's special elixir); Julien Advent; Rick's Café Imaginaire; stuffed baby Morlock; baby Eloi; Jimmy Thunder; the Deep School; Lord Orlando; the Bride of Frankenstein; the Baron Frankenstein; the Schalcken Affair; the Lovett Pie Shop fiasco; the Family of Immortals; the Drood Family; Eddie Drood; the Mirror of Dorian Gray; Leo Morn; Old Father Time; black centipede meat; Juliet, Advent's ex-lover, who runs a nightclub called the Adamant; the Amber Prince; the Grey Fox; a TARDIS; a golden-eyed cyborg; the Linda Lovecraft Library of Spiritual Erotica; sunglasses that allow one to detect aliens trying to pass as humans; Rats' Alley; old Carnacki; the Carnacki Institute; the Regent of Shadows; Bruin Bear and the Sea Goat; and Shadows Fall.

Novel by Simon R. Green. The Maltese Falcon is from Dashiell Hammett's mystery novel of the same name. Katherine Karnstein must be a relative of vampire Carmilla Karnstein from J. Sheridan Le Fanu's Carmilla. Doctor Jekyll is from Robert Louis Stevenson's The Strange Case of Dr. Jekyll and Mr. Hyde. *Julien Advent is an alias for Adam Adamant from the British television series* Adam Adamant Lives! *Juliet is meant to be Adamant's sidekick Georgina Jones, who was played by Juliet Harmer. Rick's Café Imaginaire is owned by Rick Blaine from the classic film* Casablanca. *The Morlocks and Eloi are from H. G. Wells'* The Time Machine. *Jimmy Thunder and Leo Morn are from Green's novel* Drinking Midnight Wine. *The Deep School is from Manly Wade Wellman's tales of occult detective John Thunstone. Lord Orlando is the gender-switching immortal from Virginia Woolf's novel* Orlando. *The Bride of Frankenstein is from the titular 1935 Universal horror film. The Baron Frankenstein is one of the many descendants of the original Victor Frankenstein, from Mary Shelley's* Frankenstein. *The Schalcken affair is a reference to J. Sheridan Le Fanu's story "Schalken the Painter." The Lovett Pie Shop fiasco is a reference to the penny dreadful serial "The String of Pearls" and its stage adaptation* Sweeney Todd: The Demon Barber of Fleet Street. *The Family of Immortals, the Drood Family, Eddie Drood, the Grey Fox and the Regent of Shadows are from Green's Secret Histories series. It is mentioned the Drood Family has been destroyed except for Eddie, thus placing this book between the* Secret Histories *books* For Heaven's Eyes Only *and* Live and Let Drood. *The Mirror of Dorian Gray is a reference to Oscar Wilde's* The Picture of Dorian Gray, *although there is no supernatural mirror* in that novel. *Old Father Time, Bruin Bear and the Sea Goat, and Shadows Fall are from Green's novel* Shadows Fall. *Black centipede meat is from William S. Burroughs' novel* Naked Lunch. *The Amber Prince is Prince Corwin from Roger Zelazny's* Chronicles of Amber. *The TARDIS is from the television series* Doctor Who. *The golden-eyed cyborg is one of the Hadenmen from Green's Deathstalker series. Linda Lovecraft appeared in stories by Mike Vosburg in the anthology comic book* Star*Reach *in the 1970s. The sunglasses that allow one to detect aliens trying to pass as humans are from the film* They Live. *Rats' Alley is from T. S. Eliot's poem "The Waste Land." Old Carnacki is Thomas Carnacki, aka "Carnacki the Ghost-Finder," an occult detective appearing in short stories by William Hope Hodgson. The Carnacki Institute is from Green's* Ghost Finders *novels.*

LIVE AND LET DROOD

Eddie Drood discovers the murdered Droods and the damaged Drood Hall he has come home to are from a different dimension, meaning that his family has been sent somewhere else, and sets out to find them, going up against Unholy Crow Lee, the most evil man in the world. Appearing or mentioned are: Merlin's Glass; the Kandarian language; Walker; Castle Frankenstein; Roland the Headless Gunner; Indiana Jones; the Nightside; an ancient flame that bestows eternal youth; tana leaves; Walker; the London Knights; the Carnacki Institute; John Taylor; Dead Boy; MI13; the Walking Man; Augusta Moon; an old Transylvanian vampire count who was trying to set himself up in England; the Scooby-Doo gang; Catherine Latimer; Heather; SAS combat sorcerers; the Satan Claw; Kayleigh's Eye; the Salvation Army Sisterhood; the Traveling Doctor, who said that bow ties are cool; a monkey's paw; and Castle Inconnu.

Novel by Simon R. Green. This Merlin's Glass is an alternate universe version of the item seen in Green's Nightside novels. Walker, the London Knights, John Taylor, Dead Boy, the Walking Man, Augusta Moon, Kayleigh's Eye, the Salvation Army Sisterhood, and Castle Inconnu are also from the Nightside books. The Kandarian language is a reference to the Kandarian demons from the Evil Dead *film series. Castle Frankenstein is from Mary Shelley's novel* Frankenstein. *Roland the Headless Gunner is from Warren Zevon's song "Roland the Headless Thompson Gunner." Indiana Jones needs no introduction at this point. The ancient flame that bestows eternal youth is a reference to the fires of Kôr from H. Rider Haggard's* She. *Tana leaves are from Universal Studios' first series of Mummy movies. The Carnacki Institute, Catherine Latimer, and Heather are from Green's* Ghost Finders *novels. MI13 is a CU version of the British government agency seen in the Marvel Universe. The old Transylvanian vampire* count is probably Count Dracula. The Scooby-Doo gang is from the animated television series Scooby-Doo, Where Are You! *and its many subsequent incarnations. SAS combat sorcerers are from Warren Ellis'* comic book Gravel. *The Satan Claw is from the Marvel Comics series* Nick Fury, Agent of S.H.I.E.L.D. *The Traveling Doctor is the CU equivalent of the time-and-space traveling Doctor of* Doctor Who *fame, in this case, his eleventh incarnation. The monkey's paw is from W. W. Jacobs' story of the same name.*

March
BABYLON RISING

A man is drawn back in time to the days of ancient Babylon as part of a spell to bring an evil wizard to the present so he can summon Kandara.

Short story by John Urbancik, found in The Rise and Fall of Babylon. *Kandara is one of the Thirteen in Brian Keene's Labyrinth mythos. The story is continued in Keene's "Babylon Falling."*

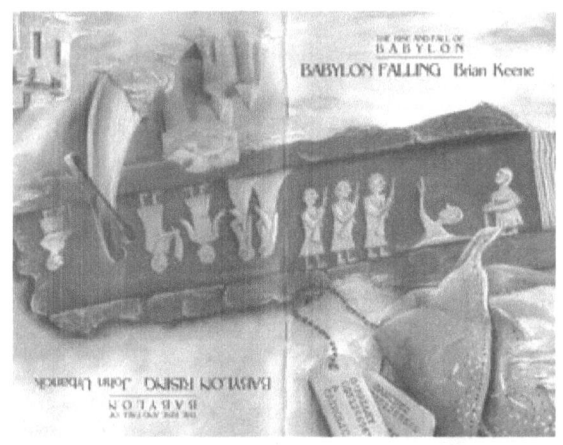

BABYLON FALLING

In Iraq, U.S. soldier Don Bloom and his infantry unit are kidnapped by remnants of Saddam Hussein's Fedayeen, and tortured by an ancient wizard as part of a ritual to summon Kandara. The *Daemonolateria* appears.

Short story by Brian Keene in The Rise and Fall of Babylon *and* Blood on the Page, *concluding the events begun in John Urbancik's "Babylon Rising." Kandara is one of the Thirteen, the villains of Keene's Labyrinth mythos; the* Daemonolateria *is a fictional book of magic that recurs in Keene's works. The name Kandara is clearly a reference to the Kandarian demons of the* Evil Dead *films.*

Spring
SPIKE: OLD WOUNDS

The vampire Spike and the Angel Investigations crew, now working for Wolfram & Hart, battle a Kandarian predator demon.

One-shot comic by Scott Tipton and Fernando Goni, IDW Publishing, 2007. The Kandarian predator demon is a shout-out to the Kandarian demons of the Evil Dead *series.*

ANGEL SPOTLIGHT: WESLEY

Charles Gunn asks Fred Burkle for the slime analysis on "the Illithid case."

One-shot by Scott Tipton and Mike Norton, IDW Publishing, 2006. Illithids are the mind-flayers from the Dungeons and Dragons *games, thus making the various* D&D *realms alternate realities to the CU.*

MONSTER HUNTER VENDETTA

Monster Hunter International (M.H.I.) continues to battle against the Old Ones. Trip Jones buys a fantasy novel by L. H. Franzibald in a hotel gift shop. A shoggoth appears, and one of the books in M.H.I.'s library is a tome written by a Mad Arab, which contains information on Shoggoths. M.H.I. has worked with Britain's Van Helsing Institute. Agent Franks is revealed to be a Frankenstein creation, though constructed by the historical alchemist Johann Conrad Dippel. The Yith are mentioned.

Novel by Larry Correia, Baen Books, 2010. The Old Ones, shoggoths, and the Yith are all from the works of H. P. Lovecraft, as is the Mad Arab, Abdul Alhazred. His book is the Al Azif, *better known as the* Necronomicon. *L. H. Franzibald is from Jerry Holkins and Mike Krahulik's web comic* Penny Arcade. *Given the surreal humor in* Penny Arcade, *this Franzibald must be a CU counterpart of the one in the universe where the comic takes place. The Van Helsing Institute must be named in honor of the monster hunting Van Helsing family, originally from Bram Stoker's* Dracula. *Johann Dippel is established as an ancestor of the more infamous Frankenstein clan in several sources.*

DEVIL TAKE THE HINDMOST

In the city of Denbrook, former journalist Damon St. Cloud seeks to avenge his family's murder. Along the way, he encounters Matthew Corrigan, Detective Christos, Frederick "the Whale" Whalen, Charybdis and Scylla, and Toulon. Kenneth Ottman and Laloosh are also mentioned.

Novel by Joel Jenkins, PulpWork Press, 2007. The city of Denbrook, created by Mike McGee, was the setting of nine serialized stories by various authors on the website Frontier Publishing. *The first section of the book, "Club Red," originally appeared on the website in 2004. Matthew*

Corrigan and Detective Christos are from Michael Franzoni's Denbrook story "Missing Persons." Frederick "the Whale" Whalen is from Derrick Ferguson's novel Dillon and the Voice of Odin. *Since Dillon is in the CU, so are the various inhabitants of Denbrook. Charybdis and Scylla, Toulon, and Laloosh are from Ferguson's as-yet-unpublished Denbrook novel* Diamondback: It Seemed Like a Good Idea at the Time. *Kenneth Ottman is from Tom Lynch's Denbrook story "Pentagram Whispers."*

CASINO INFERNALE

Eddie Drood and Molly Metcalf try to bring down the Shadow Bank, a mysterious conspiracy that bankrolls the evil schemes of villains. Appearing or mentioned are: Kayleigh's Eye; the London Knights; Dead Boy; the Nightside; John Taylor; J. C. Chance; the Carnacki Institute; Natasha Chang; the Crowley Project; Bruin Bear and the Sea Goat; Shadows Fall; Bradford-on-Avon; the Traveling Doctor, who said that bow ties are cool; a triffid; Jacqueline Hyde; the Brotherhood of the Vril; the Little Lord; and the Elder Gods.

Novel by Simon R. Green. Kayleigh's Eye, the London Knights, John Taylor, and Jacqueline Hyde are from Simon R. Green's Nightside novels. J. C. Chance, the Carnacki Institute, Natasha Chang, and the Crowley Project are from Green's Ghost Finders *novels. Bruin Bear and the Sea Goat are from Green's novel* Shadows Fall. *Bradford-on-Avon is a fictionalized version of the real place of that name, from Green's novel* Drinking Midnight Wine. *The Traveling Doctor is the CU version of the main character of* Doctor Who, *specifically his 11th incarnation. The triffid is a CU version of the plant seen in John Wyndham's apocalyptic science fiction novel* The Day of the Triffids. *The Brotherhood of the Vril is a reference to the Vril power from Edward Bulwer-Lytton's* The Coming Race. *The Little Lord is from Green's Hawk and Fisher novellas. The Elder Gods are from H. P. Lovecraft's Cthulhu Mythos.*

PROPERTY OF A LADY FAIRE

Eddie Drood seeks out the Lady Faire, an omnisexual being created by Baron Frankenstein later in his life. Also appearing or mentioned are: Harry Fabulous; the Nightside; Dagon; Cthulhu; the Painted Ghoul; MI13; the London Knights; Kayleigh's Eye; Strangefellows; Dead Boy; the Doormouse's shop; Shadows Fall; Carcosa; Sinister Albion; John Taylor; Lud's Gate; old Carnacki; the Griffin; stuffed baby Morlock; Hadleigh Oblivion; the Deep School; Rossignol; Jimmy Thunder, God for Hire; the Bride of Frankenstein; Ms. Fate; Larry Oblivion; "something from the Black Lagoon"; and the Plateau of Leng.

Novel by Simon R. Green. Baron Frankenstein is a member of the family seen in Mary Shelley's novel Frankenstein *and its many continuations. Harry Fabulous, the Painted Ghoul, the London Knights, Kayleigh's Eye, Strangefellows, Dead Boy, Sinister Albion, John Taylor, the Griffin, Hadleigh Oblivion, Rossignol, Ms. Fate, and Larry Oblivion are from Green's Nightside novels. Dagon, Cthulhu, and the Plateau of Leng are from H. P. Lovecraft's Cthulhu Mythos. MI13 is the CU version of the British Secret Service's branch that investigates "weird happenings" in the Marvel Comics Universe. The Doormouse is a member of the race first seen in Green's novel* Drinking Midnight Wine, *although he specifically and his shop are from the Nightside books. Jimmy Thunder, God for Hire, is also from* Drinking Midnight Wine. *Shadows Fall is from Green's novel of the same name. Carcosa is from Ambrose Bierce's short story "An Inhabitant of Carcosa." Lud's Gate is from Green's* Ghost Finders *novel* Spirits from Beyond. *Old Carnacki is from William Hope Hodgson's* Carnacki the Ghost-Finder. *Stuffed baby Morlock is a reference to H. G. Wells' novel* The Time Machine. *The Deep School is from Manly Wade Wellman's John Thunstone stories. The Bride of Frankenstein is from the titular Universal horror film. "Something from the Black Lagoon" is a reference to another Universal horror film,* Creature from the Black Lagoon, *and its sequels.*

June
THE DEAD DON'T DIE
Monster hunting P.I. Cal McDonald puts down a zombie outbreak in the California desert. While commenting on zombies, he mentions "what happened with radiation in Pittsburgh in the late sixties."

Short story by Steve Niles, found in his collections Dial M for Monster *and* Criminal Macabre: The Complete Cal McDonald Stories. *The incident in Pittsburgh is clearly meant as a reference to the events of the first* Night of the Living Dead *film. Although later films in the series (*Dawn of the Dead, Day of the Dead, *and* Land of the Dead*) involve the world being overrun with the walking dead, other sources, such as the* Return of the Living Dead *films and the Nathaniel Cade novels, show this particular incident was actually very isolated. Some hero must have stopped whatever caused the outbreak to spread in other universes.*

Summer
DEAD BEAT IN LA ESCA
The adventurer Dillon and rock star/mercenary Sly Gantlet manage to evade a group of would-be killers despite having downed several drugged drinks. Sly has partied in the fleshpots of cities such as Morocco, Cairo, Isthmus City, and Casablanca. When Sly challenges Dillon to an arm-wrestling

contest, Sly's date suggests they rent the best room at the Cobalt Club after he wins to celebrate.

Short story by Derrick Ferguson and Joel Jenkins in Thrilling Tales, *86th Floor Productions, 2007, reprinted in* Four Bullets for Dillon, *Pulp-Work Press, 2011, and* The Gantlet Brothers' Greatest Hits, *Pulp Work Press, 2011. Isthmus City is from the James Bond film* Licence to Kill. *The Cobalt Club is from Walter Gibson's pulp novels about a vigilante who knows the evil lurking in men's hearts. This crossover also brings in Jenkins' Gantlet Brothers, sibling musicians who moonlight as mercenaries, who appear in the novel* The Nuclear Suitcase *and the collections* The Gantlet Brothers' Greatest Hits *and* The Gantlet Brothers: Sold Out. *John Velvet from the Dillon series appears in* The Nuclear Suitcase.

THE LIBRARIAN: QUEST FOR THE SPEAR

Genius Flynn Carsen is kicked out of college, and receives a job offer from the Metropolitan Public Library. He soon discovers he has been appointed to act as "the librarian," the guardian of historical and often magical items found in a hidden section of the library. When the evil Serpent Brotherhood steals one of three pieces of the Spear of Destiny, which when combined can be used to control the world, Flynn must go on a quest to prevent them from acquiring the other two pieces. He finds the last spear piece in Shangri-La. After defeating the Brotherhood, Flynn learns the Death Scorpion Cult has stolen H. G. Wells' Time Machine. The Ark of the Covenant is also seen in the Library.

TV movie broadcast December 5, 2004. The connections to Shangri-La (from James Hilton's Lost Horizon*) and the Time Machine (from H. G. Wells' novel of the same name) bring Flynn Carsen into the CU. Various accounts set in the CU have portrayed different parties as possessing the Spear of Destiny. It has yet to be determined which, if any, of these stories features the true Spear. The Ark of the Covenant seen here is visually based on the one seen in* Raiders of the Lost Ark. *It must have been moved to the Library after the alien breach of Area 52 in the Antarctic, as seen in the comic book* Area 52.

THE GOON MEETS HELLBOY

Hellboy gets knocked on the head, and upon regaining consciousness finds himself at a different location, where he meets a zombie-killing palooka known as the Goon. After another knock on the head, Hellboy finds himself back where he was when he received the first blow to the head.

The Goon #7 by Mike Mignola and Eric Powell, Dark Horse Comics, June 2004. The exploits of Powell's adventurer the Goon take place in the present day, but in a very surreal world with 1930s trappings, and therefore likely occur in an alternate reality to the Crossover Universe. Hellboy must have somehow been transported to the Goon's universe from the CU.

MY FIRST MANIAC

While researching slashers on the internet, Cassie Hack reads about "a man who kills in dreams in Ohio . . . a masked maniac who terrorizes a small town on Halloween . . . a camp plagued for thirty years by a psycho who won't die." Among the other monsters she researches are "rabid dogs" and Hell Spawn, the info on which is accompanied by a picture of Spawn.

Hack/Slash prequel miniseries by Tim Seeley and Daniel Leister, Image Comics, 2010. The man who kills in dreams is Freddy Krueger, from the Nightmare on Elm Street film series. The masked maniac is Michael Myers from the Halloween movies. The psycho who won't die is Jason Voorhees of Friday the 13th fame. The rabid dog is the titular canine from Stephen King's novel Cujo. Spawn is a comic book character created by Todd McFarlane; this crossover brings a version of him into the CU, but does not incorporate all of the Image Comics Universe's continuity.

BLOOD IS THE HARVEST

Wynonna Earp battles a killer scarecrow in a cornfield, which she at first suspects of being "one of those crazy 'kids in the corn' things."

Comic book story by Beau Smith and Manuel Vidal in IDW's Tales of Terror, Vol. 1, IDW Publishing, 2004. "Those crazy 'kids in the corn' things" is a reference to Stephen King's story "Children of the Corn."

GHOST OF A SMILE

Carnacki Institute field agents J. C. Chance, Melody Chambers, and Happy Jack Palmer investigate a crisis at a drug research center, where super soldier experiments have turned the test subjects into godlike New People. Appearing or mentioned are: the Hogge; Frankenstein creatures; a monkey's paw, made into a Hand of Glory; the London Knights; the Droods; the Regent of Shadows; Hadleigh Oblivion; Shadows Fall; Old Father Time; and Bruin Bear and the Sea Goat.

Novel by Simon R. Green. The Carnacki Institute is named after Thomas Carnacki from William Hope Hodgson's short story collection Carnacki the Ghost-Finder. *The Hogge is a reference to the titular being from the Carnacki story "The Hog." Frankenstein creatures are a reference to Mary Shelley's novel* Frankenstein *and its continuations across various media. The monkey's paw made into a Hand of Glory is a shout-out to W. W. Jacobs' story "The Monkey's Paw." The London Knights and Hadleigh Oblivion are from Green's Nightside series. The Droods and the Regent of Shadows are from Green's Secret Histories series. Shadows Fall, Old Father Time, and Bruin Bear and the Sea Goat are from Green's novel* Shadows Fall.

FROM A DROOD TO A KILL

Eddie Drood takes action when his beloved, Molly Metcalf, is abducted by the Powers That Be to take part in the Big Game. Appearing or mentioned are: the Merlin Glass; MI 13; the London Knights; Area 52; Kayleigh's Eye; the Nightside; an old 1930s Hirondel; Queen Mab; King Oberon and Queen Titania; Saint Jude's Church; the original Fantom of the Paris Opera; Charlotte Karstein, the Wilderness Witch; Castle Frankenstein; the Nineteen Sixties Black Beauty; a shocking pink Rolls-Royce; the only occasionally successful Lotus submersible; Strangefellows; Walker; Dead Boy and Julien Advent; the *Night Times*; Shadows Fall; Bruin Bear and the Sea Goat; Old Father Time; the Carnacki Institute; Catherine Latimer; Deathstalker; Jason Royal; Castle Inconnu; Sir Kae; the Questing Beast; Lady Gaea (aka Gayle); the Doormouse and his House of Doors; Robot Archibald; Harry Fabulous; knock-off Hyde; Martian Red Weed; smoked black centipede meat; John Taylor and Shotgun Suzie; Carrys Galloway, the Waking Beauty; Bradford-on-Avon; the Hawk's Wind Bar and Grill; and Puck.

Novel by Simon R. Green. The Merlin Glass, the London Knights, Kayleigh's Eye, the Nightside, Saint Jude's Church, Strangefellows, Walker, Dead Boy, the Night Times, *Castle Inconnu, Sir Kae, the Questing Beast, Harry Fabulous, John Taylor, Shotgun Suzie, and the Hawk's Wind Bar and Grill are from Green's Nightside series. Julien Advent, a recurring character in the Nightside books, is a disguised version of the title character of the television series* Adam Adamant Lives! *The Doormouse and his House of Doors are from* the *Nightside* series, *but the group of hippies-turned-mice he belongs to first appeared in Green's novel* Drinking Midnight Wine, *which is also the source of Lady Gaea (aka Gayle); Carrys Galloway, the Waking Beauty; and Bradford-on-Avon, a fictionalized version of the real town of the same name where Green lives. MI 13 is the CU version of the British intelligence division of the same name seen in the Marvel Comics Universe. The Area 52 referenced in several of Green's works is probably the one seen in the Image Comics series* Area 52. *The Hirondel is a fictional car also driven by Simon Templar, aka the Saint, Leslie Charteris' "laughing Robin Hood of crime." Queen Mab is from William Shakespeare's play* Romeo and Juliet, *while King Oberon, Queen Titania, and Puck are from Shakespeare's* A Midsummer Night's Dream. *The original Fantom of the Paris Opera is Erik from Gaston Leroux's novel* The Phantom of the Opera. *Charlotte Karstein, the Wilderness Witch may be a relative of Carmilla Karnstein from J. Sheridan Le Fanu's classic vampire tale "Carmilla." Castle Frankenstein is from Mary Shelley's novel* Frankenstein, *of course. The Nineteen Sixties Black Beauty is the car used by the second Green Hornet, Britt Reid II, and his chauffeur/partner Hayashi Kato. The shocking pink Rolls-Royce is FAB 1, the car driven by Lady Penelope Creighton-Ward in the television series* Thunderbirds, *which takes place in the 2060s. Presumably, the Droods acquired FAB 1 via time travel. The only occasionally successful Lotus submersible is from the James Bond movie* The Spy Who Loved Me, *which bears little resemblance to Ian Fleming's original novel. Shadows Fall, Bruin Bear and the Sea Goat, and Old Father Time are from Green's novel* Shadows Fall. *The Carnacki Institute and Catherine Latimer are from Green's* Ghost Finders *novels. Deathstalker is the protagonist of a series of novels by Green set in one of many possible futures for the CU. Jason Royal is a disguised version of debonair spy Jason King from the TV shows* Department S *and* Jason King. *Robot Archibald is meant to be Robot Archie, who appeared in the British weekly comic book* Lion. *Hyde is a drug derived from the formula created by Dr. Henry Jekyll in Robert Louis Stevenson's* The Strange Case of Dr. Jekyll and Mr. Hyde. *Martian Red Weed is from H. G. Wells' novel* The War of the Worlds. *Smoked black centipede meat is from William S. Burrough's novel* Naked Lunch.

QUESTION OF SOLACE

Jack Drood, Armourer for his family, reminisces about his life as an agent, including the time he went to the Moon to recover Professor Cavor's last moonship, so it wouldn't embarrass the Americans when they arrived a few years later.

Short story by Simon R. Green in Tales of the Hidden World, *Open Road Media, 2014. The Drood family is from Green's* Secret Histories *novels, while Professor Cavor is from H. G. Wells'* The First Men in the Moon. *The events of this story overlap with* From a Drood to a Kill.

August
DARK CONGRESS

Buffy Summers, the Slayer, is recruited as the mediator of a gathering of demons and monsters, the Dark Congress, in Providence, Rhode Island. Providence was once the site of a Hellmouth that was closed by the death of H. P. Lovecraft in 1937, something that makes Lovecraft a figure of great disdain among the monsters. Among the creatures present for the Congress are "shambling shuggoths" and a race of tentacled demons called "Yurgoths."

Buffy the Vampire Slayer tie-in novel by Christopher Golden, Gallery Books, 2007. The "shuggoths" are likely shoggoths from the works of H. P. Lovecraft, and the Yurgoth demons are clearly named in honor of Yuggoth, another of Lovecraft's creations. Furthermore, the closing of a Hellmouth with Lovecraft's death fits perfectly with Lovecraft's appearance in the Supernatural *episode "Let It Bleed." This novel takes place after the final episode of* Buffy the Vampire Slayer, *"Chosen," but in a very different continuity from the official Season 8 comics, which feature the public becoming aware of Slayers and vampires, and which do not fit into CU continuity. This fact, coupled with the Lovecraftian material, leads to the conclusion* Dark Congress *details the CU version of Buffy's activities after "Chosen."*

Late September–Autumn
GHOST OF A DREAM

The field agents of the Carnacki Institute investigate a haunting at an abandoned theater that is up for renovation. Julien Advent, the Apocalypse Door, the Droods, and Area 52 are mentioned, and Alistair Gravel appears.

Novel by Simon R. Green. The Carnacki Institute is named after the title character of William Hope Hodgson's Carnacki the Ghost-Finder. *The Apocalypse Door was destroyed by the Drood family in Green's Secret Histories novel* From Hell with Love. *Julien Advent is from Green's Nightside novels; he is meant to be adventurer Adam Adamant, from the television series* Adam Adamant Lives! *The Area 52 referred to in Green's work is located in the Antarctic, and thus is probably meant to be the same one seen in the Image Comics miniseries of the same name. Alistair Gravel is probably meant to be a relative of combat magician William Gravel from Warren Ellis' comic* Gravel.

Early December
MONSTER HUNTER ALPHA

Earl Harbinger, head of Monster Hunter International and a century-old werewolf, battles agents of the Old Ones and a new breed of lycanthrope in Michigan's Upper Peninsula. The Deep Ones are discussed, and it is mentioned every nation with a Navy has programs to eradicate them.

Novel by Larry Correia, Baen Books, 2011. These references further solidify the presence of Monster Hunter International in the CU.

2004

Winter–Autumn
DILLON AND THE PIRATES OF XONIRA

Dillon battles Professor Alonzo Sunjoy, who is instructed to cut the engines of his hydrofoil by a member of the Advanced Counter Espionage Syndicate in a Scorpion Attack Helicopter. Some time later, Dillon is asked to investigate piracy on the island of Xonira by the Braithwaite group, which was founded in 1973 by a man heavily involved in world politics who thought globally, although he worked for the British government. Dillon asks for a Black Yukon Sucker Punch, and travels to Xonira in a high-tech submarine, the *Morgan Adams*. Dillon tells his friend and comrade Eli Creed to fly to MARDL and stay there until he can arrange other accommodations for them. Dillon types a code into his Worldstar satellite phone that lets the *Morgan Adams* know he has arrived safely on Xonira. The Pirate Emperor uses the Bonetti Defense during a sword fight with Dillon.

Novel by Derrick Ferguson, PulpWork Press, 2012. The Scorpion Attack Helicopter is from the movie Fire Birds. *Braithwaite is the British agent who recruits Lee to travel to the evil Han's island and investigate his criminal activities in the 1973 film* Enter the Dragon. *The Black Yukon Sucker Punch is a drink from the television series* Twin Peaks. *The* Morgan Adams *is named after the pirate played by Geena Davis in the movie* Cutthroat Island. *MARDL (Miami Aerodrome Research & Development Laboratories) is from the Challenger Storm novels by Don Gates. The Worldstar satellite phone may be a reference to Pamela Fryer's novel* The Midnight Effect. *The Bonetti Defense is from William Goldman's book* The Princess Bride, *as well as Rob Reiner's film adaptation.*

February
WAR CRY

Harry Dresden and the White Council try to keep a shoggoth in suspended animation away from the Red Court of vampires.

Five-issue The Dresden Files *miniseries by Jim Butcher, Mark Powers, and Carlos Gomez, Dynamite Entertainment, 2014. This story takes place four months after the novel* Dead Beat.

Spring. Events of *Terminal* by Brian Keene.

Spring
THE ADVENTURES OF SHARKBOY AND LAVAGIRL IN 3-D
A bag of Big Kahuna Burgers is seen on the dock where Max first encounters his imaginary superhero Sharkboy, who has been brought to life.

2005 feature film directed by Robert Rodriguez. Big Kahuna Burger is a fictional fast food chain that is best known for its appearance in Quentin Tarantino's film Pulp Fiction, *and has appeared in several more films made by Tarantino, Rodriguez, and others.*

DEER WOMAN

Detective Dwight Faraday, investigating a series of murders committed by (unknown to him) the deer woman of Native American lore, suggests to his chief the killer may be a new type of animal, citing a series of brutal animal attacks in London in 1981 that were linked to a freakish wolf that was gunned down in Piccadilly Circus. Later, Faraday and his colleague Officer Hood visit a casino, where a mechanical deer announces Murph and the Magictones will be performing that night.

Episode of the anthology television series Masters of Horror *directed by John Landis, broadcast December 9, 2005. The wolf attacks in 1981 are a reference to Landis' film* An American Werewolf in London, *which is already in the CU. Murph and the Magictones are from Landis' film* The Blues Brothers, *bringing in Jake and Elwood Blues.*

DILLON AND THE ALCHEMIST'S MORNING COFFEE
The Alchemist's Morning Coffee is a method of encoding digital information in human DNA devised by Dr. Alejandro Candu of the Henderson Institute of Alternative Technologies. The nation of Khusra is mentioned. Dillon's friend Wyatt Hyatt has been hacking into government agencies' computers since he was a kid, including hacking into CTU's computer core when he was thirteen. Dillon mentions another friend, Elisa Hill.

Short story by Derrick Ferguson in Black Pulp, *Tommy Hancock, Gary Phillips, and Morgan Minor, eds., Pro Se Press, 2013. This story takes place during the eight-month gap between Chapters 1 and 2 of* Dillon and the Pirates of Xonira. *The head of the Henderson Institute of Alternative Technologies is Dr. Sylvester Henderson, whose brother Mongrel is the protagonist of a series of stories by Ferguson in Airship 27 Productions'* anthology series Mystery Men (& Women). *Ferguson's 1930s adventurer Fortune McCall is a Prince of Khusra's Royal Family. The CTU (Counter Terrorist Unit) is from the television series* 24, *which features fictional U.S. Presidents and massive terrorist attacks, including a nuclear device being detonated in Los Angeles. Presumably, as with the Spider novels, the true details of Jack Bauer's adventures have been exaggerated and distorted for dramatic effect. Elisa Hill is the main character of Percival Constantine's* Myth Hunter *series.*

THE LIBRARIAN: RETURN TO KING SOLOMON'S MINES

Flynn Carsen and archaeologist Emily Davenport strive to prevent a thief from plundering the treasures of King Solomon's Mines. While traveling to the mines, they pass the Breasts of Sheba and Three Witches Mountain.

This TV movie, originally broadcast December 3, 2006, takes place a year after The Librarian: Quest for the Spear. *The Breasts of Sheba and Three Witches Mountain are from H. Rider Haggard's first Allan Quatermain novel,* King Solomon's Mines. *Solomon's treasure must have been returned to the African mines from the Pacific island where it was kept for a time, as seen in the* Tales of the Gold Monkey *episode "Legends Are Forever."*

MARRIAGE CAUSES CANCER IN RATS

A man is haunted by his family after paying Tony Genova and Vincent Napoli to murder them.

Short story by Brian Keene, found in his collections The Cage *and* Blood on the Page. *Tony and Vince appear throughout Keene's multiverse, in the worlds of his Clickers novels and the short story "The Siqqusim Who Stole Christmas." These versions are the ones native to the CU.*

REBORN

Illyria, the fallen Old One, is recruited by the Hierarchy of Bete Noir, the secret City that Shapes the World, to destroy Liandra, the Fallen Angel and the city's "court of last resort." The Hierarchy is mentioned to be the oldest client of the evil law firm Wolfram & Hart. Illyria and Liandra fight, but end up forming an uneasy alliance as they are mystically transported around the world and finally to a post-apocalyptic future before returning to Bete Noir in the present.

Fallen Angel *miniseries by Peter David and J. K. Woodward, IDW Publishing, 2009. This crossover links Peter David's* Fallen Angel *comic series to Illyria and Wolfram & Hart from the TV series* Angel, *and thus to the CU. Since time flows differently within Bete Noir than it does in the rest of the world, dating within the* Fallen Angel *series can be difficult; however, using Illyria's perspective, this crossover happens a few days after the* Angel *episode "Time Bomb."*

SPIRITS FROM BEYOND

Carnacki Institute field agents J. C. Chance, Melody Chambers, and Happy Jack Palmer investigate a haunted village inn. Happy recommends turning a case involving Druids over to the Droods, but Melody says they're scarier than the Druids ever were. J. C. says refugees from the Nightside hide out in London Undertowen. The trio visits the Institute's Secret Libraries, where the Empty Librarian, so called because he appears to be a sentient empty suit, tells them the Libraries' Index, which is much bigger inside than out, was made by the Traveling Doctor. Among the items in the Libraries are the Siggsand Manuscript, a single marble finger, a brass mezzotint, a bottle of comet wine, and the Sword Sacnoth. Happy, who uses various drugs to cope with his powerful telepathy, has been experimenting with stronger and stranger things, including mongoose blood, green tea, and even diluted doses of Dr. Jekyll's elixir.

Novel by Simon R. Green, taking place six months after Ghost of a Dream. *The Carnacki Institute is named for occult detective Thomas Carnacki from William Hope Hodgson's* Carnacki the Ghost-Finder. *The Siggsand (or Sigsand) Manuscript is also from the Carnacki stories. The Drood family is featured in Green's* Secret Histories *novel series. The Nightside is the setting of another series by Green, featuring private eye John Taylor. The Traveling Doctor is the CU counterpart of the Doctor of* Doctor Who *fame. Apparently the Index was built along similar principles to the Doctor's TARDIS. The single marble finger is from E. Nesbit's story "Man-Size in Marble." The brass mezzotint is probably a reference to M. R. James' story "The Mezzotint." Comet wine is real, but given the presence of a bottle in the Libraries of the paranormal-investigating Carnacki Institute, this is likely a reference to Ray Russell's story "Comet Wine," inspired by the Faust legend. Two characters in "Comet Wine," Sir Robert Cargrave and Lord Henry Stanton, also appear in Russell's stories "Sardonicus" and "The Vendetta"; all three stories are included* in a collection entitled Haunted Castles. *The title character of "Sardonicus" is mentioned in Kim Newman's story "The Mark of Kane," confirming all three stories in the CU. The Sword Sacnoth is from Lord Dunsany's story "The Fortress Unvanquishable, Save for Sacnoth." In the 1940s, a transfusion of mongoose blood turned Bob Frank into the super-fast costumed crimefighter known as the Whizzer, who appeared in the titles* USA Comics *and* All-Winners Comics, *both published by Timely Comics, later known as Marvel Comics. Green tea is real, but the reference here is an allusion to J. Sheridan Le Fanu's story of the same name. Dr. Jekyll's elixir is from Robert Louis Stevenson's* The Strange Case of Dr. Jekyll and Mr. Hyde, *of course.*

WRIT IN BLOOD

Immortal occult detective Jonathan Crowley encounters a Deep One.

The first novel in James A. Moore's Serenity Falls Trilogy. *Besides the Trilogy, Crowley is featured in other novels and stories by Moore. The run-in with a Deep One (from Lovecraft's "The Shadow Over Innsmouth") brings him into the CU.*

April 26–30
RECALLED

A man using the name Theodore Gordon attempts to turn the residents of a suburban neighborhood against each other, but winds up being thwarted and exposed by Repairman Jack.

Short story by F. Paul Wilson in He Is Legend: An Anthology Celebrating Richard Matheson, *Christopher Conlon, ed., Gauntlet Press, 2009; reprinted in* Quick Fixes: Tales of Repairman Jack, *2011. This story is a sequel to Richard Matheson's "The Distributor," Theodore Gordon's first appearance.*

Summer
IN MEDIA RES

The Perhapanauts, a government-sponsored group of monsters who hunt monsters themselves, roust a chimera from the Blue Ribbon Laundry.

The Perhapanauts #1 by Todd Dezago and Craig Rousseau, Dark Horse Comics, 2005. The Blue Ribbon Laundry is from the works of horror writer Stephen King, appearing in Carrie, *"The Mangler," and* Roadwork.

October
BRIMSTONE

Aloysius Pendergast encounters Count Isidor Ottavio Baldassare Fosco.

Novel by Douglas Preston and Lincoln Child. Count Fosco is identical in name, appearance, and personality to Count Fosco from Wilkie Collins' novel

The Woman in White, *which he actually refers to at one point. Therefore, the contemporary Fosco is probably a descendant of his earlier namesake.*

2005

Winter
KANKICHI RYOTSU VS. LUPIN III

Police officers Kankichi "Ryo-san" Ryotsu, Keiichi Nakagawa, Reiko Akimoto, and Bucho attempt to thwart Lupin III and his gang's theft of a diamond from a museum.

Story in the one-shot manga *special* Super Kochikame, *featuring crossovers between the characters of Osamu Akimoto's comedic* manga Kochikame *and characters from other series. Since "Monkey Punch's" Lupin III is in the CU, so are the characters from* Kochikame. *The other stories in* Super Kochikame *had Ryo-san and company meeting the main characters of Takao Saito's* Golgo 13, *Yoshinori Nakai and Takashi Shimada's* Kinnikuman, *Akira Toriyama's* Dragon Ball, *Yoshio Sawai's* Bobobo-bo Bo-bobo, *Usuta Kyosuke's* Pyu to Fuku! Jaguar, *Amon Dai's* Taizou Mote King Saga, *and Kōji Ōishi's* Maison de Penguin. Golgo 13 *fits easily into CU continuity, but the other series are far too outlandish to be easily included, and therefore only the Lupin and Golgo crossovers will be treated as taking place in the CU.*

Early Spring
DANGERGIRL AND THE ARMY OF DARKNESS

The ladies of DangerGirl team up with Ash Williams when the *Necronomicon Ex Mortis* falls into the wrong hands.

Miniseries by Andy Hartnell and Chris Bolson, Dynamite Entertainment, 2011–2012. Both the DangerGirl organization and Ash have independent ties to the CU; this crossover confirms their coexistence. This story explains the presence of the Necronomicon Ex Mortis *(not to be confused with the similarly-named* Necronomicon *penned by Abdul Alhazred) in DangerGirl member Abbey Chase's home during the events of the* DangerGirl: Back in Black *miniseries, which took place in*

Spring 2005. Thus, I have placed this story before that one and after the "Army of Darkness vs. Re-Animator" storyline, which took place in winter of that same year and depicted Ash escaping from an asylum. The miniseries DangerGirl: Revolver *takes place after* DangerGirl and the Army of Darkness, *and claims Abbey has been a DangerGirl member for nearly five years. However, Abbey joined the group in the autumn of 1997, during the events of the original* DangerGirl *miniseries. Given its connection to other stories,* Revolver *cannot take place in 2002. Furthermore, the presence of what appears to be an iPhone places* Revolver *no earlier than 2007. Therefore, it is more likely* Revolver *takes place in the autumn of 2007, and Abbey actually had been an agent of DangerGirl for ten years.*

Spring
NEVERMORE

Among the members of a small network of cops who help out Hunters protecting people from supernatural threats is "a woman in Chicago named Murphy."

A Supernatural *tie-in novel by Keith R. A. DeCandido. Murphy is Karrin Murphy from Jim Butcher's* Dresden Files *book series. This novel takes place during Season 2 of* Supernatural, *between the episodes "Crossroads Blues" and "Croatoan."*

EZRA VS. 10TH MUSE

The 10th Muse is sent back in time by her mother to ensure Perseus receives the credit for Medusa's death, rather than the legendary being's actual killer, the female demon hunter known as Ezra.

One-shot comic by Sean O'Reilly and Vicente Cifuentes, Arcana Studio, 2006. The 10th Muse is already in the CU; this crossover brings in the immortal Ezra, who is featured in Sean O'Reilly's series Kade, *as well as spin-off stories of her own.*

May
RED EYE

L.A. cop Harry Bosch travels to Boston to collect DNA from a suspect in a 15-year-old cold case, and winds up working with private eye Patrick Kenzie, who believes the same individual is responsible for the recent kidnapping of a young girl.

Short story by Dennis Lehane and Michael Connelly in FaceOff, *David Baldacci, ed., Simon & Schuster, 2014. Connelly's L.A. cop Harry Bosch is already connected to the CU, and this crossover brings in Lehane's Boston P.I. Patrick Kenzie.*

BLACK ORDER

Gray Pierce, lead agent of Sigma Force, a division of DARPA, visits a bookstore in Copenhagen that is owned by an ex-lawyer from Georgia. Sigma's director, Painter Crowe, begins a romance with Dr. Lisa Cummings.

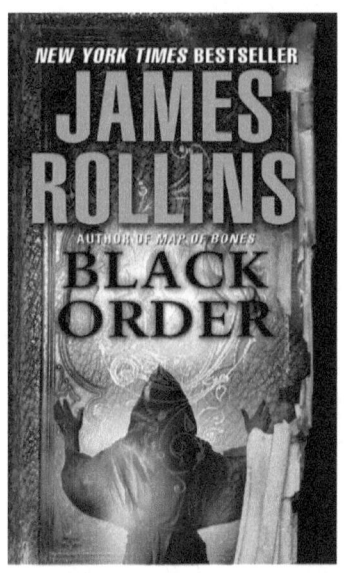

Novel by James Rollins. The ex-lawyer is Cotton Malone, who appears in novels by Steve Berry. Since Malone is in the CU (see the 2010 entry for "Extenuating Circumstances,") this crossover brings in Sigma Force. Dr. Cummings first appeared in Rollins' non-series novel Deep Fathom, *which depicts the Earth suffering massive natural disasters due to solar flares. Obviously, Rollins must have exaggerated the apocalyptic nature of the true events, just as the authors of the Spider pulp novels did. Rollins and Grant Blackwood are the coauthors of a spin-off series featuring ex-army ranger Captain Tucker Wayne and his military working dog Kane.*

Summer

BEHIND THE MASK: THE RISE OF LESLIE VERNON

Aspiring slasher Leslie Vernon seeks to follow in the footsteps of the great slashers that came before him. Footage is shown of Camp Crystal Lake, the town of Springwood, Ohio, and Haddonfield, Illinois as places that have suffered slasher attacks. Jason Voorhees, Freddy Krueger, Michael Myers, and Chucky are mentioned by name as existing. A Lament Configuration can be seen in the house of Leslie's friends Eugene and Jamie. Leslie has a bottle of Stay Awake medicine on his mantlepiece.

2006 horror film. The references connect Vernon to most of the important slasher series: Friday the 13th *(Jason Voorhees and Crystal Lake),* A Nightmare on Elm Street *(Freddy Krueger, Springwood, and Stay Awake),* Halloween *(Michael Myers and Haddonfield), and* Child's Play *(Chucky). The Lament Configuration is from the* Hellraiser *movies, based on Clive Barker's story "The Hellbound Heart." Of interest, one deleted scene has Leslie mentioning he spent some time in Texas, helping a fellow slasher who was trying to "reinvent his thing," a reference to Leatherface from the* Texas Chainsaw Massacre *movies, and a nod to both the originals and the 2003 remake. Some references in the film do seem to imply slashers lack supernatural powers, but this can be seen as Leslie simply using showmanship and stage magic to make up for abilities he lacks; this is backed up by a reference to Leslie Vernon in the ghost-slasher film* Hatchet II.

THE TWO-MINUTE RULE/THE WATCHMAN

On the run from a hit squad, Joe Pike and the woman he's protecting abandon his red Jeep Cherokee in a grocery store parking lot. It is stolen by ex-con Max Holman. It is mentioned Holman used to steal cars for two Hispanic gangsters named the Chihuahua Brothers.

Two novels by Robert Crais. The Watchman *is the first Joe Pike novel. Joe Pike is the partner of Crais' P.I. Elvis Cole. Pike appears in all the Elvis Cole books and Cole in all the Joe Pike books.* The Two-Minute Rule *is a standalone novel featuring former bank robber Max Holman. The Jeep Cherokee links the two books. The Chihuahua brothers are mentioned in Crais' Elvis Cole novel* L.A. Requiem.

SOMETHING WICKED

It is mentioned the monster Sam and Dean Winchester are tracking previously hit Ogdenville, Brockway, and North Haverbrook.

Episode of the television series Supernatural *broadcast April 6, 2006. Ogdenville, Brockway, and North Haverbrook must be the Crossover Universe versions of the towns of those names mentioned in "Marge vs. the Monorail," an episode of the animated series* The Simpsons.

THE HOLIDAY RUNNER

Cops Kankichi Ryotsu and Keiichi Nakagawa vacation in France, where Ryotsu's luggage gets mixed up with Golgo 13's. The duo races to catch up with the assassin.

This story in the one-shot manga *special* Super Kochikame *brings Takao Saito's character Golgo 13 into the CU.*

MONSTER HUNTER LEGION

Monster Hunter International and other like-minded organizations come together for a conference in Las Vegas, which is disrupted when a creature created as a weapon during World War II is released and rampages across the Nevada desert. Agent Franks is a Frankenstein creation, albeit constructed by the alchemist Johann Dippel. The Great Old Ones and shoggoths are also mentioned. Two M.H.I. members comment that with huge P.U.F.F. bounty on the monster, "it's more likely to be Godzilla." "Or Dracula riding Godzilla."

Novel by Larry Correia, Baen Books, 2012. Johann Dippel was a historical figure, and is established as an ancestor of the Frankenstein family in several sources. The Great Old Ones and shoggoths are from the Cthulhu Mythos. There is a version of Godzilla in the CU, as seen in Emmanuel Gorlier's story "Twilight" and Nick Pollotta's novel Doomsday Exam, *but he seems to have spent most of his existence in captivity, given that the massive destruction seen in the Godzilla movies is not compatible with CU continuity.*

MONSTER HUNTER NEMESIS

Agent Franks of the Monster Control Bureau, a Frankenstein monster built by the alchemist Johann Dippel, battles a cult trying to raise an Old One off the coast of California. Some of the cultists are Deep One hybrids. There is a reference to shoggoths. Special Task Force Unicorn has access to a werewolf disabling poison made from a rare plant that only blooms on out of the way mountains under a full moon.

Novel by Larry Correia, Baen Books, 2014. Johann Dippel is an historic figure who has been identified as an ancestor of the Frankenstein family in several sources. The Old Ones, the Deep Ones, and the Shoggoths are from the works of H. P. Lovecraft. The rare plant is the Mariphasa plant from the movie Werewolf of London.

UNEARTHED

In a flashback to France in 1985, Atomic Robo battles his old foe Heinrich von Helsingard, whose brain has been placed in a cybernetic body, alongside Roadblock, Scarlett, and Bazooka.

Atomic Robo #5–6 by Brian Clevinger and Scott Wegener, Red 5 Comics, February–March 2008. Roadblock, Scarlett, and Bazooka are from the toy line G.I. Joe: A Real American Hero. *The Joes' British counterpart, Action Force, is already in the CU through references to Fu Manchu and Denis Nayland Smith. The Joes will also later meet the DangerGirl team.*

HATCHET II

Marybeth Dunstan, the last survivor of a group of tourists slaughtered by the ghostly slasher Victor Crowley, returns to the bayou with a group of hunters and gunmen to end his threat once and for all. The Jack Chop is sold at Reverend Zombie's store, and the TV in there shows Parker O'Neil saying she's never going skiing again. Chad asks if Crowley is "like Jason Voorhees or something?" and refers to the town of Glen Echo and a man called Leslie Vernon.

Film directed by Adam Green, 2010, picking up immediately after the first Hatchet *film. The Jack Chop is from Green's short film of the same name, while Parker O'Neil is from his film* Frozen. *The reference to Jason*

Voorhees from the Friday the 13th *series can easily be interpreted as to a real slasher. The town of Glen Echo and Leslie Vernon is from the film* Behind the Mask: The Rise of Leslie Vernon, *which takes place in the CU through references to Jason and other slashers who have already been included. Further bolstering the inclusion of the* Hatchet *series in the CU is a later battle between Crowley and Cassie Hack and Vlad of* Hack/Slash *fame.*

September
A RARE MOMENT

Bianca Jones has just returned to Baltimore from post-Hurricane Katrina New Orleans, where she battled zombies alongside London's people, among others. Crime scene specialist Joe Russo speculates the murders of three teens may have been perpetrated by disciples of Dagon or those things from Innsmouth. He remarks if the seaweed recovered from the crime scene is not indigenous to the area, he will send it to Arkham University for analysis.

Short story by John L. French in Here There Be Monsters, *Dark Quest, 2010. Dagon, Innsmouth, and Arkham are, of course, from H. P. Lovecraft's Cthulhu Mythos. London is C. J. Henderson's private investigator Teddy London, who has had frequent run-ins with beings from the Mythos.*

Autumn
THE LIBRARIAN: CURSE OF THE JUDAS CHALICE

Flynn Carsen battles the vampire Vlad Dracula, who has rejuvenated himself by drinking from the Judas Chalice.

TV movie broadcast December 7, 2008. Supposedly, Dracula was left crippled and stripped of most of his power after drinking from the corpse of a cholera victim hundreds of years ago. This "Dracula" is most likely a "soul-clone" of the true Count.

December
THE COLD MOON

Lincoln Rhyme meets California Bureau of Investigation agent Kathryn Dance.

Novel by John Sandford. Kathryn Dance went on to be the protagonist of three novels of her own, The Sleeping Doll, Roadside Crosses, *and* XO. *Both* The Sleeping Doll *and* XO *had appearances by Lincoln Rhyme.*

PREFACE

Mark Badbury recalls visiting a quarry with Clive Pike and Gary Drake in 1984 or 1985.

Short story by David Mitchell published in The Daily Telegraph, *April 29, 2006. Mark Badbury and Gary Drake are from Mitchell's novel* Black Swan Green, *which takes place in 1982. Clive Pike also appeared in* Black Swan Green, *but made his first appearance as an adult in Mitchell's story "Acknowledgments."*

2006

Winter
ONE NIGHT IN CHINATOWN

Ex-Sheriff Donna Fargo, who now works for supernatural experts Doctors Blakely and Boles, teams up with Lai Wan to battle a demon, and later enters the dreamplane with her to battle the person responsible for said demon's presence.

Short story by C. J. Henderson and Bruce Gehweiler in Lai Wan: Tales of the Dreamwalker, *Marietta Publishing, 2007. Lai Wan first appeared in Henderson's books about private eye Teddy London before spinning off into her own series of stories. The dreamplane also appears in the Teddy London series. Henderson and Bruce Gehweiler's Blakely and Boles stories are collected in* Where Angels Fear.

March
DARK HOLLOW

Mid-list writer Adam Senft finds himself battling a malignant satyr, Hylinus, after it is summoned in the area of LeHorn's Hollow and begins hypnotizing and raping the women of rural Pennsylvania. Senft once dated Becky Schrum. There is a reference to a group of deer hunters that died in a mysterious fire near the Hollow. Detective Hector Ramirez appears, and mentions his involvement in a strange bank robbery case two years earlier. Nelson LeHorn's copy of the *Daemonolateria* plays a major role in the story, and LeHorn's diary, written in 1985, states: "I've heard tell of a fellow down south, a Korean War vet. Folks call him Silver John. Walks the Appalachians with a silver-stringed guitar and works some really strong powwow. Hear tell he's got a real nice singing voice, too. But I don't think he's ever made it this far north. Sticks below the Mason-Dixon. And there was an old Amish fella, but he passed on five years ago." The diary also tells the fate of another occultist, Saul O'Connor, who was found dead covered in a strange fungus. Nodens and the rest of the Thirteen are mentioned.

Novel by Brian Keene. Becky Schrum is a minor character from Keene's novel Ghoul. *The fate of the deer hunters is revealed in Keene's story "Red Wood," which also marks the first appearance of LeHorn's Hollow, a major setting in Keene's work, including* Ghost Walk, *"Bunnies in August," and "The Ghosts of Monsters." Hector Ramirez and the strange bank robbery are from Keene's novel* Terminal. *The* Daemonolateria *is a fictional book of magic that appears throughout Keene's works. Nelson LeHorn, the original summoner of Hylinus, also appears in Keene's short story "Stone Tears." Although Keene's Lovecraft references often seem at odds with other sources, and are thus only a tenuous link to the CU, the reference to Manly Wade Wellman's wandering occult hero Silver John ties the main Keene-verse more solidly into the CU. The "old Amish fella" is Amos Stoltzfus, the father of Keene's ex-Amish magus Levi Stoltzfus, who appears in* Ghost Walk, A Gathering of Crows, *"The Witching Tree," and "Last of the Albatwitches." Saul O'Connor's story is told in Keene's story "The Burn Barrel." The weird fungus is a creation of Behemoth of the Thirteen, and can be seen at work in an alternate universe in Keene's* Earthworm Gods *trilogy. Nodens is neither the original Celtic deity nor the Elder God of the Cthulhu Mythos, but rather the greatest among the Thirteen, the main villains of Keene's Labyrinth mythos.*

Spring
KONI WAVES/DEMONSLAYER

Koni Kanawai, aka Koni Waves, a former exotic dancer-turned member of the Honolulu P.D.-turned private investigator, teams up with Demonslayer to battle a mysterious woman called Genesis, as well as Puea, the Hawaiian god of darkness, and Prince Hopohopo, a practitioner of "the dark arts," both of whom were freed by Genesis from imprisonment within a Tiki statue.

One-shot by Mark Poulton, Stephen Sistilli, and Dexter Weeks, Arcana Studio, June 2007. A prologue, "Hog Wild" by Mark Poulton and Jon Landry, appeared in Dark Horrors Anthology Volume I, *Arcana Studio, December 2006. Demonslayer is already in the CU through an encounter with the 10th Muse; therefore, this crossover brings in Koni Waves.*

DÉNOUEMENT
Former school headmaster Graham Nixon finds his plane ride is not what he thought it was.

Short story by David Mitchell in The Guardian, *May 26, 2007. Nixon first appeared in Mitchell's story "Acknowledgments," and also appeared in the novel* Black Swan Green.

NOT WHAT ONE DOES
The psychometrist Lai Wan is hired by what appears to be Agent Jack Dixon of the National Security Agency to become involved in a case concerning a shoggoth. She soon finds the shoggoth has been impersonating the real Agent Dixon.

Short story by John Sunseri and C. J. Henderson in Lai Wan: Tales of the Dreamwalker, *Marietta Publishing, 2007. Dixon also appears in the collection* The Spiraling Worm, *consisting of seven interconnected stories by Sunseri and David Conyers. The book also features Major Harrison Peel of the Australian Army's intelligence division, who appears in several of Conyers' Cthulhu Mythos stories.*

DON'T JUDGE A BOOK BY ITS TITLE
Ash Williams travels to France, searching for the *Necronomicon.* Ash reached out to several people in the paranormal community for leads on the book, including some Ghostbusters in New York and an elderly Frenchman called the Sâr Dubnotal. Inside the cabin where he believes the *Necronomicon* to be, he drives off a creature called Baal, ending its alliance with the vampire Countess Irina. Irina's giant servant says the book Ash seeks is the *Necronomicon Ex Mortis*, while the book Irina holds is the *First Necronomicon*, written by the Mad Arab Abdul Alhazred. When Irina asks if he is "the one destined to fight the forces of darkness," Ash responds, "The same . . . although I did hear something about a girl named Buffy who hangs out with the band Slayer, I think."

Short story by Matthew Dennion in Tales of the Shadowmen Volume 11: Force Majeure, *Jean-Marc and Randy Lofficier, eds., Black Coat Press, 2014; reprinted in French in* Les Compagnons de l'Ombre (Tome 16), *Jean-Marc and Randy Lofficier, eds., Rivière Blanche, 2015. Ash Williams and the Necronomicon Ex Mortis are from the* Evil Dead *film series. Although this story supposedly takes place in 1993, shortly after the third Evil Dead movie,* Army of Darkness, *this cannot be correct. In the CU, the films take place from 1982–1983, and Ash spent over twenty years in a mental institution after the events of the comic book miniseries* Army of Darkness: Shop 'til You Drop Dead, *only to escape in 2005, as seen in* Army of Darkness vs. Re-Animator. *Furthermore, 1983 would be well before Buffy Summers (from the movie and*

TV series Buffy the Vampire Slayer*) discovered she was the latest in a long line of Slayers. Therefore, I have placed this story in 2006, a year after Ash escaped from Arkham Asylum in Massachusetts. The Ghostbusters in New York are from the movie* Ghostbusters *and its sequel, as well as the cartoon* The Real Ghostbusters. *The animated series* Extreme Ghostbusters *is set in the 1990s, and features a younger group of investigators who have taken up the mantle of the retired original Ghostbusters. Ash probably contacted the latter-day team. The Sâr Dubnotal is an occult investigator who appeared in a French pulp series. Baal is from Renée Dunan's novel of the same name, which has been translated by Brian Stableford for Black Coat Press. Countess Irina Karlstein is from the film* Female Vampire. *In the movie, which was made and takes place in the 1970s, Countess Irina is mute. How she gained the ability to speak is unknown. The* Necronomicon *penned by Abdul Alhazred is from H. P. Lovecraft's Cthulhu Mythos, of course.*

PASSIONS

Kay Bennett Crane helps Tabitha Lenox rescue her daughter Endora from the 10th dimension, which is sandwiched between Oz and Narnia.

Untitled episode of the daytime television drama Passions *broadcast June 25, 2007. The Oz and Narnia references bring this series into the CU. Tabitha's parents were a human named Darrin and a witch named Samantha. The television series* Bewitched *featured a mortal named Darrin Stephens who was married to a witch named Samantha. Eventually, they had a daughter named Tabitha. Samantha's mother was named Endora. A 1999 episode of* Passions *featured Dr. Bombay from* Bewitched, *establishing both shows take place in the same universe. Tabitha Stephens, who was born in the 20th century, is clearly not the same person as Tabitha Lenox, who is over 300-years-old. However, there may be some relationship between their two families.*

April
FIX

Repairman Jack has a chance encounter with a female spy known only as Chandler, and winds up working with her to prevent a deadly toxin from being unleashed on New York City.

A Kindle Worlds novella by F. Paul Wilson, J. A. Konrath, and Ann Voss Peterson. Wilson's "fixer" Repairman Jack is already in the CU, and this crossover brings in the main character of Konrath and Peterson's Codename: Chandler *series. Through various crossovers, the inclusion of Chandler brings the following works into the CU: Konrath's respective series featuring Harry McGlade, Phineas Troutt, and Jacqueline "Jack" Daniels, and his novel* Disturb; *Konrath's* Afraid, Endurance, Trapped, *and* Haunted House, *all written as by Jack Kilborn; Peterson's* Val Ryker *series;* Blake

Crouch's Abandon, Famous, *and* Snow-
bound, *the Andrew Z. Thomas series, and
the Letty Dobesh series; Garth Perry's A. J.
Rakowski stories; Henry Perez's Alex
Chapa novels; Jeff Strand's Andrew Mayhem
series; Tom Schreck's* Duffy Dombrowski
Mysteries; *Bernard Schaffer's* Superbia
*trilogy; Tracy Sharp's Leah Ryan series;
Jude Hardin's Nicholas Colt series and the
spinoff* Jack Reacher Files *series, set in the
same continuity as Lee Child's Jack Reacher
series; Iain Rob Wright's Sarah Stone series;
Crouch, "Kilborn," Strand and Wilson's
novel* Draculas, *which mentions* The
National Tattler, *a fictional tabloid from
Thomas Harris' novel* The Silence of the
Lambs; *Gary Ponzo's Nick Bracco series;*

*John W. Mefford's Booker series; Felipe Adan Lerma's Samantha LaCroix
series; Erik Williams' novel* Progeny; *David MacInnis Gill's Boone Childress
Mysteries; Nick Andreychuk's Earl Stack stories; Paul Seiple's James Beamer
thriller series; Mark Terry's Derek Stillwater series; Bryan Higby's OzValt
Grant series; H. L. LeRoy's Jillian Varela series; Gordon Hopkins' Gil
DiMauro series; Silas Payton's Bill Roberts series; T. M. Bilderback's Justice
Security series; James A. Moore and Charles R. Rutledge's Griffin and Price
series, which has a number of ties to the CU; Steve DeWinter's Peacekeepers
X-Alpha series; Linda Style's Street Law series; and Tim Tresslar's Fight Card
novel* Blood Feud. *The Clayton family seen in Schaffer's* Guns of Seneca 6
series is descended from Superbia's *Cole Clayton, while the hero of Konrath's*
Timecaster *series (written as "Joe Kimball") is Jack Daniels and Phineas
Troutt's grandson, and a recurring villain in that series is descended from
characters in* Afraid *and* Haunted House. *Both series take place in alternate
futures to the CU.*

April 18–21
THE VENETIAN BETRAYAL
      Cotton Malone battles Irina Zovastina, supreme minister of the Central
Asian Federation. Zovastina was previously suspected of being behind the
theft of several endangered animals, a crime that was investigated by Painter
Crowe at Sigma.
      Novel by Steve Berry. James Rollins' Sigma Force novel Black Order
*had a reference to Malone. This crossover further cements Cotton Malone
and Sigma's coexistence within the CU.*

May
BLACK MAGIC WOMAN

Supernatural investigator Quincey Morris and white witch Libby Chastain battle a practitioner of black magic who is continuing her family's vendetta against the descendants of the woman who exposed her ancestress as a witch during the trials in Salem. Quincey owes a debt to a man named Jack, whose crew travels in semis and four-wheel-drive jeeps. Quincey thinks none of the experts who have written about the vampire's nature, such as Van Helsing, Blake, and Tregarde, have been able to explain why the undead are vulnerable to certain natural substances. A flashback details Quincey's namesake and great-grandfather's death while helping to kill Dracula, as well as the aftermath of those events. Morris once spent an hour in a townhouse in Washington's Georgetown section where two Jesuit priests died performing an exorcism to save a young girl. Quincey and Libby visit occult investigator Barry Love, whose bookshelves hold two different editions of the Bible, Stone's *Practical Demon-Hunting*, the *Bhagavad-Gita*, Newman's *The Vampire in Victorian England*, Wellman's biography of John the Balladeer, books by Hegel and Sartre, Black's *Approaching the Millennium*, and the third edition of *Investigating the Occult: Principles and Techniques* by Scully and Reyes. Later, the black witch uses her magic to force the driver of an SUV to attempt to run over Quincey and Libby. The SUV smashes through the front of Del Floria's Tailor Shop. After Libby is hospitalized, a pair of N.Y.P.D. detectives question Quincey about the "accident." One is named Clark, while the other's last name is something that ends with "witz."

Novel by Justin Gustainis, 2008. The modern-day Quincey Morris is a descendant of the courageous Texan of the same name in Stoker's Dracula. The original Quincey's wife died in childbirth, thus explaining his bachelorhood in the original novel. Jay Lindsey notes, "There is some conflict with Quincey Morris, Vampire, by P. N. Elrod. In Gustainis' book, Morris is survived by his parents and one son. In Elrod's account, Morris claims his parents died long before. I think we can get around that, though. Given that the Morris family picked up a generational monster hunting legacy, it's obvious that at some point the original Quincey, in his new state of undeath, attempted to make contact with his parents and son, and it did not go well.

A century later, while relating his account to Elrod, vampire Quincey chose to gloss over those painful memories." Jack is vampire hunter Jack Crow from John Steakley's novel Vampire$. Van Helsing needs no explanation at this point. Blake is a reference to the protagonist of Laurell K. Hamilton's Anita Blake: Vampire Hunter novels. However, Blake's exploits take place in a world where the existence of the supernatural is widely known. The Blake referenced here must be her CU counterpart, whose exploits are vastly different from the "Blake-verse's" Anita. Diana Tregarde appears in a series of novels by Mercedes Lackey. The two Jesuit priests are from William Peter Blatty's novel The Exorcist. Barry Love is a disguised version of Harry D'Amour, a private investigator specializing in the occult in novels and stories by Clive Barker. Stone is Ezekiel Stone from the television series Brimstone. Newman is doubtless the CU counterpart of Kim Newman. The exploits of Manly Wade Wellman's John the Balladeer, aka Silver John, are well-established as part of the CU. Black is Frank Black from the television series Millennium. Scully and Reyes are FBI Agents Dana Scully and Monica Reyes from The X-Files. Earlier in the book, Special Agent Dale Fenton refers to The X-Files as a television series; presumably, this was a spin-off of the movie starring Garry Shandling and Téa Leoni. Del Floria's Tailor Shop houses the secret entrance to the headquarters of U.N.C.L.E. The N.Y.P.D. detectives are John Clark, Jr. and Andy Sipowicz from the television series NYPD Blue.

May 13–September
SILENCE

Private eye Jack Till must save a woman he helped six years ago from assassins Paul and Sylvie Turner. Paul used to receive most of his referrals from the bartender at the Palazzo di Conti restaurant, which was rumored to be a remote outpost for members of the Balacontano family who came west on business.

Novel by Thomas Perry. The Balacontano crime family is from Perry's novels dealing with the assassin known as the Butcher's Boy. The Butcher's Boy appears under the pseudonym "the Grocer's Boy" in Justin Gustainis' novel Sympathy for the Devil, *part of his Morris and Chastain Supernatural Investigations series, which has many crossover references bringing it into the CU. This reference brings in Jack Till as well.*

Summer
FAIRWAY, MY LOVELY

Andy Barker, an accountant doing side work as a private investigator, investigates the death of his client, Guy Halverson, who owned a company called Doublemeat Enterprises.

Episode of the television series Andy Barker, P.I., *written by Jane Espenson, Alex Herschlag, and Daniel Hsia, broadcast March 22, 2007. Espenson also wrote the* Buffy the Vampire Slayer *episode "Doublemeat Palace," in which Buffy got a job at the titular fast food restaurant, only to discover her co-workers were being made into burgers. It is mentioned in "Fairway, My Lovely" that Doublemeat Enterprises owns at least one condo; they likely own the Doublemeat Palace as well. This crossover brings* Andy Barker, P.I. *into the CU. Detective Angel Batista ate two Doublemeat burgers in "Truth Be Told," an episode of* Dexter, *confirming that series in the CU.*

SHI/10TH MUSE: VOWS

The demigoddess known as the 10th Muse attempts to prevent Shi from killing a Yakuza who has entered the Witness Protection Program. They are soon forced to team up against the Muse's sister Tragedy.

One-shot by Paul Storrie, Nadir Balan, and Joey Campos, Bluewater Comics, June 2007. This crossover brings the 10th Muse into the CU.

BLOODY LIARS

Sergeant Major William Gravel, SAS member and combat magician, is ousted from the Minor Seven, a group of "occult detectives," and is forced to kill his corrupt former teammates, who are planning to use pages from the Sigsand Manuscript for their own nefarious purposes. The Manuscript's previous owner, Thomas Carnacki, appears in a flashback.

Gravel #0-7 by Warren Ellis, Mike Wolfer, Raulo Caceres, and Oscar Jimenez, 2007–2008. The connection to William Hope Hodgson's occult detective Carnacki brings William Gravel into the Crossover Universe. His presence in the CU is further solidified by a reference in Justin Gustainis' novella Midnight at the Oasis. *Gravel says Carnacki died in 1923, and another member of the Minor Seven named Sykes reveals his death was caused by cancer brought about by exposure to radiation from the sleuth's electric pentacle and other devices. However, several accounts set after 1923 feature a still-living Carnacki; furthermore Simon R. Green's Nightside novels indicate Carnacki served as a mentor to the protagonist of that series, P.I. John Taylor, who is active in the 21st century. Therefore, the accounts of Carnacki's death in 1923 must be false. Since Taylor would have been born in the 1970s, Carnacki must have had his lifespan extended somehow. The Nightside books also have a number of references to combat magicians, further cementing William Gravel's presence in the CU. Josh Reynolds' Royal Occultist stories place Carnacki's death in 1918, but I have previously speculated Carnacki merely faked his death in that year.*

July

THE JUDAS STRAIN

Joe Kowalski joins Sigma Force.

Novel by James Rollins. Kowalski first appeared in Rollins' non-series novel Ice Hunt.

Summer

TWO RED EYES

The ancient vampire "Nosferatu" travels to Los Angeles and picks a fight with monster hunting P.I. Cal McDonald.

Four issue comic miniseries by Steve Niles, Dark Horse Comics. "Nosferatu" is clearly Graf Orlok, the vampire from F. W. Murnau's film Nosferatu, ein Symphonie des Grauens.

BAD LUCK AND TROUBLE

Jack Reacher is broke and stranded in Portland, Oregon, after spending two nights with an assistant district attorney named Samantha.

Novel by Lee Child, 2007. Jack Reacher is in the CU through a reference in Stephen King's novel Under the Dome. *Samantha is Samantha Kincaid, a deputy district attorney in Portland who is the main character of a series of novels by Alafair Burke.*

DILLON AND THE LAST RAIL TO KHUSRA

Dillon is hired to act as a bodyguard for Princess Salena of the North African country of Harak aboard a train to Khusra. Dillon is rumored to have encountered Li Shoon once or twice. John Velvet of the American intelligence agency the Machine gives Sly Gantlet a special visa to perform in Khusra.

Novel by Derrick Ferguson, Pulpwork Press, 2014. Ferguson's 1930s adventurer Fortune McCall is a prince of the royal family of Khusra. Li Shoon, a Yellow Peril villain created by H. Irving Hancock, appeared in Detective Story Magazine *in 1916–1917. Sly Gantlet and his brothers are rock stars who also act as mercenaries in books by Joel Jenkins; Sly first met Dillon in Ferguson and Jenkins' story "Dead Beat in La Esca."*

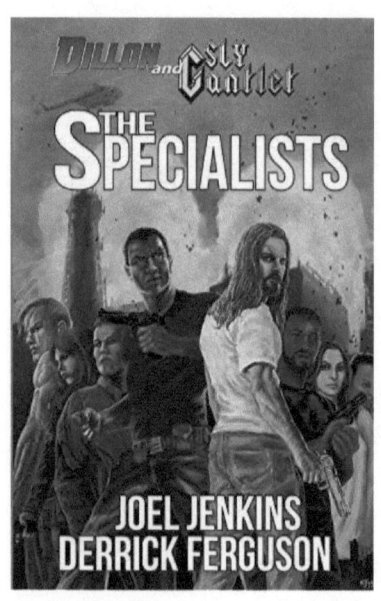

DEAD BEAT IN KHUSRA

Dillon, spending a few days in Khusra after his latest adventure, reluctantly teams up with Sly Gantlet when his old flame and Sly's current lover, Princess Sathyra of Tosegio, is kidnapped. Appearing or mentioned are: a member of the Khusran royal family who achieved some notoriety adventuring around the world back in the 1930s and '40s; a Forrester tux; U.N.C.L.E.; F.L.A.G.; Globex; Thema Sidibe (aka Tracy); the "Long Noodle" plague; Jekyll Island beer; Madeline Scocco; the Otwani tribe; *Cry, Cry Again*; *See You Next Wednesday*; Comanapracil; Al-Julhara; and the Willis-Brennan JJ/59 aircraft, aka the Skyspear.

Novella by Joel Jenkins and Derrick Ferguson in The Specialists, *Pulp-Work Press, 2015. Dillon is the protagonist of a series of novels and short stories by Ferguson, while Sly Gantlet and his brothers, rock stars who double as mercenaries, appear in books by Jenkins. This story takes place immediately after Ferguson's novel* Dillon and the Last Rail to Khusra. *Dillon and Sly first met in Jenkins and Ferguson's story "Dead Beat in La Esca." The member of the Khusran royal family who achieved some notoriety adventuring around the world back in the 1930s and '40s is Fortune McCall, the hero of another series of stories by Ferguson. Thema Sidibe, Fortune's cousin, used the name Tracy Scott in that era during her adventures alongside him. The "Long Noodle" plague and the Otwani tribe are also from the Fortune McCall tales. Madeline Scocco is the granddaughter of Ronald Scocco, one of Fortune's aides. The Forrester tux is a reference to the Forrester family that owns the fashion house Forrester Creations on the soap opera* The Bold and the Beautiful. *U.N.C.L.E. is from the television series* The Man from U.N.C.L.E., *of course. F.L.A.G. is from the TV series* Knight Rider. *Globex is from "You Only Move Twice," an episode of the long-running animated sitcom* The Simpsons. *Since that show is too overtly absurd in its events to be incorporated into CU continuity, Globex must exist in both the CU and the Simpsons' native universe. Jekyll Island beer has appeared in several TV series, including* Burn Notice, Dexter, *and* Lost. Cry, Cry Again *is a fictional movie from the* Seinfeld *episode "The Little Kicks." * See You Next Wednesday *is a film that appears or is mentioned in several of John Landis' films, including* An American Werewolf in London, The Blues Brothers, *and* Trading Places. *Comanapracil is a drug seen in*

"Believe in the Stars," an episode of the sitcom 30 Rock. *Al-Julhara is from the movie* The Jewel of the Nile, *a sequel to* Romancing the Stone. *The Willis-Brennan JJ/59 aircraft is a reference to Willis Aircraft Company owner Leland Willis and his employee Lt. Col. Matt Brennan from the film* Chain Lightning. *Matt must have become a partner in the company after the movie's events.*

September
HEART-SHAPED BOX

Things take a paranormal turn for the worse when aging rocker Judas Coyne purchases a ghost online; other items among his collection of the strange and macabre include books by Aleister Crowley and Charles Dexter Ward.

Novel by Joe Hill. Ward is the main character of H. P. Lovecraft's The Case of Charles Dexter Ward, *linking Joe Hill's interconnected works to the Cthulhu Mythos, and thus the CU.*

Early Autumn
THE FIRST COMMANDMENT

CIA paramilitary operative Rick Morrell tells his subordinate Mike Raymond he is going to call in a favor from an ex-Department of Justice operative turned book dealer named Malone to verify whether or not former Navy SEAL and current Secret Service agent Scot Harvath is in Zurich.

Novel by Brad Thor. Malone is Cotton Malone, who appears in thriller novels by Steve Berry. Since Malone is in the CU, this reference brings in Scot Harvath. Harvath also has a cameo in Thor's novel The Athena Project, *which features characters first introduced in the Harvath novel* Foreign Influence.

Late Autumn
CHUCK VERSUS THE SIZZLING SHRIMP

Geek turned spy Chuck Bartowski helps a rogue Chinese agent rescue her brother from triads led by the wheelchair-bound Ben Lo Pan.

Episode of the television series Chuck *broadcast October 22, 2007. Ben Lo Pan is played by James Hong, who played the sorcerer Lo Pan (alias David Lo Pan) in the film* Big Trouble in Little China, *as well as "Here There Be Dragons," an episode of the television series* The Chronicle. *In the latter, he served as a businessman and crime lord in New York. Perhaps Lo Pan relocated from New York to Burbank in the years following his encounter with the staff of the* Chronicle, *changing his alias' first name and taking control of the triads there. In* Big Trouble in Little China, *one of Lo Pan's forms was a crippled old man. The appearance he used in Burbank was likely a variant on this persona. This connection strengthens the place of* Chuck *in the CU.*

269

December 25–26
THE SHADOW KILLERS
Professional assassin Monica Killingsworth protects a little girl from her fellow contract killers. The Gantlet Brothers and Dillon are mentioned.

Story by Joel Jenkins in PulpWork Christmas Special 2013, *Pulpwork Press. Monica Killingsworth is from Jenkins' Gantlet Brothers stories. Dillon is an adventurer created by Derrick Ferguson.*

2007

Winter
THE PATH
Jordan Wethersby, the head partner in the law firm that employs the formerly precognitive Eli Stone, confronts a group of clients at the Credit Dauphine bank, which is soon devastated when a crane crashes into the building.

Episode of the television series Eli Stone *broadcast October 14, 2008. Credit Dauphine was the front for the agency that employed Sydney Bristow and her father Jack on* Alias. *Jack Bristow was played by Victor Garber, who also played Jordan Wethersby. It is unknown whether there is any connection between the two, although they are definitely not the same person. This crossover brings Eli Stone into the CU.*

IN CUPBOARDS AND BOOKSHELVES
Hellboy's latest case brings him to Cedar Hill, Ohio.

Short story by Gary A. Braunbeck in Hellboy: Oddest Jobs, *Christopher Golden, ed., Dark Horse Books, 2008. The town of Cedar Hill, Ohio is featured in a series of short stories, novellas, and novels by Braunbeck.*

THE SINO-MEXICAN REVELATION
The Middleman and his sidekick Wendy Watson visit Schlermie Beckerman Memorial Square and Alfred Necessiter Memorial Hospital.

Episode of the television series The Middleman *broadcast June 30, 2008. The Middleman is based on Javier Grillo-Marxuach and Les McClaine's comic book of the same name. One of the stories in the comic is "The League of Professional Jealousy," which features Abraham Van Helsing, Phileas Fogg, and Nikola Tesla teaming up in 1897 to kill the Middleman of that era for beating them to the punch on their achievements (slaying Dracula, making it around the world in 73 days, etc.), and ends with him making an enemy of Holmes and Watson by solving the Baskerville case before them. Given that the TV series has several crossover nods of its own, we can assume it, rather than the comic book, is in the CU. It is worth* noting that the comic versions of the Middleman and his sidekick Wendy Watson met their TV counterparts in the graphic novel The Pan-Universal Parental Reconciliation. The group the Middleman works for, the O2STK (Organization Too Secret to Know), is mentioned in an episode of The Librarians, a spin-off of The Librarian TV movies, strengthening the argument that a version of The Middleman exists in the CU. Schlermie Beckerman and Alfred Necessiter are from the movie The Man with Two Brains.

THE MANICOID TELEPORTATION CONUNDRUM

The Middleman has a rendezvous with Wendy Watson at Lyon Estates. Wendy discovers a bomb is hidden at Twin Pines Mall. Ida, the Middleman's android assistant, says a headless murder victim lived at Eastwood Ravine Drive.

Episode of The Middleman broadcast July 7, 2008. Lyon Estates and Twin Pines Mall are from the film Back to the Future. Eastwood Ravine Drive is named after the Eastwood Ravine from Back to the Future Part III. Since the Back to the Future movies have been shown as taking place in the CU, we have further evidence The Middleman does as well.

Early March
BACKUP

The spirit being named Bob mentions the Necronomicon, referring to the White Council's publication of it in order for its summoning rituals to be diffused and weakened.

Short story by Jim Butcher in Side Jobs: Stories from the Dresden Files, 2010.

Spring
SALAMANDER BLUES

Hellboy encounters a group of mermen who are holding people hostage, and concludes the National Guard is not coming, and neither is the army or the FBI or Black Lodge or any of the other alphabet-soup agencies.

Short story by Brian Keene in Hellboy: Oddest Jobs, Christopher Golden, ed., Dark Horse Books, 2008. Black Lodge is a covert occult organization that exists across Keene's multiverse, including several works that have been incorporated into the Crossover Universe.

THE ECTOPLASMIC PANHELLENIC INVESTIGATION

Eleanor Draper's honors include the Egon Spengler Memorial Award and the Ivo Shandor Medal.

Episode of The Middleman *broadcast August 4, 2008. Egon Spengler and Ivo Shandor are from the movie* Ghostbusters.

THE HUNTERS WITHIN THE CORNERS

The masked vigilante Skaramine battles August Shorer, the last of Keziah Mason's students and coven. Skaramine was mentored by an old man named Kent, who gave him his twin Colt .45s, and taught him how to heal his own wounds, change his appearance, blend into the shadows, and throw his laugh. Kent is said to have been "a shadow hunting shadows" in another era. Shorer is served by rat-things with humanoid faces, as well as the Tcho-Tcho, children of man and the dwarven Miri Nigri, favored scions of his patron, Chaugnar Faugn. Shorer is ultimately killed by a Hound of Tindalos.

Short story by Douglas P. Wojtowicz in Cthulhu Unbound Volume 2, *Thomas Brannan and John Sunseri, eds., Permuted Press, 2008. Keziah Mason is from H. P. Lovecraft's story "The Dreams in the Witch House." The Rat-Servitors are of the same race as Brown Jenkin, Mason's familiar. Based on the descriptions, Kent probably needs no further introduction. The Tcho-Tcho race appears in August Derleth's contributions to Lovecraft's Cthulhu Mythos. The Miri Nigri and Chaugnar Faugn are from Frank Bel-knap Long's* The Horror from the Hills, *a novel based on Lovecraft's Cthulhu Mythos. "The Hounds of Tindalos" is another story by Long.*

DEAD BEAT IN THE GOBI DESERT

Dillon and Sly Gantlet steal a biological weapon from a Russian military base, only to find the scientist who created the mutagen's daughter inside the container. They must contend with a blizzard, Russian Special Forces, and a band of cannibals to complete their mission safely.

Novella by Joel Jenkins and Derrick Ferguson in The Specialists, *PulpWork Press, 2015. This story takes place an unspecified amount of time after "Dead Beat in Khusra."*

April 9–May 1
EVIL WAYS

Quincey Morris and Libby Chastain battle the vile Walter Grobius, who has purloined a copy of Abdul Alhazred's *Book of Shadows* from an Iraqi muse-um. An extremely dangerous occultist named Janos Skorzeny is mentioned. Quincey tells FBI Special Agent Dale Fenton he knew Will Graham and asks if Jack Crawford is still in charge of the Bureau's Behavioral Science Unit, only to be told Crawford died of a heart attack some years back. Quincey asks if Fenton is "from the X-Files." Fenton replies the X-Files Unit is a myth in a manner that suggests he is quoting somebody. Quincey subsequently heads to Chicago to meet with Harry, the city's resident wizard, who has problems with machinery. Quincey suggests to Libby she ask their old acquaintance Barry Love to help her with Grobius' henchmen, who are preying on Libby and other members of her coven; Libby says she already called him, and his answering service says he is out of the country, date of return unknown. Fenton's partner Colleen O'Donnell says she thought Quincey was just a hustler "like that 'Ghost Whisperer' clown."

Quincey and Libby visit a pub whose owner, Mac, gives them a letter from Harry, explaining he had to miss their appointment because he was called away on Council business. One of Quincey's other Chicago contacts is a reporter named Carl, who monitors supernatural occurrences in the city, despite his boss Tony repeatedly trying to dissuade him from doing so. Quincey and Libby visit the Ouroboros Bar and Grill in Cleveland, which is owned by a psychic sensitive named Frank, who has a daughter in college named Jordan. He states that about ten years ago he used to work with a group of people who believed the new millennium would bring about a major supernatural catastrophe. The group managed to prevent this before falling apart. Quincey and Fenton compare Grobius to Keyser Soze. Quincey and Libby's ally Hannah Widmark, aka "the Widowmaker," had as a mentor "a shadowy, enigmatic man named Cranston," who taught her to fire a pair of .45s, had a weird laugh, and once told her, "the weed of Satan bears bitter fruit." A college professor mentions that Sharon Purcell, alias Shari Sexpert, is giving a talk on campus.

Novel by Justin Gustainis, 2009. Abdul Alhazred is most famous as the author of the Necronomicon *in the Cthulhu Mythos. While some characters in this novel refer to the* Necronomicon *as fictitious, Quincey's friend John Wesley Hester counsels him not to be sure of that. There are two villains named Janos Skorzeny in horror fiction: one is the vampire battled by Carl Kolchak in Jeff Rice's book* The Night Stalker *and its TV movie adaptation, while the other is a malevolent lycanthrope in the television series* Werewolf. *The occultist Janos Skorzeny may be a relative of one or both of his namesakes. Will Graham and Jack Crawford are from Thomas Harris' Hannibal Lecter novels. Graham appears in* Red Dragon, *while Crawford appears in that novel,*

The Silence of the Lambs, *and* Hannibal, *the latter of which depicts his fatal heart attack. Given references to Dana Scully and Monica Reyes as real people in the first novel in this series,* Black Magic Woman, *Agent Fenton is obviously providing Quincey with misinformation when he dismisses the X-Files as fictional. Harry is Harry Dresden from* The Dresden Files, *a series of urban fantasy novels by Jim Butcher. Harry frequents the pub McAnally's, and is a member of the White Council, which governs the world's wizard community. Barry Love is a disguised version of Harry D'Amour, Clive Barker's occult detective. "That 'Ghost Whisperer' clown" is a reference to Melinda Gordon from the television series* Ghost Whisperer. *Carl is clearly meant to be Carl Kolchak, whose boss is Tony Vincenzo, although both Carl and Tony would be a bit long in the tooth by this time. However, the 2005 television series* Night Stalker *featured much younger versions of Carl and Tony based in Los Angeles. It has been conjectured the Carl Kolchak seen in that series is the nephew of the elder Carl, in which case maybe the younger Tony is Tony Vincenzo Jr. Perhaps the two relocated from Los Angeles to Chicago sometime in the three years since their last recorded appearance. Frank is Frank Black from the television series* Millennium. *Keyser Soze is the villain of the film* The Usual Suspects. *Hannah Widmark's mentor is a well-known shadowy pulp hero, of course. Shari Sexpert is a character from Gustainis' earlier novel* The Hades Project.

Summer
BUMPED

Cassie and Vlad investigate the murders of several environmentalists, and wind up face-to-face with the culprits: undead slasher Edgar Dill and his Treehuggers, animated wooden statues carved by Dill himself.

Hack/Slash: The Series *#12–13 by Mark Kidwell, Tim Seeley, and Emily Stone, Devil's Due Publishing, May–June 2008. Edgar Dill is from Kidwell's comic book* Bump; *this crossover brings him into the CU.*

THE DREAMSCAPE

Olivia Dunham of the FBI's Fringe Division, investigating the death of a Massive Dynamic employee who jumped out of a window after being attacked by butterflies, discovers the deceased man had an unused Oceanic Air ticket for travel from New York to Omaha.

Episode of the television series Fringe *broadcast November 25, 2008. Oceanic Air must be another name for Oceanic Airlines, a fictional company seen in many TV series and movies, most notably* Fringe *creator J. J. Abrams' series* Lost. *It was also mentioned in Win Scott Eckert's story "The Eye of Oran." This crossover brings* Fringe *into the CU. Several episodes of* Fringe *feature Slusho, a fictional soft drink seen in a number of Abrams productions, including* Alias, Cloverfield, *the 2009 reboot of the* Star Trek *film franchise and its sequel,* Star Trek: Into Darkness, *and* Super 8, *as well as the non-Abrams TV show* Heroes. Alias *is already in the CU, and* Super 8 *could also fit into CU continuity. However, the very public level of destruction caused by the monster in* Cloverfield *is incompatible with the CU, and the 2009* Star Trek *film and* Into Darkness *explicitly take place in a divergent timeline from the one in which the previous* Star Trek *TV series, films, books, and comics occur.*

THE X-FILES: I WANT TO BELIEVE

A woman referred to as "Special Agent in Charge Fossa" appears.

Feature film directed by Chris Carter. Fossa is played by Sarah-Jane Redmond, who played an enigmatic woman named Inga Fossa in Carter's short-lived TV series Harsh Realm. *Since we never learned Inga's motivations or who she worked for, there's no reason to think the characters aren't the same, or at least related.*

THE CLOTHARIAN CONTAMINATION PROTOCOL

A NASA employee is named Lethbridge-Stewart. A "Zygon-Rated" containment box appears. The Nakatomi Protocol expands the vents in Middleman HQ to human size, allowing the Middleman to crawl through them in case of an emergency. A Clotharian bomb has writing on it in Aurebesh.

Episode of The Middleman *broadcast August 25, 2008. Lethbridge-Stewart is probably related to the CU counterpart of Brigadier Alistair Gordon Lethbridge-Stewart from* Doctor Who. *The Zygons are an alien race also seen in* Doctor Who. *The Nakatomi Protocol appears to have been inspired by John McClane crawling through the vents of the Nakatomi Plaza building, as seen in the movie* Die Hard. *The Aurebesh language is from the* Star Wars *film series.*

THE PALINDROME REVERSAL PALINDROME

The Middleman and Wendy Watson investigate the theft of a Beryllium Sphere and an Oscillation Overthruster. A collection of stolen doll eyes is made of polydichloric euthimal. The Middleman has a phased polaron cannon in his weapons archive.

Episode of The Middleman *broadcast September 1, 2008. Beryllium spheres are from the movie* Galaxy Quest, *while the Oscillation Overthruster is from the movie* The Adventures of Buckaroo Banzai Across the Eighth Dimension. *Polydichloric euthimal appears in the movies* Outland, *Termi-nator 2: Judgment Day, and* The Relic, *based on Douglas Preston and Lincoln Child's novel* Relic. Outland *must take place in an alternate future. The future seen in the Terminator movies is also an alternate timeline to the established future of the CU. The novel* Relic *has already been established as taking place in the CU, so the events of the movie must occur in an alternate reality as well. Phased polarons are from* Star Trek.

October
DEEPER

Captain Joe Bierden takes a research team, including parapsychologists Jacob and Mary Parsons, to the town of Golden Cove to embark upon a month-long diving expedition, only to encounter the Deep Ones and ghostly pirates. Joe's wife is from Black Stone Bay.

Novel by Joe Bierden, edited by James A. Moore, Necessary Evil Press, 2008. Golden Cove is allegedly built on the site where Innsmouth once stood, before it was completely demolished by the FBI in their raid on the town. Since Innsmouth is shown as still existing after the events of Lovecraft's story in several accounts, this must be fictionalization. More likely, Golden Cove is actually a neighboring town to Innsmouth, since many of its citizens possess "the Innsmouth look." Jacob and Mary Parsons first appeared in The Pack, *the second novel in Moore's* Serenity Falls Trilogy. *Black Stone Bay is the setting of Moore's novels* Blood Red *and* Blood Harvest.

Late October 2007–Spring 2013
THE SPECIALISTS

Dillon, Sly Gantlet, and Dillon's reformed foe Frederick Whalen are among the individuals recruited by the American Intelligence Machine (AIM) for a suicide mission in Kalmykia. Omega Elite, Li Shoon, Denbrook, and Moldavia are mentioned.

Novella by Joel Jenkins and Derrick Ferguson in The Specialists, *PulpWork Press, 2015. Dillon encountered Frederick Whalen in Ferguson's novel* Dillon and the Voice of Odin. *Whalen later encountered Damon St. Cloud in the city of Denbrook, as seen in Jenkins' novel* Devil Take the Hindmost. *Denbrook, created by Mike McGee, was the setting of serialized novels by several authors on the* Frontier Publishing *website. Omega Elite is mentioned in several of Ferguson's stories. Li Shoon is a "Yellow Peril" villain created by H. Irving Hancock for the pulp magazine* Detective Story Magazine. *Moldavia is a fictional country from the television series* Dynasty, *bringing that show and its spin-off,* The Colbys, *into the CU.*

October 31, 2007–January 21, 2009
SYMPATHY FOR THE DEVIL

Quincey Morris and Libby Chastain attempt to prevent presidential candidate Howard Stark, who has been possessed by the demon Sargatanas, from winning the election and destroying the Earth. The tabloid *The National Tattler* is mentioned several times, and FBI agents Colleen O'Donnell and Melanie Blaise discuss the female agent who shot Buffalo Billy. During the Maine primaries, Stark attends a meet-and-greet at the IHOP in Derry, and later hosts a town hall meeting in the auditorium of Bannerman High School in Castle Rock. Quincey says many weird things have occurred in Castle Rock, and suggests it may be a nexus of supernatural activity. Malachi Peters, a CIA assassin who was killed in 1983 and ended up in Hell because he enjoyed his work too much, has been sent back to Earth to assassinate Stark. He reminisces about his old boss, "an enigmatic man known only as Mac," who always referred to a hit as a "touch." Quincey and Libby discuss other supernatural investigators, including a woman named Anita and Jill Kismet. An assassin called the Grocer's Boy, whose father was an assassin himself and had a cover identity as a grocer, is hired to murder one of Stark's fellow candidates. Peters is told by a demon using the name Ashley she can make his sniper rifle invisible using a variation of the Tarnhelm effect.

Novel by Justin Gustainis, 2011. The National Tattler is from the Hannibal Lecter novels by Thomas Harris, as is Agent Clarice Starling, who shot serial killer Buffalo Bill in The Silence of the Lambs. *The Maine towns of Derry and Castle Rock appear in many novels and short stories by Stephen King. Bannerman High School is named after the late Sheriff George Bannerman from King's* The Dead Zone *and* Cujo. *Mac is Matt Helm's boss in Donald Hamilton's novels. Hamilton portrayed Helm as a member of a separate organization from the CIA, so perhaps the references in the series to Peters being a former CIA agent are an error or fictionalization on Gustainis' part, and he was actually a member of the same agency as Helm. Anita is a reference to Laurell K. Hamilton's vampire hunter Anita Blake, while Jill Kismet appears in novels by Lilith Saintcrow. The Anita Blake and Jill Kismet series both portray the general public as being aware of the existence* of the supernatural, which is incompatible with CU continuity; the Blake and Kismet mentioned in this novel, therefore, must be versions unique to the CU, who have had very different adventures from their better-known counterparts. The Grocer's Boy is meant to be a pastiche of the hitman known as the Butcher's Boy, who appears in novels by Thomas Perry. Indeed, Gustainis refers to him (possibly accidentally) as the Butcher's Boy at one point, and therefore it can be assumed for CU continuity he is in fact a disguised version of Perry's assassin. The Tarnhelm effect is a spell used to make specific objects or people invisible to others in the Lord Darcy stories by Randall Garrett. Since the Lord Darcy tales take place in an alternate reality where Richard the Lionheart did not die in 1199 and the world is governed by laws of magic rather than physics, the Tarnhelm effect must exist in both the CU and Lord Darcy's universe.

THE LAST PATRIOT

Scot Harvath once did a short stint with storied U.S. operative Painter Crowe and his elite Sigma Force unit.

Novel by Brad Thor. Painter Crowe and Sigma Force appear in novels by James Rollins.

Autumn. After the murder of their father, the Locke children move with their mother to Keyhouse in the town of Love-craft, Massachusetts, where they discover magic keys that have various magical effects, in Joe Hill's comic series *Locke & Key.*

TAG TEAM MATCH WITH HELL

Agents Karver and Mandi Cobb of the Department of Mystic Affairs, the psychometrist Lai Wan, and Baltimore police detective Bianca Jones team up to deal with a group of alleged child pornography stars who are actually adults who have kept their bodies eternally young via a demonic pact.

Short story by Patrick Thomas, C. J. Henderson, and John L. French in Dead to Rites: The DMA Casefiles of Agent Karver, *Padwolf Publishing, 2010. Karver first met Bianca in French and Thomas' novel* Rites of Passage. *Bianca first met Lai Wan in French and Henderson's story "Innocent Monsters." Lai Wan first met Karver and Mandi in Thomas and Henderson's story "Family Ties" (aka "The Ties that Bind.")*

December 11–22
THE CHARLEMAGNE PURSUIT
Edwin Davis, a deputy national security advisor to the president, asks Stephanie Nelle, Cotton Malone's former boss, for help, telling her Scot Harvath already turned down the request.

Novel by Steve Berry. Secret Service agent Scot Harvath appears in a series of novels by Brad Thor. Malone was previously mentioned in the Harvath novel The First Commandment. *The death of Malone's father, which occurred in 1971, is said to have been thirty-eight years ago. However, a year of 2009 would place the events of this novel after its year of publication, 2008. Additionally, the dates given fit 2007 rather than 2009. Therefore, I am regarding the references to thirty-eight years having passed as an error, and placing it in 2007, thirty-six years after the death of Malone's father.*

December 24
CHUCK VERSUS SANTA CLAUS
A member of the malevolent espionage agency FULCRUM takes hostages at the Buy More electronics store where Chuck Bartowski works. One of the cops trying to defuse the situation is Sgt. Al Powell, cousin of Buy More's proprietor, Big Mike.

Episode of the television series Chuck *broadcast December 15, 2008. Sgt. Powell first appeared in the films* Die Hard *and* Die Hard 2. *Since* Chuck *takes place in the CU, so does the* Die Hard *series.*

2008

Winter
LUPIN III VS. DETECTIVE CONAN (RUPAN SANSEI VS. MEITANTEI CONAN)
Arsène Lupin III and amateur sleuth Shinichi Kudo, aka Conan Edogawa, become involved in an investigation into the death of Queen Sakura and Prince Gill of the kingdom of Vesparand. Conan's best friend and would-be love interest, Ran Mori, is a dead ringer for Princess Mira.

Anime special directed by Hajime Kamegaki broadcast March 27, 2009. Shinichi (or Jimmy in the English dubbed version) Kudo, aka Conan Edogawa, is from Gosho Aoyama's manga Detective Conan *(aka* Case Closed*) and its anime adaptation. Philip José Farmer identified Lupin III's grandfather, Arsène Lupin, as a Wold Newton Family member, and therefore this crossover brings Conan Edogawa into the CU. Lupin and Conan encounter each other again in the film* Lupin III vs. Detective Conan: The Movie.

Edited by Joe Gentile and Richard Dean Starr

RECREATIONAL VEHICLE

A St. Louis private eye named Nudger travels to Florida to help his girlfriend's aunt and uncle, who are being blackmailed, and works with his fellow P.I. Fred Carver to resolve the situation.

Short story by John Lutz in Sex, Lies and Private Eyes, *Joe Gentile and Richard Dean Starr, eds., Moonstone Books, 2009. Lutz's P.I. Fred Carver is in the CU through a mention of Robert B. Parker's eye Spenser in his first appearance,* Tropical Heat, *as well as a brief appearance in Robert J. Randisi's Miles Jacoby novel* Hard Look. *This crossover brings in Lutz's other series P.I. character, Alo Nudger.*

April
SCRATCH

Comic book artist Evan Fisher has a run-in with Old Scratch, a giant snake that dwells in Pennsylvania's Susquehanna River. Evan co-created the comic book *United Hero Federation* with comics writer Timothy Graco, and sends his work in through Globe Package Services. During these events, a neighbor mentions the Goat-Man of LeHorn's Hollow.

Short story by Brian Keene, released as a limited edition hardcover and, more accessibly, as an e-book. Timothy Graco is the main character of Keene's novel Ghoul. *Globe Package Service is a branch of the Globe Corporation, which appears throughout Keene's various works, such as* Dead Sea. *The Goat-Man of LeHorn's Hollow is Hylinus, the villain of Keene's* Dark Hollow. *"Old Scratch" is also briefly mentioned in Keene's story "Stone Tears."*

Spring
THE LEGEND OF THE JERSEY DEVIL

When Cassie Hack and Vlad kill the Jersey Devil, they are forced to team up with the Living Corpse to defeat the Devil's angry mother, Old Mother Leeds. Cassie and the Corpse have met before.

The Living Corpse Annual #1 by Ken Haeser and Buz Hasson, Zenescope Entertainment, April 2009. The Living Corpse is John Romero, who died and was resurrected as a zombie. He fed on a family until he saw the only surviving child crying; guilt-ridden, he swore to combat all supernatural evil. This crossover brings him into the CU. The circumstances of his first meeting with Cassie are unrevealed. There must be more than one Jersey Devil, as FBI agents Fox Mulder and Dana Scully encountered one several years ago.

ENTRY WOUND

A battle between the heroes of several universes and the "sentient hyper-concept" Mary Shelley Lovecraft causes all the holiday-themed slashers of Cassie Hack and Vlad's universe to be resurrected. Lovecraft's foes include the Dusk Patrol, John Prufrock and the agents of the Lodge, the residents of the Boneyard, the Daughter of Alice Liddle, a demoness in the employ of Heaven, the Living Corpse, the Halloween Man, and the Answer. At the end of the battle, Lovecraft finds herself in Lovebunny & Mr. Hell's world. Cassie mentions fighting "that little leprechaun bastard."

A Hack/Slash one-shot written and illustrated by Tim Seeley, Devil's Due Publishing, May 2009. The Dusk Patrol is from an unpublished comic by Seeley. John Prufrock and the Lodge are from Alex Grecian and Riley Rossmo's comic Proof. The Boneyard is from the comic of the same name by Richard Moore. The Daughter of Alice Liddle is Calie Liddle from the comic book series Wonderland. The demoness is Mercy Sparx from a comic book miniseries by Josh Blaylock and Matt Merhoff. The Living Corpse is the title character of a comic book by Ken Haeser and Buz Hasson. Halloween Man is the subject of a web comic created by Drew Edwards. The Answer is from Mike Norton and Dennis Hopeless' comic of the same name. Cassie has already met the Living Corpse recently, and will later encounter Mercy Sparx; therefore, both of them appear to be native to the CU. She will also later travel to Halloween Man's alternate universe. Another Hack/Slash storyline has a reference to the Answer, confirming him as existing in the CU. It is uncertain which, if any, of the other characters are native to the CU, though in Calie Liddle's case it is unlikely. Lovebunny & Mr. Hell are from the superhero parody comic of the same name by Seeley. "That little leprechaun bastard" is a reference to the Leprechaun horror film series.

BULLETS & BRIMSTONE

Negral, a Sumerian fire god turned Hell's chief of security, meets Baltimore Police Detective Bianca Jones, who regularly combats the occult. The Department of Mystic Affairs told Bianca about Negral. Negral doubts Hex or Paddy Moran are very fond of him.

Collection of three short stories by Patrick Thomas and John L. French, Dark Quest, 2010. French's Bianca Jones is already in the CU, as is Thomas' Paddy Moran from his Murphy's Lore series. Negral (aka Hell's Detective), the Department of Mystic Affairs, and Hex have also appeared in the Murphy's Lore novels, as well as in spin-off books of their own, thus establishing Thomas' Murphy's Lore Universe is a subset of the CU.

CASTAWAYS

A group of reality show contestants on a tropical island are stalked and attacked by a tribe of degenerate, ape-like cryptids. One of the characters, Troy, is from Brackard's Point, New York, and mentions his brother Sherm, who died in a botched bank robbery in Pennsylvania. Unbeknownst to most, one of the contestants is a member of the Sons of the Constitution and plans to kill most of the crew and contestants. The Globe Corporation is mentioned to have an oil platform somewhere near the island. The cryptids' cave contains a statue of a creature with a human body but the head of a squid. The walls are decorated with drawings of a labyrinth with a great, black, red-eyed mass in the center, creatures with human bodies but the heads of swine, and a towering creature like a cross between a gorilla and a cat.

Novel by Brian Keene. Brackard's Point, New York is the setting of much of horror author Geoff Cooper's work. Sherm and the bank robbery are from Keene's novel Terminal. *The Sons of the Constitution are a right-wing terrorist militia group that recurs throughout Keene's work, such as in the story "Full of It." The Globe Corporation is another recurring element of Keene's fictional multiverse (*Dead Sea, *"Scratch," etc.) The squid monster is Keene's Leviathan, one of the Thirteen, as seen in the alternate realities of the* Earthworm Gods *books and* Clickers III: Dagon Rising. *The Labyrinth is an extradimensional realm that connects all of Keene's various works, seen best in the short story "Tequila's Sunrise" and* A Gathering of Crows. *The black mass in the center of it is Nodens, greatest among the Thirteen, from* Ghost Walk *and* Darkness at the Edge of Town. *The swine-things are from William Hope Hodgson's novel* The House on the Borderland. *The gorilla-cat creature is Meeble, another of the Thirteen, who plays a major role in "Tequila's Sunrise" and* A Gathering of Crows.

HOUSE OF THE WOLF MAN

Dr. Bela Reinhardt invites a group of connected but unsuspecting individuals to his castle, and monster mayhem ensues. Reinhardt is revealed to actually be Bela Frankenstein, son of Peter Frankenstein and a gypsy girl revealed to be the sister of Bela Blasko. A wolfshead cane appears ("a morbid keepsake") and an old gypsy verse is quoted: "Even a man who's pure in heart . . ." Among Reinhardt's books is Alhazred's *Alchemy of Transmutation*. Later, a Frankenstein Monster is released, and Dracula and his Brides show up. Reinhardt's lab contains a fossilized Gill-Man hand, as well as one of Dr. Pretorius' homunculi.

This 2009 film directed by Eben McGarr is a tribute to Universal Studios' 1940s horror films. Peter Frankenstein is from the film Son of Frankenstein. *Mark Brown conflated Peter with Dr. Frederick Frankenstein from the film* Young Frankenstein *in his essay "The House of Frankenstein" (found on the website* An Expansion of Philip José Farmer's Wold Newton Universe*). Bela Blasko is the werewolf that bites Larry Talbot in the film* The Wolf Man, *which is also the source of the wolfshead cane and the old gypsy verse.* Alchemy of Transformation's *author is Abdul Alhazred, best known as the author of the* Necronomicon *in H. P. Lovecraft's Cthulhu Mythos. The fossilized Gill-Man hand is from the film* Creature from the Black Lagoon, *while Dr. Pretorius' homunculi are from* The Bride of Frankenstein.

Summer
TURN COAT
Harry Dresden muses the universe contains "terrors that the Black-Goat-with-a-Thousand-Young wouldn't dare use for its kids' bedtime stories."

2009 novel in Jim Butcher's Dresden Files *series. "The Black-Goat-with-a-Thousand-Young" is one of the titles of the Lovecraftian entity Shub-Niggurath.*

SOMETHING'S FISHY
Cassie Hack faces off with Mary Shelley Lovecraft, who compares her to "that red devil boy with the tail" and claims she's "compelling, though maybe not so well loved as the Summers girl."

Hack/Slash: The Series *#28 by Tim Seeley and Dan Parent, 2009. Mary is comparing Cassie to Hellboy and Buffy Summers.*

A NEW DAY IN THE OLD TOWN
At a committee hearing over whether to close the FBI's Fringe Division, Senator Kenneth Taylor refers to "the old X designation."

Episode of the television series Fringe *broadcast September 17, 2009. "The old X designation" is a clear reference to* The X-Files, *thus reinforcing the inclusion of* Fringe *within the CU. Senator Taylor is played by Ken Camroux-Taylor, who played an unidentified Senior Agent on several episodes of* The X-Files. *It is possible, but unconfirmed, this agent is the same person as the future Senator Taylor. The X-Files can be seen on a television at one point in this episode; presumably, the CU version of the series is a spin-off of the movie starring Garry Shandling and Téa Leoni.*

SUPER SIDEKICK SLEEPOVER SLAUGHTER

Slasher hunter Cassie Hack and her partner Vlad battle a slasher killing a group of teens who have used a device called "the godbox" to gain superpowers and adopt the mantles of 1940s superheroes Nightmare, the Black Fury, Crash Kid, Fantomah, Flamingo, the Heap, and U.S. Jones. Crimebuster, Daredevil, and Airboy are mentioned, and pictures of those three, Black Angel, Judy of the Jungle, and Captain Fight are shown. Nightmare's sidekick Sleepy appears in flashback. The original Fantomah was imprisoned by the Crime Cabal, which consisted of Dr. Mortal, the Great Question, Dr. Dracula, the Puzzler, and an unidentified fifth individual. Fantomah is eventually freed and takes her revenge on the current Crime Cabal.

Hack/Slash: The Series *#29-32 by Tim Seeley, Chris Burnham, Ross Campbell, Daniel Lester and Jason Millet, Devil's Due Publishing, December 2009–February 2010. Many of the characters referenced here are Golden Age comic book characters. Nightmare and Sleepy appeared in* Clue Comics, *published by Hillman. Airboy, the Heap, and the Black Angel were also published by Hillman, and are already in the CU. Crash Kid appeared in two issues of Rural Home Productions'* Cannonball Comics. *Fantomah, created by the notorious Fletcher Hanks, appeared in fifty issues of* Jungle Comics, *published by Fiction House. Captain Fight appeared in* Fight Comics, *another Fiction House title. Flamingo was a costumed aviator who appeared in the Aviation Press title* Contact Comics. *The Black Fury appeared in Fox Features Syndicate's titles* Fantastic Comics, V . . . -Comics, *and* Blue Beetle. U.S. Jones *appeared in* Wonderworld Comics *and two issues of his own series, both also published by Fox. The villainous Dr. Mortal was the subject of his own strip in Fox's* Weird Comics *and* The Flame. *Bart Hill, aka Daredevil, appeared in* Silver Streak Comics *and his own series, both published by Lev Gleason, and is not to be confused with the later masked vigilante who called himself Daredevil, Matt Murdock. Crimebuster appeared in every issue of* Boy Comics, *another Lev Gleason title. Dr. Dracula was the archnemesis of Captain Battle, who appeared in* Silver Streak

Comics *as well as his own self-titled series. Judy of the Jungle appeared in Nedor's* Exciting Comics. *The Puzzler was a foe of Nedor's best-known hero, the Black Terror. The Great Question is the arch foe of the Centaur character Amazing Man. It is as yet uncertain whether Captain Battle, the Black Terror, and Amazing Man themselves exist in the CU. I have been unable to identify the fifth member of the original Crime Cabal. With the exception of Fantomah, most of these characters have no superpowers or very low-level powers; they must be CU versions of their comic counterparts, and of course their exploits must have been less colorful than the comics depicted.*

THE MASSIVE RAT

Nicholas Briar clears a rat out from behind his fireplace. Nick thinks of the raft he and David Ockeridge built in David's dad's orchard, when they were kids in Black Swan Green. Nick denies he would, or could, bludgeon his own soon-to-be-ex-wife to death, much less their son Fred, as he lay asleep, before knocking back 120 Nurofen Expresses with a bottle of Kilmagoon.

Short story by David Mitchell in The Guardian, *August 1, 2009. Nicholas Briar, David Ockeridge, and Black Swan Green are from Mitchell's novel* Black Swan Green. *Kilmagoon whiskey appears in a number of Mitchell's works.*

PRICE TAG ATTACHED

New Orleans private eye Burleigh Drummond and Police Detective Jodie Kintyre investigate the theft of a marble heart and the murder of its seller.

E-book by Kent Westmoreland and O'Neil de Noux, 2009. Westmoreland's P.I. Burleigh Drummond is the grandson of Philip Marlowe, and therefore a Wold Newton Family member. Jodie Kintyre is the partner of Dino LaStanza, a cop featured in a series of novels by de Noux. This crossover brings LaStanza and Jodie into the CU. Half-Cajun, half-Sioux cop John Raven Beau appeared in the LaStanza novel New Orleans Homicide *before spinning off into his own series of novels. De Noux's story "Little Known New Orleans Mysteries" establishes his '40s P.I. Lucien Caye exists in the same universe as Jodie.*

SHORTS

Toe Thompson eats a cereal called Great White Bites.

Feature film directed by Robert Rodriguez. Great White Bites first appeared in Rodriguez's film Planet Terror.

August 16
MATERIAL WITNESS

Joe Ledger and his comrades in the Department of Military Sciences are dispatched to Pine Deep, Pennsylvania to deal with an author who is offering to sell a plot he devised involving a major terrorist attack to several different extremist groups.

Short story by Jonathan Maberry. Joe Ledger is already in the CU through crossovers with Lovecraft's "At the Mountains of Madness" and Larry Correia's Monster Hunter International series. This crossover brings in Maberry's Pine Deep Trilogy of novels, which consists of Ghost Road Blues, Dead Man's Song, *and* Bad Moon Rising. *This story takes place a few weeks after Maberry's first Joe Ledger novel,* Patient Zero, *which was released in 2009.*

Autumn
DUPED

The caretakers of Warehouse 13, a repository for powerful artifacts, battle the alleged spirit of Alice Liddell, which has been imprisoned in the Looking Glass for 100 years.

Episode of the television series Warehouse 13 *broadcast August 25, 2009. The connection to Lewis Carroll's Alice novels brings the Warehouse and its custodians into the CU. The Looking Glass previously appeared in the episode "Resonance," and reappeared after this episode in "The Ones You Love" and "Fractures," the latter of which also featured Alice. The spirit may actually be impersonating Alice, as its account of its youth does not match with what is known of the life of the CU version of Alice Liddell. A behind-the-scenes video for* Warehouse 13 *reveals the Warehouse contains Ralph Kramden's bowling ball and Rosemary's baby carriage, referring to the television series* The Honeymooners *and Ira Levin's novel* Rosemary's Baby, *respectively. The show's website mentions Gordon Gekko's cell phone as an artifact in the Warehouse, bringing in the films* Wall Street *and* Wall Street: Money Never Sleeps. *Furthermore, a SyFy Channel "digital press tour" video reveals the Maltese Falcon is another artifact contained within the Warehouse.*

KILL WHITEY

Larry Gibson, an employee of Globe Package Service, finds himself in trouble with the Russian mob, in particular one Zakhar "Whitey" Putin, a descendant of Rasputin with superhuman abilities. The Sons of the Constitution are mentioned. Whitey's organization was at one time in competition with the Marano crime family; it's mentioned Marano's top guy, Tony Genova, disappeared some time before. Larry used to work with a guy named Sherm, who was killed in a botched bank robbery. Bathroom graffiti at the Odessa includes the name Kaine, as well as the phrase "Jesus saves, but Ob rulez." The Kwan and Black Lodge are mentioned. Whitey's group disposes of bodies in LeHorn's Hollow. Whitey refers to himself as "Homo superior." When police dredge Lake Pinchot for Whitey's body, they instead find the body of a young girl murdered when her car broke down on an Interstate exit ramp.

Novel by Brian Keene. Globe Package Service is a branch of the Globe Corporation, which appears throughout Keene's works. The Sons of the Constitution are a right-wing terrorist organization that has appeared most prominently in Keene's novel Castaways. *Tony Genova, an enforcer for the Marano crime family, appears across Keene's multiverse, most notably in the Clickers series; the version here is the CU version, distinct from the Clickers-verse Tony. Sherm and the botched robbery are from Keene's novel* Terminal. *Kaine is a name that turns up across Keene's multiverse, in tales such as "Full of It," "Two-Headed Alien Love Child," and* Clickers vs. Zombies. *Ob is one of the Thirteen, and is the main villain of Keene's* The Rising *series. The Kwan are an occult group from the works of horror author Geoff Cooper, and play a prominent role in Keene and Cooper's novel* Shades. *LeHorn's Hollow is a major setting in Keene's works, such as "Red Wood,"* Dark Hollow, *and* Ghost Walk. *"Homo superior" is a term first used to describe superhumans in Olaf Stapledon's novel* Odd John, *and later in other works such as Marvel Comics' X-Men titles (as a scientific designation for mutants) and the television series* Bablyon 5; *at least two Marvel Comics mutants, Piotr "Colossus" Rasputin and Illyana "Magik" Rasputina, are also descendants of Rasputin; although the X-Men's stories do not fit into CU continuity, the CU obviously has a mutant descendant of the Mad Monk among its inhabitants as well. The murdered girl is implied to be a victim of The Exit, a serial killer from Keene's stories "I Am an Exit" and "This is Not an Exit," who murders people at highway exits.*

GREY MATTERS

Peter Bishop and Olivia Dunham visit Dunwich Mental Hospital in Massachusetts in the midst of a case.

Episode of Fringe *broadcast December 10, 2009. Dunwich Mental Hospital is named for the town of Dunwich, Massachusetts, from H. P. Lovecraft's "The Dunwich Horror" and other stories, further confirming* Fringe *takes place in the CU.*

October
GHOST WALK

Levi Stoltzfus, the ex-Amish magus, battles Nodens of the Thirteen near LeHorn's Hollow, with help from Maria Nasr and Adam Senft, in a battle that culminates on Halloween night. There are numerous references to the Goat-Man and the forest fire of 2006. Nodens has been known as "Shub-Niggurath," but this is not its true name; its temples can be found on "the twin moons of distant Yhe and the fungal gardens of Yaksh." There are references to Nelson LeHorn and Saul O'Connor, and LeHorn's copy of the *Daemonolateria* is featured. There is a reference to a group of hunters who died in a mysterious fire near LeHorn's Hollow. Tony Genova and Vincent Napoli are mentioned. Levi mentions various occult groups, like Black Lodge, the Kwan, and the Starry Wisdom sect. Maria Nasr places a call to retired Detective Hector Ramirez. Adam Senft was incarcerated alongside Karen Moore. A minor character, Cecil Smeltzer, thinks about his late brother Clark and his nephew Barry. Levi mentions Nyarlathotep in a spell, and also refers to the Lost Level.

Novel by Brian Keene. Nodens is not the Celtic deity, nor the Lovecraftian entity, but is instead the greatest of the Thirteen, pre-Universal beings that travel the multiverse destroying entire realities. They are the primary villains of Keene's Labyrinth saga. The Goat-Man, the fire of 2006, Nelson LeHorn, Saul O'Connor, and Adam Senft are from Keene's novel Dark Hollow, *to which this novel is a semi-sequel. While Nodens is not Shub-Niggurath, it may have disguised itself as that entity at times. Yhe and Yaksh are Cthulhu Mythos locales. The* Daemonolateria *appears throughout Keene's works, including* Dark Hollow *and* "Caught in a Mosh." *The deceased hunters are from Keene's short story* "Red Wood." *Tony Genova and Vincent Napoli are mobsters who reappear throughout Keene's multiverse. The versions mentioned here are native to the CU, but other versions can be seen in Keene's novels* Clickers II, Clickers III, *and* Clickers vs. Zombies *(cowritten with J. F. Gonzalez), and in the short story* "The Siqqusim Who Stole Christmas." *Black Lodge is a secret occult organization that also appears throughout Keene's multiverse, including the short story* "The Black Wave," *and in other universes, such as those of* Earthworm Gods II: Deluge *and* Clickers vs. Zombies. *The Kwan are from the works of horror author Geoff Cooper; they play a major* role in Keene and Cooper's novel Shades. *The Starry Wisdom sect is from H. P. Lovecraft's story "The Haunter of the Dark." Detective Ramirez appears in Keene's novels* Terminal *and* Dark Hollow. *Karen Moore and Clark and Barry Smeltzer are from Keene's novel* Ghoul. *Nyarlathotep is the crawling chaos of the Cthulhu Mythos. The Lost Level is from Keene's novel of the same name. A short follow-up story, "The Ghosts of Monsters," can be found in Keene's collections* Unhappy Endings *and* Blood on the Page, *and takes place about a year later. Keene's novel* Darkness at the Edge of Town *takes place in one of his many parallel universes, and shows what happened in a world where Levi died years earlier and was not around to stop Nodens. A follow-up story, "The House of Ushers," sees Adam Senft traveling to the version of Hell created by horror author Edward Lee in his novel* City Infernal *and its sequels.*

October 8–23
THE DOOMSDAY KEY

Monk Kokkalis, an operative for Sigma Force, tells his colleague Captain Kat Bryant Andrea Solderitch is being personally watched over by Scot Harvath, an agent Monk fully trusts to keep her safe.

Novel by James Rollins. Scot Harvath is the protagonist of a series of novels by Brad Thor. The Harvath novel The Last Patriot *contained a reference to Harvath briefly being a member of Sigma.*

2009

January
BACK IN BLACK

Jimmy Black and Greg Knightwood are not only partners in a private investigation firm, but also secretly vampires. At a strip club owned by Lilith, the biblical mother of demons, Jimmy spots "a skinny dude sitting in the corner with a leather duster and a glowing staff."

The second novel in John G. Hartness' series The Black Knight Chronicles, *published by Falstaff Books in 2010, and reissued in a revised edition published by Bell Bridge Books in 2012. The "skinny dude" is Harry Dresden, the protagonist of Jim Butcher's "urban fantasy" book series* The Dresden Files.

Late January–March
PLAY WITH FIRE

Occult detectives Quincey Morris and Libby Chastain and their allies– FBI agents Dale Fenton and Colleen O'Donnell, hitman Mal Peters, and a demon using the mortal alias Ashley –battle a cult that is literally trying to raise Hell on Earth. Quincey says one of his ancestors was a Marshal in Dodge City. Quincey and Libby help occult P.I. Barry Love clear a hell-hound out of his office. O'Donnell refers to a report written by Monica Reyes of the New Orleans Field Office. Fenton and O'Donnell's boss Susan Whitlavich became head of the Behavioral Science Unit after her own boss, Jack Crawford, suffered a fatal heart attack. Whitlavich tells Fenton and O'Donnell she's smoothed things over for them with Bernie Jenks at the Las Vegas Field Office.

Novella by Justin Gustainis, 2012. Quincey's ancestor is Marshal Matt Dillon from the radio and television series Gunsmoke. *Barry Love is a disguised version of Clive Barker's occult detective Harry D'Amour. Agent Monica Reyes is from* The X-Files. *Jack Crawford is from Thomas Harris' Hannibal Lecter novels. Crawford died of a heart attack in* Hannibal. *Las Vegas-based FBI agent Bernie Jenks met Carl Kolchak in the TV movie* The Night Stalker. *Bernie would be elderly by 2009, so this Bernie Jenks must be a relative of his, likely his grandson. The end of this novella leads directly into the next entry in the series,* Midnight at the Oasis. *However, as explained in the 2011 entry for that novella, Gustainis must have compressed the actual amount of time between the two stories.*

Winter
HACKOWEEN

A female superhuman called Brainchild recruits Cassie Hack and Vlad to travel to her alternate Earth and battle an alleged zombie slasher called Halloween Man, who is actually a superhero. After battling and slaughtering a group of zombified heroes from yet another Earth called the Revengers, the duo and Halloween Man combat each other until the necromancer Morlack reveals the truth. Cassie and Halloween Man team up to defeat Brainchild; her husband, a demon called the Elder; and the ghosts of the Revengers. After accomplishing this, Cassie and Vlad return to their world, where another extra-dimensional superhuman named Heck Gal, an agent of the BSID, requests their aid against "the zombie army of Adolf—" They refuse.

Story in the web comic Halloween Man *by Drew Edwards, David Baldeon, and Scott D. M. Simmons. Halloween Man is Solomon Hitch, who was killed by a vampire, but brought back to life via magic. He defends Solar City, TX, from supervillains and the supernatural, aided by Morlack, his scientist girlfriend Lucy, and the demigod Man-Goat. This story establishes Halloween Man's world as an alternate reality to the CU. The Revengers are alternate universe versions of the Marvel Universe super-team the Avengers. Heck Gal's name, appearance, and dialogue make it clear she is a distaff AU counterpart to Hellboy.*

AVENGELYNE VS. KONI WAVES

In Hawaii, Avengelyne battles Koni Kanawai, who has been possessed by the malevolent ancient mystic Milu.

One-shot by Mark Poulton and Stephen Sistilli, Arcana Studio, February 2010.

KNIGHT FALL

Dr. Gregory House sends members of his diagnostic team to check the apartment of their patient, a Renaissance re-enactor called Sir William, for possible causes of the faux knight's unidentified affliction. They discover a locked room filled with items relating to witchcraft, including a copy of the *Necronomicon.*

Episode of the television series House M.D. *broadcast April 19, 2010. The* Necronomicon *is from Lovecraft's Cthulhu Mythos, which is squarely in the CU. Therefore, this crossover brings in the temperamental Dr. House.*

BALL AND CHAIN

Audrey Parker, an FBI agent currently operating in Haven, Maine, and Detective Nathan Wuornos investigate a case involving men rapidly aging to death and decomposing. Nathan learns of a similar death that occurred in Derry years ago.

Episode of the television series Haven, *loosely based on Stephen King's novel* The Colorado Kid, *broadcast August 6, 2010. Derry, Maine is a recurring locale in King's fiction. Derry is also mentioned in the episode following this one, "Fur." It is worth mentioning that a flyer seen in the show's opening credits refers to "the revered Flagg," a reference to King's recurring villain Randall Flagg. These and other later connections to King's interrelated fiction bring* Haven *into the CU. This Haven appears to be a separate place from Haven Village from King's novel* The Tommyknockers, *which is located in a different part of Maine, and was destroyed at the end of the novel.*

Spring
DEXTER VS. JASON VS. HACK/SLASH

At Camp Crystal Lake, Dexter Morgan inserts a syringe into Jason Voorhees' neck, intending to place Jason on his kill table. Jason swats him aside, just as Cassie Hack and Vlad appear.

One-page online comic by Tim Seeley and Scott Allie. Jason Voorhees (from the Friday the 13th *film series) and Seeley's slasher hunters Cassie Hack and Vlad (from Seeley's comic* Hack/Slash*) are already in the CU. This crossover brings in Dexter Morgan, a blood spatter analyst for the Miami Metro Police Department, who is also secretly a serial killer targeting other murderers, from the television series* Dexter. *The television series is based on a series of books by Jeff Lindsey, which takes place in a different continuity than the TV show. Allie draws Dexter to resemble Michael C. Hall, the actor who plays him on the show, and Cassie refers to him as the Bay Harbor Butcher, a name Dex was only known by on TV, thus establishing the* Dexter *TV series as the version of his life that is in the CU, with the books taking place in an alternate universe. The outcome of these characters meeting, though no doubt violent, is unknown, but Cassie and Vlad survived, as did Dexter, and Jason almost certainly did as well.*

AS YOU WERE

Vince Teagues gives Audrey Parker the book *Misery Unchained*, a "first edition signed by the author just before that lady chopped off his foot," as a birthday gift.

Episode of Haven *broadcast September 10, 2010. The author of* Misery Unchained *is Paul Sheldon, whose foot was chopped off by his deranged fan Annie Wilkes in Stephen King's novel* Misery.

April 9, 2009–November 2011
MR. MERCEDES

A roadie at a concert for the boy band 'Round Here wears a Judas Coyne T-shirt.

Novel by Stephen King. 'Round Here was first mentioned in King's novel Doctor Sleep, *a sequel to* The Shining. *Aging rock star Judas Coyne is the protagonist of Joe Hill's novel* Heart-Shaped Box. *Both these references link this novel to the King-verse, and therefore to the CU. It is worth noting that the titular supernatural car from King's novel* Christine *and Pennywise the Clown from* It *are both referred to as movie monsters, despite both novels having already been established as taking place in the CU. Presumably these films were inspired by the real rampages of Christine and Pennywise, and were falsely assumed by most people to be completely fictional.*

May
URBAN GOTHIC

A group of suburban youths returning from a Monsters of Hip Hop concert (headlined by Prosper Johnson) become stranded in an abandoned house in the Philadelphia ghetto and hunted by subterranean mutants. The kids were present at a Ghost Walk in LeHorn's Hollow the previous Hallow-een, but it was closed down after several people were killed inside, before the kids could get in. Leo once lived with the Graco family for two weeks; the father, Timothy, wrote comic books. One of the mutants wears a shirt with the slogan I GOT CRABS IN PHILLIPSPORT, MAINE, and another wears a ball cap with the Globe Package Service logo. One of the mutants, Scug, swears to Ob.

Novel by Brian Keene. Prosper Johnson is a minor, but important, character in Keene's mythos, figuring most prominently (so far) in his story "Slouching in Bethlehem." The events behind the massacre at the Ghost Walk are told in Keene's novel Ghost Walk. *Timothy Graco is the main character of Keene's novel* Ghoul. *Phillipsport, Maine, first appeared in Mark Williams and J. F. Gonzalez's novel* Clickers; *that series (the latter books being cowritten between Gonzalez and Keene) takes place in an alternate universe, but there must be a version of Phillipsport in the CU. Globe Package Service appears in several Keene works, including "Scratch" and* Kill Whitey, *and is a branch of the Globe Corporation. Ob is one of the Thirteen, and is the main villain of Keene's* The Rising *series.*

Summer
MACHETE
Machete Cortez's wounds are treated by Doc Felix.

Feature film directed by Robert Rodriguez. Machete first appeared in the Spy Kids *movies, where he is the uncle of the title characters. Doc Felix previously appeared in* Planet Terror. *Edgar McGraw appears in a deleted scene; this is likely the same Edgar seen in* Kill Bill: Vol. 1 *and* Death Proof. *It has been conjectured that this Edgar and his father Earl are identical cousins of the Earl and Edgar McGraw seen in the* From Dusk Till Dawn *films.*

THE HAND YOU'RE DEALT
Audrey Parker reads notes about a "firebug" (pyrokinetic) on the Vermont-New Hampshire border and in upstate New York. Photographer Morris Crane refers to creatures with lobster-like claws who communicate in a clicking language.

Episode of Haven *broadcast September 17, 2010. The firebug on the Vermont-New Hampshire border and in upstate New York is Charlie*

McGee from Stephen King's novel Firestarter. *The lobster-like creatures are the Lobstrosities from* The Drawing of the Three, *the second book in King's Dark Tower series.*

THE TRIAL OF AUDREY PARKER

Audrey Parker says to her FBI supervisor, Agent Howard, "At least I'm not like that one guy you trained that was chasing aliens, what was his name?" Howard retorts, "Hey, he was a genius. What happened to him the last few years was a tragedy . . ." Little Tall Island is mentioned.

Episode of Haven *broadcast September 24, 2010. The alien-hunting FBI agent trained by Agent Howard is Fox Mulder from the television series* The X-Files. *Little Tall Island is from Stephen King's novel* Dolores Claiborne, *as well as the TV mini-series* Storm of the Century.

THE PHANTOM/CAPTAIN ACTION

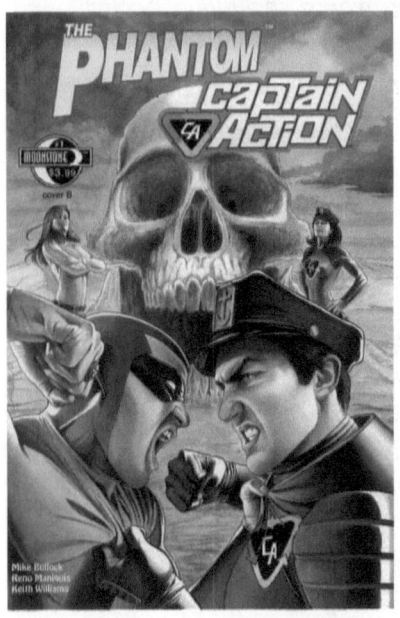

The Phantom and Captain Action (Cole Drake, the son of Miles Drake, the original Captain Action) battle a counter intelligence agency called Tatsu.

Two-issue miniseries by Mike Bullock, Reno Maniquis, and Keith Williams, Moonstone Comics, 2010. The Phantom's wife is called Diana Walker-Palmer in this story, but this must be fictionalization. The 22nd Phantom, who became active in 1989 (as seen in the Marvel Comics series The Phantom: The Ghost Who Walks) *was the grandson of the 20th Phantom and Diana Palmer. After his death in 2016, his son will take over as the 23rd Phantom. He dies in 2024, and his son becomes the 24th Phantom in 2040, as seen in the animated series* Phantom 2040.

August. Events of *Horns* by Joe Hill.

Autumn
HACK/SLASH & MERCY SPARX: A SLICE OF HELL

Cassie Hack and Vlad team up with a devil girl, Mercy Sparx, to stop a slasher that is using an angelic sword to kill people.

One-shot by Josh Blaylock, Joe Song, and Ben Ellebracht, Devil's Due Publishing, 2010. Mercy Sparx is a devil girl from Sheol, a realm between Heaven and Hell, and next door to Purgatory, who has been recruited by Heaven to track down rogue angels on Earth; she first appeared in a series of comics from Devil's Due, also penned by Josh Blaylock. This crossover links her to the CU.

CROWN OF WORMS

In Seattle, Vampirella enters into a temporary alliance with Dracula, King of the Vampires, in order to defeat a Lovecraftian worm-creature called Yag-Ath Vermellus.

Vampirella *ongoing series #1–6 by Eric Trautmann, Wagner Reis, and Fabiano Neves, Dynamite Entertainment, 2010–2011. There is also a female vampire called Le Fanu, a former servant of Dracula's, and a nightclub called Carmilla's, but these are vampiric in-joke references rather than true crossovers.*

THE DARKNESS/DARKCHYLDE: KINGDOM PAIN

Jackie Estacado, wielder of the Darkness, finds himself in the nightmare world of Kingdom Pain, where he frees Ariel Darkchylde from her slumber. Together, they battle Darkchylde's fellow coma patient Breathtaker. Their opponent is finally killed by Sara Pezzini, wielder of the Witchblade, who vaguely remembers Ariel from their previous encounter.

One-shot by Randy Queen, Image Comics, 2010. The Darkness, Darkchylde, and Witchblade all have valid independent links to the CU. The latter two previously met in a 2000 one-shot. Therefore, it is likely this crossover takes place in the CU as well.

TIME WILL TELL

Helena G. Wells tricks Myka Bering and Peter Lattimer into activating a Cavorite generator in her London home, allowing her to detain them.

Episode of the television series Warehouse 13 *broadcast July 6, 2010. According to herself, Helena G. Wells was the true author of H. G. Wells' books (including* The First Men in the Moon, *which features Cavorite), and the man history knows as H. G. Wells was actually her brother Charles. Television crossover expert Toby O'Brien suggests instead Helena is the sister of the real Herbert George Wells, and she lied to the Warehouse caretakers.*

MILD MANNERED

Among the items housed in Warehouse 13 is a bow and set of emerald arrows, a golden rope that controls the minds of those bound with it, a Norse hammer, and a purple umbrella.

Episode of the television series Warehouse 13 *broadcast July 13, 2010. All of the artifacts are references to equipment used by superheroes (or in one case, supervillains) appearing in DC or Marvel Comics. The bow and arrows belong to the DC hero Green Arrow. The golden rope is Wonder Woman's golden lasso. The Norse hammer is Thor's hammer Mjolnir. The lasso and Mjolnir were last seen in Area 52, in Image Comics' miniseries of the same name, but must have been relocated to Warehouse 13 after the alien breach of the Antarctic facility. The umbrella belongs to Batman's foe the Penguin.*

AGE BEFORE BEAUTY

Among the artifacts in Warehouse 13 is the portrait of Dorian Gray.

Episode of the television series Warehouse 13 *broadcast July 27, 2010. The connection to Oscar Wilde's* The Picture of Dorian Gray *reinforces* Warehouse 13 *in the CU.*

13.1

Global Dynamics sends Douglas Fargo to upgrade the computers at Warehouse 13. Unfortunately, a holographic AI modeled on and created by former Warehouse agent Hugo Miller takes over the Warehouse and attempts to kill those inside. Meanwhile, Pete Lattimer and Myka Bering, Secret Service agents attached to the Warehouse, attempt to recruit the institutionalized real Hugo Miller to help them resolve the situation.

Episode of the television series Warehouse 13 *broadcast August 3, 2010. Global Dynamics and Douglas Fargo are from the television series* Eureka, *which is already in the CU through a connection to* Buffy the Vampire Slayer.

CROSSING OVER

Warehouse 13 agent Claudia Donovan's arrival in Eureka coincides with objects from the past materializing in various parts of town.

Episode of the television series Eureka *broadcast August 6, 2010. This marks the second crossover between* Eureka *and* Warehouse 13.

WHERE AND WHEN

Helena G. Wells' psychic time machine includes a flux capacitor.

Episode of the television series Warehouse 13 *broadcast September 7, 2010. The flux capacitor technology invented by Wells in the 19th century would be rediscovered by Dr. Emmett Brown in the 20th century, as seen in the* Back to the Future *film series.*

THE SECRET SERVICE

Spy Jack London trains his nephew Gary in the art of espionage. After Jack is shot and killed, Gary toasts his uncle with London's own trainer,

Rupert Graves, who says, "Your uncle and I toasted a lot of old pals over the years. Steed. Gambit. Even some of the old timers like Drake and Templar."

Comic book story by Mark Millar and Dave Gibbons in CLiNT *#1–7, Titan Magazines, 2012–2013. Apparently John Steed (*The Avengers *and* The New Avengers*), Mike Gambit (also from* The New Avengers*), John Drake (*Danger Man/Secret Agent *and* The Prisoner*), and Simon Templar (aka the Saint) have all died or faked their deaths by the time this story takes place. The year is based on a reference to Elton John trying to adopt. The* Secret Service *is supposed to take place in the same universe as several of Millar's other comic books, including* Wanted, Kick-Ass, Nemesis, MPH, Superior, *and* Supercrooks. *However, including all of these series would bring in many more superheroes and supervillains than can smoothly fit into the Crossover Universe. Furthermore,* Wanted *portrays the world as secretly controlled by supervillains, which also does not fit with CU continuity. Therefore, the events of* The Secret Service *must have occurred in both the CU and the "Millar-verse."*

SPIRAL

Max Hansen has just been released from Shawshank State Prison.

Episode of Haven *broadcast October 8, 2010. Shawshank State Prison is a recurring location in Stephen King's fiction, appearing most prominently in "Rita Hayworth and Shawshank Redemption."*

November
BLOOD OATH

White House aide Zachary Barrows is assigned the job of assisting Nathaniel Cade, America's secret vampire agent. Cade's trophy room includes the skull of a Deep One from Innsmouth, parts of Brainerd's Steam Man, a large bright-gold beetle, wood from the Devil Tree of British Guiana, and a mummified monkey's paw. There are several references to the "Teenage Monster" incident in New Jersey and the "Night of the Living Dead" incident in Pennsylvania. A news report about the murder of several camp counselors outside Blairstown, New Jersey by "some bogeyman" is mentioned; there was one survivor. Cade runs up against an old nemesis, the immortal alchemist Johann Konrad Dippel. The immortal St. Germain is mentioned to have visited Teddy Roosevelt at the White House.

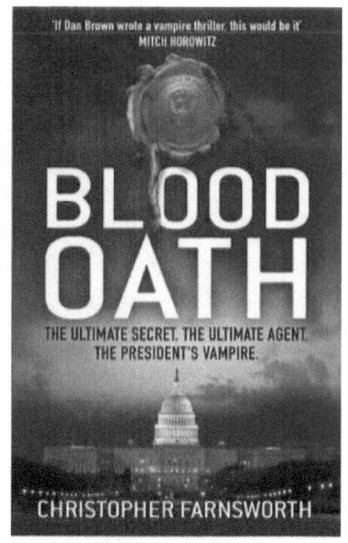

297

Novel by Christopher Farnsworth, Putnam Adult, 2010. The reference to Lovecraft's "The Shadow over Innsmouth" links the Cade novels to the CU. Brainerd's Steam Man is from "The Steam Man of the Prairies" by Edward S. Ellis. The Steam Man must have passed into Cade's hands at some point after the 1898 events of The League of Extraordinary Gentlemen, Volume I, *where it was seen in the League's headquarters. The beetle is from Edgar Allan Poe's "The Gold-Bug." The Devil Tree is from* The Devil-Tree of El Dorado: A Romance of British Guiana *by Frank Aubrey. The monkey's paw is from W. W. Jacobs' "The Monkey's Paw." The Teenage Monster incident is from the 1958 film* I Was a Teenage Frankenstein *and the Night of the Living Dead incident is, of course, from the 1968 film* Night of the Living Dead. *While George Romero's later zombie films in the series move in a decidedly apocalyptic direction, another series, the* Return of the Living Dead *movies, explains those films were based on a very limited zombie outbreak in Pennsylvania. The murders of the camp counselors are a reference to the* Friday the 13th *series of films, the first of which was shot, in part, near Blairstown, New Jersey. This novel claims Johann Konrad Dippel was the basis for the character of Victor Frankenstein in Mary Shelley's* Frankenstein. *While the Frankenstein family is well-established as part of the CU, Dippel was likely an ancestor of the clan. This is backed up by a reference to him in* The Historical Illuminatus Chronicles *as Johann Dippel von Frankenstein. While based on a historical St. Germain, the immortal St. Germain of the CU has encountered several important characters, including Dracula and Frankenstein (see Jean-Marc Lofficier, Roy Thomas, and Claude St. Aubin's comic miniseries* The Frankenstein-Dracula War*) and Spike and Drusilla (see* Spike vs. Dracula #4, *by Peter David, Joe Corroney, and Mike Ratera). The official website for the* President's Vampire *books has a timeline of Cade's universe and activities that includes a number of references that have not appeared in the books themselves yet: the founding of Miskatonic University in 1690 (from Lovecraft's Cthulhu Mythos); the Headless Horseman incident of 1790 (from Washington Irving's "The Legend of Sleepy Hollow"); the reported resurrection of a mummy from the Sabretash Expedition in 1850 (from Poe's "Some Words with a Mummy"); the Baltimore Gun Club launch on December 10, 1867 (from Jules Verne's* From the Earth to the Moon*); a police raid on the swamps near New Orleans where a cult worshipped a strange, "squid-like statue" in November, 1907 (from Lovecraft's "The Call of Cthulhu"); magician Charles Carter being suspected of the death of President Warren G. Harding on August 2, 1923 (from Glen David Gold's novel* Carter Beats the Devil, *although there was a real Carter whom Gold heavily fictionalized); the Grover's Mill intrusion event of October 30, 1938, the radio broadcast of which is considered a hoax (from*

Orson Welles' 1938 adaptation of The War of the Worlds for The Mercury Theatre); and the Vampire King encounter in Jeremiah, Massachusetts in 1975, which ended with the town being burned and removed from the maps (a disguised version of the events of Stephen King's novel 'Salem's Lot). The site also has an older version of the timeline, with three additional references: a "gray champion" appearing out of nowhere to protest British oppression of New England colonists in Boston, Massachusetts in April, 1689 (from Nathaniel Hawthorne's short story "The Gray Champion"); a demon-boy allegedly being summoned from Hell by Nazi scientists in East Bromwich, England on October 9, 1944 (a reference to Hellboy); and the Antichrist being allegedly born in 1966, either to a housewife in New York City (from Ira Levin's novel Rosemary's Baby) or adopted by a U.S. political figure overseas (from the movie The Omen). The Cade books feature a man named Samuel Curtis as the President of the United States, rather than Barack Obama. As with other works set in the CU that feature fictional Presidents, we can assume the true political details of the book are being distorted for dramatic effect.

December 24–25
THE HO HO HO JOB
Nate Ford, leader of the Leverage team, gives his teammates Christmas presents. Eliot Spencer receives a Hanzo sword.

Episode of Leverage *broadcast December 12, 2010. The Hanzo sword is a clear reference to the film* Kill Bill, *providing confirmation* Leverage *takes place in the CU.*

December 31
EARTH CALLING TAYLOR
Ryan Taylor visits his ailing father in the hospital. Ryan's mother Cynthia and older half-siblings Jason and Julia appear, and Ryan drinks Kilmagoon Special Reserve.

Short story by David Mitchell in The Financial Times, *December 30, 2010. Ryan's older half-brother Jason Taylor is the main character of Mitchell's novel* Black Swan Green, *which takes place in 1982, before Ryan's birth. Kilmagoon Special Reserve whiskey appears in several of Mitchell's works.*

Winter
THE FIREFLY

Dr. Walter Bishop, a brilliant scientist working with the FBI investigating cases involving unusual phenomena, dons a pair of glasses, one lens of which is red, the other blue. When Junior Agent Astrid Farnsworth sarcastically compliments him on this "look," he replies they were a gift from his old friend Dr. Jacoby in Washington State.

Episode of the television series Fringe *broadcast January, 21, 2011. The cult classic television series* Twin Peaks *was set in the small town of the same name in Washington State. The town's psychiatrist, Dr. Lawrence Jacoby, wore glasses identical to the ones worn by Dr. Bishop.* Fringe *is already in the CU through connections to* Lost *and* The X-Files. *The reference to* Twin Peaks *reinforces its inclusion.*

VAMPIRELLA VS. DRACULA REDUX

Vampirella does battle with Dracula once again.

#8–10 of Dynamite Entertainment's Vampirella *ongoing series by Eric Trautmann, Fabiano Neves, and Heubert Khan Michael, 2010. This encounter takes place a year after "Crown of Worms." This story ran untitled; I have taken the liberty of providing a title.*

EXTENUATING CIRCUMSTANCES

Under the pretense of seeking a new addition to her collection of erotica, sex therapist Morgan Snow visits the Copenhagen bookstore run by Cotton Malone at the request of Malone's girlfriend Cassiopeia Vitt.

Short story by M. J. Rose included in the audiobook In Session: Dr. Morgan Snow with Steve Berry's Cotton Malone, Lee Child's Jack Reacher & Barry Eisler's John Rain, *2011. The three stories involve Snow, a series character of Rose's, psychoanalyzing other thriller characters. Since Jack Reacher is in the CU, so are Snow, Malone (a former Justice Department operative turned bookseller and adventurer), and Rain.*

LYSERGIC ACID DIETHYLAMIDE

Inside William Bell's mind, Olivia Dunham encounters Bell himself, who pours her a glass of MacCutcheon Scotch Whiskey.

Episode of Fringe *broadcast April 15, 2011. MacCutcheon Scotch Whiskey is from* Lost, *reinforcing* Fringe*'s inclusion in the CU.*

April

A GATHERING OF CROWS

In Brinkley Springs, West Virginia, Levi Stoltzfus, the ex-Amish magus, battles agents of Meeble of the Thirteen. Former soldier Donny Osborne served with the likes of Tyler Henry, from York, Pennsylvania, and Don Bloom, who went AWOL and was rumored to have joined Black Lodge. Levi is familiar with Cthulhu cultists, and has an e-reader that contains scanned pages from the *Necronomicon.* A supernatural entity called "Mrs. Chickbaum" is mentioned. Nyarlathotep is named. Levi is familiar with the siqqusim. "That crazy Earl Harper wingnut" and Teddy Garnett are mentioned. Levi walks through the Labyrinth with a group of survivors, one of whom observes in the various realities zombies, "something dark in the middle of it all," goat-men, a giant monster with a squid for a head, and crab-lobster-scorpion monsters, as well as being passed by a different version of Teddy Garnett, "a real pretty black girl," "some young guy dressed up like a mobster," and an old farmer Levi believes to have been Nelson LeHorn. Levi defeats Meeble's agents by using the Labyrinth to send them to Yuggoth, domain of Behemoth of the Thirteen; while there, he glimpses the shining trapezoid.

Novel by Brian Keene. The Thirteen are the main villains of Brian Keene's Labyrinth Mythos, pre-Universal beings that travel from reality to reality destroying Earths. The Labyrinth is an otherdimensional realm that connects all of Keene's various realities. Tyler Henry was a minor character in Keene's novel Ghost Walk. *Don Bloom was the protagonist of Keene's short story "Babylon Falling." Black Lodge is a super-secret occult organization that appears throughout Keene's works, and across his multiverse. While there is no overt connection in this story, Keene's notes on his short story "Halves" claim the leprechaun "Mr. Chickbaum" from that story is connected to this "Mrs. Chickbaum." The siqqusim are the main villains of Keene's* Rising *series and the novel* Clickers vs. Zombies, *all of which take place in an AU. The Earl Harper and Teddy Garnett mentioned here are this world's versions of those characters, which originally appeared in Keene's book* Earthworm Gods; *the version of Teddy seen in the Labyrinth is probably from that world. The zombies could be from any of Keene's zombie realities. The "something dark" is Nodens of the Thirteen, from Keene's novels* Ghost Walk *and* Darkness at the Edge of Town. *The goat-men are a reference to Keene's novel* Dark

Hollow. *The squid-monster is Keene's Leviathan, of the Thirteen. The crab-lobster-scorpion monsters are Clickers, from the worlds of Keene and J. F. Gonzalez' trilogy of novels and* Clickers vs. Zombies. *The black girl is Frankie, from* The Rising *and* City of the Dead, *and the mobster is Tony Genova, from various Keene works; there's no way to know yet which of Keene's worlds they hail from. Nelson LeHorn is from Keene's novel* Dark Hollow, *which does take place in the CU. Across all levels of the Labyrinth, Frankie, Teddy Garnett, Tony Genova, and Nelson LeHorn are of the Seven, a group of people with the power to destroy the Thirteen. According to Keene, the Exit, the serial killer from his stories "This is Not an Exit" and "I Am an Exit," is also one of the Seven, and was originally supposed to appear in this tale, until Keene felt he was stealing the show. Cthulhu cultists, Nyarlathotep, Yuggoth, and the* Necronomicon *are all from the Cthulhu Mythos of H. P. Lovecraft. The shining trapezoid is almost certainly connected to the shining trapezohedron from Lovecraft's "The Haunter of the Dark."*

Spring
CALL ME MONSTER
Monster hunting P.I. Cal McDonald is recruited by none other than the Frankenstein Monster to save him from the descendants of the Frankenstein family, who consider him their property.

Criminal Macabre *story by Steve Niles, Christopher Mitten, and Michelle Madsen, found in the* Baltimore/Criminal Macabre Free Comic Book Day 2011 Flipbook, *published by Dark Horse Comics.*

ONCE UPON A TIME
Emma Swan has a Geronimo Jackson sticker on her car.

Pilot episode of Once Upon a Time *broadcast October 23, 2011. The band Geronimo Jackson is from* Lost. *Several other episodes feature Geronimo Jackson merchandise. Further* Lost *elements appearing in later episodes include the ubiquitous Oceanic Airlines, MacCutcheon Scotch Whiskey, Apollo candy bars, the television series* Exposé, *Ajira Airways, and Mr. Cluck's Chicken Shack. All of these connections to* Lost *bring* Once Upon a Time *into the Crossover Universe. The Fairy Tale Land seen in the show must be an alternate dimension to the CU. Alternate versions of various fairy tale characters, several Disney characters, the inhabitants of Oz, and Victor Frankenstein are seen in the series.*

IMPOSSIBLE LOVE
Piers Knight, a curator at the Brooklyn Museum and amateur occult detective, joins forces with Madame Sarna Raniella to free a friend's daughter from demonic possession.

Short story by C. J. Henderson in Those Who Fight Monsters: Tales of Occult Detectives, *Justin Gustainis, ed., EDGE Science Fiction and Fantasy Publishing, 2011. Madame Sarna La Raniella also appears in Henderson's short stories "To Cast Out Fear" and "Locked Room," as well as his novel* To Battle Beyond *and comic book* Kolchak: The Night Stalker– The Lovecraftian Damnation. *Piers Knight has also appeared in three novels by Henderson:* Brooklyn Knight, Central Park Knight, *and* Radio City Knight. Central Park Knight *features major destruction in New York City and the revelation of the existence of dragons to the world. This must be chalked up to exaggeration akin to the* Spider *novels.*

CONGRATS ALL AROUND

Dick Tracy calls Skeezix to congratulate him on figuring out that a fly caused his home security system to go off. Skeezix, in turn, congratulates Dick on 80 years of fine detective work.

Gasoline Alley *strip by Jim Scancarelli, October 4, 2011. This strip commemorated the 80th anniversary of the comic strip* Dick Tracy.

DECISIONS, DECISIONS

When the politician husband of one of her patients threatens her daughter Dulcie, Dr. Morgan Snow meets with assassin John Rain in hopes he will deal with the man.

Short story by M. J. Rose included in the audiobook In Session: Dr. Morgan Snow with Steve Berry's Cotton Malone, Lee Child's Jack Reacher & Barry Eisler's John Rain, *2011. In Eisler's* The Detachment, *Rain works with Military Liaison Element Ben Treven, who had previously appeared in two non-Rain novels by Eisler,* Fault Line *and* Inside Out.

FEET OF SCIRON

Hellboy recruits Foggy Dicks, a porn star that can generate ectoplasm, for a sex magic ritual in order to prevent the planet Nekrotzar from colliding with Earth, battling King Sciron in the process. Nekrotzar was drawn towards Earth by Marvin Carnacki, the current director of the Carnacki Institute, founded by his ancestor to rid the natural world of paranormal threats. Hellboy says most people think the original Carnacki was William Hope Hodgson's fictional creation, just as many other authors pretended their subjects were fictional: Arthur Conan Doyle with Sherlock Holmes, Jules Verne with Phileas Fogg, H. G. Wells with Dr. Moreau, M. P. Shiel with Prince Zaleski, and Maurice Richardson with Engelbrecht. He also says Liz Sherman and Abe Sapien are at Mount Snaefell in Iceland. Foggy replies that he remembers Verne wrote a book about two explorers. Hellboy simply smiles in response. In Nekrotzar, the monster-hunting demon receives a riverboat ride from writer Philip José Farmer, who has been resurrected there after his death. Hellboy reveals to Foggy that billions of years ago Nekrotzar actually did collide with the Earth, which was merely a cloud of stardust then. Earth congealed around Nekrotzar, trapping Sciron's palace in what would become the younger planet's crust, forty miles under what is now Iceland.

Short story by Rhys Hughes in Hellboy: Oddest Jobs, *Christopher Golden, ed., Dark Horse Books, 2008. This Carnacki Insitute is clearly a separate group from the one seen in Simon R. Green's* Ghost Finders *series. Engelbrecht is from Maurice Richardson's book* The Exploits of Engelbrecht. *The subterranean world Sciron's palace inhabits is the one seen in Jules Verne's novel* Journey to the Centre of the Earth. *Philip José Farmer, of course, revealed the existence of the Wold Newton Family to the world, and wrote several chronicles of events in the CU. Farmer's appearance here evokes his Riverworld novels, albeit as homage rather than a true crossover. This story must take place after Farmer's passing in 2009, although it was published earlier than that.*

Summer

FLYFACE AND THE FIFTH RETURN

Dick Tracy's old nemesis Flyface takes a cab, much to the chagrin of its driver, whose license reads "M. Shrevnit-."

Dick Tracy strip by Mike Curtis and Joe Staton, March 18, 2011. "M. Shrevnit-" is a reference to a trusted agent whose death in the comic book miniseries The Shadow: Blood and Judgment *was greatly exaggerated.*

BOMB QUEEN VS. HACK/SLASH

Cassie Hack, Vlad, and Pooch trace a rash of new slashers to New Port City, which is in an alternate dimension that has been devastated by a supervillain called Bomb Queen. Cassie and Vlad do battle with Bomb Queen, while Pooch defeats the demon cat Ashe, who has been sending the psycho killers to Cass' universe. Bomb Queen threatens to visit Cassie and Vlad's world when she's done with her own.

One-shot written and illustrated by Jimmie Robinson, Image Comics, February 2011. This crossover establishes Bomb Queen's universe as being part of the same multiverse as the CU.

HACK/SLASH/EVA: MONSTER'S BALL

Cassie Hack and Vlad team up with Eva, Daughter of the Dragon, and the vigilantes known as the Ghosts of Old Detroit to rescue Eva's companion Michael from Doctor Praetorius and Mary Shelley Lovecraft. A Gill-Man can be seen among the slashers whose corpses have been collected by Praetorius and Lovecraft.

Miniseries by Brandon Jerwa and Cezar Razek, Dynamite Entertainment, May–October 2011. Eva is allegedly the daughter of Dracula, though more likely "Dracula" is a "soul-clone" of the original Vlad Tepes. Similarly, although Michael is identified as Victor Frankenstein's monster, the significant difference in personality between the original monster and Michael suggests the latter was actually created by another member of the Frankenstein family. Dr. Praetorius (or Pretorius) is from the film Bride of Frankenstein. *It is unknown whether this Gill-Man is the same one that appears in* The Creature from the Black Lagoon *and its sequels.*

MYSTERY WOMAN

Fantomah manipulates Cassie Hack and Vlad into attacking the woman responsible for despoiling her jungle home. Fantomah's mistress attempts to replace her with Cassie, but Vlad convinces his friend not to abandon her humanity.

Hack/Slash #5 by Tim Seeley and Kyle Strahm, Image Comics, June 2011. Fantomah appeared in fifty issues of Jungle Comics, *published by Fiction House. She was an incredibly powerful being who dealt bizarre punishments to those who threatened the jungle where she dwelled; when she used her powers, her face sometimes assumed the form of a skull. Cassie and Vlad previously encountered her in the "Super Sidekick Sleepover Slaughter" storyline.*

FLAKEY BISCUITS MAKES THE DOUGH

Flakey Biscuits sends four fifty-pound bags of flour to B. O. Plenty and his wife Gertie to celebrate the birth of their son, but the bags get mixed up with the cocaine Flakey is manufacturing, and Tony Rockyhorror delivers the flour to their distributor.

Dick Tracy strip by *Mike Curtis and Joe Staton, May 6, 2011. Antwan "Tony Rocky Horror" Rockamora is mentioned, but not seen, in Quentin Tarantino's film* Pulp Fiction.

ONE YEAR GONE

Monster hunter Dean Winchester, despite being supposedly retired, travels to Salem, Massachusetts to retrieve a copy of the *Necronomicon*, which he believes contains a spell that can release his brother Sam from Hell.

Supernatural *tie-in novel by Rebecca Dessertine, Titan Books, 2011. This book ties the TV series* Supernatural *into the Lovecraft mythos, and thus the CU, through the appearance of the* Necronomicon; *it also hints a similar book encountered by the brothers in the episode "Swap Meat" was a watered-down version of the* Necronomicon.

CRIMINAL MACABRE/THE GOON: WHEN FREAKS COLLIDE

Paranormal private investigator Cal McDonald comes face-to-face with the Goon, and ultimately joins forces with him to defeat a man who is bringing his imagination to life with an occult tome. The man summons Hellboy, who Cal recognizes, before being defeated.

One-shot by Steve Niles, Eric Powell, and Christopher Mitten, Dark Horse Comics, August 2011. The Goon's exploits take place in an alternate universe. However, both P.I. Cal McDonald of Niles and Mitten's comic Criminal Macabre *and Mike Mignola's monster-fighting demon Hellboy (whom the Goon met in a 2004 issue of his own title) have independent links to the CU, and given Cal knows who Hellboy is, it is very likely the two were transported to the Goon's universe from the CU.*

BACK IN BLACK

Christa Lane (aka the masked vigilante known as the Silhouette) restores the wheelchair-bound James Blacker's memories of both his own crime-fighting career as Noir and their romantic relationship using a girasol necklace she wears. Christa's grandfather taught her *baritsu*. She comes from a long line of adventurers, and her father was a private investigator who died of skin cancer. Noir and the Silhouette train at the Dragon Dojo.

Short story by Brad Mengel in Pro Se Presents, *Don Thomas, Frank Schildiner, and Lee Houston Jr., eds., Pro Se Press, November 2012. Christa Lane is the daughter of Kent Lane. Kent Lane, in turn, is the son of a pulp avenger who operated in the shadows, and his most trusted female agent. Lane is the protagonist of Philip José Farmer's story "Skinburn." The girasol in Christa's necklace is likely one of the same stones her grandfather once had set into two rings. Baritsu is a Japanese wrestling style from Doyle and Watson's Sherlock Holmes story "The Adventure of the Empty House." The comic book crossover "The Conflagration Man" indicated both the shadowy avenger and Doc had learned baritsu from the creator of the style. Since Farmer's biography* Doc Savage: His Apocalyptic Life *revealed Holmes was one of Doc's teachers, the Great Detective must have taught baritsu to both heroes. The sensei of the Dragon Dojo is meant to be Richard Dragon from "Jim Dennis'" (pseudonym for James R. Berry and Dennis O'Neil) novel* Dragon's Fists *and the comic book* Richard Dragon, Kung Fu Fighter.

THE TEMPLAR SALVATION

FBI agent Sean Reilly tells his girlfriend, archaeologist Tess Chaykin, about his friend Cotton Malone, a former government agent who has retired, moved to Copenhagen, and opened an antique bookshop.

Novel by Raymond Khoury. Cotton Malone, who appears in a series of novels by Steve Berry, is already in the CU. Therefore, this crossover brings in Reilly and Chaykin.

KNOWING YOU'RE ALIVE

The man Jack Reacher is pursuing bombs the Butterfield Institute in an attempt to destroy his girlfriend's files from sessions with her sex therapist. Reacher enters the building and helps the therapist's trapped and injured coworker Morgan Snow, and while they wait to be rescued Morgan persuades Reacher to tell her about the best sex he ever had.

Short story by M. J. Rose included in the audiobook In Session: Dr. Morgan Snow with Steve Berry's Cotton Malone, Lee Child's Jack Reacher & Barry Eisler's John Rain, *2011.*

WHO, WHAT, WHERE, WENDIGO

A radio announcer refers to Lobstrosities. A truck bears the words "Pesticide-free corn, homegrown in Gatlin, Nebraska" on its side.

Episode of Haven *broadcast September 16, 2011. Lobstrosities are from Stephen King's novel* The Drawing of the Three, *the second novel in the Dark Tower series, further establishing the Territories and Mid-World as alternate universes to the CU. Gatlin, Nebraska is from King's story "Children of the Corn."*

BUSINESS AS USUAL

Nathan Wuornos makes use of a coroner from Cleaves Mills. Duke Crocker won his boat from a man in Castle Rock.

Episode of Haven *broadcast September 23, 2011. The town of Cleaves Mills is from Stephen King's novel* The Dead Zone. *Castle Rock is the setting of* The Dead Zone *and several other books and stories by King.*

July
INTERDIMENSIONAL WOMEN'S PRISON BREAKOUT

Bomb Queen and two other supervillainesses break out of the other-dimensional prison known as the White Ward and enter Cassie Hack's world to cause havoc. Cassie teams up with Samhain to bring them to justice. Hoodoo Hex is seen among the inmates of the Ward.

Hack/Slash #9-11 by Tim Seeley and Daniel Leister, Image Comics, 2011. Cassie and Vlad first encountered Bomb Queen earlier in the year. Hoodoo Hex is from Seeley's web comic Colt Noble and the Megalords.

SILENT NIGHT

Derry is mentioned as a neighboring town to Haven.

Episode of Haven *broadcast December 6, 2011. Derry, Maine is a recurring locale in Stephen King's interconnected fiction.*

August
THE WITCHING TREE

Levi Stoltzfus, the ex-Amish magus, takes on the case of a demon-possessed tree in rural Pennsylvania. Levi recalls the time a warlock from the Kwan tried to break into his home. Levi owns a few scattered pages from the dread *Necronomicon*. Maria Nasr appears. Adam Senft, Hector Ramirez, and the forest fire of 2006 are mentioned, as are a group of deer hunters who died near LeHorn's Hollow. There are the usual references to the Labyrinth and the Thirteen.

Novella by Brian Keene in the collection Is There a Demon in You? *The Kwan is an occult group from the works of horror author Geoff Cooper, including the novel* Shades, *cowritten with Keene. The* Necronomicon *is* from the Cthulhu Mythos of H. P. Lovecraft and others. Maria Nasr originally appeared in Keene's novel Ghost Walk. Adam Senft is from Keene's novels Dark Hollow and Ghost Walk; Ramirez features in both novels, as well as Keene's earlier novel Terminal. LeHorn's Hollow is a recurring location in Keene's works, originally appearing in the story "Red Wood," which is also the source of the deceased hunters.

September
LAST OF THE ALBATWITCHES

Levi Stoltzfus battles a murderous cryptid released into Pennsylvania by the Globe Corporation after being captured on an island. The serial killer known as the Exit is mentioned. There are references to Leviathan, the Siqqusim, and a race of prehistoric, aquatic reptiles known as the Dark Ones. Levi thinks about his friend Dez, a chaos mage. The Goat-Man of LeHorn's Hollow is mentioned. The *Cryptid Hunter* TV series has been in the area filming a special on the legendary giant water snake Old Scratch. Levi places a call to Maria Nasr. There is a rumor that the heads of the Globe Corporation worship a being called Kat. Levi is familiar with the infamous Crazy Bear Valley sighting.

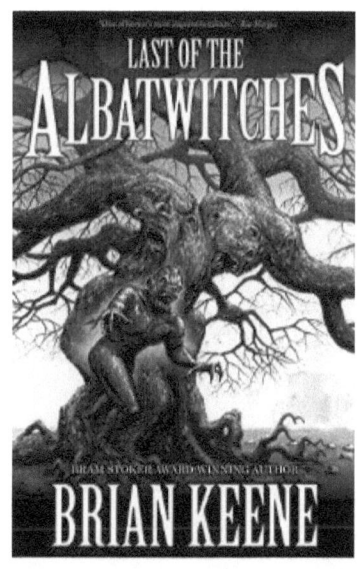

Novella by Brian Keene. The cryptid is one of the "tribe" from Keene's novel Castaways. The Globe Corporation is a recurring, if mostly background, element of Keene's fiction. The Exit is from Keene's short stories "I Am an Exit" and "This is Not an Exit." Leviathan is one of the Thirteen, and appears across Keene's multiverse, especially in the worlds of the Earthworm Gods series and Clickers III: Dagon Rising. The Siqqusim serve Ob, another of the Thirteen, and are seen primarily in the worlds of Keene's The Rising series and Clickers vs. Zombies. The Dark Ones mentioned here must be the CU versions of the Dark Ones that appear in the Clickers series by Keene and J. F. Gonzalez. Dez is the CU version of the character that appears in Keene's alternate universe novel Darkness at the Edge of Town. The Goat-Man is from Keene's Dark Hollow. Old Scratch is from Keene's story "Scratch." Maria Nasr appears in Keene's novel Ghost Walk and the story "The Witching Tree." Kat is another of the Thirteen, who has thus far not appeared directly in any of Keene's work. The Crazy Bear Valley sighting is from Keene's story "An Occurrence in Crazy Bear Valley."

THE INFORMANT

The hitman known only as the Butcher's Boy seeks revenge on the Mafia. Among the mobsters gathered for a meeting are Paul Castiglione, Phil Langusto, Salvatore Molinari, Giovanni "Chi-chi" Tasso, and Danny Spoleto, an underling for Mike Catania.

Novel by Thomas Perry. The various Mafiosi first appeared in Perry's novel Blood Money, *the third book in a series featuring Jane Whitefield, a Native American woman who helps people who need to disappear create new identities. The Butcher's Boy appeared under the alias "the Grocer's Boy" in Justin Gustainis' novel* Sympathy for the Devil, *the third entry in his Morris and Chastain Supernatural Investigations series, which has many crossover references bringing it into the CU. This crossover brings Jane Whitefield in as well.*

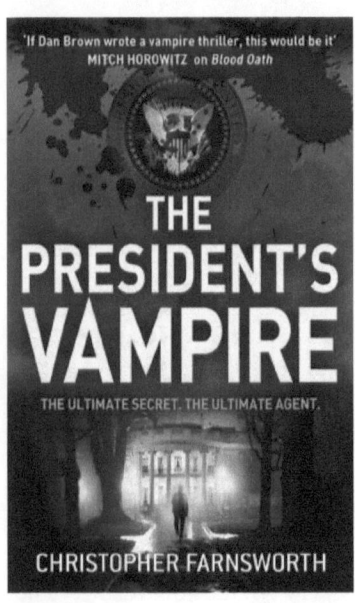

'If Dan Brown wrote a vampire thriller, this would be it'
MITCH HOROWITZ on *Blood Oath*

THE
PRESIDENT'S
VAMPIRE

THE ULTIMATE SECRET. THE ULTIMATE AGENT.

CHRISTOPHER FARNSWORTH

October

THE PRESIDENT'S VAMPIRE

Nathaniel Cade and Zach Barrows battle a threat that began in Innsmouth in 1928, and at one point Cade flashes back to his part in the Innsmouth raid. In Cairo, Egypt, Cade meets a man called Flint, who was once "The World's Greatest Secret Agent," and in his time handled "plots that never made the news: secret space missions, vanishing islands, strange weapons and deadly assassins with steel teeth." Other references include: a series of "vampire murders" in Providence, Rhode Island in 1928, during which Benjamin Franklin's corpse was stolen; the "Christmas Invasion" of Kingston Falls, Indiana; the Pabodie Expedition to the Mountains of Madness; a wave of sleeping deaths in Springwood, Ohio; the horror at Red Hook, New York in 1925; a mysterious creature that terrorized Dunwich, Massachusetts in 1928; a Gill-Man that escaped into the Everglades after being captured in the Amazon in the 1950s; a 1951 Antarctic expedition, following in the footsteps of the Pabodie expedition, that discovered an alien craft; the Pod People incident in the 1950s; and rumors of a shadowy figure that preyed on criminals in the 1930s and '40s.

Novel by Christopher Farnsworth, Putnam Adult, 2011. This novel goes into greater depth regarding Cade's involvement in Lovecraft's "The Shadow over Innsmouth." Flint is clearly secret agent Derek Flint from the films Our

Man Flint *and* In Like Flint; *the references to his past missions seem to indicate some of the adventures attributed to British agent James Bond in film were in fact Flint's cases. The "vampire murders" and the theft of Benjamin Franklin's corpse are references to Lovecraft's* The Case of Charles Dexter Ward. *The "Christmas Invasion" of Kingston Falls is a direct reference to the 1984 film* Gremlins. *The Pabodie expedition is from Lovecraft's* At the Mountains of Madness. *Springwood's dream killer is Freddy Krueger, from the* Nightmare on Elm Street *films. The Red Hook reference is to Lovecraft's "The Horror at Red Hook," and the Dunwich reference is to Lovecraft's "The Dunwich Horror." The Gill-Man is from Universal's* Creature from the Black Lagoon *movies. The 1951 Antarctic expedition is a reference to the film* The Thing from Another World, *based on John W. Campbell's story "Who Goes There?" The events are different enough in their portrayal to be treated as separate incidents, at least for our purposes. The Pod People incident is a reference to the film* Invasion of the Body Snatchers, *based on Jack Finney's novel* The Body Snatchers. *Finally, the shadowy figure that terrorized the criminal underworld likely needs no further explanation.*

October 31
COLD DAYS

Queen Mab of the Fae tests Harry Dresden by making a number of creative attempts to murder him, which he must survive. A ticking crocodile is mentioned as one of them.

Novel by Jim Butcher, 2012. Queen Mab, a recurring character in Butcher's The Dresden Files *book series, is originally from William Shakespeare's play* Romeo and Juliet. *The ticking crocodile must be the same one seen in J. M. Barrie's* Peter Pan.

Autumn
LOVE SICK

Former Warehouse 13 agent Hugo Miller returns from the town of Eureka, citing the many explosive events that occur there as the reason he has come back.

Episode of the television series Warehouse 13 *broadcast July 25, 2011. Miller previously left for Eureka (from the television series of the same name) in the episode "13.1."*

NEVER LET ME GO

Dr. Vanessa Calder travels to Fenton, PA, to investigate a series of bizarre deaths, and encounters Dr. Lee Rosen and his team, who are themselves looking into the emergence of superhumans called "Alphas."

Episode of the television series Alphas *broadcast August 8, 2011. Dr. Calder previously appeared on three episodes of* Warehouse 13, *which is in the CU through multiple connections. In the last episode of the show's first season, "Original Sin," the existence of Alphas is revealed to the world. This does not fit with CU continuity, and therefore it can be assumed the events of "Original Sin" and subsequent episodes take place in a universe which diverges from the CU at that time.*

DON'T HATE THE PLAYER

Warehouse 13 representatives Claudia Donovan, Myka Bering and Pete Lattimer travel to Palo Alto to aid Douglas Fargo and a friend of his, who are trapped inside a virtual reality game.

Episode of the television series Warehouse 13 *broadcast August 15, 2011. This marks the third crossover between* Warehouse 13 *and* Eureka.

DICK TRACY VS. ABNER KADAVER

Dick Tracy tells cartoonist Vera Alldid his favorite comic strip was *Fearless Fosdick.* Dick calls journalist Hank O'Hair of *The Daily Flash* to ask her about a dead criminal found at Abner Kadaver's Halloween attraction. Hank says the criminal's name turned up in connection with a story Brenda was investigating. Sam Catchem tells Dick his own favorite strip was always *Derby Dugan.*

Dick Tracy *strip by Mike Curtis and Joe Staton, October 30–December 1, 2011. Fearless Fosdick, a fictional comic strip parodying* Dick Tracy *in Al Capp's comic strip* Li'l Abner, *is mentioned in the November 2 strip. Hank O'Hair is from the comic strip* Brenda Starr, Reporter, *and appears in the strip on November 10.* Derby Dugan *is a fictional strip from Tom De Haven's* Funny Papers *trilogy of novels, consisting of* Funny Papers, Derby Dugan's Depression Funnies, *and* Dugan Under Ground. *Sam mentions* Derby Dugan *in the November 16 strip.*

Autumn 2010–Spring 2011
BLOOD AND BULLETS

Deacon Chalk has hunted monsters ever since a member of the race of angel/human hybrids known as the Nephilim killed his family. Deacon states, "There are few proclaimed vampire slayers and they range all kinds. Anita out in St. Louis, but she has a lot of stuff going on, not just vampire executions. Cat and Bones run their crew killing vampires and do a fine job of it. I hear whispers about the Blue Woman now and again, but it's hard to pull the fact from the fiction on that one. There's some folks in California. In L.A. and a small town east of it, who do mostly vampire slaying, but I haven't met them yet. The black guy and old man combo who roam around do nothing but vampires. From what I hear they have a personal stake in it, so to speak. Sam and Dean will tussle with a vampire, but usually they are chasing down demons."

Novel by James R. Tuck. Anita is the main character of Laurell K. Hamilton's Anita Blake: Vampire Hunter *series, which takes place in an alternate reality where humans know the supernatural is real. However, Justin Gustainis' Morris and Chastain Supernatural Investigations series has established Anita does have a CU counterpart, who has doubtless had very different adventures than Hamilton's version. Dhampir Catherine "Cat" Crawfield and vampire bounty hunter Bones are from Jeaniene Frost's* Night Huntress *series of novels. Vlad Tepesh appears in Frost's series, but he hates the name Dracula and possesses pyrokinetic abilities. This is probably a "soul-clone" of the original Dracula, who somehow developed pyrokinetic talents that the true Vlad Tepes lacks. The Blue Woman is Nancy A. Collins' monster hunting vampire Sonja Blue. The small town east of L.A. is Sunnydale, the home of Buffy Summers on the television series* Buffy the Vampire Slayer. *The Los Angeles reference is to the titular vampire from* Buffy's *spin-off* Angel. *The black guy and old man combo are Marvel Comics' vampire hunter Blade and his mentor Abraham Whistler, the latter of whom debuted in the cartoon* Spider-Man: The Animated Series *and went on to appear in the Blade film series. Sam and Dean are monster hunting brothers Sam and Dean Winchester from the television series* Supernatural.

December
NIGHT GAUNTLET

Dr. Emil Hesychius' former office at the University of Texas is covered with souvenir postcards from many places, including: Derry, Maine; Arkham, Massachusetts; Glory, West Virginia; Sesqua Valley, Washington; Brichester, England; Binger, Oklahoma; Mirocaw, Idaho; Crouch End, England; Telfer, Australia; and Nan Madol, Federated States of Micronesia. Hesychius went on a shooting spree from the top of the University's clock tower, claiming he was shooting "nightgaunts." John Giloh and Dr. Susan Derby go on a date to see *Red Dreams*, a Korean horror film directed by Harry Chang. Susan, a member of the Derby-Pickman clan, shows John the Sign of Koth.

Round-robin story by Walter C. Debill, Jr.; Richard Gavin; Robert M. Price; W. H. Pugmire; Jeffrey Thomas; and Don Webb, The Magazine of Fantasy and Science Fiction, March–April 2011. Derry, Maine is featured in many of Stephen King's works. Arkham, Massachusetts is the site of many of H. P. Lovecraft's tales of the Cthulhu Mythos. Glory, West Virginia is a recurring setting in the works of author Davis Grubb. Sesqua Valley, Washington appears in Cthulhu Mythos tales by W. H. Pugmire. Brichester, England is part of the Severn Valley in Mythos fiction by Ramsey Campbell. Binger, Oklahoma is a real place that appears in Lovecraft and Zealia Bishop's story "The Mound." Mirocaw, Idaho is from Thomas Ligotti's Mythos story "The Last Feast of Harlequin." Crouch End, England is a real place that served as the setting for Stephen King's Mythos story "Crouch End." Telfer is a real place located in Australia's Great Sandy Desert, the latter of which was referenced in Lovecraft's story "The Shadow Out of Time." Nan Madol, Federated States of Micronesia is a real place that was the setting for A. Merritt's The Moon Pool. The nightgaunts and the Sign of Koth are from Lovecraft's Dream Cycle stories. Rick Lai writes, 'Red Dreams is from the prologue to Ramsey Campbell's 'The Franklyn Paragraphs.' This prologue is generally printed on a page preceding the story, and sometimes has the title 'Errol Undercliffe: A Tribute.' Undercliffe is a fictional horror writer whose short story was the basis for Red Dreams." Dr. Susan Derby is probably related to the namesake of the Nathaniel Derby Pickman Foundation from Lovecraft's "At the Mountains of Madness."

December 18–27

WHISPERS UNDER GROUND

Police Constable and sorcerer's apprentice Peter Grant, who handles occult crimes for the London Metropolitan Police alongside Inspector Nightingale, who is also a wizard, is served a beer called a "Mac," which comes in a brown bottle, and is from a microbrewery in America. He concludes it would probably taste better at room temperature.

The third novel in Ben Aaronovitch's Rivers of London series, Del Rey, 2012. Mac's beer is the specialty of bar owner McAnally in Jim Butcher's series The Dresden Files, bringing Peter Grant into the CU.

December 24–25
DILLON AND THE NIGHT BEFORE CHRISTMAS
A depressed Dillon tells a mysterious woman no matter how many lives he saves, there will always be villains threatening the world, such as Li Shoon. Dillon has had work done on his plane at the Miami Aerodrome Research & Development Laboratories.

Story by Derrick Ferguson in PulpWork Christmas Special 2012, *Pulp-Work Press. Li Shoon is a "Yellow Peril" villain who appeared in stories by H. Irving Hancock in* Detective Story Magazine *in 1916–1917. The Miami Aerodrome Research & Development Laboratories (MARDL) is from Don Gates' Challenger Storm books.*

Christmas
THE GREATEST GIFT
Among the artifacts in Warehouse 13's Christmas section is a leg-shaped lamp.

Episode of the television series Warehouse 13 *broadcast December 6, 2011. The leg lamp is identical to that won by Ralphie Parker's father in the film* A Christmas Story. *Since the Old Man's major award was destroyed by Ralphie's mother, the same company that gave it out as a prize must have released another lamp in the decades between the film's events and this episode, one which had properties unusual enough to merit storage in Warehouse 13.*

2011

Winter
DICK TRACY VS. BLACKJACK
Dick Tracy calls Hotshot Airlines and speaks to Hotshot Charlie, who has had dealings with a bank robbed by Blackjack. Charlie asks his secretary, Wingy Plenty, if Bitsy Beekman has called in yet.

Dick Tracy *strip by Mike Curtis and Joe Staton, March 28–30, 2012. Charles C. "Hotshot Charlie" Charles is from Milton Caniff's classic comic strip* Terry and the Pirates. *Bitsy Beekman is from another Caniff strip,* Steve Canyon. *Wingy Plenty is a character introduced in* Dick Tracy *in 1953.*

GRAND DESIGNS
Don Quixote's lance is used to stop the powerful winds generated by Miguel de Cervantes' windmill.

Warehouse 13 *webisodes. The connection to Miguel de Cervantes' Don Quixote further cements Warehouse 13 in the CU.*

Late Winter
THE ROOK

Myfanwy Thomas is a member of the Checquy, a British agency dedicated to protecting the world from supernatural threats. She writes letters to her future self after hearing a prophecy she will lose her memories soon. Mentioned in the letters are: Brigadoon; Groke; Scabmettler; Marshwiggle; Hattifattener; Panwere; Flukeman; Morlock; Aufwader; Balrog; cat in shoes; creepy blond kids wandering around in Winshire; talking mice that infested Lewisham; a two-door wardrobe in the spare room of a country house; and a couturier in Gloucestershire who had been imprisoned for using rodents as indentured servants.

Novel by Daniel O'Malley. Brigadoon is from Alan Jay Lerner and Frederick Loewe's titular musical. The Groke and the Hattifatteners are from Tove Jansson's Moomin books. The Scabmettlers are from China Miéville's novels about the fantasy world of Bas-Lag. Marshwiggles and the two-door wardrobe are from C. S. Lewis' Narnia books. The Panweres mentioned here must be CU versions of the race seen in Laurell K. Hamilton's Anita Blake, Vampire Hunter *books, which take place in an alternate reality where the world is aware vampires and other supernatural beings really do exist. The Flukeman is from "The Host," an episode of* The X-Files. *Morlocks are from H. G. Wells'* The Time Machine; *since they are mentioned as having visited Bath before the events of this book, a group of Morlocks must have traveled or been transported back in time from their native era. Aufwaders are from Robin Jarvis' Whitby Witches books, while the talking mice in Lewisham are a reference to Jarvis' Deptford Mice series. Balrogs are from J. R. R. Tolkien's fantasy saga* The Lord of the Rings. *Cat in shoes is a reference to the fairy tale* Puss in Boots. *The creepy blond kids wandering around Winshire are from John Wyndham's book* The Midwich Cuckoos. *The couturier in Gloucestershire who used rodents as indentured servants is a reference to Beatrix Potter's children's book* The Tailor of Gloucester.

DOUBLE JEOPARDY

Duncan Fromsley is transferred from Shawshank State Prison.

Episode of Haven *broadcast October 19, 2012. Shawshank State Prison appears in "Rita Hayworth and Shawshank Redemption" and other novels and stories by Stephen King.*

SARAH

Roy Crocker's wife and son live near Derry, Maine.

Episode of Haven *broadcast November 16, 2012. Derry, Maine is a recurring locale in Stephen King's interrelated fiction.*

March 8
HATCHET/SLASH

A vengeful former victim of the deformed ghostly slasher Victor Crowley manipulates Crowley into killing her former friends who left her for dead, and also lures Cassie Hack and Vlad to New Orleans to kill Crowley himself. Cassie, initially unaware of the exact nature of the threat they've been asked to deal with, hopes it's not "that f***ing Good Guy doll again."

Hack/Slash Annual 2011 by Benito Cereno and Ariel Zucker-Brull, Image Comics, November 2011. Victor Crowley is from the film series Hatchet. *The Good Guy doll is Chucky, from the* Child's Play *film series; Cassie and Vlad previously encountered him in the* Hack/Slash vs. Chucky *one-shot. This story takes place during Mardi Gras.*

Spring
WHAT HAPPENED TO FREDERICK

Regina Mills gives her adopted son Henry the handheld video game *Space Paranoids* as a gift.

Episode of Once Upon a Time *broadcast February 19, 2012. Space Paranoids is from the movie* Tron. *Since* Once Upon a Time *takes place in the CU, so do* Tron *and its sequel,* Tron: Legacy. *Another episode, "Welcome to Storybrooke," features a park bench that bears the logo of ENCOM, the company that released* Space Paranoids.

WITCHBLADE/RED SONJA

The wielder of the Witchblade, Sara Pezzini, battles the fallen angel Ragniel, who has abducted Sara's infant daughter Hope with the goal of eventually producing offspring by her, so as to take his revenge on God and man. Contacting the embodiment of her predecessor Nissa's memories via the Witchblade, Sara decides the Witchblade must influence its own past by joining with Nissa's onetime ally, the warrior woman Red Sonja, who uses it to kill several of Ragniel's past self's minions. Sara soon encounters the embodiment of Sonja's own memories, and persuades Sonja to lend her Hyrkanian blade to her in order to destroy Ragniel. Sara kills him once and for all.

Five-issue miniseries by Doug Wagner and Cezar Razek, Dynamite Entertainment, 2012. Sonja and Nissa's battle with Ragniel occurred c. 10,000 B.C.E.

DANGERGIRL/G.I. JOE

The agents of DangerGirl and G.I. Joe team up to battle the Joes' archenemy, the terrorist organization Cobra, which has hijacked several missiles.

Five-issue miniseries by Andy Hartnell, John Royle, Philip Moy, and Jeffrey Moy, IDW Publishing, July–November 2012. This crossover confirms the members of G.I. Joe are in the CU.

AN EVIL WITHIN

Pete Lattimer and Myka Bering travel to Philadelphia, where H. P. Lovecraft's Silver Key is causing people to hallucinate monsters.

Episode of the television series Warehouse 13 *broadcast July 30, 2012. The Silver Key is from Lovecraft's stories about the Dreamlands.*

THE MYSTERIOUS MAID

The grave of Mysta "Moon Maid" Tracy, Junior Tracy's deceased first wife, is visited by a woman resembling Mysta herself and wielding a sledgehammer. The grave is at Wildwood Cemetery.

Sunday Dick Tracy *comic strip by Mike Curtis and Joe Staton, September 29, 2012. Wildwood Cemetery also hosts the grave of the supposedly dead Denny Colt, aka the Spirit.*

MONSTER BAITING

An ailing Vlad is visited and diagnosed by occult physician Dr. Vincent Morrow.

Hack/Slash #12–15 by Tim Seeley, Daniel Leister, and Emilio Laiso, Image Comics, January–April 2012. Dr. Vincent Morrow, who appears in #13, is the protagonist of Brandon Seifert and Lukas Ketner's series Witch Doctor, *which is also published by Image.*

QUEEN OF WANDS

A man named Artie and a woman named Claudia collect an artifact from Barbara Everette and an Opus Dei strike team. A group of Asatru covering the Caucasus, led by a demon-possessed former SEAL, is mentioned.

The second novel in John Ringo's Special Circumstances *series, Baen Books, 2012. Artie and Claudia are Artie Nielsen and Claudia Donovan from* the television series Warehouse 13. *The group of Asatru is the Keldera, while their leader is Michael Harmon; both are featured in Ringo's Paladin of Shadows series. Since Warehouse 13 takes place in the CU, so do both of Ringo's series.*

May 1, 2011–September 11, 2012
MIDNIGHT AT THE OASIS

Quincey Morris and Libby Chastain battle a Middle Eastern terrorist cell that has acquired control of an afreet. A Navy SEAL and combat magician volunteered to spend six months in the U.K. under the tutelage of an ex-SAS sergeant major, who was said to be the greatest combat magician living. Quincey and Libby's ally, FBI agent Colleen O'Donnell, mentions a blood spatter analyst named Morgan who worked on a case in Chicago. Quincey and Libby discuss the time they traveled to London for "that Castor thing." Quincey meets with another colleague, Barry Love, who refers to rumors of an afreet driving a cab in New York for a while. Quincey and Barry set up a meeting at Strangefellows Bar and Grill; Quincey says there's another bar of that name in the U.K., and Barry knows a man in the same line of work as them named John who hangs out at the English bar. When Quincey arrives at Strangefellows, Barry is talking to a werewolf named Larry Talbot. Barry tells Quincey about a vampire he once encountered named Jerry, who was fond of apples and was killed by a high school kid after going to California. As Quincey and Barry part ways, Barry says he is planning to deal with a guy called Pinhead. The terrorists use a spell called the Tarnhelm Effect to mask their breaking into a zoo, and discuss potential threats to their plot, including a magician in Chicago named Dresden and a woman named Blake in St. Louis.

Novella by Justin Gustainis, 2013. The ex-SAS Sergeant Major and combat magician is William Gravel from Warren Ellis' comic books Strange Kiss and Gravel. Morgan is Dexter Morgan, a blood spatter analyst and secret serial killer of other murderers, from the television series Dexter. However, Dexter works for the Miami Metro Police Department's Homicide division, and has never been based in Chicago. Most likely, Dexter was on loan to the Chicago Police Department for this case, and O'Donnell merely assumed he worked for the CPD full time. "That Castor thing" is a reference to Felix Castor, an occult detective created by Mike Carey. The Castor books take place in a world where the public knows supernatural beings exist, so the Castor mentioned by Quincey and Libby must be the Crossover Universe counterpart of the character seen in Carey's novels. Barry Love is a disguised version of Clive Barker's occult investigator Harry D'Amour. Pinhead is from Barker's story "The Hellbound Heart," as well as the Hellraiser film series. The afreet that drove a cab in New York City appears in Neil Gaiman's novel American Gods. The British Strangefellows is featured in Simon R. Green's Nightside books; the main character of that series is private eye John Taylor. Larry Talbot is from the classic horror film The Wolf Man *and its sequels. Jerry is Jerry Dandridge from the movie* Fright Night. *The Tarnhelm Effect is from Randall Garrett's Lord Darcy books, which take place in an alternate universe where Richard the Lionheart did not die in the year 1199 and magic has supplanted science. Obviously, the Tarnhelm Effect exists in both Lord Darcy's universe and the CU. Dresden is Harry Dresden, the protagonist of Jim Butcher's* The Dresden Files *series of novels, while Blake is Laurell K. Hamilton's vampire hunter Anita Blake. Like the Felix Castor novels, the Anita Blake novels take place in an alternate universe where the general public is aware of the existence of the supernatural. Therefore, the Anita Blake mentioned in Gustainis' Morris and Chastain Supernatural Investigations novels must be the CU counterpart of Hamilton's character. Although this novella supposedly takes place shortly after the last entry in the series,* Play with Fire, *Gustainis must have compressed the timeline of events.* Play with Fire *begins shortly after the novel preceding it,* Sympathy for the Devil, *which ends the day after Inauguration Day. The last Inauguration Day before the publication of* Sympathy for the Devil *was January 20, 2009. The inspiration for the terrorists' actions in* Midnight at the Oasis *is the death of Osama bin Laden, which occurred on May 2, 2011.*

May 7
SCIENCE FAIR
Atomic Robo and his team drive the A-Team's van, which is later stolen by Robo's foe Dr. Dinosaur.
Story by Brian Clevinger and Scott Wegener in Atomic Robo/Foster Broussard/Moon Girl Free Comic Book Day 2011, *Red 5 Comics, May 2011.*

June 30–July 12
BLOODLINE
Ex-Navy SEAL Jack Kirkland appears.
A Sigma Force novel by James Rollins. Kirkland first appeared in Rollins' non-series novel Deep Fathom.

Summer
FINAL
The TV show *Hoax Hunters* is mentioned, as is a puzzle-obsessed cult led by a self-help guru, and the *Necronomicon Ex Mortis* appears.
Hack/Slash *#20-25 by Tim Seeley and Elena Casegrande, Image Comics, 2012–2013.* Hoax Hunters *is from the comic of the same name by Michael Moreci and Steve Seeley, while the self-help guru is the title character of Mike Norton and Dennis Hopeless' comic* The Answer! *The* Necronomicon *is from the* Evil Dead *films, and its appearance here leads into the miniseries* Army of Darkness vs. Hack/Slash.

DARK SHADOWS/VAMPIRELLA

Barnabas and Quentin Collins team up with Vampirella and Pantha to battle Lady Elizabeth Bathory and her minion, who is allegedly Jack the Ripper. Vampi and Barnabas receive some last-minute assistance from Dracula.

Five-issue miniseries by Marc Andreyko, Patrick Berkenkotter, and Jose Malaga, Dynamite Entertainment, August–December 2012. This crossover confirms the Collinses, Vampirella, Pantha, and Dracula coexist within the CU. Elizabeth Bathory has made several other appearances in the CU as a vampire. Since the Ripper killings are known to have been committed by the Redjac entity, the supposed Jack the Ripper serving Elizabeth must be a copycat.

INQUISITION

Dracula's former minion Le Fanu recruits Vampirella's former partner Sofia Murray, now possessed, to do battle with Dracula himself.

Vampirella ongoing series #21–23 by Brandon Jerwa and Heubert Khan Michael, Dynamite Entertainment, 2012.

HELL ON EARTH

The Parliament of Demons seeks to give Dracula the power belonging to the god Chaos. The Parliament allows Dracula to use its forces, including the vampire Orlok, to attack Earth. The Conjuress sends her agents, including Vampirella and Pantha, to battle Dracula and company.

Vampirella #24–25 by Brandon Jerwa and Heubert Khan Michael and Pantha #5 by Brandon Jerwa and Pow Rodrix, Dynamite Entertainment, 2012. The Dracula seen here is a "soul-clone" of Bram Stoker's vampire. Orlok is from the classic silent horror film Nosferatu, *and was last seen in the miniseries* The Darkness vs. Eva: Daughter of Dracula, *where he was seemingly killed by Eva, whose father is another of the true Dracula's soul-clones. Given that he also died in the original film, which was set in 1838, Orlok must have been resurrected at least twice: once after his 1838 death via exposure to sunlight, and again after his death at Eva's hands in 2007.*

DICK TRACY MEETS GASOLINE ALLEY PART 2

Walt Wallet wins the Sunny Wheat Vitamin Flintheart look-alike contest, despite looking nothing like Vitamin. Vitamin's friend Dick Tracy reveals Walt helped him many years ago on a case, during which Walt discovered a baby girl who would become his adopted daughter Judy.

Dick Tracy *strip by Mike Curtis and Joe Staton, November 11–17, 2012. Walt Wallet is from the comic strip* Gasoline Alley. *Dick himself appeared in the latter strip in 2001 and 2011. Walt and Dick's first meeting is stated to have taken place in the spring. The strip where Walt discovered Judy was published on February 28, 1935. Most likely, Walt's meeting with Dick and adoption of Judy happened in the spring of 1934.*

BROADWAY BATES STRIKES AGAIN

Dick Tracy's old foe Broadway Bates tells his brother Oswald he is leaving the latter's hometown for his own city, "Where cops don't wear masks and capes . . . and that blasted signal isn't in the sky!" Broadway's girlfriend Belle tells him back in Oswald's city, her friend Harley dressed up to help her boss, Mr. J.

Dick Tracy *strip by Mike Curtis and Joe Staton, November 17–18, 2012. Although "Oswald" is only shown in silhouette, he is clearly meant to be Oswald Cobblepot, aka the Penguin, one of Batman's greatest foes. It is worth noting that during Broadway Bates' original 1932 appearance in* the Dick Tracy strip, *the miscreant's name was rendered in quote marks, suggesting it may have been an alias. Therefore, Broadway's true surname is likely Cobblepot. Broadway and the Penguin are virtually identical in appearance, although Oswald prefers a top hat to Broadway's bowler. Belle's friend is Harley Quinn, the Joker's henchgirl.*

THE ONES YOU LOVE

Warehouse 13 Director Mrs. Frederic and Gatherer Steve Jinks visit "The Library," a secret room in the Vatican, where they find a pack of Morley Cigarettes that was left behind four months ago.

Episode of Warehouse 13 *broadcast September 24, 2012. Morley Cigarettes have appeared in a number of TV shows and movies, and are best known as the Cigarette Smoking Man's brand of choice on* The X-Files. *Their appearance here reinforces* Warehouse 13 *'s inclusion in the CU.*

MR. BLANK

A man with many identities works for all of the various conspiracies and secret societies (and a few monsters) in Los Angeles. As a result of his work, he can find Symbionia, Thule, Shangri-La, and the entrance to the Hollow Earth on a map. The Elder Gods are mentioned, and our nameless hero mentions rumors of a Gill-Man in Reseda, though it turned out to be a mechanic with a skin condition.

Novel by Justin Robinson. Thule is a region in the far north in European folklore. Shangri-La is from James Hilton's novel Lost Horizon. *The Hollow Earth theory has been adapted in a number of works of fiction, including Edgar Rice Burroughs' series set at the Earth's core. The Elder Gods were created by August Derleth as part of Lovecraft's Cthulhu Mythos, and are inimical to the Great Old Ones. This false Gill-Man is pretending to be a member of the species seen in the film* Creature from the Black Lagoon *and its sequels.*

BORDER OFFENSIVE

Mack Bolan battles a group of "coyotes" smuggling people across the border between the United States and Mexico. An Interpol agent named Eugene Chantecoq appears.

The Executioner *#408 by Joshua Reynolds. Eugene Chantecoq may be related to Chantecoq, "the King of Detectives," from novels by Arthur Bernède, as well as the film serial* Belphégor. *This seems very likely, since Reynolds features Bernède's Chantecoq in his story "The Carolingian Stone."*

August
FINAL NIGHT

P.I. and monster hunter Cal McDonald battles vampires under the command of former Barrow, Alaska sheriff turned *nosferatu* Eben Olemaun, who seeks to resurrect his wife Stella. Cal has a framed picture of himself and the Goon in his house.

Criminal Macabre: Final Night—The 30 Days of Night Crossover *#1–4 by Steve Niles and Christopher Mitten, Dark Horse Comics, December 2012–March 2013. Both Niles' supernatural detective comic series* Criminal Macabre *and his vampire series* 30 Days of Night *have valid independent connections to the CU, and this crossover confirms both series take place in the same universe. The Goon is the title character of a comic book series written and illustrated by Eric Powell. The Goon previously met Cal in a one-shot by Niles, Powell, and Mitten. The picture was likely taken shortly after that story, which concluded with Cal and the Goon encountering Hellboy. Cal and Hellboy presumably returned to the CU from the Goon's universe soon after that.*

Late October–October 31
BLIND SHADOWS

In Wellman, Georgia, Sheriff Carl Price and private investigator Wade Griffin, join forces to avenge the death of a mutual friend, and ultimately find the murder had supernatural connections. Price and Griffin receive aid from Carter Decamp, who owns a silver-edged blade etched with Latin words, which once belonged to an old family friend, a judge from North Carolina. Another ally of theirs, Andy Hunter, calls an occult expert named Jonathan Crowley seeking help in identifying the charms on a necklace. Decamp was given a first edition of *Malleus Maleficarum* as a gift by his friend Adam. He also owns the bound manuscript for an unpublished book on demons written by a doctor named Trowbridge. The death of Griffin and Price's friend was orchestrated by the Blackbourne family, who are attempting to bring Shub Niggurath into this universe.

Novel by James A. Moore and Charles R. Rutledge, Arcane Wisdom Press, 2012. The judge is Manly Wade Wellman's occult detective Judge Keith Hilary Pursuivant. The town of Wellman is named after the author, while Carter Decamp's name is a tribute to writers Lin Carter and L. Sprague de Camp. Jonathan Crowley is a series character in James A. Moore's fiction. Adam is Dr. Adam Spektor, from Donald F. Glut's comic book series The Occult Files of Doctor Spektor. *Dr. Samuel Trowbridge is the sidekick of Seabury Quinn's occult investigator Jules de Grandin. Shub Niggurath is one of the Great Old Ones of Lovecraft's Cthulhu Mythos.*

December 24–25
DILLON AND THE NIGHT OF THE KRAMPUS

Dillon and his friends Wyatt Hyatt and Reynard Hansen battle a Krampus in Reynolds, Alaska. Dillon receives a puppy from Hoover, a man he met years ago. Dillon once sought out a man named Jim Anthony in New York to learn certain specialized knowledge from him. Professor Ursula Van Houghton, who teaches at Grand Lakes University, has been hired by the people of Reynolds to help them deal with the Krampus and recover their stolen children. Dillon took some courses in archaeology and cultural anthropology at the University of Northeastern California under Professor Sydney Fox.

Short story by Derrick Ferguson in PulpWork Christmas Special 2014, *PulpWork Press. Hoover is Alaska Jim Hoover from the German pulp magazine* Alaska Jim, Ein Held der Kanadischen Polizei. *Jim Anthony appeared in the American pulp* Super Detective. *Dillon first met Alaska Jim and Jim Anthony in the novel* The Vril Agenda, *coauthored by Ferguson and Josh Reynolds. Grand Lakes University is from the movie* Back to School. *The University of Northeastern California is from the sitcom* Undeclared. *Professor Sydney Fox is from the television series* Relic Hunter.

2012

Winter
THE IDES OF MARS
Martin Mystère finds himself in a holographic representation of Mars, where he is greeted by Colonel Bozzo and the Marchef. Bozzo is the head of the criminal organization once called the Brotherhood of Mercy or the Black Coats, now known as BlackSpear Holdings. Meanwhile, in Los Angeles, the Nyctalope prepares to do battle with the last survivor of the evil Martians he destroyed decades ago. Bozzo tells Martin some of the Martians' technology was acquired by Kiang-Ho of the Golden Belt, who was defeated by Rama Rundjee, alias Doctor Mystère, after whom Martin was named. He also says Jean de La Hire was the Nyctalope's biographer, just as Watson was Holmes,' Ponson du Terrail was Rocambole's, Burroughs was Greystoke's, and Féval was Bozzo's own. Bozzo knew Martin's ancestor Remy d'Arx very well.

Short story by Jean-Marc Lofficier in Night of the Nyctalope, *Jean-Marc and Randy Lofficier, eds., Black Coat Press, 2012; reprinted in French in* La Nuit du Nyctalope, *Jean-Marc and Randy Lofficier, eds., Rivière Blanche, 2012. Martin Mystère's exploits have been portrayed in comics by Alfredo Castelli. Colonel Bozzo (aka Colonel Bozzo-Corona), the Marchef, the Black Coats, and Remy d'Arx appear in a series of novels by Paul Féval. BlackSpear Holdings, the present-day incarnation of the Black Coats, also appears in Castelli and Lofficier's graphic novel* The Treasure of the Veste Nere *and Lofficier's novel* The Katrina Protocol. *The Nyctalope was the hero of French pulp stories by Jean de La Hire. Kiang-Ho of the Golden Belt is the archenemy of Philip Reade's dime novel boy inventor (or "Edisonade") Tom Edison Jr. Doctor Mystère's adventures were recounted by Paul d'Ivoi; Castelli has established the Doctor's adopted son Cigale is Martin Mystère's great-great-grandfather.*

PROPHECY
Kulan Gath travels to the 21st Century, planning to use a mystic dagger to bring about the end of the world prophesied by the Mayans. Red Sonja is also brought forwards in time, and teams with Dracula, Vampirella, Pantha,

Dr. Herbert West, Eva, Athena, and Ash Williams to defeat Gath. In a series of flashbacks to 1890, Sherlock Holmes and Dr. Watson team up with Allan Quatermain to battle Dorian Gray, who possesses the same dagger wielded by Gath. As Sonja is thrown forwards and later backwards through the timestream, Indiana Jones, the Three Musketeers, Quasimodo, the Phantom, Jungle Girl, Flash Gordon, the Green Hornet and Kato, the Lone Ranger and Zorro, a group of superheroes, and Evil Ernie can be seen.

Seven-issue miniseries by Ron Marz and Walter Geovani, Dynamite Entertainment, 2012–2013. This story confirms Red Sonja, Kulan Gath, Dracula, Vampirella, Pantha, Dr. West, Eva, Ash Williams, Holmes and Watson, Allan Quatermain, Dorian Gray, Indiana Jones, the Musketeers, Quasimodo, and the Phantom coexist in the CU. This crossover also brings in Dynamite Entertainment's version of the Greek goddess Athena. The Dracula seen here is a "soul-clone" who has encountered Vampirella many times. Given that he does not recognize Eva, who claims to be his daughter, or Ash, who previously ran into Eva and her father, it is likely Eva's father was a different soul-clone. This version of Herbert West has previously encountered Ash. I. Ronald Schablotski has theorized this Herbert is the grandson of the title character of H. P. Lovecraft's "Herbert West—Reanimator." Quatermain's physical appearance and explanation for faking his death some years before are both consistent with The League of Extraordinary Gentlemen. Jungle Girl is from Frank Cho's comic book of the same name. Also seen during Sonja's trips through time are: the versions of Flash Gordon seen in the Dynamite series Flash Gordon: Zeitgeist, *a reimagining of Flash's origins; Dynamite's modern versions of the Green Hornet and Kato, which do not fit into CU continuity; the Lone Ranger appearing alongside Zorro, a reference to the Dynamite miniseries* The Lone Ranger: The Death of Zorro, *also incompatible with CU continuity; the heroes of* Project Superpowers, *a revival of many superheroes from the Golden Age of comics who have fallen into the public domain, set in the present day; and Evil Ernie, whose stories take place in a world devastated by nuclear war. Sonja must be glimpsing alternate timelines as well as the CU during her travels.*

ARMY OF DARKNESS VS. HACK/SLASH

Cassie Hack is called out of retirement by Ash Williams when the remnants of the Black Lamp Society begin selling pages from the *Necronomicon Ex Mortis*. As Cassie and Ash are thrown through time by the *Necronomicon*, they pass Nightmare and Sleepy battling the Claw alongside 'Devil in the 1940s.

Six-issue miniseries by Tim Seeley and Daniel Leister, Dynamite Entertainment, 2013–2014. Nightmare and Sleepy appeared in Clue Comics, *published by Hillman. The Claw was a villain featured in the Lev Gleason title* Silver Streak Comics. *'Devil is Bart Hill, aka Daredevil, one of several heroes who fought the Claw. The shortening of his codename is done in deference to Marvel Comics' long-standing use of the name Daredevil for one of their own heroes. The abbreviated name is also used in the Dynamite series* Project Superpowers, *which does not fit into CU continuity. Nightmare and Sleepy appeared in a flashback in the* Hack/Slash *storyline "Super Sidekick Sleepover Slaughter," and Daredevil was shown in a symbolic image in that story.*

FORGET ME NOT

The Red Queen considers sending a sarlacc to kill Alice.

Episode of the television series Once Upon a Time in Wonderland, *a spin-off of* Once Upon a Time, *broadcast October 24, 2013. The versions of Wonderland and its citizens seen in this series must be some kind of counterparts to the versions seen in Lewis Carroll's books. Furthermore, the Alice seen in the series is clearly not the Alice Liddell of Carroll's books, though she probably is a native of the CU. The sarlacc is a creature from the film* Star Wars: Episode VI–Return of the Jedi.

DICK TRACY VS. THE JUMBLER

Dick Tracy battles a criminal called the Jumbler, who has modeled himself on the comic strip/word puzzle *The Jumble*. One of the Jumbler's schemes is to steal a collection of old comic books found in the walls of a pharmacy, including an issue of *Starbuck Jones*.

Dick Tracy *strip by Mike Curtis and Joe Staton, March 24, 2013. Starbuck Jones is a comic book from Tom Batiuk's strip* Funky Winkerbean. *This crossover also brings in* Funky Winkerbean*'s spin-off strip,* Crankshaft.

BLACK MASK, BIG CITY

The female vigilante known as the Pulptress battles a gang attempting to kidnap a scientist, and winds up receiving some assistance from Dillon, one of her former teachers.

Short story by Tommy Hancock in The Pulptress, *David White, ed., Pro Se Press, 2012. The Pulptress and Dillon are both already in the CU.*

BUTCHER'S FESTIVAL

The Pulptress works with the undead adventurer Brother Bones to defeat mobster Pete Malone and his brother Arnold, nicknamed "the Butcher."

Short story by Ron Fortier in The Pulptress, *David White, ed., Pro Se Press, 2012; reprinted in* Brother Bones: Tapestry of Blood, *Ron Fortier, ed., Airship 27 Productions, 2014. Brother Bones was created by Fortier, and is in the CU through a reference in Andrew Salmon's Dan Fowler story "The League of Dead Patriots."*

THE BONE QUEEN

The Pulptress encounters the Bone Queen,

Short story by Andrea Judy in The Pulptress, *David White, ed., Pro Se Press, 2012. Judy also wrote a novel, also called* The Bone Queen, *which was published by Pro Se in 2013, and gives the Bone Queen's history.*

Late February
SKIN GAME

A monster locked up under Demonreach uses the word "fthagn." Drakul is listed as one of the supernatural beings who keep a vault in Gentleman Johnny Marcone's mob bank.

A Dresden Files novel by Jim Butcher, 2014. "Fthagn" (or rather "fhtagn") is a R'lyehian word from the Cthulhu Mythos. Drakul is better known as Dracula.

Spring
VAMPIRELLA: NUBLOOD

Vampirella and her partner Criswell visit the town of Mal Navet, Louisiana, where vampires and werewolves live openly, only to find humans are being drained in order to make the vampire-oriented beverage Nublood.

One-shot by Mark Rahner and Cezar Razek, Dynamite Entertainment, 2013. Mal Navet and its natives are based on the town of Bon Temps and its inhabitants from the television series True Blood, *which in turn was based on Charlaine Harris'* The Southern Vampire Mysteries *series of novels. Both the books and the show take place* in a world where the existence of vampires and other supernatural beings is publicly known, which does not fit with CU continuity. Neither does the one-shot fit with the continuity of the books and show. There is no indication the general public is aware of the vampires in Mal Navet in Nublood. The town is probably located in a pocket universe accessible from the CU, and is the CU's equivalent of Bon Temps.

MACHETE KILLS
A Mexican bar sells Cerveza Chango beer. Desdemona uses the "crotch gun."

Feature film directed by Robert Rodriguez. Cerveza Chango beer and the "crotch gun" previously appeared in both Desperado *and* From Dusk Till Dawn.

THE RETURN OF MOON MAID
Dick Tracy calls Oliver Warbucks to verify whether Dr. Sail worked on Warbucks' Lazarus Project. Warbucks denies it, and tells Tracy if the expedition he, Punjab, and the Asp are going on fails, he may call on Dick to help him find Annie.

Dick Tracy *strip by Mike Curtis and Joe Staton, June 14–16, 2013. Oliver "Daddy" Warbucks, his adopted daughter Annie, and his employees Punjab and the Asp are from the comic strip* Little Orphan Annie, *originally written and illustrated by Harold Gray, which ended in 2010 with Annie as the captive of a terrorist called "the Butcher of the Balkans."*

BLOOD COMMUNION
Private investigator Harry D'Amour joins forces with the Female Cenobite to prevent Pinhead from remaking the world in his own twisted image.

Clive Barker's Hellraiser *#17-20 by Clive Barker, Marcio Henrique, Janusz Ordon, Giovanni P. Timpano, Jesus Hervas, and Tom Garcia, Boom! Studios, August–November 2012. This crossover links Barker's P.I. Harry D'Amour to the Cenobite Pinhead from Barker's story "The Hellbound Heart," as well as the film* Hellraiser *and its sequels. In Justin Gustainis' novella* Midnight at the Oasis, *Barry Love, a disguised version of Harry D'Amour, refers to an upcoming encounter with Pinhead. Therefore, I have placed this story sometime after D'Amour's appearance in Gustainis' story.*

MOTEL CALIFORNIA
In a flashback to March 5, 1977, werewolf hunter Alexander Argent checks into the Motel Glen Capri in Fairvale, California.

Episode of the television series Teen Wolf *broadcast July 8, 2013. Fairvale, California is the setting of Robert Bloch's novel* Psycho, *which was* brought into the CU by references in Christopher Farnsworth's novel Red, White and Blood *and "Fugue," an episode of the television series* Endeavour. *Therefore, this crossover brings* Teen Wolf *(which is inspired by, but not a remake of, the 1985 film of the same name) into the CU.*

THE OVERLOOKED

Nurse Melissa McCall says Hill Valley, the next town over from Beacon Hills, has been flooded.

Episode of Teen Wolf *broadcast August 5, 2013. Hill Valley, California is the setting of the film* Back to the Future. Teen Wolf *is inspired by, but not a remake of, the movie of the same name starring Michael J. Fox, who also played Marty McFly in* Back to the Future *and its two sequels, as Scott Howard. Since the* Back to the Future *series takes place in the CU, this reference provides further evidence the TV version of* Teen Wolf *does as well.*

COUNTDOWN

Duke Crocker says Dwight Hendrickson is in Cleaves Mills cleaning up a mess.

Episode of Haven *broadcast October 18, 2013. Cleaves Mills is from Stephen King's novel* The Dead Zone.

May–October
NOS4A2

Charlie Manx is a supernaturally-empowered revenant who kidnaps children and takes them to "Christmasland," a world he created and shaped with his mind, until he makes the mistake of going after an escaped former victim, Victoria McQueen, who has similar powers. Victoria's neighbor Sigmund de Zoet is murdered by Manx's servant the Gas Man while listening to the Berlin Orchestra's performance of Frobisher's sextet *Cloud Atlas*. Charlie knows of places like "the doors to Mid-World, or the old trail to the Treehouse of the Mind." Shawshank Prison is mentioned. The map of Manx's "United Inscapes of America" shows the Treehouse of the Mind, the Lovecraft Keyhole near Boston, and the Pennywise Circus in Maine, near the Lewiston/Auburn/Derry area. Manx is also familiar with other "special" folks, such as Craddock McDermott and the True Knot.

Novel by Joe Hill. The musical sextet Cloud Atlas, *composed by Robert Frobisher, is from David Mitchell's novel of the same name, while Sigmund de Zoet is a descendant of the title character of Mitchell's* The Thousand Autumns of Jacob de Zoet. *The doors to Mid-World are a feature of Stephen King's Dark Tower series. The Treehouse of the Mind is from Hill's novel* Horns. *Shawshank is a recurring element of King's works, most especially* "Rita Hayworth and Shawshank Redemption." *The Lovecraft Keyhole is a reference to Hill's comic book series* Locke & Key, *which takes place in Keyhouse, in the town of Lovecraft, Massachusetts. Derry, Maine, is also from King's works, and is the setting of such novels as* It *(which features the villain Pennywise the Clown) and* Insomnia. *Craddock McDermott is the villain of Hill's novel* Heart-Shaped Box. *The True Knot are the antagonists of King's* Doctor Sleep. *The comic book miniseries* Wraith: Welcome to Christmasland *is a prequel to this novel.*

Summer. Remo Williams' children, Winston "Stone" Smith and Freya, begin having adventures. (*Legacy* #1: *Forgotten Son* by Warren Murphy and Gerald Welch, Destroyer Books, 2012).

Summer
THE DEEP: HERE BE DRAGONS
The Nekton family travels the world in their advanced submarine the *Aronnax.*

Graphic novel by Tom Taylor and James Brouwer, Gestalt Publishing, 2013. The submarine is named for Professor Pierre Aronnax from Jules Verne's 20,000 Leagues Under the Sea. *The sequel is* The Deep Vol. 2: The Vanishing Island.

SUSPECT
L.A. cop Scott James joins the Metro K-9 Unit and is paired with a former bomb-sniffing dog named Maggie, who like himself suffers from post-traumatic stress disorder. Together, they investigate the death of Scott's partner. John Chen appears.

Novel by Robert Crais. John Chen also appears in Crais' Elvis Cole novels, as well as the Joe Pike series and the non-series novel Demolition Angel.

THE PHANTOM AND MANDRAKE
The Phantom and Mandrake do battle with Mandrake's brother Luciphor and a man with psychic powers called Mind Switch.

The Phantom *Sunday strip by Tony DePaul and Terry Beatty, April 21– November 24, 2013.*

SEE NO EVIL

Audrey Parker, whose original personality has come out of dormancy, searches for "Thinnys," weak spots in reality, in order to find the mysterious William.

Episode of Haven *broadcast September 11, 2014. Thinnys are from Stephen King's* Dark Tower *series, reinforcing the Territories and Mid-World as alternate realities to the Crossover Universe.*

Late August
CONGREGATIONS OF THE DEAD

Sheriff Carl Price and Wade Griffin battle the Reverend Lazarus Cotton and his congregation of vampires. Price and Griffin's ally Andy Hunter refers to an old colleague of his named Crowley. Another ally, Carter Decamp, reminds Griffin he said the Great Old Ones only have limited power on Earth because our reality is naturally resistant to supernatural forces. Griffin's girlfriend Charon recognizes copies of *Unspeakable Cults* and the *Ruthvenian* in Decamp's personal library of occult texts. Decamp says he only knows of two other surviving copies of the *Ruthvenian*, a book of lore and spells dealing with vampires, both of which are in the possession of a colleague of his. Charon remarks she thought the *Ruthvenian* was a myth like Alhazred's *Necronomicon*, but Decamp indicates the *Necronomicon* may not be mythical. Charon notes Pursuivant's *Vampiricon* suggests garlic as a means of repelling vampires.

Novel by James A. Moore and Charles R. Rutledge, Arcane Wisdom Press, 2014. Jonathan Crowley is a recurring character in Moore's fiction. The Great Old Ones are at the center of H. P. Lovecraft's Cthulhu Mythos; Price and Griffin battled one of the Old Ones, Shub Niggurath, in their first appearance, Blind Shadows. *The* Necronomicon, *penned by Abdul Alhazred, also plays a prominent role in the Mythos. Friedrich von Juntz's* Unspeakable Cults *(or* Unaussprechlichen Kulten*) is a Cthulhu Mythos tome created by Robert E. Howard. The* Ruthvenian *is a recurring book in the interconnected fiction of Donald F. Glut. Decamp's colleague who owns the other two surviving copies of the book is Dr. Adam Spektor, from Glut's comic book series* The Occult Files of Doctor Spektor. *The* Vampiricon, *authored by Manly Wade Wellman's occult detective Judge Keith Hilary Pursuivant, is mentioned in the Pursuivant stories.*

September 20–October 30
RED, WHITE AND BLOOD

Nathaniel Cade and Zach Barrows attempt to prevent the parasitic creature known as the Boogeyman from murdering the president. Among the items in Cade's trophy room are the leg of a cockroach roughly the same size as a human arm, hung on the wall with a plaque reading *Operative Samsa,*

W. Berlin, 1948; a gallon jar filled with formaldehyde holding an insect claw labeled *Delambre Remains, 1958*; and the dried-out husk of a six-foot-tall praying mantis marked *Judas Breed, Adult Stage, New York, 1997*. The Whateley farm appears in a flashback to 1890, which also mentions Crowley's conjuring of a moonchild, the bloody proof of which is all over Whitechapel. Among the places where the Boogeyman is reported or confirmed to have been encountered are Fairvale, CA; Camp Crystal Lake, NJ; and Springwood, IL.

Novel by Christopher Farnsworth, Putnam Adult, 2012. The cockroach leg comes from Gregor Samsa, the protagonist of Franz Kafka's novella "The Metamorphosis," who transformed into a human-sized insect while sleeping. Andre Delambre is the scientist who finds his atoms mixed with those of a fly in a teleporter accident in the 1958 film The Fly, *based on George Langelaan's short story of the same name. The Judas Breed of insect is from the film* Mimic, *based on Donald A. Wollheim's story. The Whateley Farm is from H. P. Lovecraft's "The Dunwich Horror." The Moonchild is from the novel of the same name by Aleister Crowley. The Moonchild conjured by Crowley is implied to have been Jack the Ripper. However, he was only thirteen-years-old when the Ripper murders took place. Perhaps the adult Crowley traveled back in time to 1888 via supernatural means. The Ripper killings were committed by the entity Redjac, whose origins are unknown, so it may indeed have been created by Crowley. Fairvale, CA is from Robert Bloch's novel* Psycho, *as well as the film adaptation by Alfred Hitchcock. Camp Crystal Lake, NJ is from the* Friday the 13th *film series, while Springwood, IL is from the* Nightmare on Elm Street *films. The implication is the Boogeyman influenced Norman Bates, Jason Voorhees, and Freddy Krueger, at least during their initial killings.*

October 31
VAMPIRELLA HALLOWEEN SPECIAL 2013

Vampirella, Dracula, and Eva join forces to battle a coven of witches seeking to resurrect an Elder God. Eva learned about the witches' plans via a prophecy in a copy of the *Necronomicon*.

One-shot by Shannon Eric Denton and Dietrich Smith, Dynamite Entertainment, 2013. The Dracula seen here is a "soul-clone" of Bram Stoker's Dracula, and has encountered Vampi many times before. Eva, Daughter of Dracula, has previously encountered the likes of Ash Williams, the Darkness, and slasher hunters Cassie Hack and Vlad. Vampi, Eva, and Dracula first joined forces in the miniseries Prophecy. *In both stories, Dracula denied being Eva's father. Most likely, she was fathered by a different soul-clone than Vampi's old foe. The* Necronomicon, *written by Abdul Alhazred, recurs throughout the Cthulhu Mythos of H. P. Lovecraft.*

Autumn
THE RESURRECTION OF ABNER KADAVER

A woman claiming to work for the Emilio Lizardo Crematorium appears at the State Prison to collect Abner Kadaver's body. Dick Tracy and his wife Tess take some time off to go fishing. A boat with the name "Swee'pea" on it is seen. Tess is offered a cup of coffee by a woman named Olive, who says Dick is out fishing with Olive's own husband at the dock. We see Dick with a man with a large forearm that has a tattoo of an anchor on it, who is holding a can of spinach. Olive and Tess discuss what first attracted them to their respective husbands, namely their chins. As they return home, the Tracys' son Joe refers to both Olive's husband and Dick being ex-Navy. Dick smokes a corn cob pipe and says, "I yam what I yam!" Dick's granddaughter Honeymoon tells him she is going to a Hong Kong Cavaliers concert on Sunday night, and she hopes to get an autograph from Perfect Tommy.

Dick Tracy *strip by Mike Curtis and Joe Staton, October 22, 2013– January 4, 2014. The crematorium, mentioned in the October 22 strip, is named after Dr. Emilio Lizardo from the film* The Adventures of Buckaroo Banzai Across the Eighth Dimension. *The couple who are also vacationing is Popeye and Oliver Oyl from E. C. Segar's classic comic strip* Thimble Theatre. *Swee'pea is the name of Popeye's adopted son. The boat appears in the October 27, 2013 strip, and Popeye and Olive first show up on October 28. The leader of the Hong Kong Cavaliers, who were mentioned in the strip on November 7, 2013, is Buckaroo Banzai himself. Perfect Tommy is the Cavaliers' rhythm guitarist, and also designed the suspension system on Buckaroo's Jet Car.*

CLIP SHOW

Sam and Dean Winchester are looking over some files in the Men of Letters bunker. Dean comments he has "Borden, Lizzie to Crane, Ichabod."

Episode of the television series Supernatural *broadcast May 8, 2013. Ichabod Crane (from Washington Irving's "The Legend of Sleepy Hollow") is treated as a real person, providing further proof the Winchester brothers are in the CU.*

December
MAYDAY

Natalia Kassle, a former traitor to the DangerGirl organization once believed dead, has been restored to health by April Mayday, who describes Natalia's history: "Moscow is where it all started for her . . . first as a Russian Intelligence officer . . . then on to become a special agent in the F.S.B . . . Federal Security Service of the Russian Federation. She became Russia's James Bond."

Four-issue miniseries by Andy Hartnell, John Royle, Jose Marzan, Jr., and Eeshwar, IDW Publishing, 2014. The comparison of Natalia to James Bond suggests the latter is a real person, further cementing DangerGirl's inclusion in the CU.

2013

Winter
INFERNAL NIGHT

Private investigator Michael Quinn and urban mercenary Repairman Jack cross paths when Jack is hired by the wealthy Jules Chastain to retrieve an ancient ring from his family mausoleum, which he is afraid to go into himself lest he suffer the wrath of Madame de Medici, the ring's previous owner.

Story by Heather Graham and F. Paul Wilson in FaceOff, *David Baldacci, ed., Simon & Schuster, 2014. Wilson's character Repairman Jack is already in the CU. This crossover brings in Graham's Michael Quinn, a private eye who works with curio shop owner Danni Cafferty in acquiring and, when necessary, destroying powerful artifacts. Madame de Medici is a recurring character of Sax Rohmer's, appearing in "The Key to the Temple of Heaven," "The Black Mandarin," and "The Treasure of Taia."*

THE BREAK-UP

Fake psychic and private investigator Shawn Spencer and his partner Burton "Gus" Guster relocate from Santa Barbara to San Francisco, although Juliet O'Hara, Head Detective and Shawn's girlfriend, tells them at a crime scene they already have a private eye that consults with the department, who is currently alphabetizing the kitchen pantry.

Series finale of the television series Psych *broadcast March 26, 2014. The San Francisco Police Department's consultant is the obsessive-compulsive Adrian Monk, from the television series* Monk. *An ancestor of Monk's was mentioned in one of Edward M. Erdelac's Merkabah Rider stories, which take place in the CU via strong ties to the Cthulhu Mythos, among many other crossover connections. Since* Monk *takes place in the CU, so does* Psych.

Spring
SLUMBER PARTY
Sam and Dean Winchester discover Dorothy Baum once traveled to Oz and fought against the Wicked Witch.

Episode of the television series Supernatural *broadcast October 29, 2013. There are multiple dimensions known as Oz; just which one this Dorothy visited is unknown.*

THE DEVIL'S BONES
In Brazil, Cotton Malone and Sigma Force's Gray Pierce join forces when the man they are both after, who has in his possession an orchid that contains a deadly neurotoxin, is captured by guerilla forces.

Story by Steve Berry and James Rollins in FaceOff, *David Baldacci, ed., Simon & Schuster, 2014. Berry's Cotton Malone series and Rollins' Sigma Force series have referenced each other in the past, but this is the first full-fledged crossover between the two series.*

IMMACULATE
Fox Mulder once again crosses paths with Frank Black, formerly of the Millennium group.

The X-Files: Season 10 *#16–17 by Joe Harris and Colin Lorimer, IDW Publishing, September–October 2014. Frank Black is from the television series* Millennium. *Some of the dangling plotlines from that show's last episode were resolved in an episode of* The X-Files *also entitled "Millennium." Frank was last seen in 2007, when he briefly encountered occult detectives Quincey Morris and Libby Chastain, as seen in Justin Gustainis' novel* Evil Ways.

IN PURSUIT OF LAMIA
Demon hunter Lucy Carnacki, the granddaughter of a ghost-finder, battles a lamia preying on a family. One of Lucy's colleagues is a Dutchman named Aaldert Van Helsing.

Short story by Lucy Carnacki, edited by Adam Millard in Blood Trails, *Miles Boothe, ed., Emby Press, 2014. Lucy Carnacki's grandfather is Thomas Carnacki, the archetypal occult detective, from William Hope*

Hodgson's Carnacki the Ghost-Finder. *Aaldert Van Helsing is a progeny of the long line of monster hunters whose most famous member is Abraham Van Helsing, from Bram Stoker's Dracula.*

WE GO BACK

Frank Martin, a professional freelance courier for hire, is tracking down an old war buddy who now works for MI6. During a conversation, Frank refers to MI6 as "the Circus."

Episode of Transporter: The Series *originally broadcast October 5, 2014. The Circus is the name used for MI6 in John le Carré's Smiley novels. Since George Smiley is in the CU, so is Frank Martin, who has appeared in three* Transporter *movies,* Transporter: The Series*, and a prequel trilogy starting with* The Transporter Refueled*. Frank Martin also had a cameo in the film* Collateral*, while the film* The Acquirer *is a spin-off starring the character of Wall Street from the first film under a new alias.*

THE ACCURSED

Vampirella battles Dr. Faustus, who has unleashed a pathogen that causes people to go on murderous rampages. Her allies include werewolf Tristan Calliet and Roderick Usher IV, who claims the story of his ancestor's demise was somewhat embellished, and his family estate still stands, though it's seen better days.

Vampirella #7-11 by Nancy A. Collins and Patrick Berkenkotter, December 2014– April 2015. Dr. Faustus is from Christopher Marlowe's play The Tragical History of the Life and Death of Doctor Faustus*. Tristan Calliet is probably a relative of Bertrand Calliet, the title character of Guy Endore's* The Werewolf of Paris*. The original Roderick Usher is from Edgar Allan Poe's story "The Fall of the House of Usher."*

BLOOD AND BONE

The Pulptress has her final battle with the Bone Queen.

Novella by Andrea Judy, Pro Se Press, 2015. The Pulptress first battled the Bone Queen in Judy's story "The Bone Queen," which is described here as having taken place nearly a year ago. Judy elaborated upon the undead Bone Queen's origins in a novel also entitled The Bone Queen.

Summer

DICK TRACY VS. SILVER NITRATE

Vitamin Flintheart is co-starring with Mary Perkins in a production at the Patterson Playhouse. Dick Tracy tells Silver Nitrate a criminal named Miles Mycroft was involved in a lost film swindle in Metropolis. Nitrate says Mycroft tried to sell him and his sister Sprocket some films in Opal City, but the deal was too shady. Sprocket tells Tracy they have a table at an old-time film convention in Star City.

Dick Tracy *strip by Mike Curtis and Joe Staton, January 5–March 19, 2014. Mary Perkins is from Leonard Starr's comic strip* Mary Perkins, On Stage *(originally titled simply* On Stage*). She first appears in the strip on January 5. The city of Metropolis is Superman's base of operations, while Opal City is the hometown of Starman, another DC Comics hero. Metropolis and Opal are mentioned in the January 10 strip. Star City, the home of a third DC hero, Green Arrow, is mentioned in the February 11 strip.*

J. STRAIGHTEDGE TRUSTWORTHY

Dick Tracy's old annoyance Vera Alldid creates a comic strip parodying the detective. Meanwhile, Daddy Warbucks tells Punjab and the Asp he is going to ask Tracy to help him find his missing adopted daughter Annie. The *J. Straightedge Trustyworthy* comic strip is picked up as an animated series by Kolossal Pictures, run by Mr. Kolossal. Outside of the Wilcox Downs racetrack, a man sells Tootsie Frootsie ice cream. Sparkle Plenty and Gravel Gertie sing Ricky Ricardo's "There's a Brand-New Baby at Our House" on the radio.

Dick Tracy *strip by Mike Curtis and Joe Staton, March 23–May 31, 2014. Daddy Warbucks, Punjab, the Asp, and Annie are from the comic strip* Little Orphan Annie, *originally by Harold Gray, which ended in 2010 with Annie in the clutches of a terrorist, "the Butcher of the Balkans." Punjab and the Asp first appear in the March 26 strip and Warbucks on March 27. Mr. Kolossal appeared in a 1935* Little Orphan Annie *storyline. The ice cream vendor, who appears in the April 18 strip, is an Italian who, under various aliases, is often seen in the company of a bespectacled cigar-chomping man with a mustache and an innocent mute. In 1936, he used the name Tony while selling Tootsie Frootsie ice cream at a race track, as seen in the movie* A Day at the Races. *Band leader Ricky Ricardo is from the classic sitcom* I Love Lucy. *The song "There's a Brand-New Baby at Our House" was written to commemorate the birth of Ricky and his wife Lucy's son Little Ricky. The song is first mentioned in the strip on May 18.*

THE EYES OF FRANKENSTEIN

Cal McDonald and Mo'Lock assist the Frankenstein Monster once again.

Comic miniseries by Steve Niles, Christopher Mitten, and Michelle Madsen, Dark Horse Comics.

GOOD AND VALUABLE CONSIDERATION

Jack Reacher and Nick Heller watch a baseball game in a Boston pub, and wind up coming to the defense of another customer against an Armenian gangster.

Story by Lee Child and Joseph Finder in FaceOff, David Baldacci, ed., Simon & Schuster, 2014. Child's ex-military policeman and adventurer Jack Reacher is already in the CU. Therefore, this crossover brings in Finder's Special Forces intelligence investigator Nick Heller.

THE QUEST FOR ANNIE

Daddy Warbucks asks Dick Tracy to help him find his missing ward Annie. Warbucks' friend the Great Am tells Tracy he reminds him of someone he met long ago named Alley. Annie is on Thunder Island, which is filled with people who have been abducted and hypnotized into thinking they're in a small town in 1944 by Axel, an old foe of Annie and Warbucks. Among the businesses on Thunder Island is Jot 'em Downs, owned by Lum Edwards and Abner Peabody. Hotshot Charlie flies a rescue mission to the island.

FACEOFF

DENNIS LEHANE vs MICHAEL CONNELLY
IAN RANKIN vs PETER JAMES
R. L. STINE vs DOUGLAS PRESTON – LINCOLN CHILD
M. J. ROSE vs LISA GARDNER
STEVE MARTINI vs LINDA FAIRSTEIN
JEFFERY DEAVER vs JOHN SANDFORD
HEATHER GRAHAM vs F. PAUL WILSON
RAYMOND KHOURY vs LINWOOD BARCLAY
JOHN LESCROART vs T. JEFFERSON PARKER
STEVE BERRY vs JAMES ROLLINS
LEE CHILD vs JOSEPH FINDER

Edited by David Baldacci

Dick Tracy strip by Mike Curtis and Joe Staton, June 1–October 12, 2014. This story resolves the dangling plotline from the last Little Orphan Annie *strip in 2010. Alley is the titular caveman from the comic strip* Alley Oop. *Lum Edwards and Abner Peabody first appeared in the radio show* Lum and Abner, *and have also appeared in movies and a comic strip. Hotshot Charlie is from Milton Caniff's classic comic strip* Terry and the Pirates.

THE LIBRARIANS AND THE APPLE OF DISCORD

The World Crime League is named as one of the factions that sent a representative to a conclave of supernatural beings. Jenkins refers to the amendment to the Wold Newton bylaws. The O2STK is also mentioned.

Episode of The Librarians *broadcast December 28, 2014. This series is a spin-off of* The Librarian *TV movies, which are already in the CU, featuring a group of librarians following in Flynn Carsen's footsteps. The World Crime League is from the film* The Adventures of Buckaroo Banzai Across the Eighth Dimension. *The Wold Newton bylaws were probably passed at an earlier conclave, which itself might have been part of a larger conclave that happened in Wold Newton, Yorkshire on December 13, 1795, as originally revealed by Philip José Farmer in* Tarzan Alive, *and elaborated on by Win Scott Eckert in "The Wild Huntsman." The O2STK (Organization Too Secret to Know) is from the TV series* The Middleman.

THE LIBRARIANS AND THE FABLES OF DOOM

Jenkins lists fifty-seven magical and/or supernatural items that could have caused fairy tale characters to come to life in the tiny Washington village of Bremen, including the Tell Tale Heart and the Veil of Scherazade.

Episode of The Librarians *broadcast January 4, 2015. Scherazade is from* The Arabian Nights, *which is in the CU via a reference to Sinbad in a storyline of the comic strip* The Phantom. *This episode also brings in Edgar Allan Poe's story "The Tell-Tale Heart." The heart being supernatural or magical in nature would explain why it kept beating even after its owner's death and dismemberment.*

FOOL'S PARADISE

Remo Williams and Chiun team up with a masked vigilante to end the threat of the sentient computer chip Friend, which has been corrupted by the caped crusader's archenemy, a psychotic clown. Mark Howard, assistant director of CURE, tells Remo, "Thanks to the run of unique characters that regularly pass through this city, your street clothes and your blurred-out features have the newscasters crediting some faceless vigilante, with the 'man in the kimono' as his partner and sensei. Richard Salamander, Rick Dragon, something like that." There is apparently some bad blood between Chiun and this latter individual. The vigilante says more than one of the defense mechanisms in his cave headquarters were designed to contend with an out-of-control extraterrestrial, should the need ever arise.

Short story by R. J. Carter in More Blood: A Sinanju Anthology, *Donna Courtois and Devin Murphy, eds., Destroyer Books, 2014. Although the masked vigilante is not referred to by name, the story makes it abundantly clear he is the Batman. Per CU continuity, this would be the as-yet unidentified fourth Batman, whose predecessors were Bruce Wayne Sr., Dick Grayson, and Bruce Wayne Jr. His archenemy is the Joker. The faceless vigilante is another DC Comics hero, the Question (although he was originally published by Charlton Comics), while his sensei is martial arts master Richard Dragon. The extraterrestrial against whose losing control Batman is taking precautions is Superman.*

ARCTIC KILL

Mack Bolan battles the Society of Thylea, a white supremacist group dating back to World War I. The society believes in the *Vril*, and their ruling body is known as the Sun-Koh. One of their henchmen is an ex-German Special Forces officer who was nicknamed "Sturmvogel." Agent Chantecoq of Interpol also appears.

The Executioner #429 by Joshua Reynolds. The *Vril is from Edward Bulwer-Lytton's* The Coming Race. *The Sun-Koh is named after Sun Koh, a German pulp character. This Sturmvogel must have been nicknamed after the German pulp character of the same name. Chantecoq, who first appeared in Reynolds' Executioner novel* Border Offensive, *is probably a relative of Arthur Bernède's character Chantecoq, "the King of Detectives."*

VIRGIN ZOMBIE

Lt. Jacqueline "Jack" Daniels of the Chicago Police Department tracks a meth cook to Wellman, Georgia, teaming up with private eye Wade Griffin in the process. They discover the cook is using a neurotoxin to create zombies. Jack mentions her friend McGlade, who is also a P.I.

A Kindle Worlds story by Charles R. Rutledge. Wade Griffin is from Rutledge and James A. Moore's novels Blind Shadows *and* Congregations of the Dead, *both of which have several links to the CU. J. A. Konrath's cop Jack Daniels has also been linked to the CU. Private eye Harry McGlade is featured in his own series of books by Konrath. The events of* Congregations of the Dead *are referred to as having occurred "last summer."*

Mid Summer
RHYMES WITH PREY

Quadriplegic New York criminologist Lincoln Rhyme teams up with the visiting Lucas Davenport of Minnesota's Bureau of Criminal Apprehension to investigate a sadistic series of murders.

Story by Jeffery Deaver and John Sandford in FaceOff, *David Baldacci, ed., Simon & Schuster, 2014. Lucas Davenport, the main character of Sandford's* Prey *novels, is already in the CU, and this crossover brings in Deaver's detective Lincoln Rhyme.*

PIT STOP

FBI Agent Sean Reilly and contractor Glen Garber race to intercept Garber's Ford F-150, which has been stolen by a man carrying a biological agent while Garber's young daughter was still in the vehicle.

Story by Raymond Khoury and Linwood Barclay in FaceOff, *David Baldacci, ed., Simon & Schuster, 2014. Khoury's FBI Agent Sean Reilly is already in the CU. This crossover brings in Glen Garber, from Barclay's novel* The Accident.

DICK TRACY IN HOOTIN' HOLLER

Dick Tracy fills in for the sheriff of Hootin' Holler when he goes on vacation. Barney Google takes Dick to the town on his horse Sparkplug. Tracy returns to his hometown when he finds his two-way wrist radio won't work in the remote area.

Dick Tracy *strip by Mike Curtis and Joe Staton, October 19, 2014, and* Barney Google & Snuffy Smith *strip by Fred Lasswell, October 20–21, 2014. This crossover confirms Barney Google and Snuffy Smith's inclusion in the CU.*

THE RETURN OF GRUESOME

Independent filmmaker Kandikane Lane is doing a documentary about Dick Tracy's friend, actor Vitamin Flintheart. She calls her sister Margot to give her the news about Vitamin agreeing to do the film. Kandikane says, "Oh hush, Margot! I don't tease you or Lois about the men in your lives. At least Vitamin doesn't wear a cape."

Dick Tracy *strip by Mike Curtis and Joe Staton, November 8, 2014. "Margot" is a reference to a female agent of a pulp vigilate who operated from the shadows. Lois is Superman's girlfriend and later wife, Lois Lane. Philip José Farmer made the tongue-in-cheek suggestion the female agent and Lois were sisters in* Doc Savage: His Apocalyptic Life.

September
DOCTOR SLEEP

Dan Torrance, now middle-aged, helps a young girl named Abra Stone, who has the shining, battle a group of psychic vampires called the True Knot. Dan remembers Dick Hallorann mentioning a man named Charlie Manx, who steals children. There are references to Castle Rock, Harlow, Gates Falls, and *Inside View*. The True Knot have sheltered in places like Jerusalem's Lot and Sidewinder. The True Knot use a computer program called Whirl 360 to locate Abra's neighborhood. The battle with the True

Knot comes to a head outside Sidewinder, Colorado, where the Overlook Hotel once stood.

Novel by Stephen King. Dan Torrance; "the shining"; Dick Hallorann; Sidewinder, Colorado; and the Overlook Hotel are all from King's novel The Shining. *Charlie Manx is from Joe Hill's novel* NOS4A2. *Castle Rock, Harlow, Gates Falls, and Jerusalem's Lot are recurring locales in King's work. The tabloid* Inside View *appears or is mentioned in a number of King's works, such as* The Dead Zone, Insomnia, *and* Bag of Bones. *Whirl 360 is from Linwood Barclay's novel* Trust Your Eyes.

Autumn

GASLIGHTED

Aloysius Pendergast fends off Dr. William Grundman's attempts to convince him his career as an FBI Special Agent investigating bizarre cases is a delusion. Grundman tells Pendergast a ventriloquist's dummy in a lab coat called Dr. Augustine he used as part of the deception was only an image implanted in Pendergast's mind, but soon after Pendergast finds Dr. Augustine sitting in the backseat of Grundman's car.

Story by R. L. Stine and Douglas Preston and Lincoln Child, FaceOff, *David Baldacci, ed., Simon & Schuster 2014. Preston and Child's Agent Pendergast is already in the CU. The dummy referred to as "Dr. Augustine" is actually Slappy, an evil ventriloquist's dummy that can be brought to life by reading the words on a sheet of paper in his pocket, from Stine's* Goosebumps *horror books for children. This crossover brings Slappy into the CU.*

THE NEXT GENERATION

Sam Catchem shows Dick Tracy's granddaughter Honeymoon the Hanukkah present his wife gave him, a vintage Derby Dugan wallet with the original magic ten spot inside.

Dick Tracy strip by Mike Curtis and Joe Staton, January 16, 2015. Derby Dugan is the title character of a fictional comic strip seen in Tom De Haven's trilogy of novels consisting of Funny Papers, Derby Dugan's Depression Funnies, *and* Dugan Under Ground.

YEAR ZERO

Mulder and Scully hunt a were-cat who can only resume its human form by killing. Later, the two visit a diner, where their waitress asks them if they would like more coffee. Scully declines, and Mulder adds, "Although it is damn good coffee, as a friend of mine in the Pacific Northwest would say."

Five-issue miniseries by Karl Kesel, Greg Scott, and Vic Malhotra, IDW Publishing, 2014. The were-cat is a member of the race seen in Paul Schrader's 1982 remake of Jacques Tourneur's film Cat People. *Although the original film has already been included in the CU, the two versions are completely different in plot details and character names, and could conceivably be included in the same universe. Mulder's friend in the Pacific Northwest is FBI Special Agent Dale Cooper from the television series* Twin Peaks.

DICK TRACY IN WESTVIEW

Dick Tracy and Sam Catchem travel to the town of Westview to attend the auction of the collection of Golden Age comic books stolen by the Jumbler. They meet Funky Winkerbean, the owner of Montoni's Pizza, and foil a bank robbery. Later, Dick and Sam deliver the comics to the auction winners.

Dick Tracy *strip by Mike Curtis and Joe Staton, January 19–24, 2015, and* Funky Winkerbean *strip by Tom Batiuk, January 19–25, 2015.*

DAWN/VAMPIRELLA

Dawn and Vampirella are captured by a demon seeking a bride, who considers the duo the most beautiful women in the world. The ladies hold a storytelling contest to determine who will go home.

Six-issue miniseries by Joseph Michael Linsner, Dynamite Entertainment. Linsner's character Dawn is already in through a crossover with Witchblade, *but this story reinforces her place in the CU.*

December
FORSAKEN

Writer Thad McAlister and his family are menaced by a witch cult from one of Thad's books, which turns out to be real. Thad's wife Rachael bought the journal in which Thad wrote the novel at *Needful Things*, a store in Castle Rock, Maine, owned by Leland Gaunt.

The first novel in J. D. Barker's Shadow Cove Trilogy, *Hampton Creek Press*, 2014. The connection to Stephen King's novel Needful Things brings this series into the CU. Although the epilogue which shows Rachael buying the book from Gaunt is stated to have taken place ten years earlier, Gaunt was only in Castle Rock in 1991, twenty-two years before the novel's main events. At one point, Rachael reads an old e-mail dated Thursday, December 3, 2014. December 3, 2014 was a Wednesday, and also after this book's publication date, and therefore the date given for the e-mail must be considered misinformation.

2014

Winter
DARK DYNASTY

The Winchester brothers discover their foes, the Styne family, are really the Frankensteins, who changed their name after Mary Shelley wrote her book about the family.

Episode of Supernatural *broadcast May 6, 2015. This revelation adds another branch to the already-vast Frankenstein family.*

Spring
HITLER ON THE HALF-SHELL

The immortal Henry Morgan works as a Medical Examiner for the NYPD. In a flashback to 1812, Henry meets Nathaniel Hawkes at the Diogenes Club in London.

Episode of the television series Forever *broadcast February 3, 2015. In "The Adventure of the Greek Interpreter," Sherlock Holmes says that his brother Mycroft was one of the founders of the Diogenes Club. Mycroft was born in 1847, thirty-five years after Henry Morgan's encounter with Hawkes. Perhaps Mycroft named his Club after an earlier one, using it as a front for British Intelligence rather than as a regular gentleman's club like its namesake.*

A FOOTNOTE IN THE BLACK BUDGET

Joe Ledger of the Department of Military Sciences' latest mission brings him to the Mountains of Madness.

Short story by Jonathan Maberry in The Madness of Cthulhu, Volume Two, *S. T. Joshi, ed., Titan Books, 2015, connecting Maberry's Joe Ledger series to Lovecraft's "At the Mountains of Madness," and therefore to the CU.*

Spring
VAMPIRELLA, KABAL AGENT

Vampirella joins the Kabal. For her first mission, she must rescue her fellow agent Beatrice Rappaccini, who has been kidnapped by the Promethean Society, which consists of Dr. Anton Moreau, Dr. John Dee, Dr. Caligari, and Victor von Frankenstein, who seek to exchange Bea for their teammate Dr. Faustus, who has been imprisoned by the Kabal. Kabal agents Tristan and Usher assist Vampi, as does Lazarus, the Walking Dead Man, one of Victor's creations.

Vampirella Annual 2015 by Nancy A. Collins and Aneke, Dynamite Entertainment, 2015. Beatrice Rappaccini is from Nathaniel Hawthorne's story "Rappaccini's Daughter." Dr. Anton Moreau must be a descendant of H. G. Wells' Dr. Alphonse Moreau who is following in his forebear's footsteps by operating on animals to give them manlike forms. Dr. Caligari is from the classic German silent film The Cabinet of Dr. Caligari. *This Victor von Frankenstein must be one of the many relatives and/or descendants of Mary Shelley's Victor who have engaged in experiments of their own. Dr. Faustus is from Christopher Marlowe's play* The Tragical History of the Life and Death of Doctor Faustus. *Werewolf Tristan Caillet is doubtless a relative of Bertrand Caillet, the title character of Guy Endore's novel* The Werewolf of Paris. *Roderick Usher IV is descended from the original Roderick Usher, from Edgar Allan Poe's story "The Fall of the House of Usher."*

Summer
SCHRODINGER'S BLOOD

Edward Delmont comes to the Sâr Dubnotal seeking help. The occult detective reveals he is being slowly drained of blood via superposition by Alinska, a vampire in the 19th century who has a grudge against his family.

Short story by Nathan Cabaniss in The Vampire Almanac (Volume 1), *Jean-Marc and Randy Lofficier, eds., Black Coat Press, 2015; reprinted in French in* L'Almanach des Vampires (Tome 2), *Jean-Marc and Randy Lofficier, eds., Rivière Blanche, 2015. Alinska is from Etienne-Léon de Lamothe-Langon's novel* The Virgin Vampire. *Edward Delmont is descended from Edouard Delmont, Alinska's fiancé who spurned her for another woman. The Sâr Dubnotal appeared in a 1909–1910 French pulp series by an anonymous author. He has apparently aged little, if at all, since the early 20th century.*

RETURN OF THE NYCTALOPE

Leo Saint-Clair, the Nyctalope, returns to the planet Rhea, which he first visited in 1935. Leo currently works for Auguste Pichenet, the head of the French Intelligence Service. Leo's lover is Gisèle d'Holbach, his liaison to French Intelligence. Rhea is revealed to have been created by a race called the Sarvants.

This novella by Jean-Marc and Randy Lofficier in Return of the Nyctalope, *Black Coat Press, 2013, is a sequel to Jean de La Hire's original Nyctalope novel* The King of the Night; *a translation and adaptation of that novel by Brian Stableford is also included in the book. "Auguste Pichenet" is an alias frequently used by Langelot, a young spy for SNIF (Service National d'Information Fonctionnelle) featured in novels by "Lieutenant X" (Vladimir Volkoff). Apparently Langelot runs SNIF himself in the 21st century. Gisèle d'Holbach is related to Langelot's fellow SNIF agent Gersende "Aspirant Mistigri" d'Holbach. The Sarvants are from Maurice Renard's novel* The Blue Peril, *which has also been translated and adapted by Brian Stableford.*

MILLENNIUM

Frank Black is aided by Fox Mulder in his efforts to keep the Millennium Group from recruiting his daughter Jordan.

Five-issue miniseries by Joe Harris, menton3, and Colin Lorimer, IDW Publishing, January–May 2015. This series is a sequel to the television series Millennium *and* The X-Files *episode of the same name, which wrapped up some dangling plot threads from that show.*

CURSE OF THE NECRONOMICON

"Myth hunter" Elisa Hill is hired by the wealthy Sebastian Clarke to locate her former lover and partner Lucas Davalos, who has gone incommunicado while tracking down the *Necronomicon* for Clarke. Elisa refers to an acquaintance of hers whose drink of choice is Demarara rum, as well as "that Diamondback character out of Denbrook."

Novel by Percival Constantine, 2015. The Necronomicon *is a staple of Lovecraft's Cthulhu Mythos. Elisa's Demerara-drinking acquaintance is Derrick Ferguson's adventurer Dillon. Diamondback is from Ferguson's as-yet unpublished novel* Diamondback: It Seemed Like a Good Idea at the Time. *The city of Denbrook, created by Mike McGee, was the setting of serialized novels by Constantine, Ferguson and other authors for the Frontier Publishing website.*

DICK TRACY VS. MR. BIGG

Dick Tracy and Sam Catchem, investigating a shooting at one of Jimmy Choo Shooz's gambling halls, run into their old foe Doubleup. On the wall are the names of three horses and their jockeys: Sparkplug and B. (the rest of the name is obscured); the Pie and M. Taylor; and Meditation and M. Dennis. Another hall has a list of horses including "-ter Ed." Dick's grand-daughter Honeymoon is visited by her friend Annie.

Dick Tracy strip by Mike Curtis and Joe Staton. Sparkplug and his owner, Barney Google, are from the comic strip Barney Google and Snuffy Smith. *The Pie and Mi Taylor are from the movie* National Velvet. *Meditation and Mame Dennis are from the movie* Auntie Mame. *"-ter Ed" is a reference to the TV series* Mister Ed. *Surely a talking horse is not so hard to believe in a universe that contains talking dogs in the form of Ralph von Wau Wau and Scooby-Doo. The title character of* Little Orphan Annie *previously appeared in a 2014* Dick Tracy *storyline.*

October 20–28
UNDER THE DOME

The town of Chester's Mill, Maine finds itself under a dome created by aliens for a little over a week. Chester's Mill, which is southwest of Castle Rock, shares a border with the towns of Motton, Harlow, TR-90, and Tarker's Mills. Jim Rennie, Dale "Barbie" Barbara, Myra Evans, and Julia Shumway appear. Shawshank State Prison is mentioned several times, as is the town of Derry. Conspiracy theorists suggest Great Cthulhu may be behind the dome. A military policeman named Jack Reacher is mentioned.

Novel by Stephen King. Chester's Mill and Julia Shumway were first mentioned in King's story "N." The towns of Castle Rock, Motton, Harlow, fTR-90, and Derry are recurring locales in King's fiction. Tarker's Mills is from Cycle of the Werewolf. *A note written by someone called Barbie to a man named Jim appears in King's novel* Desperation. *Myra Evans first appeared in* Needful Things. *Shawshank State Prison appears in a number of King's works, notably "Rita Hayworth and Shawshank Redemption." Great Cthulhu is, of course, the most famous of the Great Old Ones created by H. P. Lovecraft. Jack Reacher is the protagonist of a series of novels by Lee*

Child, and this crossover brings him into the CU. Although this novel was first published in 2009, it takes place during Barack Obama's second term as president of the United States, and therefore between 2013 and 2016. According to King, there is a great deal of national news coverage regarding the dome, as well as a military blockade, although apart from the government no one finds out about the aliens that caused it. The nationwide knowledge of the dome's existence is probably exaggeration on King's part, although enough people outside of Chester's Mill must have learned about or heard rumors of the dome to have theories as to its origins.

Autumn

CHEF MAURICE AND A SPOT OF TRUFFLE

Chef Maurice Manchot, proprietor of the *Le Cochon Rouge* restaurant in the English village of Beakley, investigates the murder of his wild herb and mushroom supplier. The elderly Miss Fey asks Chef Maurice if he's Belgian. When Maurice replies he is French, Miss Fey remarks, "I knew a Belgian once, a little fellow. He asked a lot of questions too."

Novel by J. A. Lang, Purple Panda Press, 2015. The little Belgian fellow is Hercule Poirot, bringing Chef Maurice into the CU.

December 24–25

THE DARK SIDE OF THE ROAD

Ishmael Jones, an alien posing as a human, works for a group called the Organization, which investigates the bizarre. Ishmael's boss the Colonel invites him to his family's mansion for Christmas Eve, but when Jones gets there, the Colonel is dead. In the 1980s, Ishmael and another guest, Alexander Khan, worked for Black Heir, a group specializing in handling alien affairs. Jones remembers detonating a nuclear device in the Plateau of Leng.

Novel by Simon R. Green, Severn House Publishers, 2015. Black Heir is mentioned in two of Green's Secret Histories novels, Live and Let Drood and Property of a Lady Faire. The Plateau of Leng is from the works of H. P. Lovecraft. Both these connections place Ishmael Jones in the CU.

2155

May 22–July 25

KOBAYASHI MARU

The Vulcan V'Shar install a flux capacitor in the freighter *ECS Kobayashi Maru*.

A Star Trek: Enterprise novel by Andy Mangels and Michael A. Martin. Flux capacitors are from the Back to the Future film series. They are also mentioned in the Star Trek: The Next Generation *episode "Hollow Pursuits," the* Star Trek: Deep Space Nine *episode "What You Leave Behind," and Keith R. A. DeCandido's* Deep Space Nine *novel* Gateways Book 4: Demons of Air and Darkness, *all of which take place after this book.*

2165

January–June
UNCERTAIN LOGIC

The immortal Flint, now going by the name Willem Paul Abramson, works on a neural computer, based on what his mentor in cybernetics called "bionic plasma," though "Abramson" prefers the term "bioneural gel."

A Star Trek: Enterprise–Rise of the Federation *novel by Christopher L. Bennett, Pocket Books, 2015. Flint's mentor in cybernetics is Dr. Emil Vaslovik from* Star Trek *creator Gene Roddenberry's TV movie* The Questor Tapes. *Flint used the identity of A.I. expert Dr. Emil Vaslovik in Jeffrey Lang's* Star Trek: The Next Generation *novel* Immortal Coil, *implying he may have met the 20th century android and cyberneticist.*

2264

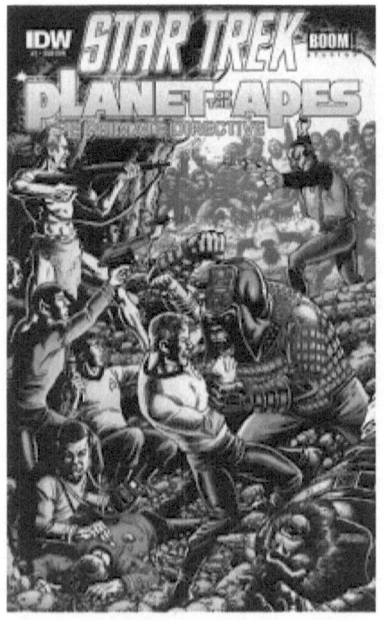

December
THE PRIMATE DIRECTIVE

The *Enterprise* crew follows Commander Kor and his men through a wormhole, ending up on an alternate Earth in the year 3878 dominated by sentient apes that have enslaved man. There, the Klingons form an alliance with the apes, while Kirk and his men befriend an astronaut named Taylor.

Five-issue miniseries by Scott Tipton, David Tipton, and Rachael Stott, BOOM! Studios and IDW Publishing, December 2014–April 2015. This story establishes the Earth on which the Planet of the Apes *films take place as an alternate reality to the CU. The story is not dated, but it takes place after the* Star Trek *episodes "Errand of Mercy" and "Mirror, Mirror," both of which occur in 2264. December 2264 is a gap in Win Scott Eckert's "The* Star Trek *Annotated*

Timeline" (found on the An Expansion of Philip José Farmer's Wold Newton Universe *website*). *In the timeline of the* Planet of the Apes *series, the appearances of Taylor and other characters from those films take place between* Planet of the Apes *and* Beneath the Planet of the Apes.

2265

HARBINGER

Cervantes Quinn uses a sonic screwdriver he stole from "a rather daft chap" on Barolia.

A Star Trek: Vanguard *novel by David Mack, Pocket Books, 2005. The "rather daft chap" is the CU version of the Doctor of* Doctor Who *fame.*

2268

STAR TREK/LEGION OF SUPER-HEROES

The crew of the starship *Enterprise* and the Legion of Super-Heroes find their worlds merged into one ruled by a tyrannical government known as the Imperial Planets. They find out the ruler of this world is the man known in the Enterprise crew's universe as Flint and in the Legion's universe as Vandal Savage. A time-traveling Q was captured by the immortal caveman, diverging and combining both timelines. Vandar the Stone, as Savage/Flint is now known shows his captives several time machines once belonging to those who tried to topple his empire.

*Six-issue miniseries by Chris Roberson and Jeffrey and Philip Moy, IDW Publishing, October 2011–March 2012. This story once again confirms the DC Universe is an alternate reality to the CU. The Legion seen here appears to be the pre-*Crisis on Infinite Earths *version of the team, at some point after the "Great Darkness Saga" storyline. The placement of this entry on the chronology reflects the Enterprise crew's point of view. The year is conjecture, but the story clearly takes place near the end of the Enterprise's five-year mission. The time machines include: Lazarus' capsule from the* Star Trek *episode "The Alternative Factor"; the Atavachron from the* Star Trek *episode "All Our Yesterdays"; Berlinghoff Rasmussen's time pod from the* Star Trek: The Next Generation *episode "A Matter of Time"; an Epoch-class timeship from the* Star Trek: Voyager *episode "Future's End"; the data disk from* Enterprise; *the Doctor and the Master's TARDISes from* Doctor Who; *the phone booth from the films* Bill & Ted's Excellent Adventure *and* Bill & Ted's Bogus Journey; *the Rocket Sled from the film* Timecop; *the DeLorean from the* Back to the Future *film series; the Cosmic Treadmill used by the DC Comics superhero the Flash; the Lazarus Pit, the source of immortality* for Batman's foe Ra's al Ghul; the *Dagger of Time* from the Prince of Persia video game series; a time bubble from the Legion of Super-Heroes stories; H. G. Wells' machine from the film Time After Time; the stopwatch from the TV series Voyagers!; the time sphere from the DC comic Rip Hunter, Time Master; and the titular conveyances from the films Hot Tub Time Machine and Stargate, H. G. Wells' The Time Machine, and the television series The Time Tunnel. *Some of these devices are known to exist in the CU, and the other ones that did not originate in DC Comics may come from the CU as well.*

2271

June
STAR TREK: THE MOTION PICTURE
"The moon Io had held some shocks for the first Earth scientists to land there, although not nearly as shattering as the earlier discovery that Earth's own moon had once served as a base for space voyagers (their identity still a mystery) who had conducted experiments with Earth's early life forms a million or more years before human history had begun."
Film novelization by Gene Roddenberry, Pocket Books, 1979. The earlier discovery is a reference to Stanley Kubrick's film 2001: A Space Odyssey.

July
THE HAUNTING OF THALLUS
A number of monsters attack the starship *Enterprise*, including Dracula. Spock cites legends Quincey Harker destroyed Dracula hundreds of years ago. The monsters are eventually revealed to have been created with a Klingon "thought-enhancer" device.
Star Trek #4–5 *by Mark Wolfman, Mike W. Barr, Dave Cockrum, and Klaus Janson, Marvel Comics, July–August 1980. This reference reinforces the place of Wolfman's Marvel series* Tomb of Dracula *in the CU. The reference to Dracula and Quincey Harker is in #4.*

2368

STAR TREK: THE NEXT GENERATION/DOCTOR WHO: ASSIMI-LATION[2]
The crew of the starship *Enterprise* teams up with a time-and-space-traveling individual from another universe named the Doctor when the Cybermen of the Doctor's world form an alliance with the Borg.

Eight-issue miniseries by Scott & David Tipton, Tony Lee, J. K. Woodward, the Sharp Brothers, and Gordon Purcell, IDW Publishing, May–December 2012. This crossover confirms once and for all most of the Doctor's exploits take place in an alternate universe to the CU, though the Doctor does have a CU counterpart in the form of Doctor Omega. At the end of this story, the Borg decide they must master time travel, foreshadowing the events of Star Trek: First Contact.

March 10, 2381–February 26, 2382

WATCHING THE CLOCK

Agent Gariff Lucsly of the Department of Temporal Investigations refers to previous temporal causality loops, including the Tigellan chronic hysteresis of Stardate 8009. Among the time travel devices in a Federation storehouse are a large, blue boxlike artifact and an ornate ancient time carriage with a large disk at its rear. Cyral Nine says agents of the Aegis such as herself "stop meddlers from tampering with history. We're not just out for general do-gooding like those damn androids." The Aegis home world is described as having silver trees and an orange sky.

A Star Trek: Department of Temporal Investigations *novel by Christopher L. Bennett, Pocket Books, 2011. The Tigellan chronic hysteresis was depicted in the* Doctor Who *serial "Meglos." Although most of the Doctor's television, novel, comic, and audio adventures take place in an alternate reality to the CU, the Doctor has been established as having a CU counterpart, and therefore some version of the events of "Meglos" must have happened there. The large blue boxlike time machine is the Doctor's TARDIS. The description of the Aegis' home world matches that of the Doctor's home planet of Gallifrey. Either the Aegis are native to the CU version of Gallifrey, or their home world is somehow connected to the Doctor's native world. The ancient time carriage with a large disk at its rear is the titular vehicle from H. G. Wells' novel* The Time Machine, *with the particular description given by Bennett being based on its appearance in George Pal's 1960 film adaptation. The do-gooding androids are a reference to the TV movie* The Questor Tapes.

353

10TH MUSE/THE LEGEND OF ISIS

The 10th Muse and her fellow goddess Isis are manipulated by a wizard on the planet Loam into battling his uncle.

Two-issue miniseries by Kenton Daniel, Benjamino Bradi, and Claudio Sepulveda, Bluewater Comics, December 2010–January 2011. The 10th Muse is in the CU through encounters in the 21st centuries with Shi and Demonslayer, among others. This crossover brings in the version of the Egyptian goddess Isis depicted in the comic book The Legend of Isis.

"The Abominable Myra Linsky Rises Again" by Chuck Miller in *Pro Se Presents*, Lee Houston, Jr., ed., Pro Se Press, August 2012. Level Twelve Magus Doctor Dana Unknown and her sidekick, ex-superhero Jack Christian, join forces with the Black Centipede and Baron Samedi to resurrect a deceased foe who has managed to create a Piecework Horror. The Black Centipede is a series character of Miller's whose exploits take place in an alternate reality to the CU. Frankenstein's Monster, Sherlock Holmes, and Professor Moriarty are mentioned.

"The Adventure of the Counterfeit Martian" by Ralph E. Vaughan in *Sherlock Holmes: The Coils of Time & Other Stories*, Dog in the Night Books, 2013. A different take on Sherlock Holmes' activities during the Martian invasion than Manly W. Wellman and Wade Wellman's *Sherlock Holmes's War of the Worlds*. Captain Philip Strange, a character created by Donald Keyhoe for the American pulp *Flying Aces*, is mentioned.

"The Adventure of the Hanoverian Vampires" by Darrell Schweitzer in *Sherlock Holmes Mystery Magazine* #2, Marvin Kaye, ed., Wildside Press, 2009. In an alternate reality where King James VII rules England rather than Queen Victoria, Sherlock Holmes and Dr. Watson battle Count Dracula.

"The Adventure of the Lost Specialist" by Christopher Sequeira in *Sherlock Holmes: The Crossovers Casebook*, Howard Hopkins, ed., Moonstone Books, 2012. Sherlock Holmes and Dr. Watson do battle with Professor Moriarty, who identifies himself as the stationmaster, and reveals both the Moriarty who Holmes dueled with at Reichenbach and Colonel Moriarty were actually his alternate reality counterparts. Moriarty than unleashes alternate versions of Holmes and Watson on the duo; one pair are meant to be Batman's foes the Joker and the Penguin, while another pair are Dracula and Frankenstein's Monster. Watson mentions Holmes' actions in the affair of the depraved Herbert West and the grave-robberies in Essex County, Massachusetts, and also refers to Victor Savage's uncle, the famous American doctor and adventurer. Given the story takes place in 1903, this most likely refers to the father of the bronze-skinned pulp hero.

"The Adventure of the Nebrodi Sapphire" by Seamus Duffy in *Sherlock Holmes in Paris*, Black Coat Press, 2013. Sherlock Holmes and Dr. Watson travel to France to thwart a scheme by Professor Moriarty involving the theft of a precious jewel. A pub in Clerkenwell called the Slaughtered Lamb is mentioned. The *Sûreté* falsely believe the *Habits Noirs* are responsible for the murder of the jewel's caretaker, and gentleman thief Raoul d'Andrésy may have hired them to commit the act. Monsieur Jerome Dubuque recounts the crimes of Vidocq and Rocambole to Holmes and Watson during dinner. The Slaughtered Lamb pub is likely a reference to the establishment of the same name in the film *An American Werewolf in London*, although that pub was in Yorkshire rather than Clerkenwell. The *Habits Noirs* (Black Coats) are a criminal conspiracy featured in a series of novels by Paul Féval. "Raoul d'Andrésy" is one of the aliases of Maurice Leblanc's gentleman thief Arsène Lupin. Rocambole is a villain turned hero in novels by Ponson du Terrail. Holmes reveals in this story the man he bested at Reichenbach was really a double for Moriarty, which contradicts multiple accounts set in the CU which make it clear the true Moriarty was the one who faced Holmes. Also, Holmes claims in this tale he has no middle name, whereas William S. Baring-Gould states his full name is William Sherlock Scott Holmes.

"The Adventure of the Other Brother" by David Marcum in *The Papers of Sherlock Holmes Volume 2*, MX Publishing, 2013. Sherlock Holmes tries to clear the name of his elder brother Sherrinford, who has been framed for murder. Sherrinford's youngest son Siger provides invaluable aid to Holmes on the case. Siger's brother Bancroft has a government position under their uncle Mycroft, though to emphasize he is his own man, he uses the last name Pons, a reference to his father's use of the false identity of Asenath Pons in 1880. Siger later becomes a consulting detective himself, eventually changing his name to Solar Pons. Many of the details of Pons' family and biography are taken from a short piece written by August Derleth himself for the collection *Four and Twenty Bloodhounds*. Besides Sherrinford Holmes, Marcum also makes use of William S. Baring-Gould's theory Nero Wolfe was the son of Sherlock Holmes and Irene Adler, but his description of the details of Wolfe's early life are irreconcilable with Baring-Gould's biography *Nero Wolfe of West Thirty-Fifth Street*. A postscript to the book in the form of a 1929 letter from Dr. Watson to Marcum's grandfather, allegedly Watson's distant cousin, describes an adventure he and Holmes had with Siger and his friend Dr. Parker, a former Belgian policeman turned consulting detective (Hercule Poirot), Holmes' son and his assistant Mr. Goodwin, a New York police inspector (Richard Queen) and his son Ellery, and a young law student from California named Mason (Perry Mason).

American Vampire, comic book series created by Scott Snyder and Rafael Albuquerque, and published by Vertigo, spanning the late 19th and 20th centuries and featuring Skinner Sweet, an outlaw who became one of the undead, and his progeny Pearl Jones, a former actress. The backup story in the first issue, "Bad Blood" by Stephen King and Rafael Albuquerque, details how Sweet became a vampire after being arrested in Sidewinder, Colorado, from King's novels *The Shining* and *Misery*. In the five-issue miniseries *American Vampire: Lord of Nightmares* by Scott Snyder and Dustin Nguyen, Sweet encounters Dracula, who is revealed to have been intercepted and imprisoned before coming to England by the Vassals of the Morning Star, a group similar to the Watchers Council from *Buffy the Vampire Slayer*. The actual novel by Bram Stoker is based on the ravings of a senile Vassal.

"An Adventure in Three Courses" by Guy Adams in *The Further Encounters of Sherlock Holmes*, George Mann, ed., Titan Books, 2014. Sherlock Holmes and Dr. Watson are invited to dinner by Colonel Sebastian Moran's sister, who, along with the other guests, seeks the Great Detective and his Boswell's deaths. Holmes uses a poison provided to him by Roger Carruthers to save the day. Carruthers is from Adams' novels *The World House* and *Restoration*. This story takes place on the first anniversary of Mary Watson's death, and Watson says he and Mary were married for twelve years. However, Baring-Gould places Watson's marriage to Mary in 1889, and her death in late 1891 or early 1892. A date of 1892 or 1893 for this story is untenable, as Holmes was in the midst of his Great Hiatus at that time, with most of the world (including Watson) believing him dead.

An Evil Guest by Gene Wolfe, Tor, 2008. A novel set in an alternate future with Cthulhu Mythos overtones. Appearing or mentioned are Vincent Palma and Tabbi Merce (from Wolfe's story "Memorare"), a mountain whose wife washes clothes (from Cory Doctorow's story "Someone Comes to Town, Someone Leaves Town"), Rusterman's restaurant (from Rex Stout's Nero Wolfe novels), a man named Cranston who could turn invisible (perhaps the radio version of a shadowy pulp hero), and Hanga the Shark God (from Wolfe's story "The Tree is My Hat.")

Angel: After the Fall, seventeen issue comic book series published by IDW, November 2007–February 2009. Angel uses a spell from the *Necronomicon Ex Mortis* (from the *Evil Dead* films) to heal himself. The city of Los Angeles is tossed into Hell and divided among warring demon lords for about six months. Even though Angel manages to alter time and keep it from happening, everyone in L.A. still remembers it, effectively revealing to the city the existence of the supernatural. The series is a prequel to the *Buffy the Vampire Slayer: Season Eight* comics, which reveal the existence of supernatural beings to the rest of the world.

"The Ape-Man of Mars" by Peter S. Beagle in *Under the Moons of Mars*, John Joseph Adams, ed., Simon & Schuster, 2012. The jungle lord finds himself astrally projected to Mars, where he winds up in combat with the planet's warlord, who resents the British's refusal to help the South during the Civil War, as well as Greystoke's attraction to his wife, a Princess. The warlord of Mars of the CU has crossed paths with the jungle lord several times; none of these stories depicted any particular animosity towards him on the warlord's part.

Aria the Scarlet Ammo, Japanese light novel series by Chūgaku Akamatsu and Kobuichi, also adapted as a *manga* and *anime*. Two of the main characters are Aria Holmes Kanzaki and Riko Mine Lupin IV, descendants of Sherlock Holmes and Arsène Lupin respectively. Riko's full name may be meant to suggest she is the daughter of Lupin III and Fujiko Mine. This series presents a very different version of Dracula than that seen in the CU. Dracula takes DNA from the blood of his victims to transform himself. Also, in this series Joan of Arc is long-lived and has freezing powers, and her twin sister was actually the one burned at the stake in her place.

The Army of Dr. Moreau, six-issue miniseries by David F. Walker and Carl Sciacchitano, MonkeyBrain Comics. In 1939, a group of British and American operatives travel to the island once owned by Doctor Meraux to stop the Nazis from using the late Meraux's secrets to create an army of beast-men. H. G. Wells' *The Island of Doctor Moreau* is stated to be a distorted account of mercenary Edward Prentiss' time on the island. Meraux's assistant was named Montague rather than Montgomery, and the beast folk never reverted to fully animalistic forms. A text piece in #2 takes the form of a report from an American member of the expedition to Colonel Eaton of U.S. Army Intelligence. Eaton must have been promoted from Major, the rank he held in 1936, as seen in the first Indiana Jones film, *Raiders of the Lost Ark*. #3's text piece continues the references to *Raiders*, being a report to General (formerly Colonel) Musgrove that refers to "the situation in Egypt" several years ago.

Artful by Peter David, 47North, 2014. The Artful Dodger and young Abraham "Bram" Van Helsing struggle against vampires seeking to rule England. The Baker Street Irregulars also appear, and it is stated their leader is always called Wiggins. Apparently the concept of the Irregulars predates Sherlock Holmes' involvement with them. In the preface, *A Christmas Carol* is described as a biographical study. David, explaining how the Dodger avoided being shipped off to Australia, writes "By now, you are doubtless becoming impatient in wondering just how it was that the Artful was walking the streets of London rather than striding the deck of a ship bound for the land of Oz (an excursion not to be confused with his later unexpected journey to the Land of Oz, an astoundingly unlikely sequence of events that will remain unexplored for the duration of this history") The portrayal of Fagin as a vampire, and the revelation in the novel's final sentence he will later become Jack the Ripper, place this novel outside CU continuity.

"Attack of the *Electric Shark*" by Aaron Smith in *Season of Madness: A Doctor Watson Adventure*, Cornerstone Book Publishers, 2009. British Secret Service agent Quincey "Hound-Dog" Harker unearths the *Nautilus* to use in battle against another submersible called the *Electric Shark*. Quincey Harker's portrayal here is irreconcilable with that in the Marvel Comics series *Tomb of Dracula*. Additionally, it is stated a long-forgotten civilization (possibly Atlantis) created both the *Nautilus* and the *Electric Shark*, which contradicts *Twenty Thousand Leagues Under the Sea* and *The Mysterious Island*.

"Bacon" by Charlaine Harris, in the collection *Strange Brew*. A witch says the only sorcerer who's gone public is in Chicago, and she hears that he's struggling. This is a reference to Harry Dresden from the *Dresden Files* series by Jim Butcher. "Bacon" is set in the continuity of Harris' *Southern Vampire Mysteries* series, which depicts vampires and other supernatural beings living openly alongside humans, and therefore takes place in an alternate reality to the CU. It is worth noting another of Harris' series characters, Lily Bard, turns up in two of the *Southern Vampire Mysteries* novels, *Definitely Dead* and *Dead Reckoning*. Harris' *Midnight, Texas* series features Bobo Winthrop from the Lily Bard series, Manfred Bernardo from the Harper Connelly books, and Sheriff Arthur Smith from the Aurora Teagarden series.

"The Baker Street Cimmerian" by Rhys Hughes in *The Mammoth Book of Best British Crime 11*, Maxim Jakubowski, ed., Robinson, 2014. A parody in which Sherlock Holmes and Conan are swapped in time and space. Conan assumes Holmes' identity and proves himself a danger to those around him, while Holmes is killed almost immediately.

"Before the War, Five Dragons Roar" by Pete Rawlik in *Tales of the Shadow-men Volume 8: Agents Provocateurs*, Jean-Marc and Randy Lofficier, eds., Black Coat Press, 2011; reprinted in French in *Les Compagnons de l'Ombre (Tome 12)*, Jean-Marc and Randy Lofficier, eds., Rivière Blanche, 2013, and *La Saga de de Mme. Atomos (Tome 8)* by Michel Stéphan, Rivière Blanche, 2014; and in *The Mark of Madame Atomos* by André Caroff, adapted by Michael Shreve, 2013. Charlie Chan, James Wong, and Kentarou Aratamoto butt heads with Dr. Yoshimuta and Ichirou Aratamoto aboard the *S.S. Claridon*. Charlie Chan is from the novels by Earl Derr Biggers. James Lee

Wong appears in several stories by Hugh Wiley. Berkford University is also from the James Wong stories. Ichirou Aratamoto is meant to be John Marquand's spy Mr. Moto, while his brother Kentarou is meant to be the film version of Mr. Moto portrayed by Peter Lorre. Dr. Kanoto Yoshimuta is the future Madame Atomos, from novels by André Caroff. The *S.S. Claridon* is from the film *The Last Voyage*. Gottfried Vanger is from Stieg Larsson's novel *The Girl with the Dragon Tattoo*. Mrs. Nora Charles is from Dashiell Hammett's *The Thin Man*. Mr. Cranston is the alias assumed by a shadow-cloaked pulp vigilante, although there is a real Cranston. Mr. Reid is Britt Reid, the Green Hornet. Oka Yuma appeared in several European pulp series. Fu Wong, the Twelve Coins of Confucius, and Keelat are from the movie *The Mysterious Mr. Wong*. "Michael Croft" is actually Mycroft Holmes. The Manchurian is Dr. Fu Manchu. Fen Chu is from the pulp *L'Enigma-tique Fen-Chu* by George Fronval. Win Lee and the map are from the James Wong film *Phantom of Chinatown*. Rawlik identifies this map with the one from Kim Ji-woon's film *The Good, the Bad, the Weird*. Wong's nephew is treasury agent Richard Wong, the pulp character created by Lee Fredericks. The Dragon Queen is from the film *Charlie Chan and the Curse of the Dragon Queen*. Egg Shen is from the film *Big Trouble in Little China*. Rawlik claims Mycroft Holmes is Charlie Chan's father; however, Dennis E. Power's essay "Asian Detectives in the Wold Newton Family" (*Myths for the Modern Age: Philip José Farmer's Wold Newton Universe*, Win Scott Eckert, ed., Monkeybrain Books, 2005) identified Chan as the son of Fu Manchu. Thus, this story must take place in an alternate universe.

The Belgian and the Beekeeper, e-book by Peter Guttridge. The French detective Jules Poiret (who is frequently confused with Hercule Poirot, a Belgian detective who recently investigated a mysterious affair at Styles) and Sherlock Holmes become involved in a sequel incident to *The Sign of The Four*, discovering Watson may not have been entirely honest in his account of the case. Jules Poiret, who may have been a partial inspiration for Poirot, is from Frank Howel Evans' *The Murder Club*. Hercules Popeau, also cited as a possible inspiration for Poirot, appears in Marie Belloc Lowndes' story "Popeau Intervenes." Georges La Touche is from Freeman Wills Crofts' novel *The Cask*. Inspector Juve and Fantômas are from Marcel Allain and Pierre Souvestre's novels. Arsène Lupin is Maurice Leblanc's gentleman thief. Joseph Rouletabille is a detective created by Gaston Leroux. Sven Hjerson is a fictional Finnish detective created by author Ariadne Oliver in Agatha Christie's works. The disturbing implications that the Agra treasure was not lost but rather stolen by Watson, who married Mary Morstan in order to capitalize on her newfound wealth, and that he may have later murdered Mary, would be enough to place this story outside CU continuity, but the metafictional piece following it, "Holmes and Watson: A Conversation," clinches it, with Watson revealing to Holmes they, Poiret, and Poirot are all fictional characters, and the many inconsistencies in Watson's accounts are really the fault of their creator.

"Big D, Little D" by Edward Morris in *The Lovecraft eZine* #18, Mike Davis, ed., October 2012. Felix Dracul attempts to take revenge on Sherlock Holmes for the death of his father, but the Great Detective and Dr. Watson have other ideas. The King in Yellow and the Goat with a Thousand Young are mentioned. This story is a followup to Roger Zelazny's novel *A Night in the Lonesome October*, which has already been placed in an alternate universe.

"Brian Keene's Alternate Universes": Jay Lindsey contributes the following:

The Rising Universe: On this level of Keene's Labyrinth, a group of scientists accidentally opened a doorway to the Void, where Ob, Ab, and Api were banished. Ob and the siqqusim start a zombie apocalypse on this world, murdering people so their bodies can be inhabited by siqqusim. After they have extinguished most human life, they depart for other realities, while Ab and the Elilum possess the plant and insect life. After them, Api and the Teraphim arrive and burn whatever's left of the world. This world is seen in Keene's books *The Rising*, *City of the Dead*, and *The Rising: Selected Scenes from the End of the World*. The author's preferred editions feature many elements of later books, including references to Adam Senft and Black Lodge.

The Dead Sea Universe: On this world, a different zombie plague, called Hamelin's Revenge since it is originally spread by rats, kills and reanimates most of humanity (and every other species) as rotted, flesh-eating zombies. This is the world of Keene's novels *Dead Sea* and *Entombed*, as well as several short stories. Richard Tyler is president in this world, just as he is in the Clickers Universe. A version of Frankie, from *The Rising*, briefly appears.

The Last Zombie Universe: This is the world of Brian Keene's comic *The Last Zombie*. This world has already seen the zombie plague come and go, with most of the undead having rotted away by now, leaving the handful of human survivors to try and rebuild society. A version of Frankie, from *The Rising*, appears.

The Clickers Universe: This is the universe of the novel *Clickers* (written by Mark Williams and J. F. Gonzalez), and its two sequels, both written by Gonzalez and Brian Keene. In this reality, America is devastated by an army of Clickers, crab-lobster-scorpion monsters swarm from the oceans along with their masters, humanoid lizards called the Dark Ones. The third book mentions giant ants in Florida, a reference to Jeff Strand's novel *Mandibles*. The Tony Genova of this reality is a major character of the books, and Black Lodge plays a huge role in the third novel.

The Earthworm Gods Universe: On this world, cultists summon two of the Thirteen, Leviathan and Behemoth. They destroy this Earth with superstorms, a global flood, and armies of monsters. This is the world of Keene's novels *Earthworm Gods* (also released as *The Conqueror Worms*), *Deluge: Earthworm Gods II*, and *Earthworm Gods: Selected Scenes from the End of the World*. The books include references to Black Lodge, LeHorn's Hollow, and other elements of Keene's wider multiverse.

Clickers vs. Zombies: This novel by Brian Keene and J. F. Gonzalez is set in a world that is invaded by Ob and the Siqqusim, at exactly the same time that massive swarms of Clickers begin pouring out of the sea, leading to zombies fighting Clickers, and, of course, the inevitable zombie Clickers. Different versions of many of Keene's characters, such as Levi Stoltzfus and Tony Genova, appear.

Darkness at the Edge of Town: This novel by Brian Keene is set in a reality where Levi Stoltzfus died years ago, and so was not around to battle Nodens in *Ghost Walk*. Nodens has utterly destroyed this world, with the exception of the small town of Walden, Virginia, which has been saved by magic, but may still be destroyed by the human survivors.

"The Siqqusim Who Stole Christmas": When Ob and the Siqqusim arrive on this reality, Ob finds himself possessing the body of Santa Claus, who has died from lack of belief. Santa-Ob fights this world's versions of Tony Genova and Vincent Napoli in Finland.

"Jack's Magic Beans": In this short story, a mysterious agent causes everyone not on Prozac to become a homicidal maniac. The Sons of the Constitution are mentioned.

"Take the Long Way Home": This tale is set on a world directly in the aftermath of the Christian Rapture. The Labyrinth and Prosper Johnson are mentioned.

"The Cage": The employees of an electronics store are taken hostage by a madman who wishes to sacrifice them to Shtar. There are references to two strip clubs: the Odessa, with ties to the Russian mob, and the Foxy Lady, with ties to the Marano crime family. The story ends with the culmination of an occult ritual, but its results are never seen. However, one of the chapters of Keene's novel *The Seven* takes place in the world of "The Cage" and reveals the ritual resulted in the Apocalypse. *The Seven* also reveals the Seven who will fight the Thirteen and maybe save the multiverse are Frankie, Tony Genova, Teddy Garnett from *Earthworm Gods*, the Exit from "I Am Not an Exit" and "This is Not an Exit," Don Bloom from "Babylon Falling," Nelson LeHorn from *Dark Hollow*, and the fallen angel Lucifer. In the fifth chapter of *The Seven*, Amun, the voice of God, claims to have been Noah's dove, Chalco's hummingbird (from "Tequila's Sunrise") and the mariner's albatross from "The Rime of the Ancient Mariner."

"A Brief History of Mystery (Men), or Where Do They All Come From?" by Erwin K. Roberts at the *Planetary Stories* website. An account of the origins of the costumed adventurer. Appearing or mentioned are: Diego (Don Diego de la Vega, alias Zorro); the *New York Clarion*, Frank Havens, the Phantom Detective and Inspector Gregg from the Phantom Detective pulp novels; the first Nick Carter; Clark Savage; Tony Quinn, aka the Black Bat; Bob Phantom, a character appearing in comics published by MLJ, later known as Archie Comics; the Phantom Bullet, a costumed crimefighter published by Timely Comics, later known as Marvel Comics; the Phantom and "Bengalia" (Bangalla); Commissioner Ralph Weston; Simon Templar; Sebastian Moran (not Sherlock Holmes' enemy, but likely a descendant); Burland and the Hoods (Kip Burland, the MLJ hero known as the Black Hood, part of a crimefighting legacy passed down through the generations of his family); the "Masked Rider of the Plains" (the Lone Ranger); Deadwood Dick; Argus the Blue Eagle, a character created by Roberts; the *Sentinel* (*The Daily Sentinel*, the Green Hornet's newspaper); Charles Foster Kane; and Jim Anthony and the Daily Star. This story portrays Don Diego de la Vega as still alive shortly before the Civil War, which contradicts the film *The Mask of Zorro,* in which Diego dies in 1842.

La Brigade Chimerique (*The Chimerical Brigade*), a French comic book by Fabrice Colin, Serge Lehman, and Gess, set in an alternate 1930s where most technology is powered by radium, and superhumans were created during World War I. Among the characters appearing are: Harry Dickson; Thomas Carnacki; Felifax (from Paul Féval *fils' Felifax the Tiger-Man*); Sun Koh; Andrew Gibberne (the son of Professor John Gibberne from H. G. Wells' "The New Accelerator"); the Nyctalope; the bronze man; the shadowy vigilante; Superman (out of costume, and using the alias "Mr. Steele"); Dr. Mabuse; Gog (from Giovanni Papin's novel of the same name); Dr. Moreau; Dr. Cornelius Kramm; Dr. Lerne; Dr. Persikov (from Mikhail Bulgakov's *The Fatal Eggs*); Gregor Samsa (from Franz Kafka's "The Metamorphosis"); Dutilleul (from Marcel Aymé's "The Man Who Could Walk Through Walls"); Fantômas; Captain Mors; Judex; Big Brother (from George Orwell's *1984*); Pierre de Givreuse (from J.-H. Rosny aîné's "The Givreuse Enigma"); a Xipéhuz (from Rosny's story "Les Xipéhuz"); Hareton Ironcastle (from Rosny's *L'Étonnant Voyage d'Hareton Ironcastle*); Doctor Flohr and the Elastic Man (from Jacques Spitz's "The Elastic Man"); Odd John (from Olaf Stapledon's novel of the same name); the Blue Angel (from the German film of the same name); and Francis Blake (from Edgar P. Jacobs' comic *Blake and Mortimer*).

"By Any Other Name" by Michael Dirda in *In the Company of Sherlock Holmes*, Laurie R. King and Leslie S. Klinger, eds., Pegasus Books, 2014. Arthur Conan Doyle's relationship with Jean Leckie hits a rough spot when he admits all the books and stories attributed to him were ghost-written by other authors. "That Blue John Gap cave-monster" (from Doyle's "The Terror of Blue John Gap"), Dr. Thorndyke, Sir Harry Flashman, the crime wave at Blandings (a reference to P. G. Wodehouse's story of the same name), and the mystery of Lord Strathmorlick's courtship (a reference to *The Courtship of Lord Strathmorlick*, a novel written by Rosie M. Banks in Wodehouse's Jeeves story "No Wedding Bells for Bingo") are mentioned.

Captain America: The First Avenger, 2011 feature film, part of the Marvel Comics Cinematic Universe. The Red Skull, on seeing the Tesseract, this universe's version of the Cosmic Cube, remarks, "And the Führer digs for trinkets in the desert," a reference to *Raiders of the Lost Ark*.

Captain Midnight, comic book series published by Dark Horse Comics, featuring the Captain returning in the 21st century after being trapped in the Bermuda Triangle during World War II. He has not aged since then. This version of the Captain is based on the Fawcett Comics series. The Captain Midnight radio show began in 1938 and ended in 1949. Therefore, the radio version of the Captain, which is the version that is in the CU, was still active after the war. Furthermore, Stephen A. Kallis, Jr.'s story "Any You Walk Away From" has the Captain active in 1971. This series is part of Dark Horse's *Project: Black Sky* imprint, which also includes the series *Blackout*, *Brain Boy*, *Ghost*, *The Occultist*, *Skyman*, and *X*, all of which are set in the same universe as *Captain Midnight*.

"Carnacki: The Parliament of Owls" by William Meikle in *The Lovecraft eZine* #18, Mike Davis, ed., October 2012. Carnacki and the sentient, talking owl Nestor, an agent of the Parliament of Owls, attempt to prevent Arthur Raffles from unleashing the forces of the Outer Darkness on Earth. Nestor explains his choice of Carnacki to aid him by saying, "The Great Detective away in France, Adamant still on ice, Hannay up and gone to Rhodesia. Fetch a closer, they said." This story utilizes concepts from Roger Zelazny's novel *A Night in the Lonesome October*, which takes place in an alternate universe. Furthermore, Raffles is portrayed as an outright villain, and is killed.

"The Case of the Ghosts at Bly" by Donald Thomas in *Sherlock Holmes and the Ghosts of Bly*, Pegasus Books, 2010. Sherlock Holmes investigates the events of Henry James' story "The Turn of the Screw" alongside Inspector Alfred Swain, a series character created by Thomas. One of the Swain novels is

Jekyll, Alias Hyde, which reveals Dr. Henry Jekyll and Mr. Edward Hyde were actually two separate people, and Hyde was blackmailing Jekyll. Therefore, the Inspector Swain books must take place in an alternate reality to the CU.

"The Case of the Lost Soul" by Paul Kane in *The Mammoth Book of Sherlock Holmes Abroad*, Simon Clark, ed., Robinson, 2015. Sherlock Holmes suggests to a would-be client he consult Carnacki instead. Holmes mentions "that business with Lord Blackwood and his toxin derived from the nectar of the rhododendron," a reference to Guy Ritchie's film *Sherlock Holmes*. Both that film and its sequel, *Sherlock Holmes: A Game of Shadows* differ from the continuity of Doyle's tales in a number of respects, including Holmes meeting Mary Morstan under completely different circumstances and different events leading up to Holmes' duel with Professor Moriarty at the Reichenbach Falls. Watson refers to a case undertaken for Sir Henry Baskerville in South Africa some fifteen years ago, a reference to Mark Morris' story "The Crimson Devil," also included in *The Mammoth Book of Sherlock Holmes Abroad.*

"The Case of the Night Crawler" by George Mann in *Encounters of Sherlock Holmes*, George Mann, ed., Titan Books, 2013. Dr. Watson works with Sir Maurice Newbury, agent of the Crown, and Newbury's assistant Veronica Hobbes to investigate a bizarre creature spotted by a friend of Watson's. Newbury and Hobbes are the protagonists of a series of novels by Mann which take place in a Steampunk London where Queen Victoria is kept alive by a crude life-support system, airships are common, and automatons perform menial jobs for lawyers, the police, and journalists. This level of publicly available advanced technology in the Victorian Era is incompatible with CU continuity. Other works by Mann set in the same universe as the Newbury and Hobbes tales include his Holmes novels *The Will of the Dead* and *The Spirit Box*, the Doctor Who audiobook *Paradox Lost*, and his books *Ghosts of Manhattan* and *Ghosts of War*, featuring the Ghost, a vigilante active in 1920s New York. Zenith the Albino also has a counterpart in this universe, as seen in the story "The Albino's Shadow."

"The Case of the Tell-Tale Hands" by Donald Thomas in *Sherlock Holmes and the King's Evil*, Pegasus Books, 2009. Sherlock Holmes and Dr. Watson investigate the bizarre behavior of Lord Arthur Savile. This story incorporates Holmes and Watson into the events of Oscar Wilde's short story "Lord Arthur Savile's Crime." However, Thomas' story takes place in 1901, whereas Wilde's tale was first published in 1887. Additionally, Savile's motivation for killing palmister Septimus R. Podgers differs from that stated in Wilde's story, despite the fact Wilde showed the murder from Savile's point of view.

"Catspaw" by David McDonald in *Tales of the Shadowmen Volume 8: Agents Provocateurs*, Jean-Marc and Randy Lofficier, eds., Black Coat Press, 2011. In 1893, Harry, Ballantine, and Jean Saint-Clair battle Dr. Moreau in Afghanistan. Harry is the son of Harry Flashman from Thomas Hughes' *Tom Brown's Schooldays* and the Flashman novels by George MacDonald Fraser. Sgt. Ballantine is an ancestor of Bill Ballantine, companion to Henri Vernes' hero Bob Morane. Jean Saint-Clair is the father of Jean de La Hire's proto-superhero the Nyctalope. Oxus, Fulbert, and the Hictaner encountered Jean de Saint-Clair in Jean de La Hire's *The Man Who Could Live Underwater*; Oxus went on to appear in *The Nyctalope on Mars*. Dr. Moreau is from H. G. Wells' *The Island of Doctor Moreau*. Karram Khan is from the film version of Talbot Mundy's novel *King of the Khyber Rifles*. Dr. Jekyll, aka Mr. Hyde, is from the novel by Robert Louis Stevenson. Ballantine says Jekyll did not commit suicide, but rather was imprisoned, and put to work by the British government on a modified version of his formula. However, *The League of Extraordinary Gentlemen, Volume I* reveals Jekyll faked his suicide and was at liberty until 1898, when he was forcibly recruited to be part of the League, apparently the first time he worked for the British government.

"Celeste" by Neil Jackson in *Gaslight Grotesque: Nightmare Tales of Sherlock Holmes*, J. R. Campbell and Charles Prepolec, eds., EDGE Science Fiction and Fantasy Publishing, 2009. Holmes and Watson investigate the salvaged ship *Mary Celeste* alongside Dr. Joseph Jephson, whose father Habakuk was one of those who disappeared from the ship in 1872. Jephson says a diary allegedly written by his father is a hoax. The diary is a reference to Arthur Conan Doyle's story "J. Habakuk Jephson's Statement." Both Doyle's and Jackson's stories offer different solutions to the mystery of the historical *Mary Celeste* than Philip José Farmer's *The Other Log of Phileas Fogg*, and therefore neither can take place in the CU. Doyle's story also takes many liberties with the known true facts of the case.

Codename: Action, five-issue miniseries by Chris Roberson and Jonathan Lau, Dynamite Entertainment. A government agent teams with Operator 5, the Green Hornet and Kato, the Green Lama, the Spider, Daredevil (the Golden Age comic character published by Lev Gleason, not the Marvel superhero who debuted in 1964), Black Venus, and the American Crusader to battle a plot by the terrorist group Hexagon. At the end of the series, the agent dons the name and costume of Captain Action. This series does not fit with the continuity of the Captain Action comics published by Moonstone, which are already connected to the CU via crossovers with the Phantom, the Green Hornet, and Honey West and Derek Flint. Additionally, the Spider's look, as with his other incarnations in Dynamite's titles, is based on the serial

The Spider's Web, rather than the fangs, hunchback, and fright wig described in the pulps. Finally, while Operator 5 is portrayed as a veteran agent, the Green Lama, the Spider, Daredevil, Black Venus, and the American Crusader are depicted as contemporary adventurers rather than 1930s and '40s heroes.

"The Comfort of the Seine" by Stephen Volk in *Gaslight Arcanum: Uncanny Tales of Sherlock Holmes*, J. R. Campbell and Charles Prepolec, eds., EDGE Science Fiction and Fantasy Publishing, 2011. Holmes recounts his time in Paris, where he learned the art of detection from the supposedly deceased Edgar Allan Poe, then living under the name Dupin. Among the cases they investigated were the affair of the so-called "phantom" of the Paris Opera and the case of the *horla* and its tragically afflicted seer. These are references to Gaston Leroux's *The Phantom of the Opera* and Guy de Maupassant's "The Horla." Dupin is portrayed as a completely fictional character created by Poe, and therefore this story must take place in an AU.

"A Counting Game" by Derek Ferreira in *The Lovecraft eZine* #18, Mike Davis, ed., October 2012. A vampire slayer named Abraham (Van Helsing) takes the place of the Count (Dracula) in the Game, which has Openers and Closers. The Game is from Roger Zelazny's novel *A Night in the Lonesome October*, which takes place in an AU. The Detective and his companion (Sherlock Holmes and Dr. Watson) appear. Abraham's familiar, a rooster named Hahn, can do a pretty passable R'lyeh if he ever takes a wrong turn in the dreamworld.

Creeping Dawn: The Rise of the Black Centipede by Chuck Miller, Pro Se Press, 2011. The vigilante known as the Black Centipede makes his debut in Zenith City, battling the evil Doctor Almanac. The Centipede refers to Professor James Moriarty as one of the many people he encountered during his career as a crimefighter. The future Centipede became friends with Howard Lovecraft as a young man after writing to him about the *Necronomicon*. Miskatonic University is mentioned as fictional. After a comment by the Centipede-to-be, Howard changes the unwieldy title of a story he's working on to "The Call of Cthulhu." A crimefighter in New York who laughs a lot and has his own radio show is referenced twice, and likely needs no additional explanation. William Randolph Hearst refers to a certain Chinaman who should trademark the word "insidious," a reference to Dr. Fu Manchu. The Centipede's enemy Bloody Mary Jane Gallows fed Doctor Almanac Henry Jekyll's serum, turning him into a villain. The sequel is *Blood of the Centipede*, 2012, in which the Black Centipede travels to Hollywood to act as a consultant on a movie adaptation of the pulp magazine very loosely based on his exploits, and winds up battling the returning Jack the Ripper. The Ripper possesses the *Necronumericon*, another book written by Abdul Alhazred, author of the *Necronomicon*. The Centipede refers to "that guy that lives in the Empire State Building," whom Amelia Earhart describes as "Doc Do-Good." This is a reference to the golden-eyed pulp superman. One of the stars of the Black Centipede movie is Nora Desmand, who is meant to be Norma Desmond from Billy Wilder's 1950 film *Sunset Boulevard*. The Centipede works with Lieutenant "Big Jack" Matteo of the L.A.P.D., who is meant to be the father of Lieutenant Jack Matteo from the *Kolchak: The Night Stalker* episode "The Vampire." Sherlock Holmes is mentioned in a flashback to the Ripper's murder of Mary Jane Kelly. Amelia refers to "that fellow in New York—the one with the chronic private joke," who has several agents, a reference to the pulp hero who operated in the shadows. The Centipede's foe Baron Samedi lists individuals who, like the Centipede, played with forces they didn't fully comprehend, including Faust, Prometheus, and Victor Franken-stein. The third book in the series is *Black Centipede Confidential*, 2015, in which the Centipede battles Professor James Moriarty, who has assumed the mantle of Lord of Vampires after killing the previous holder of the title, Count Dracula. Among the Centipede's allies in his conflict with Moriarty are J. Alfred Prufrock (from T. S. Eliot's poem "The Love Song of J. Alfred Prufrock"); Gregor Samsa (from Franz Kafka's "The Metamorphosis"); Walter Gibson and Lester Dent, who describe their working relationships with the men whose lives they fictionalize; the faceless assassin Anonymoushka, actually Vionna Moriarty, the Professor's daughter, who will later use the name Vionna Valis, as seen in Miller's book *Vionna and the Vampires*; and an elderly Sherlock Holmes. Moriarty's own allies include Herbert West. Jack Matteo and the Jekyll formula are mentioned. The portrayal of Moriarty as a vampire, Holmes' death, and the revelation Moriarty is really Holmes' older brother Sherrinford all conflict with Holmes and Moriarty's established history in the CU. Combined with the portrayal of Miskatonic University and implicitly Cthulhu as fictional in *Creeping Dawn*, the Black Centipede's exploits and other related stories by Miller must take place in an alternate universe.

Le Crime Etrange de Mr. Hyde (*The Strange Case of Mr. Hyde*) by Jean-Pierre Naugrette, Babel No. 336, 1998. An alternate take on Holmes vs. Jekyll & Hyde. A sequel, *Les Hommes de Cire* (*The Wax-Men*), Ed. Climats, 2002, features Holmes and Watson attempting to protect the late Dr. Jekyll's solici-tor, Mr. Utterson, from the mysterious "Dr. F," who may be the reincarnation of Hyde. A third book, *Les Variations Enigma* (*The Enigma Variations*), Terre de Brume, 2006, takes place throughout Europe between May and autumn of 1899, and features Holmes and Watson investigating a plot against Queen Victoria on behalf of the King of Bohemia. Hyde is now working for "Prof. M" (implicitly Moriarty), and was brought back to life by Dr. F, who is implied to be Dr. Frankenstein. Also appearing is Irene Adler, whose husband, Godfrey Norton, betrayed M's conspiracy and was murdered by Hyde. Among those attending the premiere of Edward Elgar's *Enigma Variations* in London on June 19, 1899 are: Sir Henry Baskerville, Dr. Mortimer, Sebastian Moran, Inspector Lestrade, and Sir Reginald Musgrave (all from the Holmes stories); Lord Falconbridge (likely a descendant of the title character of Arthur Conan Doyle's short story "The Lord of Falconbridge," which takes place in 1818); Lady Windermere, Sophia of Carlsruhe, the Duchess of Paisley, and Lord Arthur Savile (from Oscar Wilde's "Lord Arthur Savile's Crime"); Lady Verinder and Franklin Blake (from Wilkie Collins' *The Moonstone*); and Professor Higgins and Colonel Pickering (from George Bernard Shaw's *Pygmalion*).

The Cthulhu Encryption by Brian Stableford, Borgo Press, 2011. Auguste Dupin attempts to decipher the Cthulhu Encryption, etched in the skin of a dying woman, which will reveal the location of a fabulous treasure. Along the way, he encounters malevolent shoggoths. Jana Valdemar is mentioned. She first appeared in Stableford's novel *Valdemar's Daughter*, and is the daughter of the title character of Poe's "The Facts in the Case of M. Valdemar." The events of Stableford's "The Legacy of Erich Zann" are mentioned. In that tale, Dupin investigated the disappearance of the title character of Lovecraft's "The Music of Erich Zann." The graphic novel *The Irregulars . . . In the Service of Sherlock Holmes* is set in 1896, well after the 1840s setting of "The Legacy of Erich Zann," and has an appearance by Zann himself, presumably prior to the events of Lovecraft's tale.

"Cutting the Mustard," *X-Factor* #71 by Peter David, Larry Stroman, and Al Milgrom, Marvel Comics, October 1991. Valerie Cooper, the government liaison to the mutant superteam known as X-Factor, says "I have a brother who's an FBI agent, and I am so tired of him telling me about these exciting cases he gets . . . like for instance, this girl they found. She was dead . . . wrapped in plastic . . ." The implication is Val's brother is Special Agent Dale Cooper from the television series *Twin Peaks*. The existence of X-Factor and other mutant superhero teams is not compatible with CU continuity. In addition, Scott Frost's book *The Autobiography of FBI Special Agent Dale Cooper: My Life, My Tapes* explicitly states Dale's only sibling is an older brother named Emmet.

Death Comes to Pemberley by P. D. James, Knopf, 2011. In 1803, Mr. Fitzwilliam Darcy and his wife Elizabeth become involved in the mystery of the murder of Elizabeth's sister Lydia's husband George Wickham. Mr. and Mrs. Knightley (from Jane Austen's novel *Emma*) are described as the most important people in Highbury, and Wickham's last employer is identified as Sir Walter Elliot (from Austen's novel *Persuasion*). Miss Caroline Bingley is still alive at the time of the novel's events, which does not fit with her death in 1795 in Win Scott Eckert's story "The Wild Huntsman."

"Death to the Heretic!" by Paul Hugli in *Tales of the Shadowmen Volume 7: Femmes Fatales*, Jean-Marc and Randy Lofficier, eds., Black Coat Press, 2010; reprinted in French in *Les Compagnons de l'Ombre (Tome 8)*, Jean-Marc and Randy Lofficier, eds., Rivière Blanche, 2011; and in *The Nyctalope Steps In*, Jean-Marc and Randy Lofficier, eds., Black Coat Press, 2011. In October 1929, Bruce Wayne and his butler Alfred Pennyworth, Dr. Henry "Indiana" Jones Jr., Leo Saint-Clair (aka The Nyctalope), and Radcliffe and Amelia Peabody Emerson battle the mad Prof. William Omaha McElroy in Egypt. Bruce Wayne, Alfred Pennyworth, and Indiana Jones need no introduction. The Nyctalope is from the novels by Jean de La Hire. Archaeologist Amelia Peabody Emerson is the protagonist of a series of mystery novels by Elizabeth Peters, which is also the source of her husband Radcliffe and their son Walter "Ramses" Emerson. Professor William Omaha McElroy is better known as the villain King Tut from the 1966–1968 *Batman* television series. Indy searched for the Ark of the Covenant and the Silver Chalice of Christ in *Raiders of the Lost Ark* and *Indiana Jones and the Last Crusade*, respectively. The Cross of Coronado is also from *Last Crusade*. The Ibis Stick is the magical wand wielded by the Fawcett Comics character Ibis the Invincible, though the comics spell the wand's name as "Ibistick." The pilot named Allard Bruce met once is a well-known shadowy pulp vigilante. Doctor Hugo Strange is a recurring Batman foe. Wentworth Works is presumably owned by Richard Wentworth, aka the Spider. Boxer Ted Grant is the alter ego of the DC Comics superhero Wildcat. Indy's comment aliens visiting Earth would likely be "some super-race with powers and abilities beyond those of mortal men" evokes Superman. Doctor Francis Ardan is from Guy d'Armen's novel *Doc Ardan: City of Gold and Lepers*, translated and adapted by Jean-Marc and Randy Lofficier, and is implicitly the American pulp hero commonly nicknamed "Doc." Arkham Asylum is where many of Batman's greatest foes are incarcerated. There are several scenes in this story foreshadowing Bruce Wayne's future career as Batman. However, Bruce's age in the story is not consistent with CU continuity. It is stated Bruce's parents were killed seven years ago, shortly after his thirteenth birthday. This would suggest Bruce is twenty-years-old during the events recounted by Hugli and thus born around 1909. However, Chris Roberson's story "Penumbra" (*Tales of the Shadowmen Volume 1: The Modern Babylon*, Jean-Marc and Randy Lofficier, eds., Black Coat Press, 2005) implies Bruce was born in October 1916, which would make him only 13 when Hugli's story takes place. Furthermore, the comic book story "The Night of the Shadow" (*Batman* #259, November–December 1974, DC Comics) shows Bruce's parents died shortly after he and his father were rescued by the shadowy vigilante. Win Scott Eckert has placed Thomas and Martha Wayne's deaths in 1929. Changing the year of the story is untenable because Bruce learns at the end the stock market has crashed; therefore, this story must take place in an AU.

The Deception at Lyme (Or, The Peril of Persuasion) by Carrie Bebris, Tor Books, 2011. Fitzwilliam and Elizabeth Darcy meet characters from Jane Austen's novel *Persuasion*. In *The Suspicion at Sanditon (Or, The Disappearance of Lady Denham)*, (Tor Books, 2015), the Darcys become embroiled in a mystery involving characters from Austen's unfinished novel *Sanditon*. The dates given in Bebris' *Mr. and Mrs. Darcy Mysteries* series are inconsistent with the CU, in which the events of *Pride and Prejudice* take place in 1792–1793.

Defenders, twelve-issue series by Matt Fraction, Terry Dodson, Rachel Dodson, Michael Lark, Stefano Gaudiano, Brian Thies, Mitch Breitweiser, Victor Ibanez, Tom Palmer, Terry Pallot, Jamie McKelvie, Mike Norton, and Mirco Pierfederici, Marvel Comics, February 2012–January 2013. Flashbacks feature a group of adventurers composed of Captain Nemo, Leonard McKenzie and Princess Fen (Prince Namor the Sub-Mariner's parents), Judex, Musidora (named after the actress of the same name, and based on her character of Irma Vep from *Les Vampires*), Ivar the Strong (an original character), Farraday Bobbs (a photographer and reporter created by Frank L. Packard), and Orissa Kravinov (based on Orissa Kane from L. Frank Baum's novels *The Flying Girl* and *The Flying Girl and Her Chum*). As a superteam, the Defenders do not fit into CU continuity, although the point is moot since the series ends with its events being erased from the timeline.

"Diplomatic Freeze" by David McDonald in *Tales of the Shadowmen Volume 9: La Vie en Noir*, Jean-Marc and Randy Lofficier, eds., Black Coat Press, 2012; reprinted in French in *Les Compagnons de l'Ombre (Tome 12)*, Jean-Marc and Randy Lofficier, eds., Rivière Blanche, 2013. Jean Saint-Clair leads an expedition to the Arctic Circle which seeks to forge an alliance between the French government and the Lizard People. Jean Saint-Clair is the father of Leo Saint-Clair, aka Jean de La Hire's adventurer the Nyctalope. Major Flashman is the son and namesake of Harry Flashman from Thomas Hughes' *Tom Brown's Schooldays* and the Flashman novels by George Mac-Donald Fraser. Sgt. Ballantine is the ancestor of Bill Ballantine, companion to Henri Vernes' adventurer Bob Morane. Saint-Clair, Flashman, and Ballantine previously worked together in McDonald's story "Catspaw" (*Tales of the*

Shadowmen Volume 8: Agents Provocateurs, Jean-Marc and Randy Lofficier, eds., Black Coat Press, 2010). The Lizard People, Jean-Louis de Venasque, Professor Valenton, and Jacques Ceintras are from Charles Derennes' *The People of the Pole*. The Black Coats are a criminal conspiracy featured in a series of novels by Paul Féval. Marcel Gioja is a descendant of Annibal Gioja from the Black Coats novels. King Kull is the main character of many stories by Robert E. Howard.

Django/Zorro #1–7 by Quentin Tarantino, Matt Wagner, and Esteve Polls, Vertigo and Dynamite Entertainment, November 2014–May 2015. Django Freeman teams up with the aging Don Diego de la Vega to battle the self-styled "Archduke of Arizona." This story takes place after the events of Tarantino's film *Django Unchained*, which occurred in 1858–1859. However, the film *The Mask of Zorro* has Don Diego definitively dying in 1842.

Doc Savage Annual 2014 by Shannon Eric Denton and Roberto Castro, Dynamite Entertainment. In the opening captions, Doc says, "Unlike a few of my associates, I embrace the light rather than the shadows . . . I don't want to believe there is a vast web of evil forcing me to adopt sinister methods in order to confront those who live its embrace . . . no desire to fight evil by impersonating it." Doc is alluding to his contemporaries: the pulp vigilante who operates from the shadows, the Spider, and the pale-skinned avenging hero. Later, Doc receives a letter in a pneumatic tube and says "Looks like we have a message . . . provided we're not getting Allard's mail again." Allard is the shadowy pulp hero's real surname in the pulps. Doc uses slang in this story, something he seldom did in the original stories, and is shown as going into a bloody rage against German soldiers over the death of a friend in a flashback to World War I, which seems wildly out of character. One of Doc's aides says "It kinda looked cool," despite the fact the word "cool" was not used in that context in 1930, when this story takes place, and Ham refers to him as "Clark," something unheard of in the original pulps. Most significantly, it is implied the villain of this piece was responsible for the death of Doc's mother, which does not fit with Farmer's account of her death in *Doc Savage: His Apocalyptic Life*.

Doc Savage: Skull Island by Will Murray, Altus Press, 2013. In 1933, Doc Savage returns to the Empire State Building and sees the corpse of King Kong. He tells his men of a previous encounter with the giant ape. In 1920 the search for Doc's grandfather Stormalong Savage led Doc and his father to Skull Island. In *Tarzan Alive* and *Doc Savage: His Apocalyptic Life*, Philip José Farmer identified the 6th Duke of Greystoke as Doc's paternal grandfather; Stormalong Savage bears no resemblance to the Duke. Furthermore,

Doc's mother is identified as Kendra Robeson, rather than Arronaxe Larsen as in the CU. Murray treats Sherlock Holmes, Captain Nemo, Wolf Larsen, Tarzan, and Nick Carter as fictional characters. Finally, Farmer's "After King Kong Fell" also recounts Doc's arrival at the Empire State Building in the aftermath of Kong's fatal plunge, but that story takes place in 1931, and the exact details are different. Given these factors, this novel cannot be incorporated into CU continuity.

"Dracula on the Rocks" by Carole Nelson Douglas in *Celebrity Vampires*, Martin H. Greenberg, ed., DAW Books, 1995. Irene Adler encounters Count Dracula in Warsaw, 1886. Douglas' Irene Adler novels have Irene happily married to Godfrey Norton until at least 1889, which does not fit with William S. Baring-Gould's take on their marriage in *Sherlock Holmes of Baker Street*.

The Dragon Lives Again (aka *Li san jiao wei zhen di yu men* and *Deadly Hands of Kung Fu*), 1977 feature film directed by Kei Law. After his death, Bruce Lee finds himself in the underworld, where he teams up with Popeye, Caine (from *Kung Fu*), and the One-Armed Swordsman (the protagonist of a Hong Kong film series) to battle "the Exorcist," "the Godfather," James Bond, Emmanuelle (the main character of a series of erotic films), Clint Eastwood (dressed as the Man with No Name), Zatoichi, and Dracula (who leads an army of zombies that look suspiciously like guys in skeleton costumes). This film was part of the "Bruceploitation" subgenre that had actors playing Bruce Lee after his death in unauthorized martial arts films. The film explains the difference in Lee's appearance (and, one presumes, the other characters') via a character stating human beings' features change when they die and enter the underworld.

"A Dream of Flying," story written and illustrated by Stan Sakai in *Rocketeer Adventures 2* #1, IDW Publishing, March 2012. Flying through a rural area, the Rocketeer is attacked by a young man with red hair wielding a shotgun. After Cliff falls through the roof of a barn, the redhead demands his rocket pack, saying he'll disassemble it to see how it works and build a better one. Cliff's enemy is attacked from behind by a young boy with a spit curl in his black hair, and Cliff delivers a knockout blow to the would-be thief. The boy says of the thief, "Pa always said that Lex is a bad apple." He expresses excitement at Cliff's ability to fly, and says he has always dreamed of doing so himself, but it's impossible. Cliff takes off into the air with the ecstatic boy in his arms, then brings him back to the ground and flies off into the distance. The boy's parents arrive home from shopping to find him with a sheet tied around his neck, proclaiming he flew. When his mother comments on the boy's imagination, his father says, "Now, Martha, a bit of imagination is good for a boy his age." The boy plays happily, saying "Up, up, and away!" as his dog follows him. The boy is clearly a young Clark Kent, and this takes place before he discovers his superpowers. However, the CU version of Clark was already a grown man and active as Superman by the time Cliff Secord became the Rocketeer, thus placing this story in an AU.

"The Earth Abideth Forever" by Jean-Marc Lofficier in *The Shadow of Judex*, Jean-Marc and Randy Lofficier, eds., Black Coat Press, 2013; reprinted in French in *L'Ombre de Judex*, Jean-Marc and Randy Lofficier, eds., Rivière Blanche, 2013. Billions of years in the future, in the city of Diaspar, the Central Computer created by Yarlan Zey revives Judex so he can once more battle the forces of injustice. Diaspar, the Central Computer, and Yarlan Zey are from Arthur C. Clarke's *The City and the Stars*.

"Elementary My Dear Watson," an episode of the British anthology comedy TV series *Comedy Playhouse* broadcast January 18, 1973. A broad parody in which Sherlock Holmes (played by John Cleese) battles Fu Manchu.

"The Elphberg Red" by Nicholas Boving in *Tales of the Shadowmen Volume 8: Agents Provocateurs*, Jean-Marc and Randy Lofficier, eds., Black Coat Press, 2011; reprinted in French in *Les Compagnons de l'Ombre (Tome 11)*, Jean-Marc and Randy Lofficier, eds., Rivière Blanche, 2013. Rudolf Rassendyll, Doctor John Watson and Inspector Mackenzie attempt to recover the Elphberg Red, a jewel belonging to the Ruritanian royal family, from Rupert of Hentzau and Joséphine Balsamo, Countess Cagliostro. Rassendyll, Ruritania, Colonel Sapt, Rupert, and Queen Flavia are from Anthony Hope's novels *The Prisoner of Zenda* and *Rupert of Hentzau*. Dr. Watson, Mrs. Hudson, Sherlock Holmes, the Baker Street Irregulars, and Wiggins are from the Sherlock Holmes stories. Inspector Mackenzie, Milchester Abbey, Lady Melrose, Raffles, Bunny Manders, and Baird are from the stories by E. W. Hornung. Joséphine Balsamo and Arsène Lupin are from the novels by Maurice Leblanc. Sir Edward Lytton is the grandfather of Sir Charles Lytton, aka the Phantom, from the Pink Panther movies. This story takes place between *Prisoner of Zenda* and *Rupert of Hentzau*, as well as the two Lupin novels featuring Joséphine Balsamo, and the year is given as 1897. However, *Rupert of Hentzau* takes place in 1890, and both Rassendyll and Rupert die in the novel. Lupin did not meet Joséphine until 1894, thus making it impossible to move this story prior to 1890.

"The Empire of the Necromancers Part VI: The Necromancers of London," short story by Brian Stableford in *Tales of the Shadowmen Volume 7: Femmes Fatales*, Jean-Marc and Randy Lofficier, eds., Black Coat Press,

2010; collected in Black Coat Press' *Frankenstein in London*. Characters from the works of Paul Féval (*John Devil, Revenants, The Vampire Countess*, and the Black Coats series), as well as Victor Frankenstein and "Lazarus" (aka Frankenstein's Monster, both from Mary Shelley's *Frankenstein*), and Giuseppe Balsamo (from Alexandre Dumas' *Joseph Balsamo*) appear.

"The Evil of Atlantis" by Frank Schildiner in *Ravenwood: Stepson of Mystery Volume One*, Ron Fortier, ed., Cornerstone Book Publishers, 2010. Ravenwood battles the Atlantean priest Sun Koh, who is attempting to summon the Black Pharaoh, aka Nyarlathotep. Occult detective Ravenwood was created by Frederick C. Davis and appeared in his own stories in the *Secret Agent X* pulp magazine. Sun Koh appeared in a German pulp magazine (or "heftroman") by Paul Müller. Jan Mayen, who was also the subject of a series by Müller, crossed over with Sun Koh on more than one occasion. Nyarlathotep, Hastur, the *Necronomicon*, the Mad Arab (Abdul Alhazred), and the Deep Ones are from the Cthulhu Mythos fiction of H. P. Lovecraft. The black lotus drug appeared in Robert E. Howard's series of stories about the barbarian Conan, as well as his tales of police detective Steve Harrison. Atlach-Nacha is from Clark Ashton Smith's Cthulhu Mythos story "The Seven Geases." In this story, Sun Koh is depicted as a minion of the Great Old Ones rather than the strong-willed character he is portrayed as in the pulps and other stories involving the Nazi superman.

"The Executioner" by Lawrence Connolly in *Gaslight Arcanum: Uncanny Tales of Sherlock Holmes*, J. R. Campbell and Charles Prepolec, eds., EDGE Science Fiction and Fantasy Publishing, 2011. Frankenstein's Monster revives Sherlock Holmes and Professor Moriarty after their fatal battle at Reichenbach Falls.

"Eye of the Gorgon," *Batman Incorporated* #2 by Grant Morrison and Chris Burnham, DC Comics, August 2012. A retelling of the life story of Talia al Ghul, daughter of Batman's enemy Ra's al Ghul, and mother of his son Damian, the current Robin. As a birthday gift, Ra's gives his daughter a base that "once belonged to the infamous Devil Doctor of Limehouse himself." This is, of course, Fu Manchu, who has often been cited as one of the primary inspirations for the character of Ra's al Ghul. This series is part of DC's "New 52," a company-wide "reboot" of its titles with a brand-new continuity, and likely takes place outside CU continuity as well. This issue also continues the plot from the first, which had an appearance by the superteam known as the Outsiders, providing further proof this series takes place in an AU.

Femme Fatale, novel by Carole Nelson Douglas, Forge Books, 2003. It is revealed Irene Adler took her alias from a man named Adler who used mesmerism to bring her skill at singing opera to the forefront. Later using the name Svengali, Adler used his talents to turn an artist's model named Trilby into the supreme soprano of the age. Svengali and Trilby O'Ferrall are from George du Maurier's novel *Trilby*.

The Fifth Heart, a Sherlock Holmes pastiche by Dan Simmons, Little, Brown and Company, 2015. Colonel Moran is identified as Colonel John Sebastian "Tiger Jack" Moran, the same full name and nickname given for him in George MacDonald Fraser's *Flashman and the Tiger*. Inspector Hanaud (a detective seen in novels by A. E. W. Mason) and Hercule Poirot are mentioned, and the Lakota Indian Paha Sapa from Simmons' novel *Black Hills* appears. The revelations in this novel about Holmes and Moriarty place it in an alternate universe.

"File 4: The Adventure of the Sussex Vampire," story by Kaoru Shinitani in *Christie High Tension Volume 2*, part of a *manga* (known as *Young Miss Holmes* in America) featuring Crystal Margaret "Christie" Hope (Holmes in the American version), the mystery-solving 10-year-old niece of Sherlock Holmes. This particular story has a cameo by Mina Tepes from Nozomu Tamaki's *manga Dance in the Vampire Bund*. In that series, Mina, the queen of all vampires, reveals the existence of the undead to the world, and therefore both *Dance in the Vampire Bund* and *Christie High Tension* must take place in an alternate reality.

Flash Gordon: Zeitgeist, ten-issue miniseries by Eric Trautman, Alex Ross, Daniel Indro, and Ron Adrian, Dynamite Entertainment. A reimagining of Flash Gordon's first trip to Mongo. The Phantom and Mandrake make cameo appearances in the fourth issue.

"The Frequency of Fear" by Micah S. Harris in *Tales of the Shadowmen Volume 10: Esprit de Corps*, Jean-Marc and Randy Lofficier, eds., Black Coat Press, 2013; reprinted in French in *Les Compagnons de l'Ombre (Tome 14)*, Jean-Marc and Randy Lofficier, eds., Rivière Blanche, 2014. Detective Teddy Verano and psychic Winnie Innsmouth battle rogue members of a government project, who are working with a *dugpa* to create enough fear to open a doorway to the Black Lodge. Winnie Innsmouth is from a planned supernatural comic book series; Harris created the character, Mark Schultz suggested her surname, and Loston Wallace drew her and finalized her look. Teddy Verano and Edwige Hossegor (aka Mephista) are from books by Maurice Limat. The Innes family is from Edgar Rice

Burroughs' novels taking place in the Earth's core. Michel Delassalle is from the movie *Diabolique*. Dr. Karl Mantell is from the movie *Fear Chamber*. Dr. Warren Chopin (aka Chapin) and the Tinglers are from the movie *The Tingler*. Colonel Whiteshroud is from the short-lived series *Monster Hunters*, published by Charlton Comics. Innsmouth and the Zadoks are from H. P. Lovecraft's "The Shadow over Innsmouth." The meteor shards in New England are from Lovecraft's "The Colour Out of Space." Arkham, Massachusetts is a staple of Lovecraft's Cthulhu Mythos. The *dugpas*, the Black Lodge, and the White Lodge are from Talbot Mundy's novel *The Devil's Guard*, as well as the TV series *Twin Peaks*. Garland Briggs is also from *Twin Peaks*. Dr. Nolter is from the movie *The Mutations* (aka *The Freakmaker*). Dr. Shiragami is from the movie *Godzilla vs. Biollante*. Dr. Lorca is from the movie *Mad Doctor of Blood Island*. Harrison Chase is from the *Doctor Who* serial "The Seeds of Doom." Gilles Novak is from novels by Jimmy Guieu. Hareton Ironcastle and the Mineral-Vegetable King are from J.-H. Rosny aîné's *L'Étonnant Voyage d'Hareton Ironcastle*, as well as Philip José Farmer's translation and adaptation, *Ironcastle*. Dr. Duryea is from the movie *Dracula vs. Frankenstein*. Sally Hardesty is from the film *The Texas Chainsaw Massacre*. The government's *Scanners* program is from the movie *Scanners*. The story implies *The Texas Chainsaw Massacre* was a distorted fictionalization of the abduction of Sally Hardesty, and her subsequent death at the hands of Delassalle's chainsaw-wielding henchman Buzz. However, there are several crossovers bringing *The Texas Chainsaw Massacre* and its sequels into the Crossover Universe, making "The Frequency of Fear's" version of the true events that inspired the film irreconcilable with established CU continuity.

Friday the 13th, 2009 feature film, a reboot of the horror franchise. An obnoxious jock named Trent is one of Jason Voorhees' victims. This is meant to be Trent DeMarco from the movie *Transformers*, directed by *Friday the 13th* producer Michael Bay. Travis Van Winkle played Trent in both films. The events of the *Transformers* films, involving giant shape-changing robots engaging in very public and destructive battles, are incompatible with CU continuity.

Ghostbusters, comic book series released by IDW Publishing, based on the film series. In the one-shot *What in Samhain Just Happened?* by Peter David, Kathleen David, and Dan Schoening, 2010, a television producer seeks out the Ghostbusters to clear a ghost out of his home, so he can capture the bust on film. A DeLorean appears outside the 'Busters' firehouse. This is probably the car from the *Back to the Future* film series. After the Ghostbusters turn him down, the producer mentions he's heard of two brothers who are good at handling ghosts, "Remington . . . something like that," a reference to the Winchester brothers from the television series *Supernatural*. A copy of the *Necronomicon* also appears whose look is based on *The Real Ghostbusters* episode "Collect Call of Cthulhu." In "The Man from the Mirror," *Ghostbusters* #1–4 by Erik Burnham, Tristan Jones, and Dan Schoening, September–December 2011, KITT, the car driven by Michael Knight on the television series *Knight Rider*, appears. The Ecto-1a zooms past Axel Foley from the *Beverly Hills Cop* film series. The Blues Brothers' Bluesmobile is seen parked in front of the left foot of Ray Stantz, who has been turned into a Stay-Puft Marshmallow Man-like creature. The A-Team's van passes the Ghostbusters as Ray Stantz fixes a flat tire on the Ecto-1, with B. A. Baracus telling them they suck. In "Mass Hysteria," *Ghostbusters* Volume 2 #13–20 by Erik Burnham and Dan Schoening, February–September 2014, a god erases Winston Zeddemore's marriage by altering everyone's memories. The other Ghostbusters mention they've heard of similar things happening in Portland and to a photographer in Queens. The Portland reference is to Nick Burkhardt's fiancée Juliet's story arc in the second season of the television series *Grimm*. The photographer in Queens is Peter Parker, aka Spider-Man, who made a deal with the demon Mephisto to erase his marriage to Mary Jane Watson in order to save his Aunt May's life in the comic book storyline "One More Day." In *Teenage Mutant Ninja Turtles/Ghostbusters* #1–4 by Erik Burnham, Tom Waltz, Charles Paul Wilson III, Cory Smith, and Dan Schoening, October 2014–January 2015, the Ghostbusters team up with a quartet of masked anthropomorphic turtles from another reality to battle a centuries-old ghost. IDW's *Ghostbusters* comics feature reinterpreted versions of characters from *The Real Ghostbusters* and its sequel series, *Extreme Ghostbusters*. Since both animated series are definitely CU canon, IDW's comics featuring the 'Busters must take place in an alternate reality to the CU. This placement is cemented by the miniseries *Ghostbusters: Get Real*, which features IDW's 'Busters encountering their counterparts from *The Real Ghostbusters*, who are explicitly shown to exist in an alternate universe.

"Gilgamesh Revisited" by Matthew Baugh in *Tales of the Shadowmen Volume 11: Force Majeure*, Jean-Marc and Randy Lofficier, eds., Black Coat Press, 2014; reprinted in French in *Les Compagnons de l'Ombre (Tome 16)*, Jean-Marc and Randy Lofficier, eds., Rivière Blanche, 2015. A retelling of the Gilgamesh myth, with the characters altered to parallel characters from the CU. Gilgamesh parallels Doc Ardan from Guy d'Armen's *Doc Ardan: City of Gold and Lepers*; Jean-Marc and Randy Lofficier's adaptation and translation of that novel implied Ardan was really an American bronze-skinned pulp hero. Ut-Napishtim parallels Ardan's foe Doctor Natas, whom the Lofficiers conflated with Sax Rohmer's master villain Doctor Fu Manchu. Enkidu resembles Zembla, a jungle hero appearing in French comic books. Shamhat is analogous to Queen Antinea from Pierre Benoit's novel *L'Atlantide*. Humbaba is based on King Kong. Shangri La (from James Hilton's novel *Lost Horizon*) is also mentioned.

"The Girl from Odessa" by David McDonald in *Night of the Nyctalope*, Jean-Marc and Randy Lofficier, eds., Black Coat Press, 2012; reprinted in French in *Les Compagnons de l'Ombre (Tome 11)*, Jean-Marc and Randy Lofficier, eds., Rivière Blanche, 2013 and *L'Almanach des Vampires (Tome 2)*, Jean-Marc and Randy Lofficier, eds., Rivière Blanche, 2015; and in *The Vampire Almanac (Volume 1)*, Jean-Marc and Randy Lofficier, eds., Black Coat Press, 2015. Leo Saint-Clair (aka the Nyctalope) runs into Colonel Harry Flashman II and Sergeant Ballantine, old friends of his father. Both Leo and Harry are meeting with Countess Anastasiya Belinskya in hopes of obtaining documents that will be of use to their respective governments. The Nyctalope's adventures were chronicled by Jean de La Hire. Harry Flashman II is the son of Harry Flashman from Thomas Hughes' *Tom Brown's Schooldays* and the Flashman novels by George MacDonald Fraser. Sergeant Ballantine is an ancestor of Bill Ballantine, a comrade of Bob Morane in novels by Henri Vernes. Harry II and Ballantine worked with Leo's father Jean in McDonald's stories "Catspaw" (*Tales of the Shadowmen Volume 8: Agents Provocateurs*, Jean-Marc and Randy Lofficier, eds., Black Coat Press, 2011) and "Diplomatic Freeze" (*Tales of the Shadowmen Volume 9: La Vie en Noir*, Jean-Marc and Randy Lofficier, eds., Black Coat Press, 2012). Countess Belinskya is a relative of the Belinskyas seen in the film *The White Countess*.

Gotham by Gaslight, an "Elseworlds" graphic novel by Brian Augustyn and Mike Mignola, DC Comics, 1989. In 1889, Bruce Wayne returns to Gotham City and takes on the mantle of Batman, and soon finds himself hunting Jack the Ripper, who has fled England. In Austria, Sigmund Freud tells Bruce, "A good student, you have been. My friend, the English detective, said much the same thing," a clear reference to Sherlock Holmes.

"The Great and Groovy Game" by Joshua Wanisko in *The Lovecraft eZine* #18, Mike Davis, ed., October 2012. A woman named Charlotte and Arachne the Weaver, closers in the Great Game, encounter the openers Pig Boy and the Prescient Pig. The Great Game and its openers and closers are from Roger Zelazny's *A Night in the Lonesome October*, which has been placed in an alternate universe. The quote "If one imaginary thing exists, then all imaginary things must exist" is from Zelazany's book *If at Faust You Don't Succeed*. The driver in the Dodge Challenger (Kowalski) and Super

Soul are from the movie *Vanishing Point*. Innsmouth and the Deep Ones are from H. P. Lovecraft's "The Shadow over Innsmouth." Van Owen is from Warren Zevon's song "Roland the Headless Thompson Gunner."

"The Green Eye" by Nicholas Boving in *Tales of the Shadowmen Volume 10: Esprit de Corps*, Jean-Marc and Randy Lofficier, eds., Black Coat Press, 2013; reprinted in French in *Les Compagnons de l'Ombre (Tome 14)*, Jean-Marc and Randy Lofficier, eds., Rivière Blanche, 2014. A sequel to Boving's "The Elphberg Red." Rupert of Hentzau recruits Phileas Fogg and his cousin Rebecca to transport him across India in Fogg's airship, the *Aurora*. Rupert of Hentzau is from Anthony Hope's *The Prisoner of Zenda*. Phileas Fogg and his servant Passepartout are from Jules Verne's *Around the World in Eighty Days*. The airship *Aurora* and Rebecca Fogg are from the television series *The Secret Adventures of Jules Verne*. Also appearing or mentioned are: Countess Joséphine Balsamo, Arsène Lupin's foe; Daniel Dravot and Peachy Carnehan from Rudyard Kipling's "The Man Who Would Be King"; Maboub Ali and Colonel William Creighton from Kipling's *Kim*; Carew and the Idol's Eye from J. Milton Hayes' poem "The Green Eye of the Little Yellow God"; A. J. Raffles, E. W. Hornung's gentleman thief; and Amanda Darieux from the television series *Highlander: The Series* and *Highlander: The Raven*.

H.: The Story of Heathcliff's Journey Back to Wuthering Heights by Lin Haire-Sergeant, Pocket Books, 1992. Heathcliff (from Emily Brontë's novel *Wuthering Heights*) discovers he is the biological son of Mr. Edward Rochester and his first wife, Bertha Mason (from Emily's sister Charlotte Brontë's novel *Jane Eyre*). However, the events of *Wuthering Heights* take place decades before those of *Jane Eyre*, creating a chronological issue that cannot be resolved.

The Halflife Chronicles, novel series by Wm. Mark Simmons. Chris Cséjthe finds his life turned upside down when he discovers vampires, werewolves, and other supernatural creatures exist, and he himself is now halfway through the transition between human and vampire. Dracula appears prominently in the first novel, *One Foot in the Grave*, as do tanis leaves, legends of which inspired the tana leaves in Universal Studios' Mummy movies. A vampire named Barnabas who carries a wolf's head cane appears; this is Barnabas Collins of *Dark Shadows* fame. A New Orleans vampire enclave with literary pretensions is mentioned, a reference to Anne Rice's *The Vampire Chronicles*. In the fourth book, *Dead Easy*, Chris encounters the Great Old Ones and Captain Nemo. Nemo tells Chris Professor Aronnax was fictional and Verne made *The Mysterious Island* up out of whole cloth. Nemo died in the 19th century, and was later resurrected as a rakshasa, a spirit being from Hindu mythology. Several individuals experienced in dealing with the supernatural are mentioned:

a wizard in Chicago (Harry Dresden from Jim Butcher's *The Dresden Files* novel series); a necromancer in St. Louis (Anita Blake from novels by Laurell K. Hamilton); a waitress in Bon Temps (Sookie Stackhouse from Charlaine Harris' *Southern Vampire Mysteries*); a weather warden (Joanne Baldwin, the protagonist of a series by Rachel Caine); and a guardian in London (Aisling Grey from novels by Katie MacAlister). Simmons' take on Captain Nemo is very different from his established history in the CU. Combined with the fact both Sookie Stackhouse and Anita Blake's exploits take place in worlds where the public is aware vampires and other supernatural entities are real, this places *The Halflife Chronicles* in an alternate universe.

"His Last Vow," episode of the television series *Sherlock*, a reimagining of Sherlock Holmes as a 21st century detective. Mycroft Holmes says a colleague of his thinks Britain sometimes needs a "blunt instrument," but his brother Sherlock is a "scalpel wielded with precision." Mycroft's colleague is M, who referred to James Bond as a "blunt instrument" in the 2006 film version of *Casino Royale*.

"Hounded" by Stephen Volk in *Gaslight Grotesque: Nightmare Tales of Sherlock Holmes*, J. R. Campbell and Charles Prepolec, eds., EDGE Science Fiction and Fantasy Publishing, 2009. Dr. Watson attends a séance where the Hound of the Baskervilles is conjured up. The late Sherlock Holmes forced Watson to write a mostly fabricated account of their encounter with Hound, including the false claim the beast was not in fact supernatural in origin. The spiritualist's house contains a painting of a unicorn by Harvey Deacon and books by, among others, occultist Paul Le Duc; both individuals are from Arthur Conan Doyle's short story "Playing with Fire." Professor George Challenger is mentioned as a believer in spiritualism. A reference to Rudolph Valentino places this story sometime between the 1914 events of "His Last Bow" (1914 also being the year Valentino began acting) and the star's death in 1926.

"Hyde & Seek" by Aaron Smith in *Dr. Watson's American Adventure*, Airship 27 Productions, 2012. British agent Quincy "Hound-Dog" Harker battles a mad scientist who has recreated the serum developed by the man who was given the pseudonym of Dr. Henry Jekyll by Robert Louis Stevenson. Harker is assisted by a Swiss female police inspector and Dr. John Seward, an old family friend.

"I Spy Something . . . Boo!" *Scooby-Doo Team-Up* #11 by Sholly Fisch and Dario Brizuela, DC Comics, September 2015. Scooby and the gang team up with Secret Squirrel and Morocco Mole to apprehend a ghost that repeatedly attempts to disrupt a treaty between two rival nations. Jonny Quest is mentioned. Secret and Morocco are anthropomorphic animals, and therefore I place this story in an AU.

"The Icon Crackdown" by Michael Moorcock in *Tales of the Shadowmen Volume 10: Esprit de Corps*, Jean-Marc and Randy Lofficier, eds., Black Coat Press, 2013; reprinted in French in *Les Compagnons de l'Ombre (Tome 13)*, Jean-Marc and Randy Lofficier, eds., Rivière Blanche, 2014. A Jerry Cornelius tale set in an alternate reality where Texas has seceded from the United States, among other differences from the CU. Sexton Blake appears, as does Jacques Collin (from Balzac's *La Comédie Humaine*). Judex, Sherlock Holmes, the Ace of Spades (a comic book character created by Hugo Pratt), Fantômas, Tigris (the hero of a series of novels by Marcel Allain), Monsieur Zenith, A. J. Raffles, and Arsène Lupin are mentioned.

The Inferior Five #1–10, comic book series published by DC Comics, March–April 1967–September–October 1968, featuring a team of incompetent second generation superheroes. Parodies of various CU characters appear, including Reed Victor, the Yellowjacket, and his chauffeur Plato (Britt Reid, the Green Hornet, and Kato); Caesar Single and Kwitcha Belliakin of C.O.U.S.I.N.F.R.E.D. (Napoleon Solo and Illya Kuryakin of U.N.C.L.E.); John Claypool, Lord Gravestone, aka Darwin of the Apes (the jungle lord); Sir Chauncey Berkeley, the Crimson Chrysanthemum (Sir Percy Blakeney, the Scarlet Pimpernel); and Allergy Queen (Ellery Queen).

Jack the Ripper, an 1889 stage play by Gaston Marot and Louis Pericot, adapted by Frank J. Morlock in *Sherlock Holmes vs. Jack the Ripper*, Black Coat Press, 2011. Another Holmes vs. the Ripper story. Nick Carter appears, and the Gentlemen of the Night (from Paul Féval's *Les Mystères de Londres*) are mentioned.

Jason X: Death Moon by Alex Johnson, Black Flame, 2005. One legend about Jason Voorhees states his great-great-great-great-grandfather Jebediah Voorhees was a warlock who possessed a copy of the *Necronomicon Ex Mortis* (from the *Evil Dead* films). After his seeming death in 1667, the book was eventually passed down to Jason's father Elias, who accidentally summoned a demon with it that allegedly possessed Jason. This novel is a tie-in to the movie *Jason X*, which has Jason being brought out of cryogenic suspension in 2455, when the Earth has been overcome by pollution and humans have relocated to a new planet called Earth Two. This does not fit with the future of the CU's Earth seen in other stories set in the 25th Century or later, and therefore *Jason X* must take place in an alternate timeline.

However, the historical details about Jebediah Voorhees are probably true in CU continuity as well. They would explain the presence of the *Necronomicon Ex Mortis* in the Voorhees home in the movie *Jason Goes to Hell: The Final Friday*, as well as how Jason keeps coming back from the dead.

"The Jasoom Project" by S. M. Stirling in *Under the Moons of Mars*, John Joseph Adams, ed., Simon & Schuster, 2012. The warlord of Mars' great-grandson has an adventure, and travels to Earth, which is under attack by lunar menaces (from Burroughs' *The Moon Maid* and sequels). There, he meets the jungle lord, who suggests they head to the world at the Earth's core. The Moon series takes place in an alternate reality to the CU.

"Judex Rules" by Rick Lai in *The Shadow of Judex*, Jean-Marc and Randy Lofficier, eds., Black Coat Press, 2013; reprinted in French in *L'Ombre de Judex*, Jean-Marc and Randy Lofficier, eds., Rivière Blanche, 2013. In two different realities, Judex and Ragging Rassendyll intervene in the vigilantes Umbra and Araneus' duel to decide who will protect New York. Fantômas is the master criminal featured in novels by Marcel Allain and Pierre Souvestre. Mike Volny is from *The Untouchables* episode "The Night They Shot Santa Claus." Joe Kulak appeared in six episodes of the same series. Malay John's is from *The Further Adventures of Jimmie Dale* by Frank L. Packard. Jimmie Dale is also known as the Gray Seal. Malay Jack's is from Sax Rohmer's stories "Kerry's Kid" and "Tcheriapin." Ali of Cairo is from Rohmer's "The Man with the Shaven Skull." All three stories appear in the collection *Tales of Chinatown*. Araneus is better known as Richard Wentworth, aka the Spider. Hanoi Shan is from H. Ashton-Wolfe's *Warped in the Making* and *The Thrill of Evil*. Théophraste Lupin is the father of Maurice Leblanc's gentleman thief Arsène Lupin. Darlla Rassendyll, aka the Revenant, is from the *Shadows of the Opera* books by Lai. The Black Coats are from the novels by Paul Féval. Henri de Lagardère is from Féval's *Le Bossu*. Fergus O'Breane is from another Féval novel, *The Mysteries of London*. Ragging Rassendyll is meant to be Robert J. Hogan's pulp aviator G-8. Umbra is meant to be the well-known pulp hero of the shadows; in *Doc Savage: His Apocalyptic Life*, Philip José Farmer gave his true name as Allard Kent Rassendyll, and identified him as the brother of Bruce Hagin Rassendyll (aka G-8) and the half-brother of Richard Wentworth. The giant ape killed by Ragging Rassendyll is King Kong; Jim Harmon first proposed G-8 was one of the pilots that killed Kong in his article "The Life Story of King Kong." Philip Strange appeared in pulp stories by Donald E. Keyhoe, while Pierre d'Artois' pulp exploits were chronicled by E. Hoffmann Price. Vautrin is from Honoré de Balzac's *La Comédie Humaine* cycle of novels. Philo Vance is a detective appearing in books by S. S. Van Dine. Ellery Queen is a noted mystery writer and amateur sleuth. Rocambole is from the novels of Ponson du Terrail. Chéri-Bibi appears in novels by Gaston Leroux. In this story, Al (Allard Kent) Rassendyll is depicted as the alternate reality counterpart of Kenton (Kent) Allard, the son of Théophraste Lupin and Darlla Rassendyll. The Araneus of Kenton Allard's world chooses to operate in Los Angeles instead of New York, although Umbra agrees to let him operate in the city when he is out of town. Farmer's genealogy for Allard Kent Rassendyll in *Doc Savage* is portrayed as based on visions of Al Rassendyll's reality suffered by the Ragging Rassendyll of Kenton Allard's world, who provided misleading information to Farmer at Allard's request, having first told him Araneus, Ragging, and Kenton were all the same person, as Farmer originally wrote in *Tarzan Alive*. The other world's Umbra (Al Rassendyll) gave up his crimefighting activities in New York until Araneus retired in the 1940s, at which point he embarked on adventures analogous to the Shadow novels by Bruce Elliott, which portrayed the hero as operating almost entirely without a disguise. Neither reality's history fits with the established continuity of the CU.

Justice, Inc., six-issue miniseries by Michael Uslan and Giovanni Timpano, Dynamite Entertainment, 2014–2015, a sequel to Uslan's miniseries *The Shadow/Green Hornet: Dark Nights*. The Shadow, Doc Savage, and the newly minted Avenger battle Rodil Mocquino and John Sunlight, who seek to master time itself. In #3, Doc says one of his ancestors was a Vandal. The implication of this statement is Doc is descended from the immortal DC Comics supervillain Vandal Savage. The Shadow compares the death of Benson's wife and daughter to "that murder case last May . . . only there the child survived while the parents were slain." The child is Bruce Wayne, later known as the Batman. In #5, John Sunlight has two-way wrist radios, which were stolen from "those detectives I killed last month," a reference to Dick Tracy and Sam Catchem. Michael Uslan's annotations in the back of the issue indicate Sunlight only thought he had killed Tracy and Catchem. In #6, a Nazi agent named Kruger appears. This is meant to be Heinz Kruger, the Nazi agent who killed Dr. Reinstein, the creator of the Super-Soldier Serum that empowered Captain America. This series offers a very different take on the circumstances of the Avenger's origin than Paul Ernst's original pulp novel *Justice, Inc.* A time-traveling Doc Savage from the 21st century appears; this is the version of Doc seen in Dynamite's *Doc Savage* miniseries. However, that series is incompatible with the details of Doc's later life given in Philip José Farmer and Win Scott Eckert's *The Evil in Pemberley House.* Also, Bruce Wayne's parents died in 1929 in the CU, not 1939. Therefore, this series must take place in an alternate universe. Benson's coining of the term "Justice, Inc." here is odd, given an office with that name on its door appeared in *Dark Nights*.

Kings Watch, five-issue miniseries by Jeff Parker and Mark Laming, Dynamite Entertainment, 2013–2014. The Phantom, Mandrake, Flash Gordon, Lothar, Karma, Dale Arden, and Dr. Hans Zarkov battle Ming the Merciless and the Cobra. The Phantom seen here is not a member of the Walker family, but rather had the identity passed to him by the last descendant of the original Phantom on his deathbed. Mandrake's wife Narda has turned evil, becoming the Cobra's henchwoman and lover. Flash Gordon and company are updated to modern times, and their first meeting here is under different circumstances than their first appearance in the comic strip. In 2015, five miniseries continuing the story appeared: *King: Flash Gordon* #1-4 by Ben Acker, Ben Blacker, and Lee Ferguson; *King: Jungle Jim* #1-4 by Paul Tobin, Sandy Jarrell, and Tadd Galusha; *King: Mandrake the Magician* #1-4 by Roger Langridge, Jeremy Treece, Felipe Cunha, and Ivan Rodriguez; *King: Prince Valiant* #1-4 by Nate Cosby, Ron Salas, and Ben McCool; and *King: The Phantom* #1-4 by Brian Clevinger, Brent Schoonover, Ryan Cody, and Scott Godlewski. Flash Gordon, Dale Arden, Dr. Zarkov, and Jungle Jim are heavily mischaracterized.

"Kovak the Night Walker" by Mark Rahner and Javier Garcia-Miranda in *Vampirella* #100, Dynamite Entertainment, January 2015. Cal Kovak, a former news reporter who frequently encountered the supernatural, tells two FBI agents (apparently Mulder and Scully) about how Vampirella always saved him from the monsters he faced back in the 1970s. Cal Kovak is based on Carl Kolchak from the TV series *Kolchak: The Night Stalker*. On the show, Kolchak always managed to get himself out of trouble without the help of Vampi.

Lady Rawhide/Lady Zorro, four-issue miniseries by Shannon Eric Denton and Rey Villegas, Dynamite Entertainment, 2015. Lady Rawhide and Lady Zorro join forces to combat a group of slavers who are taking kidnapped women to sell to a brothel. Lady Zorro is from Dynamite Entertainment's Zorro comic, which portrays Don Diego de la Vega as half-Indian on his mother's side. This does not fit with the continuity of either Johnston McCulley's original tales or the continuations by later authors, and therefore Dynamite's version of Zorro must exist in an AU.

"The Last Jest of Arsène Lupin" by David L. Vineyard in *The Many Faces of Arsène Lupin*, Jean-Marc and Randy Lofficier, eds., Black Coat Press, 2012; reprinted in French in *Les Compagnons de l'Ombre (Tome 9)*, Jean-Marc and Randy Lofficier, eds., Rivière Blanche, 2012. The seemingly dying Arsène Lupin bequeaths the treasures he has accumulated over the decades to the people of France, but persuades Indiana Jones and Dirk Pitt to solve a puzzle in order to acquire it. Pitt is the hero of a series of novels by Clive Cussler.

Also appearing or mentioned are: Sherlock Holmes; Fu Manchu; Lupin's son in New York (Nero Wolfe); Maigret; San-Antonio (the protagonist of a series of spy novels by Frédéric Dard); Colonel Bozzo-Corona; Father Brown; and Raffles. The identification of Lupin as Nero Wolfe's father rather than Sherlock Holmes places this story outside of Crossover Universe continuity.

"Last of the *Kaiju*" by John Gallagher in *Tales of the Shadowmen Volume 10: Esprit de Corps*, Jean-Marc and Randy Lofficier, eds., Black Coat Press, 2013; reprinted in French in *Les Compagnons de l'Ombre (Tome 14)*, Jean-Marc and Randy Lofficier, eds., Rivière Blanche, 2014. Doctor Omega takes Barbarella back in time to 1962, where she captures Godzilla and King Kong the Second as birthday gifts for the president of Earth. Doctor Omega and his companions, Fred and Tizairou, are from Arnould Galopin's novel *Doctor Omega*, as well as its translation and adaptation by Jean-Marc and Randy Lofficier, which implied Omega was the CU counterpart of the Doctor of *Doctor Who* fame. The Blinovitch Limitation Effect is also from *Doctor Who*. Barbarella is the main character of a science fiction comic book by Jean-Claude Forest. President Dianthus and Professor Ping are from the film version of *Barbarella*. Godzilla is the so-called "King of the Monsters" in Japanese cinema. King Kong the Second is from the film *King Kong vs. Godzilla*. Rodan is from the Japanese monster film of the same name. Angilas is from the film *Godzilla Raids Again*. Ebirah is from the film *Godzilla vs. the Sea Monster*. Stella Starr is from the science fiction film *Starcrash*. The frequent massive destruction occurring in Tokyo and surrounding environs shown in the Godzilla movies is incompatible with CU continuity, and therefore this story takes place in an alternate universe.

The League of Extraordinary Gentlemen, Volume III: Century: 1969 by Alan Moore and Kevin O'Neill, Top Shelf Productions, 2011. Mina Murray struggles with the weight of immortality as she, Allan Quatermain, and Orlando attempt to thwart Oliver Haddo's plan to possess rock star Terner (from the movie *Performance*, though there his name is spelled "Turner.") Britain's Prime Minister is Wilson, a long-lived athlete who appeared in the magazines *The Wizard* and *Hornet*, rather than Harold Wilson, the U.K.'s real prime minister in 1969. The American president is identified as pop star Max Foster, who has imprisoned non-hippies in concentration camps, a reference to Max Frost from the film *Wild in the Streets*. Additionally, a character named Tom appears; this is meant to be Tom Marvalo Riddle, alias Lord Voldemort, the archnemesis of J. K. Rowling's boy wizard Harry Potter. However, Moore has Tom stating he teaches occult studies at a school up north, whereas Rowling's novels never portrayed Voldemort as a professor at Hogwarts.

The League of Extraordinary Gentlemen, Volume III: Century: 2009 by Alan Moore and Kevin O'Neill, Top Shelf Productions, 2012. Orlando, now female, attempts to track down her long-lost companions Allan Quatermain and Mina Murray, and finally defeat Oliver Haddo's plan to unleash a Moonchild upon the world. America and Britain are at war with Q'Mar (aka Qumar, a fictional Middle Eastern country from the TV series *The West Wing*), and David Palmer (from the show *24*) has succeeded *The West Wing*'s Jed Bartlet as President of the United States. The Prime Minister of Great Britain is Tom Davis from the TV series *The Thick of It*. The M played by Judi Dench in the James Bond movies is identified as Emma Peel, whereas Raymond Benson's novel *The Facts of Death* gives her real name as Barbara Mawdsley. Bond himself is depicted as aging and decrepit, is suffering from cirrhosis, emphysema, and syphilis, and has been impersonated for decades by a series of increasingly younger agents for the purposes of national morale, a reference to the number of actors who have portrayed him on film. This does not fit with the continuity of John Gardner and Raymond Benson's continuation novels. Furthermore, the Moonchild is revealed here as Harry Potter, who massacred the other students and the faculty of Hogwarts, which contradicts the continuity of J. K. Rowling's novels.

"The League of Professional Jealousy" by Javier Grillo-Marxuach and Tom Kurzanski in *The Middleman: The Second Volume Inevitability*, Viper Comics, 2006. Dr. Van Helsing and Jonathan Harker set out to destroy Dracula, only to find they have been beaten to the punch. Soon after, Phileas Fogg returns to the Reform Club after finishing his eighty-day trek around the world, only to find out his time has been beaten by the same person who stole Van Helsing's thunder: the adventurer known as the Middleman. Van Helsing enlists Nikolai Tesla to help him and Fogg get their revenge, which involves Van Helsing spreading rumors of a demonic hound in the moors of Devonshire. However, Tesla actually helps the Middleman outwit Van Helsing and Fogg. Learning there are now reports of a seemingly real "Hound of the Baskervilles" in Devonshire, the Middleman later sends a letter to Holmes and Watson telling them he has already solved the mystery, and he is off to the high seas, where a maniac has been ramming cargo ships with a submarine. This story is a parody, and Van Helsing and Fogg are both out of character. Additionally, the year is given as 1897, whereas in the CU *Dracula* took place in 1887, *Around the World in Eighty Days* in 1872, *The Hound of the Baskervilles* in 1888, and *20,000 Leagues Under the Sea* in 1866–1868.

"The Legacy of Erich Zann" by Brian Stableford in *The Legacy of Erich Zann and Other Tales of the Cthulhu Mythos*, Wildside Press, 2012. C. Auguste Dupin chases a murderous individual seeking Erich Zann's violin and notes.

Nyarlathotep, the Old Ones, the Elder Things, and von Juntz's *Unaussprech-lichen Kulten* are mentioned, as is Abbé Apollonius, a heretic monk from Averoigne, a fictional province of France seen in several of Clark Ashton Smith's stories. An Inspector Lestrade also appears who may be a relative of Sherlock Holmes' rival. Stableford places the events of Lovecraft's "The Music of Erich Zann," including the title character's death, in the 1830s, since there are no solid chronological references in the story itself. However, the graphic novel *The Irregulars . . . In the Service of Sherlock Holmes*, which has already been incorporated into the CU, portrays Zann as alive and well in 1896.

"Legends" by Tom Johnson in *Pulp Detective* #4, Altus Press, 2010. A masked hero comes out of retirement in 1963 to bring to justice a criminal he failed to apprehend ten years ago. The hero, identified only as "the legend," has disguises representing a number of pulp heroes, including Secret Agent X, the Phantom Detective, the Black Bat, the Spider, and the shadow-cloaked vigilante. Detective-Sergeant McGrath from the Black Bat stories appears, and the Pink Ship, a dive bar appearing in other stories by Johnson, is mentioned. The legend is meant to be symbolic of any and every pulp hero.

The Limehouse Text by Will Thomas, Touchstone, 2006. It is mentioned another private enquiry agent named Hewitt sometimes takes the cases for which detective Cyrus Barker is too busy. Thomas has written a series of novels about Cyrus Barker, who is meant to be the same Barker, Sherlock Holmes' "hated rival upon the Surrey Shore," that appears in Doyle's "The Adventure of the Retired Colourman." In his story "No Ghosts Need Apply," Win Scott Eckert gives Barker's first name as Cecil. Additionally, Thomas' novel *Anatomy of Evil* features Barker pursuing Jack the Ripper. This novel does not fit with the events of Ellery Queen's *A Study in Terror*, and so the Cyrus Barker series must take place in an AU.

The Lone Ranger: The Death of Zorro, five-issue miniseries by Ande Parks and Esteve Polls, Dynamite Entertainment, 2011. In 1870, a band of ex-Confederate soldiers take over a Chumash Indian mission and institute a reign of terror upon the natives. An aging Don Diego de la Vega comes out of retirement and becomes Zorro once again to defeat them. However, the leader of the renegades shoots him in the back. The Lone Ranger and Tonto set out to avenge his death with the aid of Zorro's onetime allies *La Justicia*. *La Justicia* is from Isabel Allende's novel *Zorro*, a re-imagining of the legend. This story does not fit with the circumstances of Don Diego's death in the movie *The Mask of Zorro*. In addition, Don Diego was born in 1771 in the CU, which would make him 99-years-old at the time of this story, though he appears much younger than that.

"The Long-Suffering Landlady" by Ralph E. Vaughan in *Sherlock Holmes: The Coils of Time & Other Stories*, Dog in the Night Books, 2013. Mrs. Hudson deals with the daily stresses of being Sherlock Holmes' landlady. A package is delivered to 221B Baker Street containing a loathsome green idol that causes Mrs. Hudson to think "Blasted Cthulhu cultists!" The story is too overtly parodic to fit into CU continuity.

The Lord Darcy series by Randall Garrett, mysteries set in an alternate universe governed by the laws of magic rather than science. Some of the characters in these tales are counterparts of characters who exist in the CU: Sir Lyon Gandolphus Gray (Gandalf), Sir James le Lein (James Bond), and the Marquis de London and Lord Bontriomphe (Nero Wolfe and Archie Goodwin). The Tarnhelm Effect, a magic spell from the Lord Darcy stories, is mentioned in Justin Gustainis' Morris and Chastain Supernatural Investigations series, providing further evidence the universe in which Lord Darcy operates is an alternate reality to the Crossover Universe.

Lords of Mars, six-issue miniseries by Arvid Nelson and Roberto Castro, Dynamite Entertainment, 2013–2014. The jungle lord and and his wife are transported to Mars, where Lord Greystoke is manipulated by one of the planet's many sentient races into battling the planet's warlord. Events from the comic book series *Lord of the Jungle* and *Warlord of Mars*, which only loosely follow the events of Burroughs' books, are mentioned. Also, the jungle lord is uncharacteristically naïve here, accepting a Martian ruler's claim the warlord is evil with little evidence, apparently because he feels he fits in more on Mars than on Earth.

"Love Among the Ruins" by Evelyn Waugh, *The Complete Stories of Evelyn Waugh*, Little, Brown and Company, 1998, set in a dystopian future. Writers Parsnip and Pimpernell are mentioned as having undergone voluntary euthanasia. Both are from Waugh's novel *Put Out More Flags*.

The Luke Challenger series by Steve Barlow and Steve Skidmore, featuring Professor Challenger's grandson. The first book, *Return to the Lost World*, takes place in May–July 1933. 14-year-old Luke and his cousin Nick Malone, who is the same age, travel to Maple White Land to rescue Luke's mother, Lady Harriet Challenger, from the Sons of Destiny, a multinational group dedicated to allowing fascism to rise so they can take over the world. The second book in the series, *Return to 20,000 Leagues Under the Sea*, takes place in June–August 1934. Challenger Industries is contacted by Jessica Land, the 16-year-old great-granddaughter of Ned Land, who has found out her great-grandfather had been willed the Journals of Captain Nemo by

Professor Aaron X. Perrier (who Jules Verne disguised as Pierre Aronnax). Luke and Nick join the expedition to locate the *Nautilus* in a race against the Sons of Destiny to gain the nuclear secrets of the submarine. It is possible references to the *Nautilus* being nuclear-powered and *The Mysterious Island* being fictional are influenced by Professor H. W. Starr's essay "A Submersible Subterfuge, or, Proof Impositive." The third book, *Return to King Solomon's Mines*, takes place from December 1934–January 1935. Luke and Nick go to Ethiopia to visit Luke's mother on an archaeological dig. Accompanying them is Elsa Fairfax, great-granddaughter of Allan Quatermain. The expedition comes across Kukuanaland, and discovers the people were ruled by the reincarnation of the High Priestess Gagool after the death of King Ignosi. Nick Malone is the son of Ned Malone and the late Enid Challenger. If he and Luke are both 14-years-old in 1933, they would've been born around 1919. However, Ned and Enid fell in love during the events of Doyle's *The Land of Mist*, which Rick Lai has dated to 1926. Combined with the dismissal of *The Mysterious Island* as fictional, this argues against placement of these books in CU continuity.

"The Mark of a Woman" by Rick Lai in *Tales of the Shadowmen Volume 10: Esprit de Corps*, Jean-Marc and Randy Lofficier, eds., Black Coat Press, 2013; reprinted in French in *Les Compagnons de l'Ombre (Tome 15)*, Jean-Marc and Randy Lofficier, eds., Rivière Blanche, 2014. In 1806, Ramon Castillo attempts to murder Joséphine Balsamo as revenge for her spurning him for Diego de la Vega. Diego de la Vega is the alter ego of Johnston McCulley's Zorro. Diego's father, Don Alejandro, and Bernardo, his mute servant, are also from McCulley's tales. Ramon Castillo and Marcos Estrada are from "Auld Acquaintance," an episode of Disney's *Zorro* television series. Joséphine Balsamo's great-granddaughter and namesake is one of Arsène Lupin's greatest foes. The golden ram crest of the Cagliostros is from the animated Lupin III film *The Castle of Cagliostro*. Captain Cesar de Cabanil is from Paul Féval's novel *Captain Phantom*. Lai's story takes place before de la Vega becomes Zorro, and he and Castillo are portrayed as students at the University of Madrid; however, in the Crossover Universe, Zorro began his career in 1795, thus creating a chronological conflict that cannot be resolved.

The Martian Legion: In Quest of Xonthron by Jake Saunders, The Russ Cochran Co. Ltd., 2014. John Carter, Tarzan, Carson Napier, Doc Savage, the Shadow, Alley Oop, and David Innes have an adventure on Mars, battling Dr. Fu Manchu and others. The novel takes place in 1938, and the Shadow and Margo Lane are portrayed as a married couple, which does not fit with the continuity of either the pulp novels or accounts of the Shadow's later exploits by other authors. Tarzan and Jane have a precocious twelve-year-old second son, Conan Clayton, while Korak and Meriem have two children, Ryan and Katy. Their "canonical" son Jackie is never mentioned. Tarzan and Jane, John Carter, and the Shadow are all portrayed as extremely devout Christians, which does not square with their original appearances. Based on these factors, this book cannot take place in the CU.

Masks, eight issue miniseries by Chris Roberson, Alex Ross, and Dennis Calero, Dynamite Entertainment, November 2012–June 2013. A very loose adaptation of the Black Police Trilogy from the Spider pulp novels, featuring the Spider himself, the Shadow, the Green Lama, the Green Hornet and Kato, the Black Bat, the Black Terror, Zorro (Rafael Vega, a descendant of the original Zorro) and Miss Fury. The leader of the Black Legion turns out to be Brian O'Brien, formerly the Clock, a masked vigilante appearing in stories published by Centaur Publications and Quality Comics in the 1930s and '40s. The heroes visit a penthouse at the Empire State Building, where the Shadow remarks it is too bad the occupant of the penthouse is out of the country, as he would be a valuable ally to them in this mission. This is a reference to the golden-eyed pulp hero known as "Doc." Britt Reid meets with reporter Steve Huston, who mentions Old Man Havens. Steve Huston and Frank Havens are from the pulp exploits of the Phantom Detective. The events of this comic differ greatly from the Black Police Trilogy, including factors such as the identity of the mastermind being changed and Nita Van Sloan's role being omitted (indeed, she is never even mentioned). The Spider is wearing a version of his outfit from the movie serial *The Spider's Web* rather than the costume from the pulps. The Black Bat is given a different origin story than in the original pulps. The Green Hornet is out of character, calling criminals "mooks," and is stated to be from Chicago rather than Detroit. All of these factors serve to place this story outside CU continuity. In the sequel, *Masks 2*, an eight-issue miniseries by Cullen Bunn and Eman Cassalos, 2015, heroes from three different time periods team up to fight a villain called the Red Death, including two Green Hornets, two Katos, the Black Bat, two Miss Furys, the Shadow, the Black Terror, two Black Sparrows, the Spider, the Green Lama, Lady Satan, and Peter Cannon: Thunderbolt.

"The Masks of Hastur" by Rick Lai in *The Lovecraft eZine* #30, Mike Davis, ed., April 2014. A prequel to Lai's *Shadows of the Opera* books. Appearing or mentioned are: Mademoiselle Jeanne d'Ys, *Le Roi en Jaune*, Demhe, Alar, the Lake of Hali, the Phantom of Truth, Pelagie, Philip, the Yellow Sign, Foxhall Clifford, Richard Osborne Elliot, Yian, Cassilda, Rev. Dusenberry, Severn, and Sylvia Elven from Robert W. Chambers' *The King in Yellow*; Gaston Morrell, Jeanette le Beau, Renee, Francine Lutien and her sister Lucille, Inspector

Lefevre, Renard, and the Duc de Carineaux from the movie *Bluebeard*; Darlla Rassendyll, the future Revenant, the heroine of the *Shadows of the Opera* books, and the shadowy pulp hero's mother (the surname Rassendyll comes from Anthony Hope's *The Prisoner of Zenda*); Commissioner Mifroid, Feliciana Sorelli, and the Comte de Chagny from Gaston Leroux's *The Phantom of the Opera*; Cardec from Marie-Francois Goron and Emile Gautier's *Spawn of the Penitentiary*; Carcosa from Ambrose Bierce's "An Inhabitant of Carcosa" and *The King in Yellow*; Hastur from Bierce's "Haïta the Shepherd" and *The King in Yellow*, a curse on the citizens of the city of Hastur from James Blish's "More Light"; Jean Blanc from Paul Féval's *Le Loup Blanc*; the Black Priest from Chambers' "The Messenger"; Bayrolles from "An Inhabitant of Carcosa"; cat people from Algernon Blackwood's "Ancient Sorceries"; *Le Meneur des Loups* from Alexandre Dumas' story of the same name; Anne of the Isles from Paul Féval's titular novel; Jean Grimoire (John Grimlan from Robert E. Howard's "Dig Me No Grave"); El Hichmakani from Richard Francis Burton's *The Kasidah*; the Kuen-Yuin from Chambers' "The Maker of Moons"; Van Klopen from the works of Emile Gaboriau; *Le Taon* and Sigismond Trottier from Mary Elizabeth Braddon's *Wyllard's Weird*; Lecoq de Gentilly, an alias for Gaboriau's Monsieur Lecoq, from Fortuné du Boisgobey's *The Old Age of Monsieur Lecoq*; Citoyenne Roget from Edgar Allan Poe's "The Mystery of *Marie Rogêt*"; the Eight Towers of the Dark Star from Chambers' *The Slayer of Souls;* and *The Prophecies of the Kiot Bordjiguen* from Chambers' *The Dark Star.*

"Les Mémos Wayne" by Xavier Mauméjean in *Les Compagnons de l'Ombre (Tome 12)*, Jean-Marc and Randy Lofficier, eds., Rivière Blanche, 2013, reprinted in English as "The Wayne Memos" in *Tales of the Shadowmen Volume 10: Esprit de Corps*, Jean-Marc and Randy Lofficier, eds., Black Coat Press, 2013. Soviet Russia manipulates Bruce Wayne into becoming a costumed hero serving the cause of communism. Superman and Zorro are both mentioned.

The Mr. Brass steampunk stories by Josh Reynolds, set in an alternate reality where the Martian invasion (as seen in H. G. Wells' *The War of the Worlds*) happened in 1888 rather than 1898, and had longer-lasting consequences than it did in the CU, and featuring a Pinkerton agent who has had his brain transplanted into a clockwork body by Dr. Frankenstein (from Mary Shelley's *Frankenstein*) and the Mi-Go (from H. P. Lovecraft's "The Whisperer in Darkness.") In "Mr. Brass and the Crimson Skies of Kansas" (*How the West Was Weird: Campfire Tales*, Russ Anderson, Jr., ed., PulpWork Press, 2011), Mr. Brass must protect President Theodore Roosevelt from the murderous designs of Mr. Hyde and Hanoi Xan. Mr. Hyde is from Robert Louis Stevenson's novel *The Strange Case of Dr. Jekyll and Mr. Hyde*, while Hanoi Xan is from the movie *The Adventures of Buckaroo Banzai Across the Eighth Dimension*. Also appearing or mentioned are: the Starry Wisdom cult from H. P. Lovecraft's "The Haunter of the Dark"; Jean Robur from Jules Verne's *Robur the Conqueror* and *Master of the World*; Cavorite from Wells' *The First Men in the Moon*; James Moriarty from Arthur Conan Doyle's Sherlock Holmes stories; Doctor Alphonse Moreau from Wells' *The Island of Doctor Moreau*; the Devil Doctor (Fu Manchu) and the Si-Fan from Sax Rohmer's novels; Lehnsherr brand magnetic/electrical focusers, a nod to the Marvel Comics character Magneto, who has used the alias Erik Lehnsherr; and Whitby Asylum, Seward, and Van Helsing from Bram Stoker's *Dracula*. In "Mr. Brass and the Master of Serpents," (*Strange Trails*, James Palmer, ed., Mechanoid Press, 2013), Mr. Brass works with Bass Reeves and Harley Warren to battle worshippers of the serpent god Yig. Warren is from Lovecraft's story "The Statement of Randolph Carter," while Yig is from Lovecraft and Zealia Bishop's "The Curse of Yig," as is Dr. McNeill. Also appearing or mentioned are: Brainerd (Johnny Brainerd from Edward S. Ellis' "The Steam Man of the Prairies"); Yuggoth and Yoth (from "The Whisperer in Darkness"); Cavorite; Miskatonic University (a staple of Lovecraft's Cthulhu Mythos); the Starry Wisdom and Enoch Bowen (both from "The Haunter of the Dark"); Angel Grove (the setting of the TV series *Mighty Morphin Power Rangers* and its sequels); Tsathoggua (from Cthulhu Mythos stories by Clark Ashton Smith); the Ghost Mound, the K'n Yan, the Zamacona Manuscript, and N'kai (from Lovecraft and Bishop's "The Mound"); Robur; Mors (Captain Mors, a German pulp character); and Hanoi Xan. In "Mr. Brass and the Seven Plagues of the Devil," included in the e-book *Psychopunk: A Psychopomp Special*, Artifice Comics, 2013, Mr. Brass battles the title characters of the Hammer Dracula film *The Legend of the 7 Golden Vampires* alongside Professor Van Helsing and the Devil Doctor's son Quong Lung and his dacoits.

Mister Creecher by Chris Priestley, Bloomsbury Publishing, 2011. In 1818, Victor Frankenstein's monster befriends a young street urchin and pickpocket named Billy, who attempts to help him find his creator in order to convince Victor to make another such creature. Billy is a young Bill Sikes, from Charles Dickens' novel *Oliver Twist*. The novel definitely takes place in 1818, as Percy and Mary Shelley appear, making a visit to London that corresponds to one they made in real life in that year. Historically, the Shelleys married in 1814, when Percy was 21 and Mary 16. However, in the CU the events of *Frankenstein* take place in 1790–1800, creating a chronological conflict that cannot be reconciled.

"Moon Maid Over Manhattan" by Peter David in *The Worlds of Edgar Rice Burroughs*, Mike Resnick and Robert T. Garcia, eds., Baen Books, 2013. A sequel to Burroughs' *The Moon Maid*. Barsoom and the warlord of Mars are mentioned.

"Moreau Est Vivant!" by Michel Stéphan in *Les Compagnons de l'Ombre (Tome 13)*, Jean-Marc and Randy Lofficier, eds., Rivière Blanche, 2014; reprinted in English as "Moreau Lives!" in *Harry Dickson vs. the Spider*, Jean-Marc and Randy Lofficier, eds., Black Coat Press, 2014. The jungle lord's wife asks Harry Dickson to look into her husband's sudden attraction to Lota, a panther-woman created by Doctor Moreau. The jungle lord and his wife are from Edgar Rice Burroughs' novels, of course. Harry Dickson, Tom Wills, and Georgette Cuvelier appear in pulp novels by Jean Ray. Lota is from the film *Island of Lost Souls*, the first movie adaptation of H. G. Wells' novel *The Island of Doctor Moreau*. Professor Lampini is from the Universal film *House of Frankenstein*. Nestor Burma is a private eye appearing in novels by Léo Malet. Monsieur Jackal is from Alexandre Dumas' *The Mohicans of Paris*. It is ultimately revealed the jungle lord has been deceived by Georgette, who is working with the 9th Duke of Greystoke. In CU continuity, there is no 9th Duke of Greystoke, as the jungle lord assumed the identity of his cousin, the 7th Duke of Greystoke, after the latter's death, and he and his family faked their own deaths and moved to the inner world before his son ever had a chance to inherit the title. His distant cousin Pat Wildman then became the Duchess of Greystoke.

"The Most Dreadful Monster" by Matthew Dennion in *Tales of the Shadowmen Volumes 8: Agents Provocateurs*, Jean-Marc and Randy Lofficier, eds., Black Coat Press, 2011; reprinted in French in *Les Compagnons de L'Ombre (Tome 10)*, Jean-Marc and Randy Lofficier, eds., Rivière Blanche, 2012; and in *The Revenge of Madame Atomos*, Black Coat Press, 2012. Madame Atomos believes she is the most dangerous monster created by radiation, not *daikaiju* like Gojira or Rodan. She is proven wrong when she abducts Dr. Bruce Banner. Madame Atomos is from a series of novels by André Caroff that is presently being translated into English by Black Coat Press. Gojira (or Godzilla as he's known in America) and Rodan are *daikaiju* (giant monsters) featured in films by Japan's Toho Studios. Dr. Banner is the incredible Hulk. Although a version of Gojira exists in the CU, the constant destruction wrought on Japan in his films and Rodan's are irreconcilable with CU continuity.

Mrs. Hudson and the Spirits' Curse by Martin Davies, Berkley Publishing, 2004. Sherlock Holmes and Dr. Watson hire Mrs. Hudson as their housekeeper, and become involved in the case of the Giant Rat of Sumatra. A. J.

Raffles also appears. In the original Doyle stories, Mrs. Hudson is Holmes and Watson's landlady, rather than their housekeeper. This, combined with Holmes being portrayed as a much more fallible detective than Doyle depicted him, places this novel in an AU.

"Murder Will Out," a segment of the revue film *Paramount on Parade*, 1930. A farce in which Sherlock Holmes and Philo Vance fail to give Fu Manchu credit for his murder of actor Jack Oakie, and are themselves murdered by the Devil Doctor as retribution.

My Florida Idyll: The Journal of Bloody Mary Jane, three-part *Single Shot Signature* story by Chuck Miller, Pro Se Press, 2014–2015, set in the same alternate universe as Miller's Black Centipede books. In 1892, Bloody Mary Jane Gallows, the supernaturally-created "daughter" of Jack the Ripper and Lizzie Borden, finds herself in a Florida settlement run by Cotton Mather and Juan Ponce de Leon, both of whom have drunk from the Fountain of Youth. Professor James Moriarty (who is portrayed as a vampire) and Herbert West appear, and Dracula is mentioned.

"The Mysterious Iowans" by Paul Di Filippo in *The Mammoth Book of New Jules Verne Adventures*, Mike Ashley and Eric Brown, eds., Carroll & Graf, 2005. A reporter visits the former Iowa, now the high-tech Lincoln Island run by the onetime castaways of the original island. There, he meets with Harbert Brown, one of the former castaways, who reveals he and his comrades reverse-engineered the technology of the *Nautilus* for their own technological achievements. President-for-Life Cyrus Smith introduces the journalist to the man who will be designing newer and better technology for Lincoln: Robur. There are also references to the metal adamantium from the Marvel Universe.

The Naked Monster, 2005 feature film directed by Ted Newsom. A broad farce parodying 1950s and 1960s science fiction movies, featuring many characters from those films, including Colonel Patrick Hendry and Dr. Carrington (*The Thing from Another World*), Drs. Clete Ferguson and Helen Dobson (*Revenge of the Creature*), Major Allison (*Beyond the Time Barrier*), Officer Kelton (*Bride of the Monster, Night of the Ghouls*, and *Plan 9 from Outer Space*), Dr. Sylvia Van Buren and General Mann (*The War of the Worlds*), and Professor Bradshaw (*The Indestructible Man*).

Nemo: Heart of Ice by Alan Moore and Kevin O'Neill, Top Shelf Productions, 2013. In 1925, Janni Dakkar, daughter and heir to the late Captain Nemo, follows the trail of her father's Antarctic expedition from decades ago after plundering the treasures of Queen Ayesha of Kôr. Ayesha's current patron, newspaper magnate Charles Foster Kane (from Orson Welles' film *Citizen Kane*) dispatches aging inventors Frank Reade Jr. and Jack Wright and their younger colleague "Tom Swyfte" to retrieve the Queen's belongings and deal with Janni and her crew. In the CU, Ayesha would have been dead in 1925, though her spirit would resurface in 1977, as seen in Peter Tremayne's pastiche *The Vengeance of She*. Also, Tom Swift is portrayed in an unflattering manner, making racist comments about Janni and shooting Reade in the leg with his Electric Rifle in order to slow down a raging shoggoth, effectively leaving the elder inventor to die. Swift is also seemingly driven irrevocably insane by the encounter with the shoggoth, which does not fit with his appearances in the Tom Swift Jr. novels in the 1950s-1970s. The sequel is *Nemo: The Roses of Berlin*, published in 2014 and set in 1941, in which Janni and her husband Broad Arrow Jack must rescue their daughter Hira and son-in-law Armand Robur (son of Jules Verne's Robur the Conqueror) from captivity in Nazi Germany, which is under the power of Ayesha's current benefactor, Adenoid Hynkel (from Charlie Chaplin's film *The Great Dictator*). In the process, they battle the remains of Germany's equivalent of the League of Extraordinary Gentlemen, *Die Zwielichthelden* ("The Twilight Heroes.") The Berlin of 1941 in this graphic novel is based on the titular futuristic city from Fritz Lang's film *Metropolis*. The final entry in the trilogy is *Nemo: River of Ghosts*, 2015, in which Janni, dying and experiencing visions of the ghosts of those she's lost over the years, deals with Ayesha once and for all in South America in 1975. Janni hires the super-humanly strong Hugo Coghlan, aka Hugo Hercules (the title character of a 1902–1903 comic strip by William H. D. Koerner, revealed here to really be the Celtic demigod Cuchulainn) to act as her bodyguard. Hugo says he was paid by "a Mr. Savage Senior" to kill Hugo Danner (the equally superstrong protagonist of Philip Wylie's novel *Gladiator*) soon after the Great War, though why Savage did this is not specified. Given the strong moral code he instilled in his son, it seems unlikely Doc Wildman's father, James Clarke Wildman, Sr., would put out a contract on another man's life. While Farmer identified Wildman, Sr. with James Wilder from the Sherlock Holmes story "The Adventure of the Priory School," who was guilty of kidnapping and being an accessory after the fact to murder, Farmer also says his guilt over those actions was precisely why he raised his son to be a crimefighter.

"Nextwave is Love," *Nextwave: Agents of H.A.T.E.* #6 by Warren Ellis, Stuart Immonen, and Wade von Grawbadger, Marvel Comics, August 2006. H.A.T.E. director Dirk Anger orders the release of "the Neo-Hyde Gutspawn . . . Human scum empowered by the cloned chemically-mutated cells found in the stomach walls of the corpse of Henry Jekyll himself!" Nextwave is a team composed of mostly pre-existing Marvel superheroes, and therefore this series cannot take place in the CU.

Night of the Living Deadpool #1–4 by Cullen Bunn, Joe Sabino, and Ramon Rosanas, Marvel Comics, 2014, in which a zombie apocalypse occurs, leaving the mercenary Deadpool the last remaining superhuman. In the second chapter, Deadpool and the group of survivors he's leading spend about eight weeks traveling and seeking shelter, visiting Ash Williams' cabin (from *The Evil Dead*), Hershel Greene's farm and the West Georgia Correctional Facility (*The Walking Dead*), the Monroeville Mall (*Dawn of the Dead*), the Pacific Playland Amusement Park (*Zombieland*), and the Winchester Pub (*Shaun of the Dead*).

Les Ogres de Montfaucon: Les Nouvelles Enquêtes du Chevalier Dupin (*The Ogres of Montafaucon: The New Investigations of Chevalier Dupin*), a collection of short stories featuring Edgar Allan Poe's sleuth by Gérard Dôle, Terre de Brume, 2004. In "Les Ogres de Montfaucon," Paris is struck by an epidemic of the Red Death from Poe's "The Masque of the Red Death." No date is given for these events. In "Le Vampire de Prague" ("The Vampire of Prague,") set in 1820, a twenty-year-old Dupin hunts a vampire through Europe and meets Dr. Martin Hesselius from J. Sheridan Le Fanu's "Carmilla." In "Le Drame de Reichenbach" ("The Drama of Reichenbach,") set in 1855, Dupin witnesses a duel at the Reichenbach Falls between Giacomo Moriarti, an Italian gentleman, and Sherrinford Holmes, the husband of Cornélia Vernet and father of Mycroft and Sherlock. Holmes accuses Moriarti of seducing his fiancée Cornélia ten years ago, resulting in a son, Jacques, who is being raised by Moriarti in Italy. According to Moriarti, he and Cornélia simply rescued the baby, who was a Parisian foundling, and he adopted him as his son. At the end of the duel, Moriarti falls from a cliff, and Holmes disappears. "Giacomo" is the Italian equivalent of the English name "James," while "Jacques" is the French version of that name. A birthdate of 1800 does not fit with Dupin's family history as outlined in *Tarzan Alive*, nor do the genealogies for Sherlock Holmes and Professor Moriarty given by Dôle fit with Farmer's versions.

"The Once and Future Tarzan" by Alan Gordon and Thomas Yeates in *Dark Horse Presents* #8-10, Dark Horse Comics, February–March 2012; collected with an expanded ending in *The Once and Future Tarzan*, Dark Horse Comics, November 2012. In a post-apocalyptic future, Tarzan does battle with a Cabal that seeks the secret of immortality. Tarzan is referred to by the members of an all-female tribe as "the grey-eyed god," an apparent reference to his appearance as Sahhindar, the Grey-Eyed God, in Farmer's Ancient Opar novels; however, Farmer's novel *Time's Last Gift* has Tarzan and Jane leaving Earth for good in the year 2140, and the depiction of the Earth's future in that novel and other works included in the CU does not match the world portrayed in Gordon and Yeates' story.

"Out of the Depths" by Andrew J. Wilson in *Professor Challenger: New Worlds, Lost Places*, J. R. Campbell and Charles Prepolec, eds., EDGE Science Fiction and Fantasy Fiction Publishing, 2015. In 1937, Professor Challenger and Edward Malone encounter Nazis in Maple White Land. Hobbs Lane is from the British television science fiction serial *Quatermass and the Pit*. Doctor Moreau is from H. G. Wells' novel *The Island of Doctor Moreau*. The Lidenbrock Sea is from Jules Verne's novel *Journey to the Centre of the Earth*. Medusa Von Juntz is related to Friedrich Von Juntz from Robert E. Howard's "The Black Stone." Doctor Moreau is revealed to have been Jack the Ripper, placing this story outside CU continuity.

The *Outlanders* series, written by various authors under the pseudonym "James Axler," set in a future incompatible with the one seen in the *Star Trek* franchise. In #64, *Savage Dawn* by Douglas Wojtowicz, Kondo says of a subterranean empire filled with dinosaurs, "It's amazing that no one has ever stumbled upon it." Remus replies, "Some have. But the tales were so astounding that those who lived in the world above relegated them to flights of fancy, instead of the true exploits of men such as George Edward Challenger or David Innes." In #68, *Wings of Death*, also by Wojtowicz, Kane discovers he is the reincarnation of Solomon Kane.

The Peregrine Omnibus, Volume One by Barry Reese, Pro Se Press, 2015, featuring Max Davies, aka the Peregrine, a masked vigilante based in Atlanta. In "Lucifer's Cage," the Peregrine battles an occultist who attempts to unleash Hell on Earth. The hero is part of a group of adventures called the Nova Alliance, whose other members include Leopold Grace, Clark (who operates on criminals' brains to remove the parts of the mind that compel them to commit evil deeds), and Lamont. Leopold Grace is from Reese's collection *The Family Grace: An Extraordinary History*. Clark is the bronze man. Lamont is the shadowy pulp hero who frequently assumes the identity of a millionaire named Lamont when the real Lamont is abroad. In "The Kingdom of Blood," the Peregrine encounters a female vampire named Camilla, who uses the *Necronomicon* to summon Nyarlathotep, one of the Old Ones. Camilla may be intended to be J. Sheridan Le Fanu's Carmilla. Reese's Camilla is revived merely by having a stake pulled out of her chest, but Le Fanu's Carmilla was staked, beheaded, and burned. Azathoth and Miskatonic University are mentioned. At Leopold Grace's a request, a man with dead, white features named Benson, also an adventurer, arranges to have all ongoing investigations into the Peregrine's activities by the Atlanta police ceased, in exchange for the vigilante's vow he keep the number of criminals he kills to a minimum. Benson is the avenging hero with malleable skin. A mad scientist asks the Peregrine, "Are you a killer like the one who calls himself the Spider? Or a more merciful sort, like Mr. Savage?" In "The Gasping Death," the Peregrine comes to Great City to apprehend the Moon Man, but ultimately teams up with his fellow vigilante to defeat the evil Prof. Lycos, who has been empowered by Nyarlathotep. Benson is mentioned. Lycos thinks "Unlike many other cities, there were no costumed vigilantes in this area to interfere with his scheme: nowhere to be found were the likes of the Spider, the Shadow, G-8 and his Battle Aces, or the arrogant Doc Savage." At the end of the story, the Moon Man (aka Stephen Thatcher) marries his girlfriend Sue McEwen. The circumstances of their marriage are completely different than the version depicted in Lance Curry's story "Lunar League," which has already been included in the CU. In "The Black Mass," set in an alternate 2009 where black magic is overwhelming the world, the Peregrine passes on his mantle to a successor, Ian Morris before dying. Benson is mentioned. The Peregrine gives Ian a helmet that enables him to see the future, including a battle he will have with Nyarlathotep. Fiona Grace, a member of the Grace family, appears. In "Abominations," the Peregrine must stop his former teacher, the Warlike Manchu, from unleashing a demon called the Abomination to aid him in his insidious plans. The Warlike Manchu is clearly meant to be Fu Manchu. Benson informs the Peregrine of the Warlike Manchu's presence in Atlanta. Max thinks of the other members of the Nova Alliance, including Leopold Grace, Clark Savage, and Lamont Cranston. Felix Cole, a member of the Grace family by marriage, is mentioned, as is Nyarlathotep. In "Kaslov's Flame," the hero teams with the Russian superman Leonid Kaslov to battle Rasputin and a being called the Black Flame. The Warlike Manchu and Benson are mentioned. Max's wife and sometimes partner Evelyn, an actress, was in a movie called *Ki-Gor and the Ivory Goddess*. In "Blitzkrieg," the Peregrine and Kaslov battle the Warlike Manchu and his latest protégé, Shinigami. Azathoth is mentioned, as is Felix Cole and his quest for the *Book of Eibon*, which was depicted in Reese's story "The Great Work." The Warlike Manchu's daughter Koreani appears. In Sax Rohmer's novels, Fu Manchu's daughter Fah Lo Suee used the name Koreani in *The Drums of Fu Manchu* and *The Island of Fu Manchu*. Both the Warlike Manchu and Koreani definitely die in this story. It is stated a battle wound after Koreani's birth left the Warlike Manchu unable to father any more children, which conflicts with both Rohmer's *The Bride of Fu Manchu* and the comic book series *Master of Kung Fu*. Furthermore, Koreani says she is over sixty-years-old. Since "Blitzkrieg" takes place in 1940, Koreani would have been born before 1880. However, in the CU Fah Lo Suee was born in 1896. In "Bloodwerks," the Peregrine teams up with the Domino Lady. Benson and Leopold Grace are mentioned. In "The Gorgon Conspiracy," the Peregrine faces a villain who has the power of the ancient Gorgons. Felix Cole and the *Book of Shadows*, also from *The Family Grace*, are mentioned. In "The Shambling Ones," the Peregrine and Kaslov battle Dr. Zero, who is seeking to unleash creatures called the Shambling Ones to wreak havoc on Earth. Camilla, Nyarlathotep, Leopold Grace and his father Eobard, and Felix Cole are mentioned. In "Origins," the Peregrine meets a reporter who has figured out his true identity and why he became a vigilante. The Warlike Manchu is mentioned. In "The Bleeding Hells," the Peregrine, the Black Bat, and Ascott Keane reluctantly join forces with Doctor Satan to battle an even greater threat. Leopold Grace appears, and the Warlike Manchu, Nyarlathotep, and Benson are mentioned. In "The Iron Maiden," the Peregrine's friend and ally Police Chief William McKenzie is kidnapped by the armored Nazi agent known as the Iron Maiden, who wishes to learn the location of the Sword of Hel from him. The Sword is from Reese's stories "Dogs of War" and "In the Name of Hel." Benson, Nyarlathotep, Leopold Grace, Ascott Keane, and the Black Bat are mentioned. In "The Three Skulls," the Peregrine battles a costumed Nazi called the Grim Reaper, who seeks to acquire three crystal skulls that, when joined together, are capable of destroying the world. Max, Benson, Ascott Keane, and Tony Quinn (the Black Bat's alter ego) attend William McKenzie's wedding to Kirstin Bauer, the former Iron Maiden. One of the skulls is in the possession of a professor at Miskatonic University in Arkham, Massachusetts. The Warlike Manchu and Nyarlathotep are mentioned. Leonid Kaslov says he first met the possessor of another skull about four years ago when he was investigating reports of a Deep Ones colony just off the Northeastern coast. In "Catalyst," the Peregrine and Evelyn team up with the Catalyst and Rachel Winters to battle the Black Zeppelin and Doctor Satan. Leopold Grace, Prof. Stone (a character created by Wayne Skiver), the Black Bat, *The Book of Eibon*, the Green Lama, and the Domino Lady are mentioned. In "The Lost Colony," Max investigates a case connected to the historical disappearance of the Roanoke colony. Ascott Keane appears, and Jethro Dumont (the Green Lama's alter ego) is mentioned. In "The Resurrection Gambit," the Peregrine battles the resurrected Warlike Manchu, who now possesses the Philosopher's Stone, and has an appetite for human flesh. The stories in this omnibus originally appeared in the first three volumes of a series of short story collections by Reese. In the original versions, the hero was called the Rook, rather than the Peregrine.

"The Pimpernel Problem" by Janet Pack in *Margaret Weis' Testament of the Dragon*, Harper Prism, 1997. Justin Sterling, née Sir Justinian of Sterling, aka the Wyrm, an immortal servant of the Great Dragon of the West, joins the League of the Scarlet Pimpernel in order to obtain information on those he seeks to kill, the French worshippers of the Great Dragon's enemies, the Dragons Beyond. He is prevented from murdering one such target by Sir Percy Blakeney himself. Sterling was created by Margaret Weis and David Baldwin, and also appears in the duo's book *Dark Heart*. *Margaret Weis' Testament of the Dragon* has a piece entitled "The Travels of Sir Justinian," which refers to Sterling's assassination of Don Diego Vega in Los Angeles in the autumn of 1823. The movie *The Mask of Zorro* depicts Diego's death under different circumstances in 1842, thus placing the Justin Sterling tales outside of Crossover Universe continuity.

"The Post-Modern Prometheus" by Nick Kyme in *Encounters of Sherlock Holmes*, George Mann, ed., Titan Books, 2013. Sherlock Holmes and Dr. Watson join forces with Victor Frankenstein's monster to defeat Dr. Henry Jekyll (aka Edward Hyde), who is using Frankenstein's work for his own twisted purposes. Jekyll/Hyde's presence in London after the events of Stevenson's novel and his death both conflict with *The League of Extraordinary Gentlemen*, and therefore this story must take place in an AU.

The Private Life of Dr. Watson: Being the Personal Reminiscences of John H. Watson, M.D. by Michael Hardwick. Dr. Watson recounts his life prior to his historic first meeting with Sherlock Holmes. Referring to his mother's family, the Hudsons, Watson states, "Their issue in my time included a gamekeeper with two sons of totally contrasting status. The elder, Donald, was a civil engineer. His brother, Angus, went into domestic service, rising to be a butler well known in the highest strata of London society." Angus and Donald Hudson are from the British television series *Upstairs, Downstairs*. Hardwick wrote tie-in novels for that series. Among the members of Watson's regiment in Afghanistan are Colonel Ripon and his illegitimate son, Will Gale, as well as Captain Fletcher. Ripon, Gale, and Fletcher are from the novel *For Name and Fame* by G. A. Henty. Several details in this novel conflict with Watson's CU history, placing it in an AU. Both Watson's parents are portrayed as Scottish, and he was raised in Scotland, whereas in Farmer's *The Adventure of the Peerless Peer*, Watson says he is of Scots descent on his mother's side, which suggests he does not have any such ancestry on his father's side. His middle name is given as Hudson, whereas in the CU it is Hamish. Watson also has a sexual encounter as a teen with Aggie Brown, a maid at his school. Watson later discovers this fling resulted in a son named Frank. When one of his fellow medicos tells Watson about Ripon's relationship to Gale, he describes Gale as Ripon's "bull pup," calling it an old family expression. At the end of the novel, Watson begins financially supporting

Frank; this explains why he said he kept a bull pup in *A Study in Scarlet*. However, in H. Paul Jeffers' story "The Adventure of the Old Russian Woman," which takes place in the CU, it is revealed Watson was using "keeping a bull pup" as a metaphor for having a temper.

"Professor Challenger and the Crimson Wonder" by Guy Adams and James Goss in *Professor Challenger: New Worlds, Lost Places*, J. R. Campbell and Charles Prepolec, eds., EDGE Science Fiction and Fantasy Fiction Publishing, 2015. Professor Challenger and his wife have a run-in with aliens who are planning to overrun the world with a remarkable plant. Professor Challenger is from *The Lost World* and other tales by Arthur Conan Doyle. Mycroft Holmes is Sherlock Holmes' brother. Lidenbrock is Otto Lidenbrock from Jules Verne's *Journey to the Centre of the Earth*. Cavor is from H. G. Wells' *The First Men in the Moon*. Perry is from Edgar Rice Burroughs' novels set at the Earth's core. William Dyer is from H. P. Lovecraft's "At the Mountains of Madness." Herbert is meant to be the Time Traveler from Wells' novel *The Time Machine*. Herakleophorbia IV, Bensington, and Miss Cossar's brother are from Wells' novel *The Food of the Gods*. Ryland and the Great Four are from Agatha Christie's novel *The Big Four*. The meteorite that landed in Woking in 1898 is from Wells' novel *The War of the Worlds*. This story is too overtly satirical to fit easily into CU continuity. Also, Poirot moved to England in 1916, so the portrayal of him as an agent of Mycroft Holmes in 1914 is chronologically incorrect.

"The Purloined Face" by Stephen Volk in *Beyond Rue Morgue: Further Tales of Edgar Allan Poe's 1st Detective*, Paul Kane and Charles Prepolec, eds., Titan Books, 2013, a sequel to Volk's story "The Comfort of the Seine." In Paris, young Sherlock Holmes and his mentor, C. Auguste Dupin (actually Edgar Allan Poe using the name of his own fictional creation after his alleged death) investigate the events that will later be greatly distorted as *The Phantom of the Opera*.

Raffles: The Complete Innings, a collection of novellas by Richard Foreman set early in Raffles and Bunny's careers, Endeavour Press, 2013. Sherlock Holmes, Dr. Watson, Inspector Lestrade, and Irene Adler appear. The final novella, "Raffles: Playing On," ends with Bunny marrying a Lucy Rosebery. Since such a union is never mentioned in Hornung's stories, these tales must take place in an alternate universe.

"The Railway Van that Vanished" by L. F. E. Coombs in *Sherlock Holmes at the Breakfast Table*, Robert Hale, 2013. Britain's Foreign Secretary tells Sherlock Holmes, "We have only just managed to repair the damage done to our relationship with Russia by that fool Colonel Flashman." This is a reference to George MacDonald Fraser's novel *Flashman at the Charge*, but Harry Flashman hardly did damage to Britain's relationship with Russia in that novel, and Fraser made it clear in his novels Flashman died with his undeserved reputation for honor and courage intact, at least until the publication of his memoirs.

Reanimators by Peter Rawlik, Night Shade Books, 2013. Dr. Stuart Asa Hartwell seeks revenge on Herbert West, delving into the same dark corners of science in the process. Dr. Hartwell, Dunwich, Henry Armitage, Aylesbury, William Houghton, Dean's Corners, Reverend Hoadley, Osborne's General Store, Noah Whateley, Lavinia Whateley, Wilbur Whateley, Warren Rice and Francis Morgan are from H. P. Lovecraft's "The Dunwich Horror." Robert Harrison Blake and Ambrose Dexter are from Lovecraft's "The Haunter of the Dark." Arkham, Miskatonic University, and the *Necronomicon* appear frequently in Lovecraft's Cthulhu Mythos stories. Innsmouth is from Lovecraft's "The Shadow over Innsmouth." Herbert West, St. Mary's Hospital, Allan Halsey, Eric Moreland Clapham-Lee, Sefton Asylum, Bolton, and Buck Robinson are from Lovecraft's "Herbert West—Reanimator." Doctor Waldron, Frank Elwood, Walter Gilman, Ladislas Wolejko, Professor Upham, Keziah Mason, Brown Jenkin, Dombrowski, and Joe Mazurewicz are from Lovecraft's "The Dreams in the Witch House." Soames, Ephraim Waite, Edward Derby Upton, and Edward Derby are from Lovecraft's "The Thing on the Doorstep." Gruber is from Stuart Gordon's film *Re-Animator*, based on Lovecraft's story. Dr. Rafael Carlos Garcia Muñoz is from Lovecraft's "Cool Air," though his full name is Rawlik's invention. Daniel Cain is meant to be Herbert West's unnamed assistant from Lovecraft's story; his name comes from *Re-Animator*. Megan Halsey-Griffith is based on Megan Halsey, Dean Halsey's daughter in the movie. The Darrow Chemical Company is from the movie *The Return of the Living Dead*. Paul Rigas is from the film *Man Made Monster*. Henryk Savaard is from the movie *The Man They Could Not Hang*. Richard Cardigan and the *Susan B. Jennings* are from the film *Charlie Chan in Honolulu*. Maurice Xavier and Francis Flegg are from the film *The Return of Doctor X*. Chester Armwright and Dr. Wainscott are from the book *Arkham Unveiled*, a supplement to the role-playing game *Call of Cthulhu*. Towers is from Ron Shiflet and Glynn Barrass' *Two Against Darkness*. Durden is a relative of Tyler Durden from Chuck Palahniuk's novel *Fight Club*. Alice Keezar Peaslee and her husband Nathaniel Wingate Peaslee are from Lovecraft's "The Shadow Out of Time." Laban Shrewsbury is from August Derleth's *The Trail of Cthulhu*. Kingsport is from Lovecraft's "The Festival." Arthur Jermyn is from Lovecraft's "Facts Concerning the Late Arthur Jermyn and

His Family." Englehorn is from *King Kong*; the *Adventura* is meant to be the *Venture*, the same ship later captained by Englehorn. Bull Larsen is the brother of Wolf Larsen from Jack London's *The Sea-Wolf*. Allnut is from C. S. Forester's *The African Queen*. Misty Valley is from Nancy A. Collins' *The Thing from Lover's Lane*. Witches Hollow and the Potter family are from Derleth's "Witch's Hollow." Martin's Beach is from Lovecraft's "The Horror at Martin's Beach." Alfred Morris is from the movie *The Mad Ghoul*. Evan Beaumont is from the film *The Walking Dead*. Officer Chan is Earl Derr Biggers' detective Charlie Chan. Kin Fo is from Jules Verne's *Tribulations of a Chinaman in China*. The Pan-Oceanic Banking and Insurance Corporation is meant to evoke Oceanic Airlines from *Lost* and several other TV series and movies. Dr. Vollmer is from Rex Stout's Nero Wolfe novels. Golden Goblin Press is from Robert E. Howard's "The Black Stone." Billington's Woods, Duxbury, August Dewart, and Reverend Phillips are from Derleth's *The Lurker at the Threshold*. John and Prudence Doten are from *The Lurker at the Threshold* and Robert M. Price's "Young Goodwife Doten." Goody Watkins is from Lovecraft's "Fungi from Yuggoth" and Price's "Young Goodwife Doten." Royal bee jelly is a reference to William S. Baring-Gould's *Sherlock Holmes of Baker Street*. El Mirada, Florida is from the film *Abbott and Costello Meet Frankenstein*. Doctor C is Doctor Charriere from Derleth's "The Survivor." Antoinette, the creator of the dish *Ratatouille de Ego*, is meant to be the mother of food critic Anton Ego from the animated film *Ratatouille*. Randolph Carter appears in many of Lovecraft's stories. Professor Henry Jones is Indiana Jones' father. Zorad Hoag is from Lin Carter's "Strange Manuscript Found in the Vermont Woods." Franklin Scudder is from John Buchan's *The Thirty-Nine Steps*. Kirowan is John Kirowan from stories by Robert E. Howard. Hudson University is from the television series *Law & Order* and its spin-offs. Crawford Tillinghast is from Lovecraft's "From Beyond." Morley cigarettes are from *The X-Files* and several other TV series and movies. Dr. Angell is from Lovecraft's "The Call of Cthulhu." Harley Warren is from Lovecraft's "The Statement of Randolph Carter." Dr. Valentin Gogol is from the film *Mad Love*. C. E. Winchester is a relative of Charles Emerson Winchester III from the television series *M*A*S*H*. Casey Lee is from John P. Marquand's *Your Turn, Mr. Moto*. Nick Charles is from Dashiell Hammett's *The Thin Man*. Sycamore Springs is from the film *The Thin Man Goes Home*. Hadrian Vargr is meant to be Nero Wolfe; his alias is a reference to John T. Lescroart's *Son of Holmes*, in which Sherlock Holmes and Irene Adler's son Auguste Lupa (who is meant to be Wolfe) uses a number of aliases that include the first name of one of the Caesars. The Vargr are wolves from Norse mythology. Comte de Chagny, Lady de Chagny (formerly Christine Daae), *Don Juan Triumphant*, and Lady de Chagny's admirer (Erik the Opera Ghost) are from Gaston Leroux's *The Phantom of the*

Opera. Emile Belloq is meant to be René Emile Belloq from the first Indiana Jones film, *Raiders of the Lost Ark*. Étienne-Laurent de Marigny is from Lovecraft's "Through the Gates of the Silver Key." Helman Carnby is from Clark Ashton Smith's "The Return of the Sorcerer." The *Cultes des Goules*, its author, the Comte d'Erlette; and Prinn's *De Vermis Mysteriis* appear in Cthulhu Mythos stories by Robert Bloch. *The Pretorius Commentary on the Journals of Victor Frankenstein* alludes to both Mary Shelley's novel *Frankenstein* and the film *The Bride of Frankenstein*. Erik Zann is meant to be the title character of Lovecraft's "The Music of Erich Zann." Foxfield is a town Lovecraft invented, but never used in a story; however, Robert M. Price utilized it in "The Shunpike." Zoar and Zaman's Hill are from "Fungi from Yuggoth." The Gardner Farm is from Lovecraft's "The Colour Out of Space." Dyer and Lake are from Lovecraft's *At the Mountains of Madness*. Albert Wilmarth is from Lovecraft's "The Whisperer in the Darkness." Arkham College appears in several of Lovecraft's stories. Ithaqua is from Derleth's story of the same name. Summerisle is from the film *The Wicker Man*. The Black Man is Lovecraft's Great Old One Nyarlathotep. The Panic of 1869, Ambrose Abbott, and Ezekiel Chambers are from Bloch's "The Creeper in the Crypt." The Latimers are from Marion Zimmer Bradley's *Witch Hill*. The *Cordelia Ys* is an allusion to Robert W. Chambers' *The King in Yellow*. Abigail Mason is meant to be Abigail Prinn from Henry Kuttner's "The Salem Horror." Captain Holt is the title character of Lovecraft's "The Terrible Old Man"; he was given the name Captain Richard Holt in *Kingsport: City in the Mists*, another *Call of Cthulhu* supplement. The Chau-Chaus of Liang are meant to be the Tcho-Tcho of Leng, created by August Derleth. The Jeffison family is from John Pelan and Benjamin Adams' "That's the Story of My Life." Deborah Zellaby is related to Gordon Zellaby from John Wyndham's *The Midwich Cuckoos*. Gates Falls, Maine is from Stephen King's "Graveyard Shift." The Tillinghast Building is from David Wellington's story "Cyclopean." This novel portrays Erich Zann as Erik and Christine Daae's child. If so, he would've been born in 1882, nine months after the events of Leroux's *The Phantom of the Opera*. However, Zann appears as a grown man in the graphic novel *The Irregulars . . . In the Service of Sherlock Holmes*, which is set in 1896. Additionally, Win Scott Eckert's story "The Wild Huntsman" reveals Wolf Larsen is really the immortal XauXaz, making it impossible for Bull Larsen to be his brother. *Mad Love* is an adaptation of Maurice Renard's novel *The Hands of Orlac*, which is already in the CU. Although the film makes changes to the novel's plot, such as the mad doctor's name being Gogol rather than Cerral, the man who loses his hands and has a killer's appendages grafted onto his own limbs is still a pianist named Stephen Orlac in both versions, and therefore it seems unlikely they could take place in the same universe. The novel incorporates Rawlik's short story "The Masquerade in Exile," appearing in *Tales of the*

Shadowmen Volume 7: Femmes Fatales, Jean-Marc and Randy Lofficier, eds., Black Coat Press, 2010; reprinted in French in *Les Compagnons de l'Ombre* (*Tome 8*), Jean-Marc and Randy Lofficier, eds., Rivière Blanche, 2011.

"Red Sunset" by Bob Madison in *Gaslight Grimoire: Fantastic Tales of Sherlock Holmes*, J. R. Campbell and Charles Prepolec, eds., EDGE Science Fiction and Fantasy Publishing, 2008. A private investigator asks an elderly, decrepit British consulting detective to assist him in a case involving a missing man, who upon being discovered by the American detective attacked him, forcing the detective to fire three bullets into him, which had no effect. The British sleuth deduces the younger detective works for either the Chandler or Continental agencies. The person responsible for the man's strange condition is a Romanian Count, who mentions the Dutch doctor. The elderly British detective is Sherlock Holmes. The Continental Detective Agency is from Dashiell Hammett's Continental Op stories, and the American detective is the Op himself. The Romanian Count is Dracula, while his Dutch foe is Doctor Abraham Van Helsing. This story takes place during World War II, and the P.I. claims Holmes was smuggled out of London when the Blitz began, his continued existence being considered vital to British morale. This conflicts with the events of Anthony Boucher's story "The Adventure of the Illustrious Impostor" and Manly Wade Wellman's "But Our Hero Was Not Dead," both of which portray Holmes as still residing in London in 1941. References to Marshal Antonescu's overthrow in Rumania would seem to place this story in 1944. However, Holmes says he is over a hundred-years-old. Since Holmes was born in 1854, he would be only 90 in 1944. The feebleness and brittle bones displayed by Holmes in this story are inconsistent with references in several pastiches set in the CU to his discovery of a Royal Jelly elixir that arrests the aging process. Given all these factors, this story cannot take place in the CU.

"The Resources of Mycroft Holmes" by Charlton Andrews, *The Bookman*, December 1903. Mycroft Holmes quits his government post to become a detective specializing in historical mysteries, and takes on would-be journalist Professor Mustie as his biographer. Mycroft reveals he and Sherlock are descended from Foxy Quiller, the detective from Harry B. Smith and Reginald De Koven's 1897 comic opera *The Highwayman*, which was set in the 1820s. However, the Holmes brothers' ancestry is too well-mapped in the CU for them to be descended from Foxy Quiller. Additionally, Sherlock's recent return from the dead is mentioned, which fits with the publication date of "The Adventure of the Empty House," but not with its internal dating, which places its events in 1894. Mycroft also shows contempt for his younger brother not evident in Doyle's stories or most pastiches. Finally, numerous accounts set after 1903 show Mycroft still working for the British government.

"The Return of the Sussex Vampire" by Christopher Sequeira in *Sherlock Holmes: The Game's Afoot*, David Stuart Davies, ed., Wordsworth Editions, 2008. In 1926, the elderly Sherlock Holmes and Dr. Watson investigate a case of vampirism plaguing Josiah Ferguson's daughters, similar to a case involving Josiah's nephew Bob's infant son that occurred years ago. Bob Ferguson is from Doyle's "The Adventure of the Sussex Vampire." Watson is uncertain what to do with notes from some of Holmes' cases, including that of the Nikola Formulae. This is a reference to Guy Boothby's master criminal Doctor Nikola. Watson has grown children (including at least two sons) and young grandchildren at the time of this case. However, in Farmer's *The Adventure of the Peerless Peer*, Watson states Nylepthah is the only one of his four wives to bear him a son, that child being born in November 1918. Combined with a reference to Watson attending Mycroft Holmes' funeral in 1919, this places Sequeira's tale in an alternate reality to the CU.

Rip Haywire, comic strip by Dan Thompson, featuring the titular mercenary and his talking dog TNT. In the July 6, 2009 strip, a dearth of work causes Rip to take a job as a lawn care specialist, only to wind up blowing up the Bumstead home (from *Blondie*) while attempting to uproot a stump. In the July 9–11 strips, he gets a job as a driving instructor and torments the kids from Jerry Scott and Jim Borgman's strip *Zits*. In the August 25, 2009 strip, Dick Tracy is mentioned as a real person. In the September 14–22, 2009 storyline, Rip is suspected of treason and placed in the Village, where he is tormented by a number of Number 2s, and TNT is attacked by Rover. In the July 31–August 7, 2010 strips, an unnamed Edward Cullen (from Stephenie Meyer's *Twilight* novels) appears. In the September 24, 2013 strip, Bret Maverick makes an anachronistic appearance. The various crossovers are too tongue-in-cheek to be incorporated into CU continuity.

Rot and Ruin, a novel series by Jonathan Maberry set in a world infested by zombies. The third and fourth books, *Flesh and Bone* and *Fire and Ash*, have appearances by Maberry's series character Joe Ledger. The short story "Tooth and Nail" features both Ledger and Iron Mike Sweeney from Maberry's *Pine Deep Trilogy*. Maberry's *Dead of Night* books (*Dead of Night* and *Fall of Night*) show the origins of the zombie plague seen in *Rot and Ruin*.

"Santiago Contra el Culto de Cthulhu" by Mark Zirbel in *Cthulhu Unbound Volume 2*, Thomas Brannan and John Sunseri, eds., Permuted Press, 2008.

The masked Mexican wrestler Santiago battles Cthulhu. Talking about the villains he encounters on a regular basis, Santiago says, "One week, the great-great-great-grandson of Doctor Frankenstein is trying to steal my brain to turn his monster into the World Heavyweight Champion, the next week, some voodoo priestess wants to eat my heart in order to gain control of a legion of masked wrestler zombies." Santiago's match with Cthulhu is rather tongue-in-cheek; he immediately defeats the Great Old One by punching him in the testicles.

"Satan's Signature" by Joseph Lamere in *Tales of the Shadowmen Volume 8: Agent Provocateurs*, Jean-Marc and Randy Lofficier, eds., Black Coat Press, 2012; reprinted in French in *Les Compagnons de l'Ombre (Tome 11)*, Jean-Marc and Randy Lofficier, eds., Rivière Blanche, 2013. C. Auguste Dupin comes to England and investigates Dr. Henry Jekyll alongside Sherlock Holmes. Dupin is the sleuth created by Edgar Allan Poe. Dr. Jekyll is from Robert Louis Stevenson's novel. Sherlock Holmes, his brother Mycroft, the Diogenes Club and Colonel Moran are from the stories by Arthur Conan Doyle. *L'Echo de France* is from Maurice Leblanc's Arsène Lupin novels. The Marquis Eric is better known as the Beast from Jeanne-Marie Le Prince de Beaumont's fairy tale *La Belle et la Bête* (*Beauty and the Beast*). Sunny is Solar Pons, the future Holmes-like sleuth from stories by August Derleth; his brother Bancroft is also from the Solar Pons stories. Mr. Bunbury is from Oscar Wilde's play *The Importance of Being Earnest*. Miskatonic University is from Lovecraft's Cthulhu Mythos. Lord Ruthven is from John Polidori's "The Vampyre." Alinska is from Étienne-Léon de Lamothe-Langon's *The Virgin Vampire*. Bisclavret is from the story of the same name by Marie de France. This story takes place in 1881, and "Sunny" (Solar) is stated to be fourteen-years-old, while his brother Bancroft holds a government position under Mycroft. However, according to August Derleth, Solar Pons would have been only one-year-old in 1881, and Bancroft would be only eight. Therefore, this story must be regarded as an alternate universe tale.

"Scooby-Doo, When Are You?" *Scooby-Doo Team-Up* #7 by Sholly Fisch and Scott Jeralds, DC Comics, January 2015. The Mystery, Inc. crew is pulled back in time to prehistoric Bedrock by Prof. Einstone, and accompanies the Flintstone family to the opera, where the Phantom of the Operrock shows up. *The Flintstones* is set in a prehistoric era where dinosaurs and other pre-historic animals coexist with cavemen who have many modern trappings, and therefore must be placed in an AU. At the end of the story, the Great Gazoo attempts to send Scooby and company back to their own era, but overshoots and sends them to the future era of the Jetsons, leading into "Future Shocked," *Scooby-Doo Team-Up* #8, March 2015.

Season of Madness: A Doctor Watson Adventure by Aaron Smith, Cornerstone Book Publishers, 2009. Dr. Watson teams up with Dr. John Seward to investigate a rash of madness in London. It is stated Jack the Ripper's murders happened a decade ago, which would suggest this novel takes place in 1898. However, the events of *Dracula* are described as having taken place "many months" ago, whereas in the CU it took place in 1887. Additionally, the portrayals of the Ripper, Elizabeth Bathory, and Irene Adler conflict with CU continuity, placing this book in an alternate universe.

"A Sense of Time" by Pete Rawlik in *The Lovecraft eZine* #33, Mike Davis, ed., January 2015, a Cthulhu Mythos story set in the future and involving alternate timelines. Outpost 31 in the Antarctic (from John Carpenter's film *The Thing*) and the Jonbar Hinge (from Jack Williamson's novel *The Legion of Time*) are mentioned.

The Shadow over Innsmouth, one-shot by Ron Marz and Ivan Rodriguez, Dynamite Entertainment, 2014. The Shadow and Margo Lane battle what appear to be Deep Ones in Innsmouth. The "Deep Ones" turn out to be bootleggers disguised as the creatures spoken of in the legends of the area. A surviving bootlegger refers to a Shadow, inspiring H. P. Lovecraft to write "The Shadow over Innsmouth." The implication Lovecraft's story is fictional, and based on legends rather than actual events, places this story in an AU.

The Shadow: Year One, ten-issue miniseries by Matt Wagner and Wilfredo Torres, Dynamite Entertainment. The Shadow makes his debut in New York, and battles an old foe that is precipitating a gang war. Journalist Maxwell Grant offers to be the Shadow's biographer, saying "Samuel Johnson had Boswell! Holmes had Watson!" The details about the Shadow's and Margo Lane's families given in this series conflict with their family histories in the CU. Additionally, the Maxwell Grant seen here is clearly not Walter Gibson, who in both the CU and "our" universe wrote the Shadow novels under the Grant pseudonym.

The Shadow/Green Hornet: Dark Nights, five-issue miniseries by Michael Uslan and Keith Burns, Dynamite Entertainment, 2013. In the spring of 1939, the Shadow and his agents join forces with the Green Hornet and Kato to rescue President Roosevelt from the clutches of Shiwan Khan. Roosevelt was given a silver bullet as a child by Britt Reid's great-uncle John, a Texas Ranger. John Reid is better known as the Lone Ranger. The Shadow has an office in a building that also contains offices for the Hidalgo Trading Company (from the Doc Savage pulps), Timely Comics Group (the company later known as Marvel Comics), Nick Carter P.I., Benson Industries and Justice, Inc.

(from the pulp stories of a certain pale-skinned hero), and Supersnipe Ltd. (from *Supersnipe Comics*, a comic book published by Street & Smith). A German spy named Kruger also appears; this is meant to be Heinz Kruger, the Nazi agent that killed Dr. Reinstein, the inventor of the Super-Soldier Serum that empowered Captain America. The comic book *Sting of the Green Hornet* takes place in 1942, and is clearly written as the Hornet and Kato's first meeting with the Shadow and F.D.R. This, combined with the death of Cliff Marsland at Shiwan Khan's hands, argues against placement of this comic in CU continuity.

Shadows of the Opera, Book One: The Mark of the Revenant, collection by Rick Lai, Wild Cat Books, 2010. The first story, "Acolytes of the Shadows," was reprinted in *The Shadow of Judex*, Jean-Marc and Randy Lofficier, eds., Black Coat Press, 2013, and in French in *L'Ombre de Judex*, Jean-Marc and Randy Lofficier, eds., Rivière Blanche, 2013. Policewoman Darlla Rassendyll, framed and left for dead by the Black Coats, is rescued by Erik, the Phantom of the Opera, who grooms her as his Disciple of Death, the Revenant. Erik is from Gaston Leroux's novel *The Phantom of the Opera*. The Revenant is meant to be the same character as the Man in the Felt Hat from the same novel. Other characters from Leroux's novel are: Morgane Giry, Commissioner Mifroid, Feliciana Sorelli, Count Philippe de Chagny and his brother Raoul, Joseph Bouquet, Christine Daae, Firmin Richard, Carlotta, Darius, Laurent Remy, Meg Giry, and Jammes. El Hichmakani (aka Haji Abu) is from Richard Francis Burton's *The Kasidah*, and is mentioned under the variant name Hajji Abu as one of the bronze-skinned superman's instructors in Philip José Farmer's novel *Escape from Loki*; here, he is conflated with the Persian from *The Phantom of the Opera*. Francine Letaine, Gaston "Bluebeard" Morrell, and Inspector Jacques Lefevre are from the film *Bluebeard*. Antoine Dragone is meant to be Anthony Draco from the film *Chamber of Horrors*. William Rassendyll is from Anthony Hope's *The Prisoner of Zenda*. Armande Kent is meant to be Armande the courtesan from Émile Zola's *The Mysteries of Marseilles*. Eugene Rougon is from Zola's *His Excellency* and other novels in the Rougon-Macquart cycle. Leon Fauchery is from Zola's *Nana*, as is Anna Coupeu. Claudette Piedefer is the niece of Laure Piedefer, and Clotilde Bron the daughter of Madame Bron; the elder Piedefer and Bron are both also from *Nana*. Charles Blanton is a conflation of the coachman Charles from *Nana* with Blanton the Frenchman from Walter Gibson's Shadow novel *Mobsman on the Spot*. Henri Jaraud is meant to be Henry Jarrod from the film *House of Wax*. Joseph Balsamo, Count Cagliostro is an historical figure who also appears in fiction by Alexandre Dumas. Gloria Scot is meant to be Joséphine Balsamo II, whose daughter and namesake is Arséne Lupin's archnemesis in novels by Maurice Leblanc. Leonard, Théophraste

Lupin and Henriette d'Andresy (Arséne's parents), Victoire, and the Dreux-Soubise family are also from the Lupin books. The golden ram crest of the Cagliostros is from the animated Lupin III film *The Castle of Cagliostro*. Dr. Villagos, Countess Yalta, and Maxime Dorgères are from Fortuné du Boisgobey's *The Lost Casket* (aka *The Severed Hand*). Lady Judex is the Countess de Trémeuse, the mother of the title character of Louis Feuillade's film serial *Judex*; in the novelization of the serial by Arthur Bernède, she is identified as the former Julia Orsini, who married Pierre de Trémeuse. The Callyx Bar is also from *Judex*. Lee is the father of the title character of *The Complete Adventures of Judith Lee* by Richard Marsh. Lucien Gevrol is the son of Inspector Gevrol from Emile Gaboriau's *L'Affaire Lerouge* and *Monsieur Lecoq*. Van Klopen, Victor "Toto" Chupin, Baptiste Mascarot, Lecoq, Arthur Gordon, Paul Violaine, and Flavie Mascarot are also from Gaboriau's interconnected fiction. Monsieur Jim Nemo is meant to be Professor James Moriarty, Sherlock Holmes' archenemy; in his article "A Submersible Subterfuge, or, Proof Impositive," Professor H. W. Starr conflated Moriarty with Captain Nemo from Jules Verne's *20,000 Leagues Under the Sea*, a theory adapted by Philip José Farmer for his book *The Other Log of Phileas Fogg*. Moriarty was identified as a member of the Black Coats by Jean-Marc Lofficier in a comic strip reprinted in *Strangers: Homicron* (Hexagon Comics, 2008). Other references from the Holmes canon include Ronder's Circus from "The Adventure of the Veiled Lodger," Francois Le Villard from *The Sign of the Four*, Larry Parker from "The Adventure of the Empty House," and Klopman the Nihilist from "His Last Bow." The Black Coats; the All-Father (Colonel Bozzo-Corona); the Scapular of Mercy; Marguerite Sadoulas, the Countess of Clare; the Cadet Gang; *Coeur d'Acier*; Mathieu d'Arx and his son Remy; Maurice Pagès; Andre Maynotte; and *L'Epi-Scié* are from novels by Paul Féval. Ida Similor is the daughter of Saladin from the Black Coats books. Lady Judex's mother Leocadie Pagès is Maurice Pagès' daughter by his love interest Valentine, and is named after strongwoman Leocadie Samayoux, another character from the Black Coats series. The Gentlemen of the Night are from Féval's *The Mysteries of London*. The Wolves are from Féval's *Le Loup Blanc*. Count Salvatore Corbucci and Stefano are from the Raffles stories by E. W. Hornung. Erlik Khan is from Turkic and Mongolian folklore; a widespread cult devoted to him appears in Robert E. Howard's stories about Francis X. Gordon, Wild Bill Clanton, and Steve Harrison. "A similar box" is a reference to Howard's Conan novel *The Hour of the Dragon*. "Hyborian lore" is also a reference to the Conan stories. Yolgan is from Howard's "The Daughter of Erlik Khan." The Montour Academy of Fencing and Boxing is named after the werewolf from Howard's "Wolfshead." The Black Lotus is from the Conan and Steve Harrison stories, as well as the Wu Fang pulp novels by Robert J. Hogan. The Purple Heart of Erlik Khan is from the Howard story of the same name. Zukala is from a series of poems by Howard. Here, Zukala is conflated with the King in Yellow (from Robert W. Chambers' collection of the same name), the god Koth from Howard's story "The Fire of Asshurbanipal," and Melek Taos from Howard's "Dig Me No Grave." John Grimlan is also from "Dig Me No Grave." Thuria, Lemuria, and the Serpent Ones (aka the Serpent Men) are from Howard's stories of King Kull. The Wolf People are from Howard's "The Children of the Night." The Ape Lords are from Howard and L. Sprague de Camp's "The Curse of the Golden Skull." The Akaanas are from Howard's "Wings in the Night." Arabu and Lilitu (another name for Lilith) are from Howard's "The House of Arabu." Xultha and Na-Hor are from Howard's "The Isle of the Eons." The Pickaxe of Burial is from the 1939 film version of Rudyard Kipling's *Gunga Din*. Vautrin, Janine Cibot, Madome Remonencq, Elie Magnus, and Cesarine Popinot are from Honoré de Balzac's *La Comédie Humaine* cycle of novels. The Russian aristocrat who committed suicide by throwing herself in front of a locomotive is the title character of Leo Tolstoy's novel *Anna Karenina*. Valorie Varno (aka the Green Lamia and the Jade Seraph) is a relative of magician Val Varno from Walter Gibson's Shadow novels *Murder by Magic* and *Crime Out of Mind*. The Purple Sacrament is based on a purple elixir used by the shadowy pulp vigilante and his agents in the pulp novels. Sara Balsamo is meant to be Madame Sara from L. T. Meade and Robert Eustace's *The Sorceress of the Strand*; her alias of Sarah Warrender is meant to imply she is the mother of Ms. Warrender from Arthur Conan Doyle's "Uncle Jeremy's Household." Count Corbucci's daughter Catarina is meant to be Madame Koluchy from Meade and Eustace's *The Brotherhood of the Seven Kings*. The Draconic crest is a reference to the god Draco from Peter Tremayne's Dracula novels. The Mato Grosso pestilence is from Harold A. Davis' Doc Savage novel *The Green Death*, while the ship *Peterpence* is a reference to Lester Dent's Doc Savage novel *The Black, Black Witch*. Marcellina and Friedrich Hohner are from the film *The Climax*. The Mohicans are from Alexandre Dumas' *The Mohicans of Paris*. The Mohicans in Lai's novel all take their aliases from fictional Native Americans that are real within the context of the book: Uncas and Chinachgook from James Fenimore Cooper's *The Last of the Mohicans*; Keoma from Enzo G. Castellari's Spaghetti Western of the same name; Navajo Joe from Sergio Corbucci's Western; Shuhshuhgah from Russell Thorndike's *Doctor Syn on the High Seas*; Sierra Chariba from the film *Major Dundee*; Uruwishi from Louis L'Amour's *Bendigo Shafter*; Ashawaikie from L'Amour's *Down the Long Hills*; Ma-ga-ska from L'Amour's *Tucker*; and Benactiny from L'Amour's *Conagher*. Carola Stanley is meant to be the mother of Hagar Stanley from Fergus Hume's *Hagar of the Pawn-Shop*. The German mercenary is the title character of the film *Captain Kronos–Vampire Hunter*, while Carola's gypsy ancestor is Carla from the same film. In James Clavell's *Tai-Pan*, the silver lotus is the symbol of the pirate Wu Fang Choi, hence the reference to Silver Lotus Exporters. The Wu Fang Clan is based on a theory by Lai the villains named Wu Fang appearing in fiction by Arthur B. Reeve, Harold Lamb, Robert J. Hogan, and John Marquand, among others, are all descended from Wu Fang Choi. The name of the Clan also evokes the historical group of martial artists known as the Wu Tang Clan, who appeared as villains in films made by the Shaw Brothers. Gloria Scot's father is meant to be Count Cagliostro from the films *The Bloody Vampire* and *The Invasion of the Vampires*. *La Carne* is meant to be Sylvie Karnes from Louis L'Amour's novel *Mustang Man*; Nolan is Nolan Sackett from the same book. The La Salle sisters are the aunts of the Tocsin from Frank L. Packard's Jimmie Dale stories. Felix Drubarde, Sigismund Trottier, and *Le Taon* are from Mary Elizabeth Braddon's novel *Wyllard's Weird*. Irene Tupin and Madame Fourneau are from the film *La Residencia* (aka *The House That Screamed*). The Revenant's alias of Augustine d'Erlette is derived from the Comte d'Erlette, author of the *Cultes des Goules*, from Robert Bloch's "The Suicide in the Study"; Bloch derived the Comte's name from his fellow Lovecraft disciple August Derleth. The Bazarov Medical Institute for the Eradication of Typhoid is named after Yevgeny Vassilievitch Bazarov from Ivan Turgenov's novel *Fathers and Sons*. Antonio Nikola and his cat Apollyon are from the Doctor Nikola novels by Guy Boothby. The Oracle of Benares is from the first Nikola novel, *A Bid for Fortune*. Guzman de Silvestre is from Boothby's novel *The Kidnapped President*; Lai conflates him with Nikola's stepbrother, who used the alias of Don Jose de Martinos in *Farewell, Nikola*. Both characters were described as former dictators of the fictional South American republic of Equinata. Katherine Washburn is a relative of Curly and Duke Washburn from the films *City Slickers* and *City Slickers II: The Legend of Curly's Gold*. Dao Chang of the Tiger Clan is from the martial arts movie *Crippled Avengers*. Auburt Thun is from Jules Verne's story "Master Zacharius." Ximes is from Clark Ashton Smith's story "The Holiness of Azédarac." Avalzant and Yamil Zacra are from Smith's story "The Infernal Star." The Duke of Gerolstein and his daughter Amelia are from Eugène Sue's *The Mysteries of Paris*. Hafsa Barbarossa is a member of the Barbarossa pirate clan from "Loring Brent's" (pseudonym for George F. Worts) stories about Peter the Brazen. The Ung cult is also from the Peter the Brazen stories. Nyogtha is from Henry Kuttner's "The Salem Horror." Sardopolis is from Kuttner's "Cursed Be the City." Garoth is from R. H. Barlow's stories "The Misfortunes of Butter-Churning," "The Temple," and "The Adventures of Garoth." Malachi is meant to be Professor Malaki from the film *Dark Intruder*. Jackson Drail and *The Cabala of Demonic Possession* are also from *Dark Intruder*. The Tattered King, *Le Roi en Jaune*, the Pallid Mask, and the Yellow Sign are from Chambers' *The King in Yellow*. Eveline Sincaul Bayrolles is from Ambrose Bierce's "An Inhabitant of Carcosa" and Michael D. Winkle's "Typo." *The Revelations of Hali* is also from "Typo." Although Bierce portrayed Carcosa as a terrestrial city, Robert W. Chambers portrayed Carcosa as a city on another planet in *The King in Yellow*; this city was vaguely referenced by August Derleth in his own Cthulhu Mythos stories. In his novel *The House of the Toad*, Richard Tierney says there are two cities named Carcosa, one on Earth and another on alien planet. Lai conflates the terrestrial Carcosa with the city of Koth from Robert E. Howard's Conan stories; the earthly Carcosa was named after the city in space where Zukala-Koth lives. The Yellow Sign of Zukala-Koth is based on *The House of the Toad*, which conflated the Yellow Sign from *The King in Yellow* with the Sign of Koth from H. P. Lovecraft's "The Dream-Quest of Unknown Kadath" and *The Case of Charles Dexter Ward*. The ship *Vathek* is named after the title character of William Beckford's novel. Atlanaat is from the Ismeddin stories by E. Hoffmann Price. Zemargad is from Price's "The Queen of the Lilin." The Red Offering is from the story of the same name by Lin Carter. Slidith is from Carter's tales of Thongor of Lemuria. The Marie Gilbert School is from the film *Madeline*. The Dark Shamblers are from H. P. Lovecraft and Hazel Heald's "The Horror in the Museum." Hastur is from Ambrose Bierce's "Haita the Shepherd," Chambers' *The King in Yellow*, and Lovecraft's "The Whisperer in Darkness." Martin Hewitt is a detective in stories by Arthur Morrison. Honoria Hornblower is a descendant of C. S. Forester's Horatio Hornblower, while Margot Blakeney is a descendant of Baroness Orczy's Sir Percy Blakeney, alias the Scarlet Pimpernel. John Blakeney's *The Life and Exploits of the Scarlet Pimpernel* described Sir Percy's naval exploits. Inspector George Marsden Plummer is a future nemesis of Sexton Blake. The Lake of Doomed Souls is from Brian Lumley's Titus Crow novels. Surama is from H. P. Lovecraft and Adolphe de Castro's "The Last Test." Atlantida is from Pierre Benoit's *L'Atlantide*. The curse on the people of the city of Hastur that causes them all to wear the Pallid Mask is from James Blish's story "More Light." The Byakhee are from Cthulhu Mythos stories by August Derleth. The second volume is *Shadows of the Opera: Retribution in Blood*, Black Coat Press, 2013. Appearing or mentioned are (not counting those references also in the first volume): Jim Nemo's daughter Trickie (Patricia Donleavy from Laurie R. King's *The Beekeeper's Apprentice*); the Neptune Society, a precursor to the group of scientists seen in *The Man from U.N.C.L.E.* episode "The Neptune Affair"; Urania Caber (Urania Moriarty from Philip José Farmer's *Doc Savage: His Apocalyptic Life*); Urania's son, Jim's namesake (Dr. Caber from Lord Dunsany's Jorkens books; Farmer identified Caber as Urania Moriarty's son by John Clay); the Brotherhood of the Seven Kings, from L. T. Meade and Robert Eustace's novel of the same name; Cocotte,

Piquepuce, Landerneau, and Captain Pattu, descendants of the characters of those names seen in the Black Coats novels; Chantal Lebrue, a relative of a similarly-named agent of the shadowy pulp hero; John Clay from Doyle's "The Adventure of the Red-Headed League"; St. Swithin's from the Doctor novels by Richard Gordon; Brendan McGinty, a relative of Boss Jack McGinty from Doyle's *The Valley of Fear*; Armand Zeck, an ancestor of Arnold Zeck from Rex Stout's Nero Wolfe novels; Marguerite Blakeney from the Scarlet Pimpernel novels; Marguerite's husband's mistress (Alice Clarke Raffles from Farmer's *Tarzan Alive*; Win Scott Eckert first proposed the unique relationship between the Blakeneys and Alice in his story "Is He in Hell?"); the Vicomte (Annibal Gioja from the Black Coats novels); the Royal Palace Hotel from the first Fantômas novel; Lecoq, Dr. Samuel, Julie Maynotte, Abel and Rose Lenoir, Roland and Nita Fitzroy de Clare, Echalot, Coyatier, Pistolet, Cadet-l'Amour, Reynier, Le Manchot, Julien Lenoir, Inspector Francis Badoît, Clotilde Morand Stuart de Clare, *The Brigand's Painting*, and Count Biffi from the Black Coats books; Vladimir Donevitch, a member of the Donevitch family from the Nero Wolfe novel *Over My Dead Body*; Joseph Bridau from *La Comédie Humaine*; Bartol Djanko, the brother of the title character of the Spaghetti Westerns *Django* and *Django Strikes Again*; Bel Demonio from Féval's *The Companions of Silence*; the Six Vigilant Men, the fathers or grandfathers of Edgar Wallace's Four Just Men; Master Chun from *Chamber of Horrors*; the London barber who cut the throats of his patrons (Sweeney Todd, the Demon Barber of Fleet Street); the four musketeers and Milady de Winter from Alexandre Dumas' *The Three Musketeers*; the Salazar family, relatives of Isadora Klein from Doyle's "The Adventure of the Three Gables"; Dora Marley, a relative of one of Doc's aides; Anatole and Rolande Cerral, the father and aunt respectively of the doctor from Maurice Renard's *The Hands of Orlac*; Puma, who derives his nom de guerre from the Comanche chief from the movie *McClintock*; Two-Knife, whose own alias is taken from the Apache chief from the movie *The Gatling Gun*; Major Marcus Huret, a relative of Huret the boulevard assassin from Doyle's "The Adventure of the Golden Pince-Nez"; Jack Capper, a descendant of John Capper from Robert Louis Stevenson's *The Black Arrow*; Meaghan and Desdemona Cullin, relatives of Monk Cullin from Lester Dent's Lynn Lash story "The Sinister Ray"; Magna Sark (Magna Island from Lester Dent's Doc Savage novel *The Sea Magician*, which was based on the real island of Sark); an English earl (the Earl of Mayfair) and the law firm Mason, Smith, and Mason from the Doc Savage novel *Bequest of Evil* by William G. Bogart; the name Paris Mason, meant to evoke Erle Stanley Gardner's attorney Perry Mason; the false story of Confederate spy Belle Boyd's father being murdered by abolitionists, a reference to J. T. Edson's novels about Belle Boyd, which change the historical details of Belle's father's death and her motivation for becoming a spy ("Jon Dest" is an anagram for "J. T. Edson"); Lee Bailey from the Western *Hannie Caulder*; Gunsight Eyes (a combination of Colonel Mortimer from *For a Few Dollars More* with Sabata from the films *Sabata* and *Return of Sabata*; actor Lee Van Cleef played both roles); Linus Jerome Carradine from the Spaghetti Western *Johnny Yuma*; La Frenaie wine from Clark Ashton Smith's Averoigne tales; the Pallid Mask, aka Juan North, Django, and Antoine Boucher (Fantômas, the Lord of Terror in novels by Marcel Allain and Pierre Souvestre); Wolf Hunter, who derives his alias from the Tonkawa chief from Robert E. Howard's "Graveyard Rats"; Moreau from H. G. Wells' *The Island of Doctor Moreau*; Jabez Marriott and Ratina from the film *The Brigand of Kandahar*; the hidden city of intelligent albino apes from H. P. Lovecraft's "Facts Concerning the Late Arthur Jermyn and His Family"; the men who assumed Django's name to enhance their own reputations (a reference to the many unauthorized "sequels" to Sergio Corbucci's *Django* made in Italy); Major Huret's two fellow assassins who died seeking Benito Juarez's gold (Colonel Michel Sévigny and Jean-Paul from the Spaghetti Western *Run Man Run*); the Phantom of Truth from *The King in Yellow*; Randolph Mason, an attorney from a series of books by Melville Davisson Post; King Marley from the Spaghetti Western *His Name Was King*; Minnie Warrender, a combination of the Minnie Warrender mentioned in Doyle's "The Adventure of the Mazarin Stone" with Miss Warrender from "Uncle Jeremy's Household"; Mola Singh, a nephew of Ramdeen Singh from "Uncle Jeremy's Household"; a high priestess of Astarte (Samarra from the film *The Prodigal*); Achmet Genghis Khan, Ethel Thurston, and Hugh Lawrence from "Uncle Jeremy's Household"; the Thuggee's ancestral kingdom (Pankot from the film *Indiana Jones and the Temple of Doom*); Colonel Savage from John Masters' *The Deceivers*; Julius Von Herder, Colonel Sebastian Moran and the Earl of Mayntooth from Doyle's "The Adventure of the Empty House" (Von Herder's first name is meant to imply he is the father of the title character of Ian Fleming's *Dr. No*); Derrick Stewart (Dr. Fu Manchu); Norman Head from *The Brotherhood of the Seven Kings*; Horace Dorrington from Arthur Morrison's *The Dorrington Deed Box*; John Macklin from Guy Boothby's *In Strange Company*; Ju Hai Van Eeden, a combination of Ling Ju Hai from *Doc Savage: His Apocalyptic Life* with the Chinese mother of Ah Ling (aka Hendrik Van Eeden) from Philip Pullman's Sally Lockhart novels; the Red Dragon Tong from the film *The Terror of the Tongs*; Gruesome Clayton (Sir William Clayton from *Tarzan Alive* and *Doc Savage: His Apocalyptic Life*); the Green-Eyed Devil (Dirk Struan from James Clavell's *Tai-Pan*); the Chang Li from the Wu Fang pulp novels by Robert J. Hogan; the Chuen Gin Lou from Donald E. Keyhoe's Dr. Yen Sin novel *The Mystery of the Golden Skull*; the Yat Soy from Robert E. Howard's "Lord of the Dead"; the Yo Thans from Howard's "The Sign of the Snake"; the Si-Fan from the Fu

Manchu series; Culverton Smith from Doyle's "The Adventure of the Dying Detective"; Minnie Warrender's alias of Mrs. Stewart from "The Adventure of the Empty House"; Karah, who is meant to be the mother of Cecily "Karah" Kennet from August Derleth's Solar Pons story "The Adventure of the Camberwell Beauty"; Mina (Yasmeena from Robert E. Howard's El Borak stories); Count Negretto Sylvius, Mrs. Harold, the Blymer estate, and Sam Merton from "The Adventure of the Mazarin Stone"; Dr. Archibald McDonald from Doyle's "Our Midnight Visitor"; Inspector Frederick MacStruan Jr., the son of Sir Frederick MacStruan from *Tai-Pan*; the Netherland-Sumatra Company and Baron Maupertuis from Doyle's "The Adventure of the Reigate Squire"; Noel Moriarty and Fred Porlock from *The Valley of Fear*; Sherlock Holmes and Dr. Watson; Professor Moriarty and Noel's father (Dr. Noel from Robert Louis Stevenson's "The Suicide Club"); Fu Hsi (Fo-Hi from Sax Rohmer's *The Golden Scorpion*); the Black Star from "The Daughter of Erlik Khan"; Renee Zayata, a relative of Henri Zayata from the Shadow novel *The Crime Cult*; Yuan Li from George Fielding Eliot's "The Copper Bowl"; Ali Khan from *The Golden Scorpion*; the Brotherhood of the Lotus from "The Adventure of the Camberwell Beauty"; Huan Chow Lee (a combination of John Ki/ Sam Pak from Rohmer's *The Trail of Fu Manchu* and *President Fu Manchu* with Chow Lee from the Shadow novel *Six Men of Evil*; the surname Huan is meant to imply he is the father of Huan Tsung Chao from *Shadow of Fu Manchu*, "The Wrath of Fu Manchu," and *Emperor Fu Manchu*); the Diogenes Club and Mycroft Holmes; Catherine Cusack, James Ryder, the Hotel Cosmopolitan, the Blue Carbuncle, the Countess of Morcar, and John Horner from Doyle's "The Adventure of the Blue Carbuncle"; the Cullin cousins' grandparents (Desmond Collins and Leticia Faye from the television series *Dark Shadows*); Andreina Cortina and her father Faustine Cortina, relatives of the female Faustine Cortina from Maurice Leblanc's *La Cagliostro Se Venge*; Professor Marguerite Chavain (based on a reference made by Madame Fourneau in *La Residencia* to her prize student, a botanist); the Fourneau College, Louis "Luis" Fourneau, Catherine Lineaire, Suzanne Noel, Henri, Terese Grévin, Pedro Baldie, Brechard, and Bernard Moreau from *La Residencia*; Francesca Delacourt from L. T. Meade and Robert Eustace's *The Lost Square*; Madame Nemo's thrush analogy, an allusion to THRUSH from *The Man from U.N.C.L.E.* (in his tie-in novel *The Dagger Affair*, David McDaniel implied THRUSH arose from the ashes of Professor Moriarty's organization); Lucretia Venucci from Doyle's "The Adventure of the Six Napoleons"; Reginald Crawshay from E. W. Hornung's Raffles stories "Gentlemen and Players" and "The Return Match"; Ludovic Imbert from Maurice Leblanc's Arsène Lupin story "Madame Imbert's Safe"; a statue of a black falcon (the Maltese Falcon, from Dashiell Hammett's novel of the same name); Shintaro Olaki from H. C. "Sapper" McNeile's *Bulldog Drummond*;

Madame Vabre and the Institution Bachelard from Émile Zola's *Pot-Bouille*; Maître Forrestier from Cole Porter's musical *Can-Can*; Sophy Kratides, Wilson Kemp, Harold Latimer, Paul Kratides, and Melas from Doyle's "The Adventure of the Greek Interpreter"; Asenath Pons, the father of August Derleth's detective Solar Pons; the Wrykyn Prepatory School from the works of P. G. Wodehouse; Duckworth Dreux (or Drew) from *Secrets of the Foreign Office* by William Le Queux; Mycroft Holmes as an earlier M (from the James Bond books) in the Secret Service than Sir Miles Messervey, a concept first expounded in John Lescroart's *Son of Holmes*; Monsieur Brenner, an ancestor of Fritz Brenner, Nero Wolfe's chef; Rudolf Rassendyll, Ruritania, the Elphbergs, and Zenda from *The Prisoner of Zenda* and *Rupert of Hentzau*; Digby Fell, the father of John Dickson Carr's sleuth Dr. Gideon Fell; Henri Radin from "The Grim Reaper," an episode of the anthology television series *Thriller* written by Robert Bloch; Gabrielle Damiens from Baroness Orczy's Scarlet Pimpernel novel *Mam'zelle Guillotine*; Andreas of Hungary (Andreas Petofi from *Dark Shadows*); Cornelia Vadarasse, César Cascabel, and Sandre Cascabel from Jules Verne's *César Cascabel*; Kaitlin de Winter (Kitty Winter from Doyle's "The Adventure of the Illustrious Client"); Georges Du Roy from Guy de Maupassant's *Bel Ami*; Rosette Trevor, the mother of Gertrude Trevor from Guy Boothby's *Farewell, Nikola*; the Iga ninjas, a historical ninja clan that is featured in the Japanese television series *Shadow Warriors*; Ladeau, Friedrich von Junzt, and *Nameless Cults* from Howard's "The Black Stone"; the Great Vampire and his Sisters of the Night (Dracula and his Brides; the term "Great Vampire" comes from Louis Feuillade's serial *Les Vampires*); Alexis Duvalier, the twin sister of Angelique Bouchard from *Dark Shadows*, and a counterpart of Alexis Stokes Collins from the "Parallel Time" reality seen in that series; Armond du Moliere from the film *Devils of Darkness*; Glyu-Uho, Sin, Ai, and the Elder Gods from August Derleth and Mark Schorer's "The Lair of the Star-Spawn"; Vathelos the Blind and the Zugites from Howard's Conan story "Black Colossus"; a Seed of Glyu-Uho (the Wold Newton meteorite); a member of the Cult of the Undead (Countess Nadine Carody from the film *Vampyros Lesbos*; Win Scott Eckert identified the Countess as present at the Wold Newton conclave in his Wold Newton Origins stories); the Three Matrons of Darkness (the Three Mothers from Dario Argento's films *Suspiria*, *Inferno*, and *Mother of Tears*); Bibi-Lupin from *La Comédie Humaine*, conflated here with Louis Lupin from *Tarzan Alive*; Delapalme and Lagardère from Féval's *Le Bossu*; Henri de Belcamp from Féval's *John Devil*; Raymond de Grandin, a descendant of Ramon Nazara y de Grandin from Seabury Quinn's "Fortune's Fools"; Ithaqua from August Derleth's titular story; a famous Antarctic explorer (the title character of Edgar Allan Poe's *The Narrative of Arthur Gordon Pym of Nantucket*); Enrique Basilio, the great-grandson of Andres Basilio from the

Disney *Zorro* television series; Raquel Valencia, whose name is meant to evoke Nina Valencia from ther Shadow novel *Washington Crime*; the Cypriote (Princess Nellifer from the film *Land of the Pharaohs*); Brigadier Gerard from the books by Doyle; Colonel Despienne and Captain Tremeau from the Gerard story "How the Brigadier Was Tempted by the Devil"; the Brothers of Ajaccio from "How the Brigadier Slew the Brothers of Ajaccio"; Set from Robert E. Howard's "The Phoenix on the Sword"; the Aklo tongue from Arthur Machen's "The White People" and Lovecraft's "The Dunwich Horror" and "The Haunter of the Dark"; Bruno Relli, the father of E. Varelli from Argento's Three Mothers trilogy; Steve Dixie from "The Adventure of the Three Gables"; Brichester University from Cthulhu Mythos tales by Ramsey Campbell; the Countess (Countess Natalie du Pres from *Dark Shadows*; Angelique Bouchard was revealed to be the half-sister of Josette du Pres, and therefore the Countess' niece, in the novels *Angelique's Descent* and *The Salem Branch*, both of which were written by Lara Parker, who played Angelique on the series); Herbert de Lernac and Louis Caratal from Doyle's "The Lost Special"; the child Joséphine Balsamo abandoned from Jean-Marc and Randy Lofficier's "The Death of Countess Cagliostro"; Noel Moriarty and Madame Koluchy's son (Dominick Medina from John Buchan's *The Three Hostages*); and the Order of the Serpent Heart, which is meant to be the secret society that appears in H. Rider Haggard's *Heart of the World*. A future volume will establish the Revenant and Théophraste Lupin are the parents of the shadow-cloaked vigilante; however, this contradicts the genealogy laid out in *Doc Savage: His Apocalyptic Life*. Additionally, the genealogy given for Fantômas in *Retribution in Blood* conflicts with the one provided in Jean-Marc and Randy Lofficier's translation and adaptation of Arnould Galopin's *The Man in Grey*.

"Shadows Reborn" by Rick Lai in *Tales of the Shadowmen Volume 11: Force Majeure*, Jean-Marc and Randy Lofficier, eds., Black Coat Press, 2014. Thelda Bouchard becomes a member of the vigilante *L'Ombre*'s organization, impersonating Maggie Lane Dale, but an act of murder on Thelda's part causes *L'Ombre* to seek revenge on her. *L'Ombre* is meant to be the pulp hero of the shadows. Thelda Blanche Bouchard (aka Angelique Blanchet) is from Walter Gibson's Shadow novel *The Death Tower*. The Seven Silent Companions are from *The Death Tower* and its sequel, *The Silent Seven*. The addition of the word "Companions" to their name implies a connection to the Companions of Silence from Paul Féval's novel of the same name. Roger Crowthers is also from *The Death Tower*; here, he is conflated with Roger from Gibson's short story "The Purple Girasol," which is also the source of Roger's uncle, Jethro Clayton. Margot Phoebe Lane Dale is meant to be the shadowy pulp hero's trusted female agent; her middle name is derived from the movie *International Crime*, in which his companion is named Phoebe Lane. The Szinca Girasols are also from Gibson's novels, as is the Major turned Police Commissioner. Luther Burbank is meant to be an agent of the shadowy pulp vigilante. The Aldebaran Hotel is from the Shadow novel *Green Eyes*. Humbert Kenneth Allard is H. Kenneth "Kent" Allard from Karl Edward Wagner's story "Sticks." The Black Coats, Colonel Bozzo-Corona, and Marguerite Sadoulas are from novels by Paul Féval. Pierre "the Spotter" Lecoq is a conflation of the radio and film character the Whistler with the criminal called Spotter in Walter Gibson's pulp novels; he bears the soul of the late Lecoq de la Perière of the Black Coats in a new body. Other references from the Whistler movies include: the Ramsey Arms, the Standard Savings Bank, M. K. Simmons, and the Club Royale (*The Mark of the Whistler*); Noel J. Hendricks, Nurse Carroll, and Dr. Crawford (*The Power of the Whistler*); the Crow's Nest, Lefty and Toni Vigran, and Dr. Ira Burbank Franklin (*The Whistler*); Mrs. Harrison and Joe Conroy (*The Secret of the Whistler*); Alice Duprès (*The Return of the Whistler*); John Sinclair (*Voice of the Whistler*); Don Parker and Jerry Mason (*The Thirteenth Hour*); and Don Gale (*Mysterious Intruder*). The Gray Seal (James Dale) and the Tocsin (Marie LaSalle Dale) are from books by Frank L. Packard. The Revenant is from Lai's *Shadows of the Opera* books, and is meant to be the unnamed "shade" from Gaston Leroux's *The Phantom of the Opera*. Mimile Justin, the Secret Raiders, and *N'a-qu'un-Chasse* are from Louis Feuillade's serial *La Nouvelle Mission de Judex*, a sequel to the earlier *Judex*, and its novelization by Feuillade and Arthur Bernède. Lai conflates Justin with Charlie Cook from *The Thirteenth Hour*. District Attorney Bryan and Rhea Gutman are from Dashiell Hammett's novel *The Maltese Falcon*. Lee Gentry is from the movie *Crime Without Passion*. Bernard Sutton is from Max Pemberton's book *Jewel Mysteries I Have Known*. Juan Gonzalles is from Robert E. Howard's story "The Thing on the Roof." *L'Ombre*'s alias of Alaric Kentoff is derived from Colonel Kentov, the alias used by the shadow-cloaked hero in Philip José Farmer's novel *The Adventure of the Peerless Peer*. Sanger Rainsford is from Richard Connell's story "The Most Dangerous Game"; Lai's story implies "Rainsford" is the literary pseudonym of the millionaire frequently impersonated by the shadowy hero who can see the evil in men's hearts. Arsène Lupin is Maurice Leblanc's gentleman thief. Sonia Kritchnoff, the Blue Diamond, and the Black Pearl are from the Lupin tales. The Countess Cagliostro is one of Lupin's greatest foes. The pseudo-psychiatrist confined in a Berlin asylum is Doctor Mabuse, from fiction by Norbert Jacques and a German film series. William Lane is from Edgar Wallace's novel *The Feathered Serpent*. Benjamin Gibson is from the Ragged Dick stories by Horatio Alger. The member of Thelda's family who was allegedly stabbed to death is Angelique Bouchard from the television series *Dark Shadows*, whose stabbing was described by Lara Parker in the novel *Angelique's Descent*, which also revealed Angelique was the half-sister of Josette du Pres. Margo Channing is from the movie *All About Eve*, based on Mary Orr's story "The Wisdom of Eve," in which the character is instead named Margola Cranston. Captain "Ragging" Rassendyll is Robert J. Hogan's pulp hero G-8, whose real name was given as Bruce Hagin Rassendyll in Farmer's biography *Doc Savage: His Apocalyptic Life*. Yian is from Robert W. Chambers' "The Maker of Moons." The monstrous beast is King Kong, from the film of the same name. Captain Jack Driscoll is also from *King Kong*. Jim Harmon's "The Life Story of King Kong" identified G-8 as the leader of the group of pilots who killed Kong. Ed Somers is from the movie *Destination Big House*. Doc is Lester Dent's bronze-skinned pulp hero. Pat is Doc's cousin, while Sunlight is Doc's greatest foe. Nero and Marko are Nero Wolfe and Marko Vukcic from Rex Stout's detective novels. The thirteen-year-old boy from Illinois is Tim Howller from Farmer's story "After King Kong Fell." Lai's account of Doc's arrival at the Empire State Building blends events from "After King Kong Fell" and Will Murray's novel *Doc Savage: Skull Island*. Emile Bouchard is from "Murder Under Glass," an episode of the television series *The Untouchables*. Rip Van Winkle is from Washington Irving's story of the same name. Kenton Lane is meant to be private eye Kent Lane, the son of the shadowy vigilante and his female agent, who is the main character of Farmer's story "Skinburn." Black Spear Holdings is the name by which the Black Coats are known in the 20th and 21st centuries in Jean-Marc Lofficier's fiction. Madame Palmyre is from Renée Dunan's novel *Baal*. Robert Bianchini Drake is meant to be Bob, the narrator of Robert Bloch's story "The Dead Don't Die." His middle name is meant to suggest he is the son of Clara Bianchini and the grandson of Robert Bianchini from *La Nouvelle Mission de Judex*, while his surname of Drake is derived from the Drake brothers in the TV movie adaptation of Bloch's story. *L'Ombre*'s new alias of Frédéric-Jean Orth is the real name of a hero, also known as *L'Ombre*, appearing in novels by Alain Page. This story is based on the premise the woman identified as the shadow-cloaked hero's female agent in Farmer's *Doc Savage: His Apocalyptic Life*, "After King Kong Fell," and "The Long Wet Purple Dream of Rip Van Winkle" was really Thelda Bouchard, who impersonated her just as the shadowy hero impersonated a New Jersey millionaire. Kent Lane is portrayed as the result of Thelda's sexual encounter with Rip Van Winkle, rather than being the son of the shadowy hero and the real Maggie Dale. *L'Ombre* is identified as the son of the Revenant and the half-brother of Arsène Lupin, a different genealogy than the one given in *Doc Savage: His Apocalyptic Life*. Furthermore, the idea that he and Frédéric-Jean Orth are the same person contradicts the revelations about the latter's background in Dennis E. Power's story "The Judex Codex." Therefore, this story must take place in an alternate universe.

Sherlock Holmes & the Coils of Time by Ralph E. Vaughan, Gryphon Books, 2005; reprinted as "Sherlock Holmes: The Coils of Time" in *Sherlock Holmes: The Coils of Time & Other Stories*, Dog in the Night Books, 2013. Sherlock Holmes, the Time Traveler, and a Scotland Yard inspector travel to the future to prevent the birth of the Morlocks. Charles Marlow (from Joseph Conrad's "Youth," *Heart of Darkness, Lord Jim*, and *Chance*), Martin Hewitt (Arthur Morrison's sleuth) and Sebastian Zambra (a detective created by Headon Hill) are mentioned. The Time Traveler's real name is given as Moesen Maddoc rather than Bruce Clarke Wildman, thus placing this novel in an AU.

"Sherlock Holmes and the Great Game" by Kevin Cockle in *Gaslight Arcanum: Uncanny Tales of Sherlock Holmes*, J. R. Campbell and Charles Prepolec, eds., EDGE Science Fiction and Fantasy Publishing, 2011. Holmes, discussing his fictionalized exploits with Watson, refers to "Challenger's nonsense." This story portrays Holmes as having been granted insights by a mystic Zulu dagger given to Watson in Afghanistan rather than being a natural deductive genius, and therefore cannot take place in the CU.

Sherlock Holmes and the Zombie Problem by Nick S. Thomas, SwordWorks Books, 2010. An alternate version of "The Final Problem" with Moriarty unleashing zombies upon England. Phileas Fogg and Passepartout also appear.

Sherlock Holmes: The Breath of God by Guy Adams, Titan Books, 2011. Sherlock Holmes, Dr. Watson, and Thomas Carnacki against Aleister Crowley, Julian Karswell, and Dr. John Silence. Carnacki is the archetypal occult detective, created by William Hope Hodgson. Karswell is from M. R. James' story "Casting the Runes," though his first name of Julian comes from Jacques Tourneur's film version of the story, *Night of the Demon*. Dr. Silence is another occult investigator appearing in six stories by Algernon Blackwood. There are also references to Dr. Hesselius (from "Green Tea" and other stories by J. Sheridan Le Fanu), Lawrence Van Helsing (from Hammer Studios' *Dracula* films), Charles Kent (from the Hammer film *Dracula: Prince of Darkness*), and Mocata Grange (from Adams' Big Finish audio play *Iris Rides Out*, featuring Carnacki and Iris Wildthyme, a character created by Paul Magrs for his *Phoenix Court* novels, who was revealed to be a Time Lady in his tie-in fiction for *Doctor Who*; the name Mocata Grange is an allusion to the occultist Mocata from Dennis Wheatley's novel *The Devil Rides Out*). This novel takes place December 27, 1899–New Year's Day, 1900. However, Dr. Silence's portrayal as a villain (albeit misguided rather than truly malevolent) and his death do not fit with Blackwood's tales. Additionally, Kim Newman's serial novella "Seven Stars" establishes that in the CU, Dr. Silence was still alive and active in 1942. The sequel is *Sherlock Holmes: The Army of*

Dr. Moreau, Titan Books, 2012, in which Holmes and Watson do battle against creatures created by, apparently, the still-living Doctor Moreau (from H. G. Wells' *The Island of Doctor Moreau*). Also appearing are Professor Challenger (from Doyle's *The Lost World* and other stories), Professor Cavor (from Wells' *The First Men in the Moon*), Perry (from Edgar Rice Burroughs' novels set at the Earth's core), Professor Otto Lidenbrock (from Jules Verne's *Journey to the Center of the Earth*, referred to here as Oliver Lindenbrook, the name used in the 1959 film version of Verne's novel), Roger Carruthers (from Adams' novels *The World House* and *Restoration*) and Norman Greenhough (from the film *Without a Clue*, a comedy in which Dr. Watson hires an actor to play the part of his fictional detective, Sherlock Holmes).

Sherlock Holmes: The Gods of War by James Lovegrove, Titan Books, 2014. In Late September 1913, Sherlock Holmes and Dr. Watson battle a murderous cult seeking to engineer a World War. Holmes describes the time he met Dupin, who failed to impress him. One of the cultists is descended from Sir Nigel Loring, but the reference is to the historical knight of that name, not Doyle's heavily fictionalized version. The foreword, allegedly written by Watson in 1923, claims Holmes is now deceased, and it is stated within the main text Mycroft died seven years ago (that is, in 1906). Watson also describes Mary Morstan as his first wife, whereas in the CU she was his second wife. All these factors place this book in an AU.

"Sleep No More" by Paul Hugli in *Tales of the Shadowmen Volume 8: Agents Provocateurs*, Jean-Marc and Randy Lofficier, eds., Black Coat Press, 2011; reprinted in French in *Les Compagnons de l'Ombre (Tome 11)*, Jean-Marc and Randy Lofficier, eds., Rivière Blanche, 2013; and in *Harry Dickson vs. the Spider*, Jean-Marc and Randy Lofficier, eds., Black Coat Press, 2014. A sequel to Hugli's story "Death to the Heretic!" (*Tales of the Shadowmen Volume 7: Femmes Fatales*, Jean-Marc and Randy Lofficier, eds., Black Coat Press, 2010). Richard Wentworth, Harry Dickson, and Dr. Jeffrey Fairchild battle Tang-Akhmut and Georgette Cuvelier, alias the Spider. Richard Wentworth, Tang-Akhmut, Nita Van Sloan, and Commissioner Kirkpatrick are from the Spider pulp novels by Norvell Page. This story reveals the inspiration for Wentworth's crime fighting alias. Harry Dickson, Georgette Cuvelier, and Professor Flax appear in French pulp novels by Jean Ray and others. Dr. Jeffrey Fairchild, his brother Robert, and the Scorpion are from the short-lived pulp magazine *The Scorpion*, though the Scorpion was called the Octopus in his first appearance. Leo Saint-Clair is better known as the Nyctalope in novels by Jean de La Hire. Imhotep is from the Universal Pictures film *The Mummy*. Dr. Anton Phibes is from the films *The Abominable Dr. Phibes* and *Dr. Phibes Rises Again*. The giant pod plants are from

Jack Finney's novel *The Body Snatchers*. Wentworth's half-brother Kent is Allard Kent Rassendyll, as theorized by Philip José Farmer in *Doc Savage: His Apocalyptic Life*. However, Hugli gives Wentworth an uncle, Cyril Wentworth, whose existence does not fit with Wentworth's paternal genealogy as outlined by Farmer. The Interocitor is from Raymond F. Jones' novel *This Island Earth* and its 1955 film adaptation. Billy Brown and the Consortium for Law-enforcement Action for the Sake of Humanity (CLASH) are from *Mister Song*, a backup feature appearing in the French comic book *Wampus* in 1969. Margaret White; her daughter Carietta ("Carrie"); Ewen High School; and Chamberlain, Maine are from Stephen King's novel *Carrie*. Ted White is better known as the French comic character Homicron. Both Mister Song and Homicron were published by Editions Lug, and have been part of a recent revival of that company's characters spearheaded by Jean-Marc and Randy Lofficier.

Sleepy Hollow: Children of the Revolution by Keith R. A. DeCandido, Broadway Books, 2014, a tie-in novel for the television series *Sleepy Hollow*, in which Ichabod Crane is reinterpreted as a Colonial soldier who comes back to life in the 21st century after being killed by the Headless Horseman in 1781. He battles the Horseman, who also has been resurrected, and two occult groups who seek to bring about the apocalypse. Tobin's *Spirit Guide*, a book from the movie *Ghostbusters*, is mentioned in the novel.

"Slouching Towards Camulodunum" by Micah S. Harris in *Tales of the Shadowmen Volume 7: Femmes Fatales*, Jean-Marc and Randy Lofficier, eds., Black Coat Press, 2010; completed in *Tales of the Shadowmen Volume 8: Agents Provocateurs*, Black Coat Press, 2011; reprinted in French in *Les Compagnons de l'Ombre (Tome 9)*, Jean-Marc and Randy Lofficier, eds., Rivière Blanche, 2012; and in *Slouching Towards Camulodunum and Other Stories*, Minor Profit Press, 2014, and *Sâr Dubnotal 2: The Astral Trail*, Jean-Marc and Randy Lofficier, eds., Black Coat Press, 2015. Takes place in the same alternate universe as Harris' novel *The Eldritch New Adventures of Becky Sharp*. Appearing or mentioned are: the Sâr Dubnotal, Naini, Rudolph, Ranijesti, and Gianetti Annunciata from a French pulp series penned by an anonymous author (possibly Norbert Sévestre); Helen Vaughn, Villiers, Clarke, "Memoirs to Prove the Existence of the Devil," Robert Matheson, Caermaen, and Pan from Arthur Machen's short story "The Great God Pan"; Rebecca "Becky" Sharp from William Makepeace Thackeray's *Vanity Fair*; Jacques Courbe and St. Eustache from Tod Robbins' story "Spurs," the inspiration for Tod Browning's film *Freaks*; Francis Aytown, a "deleted" character from Bram Stoker's *Dracula*; Randolph from Douglas Sirk's film adaptation of Lloyd C. Douglas' novel *Magnificent Obsession*; Richard Upton Pickman from Lovecraft's "Pickman's Model"; Pierre Rodin, a descendant of Henri Rodin from "The Grim Reaper," an episode of the anthology television series *Thriller*; the Judge's House in Benchurch from Stoker's "The Judge's House"; Charles Delaware Tate from the television series *Dark Shadows*; Basil Hallward, Dorian Gray, and Lord Henry Wotton from Oscar Wilde's *The Picture of Dorian Gray*; Leng and Kadath from Lovecraft's Cthulhu Mythos; Becky's daughter Annie (Ann Darrow from *King Kong*); Nodens from both "The Great God Pan" and Lovecraft's Cthulhu Mythos; L'Mur-Kathulos from Robert E. Howard's story "Skull-Face"; Tulu, aka Cthulhu; and the Red Shoes from Hans Christian Andersen's fairy tale of the same name.

Spider-Man: The Sinister Six, novel trilogy by Adam-Troy Castro. Spider-Man battles the Sinister Six, a team composed of his greatest foes, currently working under the orders of the Gentleman, a villain with ties to Spidey's past seeking revenge. Numerous characters from other works of fiction appear or are mentioned. References in *The Gathering of the Sinister Six* include: a certain London mathematician (Professor Moriarty); the Gruber Brothers (Hans and Simon Gruber from the Die Hard films); Carmen (Carmen Sandiego, from various computer and video games and spin-offs in other media); a long-lived Oriental gentleman (Dr. Fu Manchu); Lex (Lex Luthor, Superman's archenemy); Auric (Auric Goldfinger, from Ian Fleming's James Bond novel *Gold-finger*); and Henry the waiter (from Isaac Asimov's Black Widowers books). Appearing or mentioned in *The Revenge of the Sinister Six* are: Herr Taubman (an alias used by the Deaf Man in Ed McBain's 87th Precinct novels); the Wrightsville billionaire Diedrich Van Horn (from the Ellery Queen novel *Ten Days' Wonder*); the scarred, wheelchair-bound man who went by the name Ernst (Ernst Stavro Blofeld, leader of S.P.E.C.T.R.E. in Ian Fleming's James Bond novels); Ras (Batman's foe Ra's al Ghul); Soze (Keyser Soze from the movie *The Usual Suspects*); Hannibal (Dr. Hannibal Lecter, from Thomas Harris' novels); Mr. Glass (Elijah "Mr. Glass" Price from the film *Unbreakable*); Napier (Batman's archenemy the Joker, whose real name was given as Jack Napier in Tim Burton's 1989 film); Randolph and Mortimer (Randolph and Mortimer Duke from the movies *Trading Places* and *Coming to America*); and Sipowicz (Detective Andy Sipowicz from the television series *NYPD Blue*). Characters appearing or mentioned in *The Secret of the Sinister Six* include: Ugarte (from the classic film *Casablanca*); Belloque (a reference to Dr. René Belloq from *Raiders of the Lost Ark*); Dr. Christian Szell (from William Goldman's novel *Marathon Man*); Detective Briscoe (Lenny Briscoe from the TV series *Law & Order*); Casper Gutman (from Dashiell Hammett's *The Maltese Falcon*); a tall Texan preacher and a spiky-haired Irishman in nearly opaque shades (Jesse Custer and Cassidy from Garth Ennis and Steve Dillon's comic book *Preacher*); a female FBI agent named Starling (Clarice

Starling from Thomas Harris' novel *The Silence of the Lambs*); Matt Gunderson (the son of Chief Marge Gunderson from the movie *Fargo*); D. W. Jaxon (Downwind Jaxon from Zack Mosley's comic strip *Smilin' Jack*); Professor Fate (from the movie *The Great Race*); a lady opium smuggler in China (the Dragon Lady from Milton Caniff's comic strip *Terry and the Pirates*); an ad exec named Thornhill (Roger Thornhill from Alfred Hitchcock's film *North by Northwest*); and a group of youngsters traveling in a van with a dog (Scooby-Doo and company). There are a few factors preventing the placement of these novels within Crossover Universe continuity, chief of which is the 1990s setting. In the CU, Spider-Man started his career in the 1960s, and therefore would be somewhat long in the tooth by the time this trilogy takes place. Also, there is a chronological problem with the implication Matt Gunderson is the child Marge Gunderson is pregnant with in *Fargo*, since that film takes place in 1987. The large number of references to Marvel Comics continuity are also problematic, particularly references to superteams such as the Avengers and the X-Men.

Star Trek: Into Darkness, 2009 feature film directed by J. J. Abrams. A sequel to Abrams' 2009 *Star Trek* film, which takes place in a divergent timeline from the "mainstream" Trek universe/Crossover Universe. Montgomery "Scotty" Scott and Keenser visit a bar by the Port of San Francisco where the tables have a rotating light-up billboard for Slusho, a fictional soft drink appearing in other Abrams productions, including *Fringe*, *Super 8*, *Cloverfield*, *Alias*, and the 2009 *Star Trek* film, as well as the television series *Heroes*, which was not created by Abrams.

Star Trek/Green Lantern: The Spectrum War, six-issue miniseries by Mike Johnson and Angel Hernandez, IDW Publishing, 2015. The *Enterprise* crew of the divergent universe seen in the films *Star Trek* (2009) and *Star Trek: Into Darkness* encounter Green Lantern Hal Jordan and the surviving members of six other Corps bearing different-colored rings that allow them to harness the powers of the Emotional Spectrum, who were sent there from their own reality (a possible future of the DC Comics Universe) to escape the wrath of the embodiment of Death known as Nekron, who instead follows them to this new universe.

Stoker and Holmes, a novel series by Colleen Gleason so far consisting of *The Clockwork Scarab*, *The Spiritglass Charade*, and *The Chess Queen Enigma*, set in a Steampunk London and featuring Alvermina "Mina" Holmes, Mycroft's daughter and Sherlock's niece, and Evaline Stoker, sister of Bram and descendant of Victoria Gardella Grantworth from Gleason's series *The Gardella Vampire Chronicles*.

"Stone Cold Killer" by Matthew Dennion in *Harry Dickson vs. the Spider*, Jean-Marc and Randy Lofficier, eds., Black Coat Press, 2014. Dr. Abraham Van Helsing and his assistant Mina Harker battle Lady Rook, who has been turning men's insides into stone. Lady Rook, aka Euryale Ellis, will later battle Harry Dickson, as seen in Jean Ray's pulp novel *The Return of the Gorgon*. Detective Juve also appears; as Inspector Juve, he will later become Fantômas' archenemy. Mina Harker is portrayed as a vampire, placing this story in an alternate universe.

The Strange Case of Mr. Hyde, miniseries by Cole Haddon and M. S. Corley, Dark Horse Comics, April–July 2011. Inspector Thomas Adye releases Henry Jekyll, alias Edward Hyde, from his imprisonment beneath Scotland Yard headquarters to help him track down Jack the Ripper. Jekyll's friend Moreau appears in a flashback and Jekyll refers to his experiments on his pet beasts. At the conclusion of this tale, Adye begins investigating reports of an invisible man. The implication seems to be Adye is the Colonel Adye seen in H. G. Wells' *The Invisible Man*. However, Wells' Adye was the chief of police for Port Burdock, rather than being based in London. According to this story, Hyde was arrested five years ago for his crimes, and Scotland Yard allowed the public to believe him dead. Also, Jekyll's former friend Gabriel Utterson is identified as the Ripper. These details conflict with CU continuity.

Sun Koh: Heir of Atlantis Vol. 1, a collection of stories by Dr. Art Sippo, Age of Adventure Press, 2010. The Aryan Atlantean prince Sun Koh arrives in our era from 10,853 years in the past, and is recruited by the German Thule Society, affiliating himself with the Nazi party in the hopes of reestablishing his own race as the dominant one in the world. Sun Koh was the subject of the *heftro-man* (pulp magazine) *Sun Koh, die Erbe von Atlantis* by Paul Müller, who wrote the magazine under the house name Lok Myler. The Basilisk race of Lemuria is a reference to the Dragon Kings from Lin Carter's Thongor novels. The things in Antarctica allude to both H. P. Lovecraft's *At the Mountains of Madness* and John W. Campbell's "Who Goes There?" The product of Sun Koh and Lady Felicity Knight's sexual encounter is Emma Knight, who will grow up believing Felicity's husband, Sir John Knight, is her father. Emma will later marry Peter Peel, and after his apparent death become a "talented amateur" working with British agent John Steed, as seen in the classic television series *The Avengers*. Jan Mayen was, like Sun Koh, the subject of a German pulp series by Paul Müller, *Jan Mayen, der Herr der Atomkraft*, and the two series had a few crossovers. Ludwig Minx appeared in two other *heftroman* series, *Minx der Geisterbeschwörer* and *Minx der Geister-sucher*. Rolf Karsten appeared in the magazine *Rolf Karsten, der Schrecken der Berliner Unterwelt*. Alaska-Jim Hoover appeared in the magazine *Alaska Jim,*

Ein Held der Kanadischen Polizei, written by "Big Ben" (pseudonym for Willi Richard Sachse) and F. L. Barwin (pseudonym for Lisa Barthel Winkler and Fritz Barthel). Alaska-Jim met Sun Koh in the 49th issue of Koh's series. Rudolph "Sturmvögel" Rauhaar was the hero of the magazine *Sturmvögel, Mit Buchse und Toboggan durch die Arktis, Abenteuer zwischen Urwald und Prairie.* In the 199th issue of Alaska-Jim's magazine, he and Sturmvögel crossed paths. Robur the Conqueror is from Jules Verne's novel of the same name, as well as its sequel, *Master of the World.* The Sikh is Captain Nemo (aka Prince Dakkar) from Verne's *20,000 Leagues Under the Sea* and *The Mysterious Island.* The Agarthic master descended from Genghis Khan is one of the shadowy vigilante's greatest foes. The Atlantean cache in the Andes is intended to be the ultimate source of much of the exotic technology wielded by the foes of the bronze-skinned superman of the pulps who was frequently called "Doc" (who is also the bronzed man appearing in Sun Koh's vision during coitus with Shani). The errant British Lord who discovered an Atlantean outpost is the jungle lord, who discovered the city of Opar in 1910. Xaux is an alias for XauXaz, from Philip José Farmer's *Secrets of the Nine* trilogy. Dr. Günter Asch, one of Doc's former tutors, battled the bronze man in Mike W. Barr, Gabriel Morrissette, and Rick Magyar's story "The Olympic Peril" (*Doc Savage Annual #1*, DC Comics, 1989). The Ch'iny'n are meant to be the same race as the K'n-yan from H. P. Lovecraft's revision of Zealia Bishop's story "The Mound." Dr. Jonas Sown and his emotion-controlling device appeared in in Lester Dent's *The Screaming Man* and Will Murray's *The Frightened Fish.* "Pyrrhon Quick" is meant to be a grown-up version of Howard R. Garis' boy inventor Tom Swift; Sippo conflates Swift with one of Doc's aides. Dr. Sippo's book presents a very different version of Sun Koh and the Atlantis he hails from than the one seen in Win Scott Eckert's "Captain Midnight at Ultima Thule," which has already been incorporated into the Crossover Universe.

"A (Super) Friend in Need," *Scooby-Doo Team-Up* #6 by Scholly Fisch and Dario Brizuela, DC Comics, November 2014. Scooby and the gang help the Super Friends and Supergirl deal with a seeming haunting at the Hall of Justice, which turns out to actually be the work of the Legion of Doom.

Suspects by David Thomson, a collection of short biographies of characters from various films, mainly but not entirely from the noir genre, showing how their lives intersect. The characters covered are: Jake Gittes, Noah Cross, and Evelyn Cross Mulwray (*Chinatown*); Ilsa Lund, Victor Laszlo, and Richard Blaine (*Casablanca*); John Clay (*The Killing*); Axel Freed (*The Gambler*); Eileen Wade (*The Long Goodbye*); David Staebler (*The King of Marvin Gardens*); Judy Rogers (*Rebel Without a Cause*); Kit Carruthers (*Badlands*); Waldo Lydecker, Laura Hunt, and Mark McPherson (*Laura*); Helen Ferguson

(*No Man of Her Own*); Dickson Steele and Laura Gray (*In a Lonely Place*); Roy Earle and Marie Garson (*High Sierra*); Henry Oliver Peterson and Gwen Chelm (*Beat the Devil*); Alma McCain (*I Walk the Line*); David John Locke (*The Passenger*); Maureen Cutter (*Cutter's Way*); Al, Pete "Swede" Lunn, and Kitty Collins (*The Killers*); Joe Gillis, Max von Mayerling, and Norma Desmond (*Sunset Boulevard*); Guy Haines and Bruno Anthony (*Strangers on a Train*); Amy Jolly (*Morocco*); Julian Kay (*American Gigolo*); Walter Neff, Phyllis Diedrichson, and Wilson Keyes (*Double Indemnity*); Debby Marsh (*The Big Heat*); Harry Lime (*The Third Man*); Kay Corleone (*The Godfather* and *The Godfather Part II*); Skip McCoy (*Pickup on South Street*); Cora Papadakis and Frank Chambers (*The Postman Always Rings Twice*); Jimmy Doyle and Francine Evans (*New York, New York*); John Converse (*Who'll Stop the Rain*); Jack Torrance (*The Shining*); Vivian Sternwood (*The Big Sleep*); L. B. Jeffries and Lars Thorwald (*Rear Window*); Alicia Huberman and Alexander Sebastian (*Notorious*); Walker and Chris Rose (*Point Blank*); Ma Jarrett and Cody Jarrett (*White Heat*); Brigid O'Shaughnessy and Casper Gutman (*The Maltese Falcon*); Elsa Bannister (*The Lady from Shanghai*); Adeline Loggins (*Paper Moon*); Jay Landesman Gatsby (*The Great Gatsby*); Norman Bates (*Psycho*); Dolly Schiller (*Lolita*); Bernstein, Susan Alexander Kane, Raymond, and Mary Kane (*Citizen Kane*); Sally Bailey (*Atlantic City*); Gilda Farrell (*Gilda*); Hank Quinlan and Ramon Miguel Vargas (*Touch of Evil*); Jeff Bailey (*Out of the Past*); Bree Daniels and John Klute (*Klute*); Mary Ann Simpson (*Body Heat*); John Ferguson and Judy Barton (*Vertigo*); Smith Ohlrig (*Caught*); Howard (*Melvin and Howard*); Harry Moseby and Paula Iverson (*Night Moves*); Travis Bickle (*Taxi Driver*); Frederick Manion (*Anatomy of a Murder*); and George Bailey (*It's a Wonderful Life*). Thomson conflates three of the characters covered with other characters played by the same actors: Amy Jolly, played by Marlene Dietrich, with Lola Lola (*The Blue Angel*) and Tanya (*Touch of Evil*); Wilson (originally Barton) Keyes, portrayed by Edward G. Robinson, with Mr. Wilson (*The Stranger*) and Christopher Cross (*Scarlet Street*); and Walter Neff, played by Fred MacMurray, with Skid Johnson (*Swing High, Swing Low*). Other film and book characters mentioned but not given full biographies include: Gregory Arkadin (*Mr. Arkadin*); Powell (the Reverend Harry Powell, *The Night of the Hunter*); the de Winters (*Rebecca*); Norman Clyde (*The Locket*); Falco (Sidney Falco, *Sweet Smell of Success*); Glenn Kelly and Barbara Jean (*Nashville*); Baron von Rauffenstein (*La Grande Illusion*); Martin Daugherty and Billy Phelan (from William Kennedy's novel *Billy Phelan's Greatest Game*); Jonathan Shields (*The Bad and the Beautiful*); and Sergius O'Shaughnessy (from Norman Mailer's novel *The Deer Park*). Several factors prevent placement of this novel in CU continuity. A number of characters have their first or last names changed from the original films. The details of Jake Gittes' later life contradict the events of *Chinatown*'s sequel, *The Two Jakes*, just as Kay Corleone's fate conflicts with *The Godfather Part III*, since both films were released a few years after the publication of Thomson's novel. The details of Ilsa Lund, Victor Laszlo, and Rick Blaine's lives conflict with the versions given in Michael Walsh's novel *As Time Goes By*, an authorized sequel to *Casablanca*. The events of *The Big Sleep* and *The Long Goodbye* are placed in the 1940s and 1970s respectively, when those films were released, yet there is no explanation given for Philip Marlowe's seeming lack of visible aging over three decades. *Point Blank* is a film adaptation of the novel *The Hunter* by Richard Stark, a pen name for Donald E. Westlake; director John Boorman renamed Westlake's thief Parker, who is in the CU, as Walker. Rather than meeting an angel named Clarence on Christmas Eve, George Bailey had sex with his sister-in-law Laura Hunt, who gave him the money to save the Bailey Building & Loan from ruination. Sally Bailey (whose last name is actually given as Matthews in *Atlantic City*) and her sister Chrissie, Harry Moseby, and Travis Bickle are identified as George and Mary Bailey's children, and yet the four children they have in *It's a Wonderful Life* are never mentioned. Thomson identifies Bedford Falls as being in Nebraska, even though the movie places it in New York State, and refers to Glenn Kelly shooting Barbara Jean, despite the fact in *Nashville*, she is shot by Kenny Frasier, whom Kelly disarms. Thomson's novel *Silver Light* is a sequel of sorts, featuring characters from several movie Westerns: Matthew Garth, Tom Dunson, Tess Millay, Cherry Valance, and Frank Melville (*Red River*); Ethan Edwards and Debbie Edwards (*The Searchers*); Ransom Stoddard, Hallie Stoddard, Liberty Valance, and Tom Doniphon (*The Man Who Shot Liberty Valance*); John McCabe and Mrs. Miller (*McCabe and Mrs. Miller*); Mrs. John T. Chance (*Rio Bravo*); David Braxton and Jane Braxton (*The Missouri Breaks*); James Averill I and Nate Champion (*Heaven's Gate*); and Travis Blue and Denver (*Wagonmaster*). Noah Cross also appears.

Swords of Sorrow, a crossover event from Dynamite Entertainment featuring various heroines and anti-heroines, 2015. Titles include *Swords of Sorrow #1–6* by Gail Simone and Sergio Fernandez Davila, *Swords of Sorrow: Chaos! Prequel* by Mairghread Scott and Mirka Andolfo; *Swords of Sorrow: Masquerade and Kato* by G. Willow Wilson, Erica Schultz, and Noah Salonga; *Swords of Sorrow: Vampirella & Jennifer Blood #1–4* by Nancy A. Collins and Dave Acosta; *Swords of Sorrow: Black Sparrow & Lady Zorro Special* by Erica Schultz and Cristhian Zamora; *Swords of Sorrow: Dejah Thoris & Irene Adler #1–4* by Leah Moore and Francesco Manna; *Swords of Sorrow: Red Sonja & Jungle Girl #1–4* by Marguerite Bennett and Mirka Andolfo; *Swords of Sorrow: Pantha & Jane Porter Special* by Emma Beeby and Rodrigo Ramos Rodolfo; and *Swords of Sorrow: Miss Fury & Lady*

Rawhide by Mikki Kendall and Ronilson Freire. The Kato seen in this series is Mulan Kato from Dynamite's *Green Hornet* comic, which ignores the continuity of NOW Comics' version of the Green Hornet. Lady Zorro first appeared in Dynamite's *Zorro* ongoing series, which portrays Zorro as half-Native American, a conflict with numerous other accounts of his background. Therefore, this series has to take place in an AU.

"Sycorax" by Matthew Baugh in *Of Monsters and Men*, Tommy Hancock and Joe Gentile, eds., Moonstone Books, 2014. Captain Future battles the witch Sycorax on Titan. Captain Future appeared in pulp stories by Edmond Hamilton. Sycorax and Setebos are from William Shakespeare's *The Tempest*. Segir and Black Pharol are from C. L. Moore's Northwest Smith stories. Tsathoggua is from Cthulhu Mythos fiction by Clark Ashton Smith. Jekkara (spelled Jakkara here) is from Leigh Brackett's Mars stories. The Greymalkin, a large catlike creature found on the moons of Saturn, is meant to be the cat from Saturn referred to in H. P. Lovecraft's "The Dream-Quest of Unknown Kadath." The Captain Future stories take place in an alternate universe where all the planets in the Solar System are inhabited by various sentient species in the 21st century.

"Teen Titans–Ghost!" *Scooby-Doo Team-Up* #4 by Sholly Fisch and Dario Brizuela, DC Comics, July 2014. The Mystery, Inc. gang meet the version of the DC comics superteam the Teen Titans seen in the cartoon *Teen Titans Go!* They initially investigate a seeming haunting at Titans Tower, then help the Titans get rid of Raven's uncle Myron the Mildly Irritating.

Terovolas by Edward M. Erdelac, JournalStone, 2012. Dr. Abraham Van Helsing travels to Texas to deliver the cremated remains of Quincey Morris to his brother Coleman, encountering werewolves in the process. Van Helsing twice refers to an adventure he had with his colleague Hamish and his famous friend, the Great Detective. Apparently Van Helsing prefers calling Dr. John Hamish Watson, Sherlock Holmes' best friend and biographer, by his middle name. The afterword describes how Erdelac discovered Van Helsing's papers at the University of Chicago in 1997. The papers had been earmarked for the Ravenwood Collection. The Collection is named for Abner Ravenwood, Indiana Jones' archaeology professor at the University of Chicago and the father of his future wife Marion. Among the names listed in the acknowledgments are Dr. Byron McFynn Jr., History Department, Marshall College, Connecticut (the school Indy taught at); Professor Stanislaus Laff, History Department, Empire State University, New York City, New York (the college attended by Peter Parker, aka Spider-Man); and Professor William Wallace Spates III (the grandson of Professor Alfred William Wallace Spates from Erdelac's Merkabah

Rider books, himself based on a reference to "Spates's catalog" in the movie *Ghostbusters*), Special Collections, Miskatonic University, Arkham, Massachusetts (the site of numerous Cthulhu Mythos stories by H. P. Lovecraft and others). Quincey Morris' body being recovered and cremated does not fit with the events of P. N. Elrod's novel *Quincey Morris, Vampire*.

"The Three Lives of Maddalena" by Michel Stéphan in *Tales of the Shadowmen Volume 7: Femmes Fatales*, Jean-Marc and Randy Lofficier, eds., Black Coat Press, 2010; reprinted in French in *Les Compagnons de l'Ombre (Tome 6)*, Jean-Marc and Randy Lofficier, eds., Rivière Blanche, 2010, and *L'Almanach des Vampires*, Jean-Marc and Randy Lofficier, eds., Rivière Blanche, 2014; and in *The Vampire Almanac (Volume 1)*, Jean-Marc and Randy Lofficier, eds., 2015. Maddalena Ernestine introduces Carmilla to Victor Frankenstein. Dr. Pretorius and Karl are mentioned. Victor Frankenstein is from Mary Shelley's novel. Carmilla is from the short story by J. Sheridan Le Fanu. Maddalena Ernestine is the name of the deceased woman used to create the Bride of Frankenstein in the eponymous film. Dr. Pretorius and Karl are also from *The Bride of Frankenstein*. In the film, the Bride is created by Henry Frankenstein, who in the CU is a descendant of Victor, as explained in Mark Brown's article "The House of Frankenstein" (which can be found at Win Scott Eckert's website *An Expansion of Philip José Farmer's Wold Newton Universe*). Therefore, this story must take place in an AU.

"The Tragic Affair of the Martian Ambassador" by Eric Brown in *Encounters of Sherlock Holmes*, George Mann, ed., Titan Books, 2013. Sherlock Holmes investigates the death of Mars' Ambassador to the British Empire. H. G. Wells and his fiancée Rebecca West appear. This story takes place in an alternate reality where the Martians from *The War of the Worlds* made a second, peaceful voyage to Earth, and settled there after overcoming their vulnerability to terrestrial germs.

"Training Day" by Matthew Dennion in *The Shadow of Judex*, Jean-Marc and Randy Lofficier, eds., Black Coat Press, 2013; reprinted in French in *L'Ombre de Judex*, Jean-Marc and Randy Lofficier, eds., Rivière Blanche, 2013. Judex, Arsène Lupin, and Kent Allard come to Professor George Edward Challenger's aid against Grun and Lorenzo Prunesti. Professor George Edward Challenger appears in *The Lost World* and other novels and stories by Arthur Conan Doyle. The God-Stone of Sarek is from Maurice Leblanc's Arsène Lupin novel *The Secret of Sarek*. Herr Grun is a recurring foe of Robert J. Hogan's heroic World War I aviator G-8. Lorenzo Prunesti will later battle Dick Tracy as Pruneface; the Nazi spy's real name was revealed by John Moore and Kyle Baker in their comic book prequel to the 1990 *Dick Tracy* movie. Chen Zhen was played by Bruce Lee in the Chinese martial arts film *Fist of Fury* (aka *The Chinese Connection*). *Fist of Fury* depicts Zhen as having been trained by Huo Yuanjia, a historical martial artist and co-founder of the Chin Woo Athletic Association. Pai Mei is a legendary Chinese martial artist who appeared in several films produced by the Shaw Brothers, as well as Quentin Tarantino's film *Kill Bill: Vol. 2*. Kent Allard will later become the pulp hero of the shadows, adopting some of Lupin and Judex's methods for his own war on crime. Bruce Wayne will later adopt the mantle of the Batman. Chris Roberson's story "Penumbra" (*Tales of the Shadowmen Volume One: The Modern Babylon*, Jean-Marc and Randy Lofficier, eds., Black Coat Press, 2005) depicted the first meeting between Allard and Judex, and suggested Bruce Wayne may have been Allard's illegitimate son. Inspector Jules Maigret is the main character of detective novels by Georges Simenon. This story takes place in 1927. However, Denny O'Neil, Irv Novick, and Dick Giordano's comic book story "The Night of the Shadow" includes a flashback revealing the young Bruce Wayne and his father Thomas were saved from criminals by the Shadow sometime before the murder of Thomas and his wife Martha at the hands of Joe Chill. "The Night of the Shadow" also places the Wayne murders twenty-five years before its main events, which based on other chronological evidence in the story means Thomas and Martha were killed in 1929, two years after the events of this story. The 1929 date for the flashback in "The Night of the Shadow" is borne out by Rick Lai's *Chronology of Shadows: A Timeline of the Shadow's Exploits* (Altus Press, 2007), which places the hero's debut in that same year. The chronologies of the two stories cannot be reconciled, and therefore "Training Day" is being placed in an alternate universe.

"Twenty to Life in the Lonesome October" by Evan Dicken in *The Lovecraft eZine* #18, Mike Davis, ed., October 2012. Imprisoned in Newgate Reformatory, the Frankenstein Monster battles the god Donar. Alhazred, Friedrich Von Juntz's *Unaussprechlichen Kulten*, and Sarnath are mentioned. This story is connected to Roger Zelazny's novel *A Night in the Lonesome October*, which has already been placed in an AU.

"Two Outs, Bottom of the Ninth" by Aaron Smith in *Lance Star: Sky Ranger Volume 2*, Ron Fortier, ed., Cornerstone Book Publishers, 2009. The aviators known as the Three Mosquitos are told by their superior, General Saunders, that a company of British soldiers led by First Lieutenant Harker will defend a French village while they are off on a mission. Smith also writes the Hound-Dog Harker stories, featuring a grown version of Quincey Harker, son of Jonathan and Mina Harker from *Dracula*, as a British Secret Service agent. Quincey's depiction in Smith's stories is irreconcilable with that in the Marvel Comics series *Tomb of Dracula*, and therefore those stories cannot take place in CU continuity.

"Unquiet Wedding" by Maurice Richardson in *The Exploits of Engelbrecht*, 2001. The wedding of Dracula's Daughter, Lamia, and the Son of Frankenstein brings together a number of individuals as hosts and guests. Hosting the happy event are Count Dracula and Frankenstein's Monster, as the fathers of the bride and the groom, and Professor Moriarty, as a senior advisor to the family. Wedding guests include: Sherlock Holmes, Mycroft Holmes, Dr. Watson, Inspector Lestrade, Colonel Sebastian Moran, and Dr. Grimesby Roylott; A. J. Raffles and Bunny Manders; Bulldog Drummond, Phyllis Drummond, and Irma Peterson; Count Fosco and Sir Percival Glyde (from Wilkie Collins' *The Woman in White*); Ellery Queen Senior and Junior; Hercule Poirot and Captain Hastings; Inspector French; Dr. Adolph Grundt, aka "Clubfoot"; Doctor Nikola; Mrs. Bradley; Father Brown; Lord Peter Wimsey; Lemmy Caution and Slim Callaghan (the protagonists of two separate series of novels by Peter Cheyney); Detective Val Fox and Joey the Parrot (from the British comic *The Rainbow*); the Beetle; Rin Tin Tin; and the Jackdaw of Rheims (from the poem of the same name by Richard Harris Barham).

The Venture Bros., animated television series created by Jackson Publick and Doc Hammer. Jonny Quest (referred to as "Action Jonny") appears, and is portrayed as a homeless junkie with a grudge against his father. The recurring villain Phantom Limb is descended from Fantômas. In the episode "Self-Medication," Jonny says he got an STD from Velma of *Scooby-Doo* fame. The show is too overtly parodic to fit smoothly into CU continuity.

Victorian Undead, six-issue miniseries by Ian Edginton and Davide Fabbri, WildStorm Comics, January–June 2010. In 1898, London is devastated by zombies ("revenants") resurrected by Professor Moriarty, forcing Sherlock Holmes and Dr. Watson to come to the city's aid. The very public mass destruction wrought by the revenants is incompatible with CU continuity, as are the portrayal of Moriarty as having become a revenant himself after the duel at Reichenbach and the death of Colonel Sebastian Moran. Two sequels followed. The first is the one-shot *Victorian Undead Special: Sherlock Holmes vs. Jekyll/Hyde* by Ian Edginton and Horacio Domingues, December 2010, in which Holmes battles Dr. Henry Jekyll, who transforms into the revenant Mr. Edward Hyde. The second follow-up is the five-issue miniseries *Victorian Undead II: Sherlock Holmes vs. Dracula* by Ian Edginton, Davide Fabbri, Tom Mandrake, and Mario Guevara, January–May 2011, in which Holmes and Watson must join forces with Van Helsing and crew to destroy Dracula. The sequels differ radically from the events chronicled in *The Strange Case of Dr. Jekyll and Mr. Hyde* and *Dracula* respectively, providing further evidence the *Victorian Undead* comics take place in an alternate reality to the Crossover Universe.

"Villains, By Necessity" by Pete Rawlik in *Tales of Jack the Ripper*, Ross E. Lockhart, ed., Word Horde, 2013. Former Inspector Thomas Newcomen, who lost his job after he botched the case of Dr. Jekyll and Mr. Hyde, is asked to end the Ripper murders by a Chinese Doctor (Fu Manchu) and an Irish Professor (Moriarty). Newcomen was recommended to the Professor by the former's one-time commanding officer in Afghanistan, the Colonel (Sebastian Moran). The Professor says he and the Doctor have ties to the Continental Agency (from Dashiell Hammett's Continental Op stories), and the Gentleman Thief (A. J. Raffles) has supplied them with copies of all the evidence and files pertaining to the case. He also says their logicians, Mr. Fogg and Mr. Loveless, have identified those responsible for the killings, as well as their motives and hiding place. A man they recently recruited from Paris, who is an expert in the art of remaining unobserved, as well as on subterranean labyrinths (Erik the Opera Ghost), has the culprits under observation. The Professor assures Newcomen London has not been beset by the Dowager Calipash and her daughters (from Molly Tanzer's collection *A Pretty Mouth*), and adds the killers are Edward Hyde's four-year-old offspring by several prostitutes. This does not fit with CU continuity, in which the Ripper killings were committed by the Redjac entity.

Vionna and the Vampires by Chuck Miller, Pro Se Press, 2014. Private eyes Vionna Valis and Mary Kelly (a victim of Jack the Ripper who was resurrected by the vigilante known as the Black Centipede) join forces with the ghost of Sherlock Holmes to battle the Lord of the Vampires, Professor James Moriarty. Moriarty formerly served the previous Lord, Count Dracula, before betraying and killing him. One of Moriarty's vampire henchmen is a Chinese man who claims to have once been played by Boris Karloff, implicitly Fu Manchu. Holmes and Moriarty's fates in this story are irreconcilable with their established history in the CU. Combined with the unlikelihood Fu Manchu would stoop to being Moriarty's crony and the revelation Moriarty is really Holmes' oldest brother Sherrinford, this book, as well as the Black Centipede novels by Miller, must take place in an AU.

The Walking Dead, television series based on the comic book created by Robert Kirkman, in which the Earth is overrun by zombies ("walkers"). In the episode "Save the Last One," Dale Horvath has a pack of Morley Cigarettes, a brand seen in *The X-Files* and several other TV series and movies. In "Bloodletting," Blue Sky, the blue-tinted, incredibly pure and potent form of crystal meth made by Walter White on the television series *Breaking Bad*, can be seen among Merle Dixon's drug stash. In "No Sanctuary," the crate from the Horlicks University expedition to the Antarctic (from "The Crate," a segment of the anthology film *Creepshow*) can be seen. The show has spawned a prequel series, *Fear the Walking Dead*.

"The Warlord of Vaha" by Michel Vannereux in *Tales of the Shadowmen Volume 8: Agents Provocateurs*, Jean-Marc and Randy Lofficier, eds., Black Coat Press, 2011. The warlord of Mars finds himself transported from his adopted planet to Vaha, where he battles cultists alongside his fellow Earthman Cal. The warlord of Mars was created by Edgar Rice Burroughs. Cal's adventures on the planet Vaha were chronicled in five novels by P.-J. Herault. Sinharat is from Leigh Brackett's Eric John Stark novel *The Secret of Sinharat*. The Erloor are from Gustave Le Rouge's novels *Le Prisonnier de la Planète Mars* and *La Guerre des Vampires*. The Cal novels take place several millennia in the future.

Warriors of Mars, five-issue miniseries by Robert Place Napton and Jack Jadson, February–October 2012. The warlord of Mars meets Gullivar Jones, who has been transported to Carter's time from Mars' past, where he was brought in turn from post-Civil War Earth by a flying carpet. In the CU, Gullivar Jones was transported to Mars in the 1890s, rather than the 1860s or 1870s. Additionally, the Hither people from Arnold's novel are conflated with Burroughs' Red Martians, which does not fit with either Edwin L. Arnold's book *Lieutenant Gullivar Jones: His Vacation* or *The League of Extraordinary Gentlemen, Volume II*.

The Web Weaver, a Sherlock Holmes pastiche by Sam Siciliano, Titan Books, 2012, a sequel to *The Angel of the Opera*, which has already been placed in an AU. The Duke of Denver, presumably Lord Peter Wimsey's father or grandfather, is mentioned.

The Weird Company by Pete Rawlik, Night Shade Books, 2014, a sequel to Rawlik's novel *Reanimators*. A group of bizarre individuals combat the creatures unleashed by the Lake expedition to Antarctica. Robert Harrison Blake is from H. P. Lovecraft's "The Haunter of the Dark." Innsmouth, Robert Martin Olmstead, the Deep Ones, Walter, Lawrence, Y'ha-nthlei, Pth'thya-l'yi, Joe Sargent, the Marsh family, the Eliot family, the Gilman family, Captain Obed Marsh, Matt Eliot, Barnabas, the Manuxet, Devil Reef, Dagon, and Mother Hydra are from Lovecraft's "The Shadow over Innsmouth." The Miskatonic University Expedition to the Antarctic, Pabodie, Thomas Gedney, Lake, Atwood, Mills, Boudreau, Fowler, Orrendorf, Watkins, Moulton, Carroll, Captains Douglas and Thorfinnssen, Sherman, Gunnarson, Larsen, Dyer, Danforth, Ropes, Williamson, the Pickman Foundation, and the *Arkham* are from Lovecraft's *At the Mountains of Madness*. The Secondary Magnetic Expedition of 1936, Van Wall, McReady, Garry, and the blue-skinned shapeshifting creature are from John W. Campbell's novella "Who Goes There?" Dr. Wingate Peaslee, Nathaniel Wingate Peaslee, Hannah Peaslee, the flying polyps, and the Yith are from Lovecraft's "The Shadow Out of Time." The Elder Things, the *Necronomicon*, Alhazred, Cthulhu, shoggoths, Arkham, Kingsport, Yog-Sothoth, R'lyeh, Shub-Niggurath, Nodens, and the Pnakotic Manuscripts all have recurring roles in Lovecraft's Cthulhu Mythos. Professor Wilmarth is from Lovecraft's "The Whisperer in Darkness." Ludwig Prinn is from Robert Bloch's "The Shambler from the Stars." The Q'Hrell are a conflation of the Elder Things with the Krell race from the movie *Forbidden Planet*. The great machine of Altair is also from *Forbidden Planet*. Ephraim Waite, Asenath Waite, Moses Sargent, Crowninshield Manor, the Hall School, and Kamog are from Lovecraft's "The Thing on the Doorstep." Reverend Ward Phillips, the Lurker at the Threshold, and Billington are from August Derleth's novella *The Lurker at the Threshold*. Joseph Curwen, Simon Orne, Edward Hutchinson, Dr. M. B. Willett, Peck, Lyman, Waite, and Count Ferenczy are from Lovecraft's *The Case of Charles Dexter Ward*. Von Junzt is from Cthulhu Mythos stories by Robert E. Howard. The Sandwin Family is from Derleth's "The Sandwin Compact." Falcon Point is from Derleth's "The Fisherman of Falcon Point." Zaman's Hill is from Lovecraft's "Fungi from Yuggoth." Obadiah Marsh and the *Corey* are from Derleth's "The Seal of R'lyeh." Doctor Stuart Hartwell, Armitage, Dunwich, the Whatelys, the Dunwich Horror, and Lavinia are from Lovecraft's "The Dunwich Horror." The Whitmarsh Institute is named after Doctor Whitmarsh from Lovecraft's "The Shunned House." Nora Forrest is meant to be the future Nora Charles from Dashiell Hammett's novel *The Thin Man*; in the movie *After the Thin Man*, Nora has an aunt named Katherine Forrest, suggesting Forrest may be her maiden name. Castaigne and *The King in Yellow* are from Robert W. Chambers' short story collection named for the latter. Edmund Carter, Swami Chandraputra (aka Randolph Carter), the Orinoco Clock, the Dreamlands, the Other Gods, and Ulthar are from Lovecraft's Dream Cycle stories. Muñoz is from Lovecraft's "Cool Air," while Charriere is from Derleth's "The Survivor." Frank Elwood, the Witch House, Walter Gilman, Keziah Mason, and Brown Jenkin are from Lovecraft's "The Dreams in the Witch House." Xoth, Ythogtha, and Zoth-Ommog are from Lin Carter's own contributions to the Cthulhu Mythos. The Valusians are from Robert E. Howard's Kull stories. The Cthonians are from Brian Lumley's Mythos tales. Yig is from Lovecraft and Zealia Bishop's "The Curse of Yig." Bokrug is from Lovecraft's "The Doom That Came to Sarnath." Atlach-Nacha is from Clark Ashton Smith's "The Seven Geases." The *Alert* and LeGrasse are from Lovecraft's "The Call of Cthulhu." Idh-yaa is from Lin Carter's "Out of the Ages." Yidhra is from Walter C. DeBill, Jr.'s story "Where Yidhra Walks." Ghatanothoa is from Lovecraft and Hazel Heald's "Out of the Aeons." Kingsport Head is from *At the Mountains of Madness* and "The Dunwich Horror." Megan-Halsey Griffith is based on

Megan Halsey from the movie *Re-Animator*, an adaptation of "Herbert West—Reanimator." The *Elizabeth Dane* and Blake are from the movie *The Fog*. Zkauba, the Tablets of Nhing, the Nug Soth, the Arch-Ancient Buo, Yaddith, the Dholes, Nython, and Mthura are from Lovecraft and E. Hoffmann Price's "Through the Gates of the Silver Key." Xastur is Hastur from *The King in Yellow*, which was adapted into the Mythos by Lovecraft; the variant name Xastur comes from D. J. Tyrer's story "Justified." Celeano and the Elder Gods are recurring features of Derleth's Mythos stories. The great machine of Epsilon Eridani is from the television series *Babylon 5*. Quacchil Uattus is from Smith's "The Treader of the Dust." The Hounds of Tindalos are from Frank Belknap Long's story of the same name. Tsathoggua, Abhoth, Ubbo-Sathla, and Yaksh (the native name for Neptune) recur in Clark Ashton Smith's Mythos fiction. The Dark Young is the name given to the log-like creatures from Robert Bloch's story "Notebook Found in a Deserted House" in *Cthulhu Dark Ages*, a supplement to the role-playing game *Call of Cthulhu*. The Green Abyss is from C. Hall Thompson's "Spawn of the Green Abyss." Kadath in the Cold Waste is from Lovecraft's "The Dream-Quest of Unknown Kadath." Celephais appears in both that tale and a titular story by Lovecraft. VarSuwm is a variation on the native name for Mars in Edgar Rice Burroughs' John Carter novels. L'gy'hx is the native name for Uranus in Ramsey Campbell's "The Insects from Shaggai." Thyoph is from Brian Lumley's "In the Vaults Beneath." Theodoras Philetas is from Lovecraft's "History of the *Necronomicon*."

"Will There Be Sunlight?" by Rick Lai in *Tales of the Shadowmen Volume 7: Femmes Fatales*, Jean-Marc and Randy Lofficier, eds., Black Coat Press, 2010; reprinted in French in *Les Compagnons de l'Ombre (Tome 9)*, Jean-Marc and Randy Lofficier, eds., Rivière Blanche, 2012. Jean Lumière is elected to the High Council of the Black Coats and proceeds to overthrow Colonel Bozzo-Corona. Lumière is meant to be the greatest foe of the golden-eyed pulp hero known as "Doc." The Black Coats and their leader, Colonel Bozzo-Corona, are from the novels by Paul Féval. Also appearing or mentioned are: Dr. Mabuse from Norbert Jacques' novel *Dr. Mabuse the Gambler* and films by Fritz Lang; Reverend H. Briefenstein from the film *The Return of Dr. Mabuse*; Nemirovitch Beauty Salons from *The Man from U.N.C.L.E.* episode "The Adriatic Express Affair"; Natasha Malakoff from H. C. McNeile and Gerard Fairlie's play *Bulldog Drummond Hits Out* and its novel adaptation by Fairlie, *Bulldog Drummond on Dartmoor*; the Black Pearl of the Borgias from the Sherlock Holmes story "The Adventure of the Six Napoleons"; Raffles, the gentleman thief created by E. W. Hornung; Gaspard Zemba from the Shadow novel *Zemba*; Irma Caber (Irma Peterson from McNeile and Fairlie's Bulldog Drummond novels); Dr. Caber from Lord Dunsany's Jorkens stories; Dolores Valencia (from the Shadow novel *Quetzal*; in his essay "Irma of the Ilsa" [*Rick Lai's Secret Histories: Criminal Masterminds*, Altus Press, 2009], Lai argued the villainess of the Shadow novel *Washington Crime* was actually Irma); Professor Moriarty from the Holmes stories; Peterson's Pup-Food from P. G. Wodehouse's story "The Go-Getter"; Darvin Rochelle from the Shadow novel *The Embassy Murders*; Urania Caber (also known as Urania Moriarty from Philip José Farmer's biography *Doc Savage: His Apocalyptic Life)*; Claud Caber (Bulldog Drummond's nemesis Carl Peterson combined with Claud Darrell from Agatha Christie's Hercule Poirot novel *The Big Four*,) John Clay from the Holmes story "The Adventure of the Red-Headed League"; Dr. Stewart (Fu Manchu); Karah Stewart (the mother of Cecily "Karah" Kennet from August Derleth's Solar Pons story "The Adventure of the Camberwell Beauty"; in his essay "The Legacy of Hanoi Shan" [*Rick Lai's Secret Histories: Criminal Masterminds*, Altus Press, 2009], Lai proposed Fu married Miss Warrender from Arthur Conan Doyle's story "Uncle Jeremy's Household"; Miss Warrender used the alias of Mrs. Stewart of Lauder, under which name she was murdered by Colonel Sebastian Moran, as mentioned in the Holmes story "The Adventure of the Empty House"; and their daughter Karah impersonated the male criminal Hanoi Shan from H. Ashton-Wolfe's *Warped in the Making* and *The Thrill of Evil*, rather than her father as suggested by Farmer in *Doc Savage)*; Césarine from Grant Allen's *An African Millionaire* (in *Doc Savage*, Farmer conflated John Clay with Colonel Clay from Allen's novel); Lecoq (Lecoq de la Perière from the Black Coats books); Chauvelin from Baroness Orczy's Scarlet Pimpernel novels; Sherlock Holmes; Julius Freyder from McNeile's *The Third Round* and Fairlie's *Bulldog Drummond Attacks*; Fantômas from novels by Marcel Allain and Pierre Souvestre; and Rosa (Rosa Klebb from Ian Fleming's James Bond novel *From Russia, with Love*). Further references from the Doc Savage novels: Robert Thomas from *Devil on the Moon*; El Pecoso and Goering's double from *The Munitions Master*; Hest from *The Golden Man*; Goebbels' clubfooted double from *Hell Below*; Baron Vardon from *The Golden Peril*; the Golden City of the Very Highest (the home of the Clan of the Very Highest from *They Died Twice* combined with the Golden City from H. Rider Haggard's novel *Heart of the World*); Antonia Lashley from *The Devil Genghis*, the second novel featuring Jean Lumière; the Sons of the Feathered Serpent from the first Doc Savage novel, *The Man of Bronze*, the Red Knife (Frunzoff Nosh) from *The Red Spider*; the prosecutor from Jean Lumière's first appearance, *The Fortress of Solitude*; and Stalin's aide from *Terror Wears No Shoes*. Lai's story draws heavily on Farmer's Wold Newton mythos, and he claims here Carl Peterson and Karah

Stewart are Jean Lumière's parents; however, Win Scott Eckert has strongly implied in his own fiction Lumière is the son of Doc Savage and Countess Lili Bugov.

The X-Files: Conspiracy, series of one-shots from IDW Publishing. The Lone Gunmen (who are revealed in *The X-Files: Season 10* comics to have faked their deaths) investigate a series of documents from the future that lead them to investigate a series of "urban legends" that turn out to be true, including the Ghostbusters, the Teenage Mutant Ninja Turtles, the Transformers, and the Crow. The premise of the Transformers, involving giant robots using Earth as a battleground, is incompatible with the premise the CU resembles the world outside our window, at least on the surface.

The Year of High Treason by Vithal Rajan, Rupa Publications, 2011. In 1911, Sherlock Holmes, Dr. Watson, Arsène Lupin, A. J. Raffles, Bunny Manders, Rudolf Rassendyll, Fritz von Tarlenheim, Rupert of Hentzau, Sir Denis Nayland Smith, Dr. Petrie, Fu Manchu, Kâramanèh, the jungle lord, and Michael Strogoff all become embroiled in an affair revolving around King George V's Coronation Durbar in Delhi, India. Rassendyll and Rupert died in Anthony Hope's novel *Rupert of Hentzau*, which takes place in 1890. No explanation is given for their apparent survival. Combined with the revelation Kâramanèh is not only a Tamil whose real name is Kannamma, but a loyal agent of Fu Manchu's who deceived Petrie, this places Rajan's novel outside CU continuity.

Young Nemo and the Black Knights by Michael Vance, Airship 27 Productions, 2014. In 1836, 18-year-old Prince Rajesh Dakkar and a diverse crew dubbed the Black Knights travel aboard a boat called the *Nautilus* to find the Library of Alexandria in order to acquire a manuscript that reveals Atlantean secrets Rajesh, after renaming himself Captain Nemo, will one day use to create a remarkable submarine, also called the *Nautilus*. Rajesh's collection of books includes the dark *Necronomicon* written by a mad Arab. In the CU, Prince Dakkar was born in 1808, not 1818 as stated by Vance.

The Young Sherlock Holmes Adventures: Head of the Hydra, a graphic novel by Huw-J and J. L. Straw, Markosia Enterprises, December 2010, set in a steampunk universe in 1905 that more closely resembles a Dickensian 1870s. A college-aged Sherlock Holmes is approached by Felix Leiter, who indicates he might wish to consult Holmes in the future. Leiter's card reads *Criminal -----ation Agency*. This Leiter must be a counterpart to CIA agent (and later Pinkerton) Felix Leiter from the James Bond novels. We can assume the full second word in the name of the Agency is "Investigation."

Selected Bibliography

Books

Baring-Gould, William S. *Sherlock Holmes of Baker Street: The Life of the World's First Consulting Detective.* New York: Bramhall House, 1962.

Eckert, Win Scott. *Crossovers: A Secret Chronology of the World, Volume 1.* Encino, CA: Black Coat Press, 2010.

---. *Crossovers: A Secret Chronology of the World, Volume 2.* Encino, CA: Black Coat Press, 2010.

Eckert, Win Scott, ed. *Myths for the Modern Age: Philip José Farmer's Wold Newton Universe.* Austin, TX: MonkeyBrain Books, 2005.

Farmer, Philip José. *Tarzan Alive: A Definitive Biography of Lord Greystoke,* Garden City, NY: Doubleday & Co., 1972. New York: Popular Library, 1976. New York: Playboy Paperbacks, 1981. Lincoln, NE: University of Nebraska, Bison Books, 2006.

---. *Doc Savage: His Apocalyptic Life.* Garden City, NY: Doubleday & Co., 1973. New York: Bison Books, 1975. New York: Playboy Paperbacks, 1981. Meteor House, 2013. Altus Press, 2013.

Lai, Rick. *Chronology of Shadows: A Timeline of the Shadow's Exploits.* Altus Press, 2007.

---. *The Revised Complete Chronology of Bronze.* Altus Press, 2010

---. *Rick Lai's Secret Histories: Criminal Masterminds.* Altus Press, 2009.

---. *Rick Lai's Secret Histories: Daring Adventurers.* Altus Press, 2008.

Lofficier, Jean-Marc, and Randy Lofficier. *Shadowmen: Heroes and Villains of French Pulp Fiction.* Encino, CA: Black Coat Press, 2003.

Mengel, Brad. *Serial Vigilantes of Paperback Fiction: An Encyclopedia from Able Team to Z-Comm.* Jefferson, NC: McFarland & Company, 2009.

Pearson, John. *James Bond: The Authorized Biography of 007.* New York: Pyramid Books, 1975. New York: Grove Press, 1986.

Websites

Brown, Mark. *The Wold Newton Chronicles.*
<http://www.pjfarmer.com/chronicles/>
Croteau, Michael, and Rick Beaulieu. *The Official Philip José Farmer Web Page.*
<www.pjfarmer.com>
Eckert, Win Scott. *An Expansion of Philip José Farmer's Wold Newton Universe,* aka *The Wold Newton Universe.*
<http://www.pjfarmer.com/woldnewton/Pulp2.htm>

---. *The Star Trek Annotated Timeline.*
<http://www.pjfarmer.com/woldnewton/Startrek.htm>
Holbrook, Thom. *Crossovers and Spin Offs Master Page.*
<http://www.poobala.com/crossoverlist.html>
Internet Movie Database, The. <http://www.imdb.com/>
Lofficier, Jean-Marc. *French Wold Newton Universe.*
<http://www.coolfrenchcomics.com/wnu1.htm>
Nebbett, Adrian. *Sherlock Holmes Pastiche Characters Index.*
<http://www.schoolandholmes.com/>
Nevins, Jess. *Character Lists for the Encyclopedia of Golden Age Superheroes.*
<http://jessnevins.com/encyclopedia/characterlist.html>
---. *A Page of Fantastic, Mysterious, and Adventurous Victoriana.*
<http://www.reocities.com/jessnevins/vicintro.html>
---. *Pulp and Adventure Heroes of the Pre-War Years.*
<http://www.reocities.com/jjnevins/pulpsintro.html>
---. *Some Unknown Members of the Wold Newton Family.*
<http://ratmmjess.tripod.com/wold.html>
Power, Dennis. *The Wold Newton Universe: A Secret History.*
<http://www.pjfarmer.com/secret/index.htm>
Smith, Kevin Burton. *The Thrilling Detective Web Site.*
<http://www.thrillingdetective.com/>

About the Author

Sean Lee Levin discovered Philip José Farmer's Wold Newton family writings in 2002 and has never looked back. A lifelong Chicagoan, Sean spends much of his free time reading, writing, and watching a diverse range of films. Sean was honored to serve as a continuity editor on Josh Reynolds' novella *Phileas Fogg and the War of Shadows*, published by Meteor House in 2014. *Crossovers Expanded* is his first published work, with hopefully many more to come.

Meteor House Titles

THE WORLDS OF PHILIP JOSÉ FARMER
Anthology Series edited by Michael Croteau

Volume 1: Protean Dimensions
Volume 2: Of Dust and Soul
Volume 3: Portraits of a Trickster
Volume 4: Voyages to Strange Days

WOLD NEWTON SERIES

Doc Savage: His Apocalyptic Life by Philip José Farmer

The Khokarsa Series
Exiles of Kho by Christopher Paul Carey
Flight to Opar (Restored Edition) by Philip José Farmer
The Song of Kwasin by Philip José Farmer and Christopher Paul Carey
Hadon, King of Opar by Christopher Paul Carey
Blood of Ancient Opar by Christopher Paul Carey

The Pat Wildman Series
The Evil in Pemberley House by Philip José Farmer and Win Scott Eckert
The Scarlet Jaguar by Win Scott Eckert

The Phileas Fogg Series
Phileas Fogg and the War of Shadows by Josh Reynolds
Phileas Fogg and the Heart of Osra by Josh Reynolds

SCIENCE FICTION ADVENTURE

The Abnormalities of Stringent Strange by Rhys Hughes
Airship Hunters by Jim Beard and Duane Spurlock
Dayworld: A Hole in Wednesday by Philip José Farmer and Danny Adams

NONFICTION

Crossovers Expanded, Volume 1 by Sean Lee Levin
Crossovers Expanded, Volume 2 by Sean Lee Levin

meteorhousepress.com